Lancaster Brides

Romance Drives the Buggy in Four Inspiring Novels

WANDA E. BRUNSTETTER

BARBOUR
PUBLISHING

A Merry Heart ©1997 by Wanda E. Brunstetter
Looking for a Miracle ©2001 by Wanda E. Brunstetter
Plain and Fancy ©2002 by Wanda E. Brunstetter
The Hope Chest ©2002 by Wanda E. Brunstetter

Cover image © Corbis Images

ISBN 1-58660-802-9

Scripture quotations are taken from the King James Version of the Bible.

Published by Barbour Books, an imprint of Barbour Publishing, Inc., P.O. Box 719, Uhrichsville, Ohio 44683, www.barbourbooks.com.

 Member of the
Evangelical Christian
Publishers Association

Printed in the United States of America.
5 4 3 2 1

WANDA E. BRUNSTETTER

Wanda lives in Central Washington with her husband, who is a pastor. She has two grown children and six grandchildren. Her hobbies include doll repairing, sewing, ventriloquism, stamping, reading, and gardening. Wanda and her husband have a puppet ministry, which they often share at other churches, Bible camps, and Bible schools. Wanda invites you to visit her website: www.wandabrunstetter.com

A Merry Heart

Lovingly dedicated to the memory of my sister-in-law,
Miriam (Mim) Brunstetter, who always had a merry heart.

Chapter 1

Miriam Stoltzfus took one last look around the small one-room schoolhouse, then shut the door behind her. As she stepped outside, she could hear the voices of two children playing nearby, Sarah Jane Beachy and Andrew Sepler. The children couldn't see their teacher, she knew, for if they had, they surely would not have been having such a conversation.

"I wish our teacher wasn't so cross all the time," Sarah Jane said.

"My older brother says that she is just an old maid who never even smiles," Andrew added. "I think she must have a heart of stone!"

Miriam's cheeks burned hot, and she winced as though someone had slapped her face. Perhaps some of their words were true, she reluctantly admitted to herself. At age twenty-six, she was still an unmarried woman. This was nearly unheard of among the Old Order Amish group to which she belonged. Miriam shook her head. "I am not cross all of the time, and I do not have a heart of stone," she fumed to herself. But even as she spoke the words, she wondered if they were true or not. She was glad to see that the children had now left the school yard. She did not want them to know that she had overheard their conversation, nor did she feel in the mood to hear any more such talk against herself.

The horse and buggy, hitched under a tree nearby, offered solace to the tired schoolteacher. Speaking a few words of Pennsylvania Dutch to the mare, she climbed wearily inside the box-shaped buggy. She would be glad to leave the school day behind and get home to her waiting chores.

A short time later, Miriam found her mother sitting on the front porch of their plain, white farmhouse, shelling fresh peas from their garden. "Look, Daughter, the first spring picking," Anna Stoltzfus called as Miriam stepped down from the buggy.

Miriam waved in response, then began the ritual of unhitching the horse. When she finished, she led the willing mare to the barn.

"How was your day?" Anna called when Miriam reappeared a short time later.

Miriam crossed the yard and took a seat on the step next to her mother. "*Sis gute gange*—it went well," she said in the Pennsylvania Dutch language of her people. Then changing to English, she said with a long sigh, "It is so good to be home."

Anna wiped a wisp of graying hair away from her face where it had fallen loose form the tight bun she always wore under her head covering. "Problems at school?"

Miriam sighed again and squeezed her eyes tightly shut. After a few moments, she spoke. "It is probably not even worth mentioning, Mom, but after school I overheard two of my students talking. They seem to think that I have a heart of stone." She clasped her mother's hands in her own, "Oh, Mom, do you think it is true? Am I cross all the time? Do you think I really do have a heart of stone?"

Anna frowned. "Miriam, I don't believe any Christian's heart is made of stone. However, I have noticed that you are very unhappy, and your tone of voice is a bit harsh much of the time. Does it have anything to do with William Graber? Are you still pining over him?"

The color in Miriam's oval face turned a bright pink. "Of course not! I am certainly over him."

"I hope that you are, because it would do you no good to fret and dwell on what cannot be changed."

An uncomfortable yet familiar lump had formed in Miriam's throat, and she found that she couldn't bring herself to look directly into her mother's eyes. She was afraid the hidden pain in her own eyes would betray her words.

"If your troubled spirit is not because of your old beau, then what?" her mother asked.

Miriam shrugged. "I suppose everyone feels sad and out of sorts from time to time."

"Remember what the Bible tells us," her mother reminded. " 'A merry heart doeth good like a medicine: but a broken spirit drieth the bones.' Happiness and laughter are good medicine for a troubled spirit, Miriam."

"I know, Mom. You have quoted that verse from Proverbs many times, but it's not always easy to have a merry heart." Miriam stood up, smoothing her long green cotton dress. "Now, if you will excuse me, I had best go to my room and change, and then I will help you with supper." She quickly went inside, leaving her mother behind on the porch with her head bowed in prayer.

❧

Miriam's upstairs bedroom looked even more peaceful than usual. The freshly aired quilt on the bed was neat and crisp, giving the room the sweet smell of clean, outdoor air. The bare wooden floor was shiny and smooth as glass. Even the blue washing bowl that sat on the small dresser beneath the window reassured her of the cleanliness and orderliness of the plain room. On days like today she wished she could just hide away inside the four walls of her own room and shut out the world and all its ugliness.

Miriam took a seat on the comfortable bed and pulled her shoes off with a yawn and a long sigh. *How odd that some of the young people among my faith desire to leave this secure and peaceful life for the troublesome, hectic, modern way of life. I do not believe I could ever betray the Amish faith in such a way. Modern things may have their appeal, but simplicity and humility, though they separate us from the rest of the world, are a part of our culture that I treasure.*

She fluffed up her feather pillow and stretched out luxuriously for a few moments of rest before changing her clothes. Staring up absently at the plaster cracks in the ceiling overhead, she reflected again on the voices of the two children she had heard talking about her earlier. "How little they really do know about their teacher," she whispered. "They truly believe that I have a heart of stone, but rather it is a broken and shattered heart, and I am afraid it always will be."

A tear slid down Miriam's face and landed softly on the pillow beneath her head. She longed to be loved. To feel cherished. She knew in her heart that she was capable, or at least had been capable of, returning that same kind of love to a man who was willing to give his whole heart to her. She thought she had found that man in William Graber, but she knew now that no man could ever be trusted. She would guard her heart and never let another man cause her the kind of pain she was feeling now. The reminder of her past hurts was enough to keep her from ever falling in love again.

Miriam let her mind travel back in time. Back to when she was a pupil at the one-room schoolhouse where she was now the teacher.

Chapter 2

The young Miriam sat upright at her desk, listening attentively to the lesson being taught, until a slight tug on the back of her small, white head covering caused her to turn around.

The deep green eyes of twelve-year-old William Graber met her own pale blue eyes and held them captive. Even then, at her young age, Miriam had known that it was love she felt for him. He was a good friend, but he was also the boy she hoped to marry someday.

William smiled and passed her the crumpled note he had taken from his shirt pocket.

Miriam took the note and opened it slowly, not wanting the teacher to hear the paper rumpling. She smiled as she read the words. "Miriam: I want to walk you home from school. Please meet me by the apple tree out behind the schoolhouse. Your friend, William Graber."

Miriam nodded her agreement to William; then she folded the note and placed it securely inside her apron pocket. Impatiently, she waited for the minutes on the big battery-operated wall clock to tick away.

The walk home from school with William that day was the first of many. Over the next few years, they walked together, and he continued to carry her books, as well as continued to gain her favor. Their childhood friendship grew stronger with each passing year, until by the time they were both fifteen, their relationship had turned into a trusting love and a deep commitment to one another and to their future.

Their eighth year in school was their final one, and they both spent the next year in vocational training at home. William was instructed in the best of Amish farming methods, and Miriam learned the more arduous homemaking skills. After all, it was expected that they would marry someday and settle down on a farm of their own. They would both need to be taught well in all areas of farm life, as well as learn how to run an efficient and well-organized household.

William was given a horse and courting buggy at the age of sixteen. "Miriam, will you let me give you a ride home after the singing at Schumans' tonight?" he asked after the morning church services that had been held in the home of his parents.

Miriam felt herself blush from head to toe; though she really didn't understand why. They had been close friends for such a long time, but this was to be the beginning of their official courtship. "*Jah*, William," she whispered.

How her heart swelled with joy that night, as she prepared to go to the young people's singing. She would be going with her two older brothers, Jonas and Andrew, but according to Amish custom, she would be allowed to accept a ride home from any eligible young Amish man. Since William had already asked her, the question of whom she might be traveling home with was already settled. She smiled to herself and placed her small covering securely on her head.

The singing was held in the Schumans' barn, where the young people spent several hours singing some traditional Amish hymns, playing games, and enjoying a delicious array of foods, which had been prepared by the hostess and her daughters.

Miriam was having a good time, but she could hardly wait for the evening to end so that she could be alone with William. She was also anxious to experience the thrill of riding in his new, open courting buggy.

"I am riding home with William," Miriam whispered to her friend Crystal as they waited in line for refreshments.

"*Ach*, my, now that is not such a surprise," Crystal countered. "Everyone in this county knows that you two are sweet on each other."

Miriam felt her face heat up. "Hush. We are just supposed to be friends."

"Has he asked to come calling yet?" Crystal wanted to know.

Miriam shook her head. "Not yet, but then he only got his buggy a few weeks ago."

Crystal nodded and smiled knowingly. "Your brother Jonas only had his buggy two days before he asked to call on me."

Miriam giggled. "That sounds like my bold brother Jonas all right."

"I'm so glad that my eighteenth birthday is only a few weeks away," Crystal said. "That way, if Jonas should ask me to marry him, I can be fairly certain that Papa will say, *Jah*, it is fine with me and Mom.'" She smiled happily. "I know what my answer will be as well."

"I cannot speak for your papa, of course, but I do know my brother rather well. I think he is just counting the days until you turn eighteen."

Now it was Crystal's turn to blush. "I hope you are right. Don't you wish that you and William were a bit older, so you, too, could be thinking of marriage?"

Miriam giggled again and then whispered in her friend's ear, "I think we have both already thought about it, but we still have two more years to wait. I know that my parents would never let me marry before I turn eighteen."

❧

The ride home in William's buggy was everything that Miriam had expected it to be. A gentle August breeze offered the couple a cool but pleasant trip. The horse behaved well, responding to each of William's commands without delay. At one point, William was even brave enough to rein the horse with only one hand. That left the other hand free to seek out Miriam's.

Miriam felt the color come quickly to her cheeks. She smiled and stole a quick glance at her escort. She hoped that William couldn't see how crimson her face must be in the moonlight.

William said nothing, but he smiled and tightened his hand around hers.

A short time later, as he walked her to the door, he whispered, "May I come visiting on Tuesday night, Miriam?"

Miriam nodded and ran quickly into the house. At last, they were officially courting. She felt too joyous to even utter a word.

✿

The months melted into years, and by the time the young couple had turned twenty, there was still no definite wedding plans made. Though they often talked of it secretly, William did not feel quite ready for the responsibilities of running a farm of his own. After working full-time for his father since the age of fifteen, he wasn't even certain that he wanted to farm. He knew it was expected of him, but he felt that he might be more suited to another trade.

The opportunity he had been waiting for arrived at the age of twenty-two when William was invited to learn the painting trade from his uncle Abe, who lived in Ohio. While Abe and one of his sons ran a small farm of their own, he also had a paint contracting business and needed another apprentice.

Miriam cried for days after William left, but he promised to write often and visit on holidays and some weekends. It wasn't much consolation to a young woman of marrying age. She had so hoped that by now the two of them would be married, perhaps even starting a family.

Impatiently, she waited for the mail each day, moping around in a melancholy mood when there was no letter, and lighthearted and happy whenever she heard from her beloved William. His letters were full of enthusiastic descriptions of his new job, as he explained in great detail how he had learned the correct way to use a paintbrush and apply paint quickly yet neatly to any surface. He told her about some of the modern buildings in town that they had contracted to paint. He also spoke of how he cared for her, and he promised he would be home soon for a visit.

William's visits were frequent at first, but after the first year was over, they became less and less, as did his letters. One day, on Miriam's twenty-fourth birthday, a long-awaited letter arrived with the familiar Ohio postmark. Her heart thumped wildly, and her hands trembled as she tore open the envelope. It was the first letter she'd had from him in several months, but the fact that it had arrived on her birthday caused her such joy that she nearly forgot how unhappy she had been feeling.

A sob caught in her throat, and she let out a gasp as she read the letter.

Dearest Miriam,

There are no easy words to say what must be said in this note. You have always been a dear friend to me, and I will never forget the happy times we have shared. However, I will not be coming back to Pennsylvania, as I had originally planned. I have met a girl. Her name is Lydia, and we plan to be married in a few weeks. I am sorry if I have hurt you, but it is better this way. I could never have been happy working as a farmer. I know you will find someone else—someone who will make you as happy as Lydia has made me. I will always remember you and treasure the special friendship we had as children. I wish you the very best and God's richest blessings.

Fondly,
William Graber

❧

Miriam pulled her thoughts back to the present, and a familiar sob escaped her lips. That letter from William had come over two years ago, yet if felt like yesterday. Her heart still ached when she thought of him. *How could he have found someone else?* she wondered even now. How could he possibly have thought that she would ever be happy again? How could he have referred to their relationship as a mere "childhood friendship"? He had left her with a broken heart, and she was certain that it would never be mended.

Chapter 3

In the kitchen Miriam found her mother rolling out a piecrust for chicken potpie. Mom smiled and asked, "Are you feelin' better now?"

Miriam reached for a clean apron hanging on a nearby wall peg and answered, "*Jah*, I'm fine, Mom."

"Good, because we have guests coming for supper, and it would not be good if you were gloomy all evening."

"Guests? Who's coming over?"

Mom poured the vegetable filling into the pie pan before answering. "Amos Hilty and his daughter Mary Ellen."

Miriam lifted her gaze toward the ceiling. "Oh, Mom," she groaned. "You know I am not the least bit interested in Amos. Why must you go and scheme behind my back?"

"Scheme? Did I hear that someone in my house is scheming?" Papa asked as he entered the kitchen.

Miriam put her hand through the crook of her father's arm. "Mom is trying to match me up with Amos Hilty. She has invited him and Mary Ellen to supper again. They were just here last month, Papa."

Henry leaned his head back and laughed. His heavy beard, peppered generously with gray, twitched rhythmically with each new wave of laughter. "Daughter, it is high time that you married and settled down with a good man. Amos would make you a fine Christian husband, so do not close your mind to the idea."

"I think it is her heart that is closed," Mom said softly.

"If I *should* ever decide to marry, I would at least like to be the one to select my own husband!" Miriam exclaimed. She turned away and began setting the table.

Just then, Lewis, Miriam's younger brother, came in from outside. He hung his straw hat on a wall peg and sniffed the air appreciatively. "Something sure smells mighty good, Mom!"

"We are having company for supper, so please hurry and wash up," his mother instructed.

"Who's coming?" asked Lewis.

"Amos Hilty and his daughter," Miriam answered curtly.

"Aha! I think Amos is a bit sweet on you, Sister."

Jah? Well, I am certainly not sweet on him! Just because he's a widower and his little girl needs a mother, does not mean that I am available, either! Why can't this family leave me alone? Can't you all see that I am perfectly content with my life just as it is?"

Lewis gave Mom a knowing look, and Mom smiled, but neither of them commented on Miriam's lengthy remark.

Amos Hilty and six-year-old Mary Ellen arrived at the Stoltzfus house shortly after six o' clock. He entered the kitchen carrying his straw hat in his hands, while Mary Ellen carried a basket of freshly picked radishes. She smiled and handed them to Miriam. "There are from our garden," she announced happily.

"*Danki*. I will slice a few for supper," Miriam responded. She took the basket and placed it on the cupboard, then turned back toward their guests.

Amos nodded at Miriam and gave her a broad smile. "It is good to see you, Miriam."

Miriam did not return the smile nor make any response, but rather went quickly to the cooler to get out some fresh goat's milk.

Amos shifted his long legs uncomfortably and cleared his throat. "Mary Ellen tells me that she is doing quite well in school. She says you are a good teacher."

"I do my best" was all that Miriam chose to say.

Miriam's parents and Lewis entered the kitchen from the parlor.

"Good evenin', Amos," Mom said warmly.

"Good evening to you as well. It was kind of you to have us to supper again."

"Mom knows how important good food can be for a man," Lewis said with a laugh.

"That is quite true," Amos agreed. He cast a glance in Miriam's direction, but she chose to ignore it.

"I think we should eat now," Papa said, pulling out his chair at the head of the table.

Everyone took their seats, and all heads bowed in a silent prayer of thanks for the food they were about to eat. Papa helped himself to the potpie and passed it to the guests, then followed it with a fine array of other homemade foods, including coleslaw, sourdough bread, sweet pickles, beet relish, and dilled green beans.

Miriam noticed Mary Ellen scan the table quickly. "You forgot my radishes, Teacher."

Miriam rose. "I'll see to it now." She excused herself and went to cut the radishes.

"Teacher is very pretty, don't you think so, Pappy?" Mary Ellen said in an excited tone. Miriam glanced over her shoulder. The child's blue eyes shone brightly, as she waited expectantly for her father's answer.

Amos nodded. *"Jah*, she is a fine-looking woman." He helped himself to another piece of potpie and smiled appreciatively. "The women of this house sure make a good supper."

Men! Miriam fumed inwardly. *They can't even express themselves without bringing food into the conversation. And children—they never know when to keep quiet.*

"Please, have some more coleslaw and bread," Mom offered.

"Jah. Danki!" Amos responded as he reached for the bread basket.

Papa chuckled. "You certainly do have a hearty appetite!"

Amos laughed, too. "I guess that comes from eating too much of my own cooking." He glanced at Miriam and gave her a quick wink, but she averted his gaze and stared down at her plate of food.

Miriam was relieved when supper was finally over and the men had excused themselves to go to the front parlor for a game of checkers.

Mary Ellen sat on the floor playing with Boots, the cat, while Miriam and her mother did the dishes. Miriam watched the small child out of the corner of her eye. The young girl's brown hair, braided and pinned to the back of her head, looked a bit limp, as though it might come undone at any minute. Miriam tried to visualize Amos, his large hands clumsily trying to braid his daughter's long hair. She realized that it must be difficult for him to raise the child alone. There were so many things that only a woman could do well. He did need to find another wife—but certainly not her.

After challenging Henry and Lewis to several games of checkers and winning nearly every one, Amos finally decided that it was time to go home. As he started for the door with Mary Ellen by his side, he stopped and said to Miriam, "It was good to see you again. Maybe I will come by the schoolhouse soon."

"Jah, I am sure that Mary Ellen would like that," Miriam said. She felt fairly certain that Amos had intended his remark to inform her that he would like to see her again, but without being too rude, she wanted him to be aware that she was not interested in him in any way. She could only hope that he had gotten the message and would not show up at the schoolhouse.

Chapter 4

One morning several days later, Miriam received a surprise gift. Mary Ellen was the bearer, bringing to school a small pot of newly opened heartsease. "These are from Pappy," the child explained. "He said maybe some wild pansies would make you smile. You always look so sad, Teacher. God doesn't want us to be sad. Pappy said so." She placed the pot on Miriam's desk and hurried to her seat before Miriam had a chance to respond.

Miriam studied the delicate flowers. They were lovely, and the child was kind to bring them, but Miriam was irritated that Mary Ellen's pappy could look into her heart and see her sadness. *Perhaps I do seldom smile,* she thought, *but then, there needs to be a reason to smile. If God really wants me to be happy, then why did He allow William to hurt me so?*

Miriam looked away from the pot of flowers and tried to concentrate on the day's lesson plan that lay on her desk. She had more important things to do than ponder over the unexplainable.

❧

By the end of the day, a pounding migraine headache had overtaken Miriam. Fighting waves of nausea and dizziness, she leaned against the schoolhouse door with a sense of relief as she watched all the children file outside. She would be so glad to get home again, where she could lie down and rest.

Just as she was about to close the door, a buggy pulled into the parking lot. Amos Hilty stepped out, his large frame hovering above the small child who ran to his side. With long strides, he made his way to the schoolhouse, meeting Miriam as she opened the door.

He removed his straw hat and smiled. "I came to pick up Mary Ellen, but I wanted to talk with you first."

Mary Ellen smiled up at her bearded father and reached for his large hand.

"Is there a problem?" Miriam asked.

Amos looked across the room at the flowers on Miriam's desk. "I see that you got the heartsease. Do you like them?"

"They are fine. Is there a problem?" Miriam repeated impatiently.

Amos shook his head. "Not unless you say no to my invitation."

"Invitation?"

"*Jah.* I was wondering—that is, Mary Ellen and I would like you to go on a picnic with us on Saturday afternoon. We were planning to go to the lake, and—"

"*Mir sin so froh*—we are so glad!" Mary Ellen interrupted excitedly. "It will be a lot of fun, and we will bring sandwiches and cookies. Maybe Pappy will even

17

bring some homemade root beer. He makes it really good!"

Miriam tried to force a smile. Her throbbing head was spinning again, and she steadied herself against a nearby desk. "Thank you, but I really cannot go with you. Now, if you will please excuse me, I must be going home."

Amos stood there, his mouth open slightly, but no word came out. Still holding Mary Ellen's hand, he shook his head slowly and went out the door.

As Miriam watched them go, she noticed the look of rejection on Amos's face. Placing her hands over her aching forehead, she murmured, "What is wrong with me? I know I was terribly rude to them. I did not even thank Amos for the flowers." Closing her eyes, she prayed, "Dear Lord, please take away this headache—and the pain in my heart."

❧

When she arrived home a short time later, Miriam found her mother in the kitchen, peeling vegetables over the sink.

"Sit down, Daughter. You do not look well at all," Mom said, quickly pulling out a kitchen chair.

Miriam placed the flowers on the table and flopped into the seat. "I have another one of my sick headaches, Mom. They seem to be happening more often these days."

Mom went to the woodstove and removed the teakettle, already simmering with hot water. She poured some into a cup, and dropped a tea bag inside, then placed the cup in front of Miriam. "Drink a little peppermint tea to settle your stomach, and then go on upstairs and lie down for awhile."

Miriam nodded. "That sounds nice, but what about the supper preparations?"

"I think I can manage without you this once. Anyhow, someday I will have to do it on a regular basis."

Miriam's forehead wrinkled in question.

"When you are married," Mom explained.

Miriam sighed deeply and took a sip of the soothing herb tea. "I have no plans of marriage, Mom. Not now, and not ever!"

"My, what lovely pansies!" Mom said cheerfully, trying to change the subject. "Did one of your students bring them today?"

"*Jah*. Mary Ellen Hilty brought them. She said they were a gift from her pappy. It is just another one of his tricks to gain my approval."

"Miriam, please do not be so harsh. I am sure that Amos means no harm. He likes you, and he has no doubt been very lonely since his wife, Ruth, died over a year ago."

Miriam frowned. "He actually had the nerve to come by after school and invite me to go on a picnic with him and Mary Ellen this Saturday. I suppose he thought the flowers would pave the way."

"Did you accept his kind invitation?" Mom asked hesitantly yet hopefully.

"Of course not!" Miriam stood up abruptly. "I thought I had made myself quite clear, Mom. All he wants is a mother for his child and someone to do all his

18

cooking and cleaning. Well, I refuse to be that someone!"

Mom reached out and touched Miriam's hand lovingly. "I'm sure that Amos wants more than that, Miriam. He needs a friend and companion, just as you do."

"I do not!" Miriam shouted. "I do not need anyone!" Her voice broke, and she ran quickly from the room before Mom could see the unbidden tears on her face.

Chapter 5

Early in the month of June, the farmers' market opened for business. It would remain open through the summer months and into the fall. The Stoltzfus family, though they no longer rented a booth for selling their wares, did enjoy going just to browse around and visit with many of their neighboring Amish friends and relatives. It was also an opportunity to get some good bargains on fresh produce, as well as a chance to purchase some new farming tools or look at the many handcrafted items that were for sale.

The morning sun was already giving promise of a warm day, and as they drove into the parking lot, Miriam wiped the perspiration from her forehead and sighed deeply. She hoped that this summer would not be as hot and humid as last summer had been.

Papa helped Mom down from the buggy, and she smiled up at him and took his offered arm. Then the two of them started off in the direction of the market building. Miriam stepped down, followed by Lewis, who immediately began unhitching the horse.

"I am going on ahead," Miriam told her brother.

Lewis nodded. *"Jah,* sure, leave me with all the work! I can handle it, though. You run along and have all the fun." He laughed and gave her a playful swat on the arm.

Miriam shook her head. "Brothers!" She hurried toward the market, muttering to herself as she went.

She was halfway across the parking lot when she stumbled on a broken beer bottle that someone had carelessly tossed on the ground. Her legs went out from under her, and she fell hard, landing right on the broken bottle. *"Ach,* my!" she cried. She tried to get to her feet, hoping no one had seen her calamity. She also hoped that the nasty bottle had done no real harm to her long cotton dress or her knees.

Miriam felt two strong arms pulling her to an upright position. She looked up and found herself staring right into a pair of the brightest blue eyes she had ever seen.

"Are you all right, Miss?" a young man with sandy blond hair asked as he bent down to pick up the broken bottle.

Miriam felt her face flush with embarrassment. "I—uh—I am just fine, really—thank you."

"Your dress is torn, and I see blood showing through it. Let me see your knees. You might be cut up pretty bad," the man said.

Miriam wrinkled her forehead and tried to keep her voice from sounding too sharp or too loud. "I appreciate your concern, but I am just fine." She was not about to lift the hem of her cotton dress so that a man could see her knees. She was a woman of good upbringing, and he was obviously an Englishman of modern ways. What would he know of proper modesty? Besides, she didn't even know him.

Miriam looked down at her soiled skirt and rubbed her hand against it, as though in doing so it might take away the red stain and ugly tear. She took a few tentative steps and winced, but determinedly she went on.

"At least let me offer you some assistance." The young man put one arm around her waist without even waiting for her reply. "I'll walk you to the building. I assume that's where you were heading before your little accident?"

"*Jah*, I was, but I can make it by myself." Miriam shook herself free from his grasp.

He smiled, showing his white teeth and an almost boyish grin. "My, my, I didn't know you Amish ladies could be so liberated. I thought you liked to have a man look after you."

"I am not liberated!" Miriam shouted. "But I do not need looking after, either!" Her eyes flashed, and ignoring the sharp pain in her right knee, she hurried on ahead.

The man walked on beside her. "I'm afraid we've gotten off to a rather bad start, Miss. I'm sorry if I have offended you." He smiled and reached out a friendly hand. "I'm Nick McCormick. Pretty catchy name, wouldn't you say?"

When Miriam made no reply, Nick went on, "I make it my duty to rescue fair ladies in distress."

Miriam found herself unable to keep from smiling. At least she thought it was a smile. The harsh frown was gone from her face, and she felt a bit more relaxed. She took the offered hand and shook it politely. "I am Miriam Stoltzfus, and I'm sorry if I was rude to you. Now, if you will excuse me, I really do need to catch up to my family."

"You're married, then?" Nick asked boldly.

Miriam shook her head. "I was speaking of my parents." She wondered why she was even answering this man's personal questions. It was really none of his business who she was here with or what her marital status was.

"I see," Nick replied. "Then perhaps you wouldn't mind giving me a guided tour of the place."

Miriam gave him a questioning look.

"I'm a photographer for the *Daily Express*. I'm here to take some pictures for a cover story about the Amish," he explained.

Miriam noticed his camera bag hanging over one shoulder. She didn't know why she hadn't seen it there before. Her body stiffened, and the familiar frown was back on her face again. "I have no intention of acting as a tour guide so that you can photograph my people. It is against our religion to allow our pictures to be taken."

They had reached the market, and Nick dropped the bottle into a trash can and opened the door, letting Miriam step inside first. "I'm afraid it's my turn to apologize, Miriam. In spite of what you say, I'm aware that a few Amish people do allow pictures to be taken, especially of their children. I can see that you have your guard up for some reason, and I've obviously offended you by asking for your assistance. Please accept my apologies."

"It is of no real consequence. I get my feelings hurt a lot these days," Miriam said with a shrug of her shoulders. "Good day, Mr. McCormick." She turned and limped off in the direction of the ladies' rest room.

Chapter 6

After inspecting her knees, Miriam found that only the right one was bleeding, but the cut did not appear to be too serious. She wet a paper towel and blotted the knee to stop the bleeding; then she tried unsuccessfully to get the blood off her dress. She was afraid to scrub too hard at it, for fear of tearing it more. It would have to wait until she got home to tend to it properly, she decided. She was thankful that the market had warm running water in the rest room. At home she would have had to stand at the sink in the kitchen and pump cold water for washing and then heat it on the stove if she wanted it to be warm. This was certainly much quicker and easier.

She was about to leave when the door flew open and a child burst into the room. It was Mary Ellen Hilty. "Teacher!" she cried excitedly. "I didn't know you were here today!"

"Actually, I just got here a short time ago," Miriam responded.

"Pappy will be glad to see you," the child said. "He likes you, Teacher. I can tell." Her hazel-colored eyes lit up, and her round cheeks took on a pink glow.

Before Miriam could think of a reply, Mary Ellen went on. "He thinks you cook good, too, Teacher. He said so."

Miriam tried to force a smile, but inwardly she was seething. *Of course he likes my cooking,* she thought. *He would like any woman's cooking. All he wants is a wife to take care of him and a mother for this poor little child. Well, if he thinks there is even a chance that I would marry him, he is terribly mistaken.*

"Are you happy to be out of school for the summer?" Miriam asked, hoping to change the subject to something other than Mary Ellen's pappy.

Mary Ellen smiled a wide toothless grin. She had already lost a baby tooth since school had been dismissed a week ago. "I like spending more time with Pappy, but I miss school—and I miss you, too, Teacher."

I would not be surprised if Amos told her to say that, Miriam fumed inwardly. "That was a very sweet thing to say, Mary Ellen," she forced herself to say.

"I meant it, Teacher. Some of the other children do not like you, but I think you are very smart—and pretty, too."

Another prompted compliment, Miriam thought. "Well, I must be going now, Mary Ellen. I need to look for my folks."

"Oh, they are talking to Pappy over by his root beer stand," Mary Ellen was quick to say. "Why don't you go and try some? I am sure Pappy would give you a glass for free."

"Thank you; maybe I will." Miriam left the room and turned quickly in the opposite direction, away from the side of the market where all the refreshments were sold.

She didn't have to go far before she saw a familiar face. Her best friend and sister-in-law, Crystal, was coming toward her. Holding each of her hands were her two-year-old twin boys, Jacob and John.

"Aunt Mimmy, *schussel*—hurry!" Jacob squealed.

"Aunt Mimmy, *schussel!*" John repeated.

"How are you little rascals?" Miriam asked in Pennsylvania Dutch, the only language that Amish children under school age could speak. She knelt down next to her nephews, but the pain in her knee caused her to wince. Carefully, she stood up again.

"Miriam, what is wrong? Are you hurt?" asked Crystal.

"It is not really serious. I just had a little fall outside in the parking lot. I cut up my knee a little, and I embarrassed myself some, too." She made no mention of the brazen young man who had offered her assistance. Why bring more questions from Crystal?

Crystal looked down at Miriam's dress. "You have torn your skirt. Let's go find your mom. Maybe she has something we can mend it with. Your folks are here with you, aren't they?"

"*Jah.* I was told they are over at Amos Hilty's root beer stand."

"Let's go find them, then," Crystal suggested. "Maybe after Mom fixes your dress, she will agree to watch the twins for awhile, and then we can go off by ourselves and do some shopping together. It will be just like old times."

The idea of some time alone with Crystal did sound nice, but Miriam wasn't eager to see Amos. She hesitated before answering. "Why don't you go on? I will meet you over by the quilts. I would really like to look at some that Karen Freisen has for sale."

"That sounds good, but what about your dress?" Crystal asked.

"It can wait until I go home," Miriam answered.

"Well, come with us anyway, and I will treat you to a nice cold root beer," Crystal said.

"*Schnell*—quickly, Aunt Mimmy!" John said loudly.

"*Schnell!*" echoed Jacob.

Miriam shrugged. "Oh, all right, I can see that I am outnumbered. Let's go get us some root beer."

Amos, his tall frame hovering above those around him, was pouring a glass of frothy root beer when Miriam arrived with Crystal and the twins. He handed the glass to the young boy who was his customer. When he looked up, his deep brown eyes met Miriam's. He smiled a warm friendly smile. "Hello, Miriam. It's good to see you again. Your folks were here a few minutes ago. You just missed them."

"Oh, wouldn't you know it! I wanted Anna to watch these two little guys for me," Crystal told him.

"Maybe we should go try to find them," Miriam was quick to suggest.

Jacob began pulling on his mother's skirt, and John pointed toward the root beer. "*Jah,* boys, we will have some root beer first," promised their mother.

Amos opened the spigot on the root beer keg, and then he served up four glasses of icy cold soda. Two were in large glasses for the ladies, and the twins got smaller glasses, just right for boys their size.

Frothy foam got all over John's and Jacob's noses when they took a drink and the grown-ups all laughed—even Miriam. It felt good to laugh. It was something she seldom did anymore.

After the drinks were finished and they had engaged in some polite conversation, Miriam suggested that they be on their way. Amos nodded, saying that he hoped to see her again soon.

"He is definitely interested in you," Crystal whispered as they walked away.

"*Jah?* Well, I am definitely not interested in him!" was Miriam's firm reply. "Furthermore, it troubles me the way everyone is always trying to match us up. Even his daughter, Mary Ellen, is in on the little plot."

Crystal put her hand on her Miriam's arm. "Mary Ellen is a very sweet child. I am sure that no such plotting ideas have ever entered her young little mind."

"Maybe not, but some adults, whom I will not bother to mention, are in on the plot to marry me off to Amos Hilty, and some of them are using that poor child as an instrument of their devious ways."

Crystal laughed. "How you do exaggerate, my dear friend. No one is being devious or plotting against you. We all just want your happiness. Surely you can see that."

Miriam didn't answer, and Crystal went on. "Ever since we were children, all we could think about was how we would marry someday and have a family. We both knew how happy we would be if God gave us good husbands and some fine children to raise."

"That is easy for you to say," Miriam snapped. "You are happily married to my brother Jonas, and you have these adorable twins to fill your life. I, on the other hand, am an old-maid schoolteacher, and I plan to stay that way!"

Chapter 7

The morning sun, beating against the windows, was already warming the Stoltzfus kitchen when Miriam came downstairs. She squinted against the harsh light that was streaming through an open window. Her head felt fuzzy; another pounding migraine had sent her to bed early the night before, and the unpleasant remnants of it still remained. What she really needed was something to clear her head of the dusty cobwebs that lingered there from her disturbing sleep. Perhaps she would wash her hair and then go down by the lake to dry it. Some time alone in the early morning sun would surely do some good. Papa and Lewis were already out in the fields, and Mom had gone over to her eldest son Andrew's place to help his wife, Sarah, with some baking. No one would need her for anything. This was the perfect chance to be alone so that she could think and pray.

She cut herself a thick piece of shoofly pie while she waited for the kettle to heat. She ate the molasses-filled breakfast pie hungrily, then washed it down with a big glass of fresh goat's milk taken from the cooler. The quietness of the house seemed to soothe her aching head a bit. She liked solitude. In fact, she really preferred being alone.

By the time she had finished eating, the water was warm enough. She poured it into a ceramic basin, which she placed inside the sink. After pouring some of it onto her long brown hair, she lathered up her scalp with a bar of Mom's homemade lilac soap. A hint of the perfumed flower drifted up to meet her nose, and Miriam sniffed appreciatively. She rinsed with the remaining warm water, then reached for the big towel she had placed nearby on the cupboard. She blotted her hair dry, being careful not to rub too aggressively, which she knew would only aggravate her headache.

When Miriam was satisfied that the majority of water had been absorbed from her hair into the towel, she wrapped a clean towel loosely around her head, picked up her hairbrush from the wall shelf nearby, and went out the back door.

The lake was clear and blue, and the sun had warmed the grassy shoreline. Miriam took a seat on the carpet of green and slipped off her shoes. She wiggled her toes in the grass and sighed. *Sometimes I wish I were still a child.*

She reached up and pulled the towel from her head, causing her damp hair to fall loosely about her shoulders. She shook her head several times, letting the glowing sun warm her tresses. She closed her eyes and lifted her face toward the sky.

Dear Lord, she prayed, *if only my life could be simple and pleasant, as it was when I was a small child. Why must my heart hurt so? I want to be pleasing in Your sight, yet*

I know that most of the time I fall terribly short. How can I have a merry heart, as Mom says I should, when I am so full of pain?

A tear squeezed through a closed eyelid, and Miriam reached up to wipe it away.

The crackling of a twig nearby caused her to jump. She turned and saw the lens of a camera peeking through the branches of a willow tree. When she realized that it was pointed directly at her, she gasped and jumped quickly to her feet.

Nick McCormick stepped out from behind the tree. "Sorry if I startled you, Miss."

"How dare you!" Miriam shouted. "I thought I had seen the last of you at the market yesterday."

Nick smiled sheepishly. "Uh-oh, it's the liberated Amish woman I had the privilege of helping to her feet yesterday morning. And what beautiful feet they are, too, I might add." He smiled and bowed to her. "I certainly had no idea that I'd be seeing that fair maiden again today. Especially not like this."

Miriam pulled the hairbrush from her apron pocket and began quickly brushing her tangled hair. "I must look a sight," she said, but even as she spoke the words, she wondered why she should care what she looked like. Nick McCormick was just an arrogant and very bold Englishman.

"I really do not appreciate you sneaking up on me," she continued. "And I certainly do not like the fact that you were taking my picture. I told you yesterday—"

"Yes, yes, I know. The Amish don't believe in being photographed. I heard that it's something about graven images or some other such foolishness." He smiled again and moved closer to her.

Miriam felt the need to move away from him, but she held her ground instead. Why should she give him the impression that she was nervous in his company? "It is not foolishness! The Bible tells us in Exodus twenty, verse four, 'Thou shalt not make unto thee any graven image.' We believe that includes taking photographs or displaying them."

"I can see that you certainly are well versed in the Scriptures," Nick said as he took a seat on the grass and began to advance his camera to get ready for the next picture. "Well, I say the Bible is just a lot of fairy-tale hogwash! And furthermore, I'll have you know that I've photographed several Amish children, and they didn't put up such a fuss. Is their religion any different than yours?"

Miriam sat down, making sure that she was now a comfortable distance from the insolent intruder. Her hair was almost dry, and it lay in gentle waves across her shoulders and down her back.

"Children do not always know any better," she told Nick. "Besides, you English folks usually bribe them with money or candy. They are not strong enough to say no."

Nick laughed, causing his blue eyes to twinkle. "How about you, Miss Stoltzfus? Would you allow me to photograph you for a piece of candy?"

"Don't be ridiculous! I would not allow my picture to be taken for any price!"

Miriam paused and looked the man squarely in the eyes. "Anyway, you have already taken my photograph without my knowledge or my consent. I am sure that you probably have some prize-winning shots of the silly Amish woman drying her hair by the lake."

Nick's face sobered. "I've offended you again, haven't I?"

"*Jah.* To be perfectly honest, you have," was her curt reply.

Without saying a word, Nick opened the back of his camera and removed the exposed film; then he handed it to Miriam. "Here. Accept this with my heartfelt apology for intruding on your privacy."

Miriam closed her fingers around the roll of film and smiled slightly. "Thank you for understanding, Mr. McCormick."

"I'm not sure that I really do understand. I know one thing, though—you're really beautiful when you smile," Nick told her. "And please, call me Nick," he added.

Miriam felt the heat of a blush stain her cheeks. No one had ever told her she was beautiful before. William used to say she had a kind face—but never beautiful. She looked down at her trembling hands.

"Now I've embarrassed you," he said. "I must apologize once more."

Miriam looked up. "It is just that— Well, no one has ever called me beautiful before."

Nick smiled a warm, sincere smile. "Then that was their mistake." He rose to his feet. "I'd better get going. I have to be back at the newspaper office before noon." He held out his hand. "It's been nice talking to you again. I hope this won't be the last time we meet."

Miriam shook his hand. "Good-bye, Mr. McCormick—I mean, Nick." She watched silently as he walked away and wondered why her heart was beating so rapidly against her chest.

Chapter 8

August was a hot month, and everyone found it difficult not to complain about the stuffy, humid air. There were days when not even so much as a tender breeze graced the valley.

One evening a summer storm finally brought wind and rain, but it only caused the air to be more humid than it had been before. Miriam found it even more difficult not to be cross and to complain. She sat on the front porch steps, watching the streaks of lightning brighten the sky.

"God's handiwork is a pretty picture, is it not?" said a deep voice from behind her.

She turned to see her father standing on the porch, stroking his long, full beard. He smiled at Miriam. "God is quite the artist, wouldn't you say?"

She nodded and smiled slightly. Her father had such a way with words, and such a love and understanding of God. He saw God's hand in everything around him, things that others would have simply taken for granted.

"We need a good rain," Papa said as he took a seat on the step beside Miriam.

"I suppose so, but it is making the air awfully muggy," she replied.

Jah, well we can put up with a little mugginess when the good Lord answers our prayers and brings the rain. The summer crops were in much need of a good soaking."

Miriam couldn't argue with that. She knew how important the crops of alfalfa, corn, and tobacco were to all the Amish farmers in the valley. She reached for her father's hand. "You always see the good in things, Papa."

He squeezed her hand. "As a man 'thinketh in his heart, so is he,' the Bible tells us."

Miriam couldn't argue with that, either. Perhaps that was why she was so unhappy. She thought unhappy thoughts. But how did one go about making themselves think pleasant thoughts?

Miriam shuddered as a clap of thunder sounded a bit too close to the house.

"Is something besides the storm troubling you, Daughter?" her father asked.

Of course something is troubling me. Something is always troubling me, she thought. Miriam shook her head. "Just the storm. I hope the lightning doesn't hit anyone's house or barn."

Jah, that is always uninvited," her father agreed. "But if it should happen, we will certainly rebuild." He laughed lightly. "A good barn raising is always a joy."

"A joy?" Miriam's voice was tinged with sarcasm. "You mean, it is a lot of work!"

"Jah, that, too, but working together with your friends and family is a joyous time."

Miriam didn't say anything more. What was the use in arguing with such a positive man as her father? She had to admit she admired him for his optimistic attitude. Why couldn't a little of it rub off on her?

૭❧

On Sunday, church services were held at Andrew and Sarah's home. Their farm was only about three miles from the senior Stoltzfus' place, so the ride by horse and buggy was a rather short one.

After Papa helped Mom down from the buggy, he and Lewis went to join his other sons, Jonas and Andrew, behind the barn, where the horses were all hitched in the shade. Miriam and her mother made their way to the front porch to visit with Sarah, Crystal, and some of the other women who had already arrived. The twins were playing with their cousins, Rebekah and Simon, on the front lawn, along with several other small children. It was another warm day, and Miriam was thirsty. "I am going to step inside the kitchen for a drink of water," she whispered to her sister-in-law Sarah.

Sarah, who was rocking baby Nadine, answered, "Help yourself. There is a pitcher of lemonade in the cooler, if you would rather have that."

Miriam shook her head. *"Danki,* but water will suit me just fine."

When she entered the kitchen, she thought that it was empty, but then she saw someone across the room, standing near the sink. It was Amos Hilty. He was bent over Mary Ellen, scrubbing her face with a wet washcloth. The child was wiggling and squirming, and she heard Amos say, "Mary Ellen, please stop *rutshing*—squirming!"

When the child spotted Miriam, she squealed and ran to her side. "Teacher! You look very pretty today. Doesn't she, Pappy?"

Miriam looked down at her own dark purple cotton dress with a black apron worn over the front of it. She wondered what there was about her that the child thought was pretty; in spite of herself, she remembered Nick McCormick's comment about her being beautiful. Her eyes met Amos's, and he smiled.

"Your teacher is a fine-looking woman," Amos said to Mary Ellen.

Miriam made no response.

Amos shifted his long legs as though he might be nervous. "Mary Ellen sampled some of Sarah's raspberries from the garden when we first arrived," he said. "She had sticky red juice all over her face."

Miriam nodded. "I came in for a drink of water. I will get it and be out of your way."

Amos stepped away from the sink. "Help yourself to the pump. I have done about as well as I can with this little scamp's dirty face anyway."

Miriam went to the cupboard and got out a glass; then she went to the sink, where she pumped out just enough water to quench her thirst. She wished that Amos would go outside and leave her alone, instead of standing there watching her.

"Will you sit at the table with Pappy and me during lunch after church?" Mary Ellen asked.

Miriam had to think quickly. "I believe my family is expecting me to eat with them."

"Mary Ellen, why don't you run outside and play now?" Amos said suddenly. "I want to speak with your teacher."

The child gave him a questioning look, but obediently she went out the back door, looking back over her shoulder to flash a winning smile at Miriam.

The last thing Miriam wanted was to be alone with Amos Hilty. She looked around the room, hoping that someone else would enter and rescue her from the determined man who stood by her side.

Amos pulled out a kitchen chair and motioned for her to sit down. Reluctantly, she obliged, and Amos took a seat directly across from her.

"Church will be starting soon," Miriam reminded.

Amos glanced at the wall clock. "We still have some time yet. I want to discuss something with you."

"About Mary Ellen?"

"No, about us."

"Us?" Miriam's voice sounded harsh and high-pitched, even to her own ears.

"*Jah.* It is about our relationship."

Miriam looked directly into Amos's serious brown eyes. She cleared her throat to stall for time. She wanted to be sure that her words were well chosen. "The only relationship we have is the fact that your daughter is one of my students. So, if this little talk is not about Mary Ellen, then what?"

Amos stood up and began pacing back and forth across the kitchen floor. "Miriam, surely you have been able to tell that I have an interest in you," he said.

Miriam's mouth dropped open. She hadn't expected such a bold declaration from him.

Amos hurried on. "I want to spend more time with you—to come courting. Yet every time I ask you to go someplace with Mary Ellen and me, you have an excuse why you can't. Whenever I try to talk to you, you are unfriendly and act as though you are trying to avoid me."

"I am sure that you mean well, Amos," Miriam replied, "but isn't the real truth that you really just want a mother for your little girl?"

Amos looked stunned. "Miriam, I—"

"You need not deny it, Amos Hilty," Miriam interrupted. "Everyone knows that you are a widower, without any family around to help you raise your daughter. It is understandable that you would want to find a wife to help care for her."

Amos looked down at the toes of his boots. "I—that is—I know that Mary Ellen is quite taken with you, Miriam. In fact, you are all that she talks about when she returns from school each day. However, I do have some concerns about the type of influence you could have on her young mind."

"What are you saying?" Miriam asked.

"I am saying you are quite melancholy, and I had hoped that if we started courting you might find more joy in life, and—"

"Now wait just a minute!" Miriam shouted. "Do you actually believe that you are such a wonderful person that just courting you would make me happy and delightful enough to have around your daughter?"

"That is not what I meant to say, Miriam." Amos sat back down at the table again. "I find you quite attractive, and I think we could get along rather well together if you would just give it a chance."

Miriam stood up abruptly and started across the room. She turned back and said, "There are several available Amish women in the valley, Amos. Some are a bit younger than me perhaps, but I am sure if you use your charms on one of them, you might persuade her to be your wife."

"But, I—" Amos stammered.

Miriam turned away from him and went out the door, slamming it on the way out.

Chapter 9

Heartless. . .heartless. . .heartless. . . The sound of the buggy wheels echoed in Miriam's ears as though they were calling out to her and reminding her of the heartless way she had behaved toward Amos that morning.

She probably had hurt his feelings by telling him she was not interested in him and that she knew he was only after her because of Mary Ellen, but at the time she hadn't cared about his feelings. She had such pain in her own heart because of William Graber, and now Amos was hurting her by using his child to try and gain her favor. How foolish did he believe her to be? She had been fooled by a man once, only to have her heart torn asunder. No, she would never allow herself to be hurt like that again.

When the Stoltzfus family arrived home from church, Miriam helped her mother bring their lunch dishes inside; then she hurried up to her room, saying that she wanted to change her dress. The truth was, she needed to be alone for awhile. She was beginning to feel another one of her headaches coming on, and rest was the only thing that ever seemed to help.

❧

The following day after lunch, Miriam and her mother were busy cleaning up the kitchen. The men had gone back out to the fields to work, leaving the women alone with a sink full of dirty dishes.

Mom filled the sink with hot water from the stove. "The men were certainly hungry, weren't they?" she said, as though she were trying to make some idle conversation.

"*Jah.* Just look at all the watermelon rinds in the bowl on the cupboard. I think Lewis ate three or four pieces himself."

"Our men do have some pretty hearty appetites," Mom agreed. "Speaking of men—I was talking with Amos Hilty yesterday, right after the worship service. He asked me—that is, he was wondering if I would speak to you on his behalf."

Miriam dropped the wet dishrag into the soapy water so hard that it sent several large bubbles drifting toward the ceiling. "I do not believe this!" she cried. "Doesn't that man ever give up? I thought I had made myself quite clear to him yesterday. Obviously my words must have fallen on deaf ears!"

"Now, Miriam, please calm down," her mother said soothingly. "I have probably made a mistake bringing this up, but Amos seemed very upset after he talked with you yesterday."

"*Jah,* I can just imagine."

"He is afraid you may have the wrong impression of him—of his intentions, that is," Anna continued.

"Oh, his intentions are very clear. At least to me, they are!" Miriam said loudly. "Mom, can't you see it, too? He just wants a housekeeper and a mother for Mary Ellen."

"I'm sure he wants more than that."

"Oh, *jah!* He wants someone to darn his socks and cook his meals, too. Well, that someone is not going to be me!"

Mom reached out and placed a gentle hand on Miriam's trembling arm. "Miriam, is it so wrong for a man to want those things? They are all part of the married life, you know."

"Then let him get a hired girl or someone else to help out. Just tell Amos for me that I want to be left alone!"

"I believe that he does have a hired girl come in part-time, and you know Amos has no relatives to call on. His parents are both deceased, and his two brothers have farms of their own to run. I am told that his in-laws live in another state, so—"

"I am truly sorry about all of that," Miriam interrupted, "but it is really not my problem. And it is certainly not reason enough for me to marry Amos Hilty!"

"Has he asked you to marry him?" Mom asked in a hopeful tone.

"Well, no, he just asked to come calling, but—"

"I think he only wants to establish a friendship with you for now, Miriam. In time you will both know if there is a chance for love or marriage."

"I can already tell you that there is no chance for either love or marriage. Not for me, at least," Miriam stated flatly. She marched across the room and picked up the big ceramic bowl. "I'm going out to the pasture to give these rinds to the cows."

❧

Out in the pasture, the herd of dairy cows grazed contentedly. They perked up their ears when they saw Miriam coming. She dumped the watermelon rinds over the fence, then stood watching as several of them ate greedily.

"Ach, my, you silly old cows. You carry on as though you haven't a thing to eat," she scolded. "See here, you have a whole pasture of green grass to eat!"

She lingered for awhile, watching the mothers with their young ones. She was in no hurry to get back inside to more of Mom's meddling. She was glad that September was only a few weeks away, and school would be starting up soon. She was looking forward to teaching again. Being at home all summer long gave her too much time to think. Even though there were always plenty of chores to do, it wasn't the same as keeping her brain busy. Besides, when she was around home more, Mom seemed to meddle in her life more.

Miriam leaned on the fence rail and watched with interest as a mother cow began washing her baby with her big rough tongue. For some reason it reminded her of the sight she had witnessed when she'd stepped into Sarah's kitchen and found Amos scrubbing his daughter's face. The baby cow was squirming about, just as Mary Ellen had done.

"I suppose all little ones need a mother to take care of them," she whispered. "Mary Ellen is such a sweet child. For her sake, I hope that Amos does find a suitable wife—but it certainly won't be me!"

Chapter 10

The first day of school was always a little hectic and unorganized. There were several new children in class, and since they were first graders and knew only their Pennsylvania Dutch language, they needed to be taught English. This took extra time on the teacher's part, and it meant that the older students must do more work on their own.

Mary Ellen Hilty was in the second grade and already knew her English fairly well, but still she lacked the discipline and attention span to work on her own for very long. From her seat in the second row, she raised her hand and called, "Teacher! Teacher, I need your help."

Miriam felt impatient as she frowned at the child. She was busy teaching Joanna Jost and Nona Shenk the letters of the alphabet, and she did not want to be disturbed.

"Teacher!" Mary Ellen called again.

Miriam put her fingers to her lips. "One minute, Mary Ellen. I will be with you in just a minute."

Mary Ellen nodded and smiled. She folded her hands and placed them on top of her desk, as she waited patiently.

When Miriam finished with her explanation to Nona and Joanna, she went over to Mary Ellen and squatted down beside her desk. "What is it, Mary Ellen?"

"I don't know what this word is." The child pointed to the open primer in front of her.

"That word is *grandfather*," Miriam answered. "You must learn to sound it out. Gr-and-fa-ther."

Mary Ellen looked up at Miriam. Her hazel eyes were round and large. "My grandpa and grandma Zeeman live far away. Grandpa and Grandma Hilty live in heaven with Jesus. So does Mama."

Miriam noticed a sadness about the child's face that she had never seen before. Usually there was a light in her eyes and a warm smile on her lips. For a moment she allowed herself to feel pity for the young girl. She had no one but her father to look after her. No one but him to love.

The smile was quickly back on Mary Ellen's face. "Thank you for helping me, Teacher."

Miriam touched the child's arm lightly. "You are welcome."

Back at her own desk, Miriam found herself watching Mary Ellen instead of grading the morning spelling papers that were lying before her. The child never actually looked unkempt, but her hair always showed telltale signs of not being

36

secured tightly enough in the braided knot at the back of her head. Her face was always scrubbed squeaky clean, which came as no surprise to Miriam after watching Amos wash the child's face on Sunday morning in Sarah's kitchen.

Miriam shook her head, bringing her thoughts back to the present. She had no desire to think about that day or to be reminded in any way of the things that Amos had said to her. Regardless of everyone's denial, she knew that Amos's interest in her was purely selfish. A mother for his child was what he wanted the most. Though Mary Ellen was a dear child, and Miriam had to admit that she did have a soft spot for her, it was certainly not enough reason to marry, or even to court, the girl's father. If she did ever marry, it would have to be for love, and that possibility seemed seriously doubtful.

Mary Ellen looked up then and smiled at her teacher. It was a warm, heart-melting smile, and Miriam found herself fighting the urge to go to the child and hold her in her arms. For one brief moment, she wanted to tell her that she would marry her father and be her new mama. That she would love her and take care of her needs. Instead, she just smiled back at Mary Ellen, then quickly turned her attention back to her spelling papers. What on earth had she been thinking of? she wondered. The idea was absolutely absurd!

The children always looked forward to lunchtime. When the teacher pulled the rope for the noon bell, she would be caught up in a stampede of children as they made a mad dash for their brightly colored lunch buckets. Today was certainly no exception, and Miriam fumed as she was nearly knocked over by one of the older boys.

"Slow down once!" Miriam exclaimed. "You don't need to be in such a *shussel!*"

Kenneth Freisen grunted an apology and hurried to his seat with his lunch bucket.

It only took about five minutes for the children to gobble down their lunches and scamper outside to play for the remaining twenty-five minutes of lunch break. Games of baseball, drop-the-hanky, and hopscotch could be seen being played around the school playground.

Miriam stood at the window, watching the children and wondering if the ache she felt between her temples would turn into another one of her pounding migraine headaches. The day was only half over, and already she felt physically and emotionally drained. She wondered if teaching was really her intended calling in life. She often ran out of patience with the children, and when she felt as she did today, she wondered if perhaps her mother was right. Maybe she should find a husband and settle down to be just a homemaker and wife.

"What am I thinking?" she chided herself. "Even if I did want to get married, which I do not, I am not in love with anyone, and I will never marry without love or trust—both of which I do not feel for Amos." She shrugged and decided that her mood was only because it was the first day of school; in a few days, when everything became a routine again, she would be glad she was teaching school.

Miriam's thoughts were interrupted when a ruckus broke out in the school yard outside. Several children were laughing and shouting, and many were standing around in a large circle.

Miriam hurried outside to see what the noise was all about. Several of the children pulled away from the crowd when they saw their teacher approaching.

"What is the trouble here?" Miriam asked Kenneth Freisen, who stood nearby.

"Aw, it is just some of the girls. *Sie Sin glene Bapel Meiler*—they are little blabbermouths."

Miriam pulled two of the girls aside, and that was when she saw Mary Ellen Hilty standing in the middle of the circle. Tears were streaming down her round cheeks, and she was sniffing between sobs.

"Mary Ellen, what is it? Are you hurt?" Miriam asked with concern.

"It's all right. They didn't mean it, I'm sure," Mary Ellen said quietly. She managed a weak smile through her tears.

"Who did not mean it? Did someone hurt you?"

"She is just a little crybaby," Kenneth Freisen stated. "She can't even take a bit of teasing."

Miriam eyed him suspiciously. "And who was doing this teasing, might I ask?"

"It wasn't me, Teacher. It was the girls. Like I said before, they are blabbermouths."

"Very well, which of you girls was involved, and what were you teasing Mary Ellen about?" Miriam asked impatiently. The pain in her head was increasing, and she feared the dizziness and nausea that usually followed would soon be upon her as well.

The cluster of children became suddenly very quiet. Not one child stepped forward to announce his or her part in the teasing.

Miriam frowned and rubbed her forehead. "Very well then, the entire class shall stay after school for thirty minutes."

"But, that's not fair, Teacher! Why should we all be punished for something that just a few girls said?" Kenneth said loudly.

"*Jah,* I didn't do anything, and I'll be sent to the woodshed if I'm late," Karen Lederach whined. "My papa doesn't like tardiness."

"My mama has chores waiting for me," Grace Seitz said.

Miriam looked at Mary Ellen. "What about it, Mary Ellen? Won't you tell me now who is guilty and what they said?"

Mary Ellen shuffled her feet nervously, and with tear-filled eyes, she whispered, "I'll tell you in private what they said, but I can't say who said it. It would be tattling, and Pappy doesn't like a tattletale. He has said so many times." She smiled. "Besides, the Bible tells us to do to others as we would have them do to us. I wouldn't want someone to get me in trouble."

Miriam led her inside the school building and looked down into the little girl's sad face. "All right, Mary Ellen. Please tell me now what this was all about."

Mary Ellen looked up at her. "The children notice that I don't dress like them.

My pappy. . .he doesn't always know how things should go and neither do I. Today I had my dress on backwards and I never even knew it." She bit her lip. "That's why some of the children were laughing. But please don't punish them."

Miriam nodded reluctantly. "You have set a good example for the entire class, Mary Ellen." She helped Mary Ellen to put her dress on the right way around, and then she went back outside and looked at each of the other children. "I hope you have all learned something today. No one will be required to stay after school this time, but if this ever happens again, I will punish the entire class. I don't care if you all have to go to the woodshed when you go home. Is that quite clear?"

All heads nodded in unison.

"Now get on back to your play. Lunchtime will be over soon." Miriam smiled at Mary Ellen, and the child smiled back.

She really is a dear girl. Mary Ellen, the heartsome, Miriam mused. *Even in the face of adversity, she still has a loving heart. I wonder how she does it?*

Chapter 11

The days of September went by quickly, and Miriam fell back into her role as teacher, just as she had done for the past several years. She still had days of frustration and tension, leading to her now-familiar sick headaches, but at least she was busy, and she was doing something that she felt was worthwhile and meaningful.

One afternoon, after school had been dismissed for the day, Miriam decided to pay a visit to Crystal. It had been awhile since they had taken the time for a good visit, and she was certainly in need of one now.

When Miriam pulled her horse and buggy to a stop in front of Jonas and Crystal's farmhouse, she saw Crystal outside removing her dry laundry from the clothesline. Miriam called to her, and Crystal turned and waved, then motioned for Miriam to follow her inside the house.

Crystal deposited the laundry basket on a kitchen chair and pulled out another one for her Miriam to sit on. "It's so good to see you. You have been on my mind a lot lately and also in my prayers."

"Oh, really? Why is that?"

Crystal shrugged and began to fold the clothes in the laundry basket. "I have been praying for your happiness" was her simple reply.

"Perhaps it is not meant for some to be happy," Miriam said with a deep sadness in her voice.

"I do not believe that for a moment, and neither should you," Crystal answered firmly. "We have been taught since we were children that life offers each of us choices. God gave us all the ability to choose what we will think and feel. He expects the believer to make the right choices and choose to follow Him. He expects us to be happy and content with our lives."

Miriam frowned. "That is easy for you to say. You are happily married to a man you love deeply, and you have two beautiful little boys. How could you not be happy?"

Crystal dropped the towel she was holding back into the basket and pulled out a chair next to Miriam. After taking a seat, she reached out and took one of Miriam's hands. "Please do not be envious of my life. You can have the same happiness as well."

Miriam stood up suddenly, nearly knocking over her chair. "How dare you speak to me like that! I thought that you were supposed to be my best friend!"

"I–I am," Crystal stammered.

"Then do not talk to me as though I am a child."

"I wasn't. I mean, I don't think of you as a child," Crystal said. "I was merely trying to tell you—"

"That I should marry someone?" Miriam interrupted. "Were you thinking of Amos Hilty, perhaps? Listen, I have some news for you, friend. Marrying that man would never make me happy! He does not love me. All he wants is a mother for Mary Ellen and, of course, someone to do all of his cooking and cleaning. Furthermore, I certainly do not feel any love for Amos!"

"Sometimes one can learn to love," Crystal said gently.

"Did you have to *learn* to love my brother?"

"Well, no, but—"

Miriam interrupted again. "I came here because I needed to be with my best friend. Can't we please change the subject and just enjoy each other's company?" She went to the sink and got herself a glass of water. She was beginning to feel another headache coming on.

"Of course we can change the subject," Crystal was quick to agree. "I'm very sorry if I upset or offended you. It's just that I want you to be as happy as I am."

"Please, do not worry and fret over me. I am doing just fine without a husband, and who cares if I'm not truly happy anyway? I have come to accept the fact that life is not always meant to be a bowl full of sweet cherries. I—" She broke off as she heard a horse and buggy pull into the yard, and she went to look out the window.

"Who is it?" Crystal asked.

Miriam peered out the window. "It looks like Lewis. Maybe he's looking for me. Mom probably sent him to tell me that she needs my help. It is getting pretty close to suppertime."

Crystal glanced at the clock across the room. "You're right. I'm surprised that the twins aren't up from their naps yet."

There was the sound of a man's boots on the back porch; then suddenly the back door flew open, and Lewis burst into the room.

Miriam could not remember ever seeing her younger brother look so upset before. He almost looked as though he were afraid of something. Even as a child, he had always been the brave and fearless one.

"What is it, Lewis?" Miriam cried. "You look as though you've seen something terrible."

Crystal pulled out a chair for him. "Here, you had better sit down."

"No, there is no time," Lewis said breathlessly. "We have got to go *schnell!*"

"Go where?" Miriam asked.

"To the hospital." Lewis's voice quivered, and it was obvious that he was close to tears.

"The hospital? Is someone ill? Who is it, Lewis? Tell us, please." Miriam's tone was pleading.

"It's Papa. He—he was working in the fields with me, and everything was just fine—at least I thought it was, but suddenly Papa turned very pale, clutched at his

41

chest, then he just fell over."

Miriam gasped, and Crystal waited silently as Lewis continued. "It took everything we had, but Mom and I finally got him into the buggy, and then we went straight to the hospital."

"What is it? What do the doctors say is wrong with Papa?" Miriam asked.

Lewis shook his head. "They are still running tests, but they think it might be his heart."

"A heart attack?" Crystal asked.

Lewis nodded. "Where is Jonas? He should be told, too."

"He is still out in the fields with my pa. If you and Miriam want to go on ahead to the hospital, I will send Jonas as soon as he comes back to the house."

"I'll leave my buggy here and ride with Lewis, if that's all right," Miriam said to Crystal.

"*Jah,* of course. We will see that it is brought back to your place later," Crystal answered.

Lewis reached for Miriam's arm. "I have already notified Andrew, and he is on his way to the hospital. Let's go now, before it's too late."

"Too late? What do you mean, too late? Is Papa's condition that serious?" Miriam felt the blood drain from her face and tears begin to fill her eyes.

Lewis nearly pushed her toward the door. "The doctors are not sure, but Papa isn't even conscious, and—"

"You two hurry along then," Crystal interrupted. "Jonas will be there soon. I expect him any minute."

"*Seind Papa eingedenkt in Gebeth*—remember Papa in your prayers," Miriam called over her shoulder.

Chapter 12

Papa's condition proved to be very serious. The doctors confirmed that he had suffered a massive heart attack. His wife and four children stood around his bed as the doctor gave the shocking news that because his heart was so weak, he would probably not survive the night, though they would do all they could for him.

"But how can this be?" Mom cried. "My Henry has always been a strong, healthy man!"

"Sometimes as we get older—" the doctor began.

"Older? My papa is only fifty-seven years old!" Miriam shouted. "He is not old, and he is not going to die!" She shook her finger in front of the young doctor's face.

"Miriam, please calm down," Jonas said soothingly. He put his arm around her waist and pulled her off to one side. "If it is the will of God, Papa will live. If not—"

"If not, then what? Do we all just put on a happy face and go on living as though Papa had never been a part of us?" Miriam shrieked.

"Miriam, please do not do this," Mom said tearfully. "We all need to remain calm. We need to pray for Papa."

Miriam's thoughts suddenly drew inward. How many times had she prayed over the last several years? How many of her prayers had God answered? Had He kept William from falling in love with someone else? Had He given William back to her? Surely He could have caused William to change his mind and return to Pennsylvania. Had God made the pain in her broken heart go away?

Miriam felt so weary of praying and receiving no answers. Still, she knew in her heart that prayer was the only chance her papa had now. So, she would pray, and she would even plead and bargain with God. Perhaps He would trade her life for Papa's. If she was gone, she would not be so greatly missed, but Papa was badly needed by all the family, and especially by Mom.

"I will be out in the waiting room, praying," she whispered to Mom. "Send Lewis to get me if I am needed or if Papa wakes up." She glanced at her father's still form, lying on the cold hospital bed, hooked up to machines and an IV needle. Quickly, she ran from the room.

The waiting room was empty when Miriam entered. She was glad for the chance to be alone. Silently, she began to pace back and forth, going from the window to the doorway and back again, pleading with God to heal her father.

At one point, Miriam stopped in front of the window and stared out at the street below. Several cars were parked along the curb, and several more were driving past. Some children rode bicycles on the sidewalk below. A bird flew past the window and landed in a nearby tree. The world was still going about its business as usual. It was a world that she and her Amish family had chosen to be separate from, based on the biblical teachings of nonconformity. Yet now, due to unwelcome circumstances, here they were being forced to accept the modern ways in order to provide her father with the best medical care available. Home remedies and herbal cures would simply not be appropriate for something so grave as a heart attack. But would modern medicine be enough? Could these doctors, in their fancy up-to-date hospital with all its machines and gadgets, really save Papa's life and bring him back to them again? If, by some miracle of God, he did get well enough to come home, would he ever be whole and complete, able to work on the farm again?

The waiting room door swung open suddenly, interrupting Miriam's thoughts and prayers. Jonas and Andrew both stood in the doorway, their faces pale and somber. "Papa is gone," Andrew said in a near whisper.

Papa is gone. Papa is gone. The dreaded words echoed inside of Miriam's head. Once more her prayers had gone unanswered. Once more her heart would ache with pain. It wasn't fair. Life wasn't fair! Without even a word to either of her older brothers, she ran from the room.

Tears blinded Miriam's eyes as she stumbled down the long hospital corridor. Her only thought was to run away—to escape from this awful place of death, though she had no idea where she was going. She passed by the elevator, not wanting to bother with the modern convenience, and ran quickly down two flights of stairs. She opened the door, which led outside, and was just about to step out into the evening air, when she ran directly into a strong pair of arms.

"Hey there, fair lady! You just about knocked me off my tired feet!"

Miriam looked up into the deepest pair of blue eyes she had ever seen. They were mesmerizing eyes. "Mr. McCormick!"

Nick McCormick smiled broadly, showing his straight, white teeth. "We do seem to keep bumping into each other, don't we, Miriam Stoltzfus?"

Miriam could only nod as she reached up to wipe away her tears.

"And please," Nick continued, not seeming to notice her tear-streaked face, "dispense with the formalities of Mr. and just start calling me Nick."

Miriam moved away from the tall, blond-haired man who stood in front of her, blocking the exit door of the hospital. She had no desire to make conversation with the Englishman, and she certainly did not want him to see how upset she was.

"If you will excuse me, I was on my way out," Miriam managed to say.

"I can certainly see that. You almost ran me over." Nick squinted his eyes at her. "Sorry, I didn't notice before, but I can see now that you are upset. Is there something I can do to help? I really do enjoy rescuing damsels in distress, you know." He winked.

"I—uh—am fine. I mean, I will be all right if I can just get some fresh air."

"Then air you shall have, fair lady." Nick stood to one side and politely opened the door so that Miriam could walk through.

Once outside, she took several deep breaths, allowing the cool evening air to fill her lungs and clear her head. Her legs took her quickly down the sidewalk and away from the hospital.

Chapter 13

"Slow down. What's your hurry?" Nick called as he hurried to keep up with Miriam.

Miriam turned to see him directly behind her. "I thought I was alone. I mean, I didn't know you had followed me," she stammered.

"Do you mind?" Nick asked.

"Don't you have business at the hospital?" she asked, avoiding the question.

Nick shrugged. "I was there to cover a story about an old man who was beaten and robbed at a convenience store."

"Oh, how awful! Maybe you should—"

"It can wait," Nick said quickly. "Right now, I think maybe you need someone to talk to."

"Front-page headlines or a back-page article?" Miriam asked sarcastically.

"You insult my integrity, fair lady. I have no intention of conducting a newspaper interview with you. I just thought you could use a strong shoulder to cry on and maybe even a little heartfelt sympathy."

Miriam sniffed indignantly. "What makes you think I need any sympathy?"

Nick reached down and wiped away a tear that still lingered on her cheek. "You've been crying."

Miriam knew she could not deny her tears. She also knew she really did need someone to talk to. "Jah, I have been crying," she admitted shakily. "My papa just died of a massive heart attack."

"Then shouldn't you be with your family at a time like this?" Nick asked.

Miriam nodded. "Jah, but I have no words of comfort to offer any of them. I just want to be alone."

"Oh, I see. You want to be alone in your misery, is that it?" Nick asked bluntly.

"Jah, exactly." Miriam began to walk briskly again, hoping to leave the obstinate man behind. Perhaps she did not need his listening ear after all.

But the newspaper reporter was not to be put off so easily. He kept in step with her and even offered her his arm, though she declined with a shake of her head. "Let's go somewhere for a cup of coffee," he suggested.

"I told you—"

"Yes, I know—you'd rather be alone," Nick finished her sentence. "Maybe that is how you think you feel, but I think if you search your heart, you'll discover that what you really need is someone to talk to. I promise not to include our conversation in my next article on the Amish—and I won't take any pictures." Nick laughed, and even Miriam had to smile slightly, though her throat was thick with tears.

"Oh, all right," she conceded. "I suppose a cup of coffee could do no harm."

The little café Nick picked was just a few blocks from the hospital, and it was nearly empty when they stepped inside. They took a seat at a booth in the far corner, and Nick ordered them both a cup of coffee and a piece of apple pie.

Miriam declined the pie, saying that she wasn't hungry, but Nick insisted that she needed the nourishment and that it would make her feel better if she ate something.

Miriam found the man's controlling ways to be very irritating, yet for some strange reason, she allowed him to have his way. She gave in and ate the pie, finding that she was actually hungry after all.

"Feeling better?" Nick asked as he watched her eat the piece of pie.

Miriam nodded. "At least my empty stomach does. I had no supper tonight. After school let out, I stopped to see my sister-in-law for a few minutes. I planned to be home in plenty of time to help Mom with supper, but then my brother, Lewis, came by and told us that Papa had collapsed while he was at work in the fields. We all rushed to the hospital, and—well, you know the rest."

Miriam took a deep breath and shook her head slowly. She could not believe that she was sitting here in a café, with a man she barely knew, pouring out her heart to him. Maybe that was why she felt free to do it, because she didn't really know him. He had no expectations of her. He would make no demands on her emotionally.

Nick reached out and took her hand, and she made no effort to stop him or to take her hand away. The comfort that he offered felt good. It was something she hadn't felt in a very long while.

"I think I understand how you must feel," Nick said softly. "I lost my own dad when I was just nine years old. I was an only child, and Mom and I had it pretty rough for several years."

"How did you manage?" Miriam asked.

"It was hard. We lived with my grandparents for a few years. They looked after me while Mom went back to school for some training. She became a nurse, and then she was able to support us by working at a hospital in Chicago. That's where I'm from." Nick scratched his head with his free hand and looked thoughtful. "Those were some tough times, all right, but I think they helped to strengthen me."

"Where is your mother now?" Miriam asked.

"She's still living in Chicago. When I was about fifteen, she remarried. I never got along very well with her new husband, so after I finished high school, I went to a college out of state. I majored in journalism, and after college, I worked at several small newspapers. When the newspaper here in Lancaster offered me a job, I took it." Nick smiled at her and winked. "And you know the rest of the story."

Miriam could feel her cheeks beginning to warm. It had been so long since she'd been in the company of a young, good-looking man. She had forgotten how pleasant it could feel, and now, with her heart aching, his attention was like balm. Nick McCormick had actually made her forget about her grief for a few brief moments. "Do you live in Lancaster alone, or are you—?"

"Married?" Nick finished her question.

She nodded, wondering what on earth had caused her to be so bold, or for that matter, why she even cared whether he was married or not. She quickly pulled her hand out of his and nervously reached up to straighten her head covering.

Nick laughed. "No, I'm not married. It's not that I have anything against the state of matrimony. Guess I've just never met a woman who captured my heart enough to make me want to settle down and start a family." He winked again. "Of course, any woman who could put up with me would have to be a real gem."

Miriam smiled. "I think maybe I should be getting back to the hospital now. My family might begin to think that I have deserted them."

Nick nodded, his eyes sympathetic.

"Thank you for your kindness, Mr. McCormick—I mean, Nick. I do feel better after talking to you. But the days ahead will be difficult ones." She gulped. "I don't know how we will manage without Papa—but you have reminded me that pain and death touch everyone's lives at some time or another. I feel fortunate that I'm not an only child. I know that my three brothers will help out, and at least Mom won't have to support herself. And, of course, I will be there to help with some of the extra chores."

"Do you have a job outside the home?" Nick asked.

Jah, I am a schoolteacher."

"That's right; you said earlier that you were on the way home from school when you found out about your father," Nick said. "I don't imagine that an Amish teacher makes much, though."

The magic of the moment was suddenly gone, and Miriam's mind came back into proper focus. "I make enough!" she snapped.

"No, hold your horses, fair lady. I meant no harm in asking about your wages," Nick said, holding one hand in the air, as though he was asking for a truce. "I was only trying to show my concern for your situation. If you hadn't been so quick to cut me off, I was about to say that if there is ever anything I can do to help you or your family, please feel free to call me at the newspaper office."

"That is very kind of you," Miriam said, her voice softening some, "but we Amish always help each other in times of need, and—"

"And you're not used to asking favors of modern Englishmen?" asked Nick.

"Mr. McCormick—I mean, Nick, I really do appreciate your kind offer, and I thank you for your listening ear tonight. I'll think about calling you if I should ever need your help."

Nick smiled and stood up. "I'd better pay for our eats; then I'll walk you back to the hospital."

"Really, there's no need," Miriam was quick to say. "I can find my own way back."

Nick shook his head. "You Amish are sure a proud people, aren't you? Have you forgotten that I have an interview at the hospital? I was going in as you were going out," he reminded her.

The walk back to the hospital was a silent one. When they entered the building, Miriam extended her hand to Nick. "I thank you again for your kindness to me."

Nick returned the handshake. "It was all my pleasure, Miriam. I'm only sorry for the circumstances." He squeezed her hand gently, then turned toward the information desk, then back again. "Don't forget my offer of help. Should you ever need the listening ear or the services of a worldly Englishman, just go to your nearest phone booth and call my office."

Chapter 14

The days following Papa's death were dark ones. First, there was the funeral and all the preparations that went with it. Miriam had never lost anyone close to her before. When her Grandmother Gehman died, she had only been five years old. She hardly even remembered her mother's mother at all. And Grandpa Gehman, who moved to Illinois shortly after his wife's death, had passed on nearly ten years ago, when Miriam was still a young teenage girl. She had never been close to her maternal grandfather and really did not know him very well. Neither of their deaths had affected her the way that Papa's had. Both of his parents were still alive, though living in another county with Papa's oldest brother. It was not natural for aged parents to outlive their children.

Just three short days after Papa's death, Miriam stood with her friends and family and watched as his plain pine box was taken from the horse-drawn hearse and set in place at the burial site. She closed her eyes tightly, trying to block out the memory of her final look at Papa's face. Dressed in traditional white, his body had been available for viewing during the two-hour funeral service, which was held at the Stoltzfus home before the burial. Though the local undertaker had done a fine job, Miriam's father no longer looked like himself. The stark reality that he was truly gone was more than she could bear.

Why, Lord? Why? she asked God now, as a tear slipped beneath her closed eyelids. *How could You have taken Papa from us?* She opened her eyes and glanced to her right, where she saw her mother, openly weeping as the bishop said the final words over her husband of thirty-five years. *Is Mom really strong enough to make it without Papa?* Miriam wondered. Would she herself be able to offer Mom the kind of emotional support that she would need in the days to come?

With a heavy heart and a firm resolve, Miriam decided right then that she must have a determined heart. Through her own sheer will, she needed to put her grief and pain behind her so that she could be strong for Mom and the rest of the family.

When the burial service was finally over, everyone in attendance climbed back into their waiting buggies, and forming a single line, they all followed the Stoltzfus family back to their farm, where they would spend the remainder of the day eating and offering words of comfort and encouragement to the bereaved.

Miriam didn't feel very hungry, but rather than draw attention to the fact that she wasn't eating, she put a sandwich, some dilled cucumbers, and a piece of ginger-bread cake on her plate. After picking up a glass of iced tea, she quietly made her way to the lake, where she could be alone. Friends and family had been dropping by the house for the last three days, and today all the Amish families in the valley seemed to be present. She needed some quiet time, away from all of the sympathetic looks and words that were meant to be helpful.

The lake was always beautiful in the early fall. While the days were still warm, nighttime often brought with it a light frost, gently kissing the trees with crimson color.

Something about the peacefulness of the lake made her think of Nick McCormick, perhaps the fact that she and Nick had visited with each other in this same spot several months before.

Miriam felt herself blush, just thinking about how the obstinate man had sneaked up on her with his camera, and how he had taken her picture with her hair down and uncovered. *Now wouldn't that have made a fine photo for the* Daily Express? she thought to herself.

What was there about Nick that made her feel these unexplained emotions, anyway? She had only seen him on three occasions, and each time he had succeeded in making her angry, but he'd also made her smile. She had even opened up and talked to him in spite of her great pain in losing Papa. Nick was not one of her people, yet she felt closer to him than she had to any man in such a very long time.

William Graber had been the only man Miriam had ever shared her thoughts or feelings with, and when he left her for another woman, she vowed never to let herself get close to another man. While she wasn't exactly close to Nick McCormick, she had let him a little closer to her than she had any other man since William. Was it simply because he was so easy to talk to, or was it because he was an outsider, and she knew that there was no threat of a possible commitment?

Miriam's thoughts were interrupted when a male voice suddenly called out her name. She looked over her shoulder and saw Amos Hilty heading toward the lake. He was alone and was carrying a plate of food.

"I thought you might like something to eat," Amos said when he reached the lakeshore.

Miriam held up her half-eaten plate of food. "I am afraid I have not eaten what I already have. I guess you will just have to eat it yourself."

Amos laughed and took a seat on the grass beside her. "I already had one helping, but I suppose I could force myself to eat another. All this home-cooked food sure does whet the appetite. I am not really much of a cook, so I don't enjoy my own meals very much."

If that was a hint, it is wasted on me, Miriam thought. "Where is Mary Ellen?" she asked.

"She is playing little mother to your twin nephews," Amos answered. "Since she is occupied, I decided to sneak away and check up on you."

"What makes you think I need checking up on?" Miriam asked a bit too harshly.

Amos cleared his throat. "Well, it's just that—I know what it is like to lose

51

someone close to you, and I thought that I might have some words of comfort to offer." He reached out a large, well-callused hand and touched Miriam's shoulder lightly. "I am so sorry about Henry. He will be missed by all of the Amish community, as I am sure he will be sorely missed by his family. He was a good man."

Miriam knew in her heart that Amos was only trying to console her, but for reasons unknown to even her, she felt irritation instead of comfort from his words, and even his very presence made her edgy. Somewhere in the back of her mind, she wondered if he had an ulterior motive for his kindness. If he could win her heart with sympathy, then he might be able to gain her approval and perhaps even convince her that she needed a husband. Of course, Miriam reasoned, in reality, it was he who needed a wife. Someone to cook and clean for him. Someone to be a mother to his young daughter.

Miriam stood up quickly, brushing away the pieces of grass that clung to her cotton dress. "I really should be getting back to the house. Mom may be needing me."

Amos's deep brown eyes revealed his hurt, but Miriam tried not to notice. Maybe if she gave him the cold shoulder often enough, he would finally understand that she was not now—nor would she ever be—interested in him.

"Thank you for your kindness, Amos," Miriam added briskly, "but I am going to be fine, really. Life is full of hardships and pain, but each of us has the power within us to rise determinedly above our troubles and take control."

"The power within is God," Amos reminded her.

Miriam made no reply. Instead, she turned to go, then momentarily turned back and said, "I will help my family through this great time of loss."

"But what about you, Miriam? Who will help you in the days ahead?"

"I shall help myself!" Miriam turned around again, and this time she ran as quickly as she could. She needed to be as far from Amos Hilty as possible.

"Wann du mich mohl brauchst, dan komm Ich," Amos whispered. "When you need me, I will come."

Chapter 15

The routines of life had to go on, even for those in mourning. With Papa gone, Lewis had to work twice as hard to keep up with all of the farm chores. The alfalfa fields needed one final harvesting before winter set in, and the job was just too big for one man. Even with the use of modern machinery, it would have been a challenge, but horse-drawn plows made the work harder and more time-consuming. Andrew and Jonas pitched in to help, coming over early in the morning before doing their own chores, then returning again in the evening. Some of the neighboring Amish men also came to help. Miriam wondered how long they could keep it up and still maintain their own homes and jobs. Surely their families were suffering from their absences.

Mom, too, kept busier than ever as she worked tirelessly from sunrise to sunset. While it was true there was more work to do now that Papa was gone, Miriam suspected the main reason her mother kept so busy was so she would not spend all her waking hours thinking about Papa and how much she missed him. Often in the middle of the night, Miriam would be wakened by the sound of her mother crying. Her parents had had a good marriage, and Mom would probably never get over Papa's untimely death. *If only there was some simple way to erase all the pain in one's life*, Miriam often found herself thinking.

🌺

The fall harvest was finally completed, and everyone's workload had lightened just a bit. Lewis assured his older brothers and neighbors that he could manage the farm chores on his own now. Without too much argument, they all agreed that it would not be necessary for them to come over every day. They returned to their families and their own routines, reminding Lewis that he should call on them anytime he felt the need.

One afternoon in early November, Miriam dismissed her students early because of the threat of a storm. Angry-looking dark clouds hung over the schoolhouse yard, and the wind whipped madly against the trees. A torrential rain was sure to follow. By letting the children go now, they might all make it home before the earth was drenched from above.

"I'll give you a ride home," Miriam told her six-year-old niece Rebekah. "Wait for me out by my buggy."

Rebekah smiled, *"Ich will mit dir Hehm geh*—I want to go home with you." Impulsively, she gave her aunt a hug and ran out the schoolhouse door.

Miriam hurriedly erased the blackboard and was about to write the next day's assignment on it when a loud clap of thunder sounded. The small one-room schoolhouse shook, and then a terrible snapping sound rent the air, followed by a shrill scream.

Miriam rushed to the door. A sob caught in her throat when she saw that Rebekah was lying on the ground next to her buggy, a large tree limb lying across her back. "Oh, dear God," she prayed, "please let her be all right."

Rebekah was unconscious when Miriam got to her. There was a gash on her head, with some bleeding, but Miriam could not tell the full extent of her injuries. She felt so helpless and alone. All the other children had already left for home. There was no one to help her and no one to tell her what to do. She knew that the child must be taken to the hospital to be examined, but she was afraid to move her, lest she cause more damage. She knew there was a pay telephone booth just a mile or so down the road, but if she went to call for help, Rebekah would have to be left all alone.

Miriam seldom found herself wishing for modern conveniences, but right now she would have given nearly anything if there had been a telephone inside of the schoolhouse. "Oh, Lord, what should I do?" she prayed as she wrapped a piece of cloth from her apron around Rebekah's head. The young woman with a determined heart, who only a few short months ago had decided she could handle all of life's problems on her own, suddenly realized that she needed God's help. "Lord, I do not ask this for myself, but for the dear, sweet child who lies at my feet. Please send someone now, or I must leave her alone and go for help."

Suddenly, Miriam heard the sound of an approaching buggy. She held her breath and waited as it came into sight; then she rushed toward it when it entered the school yard.

The driver of the buggy was Amos Hilty, who explained that he had come to pick up Mary Ellen because of the approaching storm.

"Oh, Amos, Mary Ellen has already gone on home. I let all the children go early because of the bad weather. But a tree limb fell on my little niece Rebekah, and now she is lying on the ground unconscious. I was so frightened to leave her alone and go for help." Miriam's voice shook with emotion, and her breath came out in short, raspy gasps.

"Let's put her in my buggy, and we will take her to the hospital," Amos suggested.

"Oh, no! I don't think she should be moved. What if something is broken? What if—"

"Very well, then, you wait right here with the child, and I will go call for help. There is a pay phone just down the road."

Miriam nodded. "Please hurry, Amos. She hasn't opened her eyes at all. I think it might be very serious."

❧

It seemed like hours until the ambulance arrived, but it had only been about twenty minutes from the time that Amos had gone. The wind was still howling, but fortunately the rain held off until right after Rebekah, who had been strapped to a hard, straight board with her neck wrapped in a large collar, was placed safely inside the back of the ambulance.

"I need to go to the hospital with her," Miriam told Amos, who had returned to the schoolhouse to offer further assistance. "But someone needs to notify Andrew and Sarah."

"You ride along in the ambulance, and I will go by my farm and get Mary Ellen; then I will go tell your brother and his wife what happened."

"My buggy. What about my horse and buggy?"

"I shall see that they get safely home for you." Amos reached out and touched Miriam's arm lightly. "Try not to worry. Just pray, Miriam. We must trust God in situations like this."

Miriam nodded and climbed numbly into the back of the waiting ambulance.

As the ambulance pulled out of the school yard with its siren blaring, Miriam looked back and saw Amos climbing into his buggy. "I never even told him thank you," she whispered.

❧

After several hours of testing, the doctor's reports were finally given to Rebekah's family. The news was very grave. The child had a concussion and a bad gash on her head where the tree limb had hit. That was no doubt the reason for her still being unconscious. But even worse news was the fact that Rebekah's spinal cord had been severely injured, and if she lived, she would never walk again.

Miriam choked back a sob when the doctor gave them the shocking news, and Sarah began to cry hysterically. Andrew put his arms around his wife and tried to comfort her, but he, too, had tears running down his cheeks. It was much too hard for any of them to accept. First Papa's heart attack, and now this. How much did the Lord think that one family could take? *Why would He allow such a thing to happen to an innocent young child?* Miriam asked herself.

"I—I am so sorry," Miriam told her brother and his wife. "If only I had not asked her to wait for me—" Her voice broke, and she ran from the room in tears.

As Miriam made her way quickly down the hospital hallway, she felt like she was reliving the past—the terrible night that she had fled the hospital when Papa died. When she opened the door that led to the street, she half expected to see Nick McCormick standing there. But he wasn't there this time to offer her words of comfort and a listening ear. Suddenly, she remembered his last words to her. "If there's anything I can do to help you or your family, please call me at the newspaper," he'd said.

Should she call? she wondered. Would Nick really be able to help her? Should she even be turning to an outsider for comfort and support? Surely it wasn't wrong to reach out for help when one was in need. Miriam turned the corner and headed for the pay phone at the end of the block. Her head was pounding, and her fingers shook as she dialed the number of the *Daily Express.*

"Hello. May I speak to Nick McCormick? He is a reporter at your newspaper," Miriam said into the receiver.

"One moment, please," the woman's voice on the other end of the phone said.

Miriam held her breath and waited anxiously until finally she heard, "This is Nick McCormick. How may I help you?"

"It is Miriam Stoltzfus, Mr. McCormick—I mean, Nick. You said that I should call if I ever needed anything."

"That I did, fair lady! What can I do for you?" Nick responded warmly.

Miriam reached up to rub the side of her pounding temple. She hoped that she wasn't about to be sick. "I—uh, that is—I need to talk. Can we meet somewhere?"

"Where are you now?" Nick asked.

"Just a block away from the hospital."

"The hospital? Are you all right?"

"It's not me. It is—" Miriam's voice broke.

"Miriam, whatever has happened, I am so sorry," Nick said softly. "Remember the little café where we had coffee a few months ago?"

"I remember," Miriam managed to say.

"Meet me there in fifteen minutes," Nick told her. "You can tell me all about it then."

Chapter 16

The café was full of people when Miriam arrived. A quick look at the clock on the far wall told her it was the dinner hour. Her eyes sought out an empty booth, but there was none. She stood there nervously, as all eyes seemed to be upon her. Was it the fact that she was wearing plain clothes that set her apart from the rest of the world? she wondered.

"May I help you, Miss?" a man's voice called from behind the counter.

"I—uh—that is, I am meeting someone, and we need a table for two," Miriam stammered.

"The tables and booths are all filled, as you can probably see, but you can take a seat on one of the stools right here at the counter, if you would like."

Not knowing what else to do, Miriam took a seat, as he had suggested. She began to look at the menu the man handed her, but nothing really appealed to her. How could she have an appetite for food when her niece was lying in the hospital, unconscious, with the prospect of being a cripple for the rest of her life? Rebekah could even die, they had been told.

Miriam looked up when a firm hand was placed on her shoulder. "Nick! How did you get here so quickly?"

Nick shook his head. "It's been over thirty minutes since we talked, and I told you fifteen. I'm actually late, fair lady, and I'm sorry to have kept you waiting."

Miriam glanced at the clock. "I guess I lost track of time."

Nick looked around. "It's really crowded in here. Was this the only seat you could find?"

Miriam nodded. "I'm afraid so. I have been waiting for one of the booths, but no one seems to be in much of a hurry to leave."

"Are you very hungry?" Nick asked.

"No, not really, but I could use something to drink, and maybe some aspirin." Miriam rubbed her forehead.

"Headache?"

She nodded. "I get really bad migraines whenever I'm under too much stress, and I don't have any White Willow Bark herb capsules with me. They usually help."

"I'll get you some iced tea to go," Nick offered. "I've got some aspirin in the glove box of my car. How about if we go for a ride? We can talk better if we have some privacy, and I don't think we'll get any in here."

"I—I suppose it would be all right," Miriam said hesitantly.

"I know that you Amish aren't supposed to drive a car, but it's okay for you to ride in one, isn't it?" Nick asked.

"*Jah,* but only when it is absolutely necessary," she replied.

"You did say that you needed to talk. That's necessary enough for me," Nick told her.

"All right then," Miriam agreed. "But I should not be gone too long. I left my brother and his wife at the hospital, and I didn't even tell them where I was going or when I would return."

"I promise not to keep you out past midnight, Cinderella." Nick winked at her gravely; then he ordered an iced tea to go.

Heat rushed to Miriam's face, and she tried to hide it by hurrying toward the door.

Nick's car was a new red and black, sporty-looking sedan. Miriam could smell the aroma of new leather as she slid into the soft passenger seat. "You have a beautiful car," she said in a near whisper.

"Thanks. Too bad it's not paid for yet," Nick answered. He reached inside the glove box and pulled out a small bottle of aspirin. "Here, take a couple of these."

Miriam took the bottle and opened it. As she swallowed the pills with the iced tea he had purchased for her, Nick turned on the ignition and pulled away from the curb. "So, do you want to tell me what's bothering you, or would you rather just ride around for awhile?" he asked.

Miriam clutched the side of her seat with one hand while hanging onto her tea with the other. "Going at this speed, I am not sure that I can think well enough to speak."

Nick smiled. "Come, come now. I'm only doing thirty-five! Now, if we were out on the tollway, I could see you getting a bit nervous. I even get stressed out sometimes during rush-hour traffic."

"I know it's silly, but remember, I am used to riding in a horse-pulled buggy," Miriam replied.

"How about if I pull over at the park, and you can just sit and relax while you tell me what has happened?" Nick offered.

"That—that would be fine, I suppose." Miriam pulled nervously on the corner of her dark green cotton dress. She wasn't used to being alone with men, other than her brothers. It made her feel a bit uneasy—especially since this particular man was not Amish and had such an unsettling way about him.

As though he could read her thoughts, Nick said, "Don't worry, fair lady, no harm will come to you. I'm your knight in shining armor. Remember that."

Miriam could feel her cheeks growing warm, but she made no reply, and she kept her face toward the window so that he would not notice.

When they pulled into a parking place at the city park, Nick rolled down the window to let in a cool evening breeze. The rain had stopped and the air felt fresh and clean. Miriam drew in a deep breath and let out a long sigh. "Thank you for taking the time to meet me, Nick. I know that you are probably a very busy man."

Nick shrugged. "I was about to call it a day anyhow. So, tell me what has happened, fair lady. Why were you at the hospital again?"

"It is my niece, Rebekah. She has been seriously injured, and it is all my fault," Miriam began somewhat shakily.

"What exactly happened?" Nick asked as he reached for the small notepad he had tucked inside the window visor.

At first Miriam barely noticed that Nick had taken a pen from his pocket and was taking notes as she continued with her story.

"When the storm was just beginning, I sent all my students home early. I told my niece that I would give her a ride home, and I asked her to wait for me outside by the horse and buggy. I never even thought about the fact that it was parked right under a tree, or that a tree branch might break, but I—"

"A branch broke and fell on the child?" Nick asked in a very professional tone.

It was then that Miriam became fully aware of his pen and paper. She gasped. "You are writing all this down?"

"Please go on. It's a very newsworthy item," Nick said.

"I will not go on!" Miriam shouted. "I did not call on you so that you could get a story for your newspaper column. When you offered to help before, I thought that included a listening ear."

"I have been listening," Nick said. "It's just that this is what I do. I—"

"I think you had better take me back to the hospital!" Miriam said loudly. "I can see now that this was a big mistake. Men are all alike. They can never be trusted!"

"Well, don't go getting yourself into such a huff." Nick placed the paper on the seat and put the pen back in his shirt pocket. "I won't write down another thing, Miriam. I didn't think you were going to get all riled up on me. I'm a reporter, so it only seemed natural to write something down that would be good as a human interest story. I'm sorry if I've offended you."

Miriam began to pull on the corner of her skirt again. She wasn't sure if she could trust his word or not. She wanted to talk, but was he really the one she should be talking to? He was, after all, nearly a stranger, and a worldly one at that.

Chapter 17

Look, I can see that you really do to need to talk, and I'm more than willing to listen," Nick assured Miriam. "No more note-taking, I promise."

Miriam gave him a half-smile and nodded. "All right. As I was about to say, the tree branch broke, and it fell across Rebekah's head and back. Amos came along then, and he went to call for help."

"Amos? Who's Amos?" Nick wanted to know.

"He is the father of one of my students. Anyway," Miriam continued, "when the ambulance arrived, I rode to the hospital with Rebekah, and Amos went to tell her parents, my brother Andrew and his wife Sarah, what had happened."

"What's the child's prognosis?" Nick asked.

"Her what?"

"Prognosis. You know, her condition."

"Oh. The doctor told us that she has a concussion, and that is the reason she is still unconscious."

"That's understandable," Nick said.

Jah, but he also said that there is some injury to the spinal cord," Miriam gulped, hardly able to speak the words aloud, "and that even if Rebekah does survive, she will probably never walk again."

"Doctors have been known to be wrong, you know," Nick said optimistically.

"I know, and I am praying for a miracle, but—"

"Oh, that's right, you Amish folks believe in all that faith stuff, don't you?" Nick asked, cutting her off.

Miriam frowned. "Faith in God is biblical, Mr. McCormick. It is not just the Amish who believe that God is in control of our lives."

"Oh, I see. I don't agree with you on something, and now it's back to calling me Mr. McCormick again."

"I think I was wrong in expecting you to help me sort out my feelings," Miriam said angrily. "You are just trying to confuse me."

"Not at all, fair lady," Nick answered. "Listen, I admire you for your faith, but it's just not for me. I'm not one to put others down for their beliefs, but I don't want to rely on anyone but myself. I don't need God or faith."

Miriam sat quietly, letting his words sink in. "You must think of me as pretty old-fashioned—in appearance, as well as my ideas."

Nick reached out suddenly and took the glass of tea from her, placing it in the cup holder on the dash. He placed her hand in his and smiled. "Fair lady, I really don't want to confuse you, but I'm afraid that you have confused me."

Miriam's skin tingled underneath his touch. She had not felt this way in many years. Not since William. "How have I confused you?" she asked breathlessly.

Nick's blue eyes gleamed, and he leaned his head close to hers. "You are so beautiful, Miriam. I find you fascinating, yet your Amish ways are a bit strange and confusing to me. I would like to find out more about you and your Amish traditions."

"What would you like to know?"

"I know you are expected to remain separate or stand apart from the rest of the world, but I really don't understand the reasons behind such a lifestyle," Nick answered.

"The Bible tells us in Romans twelve that we must present our bodies as a living sacrifice, holy and acceptable to God. It also states that we be not conformed to this world, but rather that we be transformed by the renewing of our minds," Miriam told him. "And in Second Corinthians it says that we are not to be unequally yoked together with unbelievers. Our entire lifestyle—our dress, language, work, travel, and education are all things we must consider because of this passage in the Bible. We must not be like the rest of the world. We must live as simply and humbly as possible."

"So, things like telephones in your homes, electricity, and modern things like cars and gas-powered tractors are worldly and would cause you to be part of the world of unbelievers?" Nick asked with interest.

Miriam nodded. "The Amish community can sometimes seem harsh and uncompromising, but all baptized members are morally committed to the church and its rules."

"Hmm. . .it sounds pretty hard to live like that," Nick said, "but I suppose if you are content and feel that your way of life makes you happy, then who am I to judge it as wrong?"

Miriam was tempted to tell Nick she was anything but happy and content, but she decided it was not worth mentioning. Besides, if she did, then she might have to deal with the doubts that so often swirled through her head about God and her Amish religion. She finally withdrew her hand and cleared her throat nervously.

"I really would like to help you, Miriam," Nick said earnestly.

"Just what kind of help do you have to offer?" Miriam asked.

"Well, it sounds to me like your niece is going to be in the hospital for quite awhile, and she will no doubt require a lot of physical therapy and medical care."

Miriam nodded. "*Jah*, I suppose so."

"That will cost a lot of money," Nick continued.

Miriam swallowed hard. "I suppose it will."

"If I were to write an article about the girl's accident, and it gets printed in the newspaper, people will respond to it, Miriam."

"Respond? How?"

"With money, to help out with the medical bills," he answered.

"My people do not take charity from the outside world!" Miriam snapped. "We do not even believe it is right to have medical or hospital insurance. We Amish take care of each other!"

"There you go again, getting all riled up," Nick said. "I only want to help, you know." He reached for her hand again, but she pulled it away quickly.

"I am sure that you mean well, Nick," Miriam said, "but the cost of Rebekah's medical needs is not my primary concern. Can't you understand that I am just sick about the accident? I blame myself for it, and if my niece dies, I will be accountable. Even if she survives and has to live her life as a cripple, I don't know if I can deal with it."

"Now hold on just a minute, Miriam," Nick said firmly. "There was no way that you could have known that a tree limb would fall on the child when you sent her outside. You can't go blaming yourself for something that was just a freak accident."

"But, I—" Miriam began.

Nick reached over and put a finger to her trembling lips. "You're just going to have to buck up and face this thing squarely and head-on. In matters of the heart such as this, no amount of faith in God will get you through. All of us have the strength inside to battle any of the problems that life brings our way. I truly believe that."

An unbidden tear slid down Miriam's cheek. Hadn't she decided awhile back that her own determined heart was all she could count on? Perhaps Nick was right. If faith in God really was the answer, then the terrible accident would never have happened in the first place. If living a godly life was the best way, then why had God allowed Papa to die, and why had William Graber left her? Dutifully, she had served God all of her twenty-six years, and for what? To end up an old-maid schoolteacher with no father and a crippled niece to remind her that God had let her down over and over again.

Miriam looked at Nick, so obviously sure of himself, and she resolved to be done pleading with God for His mercy and kindness. She would buck up, just as Nick suggested. She would face life head-on, by herself.

She lifted her chin, and with a look of determination, said, "I think you might be right, Nick. I can face this problem head-on. I'm ready to go back to the hospital now."

Nick started up the car's engine. "Please call me if you need some more advice or just want to talk. I really enjoy being with you." He reached for her hand one more time, and when she didn't pull it away, he placed a gentle kiss against her palm.

Miriam swallowed hard. Did he really enjoy being in her company, or was he just being polite? She was at a loss for words. Perhaps she would call on Nick McCormick again.

Chapter 18

Up at five in the morning, light the big kitchen stove, grab a jacket from the peg on the wall, head out to the chicken coop, gather eggs, slop the pigs, milk the goats. Miriam knew the routine so well that she was certain she could have done it in her sleep. It had been her routine ever since Papa died. This morning was like no other, except for the fact that the wind had picked up and it was raining slightly.

She was reminded of the day Rebekah had been injured by the falling tree limb. Could it have only happened a few weeks ago? It seemed like much longer. Perhaps that was because she kept herself so busy. Being busy seemed to help keep her from thinking too much about all of the things that caused her heart to feel so heavy.

Rebekah was still in the hospital, but she had regained consciousness. She would live, but the doctors were fairly certain she would never walk again. The doctors were fairly certain of that.

No matter how hard she tried, Miriam could not convince herself that she was not partially to blame for the accident. She had made up her mind that she would seek her inner strength, just as Nick McCormick had suggested. She must go on with the business of living, no matter how unhappy she was.

Today she planned to go by the hospital right after school let out. She would take some books to read to Rebekah and perhaps some of her favorite licorice candy as well. Maybe she would even call Nick from a pay phone and ask to meet him for coffee again. That thought caused her to quicken her step as she hurried back to the house, carrying a pail of fresh goat's milk and a basket of brown eggs. Her day was just beginning, and she still had plenty of inside chores to do before she left for the schoolhouse.

🙌

Not another headache! thought Miriam as she stood at the door watching the last of her pupils leave the school yard. "Why must I always get a migraine when I have something important to do?" she said aloud. "Well, I won't let this one stop me from going into town!"

Miriam crossed the room and opened the top drawer of her desk. Inside was a bottle of White Willow Bark herb capsules. She took two and washed them down with some cold water from her thermos bottle. Willow tea was used freely among the Amish for pain, and she could only hope that today the tiny capsules would work well. Was it the stress of going to the hospital or the fact that John Lapp had given her a hard time in class today that had brought on the headache?

It was probably a bit of both, she admitted to herself. Determinedly, she decided not to give in to the pain or to her stressful feelings. John Lapp had been punished by losing his playtime during lunch, and she would force herself to go to the hospital, no matter how much it distressed her to see her niece lying helplessly in that bed.

❧

When Miriam arrived at the hospital, Rebekah was not in her room. She was informed by one of the nurses that the child had been taken upstairs for another CAT scan and would be back in about half an hour. Miriam could either wait in Rebekah's room or in one of the waiting rooms.

She had no desire to spend any more time than was absolutely necessary in the cramped little hospital room, so Miriam left the candy and books on Rebekah's nightstand and made her way down the hall and into the large waiting area.

Except for an elderly gentleman, the room was nearly empty. Miriam took a seat and began to thumb through a stack of magazines she found on the low table in front of her. Nothing looked very interesting, and she was just about to leave the room in search of a phone so that she could call Nick when she noticed a copy of the *Daily Express* lying on the table. *Maybe one of Nick's articles is in it.* She picked up the paper and scanned the front page. After seeing nothing by Nick McCormick, she turned to page two. She stifled a gasp. There, halfway down the page, was a picture of a young girl lying in a hospital bed. It was Rebekah, and there was a four-column story to accompany the photo.

Miriam fumed as she read the author's name—Nick McCormick, reporter. "How dare he! I hoped that I could trust him!" she hissed.

Furiously, she read the entire story, pausing only to mumble or gasp as she read how Rebekah had been struck down by a tree limb during a storm that had swept the valley. The article went on to say that the small Amish girl would never walk again and that the hospital and doctor bills would no doubt be impossible for her parents to pay. The story closed by appealing to the public's generous nature and asking for charitable contributions to the hospital on the child's behalf.

Miriam slammed the paper onto the table with such force that the elderly man seated across from her jumped. She had been hoping to see one of Nick's articles but certainly not like this! With no apologies and no explanations to the man, she stormed out of the room in search of a telephone.

There was a telephone booth down the hall, and Miriam had nearly reached it when she ran into Andrew and Sarah.

"Miriam, we didn't know you were here," Andrew said. "We dropped Simon and the baby off at Mom's, but she didn't tell us you were at the hospital."

"Mom does not know," Miriam answered. "I came right after school let out, and I—"

"You look really upset. Is there something wrong? Is it Rebekah? Is she worse?" Sarah interrupted.

"No, it's not Rebekah. She's having another CAT scan done, and I was waiting until she comes out. It's what I found in the waiting room that upset me so." She reached a shaky hand up to her forehead. Her headache, which had previously eased, was back again, this time with a vengeance.

"Miriam, you are trembling," Andrew said. "What did you see in that room, anyway?"

"A newspaper article," Miriam replied.

"The news can be quite unsettling at times," Sarah agreed. "There are so many murders, robberies, and—"

"No, no, it's nothing like that," Miriam said, cutting Sarah off. "It's a story about Rebekah."

"Rebekah?" Andrew echoed. "What do you mean?"

"The article tells all about her accident and how you will not have enough money to pay all of her bills. It even suggests that people donate money to help out," Miriam explained.

"What?!" Andrew said, a bit too loudly. A nearby nurse gave him a warning look, but he did not even notice.

"But who would write such a thing, and how did they know about Rebekah's accident?" Sarah asked.

"Let's go to the waiting room, and I will show you the article," Miriam suggested. She led the way back down the hall.

The newspaper was still lying on the table, where Miriam had angrily tossed it. She reached for it and handed it to Andrew. "Look here. There is even a picture of Rebekah."

"A picture? But how?" Sarah wanted to know.

"Who is responsible for all this?" Andrew snapped.

"I am afraid that I am," Miriam replied.

Andrew raised his eyebrows. "You?"

She nodded. "It was I who told the reporter about Rebekah's accident, only I—"

"You called the newspaper and asked them to write an article about our daughter?" Sarah's expression revealed hurt and betrayal.

Miriam placed a hand on her sister-in-law's arm. "Oh, no! Please don't think for one minute that I called the *Daily Express* or that I wanted anything like this to be printed."

"Then how did the reporter know about it?" Andrew asked impatiently.

"I think I need to begin at the beginning," Miriam said.

"*Jah*, please do," Sarah told her.

Miriam suggested that they all sit down, and then she told them everything, except for the fact that she had nearly been taken in by Nick McCormick, even allowing herself to feel tingly and excited when he had kissed her hand. She would never admit that to anyone.

"I was on my way to the telephone to call Mr. McCormick and give him a piece of my mind when I ran into you two," Miriam concluded.

"Well, you need not worry about that task," Andrew stated flatly. "I'm going to call the newspaper office myself and demand a written apology for the article, as well as a retraction regarding the money needed. We do not want people thinking that we will take handouts from the rest of the world. We Amish stand together in times of trouble, and any help we might need will be given by our own kind!"

Chapter 19

The following week, a retraction on the story about Rebekah came out in the *Daily Express*. The reporter offered his apologies to all the family members he might have offended and stated that the Amish always take care of their own, so no outside help would be needed.

While it gave Miriam a sense of satisfaction that Nick McCormick had been forced to retract his story, she found that a part of her also felt sad. Not for him, but for herself. Once again, she had been let down by a man. Had she really been so naïve as to believe that Nick could have been any different than other men? To think that she had nearly phoned him to ask if they might meet again for coffee and a good talk. She chided herself for being so foolish and promised not to ever allow her emotions to get in the way of good judgment again.

Rebekah had been in the hospital for nearly three weeks already, and Miriam knew the medical bills were adding up quickly. She had a little money put aside from her teaching position, which she would give to Andrew toward the mounting bills. She also planned to sell the beautiful quilts she had made for her hope chest. Since she never planned to marry, they were useless to her now, anyway. Tourists were always on the lookout for quilts made by the Amish, so she would have no trouble selling them to the general store in town.

She knew several other Amish families had given money to help with Rebekah's hospital bills. How thankful she was that she belonged to a group of people who willingly helped one another in times of need. If she ever saw Nick McCormick again, she would tell him so, too!

❧

Whenever Miriam went to the hospital to visit Rebekah, she always took a book to read, as well as some of the child's favorite licorice candy. Today was one of those days, but Miriam found herself dreading the visit. Would she ever get over the feeling of guilt she experienced when she looked at the sweet young child, lying there so helpless in her bed? Perhaps Rebekah would be asleep when she arrived, and then she could merely leave the treat and book on the table by her bed and retreat quickly back to the protection and solitude of her home.

Miriam pulled her horse and buggy to a stop in the hospital parking lot, then got out and secured the horse to a nearby post. It was beginning to rain lightly, and she hurried toward the front door of the building.

Just as she was about to step inside, Miriam collided with a man. She looked up and found herself staring into the familiar blue eyes of Nick McCormick. "You!" she cried. "How dare you show your face at this hospital again!" She stood there trembling, fighting the urge to pound her fists against her chest.

Nick smiled at her. "Miriam, it's so good to see you, too. As usual, you look a bit flustered, but beautiful, nonetheless. Is there something I can do to help?"

"You unfeeling, arrogant man! You know perfectly well that just your presence here is irritating to me!" Miriam shouted.

Nick laughed lightly. "The last I heard, we were still living in a free country, fair lady. I have just as much right to be here at the hospital as you do. Or do you believe that only the Amish have the right to be here?"

Miriam clasped her hands tightly behind her back, trying to maintain control of herself. She had never been so close to striking anyone. Strangely, Nick McCormick seemed to bring out the worst in her, yet he also brought out the best.

"You know perfectly well what I mean," she told him. "The only reason you are here at all is just to be nosy and sneaky. I have no patience with a liar, Nick McCormick!"

"Excuse me?"

"Do not play innocent with me!" Miriam said loudly. "You know very well that I am referring to the fact that you promised not to do a story about my niece. But you went ahead and did it anyway, didn't you? Your word meant absolutely nothing, did it?"

Nick scratched the back of his head thoughtfully and gave her a sheepish grin. "Guess I'm caught red-handed. I didn't know the Amish read the *Daily Express*."

"We are not illiterate, you know!" Miriam shouted.

"No, I'm sure you're not. That's not what I meant, either," Nick said. "It's just that I thought since your religion forbids so many other worldly things, that might also include reading our worldly city newspaper."

"Never mind. I don't care in the least what you meant. I just want you to know one thing, Mr. McCormick—I am very glad that I belong to a group of people who are willing to help one another in times of need. I know that we Amish are not perfect, but we do strive for honesty, which is more than I can say for some people. And one more thing—stay away from my niece's hospital room. If you ever try going there again, I will personally report you to your superior at the *Daily Express*."

"Is that some kind of threat?" Nick asked, trying hard not to smile.

"You may call it whatever you like."

"My, my, aren't you a little feisty thing today?" He laughed lightly. "I like spunky women—but I also like women who get their facts straight."

"What is that supposed to mean?" Miriam asked.

"Fact number one is, I never actually promised you that I would not do a story about your niece," Nick said.

"But you said—"

"That I would not do any more note-taking while you were talking to me," Nick interjected. "I kept true to my word and put away my paper and pen."

"*Jah*, but you mentioned that you would like to do an article about Rebekah's accident and the cost of her medical bills, and I explained to you that would not be necessary. The Amish—"

"I know, I know. The Amish always take care of one another," Nick interrupted. "I appreciated your input, Miriam, but still I did not promise you that I would not do a story. I did what I thought best—as a reporter and as your friend."

"What kind of friend goes behind someone's back and does something sneaky?" Miriam asked.

"The kind that believes he's doing the right thing," Nick answered with conviction. He pulled Miriam aside and into the little waiting area that was just across the hall. "Listen, I really do care about you, fair lady. I thought I was doing something helpful for your family. I apologize if it upset you or if you thought I had betrayed you."

Miriam could feel her anger receding some. It was so hard to remain in control when she was in the presence of Nick McCormick. Did she really need to feel love and acceptance so badly that she would go outside her Amish faith to get it? She could not allow this Englishman to deceive her into believing that he could actually care for her.

"I really must be on my way now," Miriam said quickly, starting for the door. "I'm going to see my niece. I do appreciate your apology, but I would ask that you do not see Rebekah again or take any more pictures."

Nick opened his mouth to answer her, but Miriam turned away quickly and nearly ran up the hospital corridor.

When she entered the room, Miriam found Rebekah propped up on her pillows. *So innocent and sweet—and helpless.*

"Aunt Miriam!" Rebekah exclaimed. She smiled happily and reached a small hand out to Miriam.

"How is my best pupil and favorite niece?" Miriam asked as she took the child's hand.

"I feel better. My head don't—doesn't hurt no more. Doctor said I can go home soon," Rebekah replied.

Miriam cringed inside at the thought of Rebekah returning home as a cripple. Rebekah made no mention of it, however. Was it possible that she was not yet aware of the fact that she could no longer walk? How would the once-active six year old handle spending her days confined to a wheelchair?

"I am glad you are feeling better," Miriam said, trying to make her voice sound light and cheerful.

"Did you bring me licorice again?" Rebekah asked expectantly.

"Jah, and another book to read, too." Miriam handed the long licorice rope to Rebekah, then seated herself in the chair next to the bed. "Would you like me to read to you?"

"A man took my picture," Rebekah surprised her by saying.

"Jah, I know, but that man will never bother you again," Miriam said, and then she noticed the teddy bear sitting on the table near Rebekah's bed. She

picked it up. "Where did you get this bear, Rebekah?"

"The man," Rebekah answered.

"The man? What man?"

"The picture man."

Miriam's head was beginning to pound. She reached a trembling hand to press against the side of her forehead. So Nick McCormick must have just come from Rebekah's room when she had bumped into him at the hospital entrance. Had he come out of concern for the child? Was his gift one of genuine compassion, or had he used it to bribe the child in order to take more pictures? Now that she thought about it, Nick had been carrying his camera bag over one shoulder when they talked.

"Rebekah, did the man take any more pictures of you?" Miriam asked her niece.

Rebekah nodded. "He gave me the teddy bear and I smiled for his camera."

Chapter 20

Thirty days after Rebekah's accident, the doctors released her from the hospital to go home. She would still need to return to the hospital for physical therapy twice a week, but at least her days and nights could be spent with those whom she loved and felt closest to.

On Rebekah's first day home, Mom suggested that she and Miriam ride over to see if they could help out. "Sarah is really going to have her hands full now!" she exclaimed. "Just taking care of a baby and two other small children is a job in itself, but now this!"

Miriam nodded. "Since today is Saturday, and there is no school, I have all day."

"We shall hurry through our own morning chores, and then we will go right on over," Mom said.

Miriam reached for her jacket on the wall peg by the door. "I'll go out and feed the animals while you start breakfast."

A blast of cold air greeted her as she stepped out onto the porch. It was early December, and there was a definite feeling of winter in the air.

Miriam shivered and pulled her jacket collar up around her neck. "I hate winter!" she said grimly. The truth was, she was beginning to hate all the seasons. Perhaps it was life in general that she hated. *Is it all right for a believer to feel hate toward anything—even the weather?*

Then another thought entered her mind. Maybe she was not even a believer anymore. She was still Amish, but her faith in God had diminished so much over the last several years. She got little or nothing from the biweekly preaching services that she attended with her friends and family. She no longer even did her private daily devotions. Her prayers were few and far between, and then when she did pray, it was really more of a cry of complaint to God, rather than heartfelt prayers and petitions. Where was God anyway, and what had happened to her longing to seek His face?

Miriam trudged wearily toward the barn and forced her thoughts away from God and on to the tasks that lay before her.

As she returned to the house nearly an hour later, Miriam noticed a clump of wild pansies growing near the fence that ran parallel to the pasture. Pansies were hardy flowers, blooming almost continuously from early spring until late fall. The delicate little yellow and lavender blossoms made her think of Mary Ellen Hilty and the day that she had given her the bouquet of heartsease. *Children like Rebekah and Mary Ellen are a lot like wild pansies. They are small and delicate, yet able to withstand so much.*

Thoughts of Mary Ellen made Miriam think about Amos. She had seen him only twice since the day of Rebekah's accident. Both times had been at preaching services. It seemed strange that he had not come around. He hadn't even come over for supper at Mom's most recent invitation. Perhaps he had just been busy with his farm chores or taking care of Mary Ellen. Or maybe Miriam had finally made him understand that she really had no interest in him, and he had given up on his pursuit of her. Regardless of the reason, Miriam was glad that he was not coming around anymore. The last thing she needed was an unwanted suitor. Her life was already complicated enough.

She bent down and picked the colorful pansies. They would make a lovely bouquet to give to Rebekah.

🙒

Sarah was sitting on the front porch in tears when Miriam and Mom arrived. Mom quickly got down from the buggy and rushed to her side. Miriam followed. "What is it, Sarah? Why are you sitting out here in the cold?"

"*Seind mir einge denkt in Gebeth*—remember me in your prayers," Sarah sobbed.

"*Jah, does Kannichdu*—yes, I will," Mom answered. Then, taking up the English language again, she asked, "What is the trouble?"

"I am so happy to have Rebekah home again, but there is just not enough of me to go around. Simon is into everything, the baby always seems to need me for something, and taking care of Rebekah will be a full-time job. She's only been home half a day, and I just can't manage!" Sarah sniffed and dabbed at her damp eyes with the corner of her apron.

"There, there," Mom comforted. She put an arm around her daughter-in-law's shoulder. "We will work something out."

Miriam felt great concern for her sister-in-law. "Is there anything I can do to help?"

Mom nodded. "Please, go inside and check on the children while I speak to Sarah."

Without any further questions, Miriam did as Mom had asked. She found Rebekah sitting in her wheelchair next to the kitchen table, coloring a picture. The child looked up and smiled. "Hi, Aunt Miriam. Do you like my picture?"

Miriam nodded. "*Jah*, it is very pretty. Rebekah, where are Simon and baby Nadine?"

Rebekah pointed across the room.

Miriam gasped when she saw that three-year-old Simon had a jar of petroleum jelly and was rubbing it all over his face and hair. The baby, who was crawling on the braided rug next to Simon, had some in her hair as well.

"What in the world? How did you get this, you stinker?" Miriam said to little Simon. She reached down and grabbed the slippery jar out of his greasy hands. "This is a no-no!"

Simon's lower lip began to tremble, and tears quickly formed in the corners of his blue eyes.

"Crying will get you nowhere," Miriam scolded. "Come over to the sink with me, and let's get you all cleaned up. Then I'll tend to baby Nadine."

By the time Miriam was finished with her cleanup job on both small children, Mom and Sarah had entered the kitchen. Sarah's eyes were red and swollen, but she was no longer crying.

"Our help is definitely needed here today, and there is much to be done, so let's get ourselves busy!" Mom told Miriam.

By the time they reached home later that evening, Miriam was exhausted, and the last thing she wanted to do was chores; but farm chores did not wait, and so she climbed down from the buggy with a sigh of resignation, prepared to head straight for the barn.

"If you don't mind, I would like to talk before we start our chores," Mom said as she, too, stepped down from the buggy. "Go see if Lewis is in the barn. If he is, bring him up to the house with you. The matter I have to discuss pertains to us all."

Miriam gave her mother a questioning look, but she merely nodded, then started for the barn. What could Mom have to talk about that would affect them all? she wondered.

Lewis was grooming the horses when Miriam entered the barn leading Harvey, the big, dark brown horse that so often pulled her buggy wherever she needed to go. "Here is another one for you!" she called. "When you're done, Mom wants to see you up at the house as soon as possible."

Lewis looked up from his job. "What's up?"

"Mom has something to discuss, and she says that it pertains to all of us," Miriam explained.

"*Jah*, all right. Tell her I will be there in awhile," Lewis answered.

As Miriam left the barn, a chill ran through her entire body. She shivered and hurried toward the house. Was the evening air the cause of her chilliness—or was it the fear that she felt in her heart? Fear that whatever Mom had to tell them was bad news.

When Miriam entered the house, Mom had steaming cups of hot chocolate waiting, along with big hunks of Miriam's favorite gingerbread cake. Normally, Miriam would have dived right into one of the pieces of spicy cake, but tonight she did not feel particularly hungry. She just wanted to know what Mom had to say, and she knew that Mom wasn't about to tell her anything until Lewis joined them. She wished now that she had stayed to help him curry the horses. It would have gotten the job done more quickly.

"Is Lewis coming?" Mom asked, interrupting Miriam's thoughts.

Absently, Miriam reached for a slice of gingerbread and took a seat at the table. "As soon as he finishes with the horses."

Mom nodded and settled herself into the rocking chair near the stove. She reached into a basket on the floor and pulled out one of Lewis's socks. It had a large hole in the heel, and Miriam wondered why Mom didn't simply throw it away.

Mom's darning needle moved in and out swiftly, as she began to make small talk. "Winter is in the air. Can you feel it?"

Miriam lifted her cup of hot chocolate to her lips. *Jah,* I nearly froze to death this morning. I suppose I will have to get out my warm, heavy coat soon. A jacket just isn't enough for these crisp, cold mornings or evenings."

"The hens are not laying as many eggs, either," Mom continued. "That is a sure sign that winter is here."

Miriam sighed deeply. She was in no mood for small talk. What was taking Lewis so long, anyway?

As though on cue, the back door opened, and Lewis entered the kitchen. "Umm. . .gingerbread! I would recognize that delicious smell if I was blindfolded and clear out on the porch!" He smiled at Mom. "Miriam says that you want to talk to us?"

Mom nodded and laid the sock aside. She cleared her throat and began. "I was wondering—that is, how would you two feel about me moving in with Andrew and Sarah? I mean, could you manage on your own?"

Neither Lewis nor Miriam spoke for several moments; then Miriam broke the silence by asking, "For how long, Mom?"

"Indefinitely," Mom answered.

"Indefinitely?" Lewis echoed.

Jah. Now that Rebekah is confined to a wheelchair, and what with all the work the other two children will take—"

"But, Mom, how do you expect Lewis and me to manage here by ourselves?" Miriam asked, trying to keep her voice even.

"You are both very capable. I am sure you can manage just fine."

"I think we could do all right," Lewis said.

"That is easy for you to say!" Miriam exclaimed. "Things will not change much for you, but me—well, I will have double the work to do, and what with teaching school and all—"

"I know that my moving out will cause some discomfort for you both," Mom interrupted, "but I am badly needed over at Andrew and Sarah's."

"What about Sarah's parents? Can't they help out?" Lewis wanted to know.

"Their farm is several miles away," Mom explained. "Besides, they still have young children living at home to care for."

"It is just like you to make such a sacrifice, Mom," Lewis said. "You have such a heart of compassion."

Miriam left her seat at the table and knelt next to her mother. "It should be me that goes, Mom. I will quit my job teaching and go care for Rebekah. It was my fault that she was injured in the first place."

Mom reached out and placed a loving hand on Miriam's head. "No, it was not your fault. It was simply an accident. It was something bad that God allowed to happen. You are in no way responsible, Miriam. You are a fine teacher, and you are needed at the school. Sarah and I have already talked it over, and I have made my decision. I will be moving to their place on the weekend. I hope that I have your blessing, children."

Miriam rose to her feet. "If you are determined to go, then we shall abide by your decision."

"We will do our best to keep this place running, Mom," Lewis added.

Miriam said no more, but her private thoughts reminded her that life was not fair. There had been so many changes in the past few years, and none of them had made her happy. She lifted her chin and squared her shoulders. She would do whatever she had to in order to keep the Stoltzfus farm running. She owed Mom that much.

Chapter 21

The winter months seemed to drag by unmercifully. With all the work there was to be done, the days should have passed quickly, but Miriam's tired body and saddened soul made her feel as if each day was endless. The snow lay deep on the ground, which made the outside chores even more difficult. And the cold—Miriam couldn't remember a winter that had been as cold as this one. Was it because the temperatures often dipped below zero, or was it simply because her heart had turned so cold? she wondered.

Valentine's Day was only a few weeks away, and she knew that the boys and girls at school would expect to have a party, with refreshments and exchanging valentine hearts with one another. The last thing Miriam felt like was a party, but she would force herself to get through it somehow.

Miriam found that she missed Mom terribly. She knew that her mother was doing a good thing and her help was needed badly, but Miriam hardly ever got to see her anymore. Mom was too busy caring for Rebekah and the other two children, and Miriam had too many chores at the farm to do, also. Besides, the poor weather made it difficult and time-consuming to hitch up the horse and buggy or sleigh and get out on the roads. Only for those things that were necessary, like school and church, did Miriam go out.

Lewis had begun to see a girl whose name was Grace Zepp. He'd taken her to several singings and more recently had begun to call on her at her home. Miriam worried about him, because ever since Papa's death, Lewis had been forced to do the work of two men. Of course, she was doing the work of two women, but she wasn't taking time out for courting. Maybe it was good that Lewis was young and obviously very much in love. How else could he have managed the extra activity of courting?

❧

The schoolchildren were full of excitement on the day of the Valentine's party. Nearly everyone brought goodies. There were cookies sprinkled with red sugar crystals; cupcakes frosted in pink icing; candy hearts with silly sayings written on them; glazed, sugared, and powdered donuts; and even a big pink and white decorated cake. Miriam furnished the beverage of cold apple cider.

The party was held right after lunch. The children began by eating refreshments, followed by several games, and finally they exchanged valentine cards. Some of the cards were store-bought, but most of them had been made by hand using construction paper, glue, scissors, coloring crayons, and in some cases even delicate white paper doilies.

76

Every child had taken a cardboard shoe box and decorated it, then cut a hole in the top and placed it on their school desk. They all took turns walking around the room placing their valentines into each child's special box. Miriam had instructed the class earlier in the week that each child was expected to give a card to everyone. That way no one would be left out or go home with only a handful of valentines. She even thought to make a box for Rebekah, which she placed on her own desk, reminding the children that Rebekah was unable to finish the school year because of her accident and that she would be studying at home.

Miriam felt that some valentines, a cupcake, and a few cookies would probably cheer Rebekah up, and she planned to deliver them right after school. It had been several weeks since she'd been over to Sarah and Andrew's, and she was looking forward to a much-needed visit with both Rebekah and Mom. The chores at home would just have to wait.

Miriam looked up and forced her thoughts back to the present as Mary Ellen Hilty approached her desk. The child was holding a very large valentine heart, and she handed it to Miriam with a smile. "This is for you, Teacher. It is from me and Pappy."

Miriam nodded and tried to return the smile. *"Danki,* Mary Ellen. That was very nice of you."

"And Pappy, too," Mary Ellen reminded. "He helped me make it, and he even wrote some words on it. I think Pappy likes you, Teacher."

Miriam cleared her throat and placed the valentine on her desk. "Tell your pappy I said *danki."*

"Aren't you going to read it, Teacher?"

"Jah, but I will look at it later," Miriam replied. "Right now it is time for the class to begin cleaning up the room."

Mary Ellen gave her an imploring look, but she obediently returned to her seat.

Just when I thought that Amos had forgotten about me and given up, Miriam fumed inwardly.

She placed the valentine heart with a stack of papers that she would be taking home to correct; then she turned her attention back to the class.

❧

Snow was beginning to fall again as Miriam climbed into her buggy and headed for Andrew and Sarah's place. But today she did not care. She was not about to let a little snow stop her from a very overdue visit with her family.

She placed the stack of papers on the seat next to her and was about to pick up the reins when she noticed the red-and-white valentine heart sticking out between two pieces of paper. "I suppose I may as well read it now," she said aloud.

On the inside, there was writing on both sides of the card. She read the left side first. It was printed and obviously done in a child's handwriting.

Dear Teacher,
    I wanted to bake you some cookies, but I do not know how to bake yet.
I think you are nice and pretty, too.

Love,
Mary Ellen

Miriam sighed. "I wonder just who's idea that was?" She turned her attention to the other side of the card. It was written in cursive writing.

Dear Miriam,
    I think of you often and wonder how you are doing. Please call on me if
I can be of any help. I am praying for you and for your family.

Sincerely,
Amos Hilty

Miriam wiped the moisture from her cheek. Had the snowflakes drifted inside the buggy somehow? She thought all the windows were closed, but then she felt a familiar burning in the back of her throat and realized that she was crying. But why? she wondered. Surely Amos Hilty had no real concern for her well-being. He was only concerned about himself and his daughter. Was it possible that Amos did care for her, even in some small way? He had experienced the pain of losing someone close to him. He might have been sincere in expressing his desire to help.

Miriam sniffed and wiped away the tears. She needed to be loved so badly, but her heart would not let her trust any man. "I do not care if Amos Hilty is sincere," she told herself. "I care nothing for Mary Ellen's father." With a firm resolve not to think any further about the man, she picked up the reins and started down the snow-covered dirt trail that led to Andrew's place.

Chapter 22

Miriam's visit with Mom, Andrew, and his family had not gone very well. The fact that Miriam was still upset over the valentine she'd received from Mary Ellen and Amos was no doubt the underlying cause, but she would never have admitted it. In fact, she chose not to even mention getting the card to anyone. Why bring questions and perhaps a hopeful comment or two?

Miriam was out of sorts when she arrived, and it took very little for a disagreement to start with her brother Andrew. The argument all began when Andrew showed some concern over the fact that snow was falling hard, and he wondered if Miriam should have driven over in the bad weather. After all, he reminded her, she was a woman who was all alone, and anything might have happened between her place and theirs. The horse could have lost its footing on the icy pavement, which would probably have caused the buggy to run off the road.

Miriam argued that just because she was a woman, it did not automatically mean that she was helpless. Then, when Andrew suggested that she needed a man in her life, she really became upset. Even Mom and Sarah got into the discussion, both agreeing with Andrew and saying that a woman Miriam's age should be happily married and starting a family of her own. Miriam told them just what she thought of that idea. Instead of staying for supper as she'd planned, she went home early, not even taking the time to read a story to Rebekah.

❧

The first sign of spring came in early March, when Miriam discovered a group of little yellow crocuses poking their heads up between several clumps of grass and patches of melting snow. How she wished that the new life spring brought with it could give her a new life, too. She wanted to wake up in the morning with a feeling of joy and peace. She wanted to find a reason to begin each new day with anticipation, knowing that it truly was a day that the Lord had created and that she was going to enjoy it to the fullest.

The sound of a horse and buggy coming down the gravel drive made Miriam turn away from the flowers and look toward the buggy. She shielded her eyes against the sun, wondering who would be coming to call so early in the morning. She took a few steps toward the approaching buggy so that she could get a better look at the driver.

When the buggy was just a few feet away, it stopped and Amos Hilty stepped down. He smiled at Miriam and said, "Good morning. It certainly is a beautiful day, isn't it? There is a definite promise of spring in the air, isn't there?"

Miriam nodded and mumbled something about the crocuses she had just seen, then quickly she added, "What brings you out here so early in the day, Amos? There is nothing wrong with Mary Ellen, is there?" She really did feel genuine concern for the young girl, who always seemed so determined to make "Teacher" like her.

"No, Mary Ellen is fine. Since this is Saturday, and there is no school, I allowed her to spend last night with her friend, Becky Weaver."

"Oh, I see. Then if it's not about Mary Ellen—"

"I came by to see if Lewis has any horses he might like to sell," Amos interrupted. "I can use a—"

Now it was Miriam's turn to interrupt. "Horses? If you are looking for a new horse, then why not ask Henry Jost? He raises horses just for the purpose of selling, you know."

Jah, I know, but I thought that maybe Lewis could use the money," Amos answered.

"We are not destitute! We do not need any of your charity, either, Amos Hilty!" Miriam snapped.

"I am sorry if I've offended you," Amos said apologetically. "I don't think you need charity. It is just that with Lewis planning to get married soon, I thought he could use the extra money. I have to buy some horses anyway, and—"

"Married?! Who told you that Lewis is going to be married?" Miriam shrieked.

"He did. I thought you knew." Amos looked flustered, and he shifted nervously from one foot to the other.

"I know that Lewis has been courting Grace Zepp, but he has not said anything to me about marriage," Miriam said, trying to gain control of her voice.

"I am truly sorry. I should not have been the one to tell you," Amos apologized again. "I think maybe I have put my boot in my mouth."

"No, you were only telling me something that you thought I already knew."

"I cannot believe that Lewis hasn't told you," Amos said sympathetically.

"He probably did not want to upset me," Miriam admitted.

Amos wore a puzzled expression. "Why would it upset you if Lewis married a nice girl like Grace?"

"I have nothing against Grace Zepp," Miriam answered. "It is just that our life has been so full of changes in the last year or so. If Lewis marries Grace, it will mean more changes—especially for me."

"You mean because she will be moving into your house?" asked Amos.

Jah, I suppose she will. The farm is Lewis's now that Papa is gone. And Mom is not likely to move back, either. She is needed at Andrew's." Miriam sighed deeply, then shrugged her shoulders. "The only logical thing for me to do is move out."

"But where would you go?" Amos asked.

Miriam shrugged again. "I don't know. A boardinghouse in town, perhaps. I just know I could not stay on here. It would not be right."

"Two hens in the same henhouse? Is that it?" Amos smiled.

Miriam had to bite her lower lip to keep from smiling, too. She could almost picture in her mind Grace and her running around the kitchen, cackling and chasing each other the way that the hens in the coop often did. "No," she replied, "Grace and I would probably get on just fine together, but it would not be fair to the newlyweds to have Lewis's big sister hanging around all the time."

Amos nodded. "That is very considerate of you, Miriam. You are a good woman."

Miriam bit her lip again, only this time it was to keep from telling Amos to keep his opinions of her to himself. She felt her face grow warm, and she looked away in the hopes that Amos would not notice.

"I have embarrassed you. I am sorry," Amos said quickly. He placed a large hand on Miriam's arm and drew in a deep breath. "I think I might have an answer to your problem."

"Oh?"

Jah. You could marry me and move to my place. Mary Ellen loves you, and—"

"Marry you?!" Miriam's screech resounded in her own ears. "You must be joking!"

"No, I—that is—I have been thinking on this matter for some time now," Amos told her. "I will admit that I do have some serious concerns about your bitterness, and I have detected that you are not as interested in spiritual things as you should be, but—"

"Wait just a minute!" Miriam shouted. "My spiritual life is really none of your business, Amos! Besides, how would you know what I think or feel about God?"

Amos cleared his throat several times. "Miriam, I must admit that I have been watching you, and I have noted that during our church services, you often look absently out the window rather than concentrating on the sermons that are preached. You also do not participate in the singing of the *Ausbund*. I sense that you have become very bitter toward God. Perhaps this is because of your father's untimely death, or maybe it goes back even further to when William Graber jilted you."

"How do you know about that?" Miriam snapped.

"Miriam, this valley is not that big. There has been some talk among our people about your broken spirit and—"

"My personal life is none of your business, Amos—nor is it the business of anyone else, either! I think this discussion had better come to a close."

Amos moved toward her, but she moved quickly away. "I am sorry if I have taken you by surprise, Miriam. I would appreciate it if you would give the matter of marrying me some deep thought and prayer. I believe that we can work through your bitterness and anger together. My only concern is for Mary Ellen. You would not let your attitude affect her, would you? I do not want my child to have any feelings of distrust toward God."

Miriam shook her head. "I would never do anything to hurt Mary Ellen's belief in God. She must draw her own conclusions as she matures and is dealt more of life's harsh blows. Now, regarding your proposal of marriage—you haven't said anything about love."

"I told you that Mary Ellen loves you, and—"

"Jah, Mary Ellen, not you," Miriam was quick to say. "You are obviously not in love with me, nor I with you. Do you not think that marriage should include love?"

Amos shifted his weight nervously and pulled on the edge of his full brown beard. "I do admire you, Miriam, and I believe that given some time, love will come—for both of us. In the meantime—"

"In the meantime, nothing!" Miriam cried. "I know exactly what you want, Amos Hilty! You want a mother for your child and someone to do all of your cooking, cleaning, and all the other wifely duties that men so desperately need!"

"No, that's not all I want. Listen, you do not have to give me your answer right now, but please, at least give the matter some thought. We can both benefit from a union in marriage."

Miriam opened her mouth as if to say something, but Amos reached out and placed two fingers against her lips. "Please say no more. We can talk again later." With that, he marched off in the direction of the barn to find Lewis.

"Men!" Miriam fumed. "They would trade their heart in exchange for a live-in housekeeper!"

Chapter 23

Miriam made her way back to the house as though she were moving in slow motion. Her mind was so filled with thoughts of her conversation with Amos that her head felt like it was swimming. She wondered if he thought he would be doing her a big favor by marrying her, solving the problem of where she would live after Lewis's marriage to Grace. Actually, if she were to marry him—which she wasn't—it would be her doing him the favor. After all, she was perfectly capable of finding a place to live on her own, but Amos, on the other hand, was obviously in need of a wife and mother for Mary Ellen.

She entered the kitchen and tried to focus her thoughts on what she should be doing. Baking bread and making a pot of baked beans to take to preaching service tomorrow—wasn't that what she planned to do after her walk outside? Maybe if she got busy it would help take her mind off Amos Hilty and the fact that Lewis was going to be getting married.

"How could Lewis have kept something so important from me?" she fumed as she pulled down a tin full of flour. "Men are all alike. None of them can be trusted! I wonder who else Lewis has told, and how many other people have been hiding the truth from me. If people would talk behind my back about how William jilted me, then who knows what else they are saying?"

Miriam had her pot of beans cooking on top of the stove and four loaves of bread baking in the oven when she heard Amos's horse and buggy finally leave. She went to the window and peered out. Sure enough, two of Lewis's horses were tied to the back of the buggy. They trotted dutifully behind.

"Humph! My guess is that he wishes he had a wife as dutiful as those horses are! *Jah*, well, it will never be me!" she exclaimed. A short time later, Lewis entered the kitchen, carrying a broken harness. "Umm. . .something sure smells mighty good!"

"It's bread and baked beans for tomorrow," Miriam said coolly.

Lewis laid the harness on the table, then pulled out a kitchen chair and sat down. "Miriam, I think the two of us need to have a little heart-to-heart talk."

Oh, no—here it comes. She pulled out a chair and took a seat across from her younger brother. "If it's about you and Grace Zepp, I already know."

"Jah, Amos told me that he let the cat out of the bag." Lewis smiled, then reached for Miriam's hand. "I'm really sorry you had to hear it secondhand, Miriam. I meant to tell you. I was just waiting for the right time."

"Didn't you think I could handle it? Don't you know by now that Miriam Stoltzfus can handle anything that might come her way—even disappointments?"

Miriam's voice sounded harsh, even to her own ears.

"You are disappointed because Grace and I plan to be married?" Lewis seemed hurt, and he shook his head slowly. "I never expected you to be jealous, Miriam."

"Jealous? You think that I am jealous?"

"Well, yes, it does seem so," Lewis responded.

"You can't be serious, Lewis. I am not the least bit jealous."

"I just thought—"

"Well, you thought wrong! Personally, I never plan to marry, and I am not jealous of anyone who does!"

"Then why are you feeling disappointed?" Lewis asked.

"First of all, because you told Amos, who is not even a family member, before you told me, your only sister." Miriam paused for a breath, then continued. "And second, because with so many other changes, it is just a bit too much to take. First, Papa dies, then Rebekah gets injured. Next, Mom moves out of the house, and now I have to move out as well."

"No," Lewis said. "I don't expect you to move out, Miriam. This is your home, too, and I want you to stay here for as long as you like."

"I am sure that you are only saying that to be kind, Lewis. I would never dream of staying on here once you and Grace are married. It wouldn't be fair to either of you. And quite frankly, I'm not sure that I would enjoy it much, either."

"What do you mean?" asked Lewis.

"I have had complete control of the household for several months now, and another woman in the house would be a difficult adjustment. I have my ways of doing things, and I'm sure that Grace has hers as well."

"But, I'm sure that Grace would be most understanding," Lewis argued. "Besides, she will need your help."

Miriam shook her head. "For a time, but soon she will come to think of the house as hers, and she would want to run it her own way. It's only normal that she would, and I shall not stand in her way. Besides, you newlyweds will be needing your privacy. When is the big day, anyway? I need to know how long I have to get packed and moved."

"We had thought of waiting until fall, after the harvest, but Grace would like to be married in May if possible. Now that you have been told, we can be officially published at the preaching service tomorrow morning. I have already spoken to Bishop Benner, so it's just a matter of him announcing the date to the congregation."

"*Jah*, well, *Ich bins zufreide*—all right, I am satisfied. That will give me two months to find a place," Miriam answered.

"But where will you go?" Lewis asked with concern.

"I don't know yet, but there are two boarding homes in town. I will stop by one day next week and see if they have any rooms available."

"I suppose there's nothing I can say to change your mind?"

"No, nothing."

❧

The engagement and wedding date of Lewis Stoltzfus and Grace Zepp were officially published at the preaching service on Sunday, just as Lewis had planned.

On Monday, right after school let out for the day, Miriam rode into town, just as she had planned.

May Gate's Boardinghouse was located on a quiet street on the south side of town. It was a tall blue-and-white house, shaded by elm trees and surrounded by a white picket fence. It looked to Miriam like the perfect place to live. She would have solitude, seclusion, and no more farm duties or major household chores to take up so much of her time. Living in a boardinghouse would mean that all of her meals would be provided, and her only real responsibility would be in keeping her own room clean and tidy, and, of course, teaching at the Amish schoolhouse.

Just think of all the free time I will have for reading, quilting, and visiting friends and family, she told herself, as she mounted the front steps of the big house. She could already see herself reading to Rebekah, having long chats with Mom, and spending hours getting caught up on things with her best friend Crystal. Living in a boarding home might actually have its advantages.

Since this boarding home was run by a Mennonite woman, it would be plain, but there would still be some modern conveniences, such as electricity and up-to-date plumbing. Those were things Miriam was not accustomed to, but they were things she could probably adjust to rather well, she decided.

Miriam rapped on the front door several times and waited patiently. Finally, an older, rather heavyset woman, dressed in plain clothing similar to Miriam's, answered the door. "May I help you?" she asked.

"Are you May Gates?" Miriam questioned.

"I am," the woman replied.

"My name is Miriam Stoltzfus, and I'm looking for a room to rent. I will not be needing it until May, but—"

"I am very sorry, but all of my rooms are full right now, and no one plans to leave in the near future," May answered. "You might try Nora McCormick's Boardinghouse. It's across town, on Cherry Street."

"Jah, thank you, I will." Miriam turned and started down the sidewalk to her waiting horse and buggy.

"I hope you find something," May Gates called after her.

Miriam only nodded in response. She was beginning to feel a little anxious. What if the other boardinghouse was full, too? She hurried into her buggy, breathing a silent prayer that it wouldn't be. It was the first time she had prayed in many weeks.

Nora McCormick's Boardinghouse was a two-story brick house with a black wrought-iron fence around it. It was colder-looking than May Gate's home, but Miriam knew that she would take a room anyway, if there was one available. She rang the doorbell and waited expectantly.

A tall, slender woman of middle age answered the bell. "Good afternoon. May I help you?"

Miriam forced a smile. "Hello. My name is Miriam Stoltzfus, and I'm looking for a room to rent. I would be needing it by May."

The woman returned her smile and extended her hand. "I'm pleased to meet you, Miriam. My name is Nora McCormick. You're Amish, aren't you?"

Miriam nodded. *Jah,* I am Amish."

"I know that you Amish are usually good, God-fearing people and would probably cause me no trouble, like some previous boarders have done, and I would truly like to offer you a room. However, all of my rooms are taken at this time."

Miriam's smile faded. "Oh, I see. Is there a chance that someone might be moving out by May?"

Nora shook her head. "That doesn't seem very likely. Most of my boarders have steady jobs in the city, and they all seem quite happy living here."

"I understand. Thank you anyway." Miriam turned to leave.

"Try May Gate's place. She's across town," Nora called.

Miriam didn't even bother to answer. What point was there in telling her that she had already been to May Gate's Boardinghouse and that she, too, had no vacancies? It was beginning to look as though nothing in Miriam Stoltzfus's life would ever go as planned.

Chapter 24

Miriam had just reached the sidewalk by the curb when she bumped into a man. Her mouth dropped open. "You? Why do I always keep bumping into you?"

Nick McCormick smiled and winked at her. "I guess it's just my good fortune, fair lady. It's good to see you, Miriam. I've been thinking about you and wondering how you are doing."

"I am managing," Miriam replied curtly. She didn't want to give him the impression that she needed his shoulder to cry on again. Besides, she still had not completely forgiven him for taking Rebekah's picture or for the article that he had done for the newspaper.

"You are looking very well," Nick said smoothly. "In fact, I'd say that you are more beautiful than ever. It must be springtime. It always seems to make women their loveliest."

"Are you trying to flatter me?" Miriam asked as she felt her face turn warm.

"Not at all. I really do think you are beautiful, Miriam."

Miriam made no reply, and Nick went on. "So, what are you doing in this neck of the woods?"

"I was about to ask you the same question," she countered.

"My aunt lives here," he answered, looking up at the big brick house. "She runs a boardinghouse."

Jah, I know. I was just asking about a room. I did not know that she was a relative of yours, however."

"If you had known, would you still have come here?" Nick said with another one of his frequent winks.

"Of course I would," Miriam was quick to say. "I have nothing against you personally, Nick, though I know that we have had our share of misunderstandings."

"That is true, we have," Nick agreed. "But if you were living here in town, we could see more of each other, and then we'd be able to find out if we could ever see eye-to-eye on anything."

Miriam knew that her face was becoming redder by the minute, but there seemed little she could do about it. "I wish I could move into town," she said, "but unfortunately your aunt has no rooms available."

Nick frowned. "I'm sorry to hear that." He paused and shook his head. "Say, why do you need a room anyway? I thought you lived at your Amish homestead with your family."

"I do, but Mom has moved out in order to live with my older brother Andrew and his family. Andrew's Rebekah's father, remember?"

Nick nodded.

"Mom felt that her help was necessary since Rebekah is confined to a wheel-chair," Miriam continued. "Then in May, my younger brother Lewis is planning to be married. He will be bringing his new bride home to our house to live. So, there is really nothing left for me to do but move out."

"You mean, they're kicking you out?"

"No, no. Lewis invited me to stay on after they are married, but I don't feel that it would be the right thing to do. Newlyweds need their privacy, and I would not really feel very comfortable having another woman come into my kitchen and perhaps begin to change things around. I'm sure that Grace will want to do things her own way, and Lewis's big sister would only be in the way."

"Have you checked at the other boardinghouse in town? Maybe there's a vacancy there?" Nick suggested.

Miriam shook her head. "I've already been there. I just don't know what to do. I can't really afford to pay the high rent for an apartment, and I certainly can't buy a place of my own."

Nick smiled warmly, and his blue eyes twinkled. "You could move in with me."

"Nick McCormick, you are terrible! If you know anything at all about the Amish, you should know that we do not believe in a couple living together out of wedlock!" Miriam exclaimed.

"Who says it has to be out of wedlock?" Nick asked as he gave her another wink.

"What? What are you saying?" Miriam stammered.

"I'm saying that you can marry me," Nick answered seriously. "I'm not getting any younger, and maybe it's time I settled down with a good woman—and a beautiful one at that."

Miriam's face had grown so hot that she could feel perspiration beading up on her forehead. It was almost inconceivable that she could have had two marriage proposals in the same week—and by two men who were from opposite sides of the world, so to speak. "You are teasing me, aren't you, Nick?" she said in a near whisper.

"No, I'm not. Listen, I've surprised myself just as much as I have you by popping the question, but now that I have, I kind of like the idea," Nick said with a laugh. "The thought of coming home at night to a good home-cooked meal and a beautiful wife waiting for me is kind of appealing—even to a confirmed bachelor like me. I know we're about as different as night and day, but who knows—maybe we could make it work. We do seem to find one another easy to talk to, and it could be the adventure of our lives."

"But, but—I would have to leave the Amish faith if I were to marry an outsider," Miriam told him. "I would be excommunicated and shunned by my family and friends."

Nick reached for her hand and pulled her toward his car. "Let's go for a little ride and talk this whole thing over. I'm sure we can figure out some way to tell your folks and make them understand that it's not necessary to shun you for choosing to marry an Englishman."

Miriam's head was spinning. She felt so giddy in Nick's presence. However, there was one missing ingredient—love. She wasn't sure that the desire she felt was love. In fact, she was fairly certain that it was probably just infatuation—infatuation with something or someone that was forbidden. Still Nick's proposal was flattering, and it did make her feel good that he would make such an offer.

"You have mentioned my beauty and how nice it would be to have home-cooked meals," she said, "but you have not mentioned anything about love. Giving up my Amish faith would be a very drastic step, with many changes to make, and I certainly could never do anything so permanent unless there was a real, lasting love involved."

Nick looked down at the sidewalk for a minute as though he were trying to collect his thoughts. "If two people are attracted to each other, as I believe that we are, then what else really matters?"

"Love," Miriam responded.

"What is love anyway?" Nick asked.

"It's trust, it's friendship, it's commitment, it's a deep longing to be together, and it's a shared feeling of great emotional depth," Miriam responded. "Do you feel those things for me?"

Nick shook his head slowly. "No, Miriam, I can't honestly say that I do, but to me, they're just not all that important. I believe that two people can be happy together if they just have a genuine physical attraction, and if they are able to have fun together. Life can be a lot of fun, you know. I don't think we need to go through life with all kinds of rules and regulations controlling us. Our government and local law enforcement does enough of that for us. Our personal lives should be fun and adventuresome."

Miriam swallowed hard. She could feel tears forming in her eyes and that familiar burning at the back of her throat. She pulled her trembling hand out of his and stepped away. "I am sure that you meant well, asking me to leave my faith and marry you, but I cannot. We hardly know each other, and even if we did, I think we both know that things could never work out between us. I have strayed from my religious teachings, and my attitude toward God has changed, but I cannot and I will not let my family down by leaving our faith for a relationship that is built on nothing more than a physical attraction between two people."

"Is that your final word?" Nick asked.

"Yes, it is," she responded firmly.

"Then you will either have to get used to living with your brother and his wife or find yourself some nice Amish man to marry. Your beauty should certainly turn some man's head—someone who is worthy of you as his wife."

Miriam was tempted to tell him that she had just had such a proposal of marriage from Amos Hilty, but she decided against it, since nothing would be gained.

She could not accept either man's proposal. There was no love offered from either Nick or Amos. And she wasn't sure that she could trust either of them. Nick had already let her down once, and Amos was only looking for a mother for his child.

"I had better be getting on home," Miriam said. "I have chores that are waiting." She walked quickly to her buggy and climbed inside.

Nick followed her, and just as she was about to pull away from the curb, he called, "I wish you only the best, Miriam Stoltzfus. If you ever change your mind about us, you know where to reach me."

Nick's final words resounded in Miriam's head for the rest of the day and on into the week that followed. Her head told her that she had done the right thing in turning down his proposal, but her heart wasn't so sure. She had to find a place to live, and marrying Nick would have been her way out. But no matter how hard she tried to rationalize such a decision as leaving the Amish faith, she simply could not give in to the temptation. The Amish culture was the only way of life she had ever known. Her security and acceptance had always come through her people. Her family and friends were important to her. She could never leave them behind, not even for love, much less a physical attraction. Love and marriage were obviously not to be for her. She had come to accept that fact, and she must learn to face life alone. But where was she going to go? She would have to work on some other plan. There had to be some adequate answer to her dilemma.

꧁

Miriam sat up in bed and wiped the perspiration from her forehead. She had been dreaming. It was a strange dream about three men. First there had been William Graber, smiling and waving at her, then he drove away in his open buggy with his new bride. Then Nick McCormick came on the scene. He was following her around, with his camera pointing at her. He was laughing and calling her "fair lady." She had pulled her dark bonnet down over her face, and when she removed it again, Nick was gone, and Amos Hilty stood before her. He was holding a bouquet of heartsease pansies. *What did the strange dream mean?* she wondered now.

Miriam looked at the clock by her bedside and frowned. It was only four o'clock in the morning. She did not have to get up for another hour, yet she was afraid to go back to sleep. What if her dream continued? She did not want to think about William, Nick, or Amos. For that matter, it would suit her fine if she never thought of any man ever again!

Chapter 25

With the month of April half over and May quickly approaching, Miriam was beginning to feel a sense of panic. She had checked the classified ads faithfully every day, and not even a single room was available for rent anywhere. She had decided that maybe she could rent or buy a place after all, but the asking price of everything within her area was just too expensive. A single woman, living on the small wages she received as a teacher, could not afford any of the high-priced places that were available.

She had just about given up and had decided that for the time being she would have to stay at the house with Lewis and Grace. She hoped that the newly-weds would understand.

One morning on the way to school, Miriam passed Amos Hilty and Mary Ellen. They were obviously headed in the direction of the schoolhouse, too. Mary Ellen waved and smiled, calling out a cheery "Hello, Teacher!"

Miriam waved back and urged her horse into a trot. She didn't think it would be right for her students to arrive at school before their teacher did.

As she pulled into the school yard, she was relieved to see that none of the other children were there yet. She pulled her horse to a stop and climbed down from the buggy. She was just starting for the schoolhouse when the Hilty buggy entered the yard.

Miriam watched as Amos got out and went around to help his daughter down. In spite of her dislike for the man, Miriam had to admit that he was a good father, and Mary Ellen obviously loved him very much.

Just as Mary Ellen stepped down, her foot got caught in the hem of her dress. She looked down, and her lower lip began to quiver. "It's torn!" she sobbed. "Pappy, please don't make me go to school today. The others will laugh at me!"

The look that Amos gave his daughter turned from sympathy to frustration. "I can do nothing about your dress right now, Mary Ellen. We will take it over to Maudie Miller's right after school lets out. She can mend it for you then."

Mary Ellen shook her head and gave her father an imploring look. "No, Pappy, please!"

Miriam stepped forward. "Come inside with me, Mary Ellen. I will mend your dress."

Amos looked surprised as he turned to face Miriam. "Would you really do that for her? Do you have the necessary tools?"

Miriam gave a small laugh. "You need not be so surprised, Amos Hilty. In spite of what some may say about me, I have actually been known to do some small acts of kindness."

"I–I did not mean to say—" Amos stammered.

"Never mind, Amos. You just go on your way, and Mary Ellen will be fine." Miriam put her hand across Mary Ellen's back and guided her toward the school-house; then she turned back and called to Amos, "Oh, and by the way—you do not use *tools* to sew, but I do keep a small sewing kit full of *supplies* in my desk for just such an emergency as this."

Amos mumbled something to himself and climbed back into his buggy.

Mary Ellen's face was streaked with tears, and when Miriam reached her desk, the first thing she did was to dip a clean cloth into the bucket of water that she kept nearby. Gently, she wiped the child's face. "Now stand on this chair while I hem up your dress," Miriam instructed.

Mary Ellen gave her a questioning look.

"It would be quicker and easier if your dress was off, but some of the other children may arrive soon, and you would not want to be standing here without your dress on, now would you?"

Mary Ellen shook her head. "No, Teacher."

"Very well, then hold real still. No *rutshing* either." Miriam quickly threaded a needle and began the task of putting Mary Ellen's hem back into place.

When the job was completed, Mary Ellen smiled happily and jumped down from the chair. "Thank you, Teacher. *Es gookt verderbt schee*—it looks mighty nice."

"Jah, sis gute gange," Miriam replied, just as the door opened and three of the Hoelwarth boys burst into the room.

Miriam was glad that the sewing job had been completed. She knew that the Hoelwarth children were all teases, and they would have no doubt taunted and teased Mary Ellen if they had seen her standing on a chair getting her dress mended.

The morning went by quickly, and soon it was lunchtime. Miriam watched as Mary Ellen opened up her metal lunch box. The child ate hungrily, but Miriam was appalled at what Amos had given his daughter for lunch. The contents of the lunch box revealed a hard biscuit, some dried beef jerky, a green apple, and a bottle of water.

Miriam wondered if maybe Amos had just been in a hurry that morning, or was he completely ignorant as to a child's nutritional needs? Why had she never noticed before what Mary Ellen ate for lunch? Perhaps she brought lunches like this every day.

Miriam shook her head and sighed inwardly. *The man really does need a wife, and Mary Ellen certainly needs a mother!*

Miriam looked away from the child and directed her gaze out the window. She had to get her mind off of Mary Ellen and onto something else. She could feel one of her sick headaches coming on, and she had to do something to ward it off. Quickly, she reached into her desk drawer and retrieved a bottle of White Willow Bark capsules. The glass of water that normally sat on her desk was half full, so she popped two capsules into her mouth and swallowed them down.

Miriam was relieved when all the children had finished their lunches and filed outside to play. Now maybe she would have a few minutes of peace. But that was not to be. After only a brief time, a commotion outside ended her solitude.

When she went outside to investigate, Miriam found a group of children gathered around Mary Ellen. This was not the first time that she had witnessed some of the children picking on the child, and she wondered what the problem could be this time.

Mary Ellen lay crumpled on the ground, sobbing hysterically, while several of the older boys, including two of the Hoelwarths, were pointing at her and laughing. John Hoelwarth held a long stick in his hand and was poking Mary Ellen with it. "Get up, baby Hilty. Quit your crying. You are such a little crybaby!"

Angrily, Miriam grabbed the stick from John and whirled him around to face her. "Just exactly what is going on here, and why are you poking at a defenseless little girl?"

John shrugged and hung his head. "I was only trying to make her quit her bawling. She sounds like one of my pa's heifers."

All the children who stood nearby began to laugh.

"Quiet!" Miriam shouted. "I want to know why Mary Ellen was crying, and why you children have been teasing her again."

"Look at her hair, Teacher," Sara Kaiser answered. "She hasn't got a mama, and her papa can't fix it so that it stays up. She looks pretty silly."

Mary Ellen, who was still crying, had not moved from her spot on the ground.

Miriam bent down and pulled the child gently to her feet. "Come inside, Mary Ellen. I will fix your hair and clean you up." To the other children, she said, "You may all stay outside until I call you. Then we will discuss what has happened here." She turned and led Mary Ellen back to the schoolhouse.

It took nearly half an hour for Miriam to get the child calmed down, cleaned up, and her hair combed, braided, and back up into place again.

"Try not to let the children's teasing bother you, Mary Ellen," Miriam said softly. "Some of the older ones just like to make trouble. They like to pick on someone who is smaller and cannot defend them themselves. They will all be made to stay after school."

"Well, *wass machts aus*—what does it matter?" Mary Ellen said, trying to sound brave. "They will always tease me because I have no mama."

"Oh, no, I'm sure they understand that your mama died, and that—"

"If Mama was alive still, she would sew my dresses so the hems would always stay up. She would fix me good lunches like the others have, and she would do better with my hair. Pappy tries real hard, but he can't do some things the way a mama can," Mary Ellen was quick to say. She looked right into Miriam's eyes and her lower lip quivered slightly. "I wish you were my mama, Teacher."

Miriam swallowed hard. There was no doubt about it. Mary Ellen Hilty did need her. For that matter, Amos probably needed her, too. And as much as she hated to admit it, she needed them—or at least their home to live in. She knew she could never give up her faith to marry Nick, who she was very attracted to, but perhaps a marriage without love would not be such a bad thing if it did not mean she had to leave her faith and family. At least there would be mutual needs being met by all concerned.

It was a heartrending decision, but she knew now what she must do. She would speak to Amos this very day. She knew that she must tell him she would become his wife soon, before she lost her nerve.

Chapter 26

I will not tease" had been written on the blackboard one hundred times by each of the boys who had tormented Mary Ellen Hilty, and Miriam had kept the entire class after school and given them a lecture on kindness. She'd also reminded them of what the Bible teaches about doing unto others as we would have done unto us. It had become increasingly difficult for her to refer to the Bible, but she knew that it was the most appropriate lesson manual she could have used.

It had been a long, emotionally exhausting day at school, and Miriam was glad that it was finally over. Now she must ride over to the Hiltys' and speak to Amos before she lost her nerve. The decision to marry him had not been an easy one, and now she had a fearful heart. Her mind was so full of questions. Would he even still want to marry her? Would Mary Ellen really be happy about it? What would her own family think? And most of all, could she really make herself go through with it?

Miriam poured herself a glass of water and swallowed the two White Willow Bark capsules she had put in her mouth. If she was going to face Amos, it had better not be with a pounding headache. Then, with a sigh of resignation, she gathered up her things and headed out the schoolhouse door to her waiting horse and buggy.

❧

Mary Ellen was sitting on the front porch, playing with a yellow and white kitten, when Miriam pulled into the yard. The child waved and ran excitedly toward Miriam when she climbed down from the buggy. "Teacher, you came to visit! Look, my hem's still in place," she said, pulling at the corner of her dress.

Miriam nodded. "I see that it is, and I see that your hair is still in place as well."

Mary Ellen smiled happily. "You did a good job, Teacher. Don't tell Pappy I said so, but you're much better at fixing hair than he is."

Miriam smiled, too. She couldn't help but like the pathetic young girl. She obviously did need a woman to care for her and to train her to do all of the feminine things that her father was unable to do. "Speaking of your pappy," Miriam said, "where is he? I need to talk to him."

"He's out in the barn," Mary Ellen answered. "I can take you there, if you want me to."

"Thank you, but I think it would be best if you stayed on the porch and played with your kitten. Your pappy and I need to talk grown-up talk for a few minutes. We will join you on the porch when we are done. How does that sound?"

Mary Ellen's eyes grew large. "You are not going to tell Pappy about those boys teasing me today, are you, Teacher?"

Miriam shook her head. "No, Mary Ellen. What I have to say to your pappy has nothing to do with the Hoelwarth boys."

Mary Ellen looked relieved, and she smiled confidently. "I'll play 'til you're done talking. Then maybe we can all have cookies and milk."

"*Jah,* maybe we can," Miriam responded. She turned toward the barn then, and Mary Ellen headed for the front porch of the house.

Miriam found Amos in a horse stall, grooming one of his buggy horses. She cleared her throat loudly so he would know she had come into the barn.

Amos looked up and smiled. "What a nice surprise! It's good to see you, Miriam. I want to thank you for mending Mary Ellen's dress this morning."

Miriam nodded. "I was glad to do it."

"What brings you out our way?" Amos asked. "Did you need to speak with me about Mary Ellen?"

"No. Actually, I came here to talk about your offer of marriage," Miriam said quickly, before she lost her nerve and decided to bolt for the door.

"Have you been thinking it over?" Amos asked.

"*Jah,* I have," Miriam answered. "If the offer is still open, I will marry you Amos."

Amos dropped the currycomb he was holding and took a step toward Miriam. "*Derr Herr sie gedanki*—thank the Lord! I do not know what caused you to change your mind, but I am glad you have. I think Mary Ellen will be, also."

"Mary Ellen is the reason that I did change my mind," Miriam stated truthfully. "The child does need a woman's care. It's not that you aren't doing a fine job with her, but—"

"I think I understand what you are trying to say," Amos interrupted. "She does need a mother. She needs someone who can do all of the feminine things for her that I cannot do." He reached out and placed his hand lightly on Miriam's arm. "As you know, I do have some concerns about how your attitude might affect Mary Ellen, however."

"I would never do anything to hurt the child," Miriam was quick to say.

"*Jah,* I believe you. If there is to be a marriage, I need your word that you will not let your bitterness show to Mary Ellen. You must help me train her in God's ways, and you must set a good example for my daughter."

Miriam pulled away from his touch. She was beginning to wonder if she had done the right thing after all. Could she really keep from letting her bitter heart be noticeable to Mary Ellen? Could she set the child a good example?

Amos smiled and said softly, "I, too, need you, Miriam. I need a wife."

"Do you mean just for cooking and cleaning, or in every way?" Miriam asked boldly.

Amos shuffled his feet and looked down at the dirt floor of the barn. His face had turned slightly red, and he stammered, "I—that is—I would like a loving, physical relationship with my wife, but if you do not feel ready—"

"I am not ready!" Miriam stated, a little too harshly. "I may never be ready for that, Amos. If this will be a problem for you, then perhaps we should forget the whole idea of marriage."

"No, no. I will wait patiently, until you feel ready for my physical touch," he answered. "Until then, we will live together as friends and learn about one another. Maybe as our friendship grows, things will change between us."

"I do not want to give you any false hope, Amos. I do not think that I can ever love you," Miriam told him as gently as she knew how.

"We shall see," Amos said. "And now, let us go up to the house and tell Mary Ellen our news. I'm sure that she will be delighted."

So it was decided, just that simply. Miriam could hardly believe that Amos had accepted her conditions. *He must really be desperate for a housekeeper and a mother for his child,* she reasoned. *Of course, I had to agree to his conditions as well.*

Mary Ellen was still on the porch playing with her kitten when Amos and Miriam joined her. She looked up at them expectantly. "Can we have some cookies and milk, Pappy?"

Amos smiled down at his daughter. "That sounds like a fine idea. Let's go inside. We will sit around the kitchen table, eat our cookies, and talk. Miriam and I have something very important that we want to tell you." Mary Ellen reached for her father's hand, and they all entered the house.

It was the first time Miriam had ever been inside the Hilty house. Amos never opened it up for Sunday services, and it was obvious to her why he didn't. The house wasn't really dirty, just very cluttered and unkempt looking. If there had ever been any doubt in her mind about whether Amos needed a wife or not, it was erased now. The touch of a woman in the house was greatly needed.

Amos poured tall glasses of fresh milk, while Mary Ellen went to the cookie jar and got out some cookies that were obviously store-bought. When they had all taken seats at the table, Amos cleared his throat loudly and said, "Mary Ellen, how would you like it if Pappy got married again?"

Mary Ellen looked at him questioningly. "A new mama for me?"

Amos smiled and nodded. "A wife for me and a mama for you."

Mary Ellen turned to face Miriam. "Is it you, Teacher? Are you going to marry Pappy?"

"How would you feel about that, Mary Ellen?" Miriam asked.

Mary Ellen smiled, a smile that reached from ear to ear. She reached out and took hold of one of Miriam's hands. "I would like it very much. When can you come to live with us?"

Amos laughed. "Not until we are married, little one."

"When will that be?" Mary Ellen wanted to know.

Amos looked at Miriam, and she shrugged. "As soon as possible, I suppose."

Amos nodded in agreement. "I will speak to Bishop Benner right away. I will ask that we be published at the next preaching service."

"Maybe we could be married on the same day as Lewis and Grace," Miriam suggested. "We would be inviting pretty much the same people anyway, and if we have a double wedding, it will keep the cost of the food and everything down."

"That is a fine idea," Amos answered. "Would you like to speak to Lewis and Grace about it?"

Miriam reached for a cookie. "*Jah*, I will talk to them tonight."

Chapter 27

The date of Lewis and Grace's wedding had been set for the second Saturday of May. They were both overjoyed at Miriam's announcement that she was going to marry Amos Hilty, and they happily agreed to share their wedding day with them.

Mom was happier about the news of her daughter's wedding than anyone. Noting that they had only a few weeks, she quickly set about sewing a simple wedding dress for Miriam to wear. Miriam didn't want any fuss made, and she would have just as soon been married in one of the dresses she already owned, but Mom wouldn't hear of it. She insisted that all brides must have a new dress for their wedding day.

Miriam was certain that Mom and nearly everyone else in the family thought she was marrying Amos because she had changed her mind about him, and perhaps that she even now loved him; she had no intention of telling them anything otherwise. However, Miriam knew that Crystal, whom she had not yet told, would not be so easily deceived.

Crystal stopped by to see Miriam the day after she had already told the rest of the family. Crystal said she had left the twins with a neighbor and was wondering if Miriam would go into town to do some shopping with her.

"I really don't feel much like shopping today," Miriam told Crystal, "but thank you for thinking of me."

"Do you have some other plans for the day?" Crystal asked.

"No, not really. Just the usual work around here," Miriam answered.

"Then let's get out for awhile. It will do us both good. Besides, you stay around here working far too much," Crystal argued.

Silence filled the room as Miriam sat on the edge of her kitchen chair, blinking back the tears that had suddenly gathered in her eyes. She felt Crystal's arm encircle her shoulders.

"What is it, Miriam?" Crystal asked with obvious concern.

"Amos Hilty has asked me to marry him."

Crystal gasped. "Really? When?"

"Several weeks ago, but yesterday I gave him my answer."

"And what was your answer?" Crystal asked.

"I told him that I would marry him," Miriam said with a catch in her voice. "I know that he does not love me, Crystal. He only wants a housekeeper and a mother for Mary Ellen."

"Then why did you accept his proposal?"

"Mary Ellen needs me," Miriam stated flatly. "I know that I have said many times that I would never marry without love, but there will be love, Crystal. Mary Ellen's love for me, and my love for her."

Crystal took a seat across from Miriam. "I sense that you have some doubts."

Miriam nodded. "*Jah.*" She wiped the tears from her face with the back of her hand. "Part of it is the fact that there is no love between Amos and me, but my main concern is trust. I don't know if I can trust Amos."

"Trust him how?" Crystal asked.

"He has agreed not to force a physical relationship on me, but men are all alike," Miriam said. "Men are selfish, and—"

"Miriam, all men are not like William Graber," Crystal interrupted. "Amos Hilty appears to be a very honest man. I don't believe he will hurt you the way William did. However, since you obviously feel no love for him, and you say he doesn't love you, either—"

"He does not!" Miriam exclaimed.

"Then maybe it would be best if you do not make a lifelong commitment to him," Crystal told her. "Divorce is not an acceptable option among the Old Order Amish, as you know."

"So are you saying that I should call the marriage off?"

"I am only saying that I feel you need to give the matter much prayer and thought," Crystal answered. "I want to see you happy, and if you marry someone whom you feel no love for, how can you ever be truly happy?"

Miriam shrugged. "I have found that life is not always happy."

"Until you get rid of your feelings of mistrust and allow God to fill your heart with love and peace, you will never be happy, Miriam."

"I have learned to manage without love or happiness," Miriam replied. "Besides, if I do marry Amos, it will benefit all three of us. I won't be living here with Lewis and Grace, so they will be much happier. Mary Ellen will have a mother to care for her needs properly. And Amos will have someone to cook and clean for him."

"And what about your needs, Miriam?"

"I will be well taken care of—a roof over my head, a hardworking husband, and a child to love." Miriam paused. "I do have some serious doubts about all this, but I believe that I must go through with it. I hope that as my very best friend, you will support me in this decision. I would like you to be one of my attendants, if you are willing."

"Of course I am," Crystal assured her. "I will help with your wedding plans in any way that I can. If you are doing what you feel your heart is telling you to do, then I will support you with my love and my prayers."

Miriam stared at the table in front of her. "I am not thinking with my heart, only my head. My common sense tells me that this is the right thing to do."

With only a week before the wedding, Miriam found that she still had several things to buy in town. She was beginning to wish that she had taken Crystal up on her offer to go shopping the Saturday before. "I will just have to go alone today," Miriam told herself. "It's the last Saturday before the wedding, so I really have no other choice." As soon as her chores were done for the morning, she hitched up her horse and buggy and started for town.

The Country Store, her favorite place to shop, was unusually busy. Not only were there many Amish customers, but there were also a lot of tourists. Miriam disliked crowds, especially when she knew that the tourists would be watching her and all the other Amish who so often shopped in the little rural town. If these English people had been merely shopping, then most of them would have gone into the big city of Lancaster.

Miriam moved to the back of the store, where the household items were. There was an oil lamp on one of the high shelves that she wished to look at, but it was too high for her to reach. She looked around for the store clerk, but he was not in sight. She sighed and turned away, deciding to look at some material instead.

"Do you need some help?"

Thinking that perhaps one of the other clerks had come to her aid, Miriam turned back and said, *"Jah,* I would like to see—" Her mouth fell open. "Nick McCormick! What are you doing here?"

Nick smiled his usual heart-melting smile. "I like to come here on weekends. I get lots of story ideas from watching the people."

"You mean *my people,* don't you?" Miriam was quick to say.

Nick gave her a playful wink. "The Amish are very interesting people. Especially you, fair lady. I find you to be the most fascinating Amish woman of all."

Miriam's cheeks grew warm. Why did Nick McCormick have such a way about him? she wondered. She knew that she was considered quite plain by her own people, but in Nick's presence she actually could begin to believe that she was pretty.

"You know, I think it must be fate, us always running into each other. Maybe we really are meant to be together, Miriam," Nick said as he leaned his head very close to hers.

Miriam quickly pulled away. What if someone she knew saw her engaged in such a personal conversation with this Englishman? "We are not meant to be together, Nick."

"Your lips say so, but your eyes tell me something different," Nick whispered.

Miriam felt her hands become clammy and her heart was beating fast against her chest. She had to get away from Nick McCormick as quickly as possible. Yet she did not want to leave the store until she had completed her shopping. "If you will excuse me, I really must find a clerk to help me."

"What kind of help do you need, fair lady?" he asked smoothly.

She looked overhead at the shelf above. "I need some help getting that kerosene lamp down."

"No problem at all," Nick said. He reached for the lamp and handed it easily down to Miriam. "Here you are."

"Thank you," she replied.

"So, how are things with you these days?" Nick asked. "Did you ever find a room to rent?"

Miriam shook her head. "No. I no longer have any need of a room."

"Oh? And why is that?"

"I am getting married in a week," Miriam stated.

Nick frowned. "I see. So, who's the lucky fellow?"

"He is a very nice Amish man," Miriam answered.

"I didn't think he'd be anything but Amish," Nick countered. "I know that a girl like you could never be truly happy with someone like me, who's an outsider. You were right to turn my offer of marriage down. We both know that it probably would never have worked out for us."

Miriam was tempted to tell him that she wasn't going to be happy with Amos, either, but instead she just nodded and said, "You are right, of course. I could never be happy with someone who wasn't Amish."

Nick leaned in close to her ear and whispered, "I would ask for a kiss from the bride-to-be, but I suppose just a word of congratulations would be more appropriate under the circumstances." He smiled. "Listen, I'd like to do something for you, if you'll let me."

"What is it?" Miriam asked hesitantly.

"Let me buy that oil lamp for you. It will be my wedding present to you. Whenever you look at it, maybe you'll remember me and know that I am happy that you found someone to love you."

Miriam swallowed against the lump that had formed in her throat. How could Nick know that she had not found someone to love her—except for Mary Ellen, that is?

"Please, don't deny me this pleasure," Nick coaxed. "It would make me very happy."

Miriam shrugged. *"Jah,* I suppose it will be all right." Who was she to stand in the way of anyone's happiness?

Chapter 28

As Miriam's wedding day approached, she found herself feeling more and more anxious. She wondered at times if she could really make herself go through with it, but then she would remind herself that she really did need another place to live and that Mary Ellen desperately needed her. With those thoughts in mind, she determined in her heart to follow through with the commitment she had made to Amos.

On the day of the wedding, Miriam awoke with a headache. "Oh, no!" she groaned. "Not today!" She forced herself to get dressed and headed downstairs to the kitchen.

As she sat at the table drinking the cup of peppermint herb tea she had used to wash down two White Willow Bark capsules, she began to reflect on her life. She rubbed her forehead thoughtfully and thought about the only life she had ever known. Here at this familiar old house, all of her memories swirled around in her head. She had been born here—right upstairs in Mom and Papa's room. She had grown up here. She'd never known any other home. Now everything had changed. Papa was dead. Mom was gone, moved in with Andrew and Sarah, and she and her youngest brother Lewis were both about to be married. She would be moving away to Amos Hilty's house, where she would be his housekeeper and Mary Ellen's new mama. Lewis would be bringing a new bride to Miriam's home, and she would soon be its new mistress. Nothing would ever be the same again.

She swallowed hard, trying to force that old familiar lump out of her throat. Her eyes stung with the threatening tears. She didn't belong here anymore, but, oh, how she would miss this home.

"Good morning, bride-to-be!"

Miriam turned and saw Lewis standing in the doorway, smiling from ear to ear. *Does he actually think that my heart is happy this morning?* "Good morning, groom-to-be," she answered, instead of voicing her true thoughts.

"This is our big day, Sis. Are you feeling a bit anxious?"

Miriam nodded. *"Jah,* just a bit. And you?"

Lewis smiled. "I would be lying if I said I wasn't, but my heart is so happy that I feel like it could burst at any moment!"

"Grace is a wonderful girl," Miriam told him. "I am sure that the two of you will be very happy living here together."

"Jah, I hope we can be as happy as Mom and Papa were for so many years. I am very happy for you and Amos, too, Miriam," Lewis added. "You both deserve some real joy in your lives."

Miriam groaned inwardly, but outwardly she managed a weak smile. She was glad her brother's heart was so happy. She only wished she could feel more than an anxious heart on the morning of her wedding day.

The three-hour wedding ceremony began at nine o'clock in the morning and was similar to a Sunday morning preaching service. It was held at the home of Grace's parents, since their house was larger than the Stoltzfus home and could accommodate more guests.

Both brides, dressed in plain blue cotton dresses draped with contrasting capes and aprons, and wearing white prayer caps on their heads, appeared to be quite anxious. However, this anxiousness was for quite different reasons. Grace was anxious and excited to become Lewis's bride, while Miriam was anxious and nervous about becoming Amos's bride.

Grace had asked her sister Martha and a friend named Faith to be her attendants, and Miriam had chosen Crystal and Sarah as hers.

Lewis and Amos both wore white shirts, black trousers, and matching vests and jackets. They also had on their heads black hats with three-and-a-half inch brims.

Jonas and Andrew were Lewis's attendants, and Amos had asked two Amish men named Joseph and Philip.

The wedding included the congregational singing of several hymns from the Amish hymnbook called the *Ausbund,* a long sermon on the subject of marriage, with Scripture references taken from both the Old and New Testaments, testimonies from several of the church leaders, a time of counseling in another part of the house for the brides and grooms, and extended prayer, and, of course, the traditional wedding vows.

The vows were the part of the ceremony that Miriam had dreaded the most, knowing that both men and women of the Amish faith take their wedding vows very seriously. Divorce would not be an acceptable option if things did not go well between her and Amos. The bride and groom were expected to work out their problems, and above all else, remain true to the vows that they had spoken before God and man.

Though Miriam's intent was to remain married to Amos Hilty until death would part them, it was not going to be easy to promise to love, honor, or obey him. She might be able to honor him, and if his demands were not too great, possibly she could obey him—but love? She knew that was out of the question. She would never feel anything more than perhaps a mutual respect for Amos. She hated the idea of reciting her vows and not really meaning them, but what other choice did she have? she reasoned. She was doing the right thing for Mary Ellen, and no one but her and Amos would know this was not to be a marriage based on love.

Miriam tried to push the guilt that she was feeling aside as she took her place beside her groom. They were the older of the two couples being married, so they would repeat their vows before the bishop first.

Miriam thought that if Bishop Benner had only known about her lack of faith in God and the circumstances of her marriage to Amos, he probably would not have agreed to perform the ceremony until Miriam had come to see the error of her ways. She was glad that the man could not see into her heart and know what she was really feeling.

When the vows had been said, the bishop blessed them, and the couple sat down again. Miriam swallowed hard. It was done. There was no going back now. She was Mrs. Amos Hilty and would remain so until the day that either she or Amos died.

Amos had taken her hand as they found their way back to their seats on the backless benches. She had not resisted, since they were in full view of all the nearly two hundred guests. There had been no traditional wedding kiss, as most people outside of the Amish faith usually exchange when they become husband and wife. Kissing and other such demonstrations of affection were to be kept for private moments, when the bride and groom were alone. Only Miriam knew this was not to be the case in her own marriage. It was a marriage of convenience, not of love or even physical attraction. While Amos was not hard to look at, he certainly did not hold the appeal for Miriam that Nick McCormick had.

Now it was the younger couple's turn to stand before the bishop and say their vows. Grace smiled happily up at her groom, and the love that she obviously felt for him could be seen by all. Lewis returned her smile, and his face, too, showed love for the woman who was about to become his wife.

As Miriam watched, her eyes misted. She felt joy for her younger brother and his bride, but a heavy heart for herself. She would never know a love such as theirs. She was now a married woman, but her heart would always be empty and pained.

Chapter 29

When the final prayer had been said by the bishop, the wedding service was officially over. Everyone filed outside to wait for the meal to be served. Since there were more guests than indoor seating, groups of people took turns filing into the house to eat. Both brides and grooms were seated at a special table called the *Eck*, because it was in the corner. From their vantage place, the young couples could see all their guests and be free to visit while they ate the sumptuous wedding meal. There were platters full of fried chicken, roast beef, and ham, accompanied by large bowls of mashed potatoes, stuffing, several kinds of vegetables, coleslaw, and numerous relish trays. Coffee, tea, milk, and apple cider were also available as beverages. For dessert, there was cherry pie, donuts, fruit salad, tapioca pudding, chocolate cake, and homemade ice cream. Miriam ate until she couldn't swallow another bite. Everything tasted so good.

Mary Ellen, who was sitting next to her, smiled and said, "Can I call you Mama Mim now, Teacher?"

Miriam laughed lightly. *"Jah*, if you like, but only at home. You must still call me Teacher when you are at school."

"You mean you will be my mama and my teacher, too?" Mary Ellen asked.

"Of course I will," Miriam began.

"Now that is something Miriam and I will need to discuss later on," Amos said.

Miriam wanted to tell him there was nothing to discuss, but rather than cause a possible scene, she merely smiled and patted Mary Ellen's hand. "Why don't you run along outside and play with some of your friends?"

The child moved closer to Miriam's side and whispered, "I would much rather stay with you, Teacher—I mean, Mama Mim."

Instead of a honeymoon, most newlywed Amish couples spent their weekends visiting their extended families in order to receive gifts so that they could set up housekeeping in the proper manner. Due to the fact that Amos already had a fully stocked home, he said he didn't feel that it was necessary to receive any gifts, so he and Miriam would not be spending their weekends anywhere but in their own home.

Miriam argued with Amos, saying that Lewis and Grace were also living in a fully stocked house, and that they were planning to follow the traditional Amish custom of visiting and collecting gifts. When this statement did nothing to change Amos's mind, she tried another tactic. "Amos, we really could use a few things to make our home a bit more comfortable, such as some new blankets and quilts, perhaps some braided rugs—and even the food supply in your pantry is rather low."

"I will give you the money to buy whatever you think is needed," Amos told her firmly, making it quite clear that the subject was closed.

So this is how it is going to be, thought Miriam as she cleared away the breakfast dishes. *No wonder he could not find another wife.*

Miriam had only moved into Amos's house the day before, and already she wondered if she had made the biggest mistake of her life. Since today was an off Sunday, and there would be no regular preaching services, she and Amos could use the time to get a few things straight between them. Once the morning chores were finished, they should be able to talk without any interruptions.

Mary Ellen, who was playing on the kitchen floor with her kitten, looked up at Miriam and smiled. "I'm so glad you have come to live with Pappy and me."

Miriam smiled back but said nothing. How could she explain to the small child that she herself was anything but glad about the arrangement? Had it not been for Mary Ellen, she would probably not be standing in Amos's kitchen right now.

Amos pushed his chair away from the table and stood up. He walked across the room to the stove and removed the coffeepot. "Mary Ellen, would you please take your kitten and go outside for awhile?"

Mary Ellen looked at her father with questioning eyes. "You and Mama Mim want to be alone, don't you, Pappy?"

If only that were true. The last thing she wanted was to be alone with her new husband.

"Miriam and I need to talk," Amos told his daughter. "It is a beautiful spring day, and if you go outside to play right now, later, after the chores, we will all go on a picnic at the lake."

"Really, Pappy? I love picnics!" Mary Ellen scooped the fluffy kitten into her arms and bounded out the back door.

Amos put the coffeepot on the table and pulled out a chair for Miriam. "Please, sit down once."

"But I have dishes to do," Miriam argued.

"The dishes can wait. We do need to talk," he told her.

Miriam dried her hands on a towel and took the seat he had offered her. She knew he was right. They did need to talk, and she supposed now was as good a time as any.

Amos poured them both a cup of coffee and sat down across from Miriam. "I believe that God has brought us together, Miriam. I also believe He will bless our marriage. *Wass Got tuht ist wohl getahn*—what God doeth is well done. However, there are many adjustments that need to be made, and some of them will take some getting used to."

Miriam nodded and blew on her hot coffee. She did not voice the thought, but she certainly did not believe that God had anything to do with them being together. It was a mutual decision, made by two consenting adults, because they both needed something that the other could give.

"I believe strongly, as do most Amish men," he continued, "that the man is to be the head of the house. The Bible confirms this fact in Ephesians chapter five, verse twenty-three, where it says, 'For the husband is the head of the wife, even as Christ is the head of the church.' Therefore, while I may consult you on certain important matters, I feel that the final decisions must be made by me."

Miriam looked up from her coffee and stared directly into his dark brown eyes. "Are you sayin' I must do all you say?"

Amos reached for her hand, but she quickly withdrew it. "You promised that this would not have to be a physical union!" she shouted. "Are you not a man of your word, Amos Hilty?"

Amos stood up and began pacing the floor. "I will be true to my promise, Miriam. I will not touch you unless you ask me to. I will continue to sleep alone, just as I did last night."

Miriam thought about the night before, her wedding night. It had not been at all the way she had always dreamed of it being. After tucking Mary Ellen into her own bed, Miriam had left the child's room and slipped quietly into the bedroom across the hall. The room had previously been used for guests. Amos's room was right next to hers, and she could hear him moving about in it. She had lain awake most of the night, worrying that he might change his mind and come to her room. He had been true to his word then, but when he touched her just now, she had been greatly troubled and full of new doubts about whether he could be trusted.

"It is about other matters that I must have the final say," Amos said, interrupting Miriam's private thoughts.

"What matters are you referring to?" she asked.

He took a seat at the table again and drank some coffee before answering. "First of all, there is the matter of you continuing to teach at the school."

"What? But I thought you understood just how important teaching is to me. It's been the most important thing in my life, and—"

"I understand that, Miriam, but now you have a new life here with me and Mary Ellen. You have new responsibilities. Mary Ellen needs a full-time mother."

"I can be her mother and still be her teacher!"

"It would never work," Amos stated emphatically. "There are many things which need to be done here at home, and if you worked—"

"I could do my chores here and still teach," Miriam interrupted. "I have been doing it for several years at home."

"But you did not have a child to care for," Amos reminded her. "Also, there is the matter of how the children at school would react to having one of the other students' mothers as their teacher. They might feel that you would show favoritism toward Mary Ellen."

"I would never do that!" Miriam was quick to defend.

"Perhaps not intentionally, but some might believe you were anyway."

"But the school year is nearly over," Miriam argued. "There are only a few weeks left, and it would be difficult to find a replacement on such short notice."

Amos nodded. "You are right. I will make one concession, then. You are free to continue teaching for the rest of the school term, but the elders will meet and hire another teacher for next fall's term. I believe that I can convince them to let you stay on until then. It is not customary for us to allow married women to be the schoolteacher for our children, you know."

As though the matter was entirely settled, Amos stood up, crossed the room, removed his straw hat from the wall peg, placed it on his head, and started out the back door. He turned back just before he closed the door and said, "Do not forget about our picnic at the lake. Some fried chicken would be very nice. It is Mary Ellen's favorite."

Miriam stuck out her tongue at his retreating form. "What in the world have I gotten myself into?" she moaned.

Chapter 30

Aroutine was quickly established at the Hilty home, and Miriam found herself adapting to it, but she didn't think she could ever adapt to being a wife. Her heart longed for something more than wifely chores to do. Being a stepmother to Mary Ellen helped to fill a part of her that seemed to be missing, but there was still something else that she longed for. She didn't want to admit it, not even to herself, but she longed for the love of a man. She found Amos's presence and often his gentleness to be unnerving. It made her keenly aware of the great emptiness in her life. In the past she had managed to keep her life fairly uncomplicated because she had forgotten what love felt like. But now she had the strange sensation—a need really—to love and to be loved. Longing for love did not bring love into one's life, though, so she told herself that the best thing she could do was to keep busy. She was certainly doing a good job of that.

One evening after supper, Amos picked up his Bible to read, just as he did every night. At first, Miriam had been irritated by the practice, since she had long ago given up reading her own Bible every day. But now she found herself able to tolerate the ritual he had established. It was a time when the three of them sat around the kitchen table, reading God's Word as a family, and then taking the time to talk about what they had read. Mary Ellen usually had questions, and Amos seemed to take great pleasure in being able to interpret the Scriptures for his daughter.

"Tonight we will be reading in Proverbs," Amos said as he opened the Bible. " 'Whoso findeth a wife findeth a good thing, and obtaineth favour of the Lord.' " He looked up and smiled. "That was chapter eighteen, verse twenty-two."

Mary Ellen reached over and pulled on her father's shirtsleeve. "Mama Mim is a good wife, isn't she, Pappy?"

"*Jah*, she is," Amos answered as he looked right at Miriam.

His gaze made her feel uncomfortable, and she quickly looked away. Her slim fingers were so tightly clenched around her coffee cup that the veins on her hands stuck out.

"Is there more in the Bible about Mama Mim?" Mary Ellen asked.

"Let's see," Amos said as he began thumbing through the pages. *Jah*, here in Proverbs thirty-one, verse twenty-seven, it says, 'She looketh well to the ways of her household, and eateth not the bread of idleness.' "

Mary Ellen gasped. "Pappy, you mean that Mama Mim is not supposed to eat any bread? Won't she get awfully hungry?"

Amos laughed, and even Miriam did as well. It felt so good to laugh. It was something that she did so seldom.

Mary Ellen was looking up at her father, her hazel eyes large and expectant. Amos reached out and patted her head. "The Bible verse is not talking about real bread, Mary Ellen. The bread of idleness refers to someone who is lazy and does not work much."

Mary Ellen frowned. "But Mama Mim works all of the time. She works at school, and she works here, too. She is always busy doing something."

Amos nodded. "I know she is. In fact, that verse is saying that a good wife is not idle or lazy, and it is speaking about someone just like Mama Mim. She looks well to our house, and that means she takes good care of us. She does not eat the bread of idleness, which means that she is not lazy."

Mary Ellen smiled and took both her father's hand and Miriam's hand. "I am so glad we have Mama Mim."

Amos looked at Mary Ellen and then at Miriam and smiled. *"Jah,* I, too, am glad."

The last day of school was June sixteenth. The children were all excited, as they were about to begin their summer break, even though it meant that many of the older ones would have a lot more chores to do at home.

Miriam found herself feeling moody and depressed. This was to be her last day of teaching. She would not be returning in the fall, as she had for the past several years.

She reached into her desk drawer for some White Willow Bark capsules, feeling as though one of her headaches was coming on. She'd had a lot of sick headaches during her days of schoolteaching, she realized. Maybe once she quit, the headaches would be gone as well. Maybe staying at home and doing domestic chores all day would be less stressful.

Another thought occurred to Miriam. Amos was a farmer, and he would be in and out of the house throughout the day. She would be forced to see him more often. She was thankful that at least Mary Ellen would be there all summer long. The child would keep her busy and give her an excuse to avoid too many conversations with Amos.

She glanced at the clock and realized that it was almost time to dismiss the class. She swallowed the lump in her throat and tried to think about something else. What she really needed was a long overdue visit with Mom. She always seemed to understand her and was usually full of good advice, even if Miriam often chose not to take it.

Just before Miriam dismissed the class that afternoon, she told them that she had an announcement to make. "Today was my last day of teaching," she said, trying to make her voice sound calm and steady. "I will not be returning in the fall."

"You mean we will have another teacher?" John Hoelwarth asked, without raising his hand.

Miriam nodded. *"Jah,* that is right, John."

111

"Teacher is my mama now. That is why she is not coming back," Mary Ellen spoke up. "She will be too busy to teach. She has to take care of me and Pappy."

The class fell silent, and Miriam stood up and moved away from her desk. "I have enjoyed being your schoolteacher, and I will miss you all."

"I won't miss her," John Hoelwarth whispered to the boy in front of him. "I think she is mean, and she hardly ever smiles."

Andrew Sepler nodded and whispered back, *Jah,* she has a heart of stone, all right."

Miriam frowned at the boys. "Would you two like to share what you just said with the rest of the class?"

Andrew quickly shook his head. "No, Teacher."

"Very well, then, stop your whispering."

Both boys sat up straight and became quiet. Miriam was sure neither of them wanted to be kept after school on their last day before summer break. The truth was, she didn't choose to make an issue out of their comments, either.

Miriam looked up at the clock on the wall. "It is nearly time to go. If you will all clear out your desks, you may be dismissed a few minutes early."

Everyone hurried to do as their teacher had instructed, then one by one, they all filed out the door, laughing and calling to one another as they entered the school yard. Everyone except for Mary Ellen. She came to stand by Miriam. "I like riding home with you, Mama Mim," she said. "Pappy doesn't have to come and get me anymore." She frowned. "What about next year, when you are not my teacher? How will I get home then?"

"You will either walk with some of the older children, or I will come and pick you up. On very cold, rainy, or snowy days you will need a ride home," Miriam answered. She turned to gather up the last of her things, and as she started toward the door, she turned and looked back, letting her eyes travel around the entire schoolroom. She swallowed the irritating lump and stepped outside with Mary Ellen right at her side.

❧

Miriam found that no matter how busy she kept herself, the feeling and longing in her heart did not go away. In fact, the longer she lived under Amos's roof, the more those emotions intensified.

One day, while visiting with Mom, she was told that her newest sister-in-law, Grace, was in the family way.

"That is wonderful," Miriam told her mother, trying to sound as excited as possible. "I am very happy for Lewis and Grace."

"And what about you, Daughter? When are you going to start your family?" Mom asked suddenly.

Miriam poured herself another glass of lemonade, then replied, "I already have a family. Mary Ellen is a good child, and—"

Jah, I am sure that she is, but wouldn't you like a baby of your own?"

Miriam's eyes flooded with tears, and she quickly looked away so that Mom would not notice. How could she explain to her mother that her heart did long for a baby, but that it was an impossibility? She and Amos did not even share the same bed, and as far as she was concerned, they never would. No matter how badly she might want a baby, it was simply not meant to be.

Mom reached out and touched Miriam's arm with her hand. "I can see that I have upset you. You and Amos have only been married a little over three months. You still have plenty of time to conceive. You must remember to be patient. Children will come in God's time."

"I really must be getting home now," Miriam said. "Amos took Mary Ellen into town, and they will be arriving back home soon. I need to get supper going."

Mom nodded. "Come see us again soon, Daughter. Bring Mary Ellen next time. She can play with Rebekah."

Miriam didn't argue with her mother, though she was wondering just how much playing two little girls could do when one of them was in a wheelchair. *Jah,* I will bring Mary Ellen by soon," she said. She started for the door, then came back and impulsively gave her mother a kiss on the cheek. "Please do not say anything to Amos about me not being pregnant yet. It might upset him."

"Of course not," Mom said. "I will not mention it to anyone, but I will be praying about it. My heart longs for many grandchildren, just as I am sure that your heart longs to be a mother."

Chapter 31

The summer went by more quickly than Miriam had expected it to. There had been so much to do. Planting, weeding, and harvesting all the garden produce. Then came canning, making jellies and apple butter, besides all of the usual home and farm chores.

Mary Ellen had grown so much over the summer that Miriam had to make her several new school dresses. She hadn't realized how demanding the role of motherhood would be, but much to her surprise, she found herself enjoying it. It caused her heart to ache even more for a child of her own.

She often found herself thinking about William Graber and the love they had once shared. If they had married as planned, she would no doubt have one or two children already. She knew that she couldn't allow herself to dwell on that. The past was in the past, and now she had a new life to think about. Mary Ellen needed her, and she would be the only child Miriam would ever raise. Being around Mary Ellen had given her a reason to laugh and smile again.

Miriam even found that she was becoming more relaxed around Amos. He was a soft-spoken man with an easy, pleasant way about him. Though he wasn't what she would consider good-looking, he certainly wasn't ugly, either. Being near him did not make her heart pound wildly in her chest the way it had whenever she was with William, or even Nick, but at least she could feel respect for Amos Hilty, which was something William Graber had certainly not earned.

One evening, just a few days before school began again, Amos was reading the Bible. "We will be reading in Psalms," he said. "Chapter one hundred and twenty-seven, verses three through five say, 'Lo, children are an heritage of the Lord: and the fruit of the womb is his reward. As arrows are in the hand of the mighty man; so are children of the youth. Happy is the man that has his quiver full of them.' "

Mary Ellen gave her father a puzzled look. "What is a quiver, Pappy?"

Amos stroked his beard thoughtfully, then answered, "A quiver is a case for carrying arrows."

"Do you have a quiver, Pappy?"

Amos smiled and reached out to place a large hand on the top of his daughter's head. "I have no case full of arrows, but I do have a home, and God's Word is saying that men are happy when they have a home full of children."

Mary Ellen frowned and stuck out her bottom lip. "You only have one child, Pappy. You must be very sad."

Miriam cringed and swallowed hard. Mary Ellen had hit a nerve. At least with her, she had. Miriam was not as happy as she knew she could be. One of the reasons for this was her deep desire for a baby.

Amos pulled Mary Ellen from her chair and into his lap. "I must admit, having more children would be nice, but I am very happy with just one. If God ever sees fit to bless our home with more little ones, I will not complain, but you are all I need if He chooses not to."

Mary Ellen smiled at her father. "I hope that God does send us a baby sometime. I want a little brother or sister to play with."

The tears that had formed behind Miriam's eyes threatened to spill over, and it took all of her willpower to keep from openly crying.

"If God wishes it to be so, then it will happen in His time," Amos told the child.

"Then I will pray and ask God to hurry up!" Mary Ellen said eagerly.

Amos looked as though he was about to say something more, but instead, he closed the Bible and lifted his hand to brush the tears that had escaped from Miriam's eyes. When the back of his hand brushed against her cheek, Miriam quickly pulled away.

Amos withdrew his hand and stood up. "There are a few things outside that I must tend to," he said.

Miriam watched his retreating form with a great sadness in her heart. She felt a sense of relief that he had taken his hand away and left the room, yet it was mixed with a feeling of disappointment, too. She did not even bother to try and analyze her feelings, but she did know one thing for certain. Amos Hilty, her husband in name only, was as miserable as she was.

❧

Mary Ellen had been back in school for two weeks, and every day Miriam would either walk with the child or drive her to and from school in their buggy. She felt that the child was not yet old enough to walk alone, and she had changed her mind about letting her walk with some of the other children. Some of them who lived nearby had been among those who had teased and taunted Mary Ellen during school hours. Miriam could not take the chance that the teasing might continue on the walks to and from school. Besides, she found herself enjoying the extra time that it gave her to be with Mary Ellen when they either walked or rode together.

One afternoon, when Amos was out in the fields working, Miriam decided to leave a little early and stop and pay a call on Crystal before picking Mary Ellen up from school. She found her sister-in-law on the front porch, sweeping off the leaves that had fallen there. Crystal waved and set the broom aside. "It's so good to see you!" she called.

Miriam stepped down from her buggy and started toward the house. *"Jah,* it has been awhile, hasn't it?"

Crystal smiled and nodded. "I have been wondering about you. How are you doing now that school has started?"

Miriam plopped down on the top step of the porch and sighed deeply. "It is so hard to take Mary Ellen to school each day, then turn around and go back home to an empty house. Teaching the children has filled up my life for several years, and I must admit, I do miss it. It's hard to see Bishop Benner's daughter Linda taking my place as the new teacher."

Crystal sat down next to Miriam. "But you do have Mary Ellen to train and teach at home. The role of motherhood can be very rewarding. You will see that even more when other children come along."

Miriam gave her a questioning look. "Other children?"

Miriam shook her head, but Crystal didn't seem to notice. She continued, *"Ach,* my, you will be so busy changing diapers and doing extra laundry, you won't even have time to think about schoolteaching."

Miriam's eyes narrowed. "There will be no babies for me," she said bitterly.

Crystal reached for her hand. "Miriam, it has only been five months since you and Amos were married. Give it some time, Friend. It is God's time anyway, and it will happen when He is ready."

Miriam had confided in Crystal before the wedding, telling her why she was marrying Amos, and that there was no love between them. However, she had not spoken of the matter since then, and so Crystal obviously did not understand the full concept of things. Miriam was ashamed to tell even her best friend that she, a woman who was supposed to be a good Amish wife, was sleeping in her own bedroom, just next door to the room that her husband slept in. There had been no physical union between them, and therefore there would be no babies.

Miriam drew in a deep breath and decided that now was the time to confide in someone who might give her some understanding and sympathy. "I will never get pregnant," she whispered.

"Now, Miriam, good things come to those who wait," Crystal said with conviction.

A tear slid out from under Miriam's lashes and landed on the front of her dress. "Amos and I have not consummated our marriage."

Crystal's mouth fell open. "You mean—"

"Jah. We sleep in separate rooms. We are man and wife in name only." Miriam wiped the corners of her eyes with the backs of her hands. She hated tears. She saw it as a sign of weakness, yet she so often resorted to tears these days.

"Has Amos actually agreed to such an arrangement?" Crystal asked.

Miriam sniffed and nodded. "Of course he agreed. He knows that I don't love him, and he feels no love for me, either. Our marriage was one of convenience. He provides a home and food for me, and I cook, clean, and take care of his daughter."

Crystal placed a loving hand on Miriam's arm. "Miriam, he could have simply hired someone for those tasks. Surely Amos needs a wife and not just a housekeeper."

"Then he should have married someone else. Someone for whom he felt love." Another unbidden tear slid down Miriam's cheek. "I am afraid that I have ruined his life and mine as well."

"How can you say that? It is quite apparent that you care deeply about his daughter," Crystal said.

"*Jah,* I do," Miriam admitted. "She is a wonderful child, and I have come to love her a great deal."

"You see," Crystal said. "You just said that you have *come* to love Mary Ellen. It did not happen overnight. It happened gradually, and maybe you can learn to love Amos in the same way."

"But I—"

Crystal placed her fingers softly against Miriam's lips. "Please, do not say anything more. Just think about what I have said. Pray and ask God to fill your heart with love toward the man you have chosen to marry. I feel certain that, with God's help, things can change between you and Amos."

Chapter 32

When Miriam left Crystal's house, her heart was full of questions. She knew that Crystal cared about her and wanted her to be happy, and she even wondered if her friend could possibly be right. Could she actually learn to love Amos? Wasn't love a feeling that was simply there, or was it a matter of choosing to love, as Crystal had suggested?

Miriam tried to shake free of her thoughts and concentrate on the road ahead. The once-cloudless sky had now darkened, and soon the heavens opened up and poured forth a drenching downpour.

Miriam turned on the battery-operated windshield wipers and tried to hold the horse steady. She had left Crystal's later than she'd planned, and now she was worried that she might be late picking Mary Ellen up from school.

As the rain came down harder, the air was suddenly filled with a thunderous roar. A bolt of lightning shot across the sky, just in front of the buggy. Miriam gripped the reins tightly and strained to see the road ahead. The small battery-operated lights on the front of the buggy did little to light the way.

Miriam found herself wishing she had not spent so much time pouring her heart out to Crystal. She might have been at the school by now, and the truth about her and Amos would not have been shared, either. She felt fairly certain that she could trust Crystal to keep the information to herself, but she still wondered if telling her had been such a good idea. She didn't want Crystal's pity, and she wasn't even sure that she wanted her advice.

Another clap of thunder came, interrupting Miriam's thoughts. This one sounded closer, and she shivered, both from the cold, as well as from her fear of the storm. Suddenly, there was a loud cracking sound, and the buggy lunged to the right. Miriam pulled back on the reins, calling to the horse, "Whoa now! Steady, boy!"

The gelding whinnied loudly and reared its head. It jerked hard against the reins several times, causing the buggy to sway back and forth. It was dangerously close to the center line, and when Miriam saw the headlights of an oncoming car ahead, she gave a sharp tug on the reins. Another clap of thunder sounded, and without any warning, the horse reared up, and the buggy flipped onto its left side, along the edge of the road.

Miriam gasped and strained to see out the front window. The horse must have broken free somehow, for it was nowhere to be seen. She was pinned inside the mangled buggy, unable to open either door. She winced in pain as she pushed unsuccessfully against the door on the driver's side. Her side and shoulder hurt terribly, and she could feel a large gash on her head. She managed to rip a piece of her apron off, and she placed it against her aching head to stop the bleeding.

In spite of Miriam's predicament, her first concern was for Mary Ellen. She would be waiting for her at the schoolhouse, probably alone and frightened. *There must be some way to get out of here. Surely someone will see the buggy and stop to help. Oh, what about the horse? Is Amos's gelding all right?*

Miriam's head was throbbing. She felt helpless and alone. She was used to solving her own problems, and now she was trapped inside the buggy, unable to find an answer to her dilemma. A sense of panic began to overtake her, and she swallowed several times to keep from vomiting. "Oh, God!" she cried. "Please help me!" She closed her eyes tightly and began to think of Scripture verses she had committed to memory. "Second Timothy one, verse seven," she recited. " 'For God hath not given us the spirit of fear; but of power, and of love, and of a sound mind.' Psalm twenty-three, verse four, 'Yea, though I walk through the valley of the shadow of death, I will fear no evil: for thou art with me; thy rod and thy staff they comfort me.' Mark four, verse forty, 'And he said unto them, Why are ye so fearful? how is it that ye have no faith?' "

Miriam took a deep breath and tried to relax. A sudden sense of peace came over her. She had been so far from God for such a long time, yet now she was keenly aware that she was not alone. The Lord was with her, and she had nothing to fear. She closed her eyes and drifted into a restful sleep.

"Miriam, can you hear me? Are you all right?"

Miriam's eyes opened with a start when she heard a man's voice calling out to her. She winced in pain as she tried to sit up straight. It was impossible, and then she remembered that the buggy was on its side. Had she been asleep? For how long? Was someone calling to her?

The voice came again. "Miriam, please answer me!"

She recognized the voice this time. It was Amos. Her husband had come to her aid.

"I am here," Miriam called. "I'm hurt, but I do not think it is too serious."

"I can't get the door of the buggy open," Amos called back. "I will have to go for help. Can you hang on for a little while longer?"

Jah, I will be fine," Miriam said loudly. Then to herself, she whispered, "I am not alone—not any longer." She drifted off again.

❧

"I love you, Miriam. I love you, Miriam. . . ." The words ran through her mind again and again as she tried to become fully awake and focus on her surroundings. Where was she? Who had whispered those words of love to her? Why were her eyes so heavy? Her head was pounding, too. Was she having another one of her sick headaches? She tried to sit up but found that she was unable to. A terrible pain ripped through her left side.

"You had better lie still," a woman's voice said.

Miriam's eyes finally came fully open. "Where am I?"

The woman, who was dressed in a white uniform, placed a gentle hand on Miriam's arm and answered, "You're in the hospital. You were brought here when your buggy got turned over in the storm."

Miriam frowned as the memory of the whole ordeal came back to her. "It was so awful. The wind was blowing hard, and the lightning and thunder spooked my horse. I knew I would be late picking up my daughter, and—" Her daughter? Had she just referred to Mary Ellen as her daughter? Perhaps she was only just a stepchild, but she was the only child Miriam would ever have, and she had come to love her as a daughter.

"Mary Ellen. Is Mary Ellen all right?" Miriam asked as she tried to sit up again.

The nurse placed a firm but caring hand on Miriam again to keep her lying down. "Your husband and daughter are waiting in the visitor's lounge. They are fine and seem anxious to see you. Your family must love you very much."

The words "I love you" came back to Miriam again. Maybe Mary Ellen had said them. But why had she been called "Miriam" and not "Mama Mim"?

Miriam thought hard, trying to clear her cloudy mind. The last thing she remembered was being trapped inside the buggy. She could hear Amos calling to her and saying that he was going for help. Maybe she had fallen asleep and merely dreamed the words of love. Her heart was so full of questions.

"How did I get here?" Miriam asked the nurse.

"You were brought in an ambulance."

"When can I go home?"

"Probably in a day or so. You have a mild concussion, and the doctor wants you to be monitored for a few days."

"No wonder my head hurts so badly," Miriam said. "What other injuries do I have?"

"Many cuts and bruises, and some of your ribs are broken. That is why your side hurts so badly," the nurse explained. "You are quite fortunate, though. Your injuries could have been much more serious in an accident of that sort."

Miriam nodded. "I would like to see my family now."

"Of course. I'll tell them that you are awake." The nurse moved away from the bed and quickly left the room.

Miriam shook her head slowly. *Did I just refer to Amos and Mary Ellen as my family?* Perhaps they were the only real family she had now. Since Mom lived with Andrew and Sarah, Miriam hardly ever saw her anymore. Papa was gone, too, and their home had never been the same without him. Lewis and Grace were married and living in the home where Miriam had grown up. They were even expecting their first child. Everything had changed so, and now Miriam spent all of her time and energy taking care of her stepdaughter and her husband. *A husband in name only.* A tear slipped between her lashes and rolled onto her cheek.

Miriam's thoughts were interrupted when the door to her room opened and Amos and Mary Ellen stepped inside.

"Mama Mim!" Mary Ellen cried. "Are you all right?"

Jah, I am going to be fine," Miriam answered as the child reached her bedside.

"You are crying, Mama Mim. Does your head hurt real bad?"

"A little," Miriam admitted. She could not explain to Mary Ellen the real reason for her tears.

"We were very worried about you. You gave us quite a scare," Amos told her. Miriam studied his face. It did wear a look of genuine concern.

"How did you find me?" she asked.

"I was concerned when the storm came up," Amos said. "When you did not return home with Mary Ellen on schedule, I really began to worry. I hitched up the other buggy and started off for the schoolhouse. On the way, I came across your buggy lying on its side. I stopped to see if you were still inside; then I went to call for help."

Jah, I do remember hearing your voice," Miriam told him. "I must have dozed off. I don't remember much after that, except waking up and finding out that I was in the hospital."

Mary Ellen's eyes were large and serious. "I waited at the school for a long time. When you did not come, I got scared."

Miriam reached for the child's hand. "I'm so sorry you were frightened, Mary Ellen."

Mary Ellen swallowed hard and a tear slid down her cheek. "When Pappy sent Uncle Lewis to get me, he said that you had been in an accident. I thought you were going to die and leave me just like my first mama did. I was very sad."

Miriam squeezed Mary Ellen's hand tightly. "I am going to be just fine. I will not leave you, Mary Ellen, I promise."

Mary Ellen smiled. "I love you, Mama Mim."

"I love you, too," Miriam responded.

Chapter 33

Miriam spent three full days in the hospital, and during her stay she did a lot of thinking, praying, and soul-searching.

Amos came to visit her every day, sometimes twice a day. His daytime visits were after he had dropped Mary Ellen off at school, and in the evenings he always brought Mary Ellen along. Miriam knew that he must be getting behind on his work, because the trips to Lancaster took about an hour each time. She couldn't help but wonder why Amos was so faithful about his visits. Even her own family had not come to see her that often.

Miriam's injuries were healing nicely, and the pain in her ribs and head was beginning to improve. Her last night in the hospital was her worst, however. She had trouble falling asleep and had to ask for a sleeping pill. While waiting for it to take effect, Miriam lay in her hospital bed, staring at the ceiling and thinking about her life with Amos and Mary Ellen. Every muscle in her body felt tight.

At last, she drifted into a fitful sleep, only to fall prey to a terrible nightmare. It was a dream about Amos. He was driving the same buggy that she had been riding in the day of the accident. She watched in horror as the horse reared up, and the buggy rolled over on its side. She called out to Amos, but he made no reply. Her heart was gripped with fear that he might be dead. "Amos! Amos!" she called loudly.

"Wake up, Miriam. You are having a bad dream."

Miriam opened her eyes and saw the night nurse standing over her.

"I–I was only dreaming?"

"Yes," the nurse answered. "Sometimes the medication you took earlier can cause that. Here, take a drink of water and try to go back to sleep."

Miriam took the offered glass of water. "Thank you."

❧

Miriam awoke the following morning, knowing it was the day she would be going home from the hospital. She was anxious to go but felt confused about so many things, and she wondered just what her dream the night before had meant. Why had she had such a frightening dream about Amos?

She could feel the beginning of another headache coming on, and her hands were trembling. "What is wrong with me, Lord?" she cried. She turned over and buried her head in her pillow, giving in to the threatening tears.

❧

Miriam was dressed and waiting for Amos when he entered her hospital room later that morning. She was sitting on the edge of the bed, reading the Bible she had found in the drawer of her bed table. She looked up as Amos took a seat on the bed next to her, but she self-consciously averted her gaze, wishing she could simply disappear. She knew that she must look a sight. Her eyes were red and swollen from crying. They had been tears of confusion, of uncertainty, and of an unfilled need for love.

"Miriam," Amos said softly, "there is something we need to talk about."

Miriam forced herself to look into his eyes. "If it's about me not being able to do my chores—I am feeling well enough—"

Amos reached for her hand, and he smiled when she did not pull it away. "No, it is not about chores. I have been wondering if you have thought about what I said to you the other day?"

"What day was that?" Miriam asked.

"The day of the accident—right before I left to go get help."

Miriam gave him a puzzled look.

Amos looked deeply into her eyes. "I told you that I love you, Miriam, and I meant it, too."

Miriam swallowed hard. "I do remember hearing those words, but I thought I had just dreamed it. I was not even sure who had said the words to me."

"I have felt love for you for some time now," Amos continued, "but knowing how you feel about me, I was afraid to say anything before."

"Amos, I—"

He reached out and placed a large finger against her lips. "It is all right. You do not have to say anything. I know that you do not return my feelings of love, but I had to tell you the way that I feel. When I saw your buggy lying on its side, I was so afraid that I might lose you, and then I would never have the chance to tell you that I love you. When you did not respond, I thought that you might be angry with me for speaking the truth."

Miriam shook her head. "No, Amos, I was not angry. As I said before, I was not even certain I had heard your words at all." She paused a moment, then continued, "I only wish I—"

"It is all right," Amos interrupted again. "Maybe someday you might learn to love me as well. I am a patient man, and I'm so thankful to God for sparing your life. I need you, and so does Mary Ellen."

Miriam swallowed past the lump in her throat. "God is dealing with me, Amos," she said. "But I am not ready to make a confession of love yet."

"I understand," Amos answered.

"No, I do not believe that you really do," she said tearfully. "Real love means a yielding of the heart to another person. It means full commitment, loyalty, and trust. It is very difficult for me to trust a man, or even God. I have been hurt too many times. My heart has been filled with bitterness for a long time."

Amos nodded. "*Jah*, I know, but you have kept your promise and not let it show to Mary Ellen. I thank you for that."

Miriam sniffed loudly. "I really do love her, Amos."

"Jah, I can tell that," Amos responded. "I also know that you and your family have been through a lot over the last few years. You have suffered many hurts."

"Perhaps more than our share," Miriam agreed. "But everyone in the family seems to have dealt with it well. Everyone except for me, that is."

"Why, Miriam? Why is there so much bitterness within your heart?" he asked.

Miriam wiped away her tears, then said, "I suppose my bitterness began when William Graber moved away and fell in love with someone else. I loved him very much, and he made me believe that all men are alike. They cannot be trusted. When he broke my heart, I vowed never to allow myself to feel love for any man. I could not even trust God anymore. He could have prevented all of my pain and heartaches!" A sob caught in her throat, and Amos quickly wrapped his arms around her and held her against his strong chest.

When the sobs had finally subsided, Amos lifted her chin and looked directly into her eyes again. "I understand your pain, Miriam. When Ruth died of cancer, I thought that my whole world had been shattered. I even felt betrayed by Ruth. She had left me all alone to raise our child. I blamed God for taking her, and I was very bitter and angry toward Him. I did not know if I could trust God anymore, but I was reminded that His Word says, 'I will never leave thee, nor forsake thee.' I hung onto that Scripture, and one day I woke up and realized that Mary Ellen needed me, and that I needed her. Life does go on, whether our hearts are bitter or filled with love. It is a choice we must make. We either choose to love, or we choose to harbor bitter, angry thoughts and feelings in our heart. Proverbs fifteen, verse seventeen says, 'Better is a dinner of herbs where love is, than a stalled ox and hatred therewith.' Hatred, anger, and bitterness are all negative feelings that can make us ill. That is why the Bible says, 'A merry heart—' "

" 'Doeth good like a medicine,' " Miriam completed the verse. "Mom has quoted that to me many times. I have ignored God's desire for my heart. Lying here in this hospital bed for the past several days has given me ample time to think and to pray. I want to yield completely to God's will, but I am not sure that I can. I am so afraid of failing and never finding happiness, Amos."

Amos ran one long finger gently down Miriam's cheek, tracing a pattern where the tears had fallen. "I am afraid, too, Miriam. Afraid of being happy again, but I do love you, and I want to make you feel happy and loved as well. I want you to be my wife in every way. I want us to have children and to raise them to know God and to trust in His Son as their Savior. I want our family to be full of God's love."

Miriam nodded. "I want all that, too, Amos, but earlier this morning, I was reading in the Bible, and John chapter five, verse forty-two said, 'But I know you, that ye have not the love of God in you.' I am afraid that hit very close to home. I know that I do not truly have God's love inside of my heart. I really have never completely yielded to Him. Not even when I was baptized and taken into church membership. I did it because it was expected of me, not because I truly had faith in God or His Son Jesus."

"Then why not pray with me now?" Amos asked. "If you really want His will for your life, then you can yield to Him right here, Miriam. Jesus is waiting for you to ask Him to enter."

Miriam nodded. *"Jah,* I would like that. I have struggled and tried to do things on my own far too long. I need God's love and His power within my heart."

Amos took her hand. "Let us pray together and ask for God's forgiveness and the indwelling of His Spirit."

Miriam bowed her head and prayed aloud, "Dear God, our heavenly Father, please forgive me for the hate and bitterness that I have allowed to take over my heart. I thank You for sending Jesus to die for my sins. I accept His gift of forgiveness and love right now. Amen." She lifted her eyes to look at Amos.

He smiled a soft, loving smile that warmed the last frozen place in her heart. *"Wass Got tuht ist wohl getahn,"* she whispered.

He nodded. "Yes, what God doeth is well done."

It was then that a new realization came to her. Amos was not William Graber, or Nick McCormick, either, but he was a kind, caring man. He had told her that he loved her, and now with God's help, her yielded heart could be a loving heart.

Chapter 34

Miriam took a seat at the kitchen table and ate a bite of the scrambled eggs that were set before her. For the first time in a very long time, she actually enjoyed eating. In fact, her whole world had taken on a special glow. She felt like a freed prisoner must feel after years of confinement.

"Thank you for fixing breakfast," she said to Amos, who sat across the table from her. "You really should not have let me sleep so long. I am perfectly capable of cooking, you know."

Amos smiled and looked at her with love in his eyes. "I rather enjoyed cooking the eggs. I have not done much in the kitchen since we got married. Besides, I want you to get as much rest as possible for the next few days. The doctor's orders, you know."

Miriam smiled back at her husband and said, "These eggs are delicious. My compliments to the cook!"

"Can we have pancakes tomorrow, Pappy?" Mary Ellen asked. "Pancakes with maple syrup are my very favorite thing for breakfast!"

Amos laughed. "We shall see, Mary Ellen. We shall see." When breakfast was over, Amos excused himself to go outside and finish the morning chores.

Miriam opened her Bible for her morning devotions. She had decided to begin having a personal time with God each day. She turned to First John, chapter four. " 'There is no fear in love; but perfect love casteth out fear: because fear hath torment. He that feareth is not made perfect in love.' "

How glad she was that she'd decided to quit fearing love. She could love and be loved in return. She had nothing to fear now because she knew that she had God's love and Amos's love. The storm that had caused her buggy accident had battered her body, but the storm that had been deep within her soul for so long had battered her heart. She was grateful that she had given all of her bitterness and angry feelings to God and had asked for His forgiveness.

Miriam turned the pages in her Bible and began reading from Philippians, chapter four. In the fourth verse it read, " 'Rejoice in the Lord always: and again I say, Rejoice.' " On down, the eighth verse read, " 'Finally, brethren, whatsoever things are true, whatsoever things are honest, whatsoever things are just, whatsoever things are pure, whatsoever things are lovely, whatsoever things are of good report; if there be any virtue, and if there be any praise, think on these things.' "

"All these many years I have not been obeying Your Word, Lord," she said aloud. "I have wasted so much time thinking about all of the bad things that have happened to me that I could not even see all of the good things that You have done for me."

"Who are you talking to, Mama Mim?"

Miriam turned to see Mary Ellen standing in the kitchen doorway. She thought the child had gone outside to play. She reached her hand out to her.

Mary Ellen obliged, and Miriam pulled her onto her lap, being careful of her still-tender ribs. "I was talking to God," she answered.

"You were praying? But your eyes were open."

Miriam laughed. It hurt her ribs some, but it felt so good to laugh that she didn't mind the pain. "I suppose they were open, but I was talking out loud to God and to myself. I was thinking how fortunate I am to have you and your pappy as my family. I just wanted God to know how I feel."

"I am so glad that it's Saturday and there is no school today," Mary Ellen said eagerly. "I get to spend the whole day with my mama and my pappy!"

"Should we do something fun together?" Miriam asked.

"Let's bake cookies; then we can go to the Country Store, and after that we can go out to the barn and play with Pappy's new piglets, and—"

"Whoa! Slow down some, Daughter!" Amos called as he entered the room. "Mama Mim just got out of the hospital yesterday. She still needs to take it easy. If we do all those things in one day, we will wear her out."

Miriam looked up at Amos and smiled. "I am fine, really."

"You may feel fine, but remember what the doctor said," he reminded.

"I know, and I will get enough rest," Miriam promised. "But I'll rest after Mary Ellen and I bake some ginger cookies."

Mary Ellen's face lit up. "Ginger cookies! They are my favorite!"

Amos laughed. "I think all cookies are your favorite, Girl." He took a seat next to Miriam. "May I help, too?"

"Pappy, do you know how to bake cookies now?" Mary Ellen asked.

"Sure he does," Miriam teased. "He knows how to lick the bowl, and he is an expert at eating the cookies!" She stuck out a finger and poked Amos playfully in the stomach.

He smiled and reached for her hand. "It sure is good to have you home, Miriam Hilty."

"It is really good to be home, too," she responded sincerely.

Miriam knew her physical injuries were not the only injuries that were healing. So was her heart. She knew God cared about her, and she was glad she had finally opened up her heart to His love. Since love was a choice, and not just an emotion, she could choose to love Amos in the way a wife should love her husband. She was thankful she had chosen him and not Nick to marry. She was certain now that a mere physical attraction would not have been enough. Her thankful heart was so full of real love for Amos, for Mary Ellen, and most of all, for God.

❧

Miriam had been home from the hospital for several days and was feeling stronger and more content with her life than she had ever thought possible. Amos was very protective and would still not allow her to drive the buggy yet, so every day he drove Mary Ellen to school and picked her up again each afternoon. One morning, when he had just returned from the schoolhouse, he entered the kitchen as Miriam began making a second pot of coffee.

"I was wondering if you would have the time for a little talk?" she asked Amos as he began to remove his heavy, dark jacket.

He hung the coat on the wall peg and rubbed his hands briskly together. "That sounds good, if a big cup of hot coffee goes with it. It's pretty cold out there this morning."

Miriam smiled. "I will even throw in a few slices of gingerbread to go along with the coffee. How does that sound?"

"Mmm...sounds good to me." Amos smacked his lips in anticipation and pulled out a kitchen chair.

"I have been thinking," Miriam began. "That is, I was wondering if it would be all right if I move my things out of my room and into your room."

"Are you saying what I think you are?" Amos asked hopefully.

"Jah. I want to be your wife in every way, just as God intended that it should be, Amos," she answered.

Amos stood up and crossed the room to where she stood at the cupboard cutting the gingerbread. He turned her around to face him, and looking directly into her eyes, he asked, "Are you certain about this, Miriam? I do not want to pressure you or rush you in any way. I know that we are getting closer, but—"

Miriam placed a finger against his lips. "I want to be your wife, Amos. With God's help, I want to love you in every way that a wife should love her husband."

Amos wrapped his arms around her and held her close. Miriam could feel the steady beat of his heart against her chest. "I love you so much, Miriam Hilty," he whispered.

"I love you, too, Amos Hilty," she whispered back.

He lifted her face gently toward his, and softly, ever so softly, he placed a tender kiss against her lips.

She responded with a long sigh, and they kissed again. It was a kiss that told Miriam just how full of love her husband's heart truly was.

Chapter 35

I f love was a choice, then Miriam had made the right choice, for she found that her love for Amos was growing with each passing day. His tender, gentle way had always been there, but before she had chosen not to notice. Now she thanked the Lord daily for opening her eyes to the truth.

Miriam found that she hardly missed teaching anymore. Her days were filled with household duties she now did out of love. Amos finished his outside chores more quickly these days, which gave them more time to spend together. Often he would help her in the kitchen or with some of the heavier house-cleaning. They took time out to read the Bible together and to pray, which Miriam knew was one of the main reasons they were drawing closer to one another and to God. They also spent time talking over a cup of tea or coffee and a plate of cookies or a slice of homemade bread. When the winter weather would allow, they would go for walks hand in hand, and their evening hours were spent with Mary Ellen, playing games, putting puzzles together, reading, or working on some craft.

Miriam had one particular project that she was working on, and whenever she had a free moment, she would get out her cross-stitching, just as she had tonight.

"What are you making?" Amos asked.

"Oh, it is just a small surprise for Mom," Miriam responded with a smile.

❧

One Saturday afternoon in the middle of January, Miriam suggested that they hitch up the sleigh and go for a little ride.

"Where would you like to go?" Amos asked.

"I think it's time to pay my family a visit. Let's stop and see Lewis and Grace first. Then we can go over to Crystal and Jonas's, and last, we will call on Mom at Andrew and Sarah's. I want to take Mom the little gift I've been working on."

Amos raised his eyebrows. "A little ride, I thought you said. It sounds to me like you're planning to cover the whole valley!" He smiled at Miriam and gave his daughter a playful wink.

Mary Ellen, who was coloring a picture at the kitchen table, jumped up immediately. "*Ich will mit dir*—I want to go!"

Amos bent down and picked the child up. "Of course you may go, Daughter. It will be a fun outing for all of us."

Miriam bundled Mary Ellen into her warmest coat, cap, and mittens, while Amos got the sleigh hitched; then Miriam hurriedly gathered up three loaves of freshly baked banana bread. She planned to give one to each of the families they visited.

The sleigh ride was exhilarating, and the snow-covered landscape was breathtaking. It felt good to be out and enjoying God's majestic handiwork.

Mary Ellen, who was cuddled under a quilt next to her parents, called out, "Oh, look—there goes a mother deer and her baby. Isn't it cute?"

"*Jah*, Mary Ellen. All babies are cute," Miriam answered.

"I wish I had a baby of my own to play with," Mary Ellen said wistfully.

"Someday when you are grown-up and get married, perhaps you will," her father answered.

"But that is a long time off," Mary Ellen complained.

"Maybe Uncle Lewis still has some of those baby bunnies left," Amos said.

"Really, Pappy? Could I really have a baby bunny for my very own?" Mary Ellen's face was expectant.

"If it is all right with Mim, it is all right with me."

Miriam smiled. Amos had been calling her Mim ever since she had declared her love for him and asked to be his wife in every way. She liked the nickname that Mary Ellen had begun when they were first married. "*Jah*, if Uncle Lewis still has some bunnies left, you may have one, but only on one condition."

"What is a 'condition'?" asked Mary Ellen.

"Well, this one particular 'condition' is that you promise to help take care of the bunny," Miriam told her.

"*Jah*, I will. I promise!"

❧

Mary Ellen knelt in the hay next to her father. She would be allowed to pick out the bunny of her choice. Uncle Lewis had taken them all out of their cage so that she could have a better look.

Miriam stood off to one side, watching her step-daughter and talking with Lewis and Grace. She handed them a loaf of banana bread and leaned in close to whisper something to the young couple, but Amos and Mary Ellen were too busy laughing and playing with the black and white bunnies and didn't seem to hear what she was saying.

"I can see that everyone in your family is quite happy these days," Lewis said to Miriam.

"*Jah*, very happy," Miriam repeated.

The rabbit that Mary Ellen chose was the smallest of the litter, but it looked healthy and bright-eyed, and it was certainly playful. On the ride to Crystal and Jonas's, Mary Ellen had quite a time keeping it inside the box that she'd been given. By the time they arrived, the bunny, which Mary Ellen had already named Dinky, was tucked safely inside the child's coat pocket.

Crystal and the twins were out in the yard building a snowman when the Hilty sleigh pulled in. The boys jumped up and down, always happy to see their cousin Mary Ellen.

"I have a surprise in my pocket!" Mary Ellen called to John and Jacob.

The boys ran excitedly to meet her at the sleigh, and the three of them started off for the barn.

"Jonas is in the barn, too. He's busy working on his old plow. He wants to be sure it's usable before the spring thaw," Crystal told Amos. "I'm sure that he could use a friendly face about now."

Amos laughed. "Maybe it is time to retire that old thing. Floyd Mast has some good buys on the new ones he sells."

"I know he probably should buy a new one," agreed Crystal, "but Jonas is rather partial to the old one. It belonged to his father."

The mention of Papa caused a sharp pain in Miriam's heart. She still missed her father very much. She would always miss him, she supposed. Henry had been a devout Christian man, and for that she was very thankful. Someday they would be reunited in heaven. That was something to be thankful for, too.

"Well, then, I will go see Jonas and leave you two ladies to yourselves. I am sure that you both have plenty to talk about. Women usually do." He winked at Miriam and gave her a playful poke on the arm.

Miriam laughed and lunged for Amos, but he was too quick. His long legs took him quickly out of her reach, and soon he was out of sight, inside the barn.

"It is good to see you so happy, Miriam," Crystal said as she steered her toward the house.

Jah, I really am happy now—more than I ever thought possible. I brought you some banana bread, and I will tell you all about it over a cup of your great-tasting hot cider."

❧

The last stop of the day was at Sarah and Andrew's place. While Miriam was looking forward to seeing her brother and his family, she was most anxious to see Mom and give her the gift she had made.

It was beginning to snow again, and Amos hurried Mary Ellen out of the sleigh.

"Wait, Pappy. My bunny is still in the box. I want to take Dinky in to show Rebekah."

"I will get him," Amos told her. "You go on ahead with Mama Mim."

The warmth of the kitchen was welcoming, but the heat from the stove didn't warm Miriam nearly as much as the welcome that she and Mary Ellen received from her family.

"What brings you out on this snowy afternoon?" Andrew asked his sister.

Jah, to what do we owe this pleasant surprise?" Mom questioned.

"Oh, Amos and I just thought it would be nice to take Mary Ellen for a sleigh ride on a beautiful, snowy day." Miriam smiled at her mother and then winked at Mary Ellen.

"I've got a surprise!" Mary Ellen said excitedly. "Pappy is bringing it in."

"What is it?" asked Rebekah, who had just been wheeled into the room by her mother. "I love surprises!"

"Everyone loves surprises," Miriam said with a laugh. "I have one for Mom, too."

"So, who wants to be first?" Sarah asked as she pushed her daughter up to the kitchen table.

"Mary Ellen can," Miriam said.

"But Pappy isn't here yet," the child protested.

Just then the door opened, and Amos stepped into the room. He had Dinky inside his coat pocket, and the small rabbit's head was peeking out over the top.

"A baby bunny!" Rebekah squealed. "May I hold it, please?"

Mary Ellen reached inside her father's pocket to retrieve the ball of fur. She walked across the room and placed the little rabbit on Rebekah's lap.

Dinky's nose twitched as Rebekah stroked him behind one floppy ear. "Where did you get him?" she asked.

"Uncle Lewis gave him to me," Mary Ellen answered. "He still has three more. Maybe you would like one, too."

Rebekah looked up at her mother and then at her father with pleading eyes.

Andrew smiled. "If it is all right with your mom, it is fine with me."

Sarah nodded. "I think it will be a good idea. Of course, you must help care for it."

"Oh, I will!" Rebekah cried.

"And you must share the bunny with your younger brother and sister," her father reminded.

"I will, Papa," the child responded happily.

"Come, take off your coats and sit awhile. You must all be nearly frozen," Anna said. "I'll put some water on the stove, and we can all have some hot chocolate."

"Have you got any of those great-tasting peanut butter cookies you make so well?" Amos asked as he helped Miriam out of her coat.

"I think I might be able to find a few hiding out in the kitchen somewhere," Mom told him.

When everyone was seated, and the hot chocolate and cookies were passed around, Miriam spoke up. "It's my turn to tell you my surprise. First, I have something for all of you." She handed the banana bread to Sarah; then she reached for her coat, which was hanging on the back of her chair. She pulled a package out and handed it to Mom. "This is for you. I made it to show how much I love you."

Mom took the gift from Miriam. A small sob caught in her throat when she opened it. "Oh, Miriam, it is lovely."

"What is it? Let everyone see," Sarah said.

Mom held up the beautiful cross-stitched wall hanging. It read: "A merry heart doeth good like a medicine."

Everyone in the room said they liked it, and Miriam smiled and said, "It's so true, Mom. You have been right all along, and I just could never see it. God does want each of His children to have a merry heart." She reached for Amos's hand. "My husband helped me see the truth."

"Oh? When was that?" Mom wanted to know.

"It was just shortly after my buggy accident," Miriam replied. "I have not really had the chance to tell you all about it, but I've been working on this cross-stitch for the past few months. I wanted it to be a surprise for Mom."

"And it is a very pleasant surprise, Daughter," her mother said tearfully. "It is certainly an answer to my prayers to know that you finally do understand the importance of a merry heart."

"I know God has been calling to me for a long time," Miriam responded. "I only wish I had listened to Him sooner."

Miriam looked at Amos then. "Would you like to tell them our other surprise?"

He beamed but shook his head. "Let's let Mary Ellen tell them."

Miriam smiled. "That's a fine idea. Mary Ellen, tell everyone what our really big surprise is."

Mary Ellen giggled; then her small face grew very serious. In her most grown-up voice, she announced, "On the way here, after we left Aunt Crystal's, Mama Mim and Pappy told me that I'm gonna be a big sister!"

"Miriam, is she saying what I think she is saying?" Mom asked breathlessly.

Miriam nodded and smiled. *Jah*. I am expecting a baby in about seven months."

"Oh, Miriam, that is wonderful news!" Sarah exclaimed.

"I am so happy for you, Daughter," Anna added. "First Lewis and Grace, and now you. Oh, the rest of the family should be here to share in this joy."

"We've already stopped by to see Lewis and Grace, as well as Jonas and Crystal. They've all been told," Amos was quick to say.

"Congratulations!" Andrew said, patting Amos on the back, then hugging Miriam.

Mom dabbed at the corners of her eyes with a hanky. "*Derr Herr sie gedanki!* I only wish that Henry could be here now. He would be so glad to see how happy our Miriam is."

"Someday we will be reunited with Papa, but until then, he will always be with us—right here." Miriam placed her hand against her heart, so full of love and joy. At last she truly had a merry heart!

Looking for a Miracle

To my six wonderful grandchildren,
Jinell, Madolynne, Rebekah, Ric, Philip, and Richelle.
You are each one of God's miracles!

Chapter 1

"*Ich will mit dir Hehm geh!*" Johnny Yoder called across the room to Mary Ellen Hilty.

Mary Ellen's face flamed, and everyone else laughed. Everyone except for Rebekah Stoltzfus, that is. She sat in her cold, metal wheelchair, feeling alone and so sorry for herself. Self-pity was a common occurrence for the young Amish woman these days. Her cousin and best friend Mary Ellen had lots of suitors, including Johnny Yoder, who seemed to be her most spirited admirer and wanted to take her home. She could probably have her pick of any young man she wanted to ride home with tonight.

Rebekah and Mary Ellen were both nineteen, had become cousins by marriage, and were the best of friends. However, that's where the similarities ended. Mary Ellen had dark brown hair and hazel eyes, while Rebekah had light brown hair and pale blue eyes. Mary Ellen, who'd been the teacher at the Amish one-room schoolhouse for the last two years, was fun-loving, self-assured, and admired by nearly everyone. Why, truth be told, even her pupils loved her to pieces!

Rebekah, on the other hand, was quiet, self-conscious, and certain that no one, except her family, could possibly love her at all. She had low self-esteem and lacked the confidence usually seen in most women her age. Some said Rebekah had always been a shy, introverted child, but most knew the real reason for her inferiority complex and withdrawal from the Amish world around her. It was the simple fact that she was crippled.

The accident had happened thirteen years ago, but Rebekah still remembered it as though it were yesterday. She'd been sent outside to wait in the buggy, while Aunt Mim, also the schoolteacher, finished cleaning the schoolhouse. Aunt Mim planned to give Rebekah a ride home, but an unexpected storm blew in, bringing such strong winds that a heavy limb broke from the very tree under which Rebekah stood waiting.

The branch had fallen across Rebekah's head and neck, knocking her unconscious. When she awoke in the hospital, there were doctors and nurses aplenty standing over her bed, looking ever so serious. Her distraught parents stood nearby, too. She could still hear Mom a-weeping for all she was worth. When she'd asked what was wrong, Rebekah was informed that the blow had injured part of her spinal cord. The worst news of all was the fact that she'd probably never walk again.

The reality didn't truly sink in until she was allowed to go home, a whole month later. It was then that Rebekah came to realize exactly what her limitations would be. She'd be confined to a wheelchair, unable to run and play with the other children. She'd have to be taken by horse and buggy for physical therapy in town several times a week. Her grandma, Anna Stoltzfus, even moved into their house in order to help care for Rebekah. This gave the young girl a clue that she would always be a burden to those she loved most. She'd never be able to live a normal life—never marry or have children of her own.

Rebekah had learned to suffer in silence, because complaining would certainly do nothing to change her condition. She'd tried to put on a brave front, acting cheerful and whatnot, as though her handicap didn't matter one bit. Trouble was, it did matter, 'cause it singled her out as being different from the rest of her family and friends.

Rebekah hated to see pity on folks' faces. It wasn't their pity she wanted. What she needed was a true miracle. Some said she'd already had one miracle. Leastways, that's what everyone had called it when the physical therapist helped her stand and even take a few steps. Of course, she needed leg braces and a pair of special crutches strapped to her arms. Some miracle that was! It was a lot of work to walk, so she spent most of her time stuck in that wheelchair.

Rebekah jerked her thoughts back to the present, watching with envy as Mary Ellen skirted across the barn in a game of drop-the-hanky. As usual, she had three or four young fellas right on her heels.

Rebekah swallowed past the lump in her throat. She wouldn't give in to the threatening tears this time. Crying didn't do one bit of good, anyways. She wheeled herself over to the punch bowl instead. Maybe a cool drink would help wash away that awful, familiar lump.

"Want some punch?"

Rebekah looked up into the face of Daniel Beachy. He was one of the young men she'd recently seen talking to Mary Ellen. *"Danki,* but I can get it," she muttered.

"Ain't no bother," Daniel insisted. "I was just about to get one for myself." He ladled some punch into a paper cup, then handed it to Rebekah, in spite of her refusal. "Are you enjoyin' the singin'?" he asked.

Rebekah nodded as she took the offered punch. "It's all right, but I wish we'd do more singin' and less game playin'."

"Jah, too many games can get real tirin'," he agreed.

Rebekah thought maybe she should explain that she hadn't meant that a'tall. In fact, the reason she enjoyed singing was because it was all she could do well. Game playing, at least the kind that required running and jumping, was out of the question for someone like her. She never got the chance to express those feelings, though, because they were interrupted by Mary Ellen and Johnny Yoder.

"Rebekah, you should've heard the silly jokes some of the boys were tellin'," Mary Ellen said breathlessly. "I've laughed so much tonight, I don't think I'll have to laugh again for the rest of the month!"

Rebekah feigned a smile. *Mary Ellen looks so* schnuck, she thought with envy. Her cheeks were bright pink, and her dark brown hair was threatening to escape from the sides of the small *Kapp* she wore on her head. Mary Ellen's hazel-colored eyes shone with enthusiasm. No wonder every young Amish man in the county wanted to court her. Rebekah couldn't really be mad at her cousin, though. *Ach,* it wasn't her fault she was so much fun to be around. Maybe if Rebekah had been able to join in the fun, others would like her more, too. Could be that some of the boys might even want to court her.

"Will you be okay goin' home if I ride in Johnny's courtin' buggy?" Mary Ellen asked Rebekah.

Rebekah's eyes narrowed. "But you came with me and Simon," she reminded.

"*Jah,* I know, and I'm sure your younger brother won't mind escortin' you home." Mary Ellen laughed. "After all, he has to go to the same place you're goin'. If I go with Johnny, then Simon won't have to travel clear over to my place neither."

Rebekah shrugged her shoulders. "*Jah,* all right, go ahead and ride with Johnny then."

Was that a look of envy she saw on Daniel's clean-shaven face? Rebekah wondered. Might could be that he'd been waitin' for the chance to ask Mary Ellen if he could give her a ride home. If Daniel hadn't wasted so much time getting punch for the pitiful crippled girl, he'd already have talked to Mary Ellen by now. It would be his courtin' buggy that would carry her home, not Johnny's.

Why do I always feel so guilty about everything? Rebekah fretted. After all, it wasn't as though she'd asked Daniel to get the punch. She hadn't intentionally spoiled his chances with Mary Ellen.

Rebekah tried to shake the contrite feelings aside as she said in her most cheerful voice, "I'm gettin' kind of tired. I think I'll go find Simon so we can head for home."

"It's been a fun evening," Mary Ellen said. "Johnny and I will be leavin' soon, too, I expect."

"I'd better see if my sister, Sarah Jane, is ready to go," Daniel interjected. "My two brothers will probably have dates to take home." He glanced down at Rebekah and smiled. It was the kind of smile she'd become used to seeing—one of pity, she was downright certain of it. "*Gut Nacht,* Rebekah." He looked over at her cousin and nodded. "*Gut Nacht,* Mary Ellen."

"Good night," both girls echoed.

Mary Ellen bent down and whispered to Rebekah, "He's *schnuck,* don't you think?"

Rebekah shrugged. *If he's so cute, then why aren't you ridin' home with him?* "*Jah,* he seems to like you," she muttered, instead of voicing her thoughts.

Johnny grabbed Mary Ellen's hand. "Come on. Let's play one more game of kick the can before we head for home."

"See you in two weeks at preachin'!" Mary Ellen called to Rebekah.

"*Jah,* two weeks," Rebekah murmured.

❧

Rebekah's sixteen-year-old brother pushed her wheelchair up the wooden ramp

Papa had built several years ago. The young people found their parents in the kitchen, playing a game of Scrabble at the table.

Papa, pulling mechanically on his full, dark beard, was in deep concentration as he pondered over a possible word that could use the letters Z, T, A, O, E, L, S.

Mom looked up and smiled. Her eyes, much bluer and brighter than Rebekah's, seemed to dance in the light of the oil lamp hanging above the table. "Sit yourselves down and talk awhile. Tell us all about the singin'. Did you two have a *gut* time?"

"It was great!" Simon exclaimed, pushing a lock of sandy brown hair out of his dark eyes. "Just about every Amish teen in the valley was there. Jake Detweiler's barn might never be the same, though!" He chuckled as he opened the door of their propane refrigerator, obviously looking for something to eat.

"And you, Daughter?" Mom asked. "Did you also have a *gut* time?"

Rebekah shrugged. "It was all right, I guess."

"Just all right?" Mom questioned. "As I remember, singin's were always *wunderbaar.*" She glanced over at Papa, who was still studying the Scrabble board like his very life depended on the next move. "It was at a singin' where your papa asked me to marry him, ya know."

"*Jah,* well, I expect our family might be in for another weddin' soon," Simon said as he helped himself to a thick slice of apple-crumb pie.

"Oh? Is there somethin' you've been keepin' from us, Rebekah?" Mom asked with raised eyebrows. "*Kumme*—come now—tell us your news."

Rebekah wheeled her chair closer to the table. "*Himmel*—no, no—it's not me, Mom. I think Simon's referrin' to Cousin Mary Ellen."

"I see. So who's her lucky fellow?" Mom prompted.

"It could be anyone," Rebekah replied. "Mary Ellen's very popular with several young men. She can take her pick of whomever she pleases." She paused, drawing in a deep breath and letting it out with a little moan. "I think Daniel Beachy is the one most in love with her, but Johnny Yoder won't hardly give him a chance."

"Hmm. . ." Mom gave a slight nod of her head. "It sounds as if Mary Ellen might have to be makin' a choice then."

"She'll pick Johnny," Simon said with his mouth full of pie.

"Really, Simon, didn't you get enough food at the singin'? Sometimes I think all you ever do is eat!" Mom scolded, though she was smiling when she spoke.

"Aw, leave the boy alone, Sarah. He's growin' so fast and needs all the nourishment he can get." It was the first time Rebekah's father had spoken since their arrival. Suddenly, he slapped the table and hollered, "My word is *zealot!* The Z, which normally is worth ten points, is on a double letter square. The other letters are worth one point apiece. The L lands on a double word square, so my entire score is fifty!" He gave Mom a playful nudge on the arm. "I have only one letter left, so beat that if you can!"

Mom laughed and began to tickle his full beard, which was sprinkled with a few gray hairs here and there. "Calm down once. I concede. You've won the game fair and square, Andrew. So now you're deservin' of a reward. How 'bout a piece of pie? If your growin' son hasn't eaten it all, that is," she added with a wink.

"You two act like a couple of *kinder*," Rebekah said with a mock frown. "Watch out now, or you two children will wake up Nadine and Grandma Stoltzfus."

"We wouldn't want that, now, would we?" Papa said with a deep chuckle. "Grandma might eat all the pie before we could even make it to the refrigerator."

"Papa!" Rebekah admonished. "You know Grandma don't eat so much!"

Papa bent down and tickled her under the chin. "That's true enough, but if Simon or little sister, Nadine, should decide to help her, why, I might have to take on a part-time job just to pay for the big grocery bills."

"You are such a tease," Rebekah giggled as she propelled her chair quickly away from him.

Papa nodded. "You're right, I am. That's why your mom agreed to marry me, too. She loves to be teased!" He turned his attentions on Mom again, tickling her in the ribs and under the chin.

She tickled him right back, and soon the two of them were howling and tickling to beat the band. Rebekah was sure they would wake Grandma and Nadine.

A sudden pang of jealousy washed over her, like the rippling brook that ran across the back of their farm. Mom and Papa were chasing each other around the table now. Probably to avoid any head-on collisions, Simon had taken a seat at the table and seemed intent on finishing his pie.

Rebekah wondered how it would feel to laugh and run around with a young man—someone she loved as much as Mom loved Papa. *That would take a miracle,* she mused, *and miracles only happened back in the Bible days.* She felt herself tremble. *Or did they? God still performs some miracles today, ain't it so?*

She shook all thoughts of miracles straight out of her head. Even if it were possible, miracles were for others—those more deservin' than she. In all her nineteen years, Rebekah was sure she'd done nothing to earn any favors or miracles from God. She directed the wheelchair toward her downstairs bedroom. What she really needed was to quit thinkin' of miracles and just be alone for awhile.

❧

When she awoke the following morning, Rebekah felt physically drained and out of sorts. She hadn't slept well and had lain awake for hours, just thinking about her disability. She wondered if there was some way she could possibly fit in with the rest of the *younga* her age. Since she wasn't able to join most of their activities, she couldn't really blame them for ignoring her neither. She seemed to be more accepted by older people—especially Mom, Papa, and Grandma. Maybe it was because they couldn't do as much as the younger ones. Most of their activities, though not as restricted as Rebekah's, were still a bit hampered.

Rebekah knew her parents and grandmother loved her and were dedicated to taking care of her needs. But what would become of her when they were all gone? Would her younger brother or sister, or maybe even a cousin or niece, be stuck caring for her? There had to be some way she could provide for herself. If she had enough money, she might be able to hire a young person to do all the things she couldn't manage.

Rebekah pulled herself to an upright position, using the wooden side rails to lend the needed support. *I know I'll never have a husband or children of my own, but if I could only be financially independent, I'd be a lot less of a burden.*

Unbidden tears slipped out of Rebekah's eyes, rolling down her cheeks in little rivulets. What could one crippled young Amish woman do that would provide her with enough money to care for herself? Was it even possible, or was this all just a bunch of silly wishful thinkin'?

"I'll have to commit the problem to prayer," she whispered, closing her eyes. "What I need is a miracle, God. Do You still perform miracles? If so, could You please give me some kind of a sign? I've done nothin' to deserve a miracle, I know. I'm not askin' You to heal my crippled body or even give me a husband neither. I only want to support myself, so I'm not such a burden to others."

Silence filled her small, unadorned bedroom. Had she really expected God to answer out loud? Hadn't the bishop taught in his sermons that God often talked to people's hearts? Sometimes He spoke through others or from His Holy Word. God had spoken out loud to some people in the Bible, but they needed that type of thing back then, she reasoned. If there was any chance that God might be interested in giving her a miracle, then she'd have to learn patience, keep reading her Bible, and remember to pray every single day.

Chapter 2

A s she wheeled into the kitchen, the smoky smell of sizzling bacon assaulted Rebekah's senses, making her stomach rumble. "Where's Grandma?" Her question was directed at Mom, who stood at their old-fashioned, wood-burning cookstove.

"She's still in bed." Mom nodded toward the other downstairs bedroom. "Grandma isn't feelin' too well this mornin'. I told her we could manage and said she should rest."

Rebekah's lips puckered as her forehead wrinkled with concern. "It's not anything serious, I hope." The thought of dear Grandma being sick pulled on the young woman's tender heartstrings.

Mom flipped the bacon over. "*Ich hoff net*—I hope not. She's been a little tired the past few days. I think she tries to do too much."

Rebekah nodded. "I know she does. Ever since Grandma came to help care for me, she's done the work of two women. It wonders me so how she can keep up."

"*Jah,*" Mom agreed, "but I think keepin' busy has helped her not miss Grandpa so much."

"It was nice that Aunt Mim and Uncle Amos named their son Henry after Grandpa Stoltzfus," Rebekah added.

"I know it meant a lot to Grandma," Mom agreed.

"Do you think she should see the doctor?" Rebekah questioned with a glance at Grandma's bedroom door.

Mom shook her head. "If she's not up and around and actin' like her old self by tomorrow, I'll speak to Papa and see that he takes her to see Doc Manney."

Rebekah wheeled toward the table. "What can I do to help with breakfast?" She looked around the room. "Where's Nadine? She ain't sick, too, I hope."

"I sent her out to gather eggs." Mom piled the crisp bacon into a glass pan and popped it into the warming oven. "I'll be doin' some bakin' today, and since we're havin' eggs for breakfast, we might run short. I checked the refrigerator, and there aren't as many as I remember."

"Simon probably ate them." Rebekah giggled. "Now that it's summertime and there's more chores to do, he eats enough to choke a horse!"

Mom laughed, too. "*Jah,* he sure can put away the food these days. I do pity the poor woman my boy marries. Why, she'll hafta be cookin' from sunup to sunset."

"Maybe we should start alertin' all the eligible young women now. That way, if anyone should ever fall for my little brother, she can't say she wasn't warned!" Rebekah declared.

143

Mom smiled and reached for a jar of baking powder from the pantry. "Enough about Simon and his eatin' habits. Why don't you scramble up some eggs while I finish these biscuits?"

Rebekah grimaced. "You know it's hard for me to reach the stove from my wheelchair."

Mom turned to face Rebekah, her blue eyes looking ever so serious. "Where are your crutches and leg braces? You can stand at the stove if you're usin' them, you know."

"Aw, it's too much trouble to put them on," Rebekah whined. "Besides, the braces make my legs stiff like a doll's."

Mom shook her head and gave the strings of her white head covering a little tug. "I know they're awkward and uncomfortable, but they do allow you to stand, and even walk a short ways. It's much more'n we could've hoped for. After the accident, the doctors said you'd probably never walk again, remember?"

Rebekah's eyes filled with tears she was determined to keep from falling. She didn't think Mom needed a crybaby on her hands this morning. Besides, cryin' wouldn't make things any different. Nope, no different a'tall! "Okay, Mom, I'll go get the leg braces," she muttered.

"Maybe later," Mom said. "The *Mannsleit*—menfolk—will be in from their chorin' soon. We need to get breakfast on as quick as possible, 'cause they'll be wantin' to get out to the fields. Why don't you set the table? Nadine can cook the eggs when she comes in from the chicken coop."

Relief flooded through Rebekah as she began to set the dishes out. They were in the lower cupboards, along with the silverware, so it was something she could do without any help. She'd just put the last dish on the table when fourteen-year-old Nadine burst through the back door. Instead of a stiff organdy prayer *Kapp*, she wore a black kerchief on her pinned-up brown hair this morning.

"How'd it go in the chicken coop?" Mom asked.

"Sis gut gange," Nadine answered. "I got over a dozen eggs, so I'm thinkin' those fat hens must like summer 'bout as much as I do." She placed the basket of eggs on the cupboard and went to wash up at the sink.

"I'm glad it went well, and it's a *gut* thing they're layin' so well," Mom said. "We're havin' scrambled eggs this mornin', and I was afraid we'd run out." She motioned toward the stove. "Nadine, would you please do up the eggs? The bacon's been fried, and my biscuits are ready to go in the oven now. They should be done when you're finished."

"Jah, des Kannich du—yes, I will," Nadine said as she dashed over to the cupboard and began to break eggs into a large bowl. "How was the singin' last night?" she asked Rebekah. "I can't wait 'til I'm allowed to go." She cast a wistful look in Mom's direction.

"You'll get there soon enough, like as not," Mom stated.

"Goin' to a singin' ain't that excitin'," Rebekah said, wheeling herself over to Nadine.

"You must be jokin'! There's boys at them singin's, ain't it so?"

Rebekah lifted her gaze to the ceiling. "Of course, Silly."

"Then it'd be a whole lot of fun," Nadine persisted.

"Which is why you're not ready to go to one yet," Mom said firmly. "A young girl shouldn't be so interested in the opposite sex just yet."

"Oh, Mom," Nadine groaned, "other girls my age go to singin's. If you had your way, I'd grow up to be an old maid, just like Rebekah."

"Nadine Stoltzfus, that's an awful thing to say about your sister!" Mom scolded. "She's only nineteen and still has plenty of time to get married yet. I want ya to apologize to Rebekah and be quick about it!"

Nadine's youthful face reddened as she looked down at Rebekah. "I. . .I'm sorry. I didn't mean—"

Rebekah held up one hand. "It's all right—I am an old maid, and that's the truth of it."

"Such utter nonsense!" Mom exclaimed. "When the right man comes along and captures your heart with love, then you'll marry and start a family of your own."

Rebekah's eyes flew to her crippled legs. "Like this, Mom?" she cried, touching one knee. "What man in his right mind would be wantin' a wife who looks like me? Who'd want someone who can't do all the things a normal wife should do?" Tears of frustration slipped under her dark lashes.

Mom rushed to her and dropped down beside the wheelchair. "Oh, Rebekah, don't fret."

Rebekah leaned her head against Mom's shoulder and wept. "It's true, and you know it! No one will ever want me. I'm such a burden to my family! If only I could care for myself."

"You do, Rebekah. You've learned to dress and groom yourself, and so many other—"

Mom's words were cut off when the back door flew open and Papa and Simon came storming into the room. Their faces were as red as one of Uncle Amos's heifers, and they huffed and puffed something awful.

"Your son is gettin' too *gut* for me now, Sarah," Papa panted. "We raced all the way from the barn, and Simon nearly beat me to the back door."

"Nearly?" cried Simon. "What do ya mean, nearly, Pop? My feet hit the porch steps at least three seconds before yours did!"

Papa laughed and shrugged his broad shoulders. "Well, *wass machts aus?* I got to the kitchen first." He pounded Simon on the back. "So that means I get the first kiss!"

"The what?" Simon gave Papa a questioning look and took several steps backwards.

"Not you, Boy! I was referrin' to your *mamm.*" Papa marched across the room, drew Mom into his arms, and planted a noisy kiss right on her mouth.

"Andrew, really!" Mom exclaimed. "What kind of example are you settin' for the *younga?*"

"A good one, I hope!" With that, Papa bent down and kissed her soundly once more.

"Oh, yuk!" Simon groaned.

"I think it's kind of romantic. Don't you, Rebekah?" Nadine asked with a giggle.

Rebekah, who'd been busy drying her tearstained cheeks, could only nod.

"I think it's time for my men to get washed up," Mom announced. "Breakfast is near ready, and we need to eat so's we can get on with our day."

Get on with our day, Rebekah thought dryly. Today was just another day. Nothin' to look forward to, that's for sure. When she was a child, her disability hadn't bothered her so much; but now she was a young woman, and things were different—she was different. *Maybe if I do somethin' worthwhile today, I'll feel a bit better. As soon as breakfast is done, I'll take a tray into Grandma. Then maybe I can read to her for awhile.* Rebekah smiled to herself. Grandma wasn't feelin' well, and she could minister to her for a change.

❧

Rebekah knocked softly on Grandma's bedroom door. When there was no response, she rapped a little louder. Still no reply. She opened the door a crack and peered inside. Grandma was lying in the bed, long gray hair fanned out around her face. It was one of the few times Rebekah had seen Grandma with her hair down. Of course, Grandma was usually up and dressed way before anyone else in the family.

"Grandma, are you awake?" Rebekah called softly. "I have a breakfast tray for you." She opened the door more fully. Grandma Stoltzfus's eyes were shut, and her Bible was lying open across her chest. She looked awfully still. A strange feeling came creeping over Rebekah. Why hadn't Grandma responded? Maybe she was sicker than she'd let on. She balanced the tray carefully in her lap and wheeled toward Grandma's bed. "Grandma, can ya hear me?"

Grandma remained silent and unmoving.

Rebekah looked down at the open Bible and noticed a passage of Scripture from Proverbs had been underlined. " 'Trust in the Lord with all thine heart; and lean not unto thine own understanding. In all thy ways acknowledge him, and he shall direct thy paths,' " she read aloud.

One of Grandma's wrinkled hands lay across the open page. Rebekah reached out to touch it. Cold! It was ice cold!

"Grandma, wake up!" Rebekah shouted. "Open your eyes and look at me!"

There was no response from Grandma Stoltzfus. Her body was as lifeless as a sack of corn. She'd obviously gone to her reward in heaven and would never have to do another chore.

Rebekah dropped her head onto the bed and sobbed for all she was worth.

Mom appeared in the doorway just then. "Rebekah? What is it, Daughter?"

Rebekah jerked her head up and gulped back a hiccup. "I think she's gone, Mom. Grandma's dead."

"What?" Mom gasped. *"Ach,* my, that can't be! I spoke to her but a few hours ago." She rushed over to the bed and picked up Grandma's hand, feeling for a pulse. Glancing at Rebekah, Mom shook her head. She placed her own hand in front of Grandma's mouth and held it that way for a few seconds. "Oh, Rebekah!" she cried. "I believe you're right. Grandma's gone home to heaven."

❧

The funeral for Grandma Stoltzfus was four days later. The medical examiner, who'd come to the house to see the body and sign the death certificate, said she'd had a stroke. The family was grief-stricken, but the entire Amish community rallied to do whatever was necessary for the burial preparations, funeral service, and the meal afterwards.

The main service was held at Andrew and Sarah's house, with the funeral procession after that. The country road leading to the cemetery was lined with nearly one hundred Amish buggies. In perfect procession, they followed the horse-drawn hearse.

At the cemetery, Rebekah and the rest of the family mourned openly as Bishop Benner laid their beloved grandma to rest. She would be sorely missed, especially at the house where she'd lived for the last thirteen years.

Rebekah fought hard to keep her emotions under control. Grandma had been her primary caregiver ever since the tragic accident that left her nearly paralyzed from the waist down. She'd be missing Grandma for much more than her care, however. She'd pine for the long talks they used to have, the board games they often played, the times spent caring for Grandma's houseplants, and the meaningful hours she'd listened to her sweet grandmother read the Scriptures. There were so many precious memories.

Rebekah glanced up at the faces gathered around the plain, wooden casket. She wasn't the only one in mourning today. Aunt Mim was weeping openly as she leaned heavily on her husband's shoulder. Mary Ellen and twelve-year-old Henry stood near their parents. They had tears in their eyes as well.

To the left stood Uncle Jonas and Aunt Crystal, with their fifteen-year-old twins, Jacob and John, and eleven-year-old daughter, Maddie. Next to them were Uncle Lewis, Aunt Grace, and their children, Peggy, age twelve, and Matthew, who was seven. To the right stood Rebekah's own family—Mom, Papa, Simon, and Nadine. They were all shedding tears aplenty, too.

This was the first time Rebekah had lost someone so close. She'd only been six when Grandpa Stoltzfus died suddenly of a heart attack. She barely remembered him, and at the time of his death she hadn't been so greatly affected.

"Oh, God, why'd Ya hafta take Grandma?" Rebekah moaned. She was beginning to wonder if God even listened to her prayers.

❧

The funeral dinner was held on the lawn at Rebekah's folks' place. Picnic tables and pieces of plywood placed across sawhorses were set up to eat on. A vast array of food and beverages had been prepared and brought in by the many families in attendance.

The summer sun was blistering hot, and the air muggy and devoid of any breeze. Rebekah found solace under the branches of a large willow tree. She closed her eyes and tried to imagine a cool fall wind as she fanned her face with a napkin.

"Here, I brought ya some food."

Rebekah opened her eyes with a start. Mary Ellen was staring down at her with a look of concern. She held a plate of food in both hands.

"I. . .I'm not really hungry," Rebekah announced.

"That may be so, but you need to keep up your strength," her cousin replied.

"My strength? My strength for what—cryin'?" A fresh rush of tears seeped under Rebekah's long lashes.

Mary Ellen set the plates on the ground. She knelt next to Rebekah's wheelchair and gave her a big hug. "I know it hurts. We'll all miss Grandma, but you, probably more than anyone, will feel the greatest loss. She lived with you and has cared for you a long time. It won't be easy, but God'll give you strength. He knows what's best for each of us."

"It was best to take Grandma away?" Rebekah asked tearfully.

"Wass Got tuht ist wohl getahn," Mary Ellen replied.

"Well done?" Rebekah shrieked. "Well done for whom?"

Mary Ellen tipped Rebekah's chin up so she was forced to look directly at Mary Ellen. "For Grandma Stoltzfus, that's who."

A feeling of confusion, mixed with pain, shrouded Rebekah's soul. "What do ya mean by that? She's dead, Mary Ellen."

"I know, but the Bible says for a believer to be absent from the body is to be present with the Lord," Mary Ellen asserted. "If we could only know what heaven's really like, I think we'd all long to go there. Grandma's no longer confined in an agin' body. She doesn't have to toil here on earth or feel any physical pain no more. She's probably havin' the time of her life, walkin' all over heaven with Grandpa and Jesus right about now."

Rebekah flinched. She knew her cousin's words were true, yet it was so hard to let go of her precious grandma.

"Grieve if you must, Rebekah, but don't let your grief consume you. Grandma wouldn't want that," Mary Ellen expressed firmly.

Rebekah nodded. "I know you're right, but it's not so easy for me to feel joy the way you do. You've always been able to smile, even in the face of difficulty. I remember as *kinder,* when some of our classmates used to pick on you. Your lovin', forgivin' spirit was evident, even back then."

"My life hasn't always been easy," Mary Ellen agreed. "I lost my real mama when I was young. It was hard on Pappy, too, but he taught me how to love and laugh. Then God brought Mama Mim into our lives." She patted Rebekah's hand. "There's always somethin' for which to be thankful. Count your blessings and consider the beautiful earth that God has made."

Rebekah's head bobbed up and down. *"Jah,* that's true."

Mary Ellen got off her knees and sat on the ground beside the wheelchair. She handed a plate of food to Rebekah. "We'd better eat this before the ants find it and decide to have themselves a little picnic."

Rebekah's lips curved into a faint smile. "You're probably right. I might be willin' to share my food with one of my special aunts, but never a bunch of picnic ants!"

Chapter 3

Rebekah and Mary Ellen had just finished eating their meal when Daniel Beachy joined them under the weeping willow tree. "I'm sorry about your *mammi*—grandma," he said, dropping to the ground. "I didn't know her well, but she seemed like a right nice woman."

"*Jah*, she was the best *mammi* anyone could ever want," Rebekah agreed.

"She wasn't my grandma by blood," Mary Ellen put in, "but she always treated me as such."

Daniel removed his straw hat and wiped rivulets of sweat from his forehead. "It's a mighty warm day, ain't it so? With so many folks here, it's nice we can at least be outside."

Mary Ellen nodded. "If June's this hot and sticky, I wonder what we can expect from the rest of our summer."

"Probably more hot, muggy days," he replied with a deep chuckle.

Mary Ellen joined him in laughter. *She looks so* schnuck *whenever she laughs or even runs about playin' games and such, the way she did at the last singin',* Rebekah thought with envy. She glanced down at her lifeless legs. Two dead sticks, that's all they were. Sure weren't *gut* for nothin' much. *I'd probably never look that cute, no matter how much I laughed or smiled,* she continued to fume. *No wonder all the fellows like Mary Ellen. She's normal and can do everything a young woman's supposed to be doin'!*

"Is this a private party, or can anyone join in?" It was Johnny Yoder's smooth talk that interrupted them. He was holding a man-sized plate of crisp peanut butter cookies, and the smile he wore could have melted any size snowman. "Look here, I've brought you all some dessert." He plunked down on the grass, right beside Mary Ellen.

"Peanut butter's my favorite!" Mary Ellen exclaimed. She reached out and snatched one off the plate. "*Danki*, Johnny! I'm beholdin' to ya now."

He grinned from ear to ear. "Does that mean I'm welcome to join this group then?"

"Of course. We're glad to have your company, aren't we?" Mary Ellen glanced first at Rebekah, then over to Daniel.

Rebekah nodded. "It's fine with me."

Daniel nodded, too, but Rebekah was sure that was a look of sheer disappointment written all over his serious-looking face.

In no time at all the cookies were gone, though most of them were eaten by the two young men. Conversation didn't lag much, especially between Johnny and

Mary Ellen. Rebekah thought it most unfair that Johnny seemed to be hoggin' her friend thataway.

"The funeral service was a long one," Johnny said, to no one in particular this time.

Jah, they usually are," Daniel agreed as he leaned back on his elbows and turned his face toward the cloudless sky.

"It was almost as long as a regular preachin' service," Johnny added. He chuckled, kind of sillylike, and cast a sidelong glance at Mary Ellen. *"Es guld dem Mary Ellen wo er eikschlofe is in der Gemeh?"*

Mary Ellen jumped up, planting her hands firmly on her slim hips. "What do you mean, how about the time I fell asleep in church? I never did such a thing, and you know it, Johnny Yoder!"

"Sure you did," he teased. "You nearly fell off your wooden bench that day."

"That's not so," Mary Ellen defended. "I always pay close attention during preachin'."

"I think he's only kiddin' with you," Rebekah said, giving the ties on her cousin's head covering a little tug. "I sure don't remember you ever fallin' asleep in church."

"Me neither," Daniel put in.

Jah, well, maybe she wasn't really sleepin'," Johnny admitted. "She might've just been prayin' for a very long time." He leaned his head back and hooted until his face turned bright red and tears actually ran down his cheeks. Then suddenly, as if he'd never been joking around at all, he jumped up, grabbed Mary Ellen's hand, and started to pull her away from the others. "Why don't you take a little walk with me? We'll head on down toward the creek. Maybe that'll help cool you down some. A girl with a fiery temper needs a bit of coolin' down, don'tcha think?" he asked with a wink.

Mary Ellen folded her arms in front of her chest. "What makes you so sure I want to go anywhere with the likes of you, Johnny Yoder?"

He blinked his green eyes a couple of times and gave her a quick poke to the ribs. "Because I'm irresistible, and if you don't agree to go, then I'll be forced to get down on my knees and beg like a dog. Now you wouldn't want me to do somethin' that awful embarrassing, now, would ya?"

"Oh, all right," Mary Ellen conceded with a shrug. Her gaze fell on Rebekah, then it swung over to Daniel. "You're both welcome to come along."

"No thanks," Rebekah declined. "I'd rather stay here under this shady old tree." She glanced at Daniel, who was now lying on his back in the grass, using his straw hat as kind of a pillow. "You go ahead, if you want to, Daniel."

He crinkled his nose and waved a hand. "Naw, they don't need me taggin' along."

There was that look again, Rebekah noted. *Poor Daniel. He's so smitten with Mary Ellen that he don't rightly know what to do. What with Johnny bein' around all the time, he hasn't much of a chance at winnin' her over neither.*

Mary Ellen and Johnny said their good-byes, then walked away hand in hand. Rebekah's tender heart went out to Daniel even more as she watched them saunter off toward the creek like they didn't have a care in the world. How she hated to see anyone suffering so. She wished with all her heart there was something she could say or do to make Daniel feel a mite better. His dark eyes looked so serious and forlorn. "Why don't ya go along with them?" she suggested again. "I'm sure Mary Ellen would—"

"I'd rather not be a fifth wheel on the buggy," he interrupted. "I'd have gone if you'd been willin', but no, not alone."

Rebekah didn't understand why a grown, twenty-year-old man would need a crippled woman to tag along for moral support. Especially since it was obvious that he was smitten with Mary Ellen. He should have gathered up his courage and gone after her, for goodness' sake! At the rate Daniel was goin', Simon's prediction would come true already. Mary Ellen would most surely end up marryin' Johnny Yoder, and Daniel Beachy would be left clean out in the cold.

Rebekah drew in a breath and let it out in a long, shuddering sigh. "If I'd agreed to go along on the walk, I'd have only slowed the rest of you down."

Daniel turned his head in her direction. "I could've pushed your wheelchair, ya know. I've had lots of practice with the plow and my pop's mules, so we'd move along pretty fast."

Rebekah inwardly groaned. She'd never been compared to a team of mules before, and she wasn't so sure she liked the implication. "I think I'd better go see if Mom needs me for anything." She pointed to the plates on the ground. "Would you please hand me those, so I can take 'em inside?"

Daniel sat up and did as she asked, placing the plates in Rebekah's lap.

"Danki." She wheeled away quickly, without another word, leaving Daniel to sit there by himself.

❧

Grandma had been gone for nearly a month, yet still the pain lingered in Rebekah's heart. She missed the sweet lady so much—especially their long talks. Grandma had always been so full of good advice, and Rebekah often wondered where all that wisdom came from.

One day she was watering some of the African violets on the dressing table in Grandma's old room. Grandma had died so unexpectedly, and there had been nothing Rebekah could do about it. Now she was determined to keep those plants alive and flourishing, come what may.

As she rolled her chair toward the end of the dresser, Rebekah spotted Grandma's Bible lying on the small table next to the bed. The last time she'd seen it, it had been on Grandma's chest. Now it was closed, just like the ending chapter of Grandma Stoltzfus's life.

Rebekah reached for the Bible and held it close to her heart. Unbidden tears slipped through her thick eyelashes, and she sniffed deeply, trying to hold them at bay. She'd heard about the process of grieving for a loved one, but nothing had prepared her for this terrible, empty ache deep within her soul. She hadn't realized just how much Grandma meant to her neither. Not until the dear woman had up and died.

Why do folks always wait 'til it's too late to express their real feelin's for one another? she asked herself. *Why not tell 'em when they're still alive and can know how much you care?*

She placed the Bible in her lap and opened it to a spot where a crocheted bookmark had been positioned. It was in the exact place the Bible had been opened when Rebekah found Grandma in the deep sleep of death.

"Mom must have put this in here," Rebekah whispered. "Maybe she wanted to save the place where Grandma last read God's Word." Her eyes traveled down the page until they came to rest on the two verses Grandma had underlined. "Proverbs 3:5 and 6," she read. " 'Trust in the Lord with all thine heart; and lean not unto thine own understanding. In all thy ways acknowledge him, and he shall direct thy paths.' "

"Those are *gut* words to live by, ain't it so?"

Rebekah turned her head. Mom was standing inside the doorway. She nodded but made no reply to her mother's question. She was afraid her voice would break and she'd dissolve into a puddle of unstoppable tears.

Mom came the rest of the way into the room. She took a seat on the edge of the bed near the wheelchair, then placed a hand on Rebekah's trembling shoulder. "It's all right to grieve for Grandma, but she'd want you to go on with life and find happiness."

"Go on with life?" Rebekah nearly choked on the words. "What life, Mom? A cripple like me can never have a meaningful life! What happiness awaits someone like me?"

"Oh, Rebekah that just isn't so," Mom said softly. "You can have a meaningful life. Why, there's many people in the world who have disabilities, and most of 'em live fairly productive lives." She gently stroked the side of Rebekah's face. "You were always such a pleasant, easygoin' child. I thought you'd come to accept your limitations. However, since you've become a young woman, I've noticed a definite change in your attitude, and I'm not sure I like what I see."

Rebekah sniffed deeply, swiping angrily at the tears running down her cheeks. "When I was a little girl, you all spoiled me so. Someone was always around to care for me or just talk—the way Grandma often did. I thought somebody would always be there to provide for my needs. Now I know I'm really a burden, and someday I might not have anyone to care for me a'tall."

Mom moved from her place on the bed and knelt in front of Rebekah. She grasped her hands and held them tightly. "Losin' Grandma made us all aware of how fragile life is. None of us will live on this earth forever. Someday, each who is a believer will join Grandma in heaven." She closed her eyes for a moment, as though searching for just the right words. After a few seconds, she opened them again. "We're a close family, and I'm sure that even after your *daed* and I are both gone, someone else will take over the responsibility of your care."

"I don't want anyone to have to be responsible for me, Mom. I want to provide for myself—at least financially," Rebekah asserted. "I just don't know what someone like me can do to make enough money to accomplish that goal."

"You could sell eggs or do some handcrafts and take them to the farmers' market," Mom suggested, giving Rebekah's hand a few pats.

"Doin' small things like sellin' eggs or crafts wouldn't give me enough money," Rebekah argued. She felt as if Mom was treatin' her like a child, and it irked her to no end.

"Maybe you should pray about the matter if it means so much to you. Search God's Word for wisdom." Mom stood up. "Why don't you keep Grandma's *Biwel*? I think she'd have wanted you to have it. I know the Scriptures gave her lots of comfort, not to mention answers whenever she needed the Lord's guidance."

Rebekah thought about the underlined verses in Grandma's Bible. Maybe she would look through the rest of the Bible for other Scriptures Grandma might have highlighted. Perhaps the miracle she was looking for could be found in one of those passages.

Chapter 4

Rebekah spent the next several days looking through Grandma's well-worn Bible. On almost every page there was a verse of Scripture underlined or a little note written in Grandma's handwriting and scrawled in the margin or at the bottom of the page. There was no doubt about it—Grandma Stoltzfus lived and died by the truth of God's Word.

One morning after breakfast, Rebekah found herself alone in the house. Mom and Nadine were busy weeding the garden, and Papa and Simon were hard at work in the fields. She decided this would be a good time to read more of Grandma's Bible.

Rebekah settled herself at the kitchen table with the Holy Bible and a glass of cold lemonade. A deep sense of longing encompassed her soul as she softly prayed, "What words do You have for me today, Lord? I need to know whether You have any kind of plan for my life."

As she opened the Bible, Rebekah discovered a small ribbon marker hanging partially out. She turned the page to where the ribbon was nestled, and her eye caught another of Grandma's underlined verses in Jeremiah 31, verses 3 and 4. "The Lord hath appeared of old unto me, saying, Yea, I have loved thee with an everlasting love: therefore with lovingkindness have I drawn thee. Again I will build thee, and thou shalt be built."

Rebekah pondered the Scripture. Deep in her heart she knew God loved her, but was His Word saying He wanted to rebuild her? Did that mean her body? Now, that would take a genuine miracle! No, she was fairly sure the Scripture was referring to being spiritually renewed and rebuilt. She knew for certain that she was in need of that!

Rebekah bowed her head and closed her eyes. "Dear Father, thank You for remindin' me that You love me with an everlasting love. Please draw me closer and build me up, so's I can be a better servant. If it's Your will for me to support myself financially, then show me how. Guide me, direct me, and please, give me a true miracle. In Your Son's name, I ask it. Amen."

❒

Rebekah was watering the plants in Grandma's old room again when Mom came in and interrupted her. "*Gut,* I was hopin' to find you in here."

"What is it?" Rebekah asked with a note of concern. "Is there anything wrong?"

Mom shook her head. "I just wanted to talk to you about an idea I have."

Rebekah spun her wheelchair around so she was facing her mother. "What idea?"

"Papa and I are gonna take some fresh produce and a few other things to the farmers' market tomorrow. Since you seem so set on wantin' to make money, I thought you might like to take some flowers from the garden or maybe a few of these houseplants to sell," Mom said, pointing to an African violet.

"Sell off Grandma's plants?" Rebekah cried. "No, Mom, I could never do that! It just wouldn't be right."

"Why not?" Mom asked with a perplexed frown.

"Because they're part of her. They help keep her memory alive."

Mom's eyebrows furrowed further. "Grandma's memory will always be alive in our hearts." She patted her chest and smiled faintly. "We have many other things to remind us of her, too. I don't think Grandma would mind if you sold a few of her plants so's you could have some money of your own."

"I do want to start makin' money, but sellin' Grandma's plants?" Rebekah shook her head. "I just couldn't do that and feel *gut* about it."

Mom nodded. "I understand. Why not take cut flowers from the garden then?"

"That'd be all right, I suppose," Rebekah agreed. An idea suddenly popped into her head. "I know! I could take some starts from Grandma's plants and sell those. That way, I'll still have most of the plants. It might even be *gut* for the plants to be thinned a bit."

"I think that's a fine idea," Mom said with a nod of approval. "If you want, I'll help you get the cuttings today."

Rebekah shook her head. "Thanks for offerin', but if I'm to make the money, then I want to do all the work myself."

Mom shrugged and turned to leave. "All right then. Tomorrow you'll share our sales table at Farmers' Market," she called over her shoulder.

The market seemed unusually busy today, and the parking lot was nearly full. "It must be all the summer tourists," Papa whispered to Mom as they began unloading the market buggy.

Mom smiled. *"Jah,* business should be real *gut* today."

Rebekah was sitting in her wheelchair, holding a box of African violet cuttings. *"Ach,* my! I sure hope so," she added. "All the prunin' and pottin' I did yesterday had better pay off!"

Nadine, who stood next to Rebekah, leaned over and asked, "Want me to push you inside?"

Rebekah nodded. She hated to ask for assistance, but if she let go of the box she was holding, she'd probably end up losing the whole thing. They headed toward the big wooden building with Mom, Papa, and Simon following close behind, each carrying boxes of their own.

Once they got their table set up, the Stoltzfus family began making sales. Mom was selling vine-ripened, juicy red tomatoes and baskets of plump, sweet raspberries from her garden. Papa had made some lip-smackin' homemade root beer. Simon was selling farm-fresh brown eggs. Nadine's chocolate cupcakes and ginger cookies looked right tasty, too. Rebekah had freshly cut flowers and starts from several of Grandma's plants displayed, so she felt almost useful today.

By noontime, nearly all of Rebekah's African violet starts had been sold, and many of the cut flowers and other plants as well. It was the first time she'd ever made so much money in such a short time. It gave her an awful good feeling, way down deep inside.

"How's business?" Mary Ellen asked, stepping up to Rebekah's end of the long table.

Rebekah grinned. "Much better than I could've hoped." Just as quickly as her smile appeared, it changed to a frown. "I only wish I had more plants and flowers to sell. If the market was open five days a week, all year long, I believe I could actually make enough money to be self-sufficient."

Mary Ellen nodded. "That would be *wunderbaar gut,* all right!"

Rebekah sighed. "Even if it was open all the time, I couldn't ask anyone from the family to bring me in every day. Papa doesn't trust me to drive the buggy by myself. Besides, it's a five-mile trip from our place. My folks have lots better things to be doin' than driving me around all the time." She shrugged. "Oh, well, it was a nice thought anyways."

"You really do like flowers and plants, don't you?" her cousin asked.

Rebekah's head bobbed up and down. *"Jah,* that's for sure."

"And as you've said, you discovered today that they sell quite well," Mary Ellen remarked.

"Indeed! I've done real *gut."*

"Can you take a little break? We need to talk—in private," Mary Ellen whispered. "I think I might have a great plan for you, Rebekah Stoltzfus."

"What is it? Won't you tell me now?"

"It'll take too much time, and we'll probably be interrupted by customers if we try to talk here. Besides," Mary Ellen whispered in a conspiring tone, "I don't want anyone else to hear my idea until you've agreed to do it."

Rebekah grinned. "It's time for lunch anyways. I'll ask Nadine to watch my end of the table, then I'll get the box lunch Mom prepared. We were plannin' to eat in shifts, so I'm sure Mom won't mind if I take my lunch break with you."

Mom gave her consent for Rebekah to join Mary Ellen, and soon the young women sat outside at a picnic table shrouded in shade by a large maple tree.

"It's another hot, sticky day," Rebekah remarked. "I'm glad we have a nice tree to help keep us cool."

Mary Ellen took a big drink of foamy root beer. "Umm. . .your papa sure does make some *gut* soda! This helps put the fire out, too."

Rebekah laughed when the end of Mary Ellen's nose became covered with a frothy white head of root beer. *"Jah,* and you wear it real well, too!"

Mary Ellen smiled and swiped a napkin across her nose. "There, now do I look better?"

"Jah, but then, you always look *gut,"* Rebekah said seriously. "It's not hard to

understand why so many of the young Amish guys are always actin' like *kinder* in order to try to seek your favor."

Mary Ellen's hazel eyes took on a dreamy, faraway look, and her lips formed a contented smile. "There's only one man whose favor I seek."

Rebekah was just getting ready to ask her cousin who that one young man was when Mary Ellen abruptly changed the subject. "You didn't agree to have lunch with me so I could talk about my love life," she said. "I wanted to discuss a possible business venture with you."

"Business venture?" Rebekah repeated. "You and me?"

Mary Ellen shook her head. "No, just you. I've got my teachin' job at the school," she reminded. "Now, you've been tellin' me for weeks that you want to be self-sufficient. Isn't that right?"

Rebekah nodded. "Right as rain."

"Well, I think I have an idea that might actually work for you."

"Really? What is it? *Raus Mit*—out with it!" Rebekah cried.

"You need to make money in order to be self-sufficient, correct?" Mary Ellen asked.

"Right."

"Today you found that you have a product people will buy."

"The flowers and plants," Rebekah agreed.

"You do enjoy workin' with plants, right?" Mary Ellen prompted.

Jah, very much."

"Then all you have to do is get more plants and sell more plants!"

Mary Ellen seemed so excited that Rebekah kind of hated to burst her bubble. "That sounds *wunderbaar*, but you've forgotten one very important thing," she said soberly.

Mary Ellen's lips puckered. "Oh? What's that?"

"The farmers' market isn't open often enough. Don't forget about my problem of transportation, either," Rebekah added with a click of her tongue.

"I'm gettin' to that." Mary Ellen tapped one finger against the side of her head. "I was thinkin' that if you had a greenhouse near the front of your property, you could sell your plants and flowers from there. News travels fast here in the valley, so I'm sure folks—especially the tourists—would soon find out about it. Then you'd have a stream of customers all year-round."

Rebekah's forehead crinkled into a confused frown. "That sounds like an interestin' business venture, all right, but there's one mighty big problem."

"Oh? What's that?"

"We have no greenhouse on our property."

Mary Ellen shrugged and reached for another ham sandwich from her lunch bucket. "So you have one built."

"It's not that simple," Rebekah argued. "Buildin' a greenhouse would take time and money, too."

"Not if your family and friends did all the work," Mary Ellen stated simply.

"I'm sure my pappy would be glad to help out, and so would your other uncles and cousins. Maybe some of the neighboring Amish men would come, too." She grasped Rebekah's hand and gave it a gentle squeeze. "You've just got to ask your folks about this. Your family wants you to be happy and self-reliant. Won't you at least give my idea some thought?"

Rebekah nodded slowly. *"Jah,* I'll think about it, and pray some, too. If God wants me to do somethin' like this, then He'll show me how."

Chapter 5

The entire Stoltzfus family had been invited to a picnic at the Hiltys' farm. Family picnics were always lots of fun, and it was a good time for the busy farmers to get caught up with one another's active lives. Since preaching services in their Amish community were biweekly and this was an "off" Sunday, it was a nice way to spend the afternoon.

Mom had insisted that Rebekah wear her leg braces for at least part of the day, reminding her that she needed the exercise. As much as Rebekah disliked the cumbersome braces and the effort it took to walk, she didn't want to make a scene. With the aid of her crutches, she came hobbling up the dirt path leading to the Hiltys' front porch.

Mary Ellen had been sitting on the porch swing, but when she saw Rebekah, she jumped up and came running toward her. "Oh, it's so *gut* to see you walking today."

Rebekah scowled and shook her head. "This ain't really walkin'. I feel like one of those toy robots I've seen at the store."

"Here, let me help you up the steps," Mary Ellen offered, making no mention of Rebekah's sour mood. "We can sit on the swing and visit awhile."

Rebekah allowed her cousin to help her up the stairs, then over to the swing. "What's new in your life?" she asked, once she was seated as comfortably as possible.

Mary Ellen shrugged, but her hazel eyes sparkled as though she could hardly contain herself. "Nothin' much, except Johnny Yoder's finally asked if he can officially court me."

Rebekah had mixed feelings about this bit of news. Oh, she was happy enough for Mary Ellen. After all, she was her best friend. But deep in her soul, she felt downright disheartened for poor Daniel Beachy. Now that Johnny would be callin' on Mary Ellen, Daniel's chances of winning her over would be slim to none.

Rebekah plastered a smile onto her face, feeling more like crying with each passing moment. "I'm right glad for you."

Mary Ellen's face fairly glowed as she reached out to clasp Rebekah's hand. "And how are things with you these days? Have you thought any more about my greenhouse idea?"

Rebekah squeezed her hand in response, glad for the change of subject. "*Jah*, I have. I even talked to Mom and Papa, and they think it's a *gut* idea, too. Papa says he can begin buildin' it sometime next week." She drew in a deep breath and let it out in a rush. "Just think, I might actually be able to support myself if this business takes hold."

Mary Ellen nodded. "That would be *wunderbaar*, all right." She squinted her eyes at Rebekah. "What'll you sell? Do you have enough plants and flowers?"

"Not yet," Rebekah replied, "but with the money I made at the market, I'll be able to buy enough to get started. I can use some starts from Grandma's plants, too, and there's always fresh-cut flowers from our garden to sell."

"Sounds like you've got it all figured out," Mary Ellen noted with a grin.

Rebekah shrugged. "I'm workin' on it. In the beginning, all my profits will have to go back into the business. I'll need to buy more plants, seeds, fertilizers, pots, and potting soil. After the first year or so, I should be able to start supportin' myself, though."

Mary Ellen started pumping the swing back and forth with her strong legs— legs Rebekah would have given nearly anything to have owned.

"It's sure *gut* to see you so cheerful. You've been so gloomy lately," Mary Ellen said.

Rebekah was trying hard to think of a reply to that statement. Something that wouldn't sound too harsh, because honest to goodness, she really wasn't feelin' all that cheerful. However, she never got the chance to have her say, for Aunt Mim stepped out onto the porch, interrupting their conversation. "Ah, I see you two have found my favorite swingin' seat," she said, smiling brightly.

"Would ya like to sit here now?" Rebekah offered. "We can go someplace else to visit."

"You stay right where you are," Aunt Mim instructed, with one finger pointed at the young women. "I can't take time for sittin' just now anyways. I have to see about gettin' some food set out for this family picnic of ours."

"Is there anything we can do to help?" Mary Ellen asked sweetly.

Aunt Mim shook her head. "Maybe later. Sarah, Crystal, and Grace are here to help, so for now, you ladies just relax and do your visitin'." With a wave of her hand, Mim stepped back inside the house.

"Aunt Mim is sure one sweet lady," Rebekah said, giving Mary Ellen a little nudge with her elbow.

"*Jah.* She may not be my real mom, but she loves me like she is, just the same. I thank God for bringin' her into our lives when I was a young girl." Mary Ellen looked thoughtful. "She wasn't always so happy, though. I remember when she was our schoolteacher and some of the *kinder* used to call her an old maid with a heart of stone."

"I remember that, too," Rebekah agreed. Just thinking about it now made her wonder how many folks thought of her as an old maid. She knew her sister sure did, because she'd already said so.

"God can change hearts if we allow Him to," Mary Ellen said, breaking into Rebekah's private thoughts.

"Do you think God still performs miracles?" Rebekah asked suddenly.

Mary Ellen pursed her lips. "Of course He does, Silly. Why would you ask such a thing?"

Rebekah's eyelids fluttered, then closed. "Sometimes I think I might be able to actually feel God's presence if He gave me a really big miracle."

Mary Ellen patted Rebekah's hand in a motherly fashion. "We don't need big miracles in order to see God. He performs small miracles in people's lives nearly every day. *Es vor immerso*—it has always been this way. We don't often see the small miracles, 'cause we don't have our eyes wide open."

With those reminding words, Rebekah's own eyes flew open. "Are you talkin' about me?"

"Not specifically," Mary Ellen answered. "I'm talking about believers in general. Even when clouds of pain seem to hide God's face, we're never hidden from His miracle of love and tender care."

Rebekah tipped her head to one side as she studied Mary Ellen's serious face. "Just how did a nineteen-year-old woman get to be so smart, anyways?"

Mary Ellen smiled, bringing to the surface her two matching dimples. "I think my wisdom comes from God, but I wouldn't be teachin' school if I wasn't putting it into practice every day."

Rebekah nodded. "You're probably right. I sure hope God gives me some wisdom, and I'm hopin' it's real soon, for we grow too soon old and too late smart."

❧

There were four large picnic tables set up on the front lawn for eating and two more loaded with a wonderful array of food and beverages. Everyone seemed to be in good spirits, and hearty appetites soon devoured most of the food.

When it appeared that all were finished eating, Rebekah's papa stood up. "Attention everyone! May I have your attention?" he bellowed. The hum of talking subsided as everyone looked up at the tall Amish man with the loud, booming voice.

"Those who work hard eat hearty, and you've all done right well. Now it's time to share some *gut* news. I want you to know that my oldest daughter's about to become a businesswoman," Papa announced with a grin that stretched from ear to ear.

All eyes turned to Rebekah. She felt the warmth of a blush creep up her neck and spread clean to her face.

"Rebekah wants to open a greenhouse on the front of our property," Papa continued. "If it's to be built before summer ends, then I'll sure be needin' some help with the project."

"You can count on me," Uncle Lewis stated.

"*Jah*, me, too," Uncle Jonas agreed.

"I'd be more'n happy to help," Uncle Amos put in.

"I can help as well." This came from Amos's young son, Henry, who looked eager enough to begin building right then.

"Don't forget about us," John and Jacob said in unison.

"I'd help if I was bigger," seven-year-old Matthew spoke up.

Papa laughed. "I'll not turn away any help. *Danki*, all of you."

"I shall be grateful to everyone as well," Rebekah said, feeling tears of joy flood her eyes.

"What'll ya call this new business of yours?" Aunt Mim asked.

Rebekah sniffed and wiped her eyes with the backs of her hands. "I'm thinkin' about callin' it Grandma's Place. I'll be usin' lots of starts from her plants, and she loved flowers so. It seems only fittin' to name the greenhouse after her."

"I think it's a *wunderbaar* name!" Aunt Mim exclaimed.

"*Jah*, well, I do believe we'd better move this picnic indoors," Sarah interjected. "I just felt somethin' wet go splat on my nose!"

❧

"Papa, it riles me so that we're headin' for home. Why'd we have to leave the picnic so early, anyways?" Nadine complained from the back of their closed-in buggy. "That homemade ice cream was awful *gut*, and I wanted a second bowl."

Papa kept his eyes straight ahead, calling back to her in a booming voice, "We left because of this storm! It's gettin' worse all the time, and we need to be home to see that the livestock gets put away!"

It was obvious by the way Papa was gripping the reins that he was fighting real hard to keep the horse under control. Jagged streaks of lightning zigzagged across the sky, thunderous roars shook the evening sky, and the rain poured down in torrents.

"I'm scared," Nadine whined. "I hate lightning and *dunner*. I wish we could've stayed at Aunt Mim's house."

"We'll be home soon enough," Rebekah said, trying to soothe her little sister's nerves. "Here, take my hand."

With a grateful smile, Nadine grabbed for Rebekah's hand, saying, "*Danki.*"

"Aw, there's nothin' to be scared of," Simon asserted. "It's just a typical summer storm."

"There's nothin' typical about this weather," Mom called. "I think it'd be wise if you'd all keep quiet now. Papa needs to concentrate on the road up ahead."

Another shuddering clap of thunder sounded, and the horse whinnied loudly. "Whoa there. Steady, boy," Papa said in his most soothing voice.

They were nearing their own farm now, but just as they turned onto the gravel drive, Mom let out a shrill scream, sending shivers of apprehension up Rebekah's spine. "Fire! Fire! Andrew, our barn's all ablaze! It must've been struck by the lightnin'!"

Papa urged the horse into a fast trot. When they reached their front yard, he jumped down from the buggy. "Go get help!" he called to Mom. "Simon, you and Nadine start fillin' some buckets with water, and be quick about it now!"

"What about me?" Rebekah asked helplessly. Wasn't there something she could do to lend a hand?

"You can either go to the house or ride with me," Mom said over her shoulder.

Rebekah saw that Papa was already running toward the water trough with Simon and Nadine right on his heels. She knew how much time it took for someone to help her out of the buggy, and right now they couldn't afford to waste even one single minute. "I'll ride with you, Mom!" she hollered.

Without another word, Mom turned the buggy around and tore out of the yard at such a fast pace, Rebekah had to grab on tightly to the edge of her seat in order to keep from being thrown clean out. She turned to look out the back window. Papa, Simon, and Nadine were running frantically toward the burning barn, buckets of water in each of their hands.

Rebekah shook her head sadly. The rain had all but stopped now, though the wind was still blowing something fierce. Unless the fire department could get there quickly, which was doubtful since they didn't have a telephone, then Papa would surely lose his whole barn.

The first stop Mom made was to a pay phone, two miles down the road. She called the county fire department, then headed on over to Jonas and Crystal's place, as it was the closest.

Uncle Jonas and his boys left right away to help fight the fire, while Mom and Rebekah moved on to enlist the help of Uncle Lewis, Uncle Amos, and even young Henry.

By the time they got home, the storm had subsided. Two Lancaster County fire trucks were parked in the driveway, their red lights flashing this way and that.

One look at the barn told Rebekah all efforts had been in vain. She knew Papa had managed to save the livestock, because cows and horses were crowded into the corral. However, the barn was gone—burned clean to the ground!

Rebekah choked on a sob. "Oh, what will Papa do now?" she wailed.

Mom, whose own eyes were filled with tears, replied, "He'll do just as all other Amish men do when they lose a barn. He'll have a barn raisin'."

Chapter 6

Rebekah knew the news had spread quickly that Papa's barn was burned, for offers of help to rebuild came from far and wide, with both English and Amish promising their services.

"When is the barn raisin' gonna be?" Rebekah asked Papa at breakfast the following morning.

He looked up from the Amish newspaper he was reading. "It's set to begin on Wednesday, with the layin' of the foundation. Simon and I, and probably Amos, Jonas, and Lewis, will spend time today and tomorrow cleanin' up the mess from the fire. Many bales of hay were ruined, and those have to be disposed of, too. If all goes well, we should have it fairly well finished by Saturday, I'm a-thinkin'." Papa gave Rebekah an apologetic look. "I'm sorry, but your greenhouse is gonna have to wait a bit longer. I hope you understand."

Rebekah reached for his hand. She was disappointed, of course, but she'd never let Papa know that. "It's all right, Papa. I know you'll be busy, and the new barn's more important than anything else right now," she said with a forced smile.

"We'll all be busy during barn raisin'," Mom put in from her place at the stove. "There'll be much food to prepare for the hungry crews. Probably plenty of errands for the menfolk to run, too."

Nadine, who was sitting across the table from Rebekah, perked right up. "Will some of the boys come along to help out?"

"*Jah,* I'm sure many will come with their *daeds,*" Papa replied. "There will be plenty of work, even for the younger ones."

"Maybe I can help bring nails or other supplies to some of the workers," Nadine eagerly volunteered.

"She don't really wanna work. She just wants to flirt with all the boys," Simon teased. He was sitting closest to Nadine, and he reached out to give her arm a little jab with one finger.

"There'll be no time for flirtin', Nadine," Mom said sternly. "All of us shall work, and you'll be busy helpin' the women, not the boys."

Nadine frowned and her lower lip came thrusting out. "It just ain't fair. I always have to help the women!"

"Oh, quit your *brutzing.*"

She wrinkled her nose. "I'm not pouting."

"If you wanted to help the men, then you should've been born a boy," Simon said with a smirk covering his adolescent face.

Nadine's cheeks flamed. "Is that so? Well, let me tell you—"

"That's quite enough!" Papa shouted. He dropped the newspaper to the table and gave a warning look to Simon, then one to Nadine.

Rebekah knew Papa didn't raise his voice very often, but when he did, everyone was smart enough to keep quiet. Simon and Nadine quickly returned to the business of eating their breakfast.

Rebekah was intent on moving her pancakes back and forth across the plate. She wasn't sure why, but at least it was something to do, as she wasn't really all that hungry this morning.

Mom looked over her shoulder and said, "Rebekah, since the barn raisin' won't be for a few more days, would you like me to drive you to Lancaster? I thought you might like to pick out some plants and such for that new greenhouse of yours."

Rebekah's spirits lifted a bit. "Do you really have enough time, Mom? I know you had planned to do some bakin' today."

Mom nodded. *Jah,* but that can wait 'til tomorrow, I expect."

"Can I go along, too?" Nadine asked excitedly. "I haven't been to Lancaster in a long time."

"You'll be needed at home today," Mom said. "I have some wash that should be hung, and Papa and Simon will be workin' in the fields, so they'll expect their lunch to be made."

"Does that mean you're gonna eat lunch in Lancaster?" Nadine questioned.

Mom set another plate of steaming pancakes on the table and took her own seat. *Jah,* I expect so. By the time Rebekah and me finish our shoppin', it'll no doubt be time for the noon meal."

Nadine crinkled her nose and leered at Rebekah. "That's just not fair! Rebekah always gets to have all the fun! I wish that I—"

"What? You wish you were like me?" Rebekah snapped. "Is that what you were gonna say, Nadine? Would ya really want to be trapped in my crippled body, confined to a cold wheelchair or some dumb old leg braces? Do you think that's anything to be jealous of?" Rebekah's voice had risen at least two octaves. Her hand shook when she pointed a finger at her sister. "You don't even know what you're sayin', talkin' thataway. Why, I'd gladly trade places with you, or anyone else who could walk and run!"

Rebekah knew she was letting her emotions get the best of her, but she'd already started telling Nadine what was on her mind, so she sure wasn't about to stop now. "Someday you'll grow up and fall in love. You'll marry and have *kinder.* Your life'll be full and complete. I, on the other hand, will not marry or fall in love. I won't have my own family, and my life will never be complete." She waved her hand. "Please don't go envyin' me or anything I might be allowed to do, 'cause it's nothin' a'tall compared to what you get to do."

Everyone at the table had become deathly quiet during Rebekah's impromptu speech. By the time she'd finished, she was visibly shaking and her eyes were filled with tears.

Hers weren't the only tears being shed, however. Her sister's face was damp and flushed. "I. . .I'm so sorry, Rebekah. I. . ." Nadine choked on the words. She jumped up from the table, nearly knocking over the pitcher of milk, and fled upstairs to her room.

Papa scowled at Rebekah. "I know it's not easy bein' crippled and all, but your words were harsh and cruel. I think you owe your sister an apology. She's young and immature and doesn't fully understand what it's like to be in your situation. To her it may seem as though you get more attention and special favors. No matter how sorry you might feel for yourself, that don't give ya the right to lash out at anyone in this family."

Rebekah hung her head in shame as Papa continued his tirade. "You accused Nadine of bein' jealous, but it's obvious to me that you're the envious one. In Proverbs, chapter six, we're told that 'jealousy is the rage of a man.' It can cause us to hate instead of love—to be bitter instead of grateful." He leaned forward on his elbows, looking Rebekah straight in the eye. "You don't hate your sister, now do ya, Daughter?"

Tears were coursing down Rebekah's cheeks as she shook her head. "No, Papa, I don't hate anyone. Sometimes I hold my feelin's inside, then when they do finally come out, I speak unkindly. Please forgive me."

Papa nodded. "*Jah,* I forgive you, Rebekah. However, it's really Nadine you hurt the most."

Rebekah swallowed hard and sniffed. "I know, and I'll apologize to her as well. If you'll excuse me, I want to go to Grandma's old room. I need to spend some time alone with God. I think I'm probably owin' Him an apology, too."

❧

After searching the Scriptures and praying awhile, Rebekah returned to the kitchen. She found Nadine there, helping Mom with the dishes. Rebekah rolled her wheelchair noisily across the gray linoleum floor, and Nadine turned in her direction.

"I'm really sorry," both girls said at the same time.

Nadine dropped to her knees in front of the wheelchair and laid her head in Rebekah's lap. "I didn't mean to act so jealous and *gridlich.* Will ya forgive me?"

Rebekah placed one hand on top of Nadine's head. "I'll forgive you for being cranky, if you'll forgive me. My words were harsh and unkind, and you didn't deserve such a tongue-lashin'."

As Nadine looked up, Rebekah saw tears in her brown eyes. "I forgive you, too. I hate it when there's ugly words between us like that." Nadine's lower lip trembled. "You were right. I don't understand what it's like to be crippled. I'll try to be more understandin' from now on, though."

Rebekah smiled and patted her sister's head. "And I'll try to be more patient and lovin'."

❧

The ride to Lancaster took nearly an hour, but Rebekah didn't mind one little bit.

Since it had rained so hard the evening before, everything smelled clean and mighty fresh—like clean towels drying on the clothesline. Sometimes, right after a summer storm, the air would turn hot and muggy. Not today, though. Today was much cooler, with hardly any humidity at all.

As they pulled into the busy town of Lancaster, Rebekah's emotions soared to new heights. Opening a greenhouse of her very own would probably be the most exciting thing she'd ever done. She could hardly contain herself as Mom steered the market buggy off the main road and into Freeland Nursery's parking lot. She climbed down and secured the horse to a nearby post.

Rebekah's wheelchair was in the back of the buggy, so Mom went around to haul it out. With Rebekah helping as much as she could, she was lowered into the seat. It was a lot of work for one woman to handle, but Mom was strong and had been doing it for a good many years.

Inside the store, Rebekah wheeled up and down the aisles, inspecting a variety of houseplants and outdoor foliage as she went along. "Oh, Mom," she exclaimed, "look how many there are to choose from!"

Mom smiled. "Maybe someday you'll have nearly as many in your own place of business."

Rebekah sucked in a deep breath and let it out quickly. "I could only wish for such a miracle."

"I believe miracles are to be prayed for, Rebekah, not wished for," Mom corrected.

Rebekah shrugged. "Well, you know what I mean."

A store clerk stepped up to the two women. "Are you looking for anything in particular?"

Rebekah tipped her head back, looking into the kind eyes of the tall, gray-haired man. "I need several of your hardiest, most reasonably priced indoor and outdoor plants."

The man chuckled. "Ah, I see we have a shrewd businesswoman here."

Rebekah felt the heat of a blush sneak up her neck. She wondered if she looked old enough or smart enough to be a businesswoman. Or did this nice man merely see her as a pathetic crippled girl in a wheelchair?

She shook her head slightly, driving the negative thoughts away. "I think I do know a good bargain when I see one. So, if you'll just lead the way, I'll follow and decide what'll best suit my needs as we go along."

Rebekah was thankful that Mom walked along behind her silently, only giving an opinion when it was asked for. If this was going to be her business venture, then she had the right to do as much of it as possible on her own.

It took over an hour for her to select all the plants she wanted. The clerk was quite helpful, loading all the boxes into the back of their buggy, and even offering to help Mom with the wheelchair.

"You did *gut*, Rebekah," Mom said as she assisted her into the buggy. "You got quite a few plants for the amount of money you had. If you take some starts from them, you can probably double—or even triple—your investment in no time a'tall."

Rebekah smiled and reached over to touch Mom's arm. "You knew I was disappointed about Papa not bein' able to start buildin' the greenhouse this week, ain't it so?"

Mom nodded. *Jah,* I knew," she said, taking up the reins.

"And you thought this trip to town so's I could purchase some plants might make me feel better?"

"I sure hoped it would," came Mom's simple reply.

"Well, it worked. I do feel better!" Rebekah rubbed her stomach. "I'd feel even better if we had somethin' to eat, though."

Mom laughed. "All right then. We'll find us a restaurant and have a hearty lunch. After that, I have one more errand to run."

Rebekah tipped her head to one side. "Oh? What errand is that?"

Mom shook her head. "I'm not tellin'. It's gonna be a surprise for someone."

"A surprise? You can tell me, Mom. I won't tell anyone, I promise."

Mom clucked to the horse to get him moving forward. "Nope. My lips are sealed."

Chapter 7

Rebekah chose a Pennsylvania Dutch restaurant, telling Mom she never got tired of traditional Amish cooking. The two women were escorted to a long table, where several other people sat. This was all part of family style dining, but Rebekah felt funny about sitting next to folks she'd never even met. She knew most of them were just curious tourists wanting to check out the Plain folks, but that didn't make her feel any less self-conscious.

"Could we have a small table by ourselves?" she whispered to Mom.

"I'll ask." Mom turned to their Mennonite hostess and smiled. "Would ya possibly have a table for two?"

The young woman, who was dressed in plain clothes similar to what Rebekah and Mom wore, nodded. "Right this way." She led them to a small table near the window, handing each a menu.

Rebekah maneuvered her wheelchair as close to the table as possible. It wasn't as easy as eating at home, where the big wooden table had plenty of leg room. "I'm just not up to people's curious stares today," she said to Mom, when she'd taken a seat directly across from Rebekah.

"I don't think folks would be starin' at us," Mom replied. "This is a Pennsylvania Dutch restaurant, remember? There are several Amish and Mennonite people eatin' here." She motioned toward one of the waitresses. "Most of the help are Plain People, too."

"I know, Mom, but I was thinkin' more about them starin' at me—my disability," Rebekah said with a grimace.

Mom reached across the table to lay a gentle hand on Rebekah's arm. "I think you worry too much 'bout what people think. Not everyone in the world stares at handicapped people, ya know." She shrugged. "Even if they should stare, how can it really hurt?"

Rebekah fingered her silverware. "It makes me feel uncomfortable, that's all."

Another young Mennonite woman came to take their order, and Rebekah was glad for the interruption. She wasn't feeling much like listening to one of Mom's famous lectures just now.

"We have two choices for the Dutch family style lunch," the waitress explained. "One is roast beef with onion sauce, which also comes with baked short ribs, bread filling, mashed potatoes, fried tomatoes, dilled green beans, coleslaw, pickled beets, and brown bread." She paused a moment, then added, "The other menu includes spiced ham, chicken and dumplings, fried chicken, spiced applesauce, boiled potatoes, bread-and-butter pickles, cornmeal bread, and gingered carrots. The dessert for both meals is the same: chocolate cake, vanilla ice cream, and two kinds of pie."

"*Ach*, my! Either meal has so much food!" Mom exclaimed. "It's a hard choice to be makin'." She nodded toward Rebekah. "What would you like, Daughter?"

"I think I'll take the one that includes roast beef and bread fillin'," Rebekah replied. "I could eat tasty fillin' 'til the cows come home."

"Number one it is then," Mom told the waitress. As soon as the woman walked away, she leaned across the table and whispered to Rebekah, "Ya know, I may just have to borrow that wheelchair of yours when we leave this place."

Rebekah gave her a questioning look.

"They might have to wheel me right out of here 'cause I'll be so full," Mom said with a wink.

Rebekah giggled. It felt so good to spend the day with Mom like this. They didn't get to do lunch and shopping out so often. She could understand why Nadine might be a bit jealous.

In no time at all the food started coming. Whenever one bowl would empty, the waitress was there to fill it right up again. Rebekah and Mom ate until they couldn't take a single bite more. As they left the restaurant, Rebekah figured neither of them would ever need to eat again.

"Where would you like to go while I'm on my secret errand?" Mom asked as she helped Rebekah into the buggy.

Rebekah shrugged. "Oh, I don't know. Maybe the bookstore. I might find somethin' there on caring for plants, or possibly on business management."

"That sounds fine," Mom agreed. "I'll drop you off and be back in half an hour or so."

Rebekah smiled. "Okay, Mom."

Grossner's Bookstore was only a few blocks away, and soon they were pulling up to the brick storefront. Mom went around to get the wheelchair and help Rebekah down.

Mom walked ahead of Rebekah and opened the door to the store. "See you soon."

Rebekah waved and wheeled herself inside. There seemed to be a lot of tourists milling around today, looking at all the books that told about the Amish and Mennonite lifestyles. She moved quickly away from the group of curious people and found the shelf where all the books about plants and flowers were kept. She spotted one on the second shelf entitled *Caring for Your African Violets*. Rebekah strained to reach it, but her arm wasn't long enough. She could attempt standing, she guessed. But she'd tried that a time or two without her crutches, and usually ended up flat on the floor. Falling on her face at home was one thing, but making a complete fool of herself in front of an audience was definitely not on Rebekah's list of things to do for the day.

She glanced around, hoping to catch the attention of one of the store clerks. They all seemed to be busy helping English tourists.

"Sie Kaufen ein Buch—you are buying a book?" The Pennsylvania Dutch words came from a deep male voice.

Rebekah gave her chair a sharp turn to the left. There, looking right down on her, was none other than Daniel Beachy. He tipped his straw hat and gave her a crooked grin. "I'm surprised to see you here, Rebekah. Are ya all alone?"

"Mom's in town, too. She's on an errand, and I'm here buyin' a book." Rebekah's forehead wrinkled slightly. "At least I would be if I could reach it."

"Which one is it? I'll get it down for ya," Daniel offered.

Rebekah pointed up. *"Caring for Your African Violets."*

Daniel's long arm easily reached the book. He handed it to her with another warm smile. "Are you a plant lover?"

"Oh, yes," she said with feeling. "Especially African violets. They were Grandma Stoltzfus's favorite plant, too." She placed the book in her lap. "I hope to open a greenhouse soon, so I want to learn all I can."

Daniel's eyebrows shot up. "A greenhouse, you say? Now that does sound like an interesting business venture. Where will it be located?"

"Near the front of our property," Rebekah answered. "Of course, that won't be 'til Papa has time to build it. We lost our barn last night, so the greenhouse project will have to wait a week or two yet."

Daniel's dark eyes looked even more serious than usual. *"Jah,* I heard about the horrible fire." He shook his head slowly. "Such a shame. When is the barn raisin'?"

"The foundation will be laid on Wednesday, then the buildin' will probably begin the day after," she replied.

"Tell your *daed* he can count on my help." Daniel drummed his fingers along his rounded chin. "Hmm. . .maybe I could help build your greenhouse, too. I'm pretty handy with a hammer and saw."

"Danki. I'd sure appreciate any help I can get," she responded with a sincere smile.

Daniel shuffled his feet a few times. "Well, I'd best get goin'. I picked up some supplies for *Daed,* and he's probably wonderin' what's takin' me so long."

"I'm sorry for keepin' you," Rebekah apologized.

He chuckled and patted his stomach. "Naw, it wasn't you. I spent way too much time eatin' my noon meal. They were servin' roast beef with onion sauce at the Better Is More today. I think I ate my share and enough for about five others as well."

"Mom and I were there, too," Rebekah remarked. "We didn't see you, though."

"I was at one of them long tables," he said. "Over on the right side of the room."

Rebekah shrugged. "That's probably why we didn't see you, then. Mom and me ate at a small table by the window."

Daniel turned toward the door, then as though he might have forgotten something, he turned back around. "Say, I hear there's to be another singin' in two weeks. It's supposed to be at Clarence Yoder's. Do you plan on bein' there, Rebekah?"

Rebekah thought about the last singing she'd been at. She remembered all too well how out of place she'd felt. She shook her head. "No, I've got too much work to do if I'm gonna get all my plants ready to open for business in August." A small sigh escaped her lips. "That is, if I even have a greenhouse by then."

"The barn raisin' will only take a few days," Daniel reminded. "We should have your building up in short order after that." He turned aside, mumbling, "See you, Rebekah."

"Have fun at the singin'!" she called.

"Naw, I'm not goin' to this one neither," Daniel said just before he disappeared out the door.

"Poor Daniel," Rebekah whispered. "He likes Mary Ellen so much he just can't stand to see her flirtin' with Johnny Yoder again." She clicked her tongue. "What a shame she don't see how nice he is."

❧

The foundation for the new barn had been poured on Wednesday, and the barn raising was scheduled to begin early the following morning.

Rebekah awoke to the piercing sound of pulsating hammers, nails being pounded into heavy pieces of lumber, and the shrill hum of saws as they cut thick pieces of wood. Why, it was sure enough racket to wake up the dead!

She pulled herself upright, scooted to the edge of the bed, and dropped into the wheelchair. Her arms were strong, and she'd become quite adept at this morning ritual. It wasn't an easy task, but it was better than bothering someone else to come help.

Rebekah wheeled herself over to the window so she could look out at the side yard and see what was going on. From her downstairs bedroom, she had the perfect view of the spot where the new barn was going to be.

She pulled the dark shade to one side and took a peek. *Why, there must be over two hundred men and boys scurryin' about the place!* she mused. Some were already laying the floor beams and planks, while others paired off in groups to prepare the panels, beams, and rafters.

When she caught one of the younger men looking her way, Rebekah turned away from the window with a sigh. From this distance she couldn't be sure who'd been watching her, but she didn't need anyone's curious stares or pitying looks this morning. Besides, she should hurry and get dressed so she could help Mom.

Aunt Mim, Aunt Crystal, and Aunt Grace were already in the kitchen when Rebekah made her entrance a short time later. Nadine and their cousins Peggy, Maddie, and Mary Ellen were also helping out.

"Why'd ya let me sleep so late?" Rebekah asked Mom. "I didn't know anyone was even here 'til I woke up to the noise of hammers and saws."

"You must sleep pretty sound. They've been at it for nearly an hour already," Aunt Crystal said with a wink.

"Don't worry about it, Daughter," Mom said. "As you can see, I have plenty of help. I thought it would do you good to sleep a little longer this mornin'. We

173

did have quite a busy day in Lancaster on Monday, and you've been right occupied ever since, cuttin' and repottin' all those plants and whatnot."

"Your *mamm* was tellin' us more about your new business venture," Aunt Mim said as she made a place at the table for Rebekah to park her wheelchair. "It sounds downright excitin'—hopefully prosperous, too."

"Jah, I sure hope so," Rebekah replied, reaching for a sticky cinnamon bun.

"Rebekah's gonna use some starts off Grandma Stoltzfus's plants," Mary Ellen put in.

"Grandma was real special, and she taught me to appreciate flowers and plants," Rebekah said, reaching for a glass of cold milk.

The back door flew open, and Rebekah's fifteen-year-old twin cousins, Jacob and John, rushed into the kitchen. "We need somethin' to drink! It's already hot as an oven out there!" Jacob exclaimed, wiping his damp forehead with the back of his hand.

John nodded in agreement, his brown eyes looking ever so serious. "That's right, and when a body works hard, a body deserves a cool drink!"

Aunt Crystal smiled, like any proud mom. *"Die Buwe Kenne awer schaffe—*these boys are workers. We should give them some cold iced tea—maybe send some out for the other men, too."

"There's several jugs in the refrigerator," Sarah told the boys. "Just help yourself and take the rest outside. I think there's some paper cups on the picnic table."

John seemed to be eyeing the sticky buns on the table. "Ya wouldn't happen to have any more of those, would you, Aunt Sarah?" he asked with a nod in that direction.

She laughed. "I think there's more in the pantry. Help yourself and take some out to the workers as well."

The boys soon went back outside, and Rebekah finished eating her breakfast. "What can I do to help?" she asked Mom.

"Why don't you and Mary Ellen shell some peas for the potpies we'll be makin' for our noon meal? You can go outside on the porch, if you like."

As quickly as they could, Rebekah and Mary Ellen gathered up two hefty pans, along with the paper sack full of plump peas, and headed out the back door. Mary Ellen found a metal folding chair and pulled it next to Rebekah's wheelchair. They each held a bowl in their laps, and Mary Ellen distributed the peas equally between them.

"How's the courtship with Johnny Yoder goin'?" Rebekah asked suddenly.

Mary Ellen's face broke into a smile, her dimples growing even deeper than normal. "It's real *gut.* He's been over to see me nearly every night for the past week."

"Do you like him a lot?"

"Jah, I do," Mary Ellen replied with a slight nod. "He's really fun, and right good-lookin', don't ya think?"

Rebekah wrinkled her nose and emitted a noise that sounded something like the barn cat whenever someone stepped on its tail. "That ain't for me to be sayin'.

Johnny might not take kindly to me makin' eyes at him."

"I'm not askin' you to make eyes at him," Mary Ellen said, blinking her pretty blue eyes. "I only wondered if you think he's good-lookin' or not."

Rebekah shrugged her slim shoulders and released a small sigh. "I suppose he's all right. He's just not my type, that's all."

"Oh? Who is your type, might I ask?" Mary Ellen poked Rebekah on the arm and giggled. "Is there somethin' you're not tellin' me? Do you have your heart set on anyone special?"

Rebekah felt the heat of a blush crawl up her neck, but she gave no other indication of being flustered. "Of course not! I have absolutely no interest in any man, and none have interest in me neither!"

"Maybe they do have an interest, and you're just too blind to see," Mary Ellen remarked. "If you ask me—"

Her words were interrupted when a man's heavy boots came thudding up the porch.

"Hello, Mary Ellen. Hello, Rebekah," Daniel Beachy said with a slight nod of his head.

"Hello, Daniel. How's the work comin' along?" Rebekah asked.

Daniel yanked off his straw hat and wiped the perspiration from his forehead with the back of his hand. "It's goin' well enough. Today's sure hot and humid, don'tcha think?" His question was directed at Rebekah, and she swallowed hard as his serious dark eyes seemed to bore straight into her soul. She felt another flush of warmth but excused it to herself as the heat of the day.

"I've talked to your *daed* about helpin' with the greenhouse," Daniel said, shifting his weight from one long leg to the other. "He said he hopes to begin sometime next week."

Rebekah swallowed again. Why was Daniel bein' so nice? "I really appreciate that," she said in a near whisper. "I appreciate all who've offered to help."

Daniel stared down at his boots, rocking back and forth, kind of nervouslike. He cleared his throat a few times, then mumbled, "Well, guess I'd better get back to work now."

He was about to step off the porch when Rebekah called out to him. "Did ya get some cold tea yet?"

Daniel waved his hat at her and smiled. "I had some, *danki*." He turned and actually ran back to the job site, leaving Rebekah to wonder over his strange actions.

Mary Ellen looked over at her with a knowing kind of look, but Rebekah chose to ignore it and started shelling peas lickety-split.

"Daniel's right nice, don't you think?" Mary Ellen prompted.

Rebekah nodded but never looked up. *If ya think he's so nice, then why aren't ya givin' the poor guy a chance? If I had someone like Daniel Beachy interested in me, I sure wouldn't be wastin' my time on the likes of Johnny Yoder!*

Chapter 8

Papa new barn was fully erected and ready for hay and animals by the weekend. The men who'd helped were hardworking and faithful, in spite of the fact that they all had their own chores waiting at home by the end of each long day. Papa said he didn't feel he could ask any of them to return the following week to begin building Rebekah's greenhouse. "It just wouldn't be fair," he'd told Rebekah. However, with the help of Simon and Daniel Beachy, who'd insisted on lending a hand, the building would go up, even if it would take a little longer than expected.

At eight o'clock on Monday morning, Daniel showed up at their back door. He was holding a large clay pot, which held an equally large Boston fern. Nadine was the one to answer his knock, and she stood in the doorway with a look of utter confusion on her inexperienced face.

"I'm gonna help build the greenhouse," Daniel explained. "Is Rebekah here?"

Nadine stepped away from the door and motioned him into the kitchen. She pointed to where Rebekah sat at the table, drinking a cup of tea and writing on a tablet.

Rebekah looked up. "Oh, *Gut Morgen,* Daniel. What brings you here so early?" She eyed the plant he was holding but made no comment about it.

"This is for you," Daniel said, placing the fern in the center of the table. "It's for your new greenhouse."

"*Ach,* my, it's beautiful!" she exclaimed. "*Danki,* Daniel." Already she'd decided that the fern would not be sold. It was a gift, and she'd keep it as such.

Daniel shifted from one foot to the other, looking kind of embarrassed. "Is your *daed* still plannin' to begin work on the greenhouse this mornin'? I've come prepared to work all day."

"I think so," Rebekah replied. She was feeling kind of embarrassed herself and couldn't figure out exactly why. "Papa's out in the new barn just now, so if you want to talk with him—"

"Naw, that's okay. I'll stick around here for awhile yet," Daniel interrupted. He removed his straw hat, went to hang it on a wall peg, and shuffled toward her again. "Say, what's that you're workin' on there?"

Rebekah smiled up at him. "It's my inventory."

He squinted his dark eyes. "Mind if I take a look-see?"

Nadine had been doing dishes at the sink, and she spoke before Rebekah could respond to his question. "Would ya like some coffee or a glass of milk, Daniel?"

"Jah, that'd be fine." Daniel pulled out a chair and sat down beside Rebekah's wheelchair.

Nadine planted both hands on her hips and glared at him. "Well, which one do ya want? Milk or coffee?"

"I'll have whatever Rebekah's havin'," Daniel said absently.

Rebekah's young sister shook her head slowly. "She's drinkin' herb tea, for goodness' sake."

"Jah, tea's fine," Daniel mumbled. He glanced over at Rebekah. "Do ya mind if I see what ya have written there?"

She shrugged and pushed the tablet toward him.

He studied it intently, commenting with an occasional, "Hmm. . . Ahh. . . So. . ."

Finally, when Rebekah thought she could stand it no longer, she asked, "Well, what do you think? Does it seem like I have enough plants to open for business?"

Daniel scratched the back of his dark Dutch-bobbed head. "I suppose it'll depend on how many customers you have at first—and on what they might decide to buy. Sometimes one certain flower or plant seems to be everyone's favorite, so that'll sell rather quicklike."

Rebekah studied Daniel's face. While he couldn't really be considered handsome the way Johnny Yoder was, his dark chocolate eyes, always looking so serious, his slim angular nose, and full lips made him seem rather appealin'. At least she thought so. How foolish Mary Ellen was to pick *glushtich*—eager—Johnny Yoder over someone as kind as Daniel Beachy!

"How is it that you seem to know so much 'bout flowers and plants?" she asked, trying to keep her mind on the conversation at hand.

Daniel smiled, but before he could respond, Nadine set a cup of hot lemon-mint tea and a large slice of shoofly pie directly in front of him.

"Danki," Daniel said, never taking his eyes off Rebekah. "My uncle Jake lives in Ohio, and he owns a large greenhouse. I spent time there one summer. Even helped in the business some."

Rebekah's interest was piqued. "Really? Then you could probably give me all kinds of advice."

He bobbed his head up and down. "Why, I'd be happy to. That is, if you really want my suggestions."

"Oh, I do," she said excitedly. A bit more sedately, she added, "Of course, that's only if you have the time. I know you keep real busy helpin' your *daed* with those dairy cows and all."

"I do get some free time. Besides, my brothers, Harold and Abner, help *Daed,* too." Daniel stared down at his cup of tea, as though he might be puzzling over somethin' or other. Rebekah was about to ask him what, when he blurted out, "I wonder sometimes if workin' with dairy cows is really what I wanna do for all my life. I believe God's given us all special abilities, and I'd sure like the chance to use mine."

Rebekah tipped her head slightly, staring straight into Daniel's warm, friendly eyes. They were such caring eyes—the kind she could get lost in, if she let herself, that is. She was feeling the selfsame way about wanting the chance to use her abilities and such. *"Jah,* I think I know what you mean," she murmured.

"Rebekah, I'm done with the dishes, and I cleaned up the kitchen, too," Nadine said from across the room. "I'm goin' outside now, to help Mom with the wash."

"What?" Rebekah pulled her gaze away from Daniel and onto her sister.

"I said, I'm done here. I'm goin' out to help Mom," Nadine repeated.

"Jah, okay then," Rebekah mumbled, feeling kind of flustered.

Nadine sashayed out the door with Rebekah barely taking notice.

Rebekah and Daniel stayed deeply engaged in conversation about the plans for her greenhouse for nearly an hour. Finally, Daniel looked up at the battery-operated clock on the wall and announced, "I think I'd better get outside and see if your *daed's* ready to go to work." He smiled sheepishly. "If he hasn't already gotten half the greenhouse built while I've been in here yappin' away and borin' you with all my silly notions."

Rebekah shook her head. "No, you haven't been borin' me a'tall. I truly appreciate all your *gut* ideas."

Daniel stood up, pushing his chair back with a scraping sound. "Feel free to ask me for help of any kind once you open for business. I'd enjoy bein' around all the plants." His eyes dropped to the floor. "I. . .I'd better get goin'."

"Don't work too hard," Rebekah called as he went out the door.

With only three of them working on the greenhouse, it took a little more than two weeks to complete the project. Papa and Simon both had their chores to do, so they could only work on it part-time. Daniel, however, came over nearly every day, working for several hours at a time. Rebekah couldn't help but wonder how come his *daed* let him off the farm so much.

On the day the greenhouse was finally completed, Mom and Papa hosted a big family picnic in honor of the official opening of Grandma's Place. All the family was there, and Daniel Beachy had been invited as well. Since he'd done more than half the work, it seemed only fitting that he should be included in this special day.

Everyone was seated at the wooden tables on the front lawn. When it appeared as if they'd all had their fair share of the delectable picnic foods, Papa stood up and called for attention. "As you all know, the greenhouse is finally done. I'd like to thank my son, Simon, for his help." Simon sat to his left, and Papa patted the top of his hatless head. He glanced over at Daniel then, who was sitting beside Rebekah. "I think a very special thanks should go to Daniel Beachy, however. He came over nearly every day and did more work than anyone else."

Rebekah chanced a peek at Daniel and noticed that he was turning slightly red. He smiled but kept staring down at his plate. "I enjoyed workin' on it," he mumbled.

"Daniel not only helped build the greenhouse, but he also assisted Rebekah in settin' out all the plants and flowers she'll sell. I appreciate the fact that Clarence Beachy was so willin' to loan out his son."

Rebekah stifled a giggle behind her hand. Just thinking of Clarence loanin' Daniel out made it seem as if Daniel was sort of farm equipment, instead of someone's grown son, for goodness' sake.

"Anyway," Papa continued, "my wife has a little somethin' she'd like to give the new owner of Grandma's Place." He motioned for Mom to stand up.

"Rebekah, this is for you," Mom said as she pulled a large paper sack from behind her back. At Rebekah's questioning look, Mom handed it to her. "Go ahead, open it."

With trembling fingers, Rebekah tore open the bag. She reached inside and withdrew a large wooden plaque. Inscribed in bold, block letters was: GRANDMA'S PLACE—Proprietor, Rebekah Stoltzfus.

Rebekah let out a little gasp. "Oh, Mom, it's *wunderbaar schee*—wonderful nice!"

Mom beamed. "It's that secret surprise I was workin' on when we were in Lancaster a few weeks ago. You see now why I couldn't tell ya who it was for and all."

Rebekah nodded, reaching up to wipe away the tears of joy that had fallen onto her flushed cheeks. *"Danki* so much."

"And now," said Papa in his usual booming voice, "let's all go down to the new greenhouse and hang up the sign, because Rebekah Stoltzfus is officially in business!"

❧

The greenhouse was everything Rebekah could have hoped for. It was a wooden structure, with glass panels set in the middle section. The front of the building, which was divided by a partition, had a long counter on which people could place their purchases. A hand-operated cash register, a small calculator, some stacks of notepaper, and several pens were sitting on one end of the counter. This part of the building had a gas lamp for light and a small wooden stove for heat in the winter.

The next area of the greenhouse, which was set with glass panels, had rows of low-hanging shelves for the plants. Large hooks hung from the rafters, where other plants would be secured from wire or chains. This made the plants accessible for Rebekah, and the display would help customers see them easily as well. Due to the glass panels, this part of the building would stay quite warm. There was a small propane heater, which would supplement the sun's natural heat on colder days.

Daniel had suggested they install several small screens, which would be set in place of the glass windows during warmer weather. This would provide the necessary cross draft and help keep the room at a more even temperature.

In the very back of the greenhouse, there was a small area where Rebekah could work on repotting plants and arranging bouquets of cut flowers. It had a long, low table, as well as a small cot where she could rest whenever necessary. Papa had even plumbed in a small bathroom, which was powered by a gas generator. There was a sink, a compact propane refrigerator, and a wood-burning cookstove. Rebekah could spend the whole day there if she wanted to.

In the wintertime her store hours would be shorter, but the greenhouse should be warm and cozy. This would be a good time for her to start seeds that could be ready to repot and sell in the spring.

Jah, Papa and Daniel had thought of everything, and Rebekah was ever so grateful. She settled into her greenhouse like it had always been her home, feelin' as if her miracle might be just round the corner. Now all she needed was plenty of customers.

Chapter 9

The first official customer to visit Grandma's Place was Johnny Yoder. It was on a Tuesday morning, and Rebekah had just hung the OPEN sign on the front door of the greenhouse.

When Johnny rang the bell, which hung on a rope right outside the door, Rebekah called, "Come in!"

The door swung open, and Johnny sauntered in, holding a straw hat in one hand, his white shirttail hanging out of his dark trousers, like he hadn't even bothered to check his appearance. "*Gut Morgen. Sind deah daheen*—are you home?"

Rebekah wheeled her chair toward him, laughing. "Of course, I just told you to come in, didn't I?"

Johnny grinned and tipped the hat in her direction.

"Can I help ya with somethin'?" Rebekah asked, ignoring his immature antics.

He moved slowly about the room, as though he were checking it all out. "Say, ya wouldn't happen to have any cut flowers, now would ya?"

Rebekah giggled. "Of course. This is a greenhouse, Johnny, so I'm supposed to have flowers." That Johnny—he was such a kidder. *Maybe that's why Mary Ellen enjoys his company,* she was thinking.

Johnny chuckled. "*Jah,* I reckon that's true enough."

"Are ya needing them for any particular reason?" Rebekah asked.

When Johnny nodded, Rebekah noticed that his face had turned the color of ripe cherries. It was a surprise to see him blush thataway. "Uh, they're for your cousin, Mary Ellen. I've been courtin' her of late," he muttered.

"So I've heard," Rebekah acknowledged. She motioned him to follow as she wheeled into the part of the greenhouse where all the flowers and plants were kept. "Did ya have anything special in mind?"

He shrugged. "Not really. I thought you might have a suggestion, seeing as to how you're in the business of sellin' flowers and whatnot."

If Rebekah had known exactly how much Johnny planned to spend, it might have helped in her selection of a bouquet. However, she didn't feel it would be proper to come right out and ask such a question. Instead, she discreetly said, "I have several bunches of miniature roses. They sell for ten dollars apiece. I also have some less expensive gladiolas—or maybe some pink carnations would be more to your liking."

"I think roses would be best," Johnny asserted, his green eyes fairly dancing. "I want the gift to be really special. Somethin' that'll let Mary Ellen know exactly how much I care."

"I think a bouquet of pink and white roses will do the trick," Rebekah replied. She moved over to select the flowers, then proceeded to wrap the stems tightly together with a rubber band. A bit of tissue paper gathered around the bottom completed the arrangement nicely. "If you're not gonna give these to her right away, maybe you should put 'em in some water," she said, handing Johnny the flowers.

Johnny beamed, looking like a little boy who'd just been handed a bag of chewy, black licorice. "We're goin' on a picnic today, so I'll see her real soon, I expect." He reached into his pants pocket and pulled out a ten-dollar bill, then handed it to Rebekah.

"Danki," she replied. "I hope you enjoy your picnic, and I hope Mary Ellen likes the flowers, too."

Johnny started toward the door, then turned back. *"Es gookt verderbt schee doh*—it looks mighty nice around here. I hope your new business is a huge success." He left the building, tossing his hat in the air and whistling like a songbird on the first day of spring.

Rebekah smiled to herself as she placed the money from her very first sale into the cash register. Had it not been for the fact that she was so excited about her new business venture, she might have felt a twinge of jealousy hearing that her best friend had a picnic date. While running the greenhouse was awful nice, it sure didn't take the place of love or romance. Maybe if the business made a real go and she could support herself, she wouldn't mind missing out on courtin' so much.

❧

By the end of August, news of Rebekah's greenhouse had spread throughout much of the valley. She averaged at least twenty customers a day, sometimes even more. Her inventory was quickly receding, and she knew she'd either have to restock soon or put a Closed sign on the door.

Papa and Simon were busy harvesting in the cornfields, so Rebekah asked Mom if she'd take her to town in order to buy more plants.

The following morning, they set out right after breakfast. This time Nadine was allowed to accompany them. The young girl sat directly behind Rebekah, giggling and talking about silly stuff nonstop. Rebekah was trying hard to be patient with Nadine's prattling, but her mind was on other things—more important things than how cute Eddy Shemly was, or who'd recently gotten a new pair of roller skates. Rebekah's business mind was mentally trying to add up the estimated cost of what she might be able to purchase today. Cut flowers weren't a problem, since they still had several varieties in the garden at home. What she needed most were plants and seeds.

When Nadine took a breath between sentences, Rebekah seized the opportunity and turned to Mom. "I've made a fairly good profit durin' the last few weeks, but I'm wonderin' how much of it to put back into the business and how much I should save."

Mom kept her eyes straight ahead, as traffic was especially heavy today. "Never borrow—for borrowin' leads to sorrowin'. Spend less than you earn, and you'll never be in debt. That's the true motto of every good businessman—or woman, in your case," she said with a small laugh.

Rebekah nodded. "That's right *gut* advice. I'll try to remember it, Mom." She paused, but not for long, because she knew if she didn't speak now, she'd only be interrupted by Nadine's silly small talk again. "I've been wonderin' about somethin' else too, Mom."

"What might that be, Daughter?"

"Do you think I can really make enough money to support myself? I mean, will things work out all right if I work really hard?"

Mom smiled. " 'All things work together for good to them that love God,' " she quoted from the Bible. "I know you love the Lord, Rebekah, so you must learn to trust Him more."

Rebekah fell silent again. Trust. Now that was the hard part. When things were going along just fine, it was easy enough to trust God. But when things became difficult, it was easy to begin wavering in one's faith. She'd have to keep Grandma's *Biwel* handy in the days ahead. She knew she needed to bathe herself in God's Word every day, in order not to give in to self-pity or start fretting about the future and such.

❧

Their first stop in Lancaster was Freeland Nursery, where Rebekah selected another good supply of plants as well as several packets of seeds. This time she concentrated on indoor varieties, since winter would be coming soon, and people would most likely be wanting something to bring a bit of color and cheer into the cold, dreary winter days.

The back of the market buggy was nearly full when they left the nursery, but Rebekah still had some money left over, and she felt right *gut* about the purchases she'd made.

Next they went to the farmers' market, where Mom planned to buy some whole grains and dried beans that one of her friends was selling. Nadine was allowed to wander around the building for a time, and Rebekah wheeled off by herself, too, leaving Mom to visit with Ellie Maust and purchase her dried goods.

Rebekah hadn't eaten anything since their early morning breakfast, and she was getting a mite hungry, to say the least. She knew Mom would be taking them to lunch after errands were done, but a little snack might not be such a bad idea, either. She wheeled over to a table where they were selling everything from homemade candy to fresh salads. She really wasn't in the mood for anything as sweet as candy, but a small fruit salad looked mighty refreshing. She bought one and was heading to the corner of the room when a teenage English boy bumped right smack-dab into the front of her wheelchair.

"Why don't you watch where you're going?" he shouted, giving the chair a little shove.

Another English boy, about the same age, grabbed the handle and swung the wheelchair completely around.

183

Rebekah's head spun dizzily, and she gripped the armrests tightly, hanging on for all she was worth. "Please, stop it!" she pleaded.

"Hey, Joe, we've got ourselves one of those Plain little gals, who's crippled, no less," the first boy hollered. "She bumps right into my leg, then has the nerve to tell me to stop it. Can you believe the gall some folks have these days?"

The one named Joe let out a hoot and gave Rebekah's chair another hefty shove. She was real close to tears now, for in all the time she'd been crippled, nothing like this had ever happened before. She was scared clean out of her wits and didn't have a clue what to do!

"How about a little ride in your wheelchair?" the first boy asked. "You wouldn't mind scooting over and letting me sit next to you, now would you, Honey?" When Rebekah shook her head, he pushed the wheelchair back in the direction of his friend. It rolled with such force that her bowl of fruit salad flew right out of her lap and landed upside down on the floor with a *splat*.

"Now look what you've gone and done, Ray!" Joe cried. "The poor little thing has lost all her lunch." He leaned close to Rebekah's face and squinted his eyes like a newborn pig. "Say, tell me somethin', Honey—why do you Amish dress so funny, anyhow?"

Before Rebekah could say anything at all, Ray shouted, "Yeah, and how come you eat all that healthy food?" He poked his friend on the arm. "You know, Joe, I hear tell that the Amish grow most of their own food, just like the pioneers used to do." He wrinkled his freckled nose and stared right at Rebekah. "Why is that, little missy?"

Rebekah swallowed hard, feeling like she was going to get sick. She looked around helplessly, hoping someone might come to her aid. However, the closest table was several feet away, and the people who ran it were busy with customers.

"I. . .I've got to go find my mom," she squeaked. Her shaky voice was laced with fear—the gripping kind, that finds its way to the surface, then bubbles over like boiling water left unattended on the stove.

"Now isn't that sweet," Joe taunted. "The little lady wants her mama." He gave the wheelchair a good yank toward his friend, only it wasn't Ray who caught it by the handles. It was someone much bigger and stronger than either of the boys. Someone with a very stern look on his face.

Chapter 10

Rebekah felt as though the air had been squeezed clean out of her lungs. Daniel Beachy's serious brown eyes were looking right down at her. Since the Amish were pacifists, she knew Daniel wouldn't be apt to fight the young men who'd been taunting her so. But he sure looked like he might. Daniel's eyes were narrowed into tiny slits, and his full lips were pursed somethin' awful. Rebekah drew in a deep breath and waited expectantly to see what would happen next.

"I think you boys owe this young woman an apology, and some money to buy another salad, too," Daniel said, motioning toward the mess on the floor. His gaze went back up to the boys, and Rebekah noticed that his face was getting mighty red.

"Aw, we were just having a little fun," Ray contended. "We didn't hurt her none."

"Come on, Ray," Joe inserted, nervously shuffling his feet this way and that. "She's probably his girlfriend, so we'd better leave 'em alone to do their lovebird crooning."

Rebekah was about to inform the teenagers that she wasn't anybody's *Aldi*—girlfriend—but Daniel's booming voice cut her right off. "What about that apology and some money?" Daniel moved his body at an angle, so he was blocking the boys' way.

With a look she hoped was pleading, Rebekah tried to beseech him to drop the matter. "It's all right, Daniel. Just let 'em go."

"*Jah*, well, I don't want to see you two around here again; is that clear?" Daniel barked. His hands were planted firmly on his hips, and he was scowling something awful.

Rebekah had never seen this side of Daniel before, and his response surprised her almost as much seeing Joe and Ray tear out of there as fast as their long legs could run.

Daniel dropped to his knees beside her wheelchair, obvious concern etched on his face. "You okay, Rebekah?"

Rebekah felt herself tremble. She was closer to crying than ever now. "I. . .I appreciate you steppin' in like that, Daniel. I don't know what would've happened if you hadn't come along when you did." Her eyes glazed over, and she blinked rapidly to hold back the tide of threatening tears.

Daniel laid a gentle hand on her arm, sending a strange tingling all the way up to her neck. "I couldn't let 'em hurt you. You're a special girl, Rebekah. You sure as anything don't deserve to be taunted thataway."

The smile she gave him was one of sheer gratitude. *"Danki. Danki* so much."

Daniel's brown eyes had turned soft and gentle again, and he stayed there on his knees, looking at Rebekah like she was something real special.

She brushed an imaginary speck of lint from her long cotton dress. Anything to keep her trembling hands busy.

"Rebekah! Oh, Rebekah, do you know where Nadine is?"

Rebekah tore her gaze away from Daniel, and he jumped to his feet. Mom was heading in their direction, waving her hand and smiling all friendlylike.

"Please don't say nothin' about my encounter with those English boys," Rebekah whispered to Daniel. "Sometimes Mom's a bit overprotective. If she thought leavin' me by myself had put me in any kind of danger, she might have second thoughts 'bout lettin' me be alone in my greenhouse so much of the time."

Daniel nodded. *"Jah,* all right then. I won't say nothin'."

"Hello, Daniel," Mom said as she approached the two young people. "How's your family these days?"

He smiled warmly, never letting on that anything was amiss. "Oh, fair to middlin', thanks. I'm in town pickin' up a new harness for one of *Daed's* plow mules. I thought I'd stop by the market to see what's doin', but I was just figurin' on getting some lunch pretty soon."

Mom's face seemed to brighten. Or maybe Rebekah just thought it was so. "Would ya like to join me and the girls at the Better Is More Restaurant?" Mom asked, giving Daniel a kind of sly grin. "If we can ever find Nadine, that is."

"I haven't seen her, Mom," Rebekah said. "Not since we separated earlier."

Daniel motioned across the room. "I saw her over at Kauffmeir's root beer stand. She was talkin' to a young boy about her age." He gave Rebekah a crooked smile. "I'd sure be happy to join you ladies for lunch. The Better Is More is my most favorite eatin' spot here in Lancaster."

Mom patted Daniel's arm. "Well then, let's see if we can round up that stray daughter of mine, and we'll all go eat ourselves full!"

❧

Since summer was coming to an end, and today was a weekday, there didn't seem to be as many tourists eating at the restaurant as usual. Mom, Rebekah, Nadine, and Daniel were ushered to a table right away. It was one of the long, family style tables, but they were the only ones seated there, so Rebekah didn't mind so much. She sat on one side in her wheelchair, and Nadine sat next to her. Mom was across from Nadine, and Daniel was seated beside her, which put him directly across from Rebekah.

Rebekah glanced up several times during the meal, only to find Daniel staring at her. At least she thought he was staring. Maybe he was just in deep thought about something. Could be he was thinkin' about that incident at the market and wonderin' if he should tell Mom about it after all.

Rebekah was ever so thankful he hadn't, because it had been a stressful enough thing to go through, without havin' Mom in some kinda stew.

"How's your new business goin'?" Daniel asked, breaking into Rebekah's troubling thoughts.

"It's doin' right well. We came to town today so's I could buy more plants and several packets of seeds to start for the winter," she explained.

Daniel's eyes brightened. "I think spendin' all day with plants and flowers would be *wunderbaar schee!* I wish I could do somethin' more enjoyable like that. I've got a love for flowers that just won't quit, but *Daed* says bein' a dairyman's important work." He crinkled his nose. "My uncle in Ohio has invited me to move out there and help in his greenhouse."

"Why don't you go then?" The question came from Nadine, who, with elbows leaning on the table and hands cupped under her chin, was looking intently at Daniel.

He shrugged. "I've thought on it some, but Ohio's kinda far from my own family and friends. I don't know Uncle Jake all that well, and I'm afraid I'd be a bit lonely out there."

Mom nodded. *'Jah,* livin' near one's family is important. None of my immediate family lives close, but I sure do appreciate havin' Andrew's family to call my own. They've always been there for us, too—through good times and bad."

Rebekah's thoughts drifted back in time—back to when she'd had her accident. She still remembered how the whole family rallied with food and money for the hospital bills. That's when Grandma moved in with them, just because she had a heart full of love and wanted to help out.

"When I marry someday, I hope to teach my *kinder* the value of a lovin' family," Daniel said with a note of conviction in his voice.

If you married Mary Ellen, you'd be gettin' a wonderful family, Rebekah thought ruefully. *What a shame she's passin' up someone as* gut *as you, Daniel Beachy. Maybe when I see Mary Ellen at preachin' on Sunday, I'll tell her so, too.*

❧

The preaching service this week was held at the home of Uncle Amos and Aunt Mim. It was the first Sunday of September, and the weather was still unbearably hot, feeling sticky as flypaper hanging from the barn rafters. All the doors and windows were flung open wide, but it was much too blistering to be inside with a bunch of warm-bodied folk.

Rebekah maneuvered her wheelchair next to the backless bench where Mom and Nadine sat with several other women and girls. Her eyes scanned the room, searching for Mary Ellen. She wasn't in the usual place beside her stepmother. She didn't seem to be among any of the other young women her age, either.

"I wonder where Mary Ellen is," Rebekah whispered to Mom.

Her mother shrugged. "I don't know."

"I hope she isn't sick," Rebekah remarked.

"You can ask about her after service." Mom put one finger to her lips. "Right now, it's time to get quiet. Bishop Benner's about to begin."

The three-hour service seemed to last forever. Besides the fact that it was stifling hot, Rebekah was most anxious to talk with her cousin. She'd spent nearly an hour last night in bed rehearsing what she would tell Mary Ellen about her choice to court Johnny Yoder and not Daniel Beachy. Even if she were upstairs in her room, not feeling well, Rebekah was determined to somehow speak with her. She just couldn't bear the look of sadness that so often passed across Daniel's face. At the very least, she'd get a message to Mary Ellen to meet her at the bottom of the stairs, since climbing them was sure not possible.

"And now, before we close our service for the day," the bishop said loudly, "I'd like to announce that Johnny Yoder and Mary Ellen Hilty have asked to become officially published. Their weddin' will be on the last Thursday of November."

Bishop Benner said the closing prayer and dismissed the congregation with the following words: *"Durch Jesus Christum*—through Jesus Christ—Amen." Everyone filed out quickly. Everyone except Rebekah Stoltzfus. She just sat in her wheelchair, too stunned by the bishop's announcement to even bat an eyelash. What on earth was Mary Ellen thinkin'? How could she have agreed to marry Johnny Yoder without even consulting her best friend? Surely she would've wanted to get Rebekah's opinion on somethin' as important as this.

Rebekah shook her head slowly as a soft moan escaped her lips. So that's why Mary Ellen wasn't in service today. She knew it was customary for the bride-to-be to stay home from preachin' when she became officially published.

Rebekah drew in a deep breath and forced herself to move the wheelchair toward the front door. Mary Ellen would probably come down to join the afternoon meal. She'd no doubt be as happy as any newly engaged young woman could be. She'd expect hearty congratulations from her family and friends—especially her best friend. But how in the world could Rebekah offer such congratulations when she felt strangely betrayed by Mary Ellen?

There was a burning feeling in the back of Rebekah's throat as she wheeled onto the front porch. Was the pain she felt really because she hadn't been told about the engagement, or was it the fact that she was intensely jealous? She and Mary Ellen had shared nearly everything up to now. When they were young girls, Mary Ellen got a *Hass*—bunny. She'd seen to it that Rebekah got one, too. When they were a little older, Rebekah received a new doll. She'd asked Grandma to make one just like it for Mary Ellen.

Things had begun to change of late, though. Mary Ellen was moving on with her life, in a direction that Rebekah knew she could never take. It really wouldn't be fair to expect her cousin to give up love, marriage, and a family of her own, simply because Rebekah couldn't have those things. If Mary Ellen thought Johnny Yoder was better than Daniel Beachy, then who was Rebekah to say otherwise? She'd just have to accept it as fact, that's all.

Rebekah scanned the yard and caught sight of Mary Ellen walking across the grass with Johnny. They were holding hands and laughing like a couple of silly *kinder*. Rebekah glided the wheelchair down the ramp Uncle Amos had built her and headed in the direction of the young couple. As she drew near, Rebekah kept mentally saying, *You will be happy for your best friend. You will be happy, no matter how much your heart is breakin'.*

Chapter 11

Rebekah had nearly reached the table where Mary Ellen and Johnny sat when she was greeted with yet another surprise.

"Have ya heard the news 'bout Aunt Grace and Uncle Lewis?" her fifteen-year-old cousin John asked as he and his twin brother walked beside her.

Rebekah shook her head. "What news is that?"

"She's in a family way. They're gonna have a *buppli*—baby," Jacob put in.

Rebekah's mouth fell open. "I thought their family was complete with Peggy and Matthew. I mean, Matthew's already seven years old, and—"

"And a baby will be a real bother!" John exclaimed. "I can still remember when our little sister was born. Maddie cried all the time, she did."

Rebekah laughed. "Come on, John. You and Jacob were only four when she joined your family. You weren't much more than *bupplin* yourself, so I doubt you can even remember much about it."

"We can so!" Jacob asserted. "All Maddie ever did was eat, sleep, cry, and wet her *Vindels*. Babies are such a bother!"

"You'll change your mind someday," Rebekah said. "When you marry and start a family of your own."

"Ach, my! Now that's never gonna happen!" Johnny shook his head with vigor.

"That's right," Jacob agreed, giving his brother a slap on the arm. "John and I are gonna stay single for the rest of our lives!"

"Whatever you say," Rebekah said with a knowing smile. She grasped the wheels of her chair. "Now, if you two will excuse me, I've gotta go congratulate the happy couple." She rolled away quickly, leaving the twins by themselves.

Mary Ellen and Johnny were surrounded by several well-wishers, so Rebekah impatiently waited her turn. She'd be glad to be done with all this, so she could get off by herself. When the others cleared away, she maneuvered her wheelchair up close to the table. "Congratulations, you two." She was trying extra hard to make her voice sound cheerful, even though her heart ached somethin' awful. "You're full of surprises, that's for sure."

Mary Ellen smiled, and Johnny nodded. "It was a surprise to most, but surely not you, Rebekah," he said. "You're Mary Ellen's best friend, so she must've told you of our plans."

Mary Ellen's smile faded as she looked down at the table. "I. . .I'm afraid I didn't tell Rebekah, either."

"You didn't? Why not?" Johnny asked in obvious surprise.

Rebekah looked expectantly at her cousin. She'd been wondering the very same thing.

"Rebekah, could we speak privately for a minute?" Mary Ellen said in a whisper.

Rebekah glanced at Johnny.

Jah, go ahead. It's fine by me," he replied with a shrug.

Mary Ellen stood up. "Let's go down by the pond. I don't think anyone else is there right now, since everyone's waitin' to eat."

"That sounds fine," Rebekah agreed. She began wheeling off in that direction, and when they reached the taller grass, Mary Ellen took over pushing.

There were two ducks on the water, dipping their heads up and down and flapping strong wings as if they didn't have a care in the world.

"They look so happy," Mary Ellen said, dropping to a seat on the grass.

Rebekah shifted uneasily in her wheelchair. *Jah*, almost as happy as you and Johnny seem to be."

"Oh, we are!" Mary Ellen fairly bubbled. "I love him so much!" She looked up at Rebekah, heartfelt sorrow on her oval face. "I'm sorry for keepin' our engagement from you. It's just that—well, I was afraid you might be kinda upset."

"Upset? Why would you think I'd be upset?" Rebekah's question came out in a tone that was none too warm or friendly.

"We've always done everything together," Mary Ellen explained. "If I got a *Hass*, you got one, too."

"And if I got a doll, so did you," Rebekah put in.

Mary Ellen nodded. *Jah*, but this time I was afraid you'd be hurt that I was gettin' married and you weren't."

"That's just the way of things," Rebekah said flatly. No use tellin' Mary Ellen how she really felt. "There comes a time in life when little girls must grow up. I realize I can't have everything my friend has," she added with a curt nod.

"Oh, but you can," Mary Ellen said with feeling. "Maybe not at the exact same time as me, but someday you'll fall in love and get married, too."

Rebekah groaned. "We've had this discussion before. I'm a cripple, and no man wants to be stuck with a handicapped wife."

"Other women, some much worse off than you, get married and even have children," Mary Ellen argued.

Rebekah shrugged. "Well, *wass machts aus?* No one's in love with me." She waved a hand. "Besides, I have my new business now, and if I can become self-supportin', then I won't have need of a husband."

"Love can change all that," Mary Ellen reminded.

"As I said, there's no one to love," Rebekah asserted.

" 'Commit thy way unto the Lord; trust also in him; and he shall bring it to pass.' Psalm 37, verse 5," Mary Ellen repeated from memory.

Rebekah made no comment. Instead, she gave her wheelchair a sharp turn to the left. "We'd better be gettin' back. I'm sure they're probably servin' up the noon meal by now." She glared at Mary Ellen. "Besides, Johnny's no doubt waitin' for you."

❧

Many of the families lingered for most of the day, enjoying all the good food and the joy of just being together. It was a time for laughter and games, stories to be told and retold. No one was ever in much of a hurry to return home to the evening chores that were always waiting to be done.

However, today Rebekah was not anxious to stay around the Hilty farm and be reminded of her cousin's happiness. Even the news about Aunt Grace expecting a baby had sent a pang of regret to her tender, aching heart. It was wrong to harbor feelings of jealousy, and she knew it. She'd been unkind to Mary Ellen earlier, too, which had been equally wrong. She knew her family had no plans to leave early, but now that the noon meal was over and everyone seemed occupied, she felt the need to be alone and talk to God about things.

Rebekah wheeled off toward Aunt Mim's garden, where an abundance of flowers and herbs grew prolifically. Maybe after some time in the beauty of colors and fragrances that only God could've created, she might find forgiveness for her nasty attitude and could return to the yard feeling a bit more sociable.

There was a firmly packed dirt path in the middle of the garden, and Rebekah had no trouble navigating it with her wheelchair. She rolled right between two rows of pink roses and stopped to drink in their delicious aroma.

Closing her eyes and lifting her face toward the warming sun, Rebekah prayed first. Then she allowed her imagination to run wild. *Wouldn't it be like heaven to stand in a garden like this one and whisper words of affection to a man who'd pledged his undying love to me?* She could nearly feel his sweet breath on her upturned face as she envisioned the scene in her mind. She could almost hear his steady breathing as he held her in his arms, whispering words of endearment.

"The roses are sure beautiful this time of year, ain't it so?"

Rebekah's eyes flew open, and she whirled her chair in the direction of the deep male voice that had pulled her from a romantic reverie.

Daniel Beachy stood only a few feet away, hands in his pockets and a broad smile on his face. "I'm sorry if I scared ya. I could see you were probably meditatin' on God's special creation, but I thought you would've heard me come into the garden." He grinned, causing the skin around his eyes to crinkle. "My mom always says my big feet don't tread too lightly."

Rebekah had to smile, in spite of her melancholy spirit. "You're right. I was meditatin'." She chose not to mention what she'd been meditating on, however.

"Have you gotten any starts from your aunt's rose garden?" Daniel questioned.

She shook her head. "I've never thought to ask."

"Mim seems to like you a lot," he said. "I'm sure she wouldn't mind a'tall."

Jah, maybe I'll talk to her about it."

"You're awful quietlike today. I thought you'd be up on the lawn, joinin' in the young people's celebration," Daniel said, changing the subject.

"You mean the engagement of Mary Ellen and Johnny?"

He nodded, and Rebekah was sure that same look she'd seen on his face a few times before had cast a shadow of sadness on it now. The bishop's announcement must have jolted Daniel like it had her. He was probably hurtin' every bit as much as she, only for a different reason. She was jealous, because she'd never have the kind of happiness Mary Ellen was experiencing. Daniel probably wished it had been him, not Johnny Yoder, who'd won Mary Ellen's heart.

Rebekah swallowed hard, struggling for words that wouldn't be a lie. "Celebrations are for those who can run and play games. I'd much rather be enjoyin' these lovely flowers," she said at last.

"*Jah,* I think you might have the right idea," Daniel agreed. He looked down at the toes of his boots, then slowly raised his eyes to meet hers. "Would ya like me to push your wheelchair? We can walk around the rest of your aunt's garden."

Rebekah's first thought was to decline. She didn't need Daniel's pity. She hesitated only a moment, as pride took a backseat. "*Danki,* that'd be kind of nice."

Daniel smiled and grabbed hold of the wheelchair handles. "Hang on, Miss Stoltzfus. I've been known to be quite the reckless driver!"

The days sped by, with a delicate shifting of summer to fall. A few tourists still visited Rebekah's greenhouse, but most of her customers were Amish or English farmers who lived in the area.

Rebekah began to fret over the possibility that her business might fail. She had to remind herself frequently to pray, trust God, and search the Scriptures for His promises. Her faith was weak, and she knew it all too well.

Today was Friday, and she was lying on the cot in the back of her store, resting and attempting to seek God's will. "Dear Father," she prayed, "I'm still lookin' for a miracle. I really need to be able to support myself. I don't want to be a burden to others. Please bring in more customers, or show me what to do to make the business more successful."

The sharp ringing of the bell outside the greenhouse door pulled Rebekah from her prayer. "Come in!" she called.

As she struggled to a sitting position, she heard the door creak. Someone yelled, "Rebekah? Are ya here?"

The male voice sounded familiar, and Rebekah had to take several deep breaths in order to quiet her pounding heart. Why did Daniel Beachy make her feel so giddy? She knew he cared for her only as a friend. Daniel's kind face flashed before her eyes as she remembered that Sunday afternoon at the Hiltys', when he'd pushed her through Aunt Mim's garden. They'd laughed and talked so easily. He'd actually made her forget the pain over hearin' the news 'bout Mary Ellen's plans to be married.

Rebekah forced all thoughts to the back of her mind as she called, "I'm back here, Daniel. Just tryin' to get my crutches strapped to my arms."

Daniel poked his head around the partition and gave her a look of concern.

"Are ya all right? Why aren't you in your wheelchair? Were you lyin' down?"

Rebekah laughed. "So many questions, Daniel Beachy. And don't you go lookin' so poker-faced, now. I'm wearin' my leg braces today and usin' the metal crutches that help me stay upright." She dropped one stiff leg to the floor. "Mom hollers at me if I spend too much time in the wheelchair, so I'm tryin' to humor her today." The other leg followed the first, landing on the concrete floor with a thud. "I was only lyin' down to rest awhile, but sometimes gettin' up again ain't so easy."

Daniel moved closer to the cot. "Need some help?"

Rebekah swallowed hard. There it was again. That "I feel sorry for you" look on Daniel's face. She winced, wishing he'd just see her as a woman and not some *eledich*—pitiful—crippled girl.

"Are you hurtin'?" he asked, dropping to his knees in front of her.

She drew in a deep breath. "I'm fine, really." Her crutches were propped against the wheelchair, next to the cot. She reached for one, and bumped the other, sending it crashing to the floor. *"Immer Druwel ergitz!"* she cried.

Without waiting to be asked, Daniel lunged for the crutch. "Trouble usually has an answer, though," he said, handing it to her with a heart-melting smile.

Unexpectedly, Rebekah's eyes misted. She hated to be dependent on others, but receiving help from someone as *wunderbaar* as Daniel made it almost a pleasure. "You always seem to be around whenever I need help," she murmured.

"Jah, well, that's what friends are for," Daniel said sincerely. He looked her right in the eye. "I only wish we could be more than friends."

More than friends? What was he sayin'? Did Daniel actually see her in some other light? Somethin' that would involve more than friendship? Rebekah shifted on the cot, unsure of what to say or do next.

"Ya want to be more than friends?" she finally squeaked. "What are ya really sayin', Daniel?"

He adjusted his weight from one foot to the other. "I'm sayin' that if it were possible, I'd sure like to be your partner."

"Partner?" Rebekah could barely get the word out.

To her surprise, he laid one hand on her arm and nodded. "Jah. I'd like to be your business partner."

Business partner. The words echoed in Rebekah's head like a woodpecker thumpin' on the side of Papa's barn. She drew in a long, steady breath, hoping to calm her nerves. She should've known Daniel wasn't gonna ask her to be his marriage partner, for goodness' sake. What a dunce she was for even lettin' such ridiculous notions pop into her head. She and Daniel weren't courtin', and he'd never shown the slightest interest in a romantic sort of way neither. In fact, she was quite sure he was in love with Mary Ellen. How could she have been so stupid as to misread his intentions like that?

With the aid of her crutches, now strapped to her arms, Rebekah stood up. "Why would you wanna be my business partner anyways?" she asked pointedly.

Daniel frowned, looking as though it almost pained him to say the words. "I've told ya before that I have a love for flowers and all. Runnin' a greenhouse would be the most *wunderbaar* thing I could even imagine. I envy you so, Rebekah."

"Envy me?" she shouted. "How could anyone envy a crippled woman?" Tears gathered in the corners of her eyes, and she squinted, hoping to keep them there.

"I. . .I sure didn't mean to upset ya," Daniel sputtered.

With both crutches securely in place now, Rebekah plodded across the room. Daniel followed silently behind. When they stepped into the area where all the plants and flowers were kept, she came to an abrupt stop. "I love these green-leafed, blossomed creations of God's. I understand why you'd wanna run a greenhouse, too." She clicked her tongue. "There's two small problems, though."

His forehead wrinkled. "Two problems? What would they be?"

Rebekah held up one finger. "First of all, my greenhouse is a new business. I've only been open a few months, and it's not showin' enough profit to support two people. I'm not even sure if it's gonna support me yet," she added.

"And the second problem?" Daniel asked with a shrug.

Rebekah extended a second finger. "Probably the most obvious problem is my parents. They'd never allow such a thing."

Daniel's eyebrows shot up. "Why not?"

"We'd be spendin' many long hours together—alone—with no chaperones."

"We are adults, Rebekah," Daniel reminded. A slight smile tugged at the corner of his lips, and a twinkle danced in his usually serious brown eyes.

Why must he look at me like that? Rebekah mused. *Especially when he sees me as nothin' more than a possible business partner?* "If we were both the same sex, then maybe it wouldn't be a problem," Rebekah added.

Daniel nodded. "*Jah.* I see what ya mean."

"If it were possible," she said with feeling, "I'd actually consider becomin' partners. You know a whole lot 'bout flowers and such, and you've proved to be pretty handy to have around."

Her words brought a smile to Daniel's face. When he gave her a quick wink, her heart fluttered, and she willed it to stop as she laid one trembling hand against her chest. "So, what brings you here today, Daniel? I'm sure it was for somethin' more than to retrieve my crutch."

He chuckled. "I'm here to buy a plant for my mom. Her birthday's tomorrow, and I want to give her somethin' that will last."

"How about a purple African violet?" she suggested, moving over to the area where all the violets were kept. "I have a beautiful one that came from a start off one of Grandma Stoltzfus's plants."

Daniel bent over and scrutinized the plant in question. "I'll take it."

Rebekah giggled. "You haven't even asked the price."

He shrugged. "Well, *wass machts aus?* I like the plants, my mom needs a gift, and you probably can use the money."

Rebekah gave him a mock frown. What should she do with the likes of Daniel Beachy?

Chapter 12

The following Monday, Daniel paid Rebekah another visit. "Back so soon?" she asked when he stepped inside the greenhouse. "Did your *mamm* not like the plant you bought her? I can exchange it for somethin' else, if you like."

Daniel shook his head. "She liked it just fine." He glanced around the room, as though he might be searching for something.

"What can I help you with?" Rebekah asked, directing the wheelchair so she could see him face-on.

Daniel nodded in her direction. "I was hopin' I could help us both." He wore a boyish grin, and she could tell he was in especially good spirits this morning.

She lifted her chin slightly. "What are you talkin' about, Daniel?"

He shuffled his booted feet a few times, thumbs stuck inside his beige suspenders as though he were helping hold up his black cotton trousers. "I know I can't come here and work with you every day, but I think I've come up with a way we can both make some extra money. He wiggled his dark eyebrows. "And it'll be doin' exactly what we both enjoy."

Rebekah studied Daniel's face intently, trying to determine if he was serious or merely joking with her.

"I really do have a *gut* idea," he said, moving excitedly toward her. "Can I tell ya about it?"

"*Jah*, sure, why not?" she responded with a shrug of her shoulders.

"All right then, I'll be back."

Before Rebekah could even open her mouth to ask where he was going, Daniel spun on his heels and sauntered out the front door. In a few minutes, he reappeared, carrying a large cardboard box. He set it carefully on the floor, dropped to his knees, and jerked open the flaps.

Rebekah wheeled her chair closer, watching with interest as he pulled out several wooden bird feeders, a few whirligigs for the lawn, and some homemade flowerpots.

"Daniel, those are *wunderbaar!*" she exclaimed. "Did you make 'em yourself?"

He beamed. "In my free time I like to do a bit of woodworkin'."

"That's great, and you do a very fine job. However, I don't see what it has to do with—"

"You can try to sell these things here in your greenhouse," Daniel interrupted. "I could leave 'em on consignment, and we'd each get a percentage of the profit." His expression held so much enthusiasm, it reminded Rebekah of a small child opening his first gift on Christmas morning.

Rebekah tapped her fingers against the armrest of the wheelchair. "Hmm. . . do ya think folks comin' here would buy items like these?"

"I'm sure they would," he responded eagerly. "My uncle sells all kinds of things in his greenhouse. It only helps bring in more customers—especially the tourists. They all seem to want somethin' that's been made by one of us Plain People, ya know." He threw back his head and laughed, causing his straw hat to fall to the floor. "So, what do you say, Rebekah Stoltzfus? Shall we give 'em what they want and make a profit for both of us as well?"

Rebekah nodded slowly, trying to let all that he'd said sink into her brain. "It might work. I suppose it's sure worth a try."

Daniel reached out his hand, and long, warm fingers wrapped around hers. "Silent partners then?"

She shook on it. "*Jah,* silent partners."

Daniel made two more trips over to the greenhouse that day, bringing with him several boxes filled with wooden bird feeders and birdhouses, flowerpots, and lawn ornaments. With her permission, he placed them around the greenhouse in various eye-catching locations. He also put a few outside the building, hoping to entice customers into the store. After setting the prices for each item, he and Rebekah reached an agreement that she'd get 25 percent of all money collected from Daniel's handiwork.

Daniel suggested she stock vegetable and flower seeds, potting soil, and fertilizers to sell. Since winter would be coming soon, he also thought she should get some small holly bushes and several poinsettia plants. He even convinced her to take out a small ad in the local Amish newspaper and said he'd put up several flyers around town to advertise Grandma's Place.

Things were lookin' right hopeful for Rebekah's business, and she was gaining a new kind of self-confidence that she'd never known before. Having to deal with customers helped her feel less shy and self-conscious, too. Opening the greenhouse seemed like a real answer to prayer. It just might could be that miracle she'd been lookin' for.

The days of fall moved quickly along, and soon it was time to help with Mary Ellen's wedding. She'd asked Rebekah to be one of her attendants, along with Carolyn and Lena, two other friends.

Aunt Mim scheduled time for baking several days before the wedding, and she asked all the women in the family to help. They'd be making dozens of cakes, pies, and cookies for the wedding feast. Some of the meal would be provided by other Amish women who'd be attending the big event, but there was still much to be done.

Rebekah, Nadine, and their mom were part of the gathering, and they arrived at the Hiltys' just a little after nine on Monday morning.

Aunt Mim and Mary Ellen were already hard at work in the kitchen, and the bride-to-be greeted them at the door with a dusting of flour stuck to the end of her nose. She grabbed Rebekah's wheelchair excitedly and pushed her toward the table. "Oh, Rebekah, I'm gettin' such butterflies! I wonder if I'll be able to eat anything at all between now and Thursday."

Mary Ellen flopped into a seat at the table and poured them both a cup of raspberry tea. "Just look at me—I'm shakin' like a maple tree on a windy day," she said, extending her trembling hands across the table.

Rebekah took Mary Ellen's hands in her own. "Try not to think about it. That's what Mom always tells me whenever I'm anxious 'bout somethin' or another."

Mary Ellen snorted. "That's easy enough for you to say. You're not the one gettin' married in three days."

Rebekah was quite sure her friend's words weren't intended to hurt, but they stung like prickly nettles nonetheless. She recoiled like she'd been scratched real bad.

"Oh, Rebekah, I'm so sorry," Mary Ellen apologized. "I didn't mean—"

"It's okay," Rebekah interrupted with the wave of her hand. "I'm not the one gettin' married, and I don't even presume to know what you're feelin' right now. I was only tryin' to help quiet your nerves some."

"I know, and I appreciate it." Mary Ellen blew on her hot tea before taking a tentative sip. "I never thought I could be this happy, Rebekah. I love Johnny so much, and I know we're gonna be awful content together."

Rebekah was sorely tempted to ask Mary Ellen what there was about Johnny Yoder that appealed to her so much, but she knew that wouldn't be the right thing. Just because she saw nothin' in playful Johnny that caused her heart to skip a beat the way it so often did whenever Daniel came near, didn't mean Mary Ellen should see nothin' neither. It was more than obvious that both of the young people were deeply in love, and the reasons behind their love didn't really matter, she supposed.

"I'm truly happy for you," Rebekah assured Mary Ellen, "and I'm glad you asked me to be your main attendant."

Mary Ellen smiled, causing her dimples to expand. *"Jah,* well, who else would I ask but my very best friend?"

Rebekah smiled in return. "What do ya need me to do today? I can peel apples, roll out pie dough, or anything else that one can do from a sittin'-down position."

"Let's ask Mama Mim," Mary Ellen replied. "She's the one in charge of things."

After consulting her aunt, Rebekah was assigned the job of peeling seventy-two apples for twelve apple-crumb pies. It would take some time, all right, but she didn't mind. It gave her a chance to think about things.

Her thoughts went quickly to the new greenhouse business, which was doing better than she'd ever expected. Daniel's wooden items were selling almost as fast as he could make them. She'd taken his advice and purchased potting soil, fertilizer, and seeds, not only to use in the business, but to sell as well. She'd also placed an order for several Christmas cactus, holly plants, and poinsettias to sell during the winter months.

Rebekah's musings turned naturally to Daniel. She always seemed to be thinking about him, especially when she thought of the greenhouse. If she were truly being honest, she thought of him other times, too. Daniel's kind face was never far from her thoughts. She couldn't understand this attraction to him, because she knew it was one-sided. Truly, even if it weren't, there was no hope for any kind of future for them as a couple.

"You look like you're a million miles away," Mary Ellen said, breaking into Rebekah's thoughts.

Rebekah looked up and smiled. "I was just thinkin' about my business." She chose not to mention the part that included Daniel Beachy. There would be no point to it, and besides, why give Mary Ellen something to goad her about?

"Is the greenhouse doin' well then?" Mary Ellen asked.

Rebekah nodded. *"Jah,* right well."

"I haven't been over in quite awhile, what with all the wedding preparations and whatnot. I've heard that you have made some changes, though."

Rebekah grinned. "Daniel Beachy brought several of his handmade wooden items over to sell. The bird feeders are goin' real fast—probably because everyone likes to feed the birds during fall and wintertime. Daniel does *gut* work, and most of his things sell nearly as quick as he can make 'em." She stared off into space. "He really likes flowers and plants, so he's shown me some things about repottin', takin' cuttings, and which plants need more water than others. He's been such a big help."

Mary Ellen poked Rebekah's arm. "So, has he started callin' yet?"

"Daniel comes over to the greenhouse at least once or twice a week. He likes to see if I need any more items to sell or whether I want help with anything," Rebekah answered as she took up another apple to peel.

Mary Ellen shook her head. "No, no, not callin' at your greenhouse. Is he calling at your home? Are you two courtin', or am I not supposed to ask?"

Rebekah dropped the apple with a thud, and it nearly rolled right off the table. "Is that what you think—that Daniel and I are a courtin' couple? Do others think that as well, for goodness' sake?"

Mary Ellen shrugged. "I can't say what others are thinkin', but I for one have noticed that he seems to hang around you a lot." She raised her eyebrows. "I've seen the way you look at him, too."

"Of course he comes round," Rebekah said sharply. "I just told you, he brings things over to sell at the greenhouse." She grabbed the apple again and began attacking it with a vengeance. "Furthermore, I do not look at him in any special way. He's a *gut* friend, and there's nothin' more to it a'tall."

Mary Ellen shrugged and grabbed one of the apple slices from the bowl, popping it into her mouth. *"Jah,* all right then. Whatever you say, Rebekah Stoltzfus."

Chapter 13

Thursday morning dawned bright and clear. It was a cool, crisp, November day, but the birds were singing, and the sun shone bright, like a gleaming new penny. It was the perfect day for a wedding. Rebekah knew Mary Ellen had probably been awake since sunup, beside herself with the anticipation of her special day. And who could blame her? She was, after all, marryin' the man of her choice.

Rebekah was sitting at her bedroom window, watching two turtledoves in the old maple tree. She groaned softly. " *'Ich Will Liebe*—I Will Love.' " That was the title of one of the songs in their Amish hymnbook, the *Ausbund*. Maybe it would be sung at the wedding today.

But I'll never love—leastways not like a woman loves a man, she thought dryly. Self-pity was stealing into her heart again, and she seemed powerless to stop it.

A knock on the door caused her to jump. She lifted a hand to wipe away the tears rolling down her cheeks. "Come in."

"You didn't show up when I called for breakfast," Mom said, poking her head inside the door. "I was hopin' you weren't still asleep. We must hurry if we're to get to the weddin' by nine o'clock."

Rebekah turned the wheelchair toward Mom, forcing her lips to form a smile. *"Jah,* I'm up, and as you can see, even dressed. I guess I was too busy with my thoughts to hear your call to breakfast."

Mom moved swiftly across the room, falling to her knees in front of Rebekah's chair. "Is somethin' troublin' you *demariye*—this morning?"

Rebekah shrugged. Something was always troubling her, but she sure didn't want to talk about it. What was the point? Nothing could be changed by talking about it. "I'm fine, Mom," she replied. "I just need a little time for thinkin' and dreamin'."

Mom smiled. "I quite agree. Without dreams and goals, our lives would never move forward. I believe God has a plan for each of us, but we must be open to His will in order to discover what that plan is."

Rebekah wondered if Mom was trying to tell her something specific. It made her feel all *Verhuddelt*—mixed up. She wasn't in the mood for any lectures today; that was for sure. Besides, they had a wedding to attend. "I guess we'd better get to breakfast," she said, forcing a cheerful voice. "I'm really hungry, and we don't wanna be late for Mary Ellen's special day."

❧

The wedding, which was held at the Hilty home, began at nine o'clock sharp. The chantlike singing of several songs from the *Ausbund* started things off. Next, Bishop Benner gave a long sermon on the topic of marriage and its commitments, followed by some Scripture readings related to matrimony.

Several of the church leaders gave testimonies; then the bride and groom and their attendants were ushered to another part of the house. Mary Ellen and Johnny were taken into one of the downstairs bedrooms, while their attendants waited just outside the door.

Rebekah sat in her wheelchair, fidgeting with the corner of her dark green apron. She knew the bride and groom were receiving special counseling from the bishop. It made her wonder what rules and regulations he might give a young couple about to pledge their vows of love and fidelity for the rest of their lives. Rebekah would never know, of course, because there would be no wedding or scriptural counseling for her in the days to come. She nearly broke into tears as she glanced across the hall, where Daniel Beachy and two other young Amish men waited for the groom to reappear.

How odd, she thought, *that Johnny would ask a rival to be one of his waiters. Surely he's not tryin' to rub salt into Daniel's wounds, I hope. He has to know how much Daniel wanted to court Mary Ellen.*

Daniel must have caught Rebekah looking at him, for he flashed her a big grin. Her heart did a silly little dance, and she averted his gaze. Daniel was only being friendly, but, oh, she wished it could be more.

Suddenly, the truth slammed into her, like one of Papa's bulls runnin' at full speed. She was actually in love with Daniel Beachy! The problem was, there was absolutely nothin' she could do about it. Daniel didn't share her feelings of love, and even if he did, her disability would always stand in the way.

The bride and groom, along with Bishop Benner, finally emerged from the bedroom. Mary Ellen sent a quick smile in Rebekah's direction as they hurried back to the living room.

There were nearly two hundred guests in attendance, but not all could fit into the Hilty living room. As a result, the front sitting room, dining room, and even the kitchen had been set up with backless benches.

The bishop gave an extended prayer, then motioned for the bride and groom, who'd been sitting on opposite benches, to join him at the front of the room.

Mary Ellen, dressed in a plain blue cotton dress, draped with a contrasting cape and apron, also wore a white prayer cap on her head. Johnny wore a white shirt, black trousers, and a matching vest and jacket.

Rebekah sat nearby, listening as the young couple repeated their vows before God and those who'd come to witness this union. Her eyes stung with tears that threatened to spill over. She squeezed her eyes tightly shut, hoping to keep the dam from bursting.

Why'd she have to be crippled? Why couldn't she be like most other young women her age? She struggled against the sob rising in her throat. *Dear God,* she prayed, *please fill my life in such a way that I won't miss havin' love or marriage. Give me peace in my heart, like only You can give.*

When the wedding vows were finally over, the bishop blessed the newly married couple, and they both sat down. In a short time, the wedding feast would begin, and so would Mary Ellen's new life as Mrs. Johnny Yoder.

Everyone waited outside while tables were set up to replace the benches. Rebekah helped in the kitchen, dishing up platters of fried ham, roast beef, boiled chicken, and cold cuts. It was something she could do well, and it kept her from thinking too much, which she knew would only lead to more self-pity.

"The third group of people is finally bein' served," Mom whispered to Rebekah. "You haven't eaten since this morning's early breakfast, so why don't ya join 'em?"

Rebekah shrugged. "I'm really not all that hungry. Besides, I can snack in here."

"But you're missin' all the fun," Mom argued. "There's a lot of laughter and joke tellin' goin' on out there. I'm sure Mary Ellen's expectin' her best friend to be part of the festivities."

Rebekah sighed deeply. "Oh, all right. I'll go for a little while." Without another word, she wheeled into the dining room. The bridal party sat there, eating and visiting with their guests, as though life had never been better.

Mary Ellen saw Rebekah and motioned her over to their corner table, called the *Eck*.

Rebekah guided her chair through the crowded room and over to the table. To her surprise, Daniel was also sitting there. She steeled her heart against his lopsided smile, even managing a weak one of her own.

"You look flushed, Rebekah," Mary Ellen noted. "Have they been makin' you work in the kitchen all afternoon?"

Rebekah shook her head. "No, I wanted to help out."

"Rebekah's a hard worker," Daniel put in. "She works plenty hard in her new business, too."

"I hear that it's doin' quite well," Johnny said.

Rebekah nodded. *"Jah,* thanks to all of Daniel's wooden items and helpful suggestions." She cast another quick glance in his direction and noticed that his brown eyes fairly glowed. She wondered how he could appear so happy when he'd lost the girl he loved to his friend, Johnny.

"Rebekah," Daniel whispered, "when you're finished eating, would ya like to go for another wheelchair ride in your aunt's garden? I know most of the flowers are gone, but it's a right nice day, and the fresh air will be *gut.*"

Rebekah wondered if sitting here watchin' the newlyweds was getting to him as much as it was her. "That sounds fine to me, Daniel," she mumbled in return.

She hurried through her meal, hardly taking the time to even enjoy the succulent flavors of all the traditional Pennsylvania Dutch dishes that were set before them. She was anxious to get away from all the happy talk at the wedding table, and she was equally anxious to be alone with Daniel—even if their relationship could only be one of friendship.

When his plate was empty, Daniel stood up and turned to the newlyweds. "If you two will excuse me, I need to get some fresh air." Mary Ellen and Johnny nodded their approval, and he rushed out the door without even a backward glance.

Rebekah waited a few minutes; then she too pushed away from the table. "I think I've had enough to eat, and I'm sure you newlyweds would like to be alone for awhile." Without waiting for anyone's response, she propelled herself out the front door.

Daniel was on the porch waiting for her. "Are ya ready?" he asked with another heart-melting smile.

She nodded. "There's so much laughter and fun goin' on in there, I doubt we'll even be missed."

Daniel grabbed the handles on Rebekah's wheelchair and rolled her carefully down the wooden ramp. Soon they were on the path that led to the garden.

There were still a few chrysanthemums and geraniums in bloom, and several of the herbs were flourishing, too. Their pungent aroma drifted on the wind, and Rebekah fairly drank in the serenity of it all. "A garden is my favorite place to be," she murmured.

Jah, mine too," Daniel agreed.

They walked in silence for a time, until Daniel stopped abruptly and stepped in front of the wheelchair. "What did ya think of the weddin'?"

Rebekah answered with a shrug. "It was *gut. Wass Got tuht ist wohl getahn.*"

"So, you think God brought Johnny and Mary Ellen together?" he asked in a serious tone.

She lifted her shoulders again. "Well, I think Mary Ellen and Johnny would say so."

He blinked several times. "They do seem to be very much in love, don't they?"

"I'd say so," Rebekah replied. She wanted so badly to ask if Daniel was terribly disappointed that he hadn't been Mary Ellen's choice. However, she didn't think that would be too fittin' to say. Besides, it might make him feel worse than he already did.

Daniel went back to pushing her chair again, until he came to a small wooden bench. He stopped next to it and took a seat. "I was wonderin'," he said, looking straight ahead. "There's gonna be another singin' this Sunday night, at the Yutzys' place. Do you plan to go?"

Rebekah shook her head. "I don't think so."

He stole a quick glance at her then. "I thought I might go to this one. They'll be havin' a big bonfire, with a hot dog roast and marshmallows. It might be kind of fun and may be the last time we can have a singin' before the snow flies."

Rebekah bit down on her bottom lip. It would be fun to sit around a warm bonfire, sing some songs, and visit to beat the band. If Daniel was gonna be there, then maybe she should go, too. She nodded. *Jah*, maybe I might be there."

Chapter 14

Rebekah had second thoughts about going to the singing, but the idea of seeing Daniel again finally won out. Now she and Simon were on their way in his open courting buggy, the wind whipping against their faces and stinging their noses like a swarm of buzzin' bumblebees. The sky appeared clear and full of twinkly stars, and the air was cool and crisp as a winter apple. It was perfect weather for a bonfire.

It'll seem odd, Rebekah thought, *not to see Mary Ellen there tonight.* She and Johnny had begun their extended honeymoon, and they'd be spending the night at the home of Aunt Crystal and Uncle Jonas. They would receive a wedding present before they left the following morning, too. Probably something useful, like as not. Maybe a colorful, warm quilt, or some braided rugs for the kitchen floor. When their honeymoon of visiting family and friends was finally over, the newlyweds would live with Uncle Amos and Aunt Mim until spring. The new house their fathers were building should be completed by then.

Rebekah moaned softly. *I wonder what it'd be like to have a house of my own? Even a home right next to Mom and Papa, or one on the same property, would make me feel so* dankbaar—*thankful—and independent. Maybe if I become financially self-reliant, Papa will build me a small house. It'd have to be near family, of course. Just in case of an emergency.* Rebekah guessed she'd always need someone in the family to look out for her. *Unless I make enough money to hire one or two* mauts *to do the things I can't do myself.* She grimaced. *I guess it's not too realistic to think I could hire a maid. I'll probably never make that much money from a small business in the country.*

"Now, what's that old frown about, Sister?" Simon asked, nudging Rebekah's arm with his bony elbow. "We're on our way to a singin'. There's gonna be lots of food, fun, and games. You should be smilin', not frownin' like some old sourpuss."

Rebekah gave her brother a weak smile. *"Jah,* I know. I was just thinkin' about somethin' else, that's all."

"Like what?" he asked, flicking the reins to get the horse moving a bit faster.

"It was nothin' important."

Simon shrugged. "Well, if ya want to be an old stick-in-the-mud, then suit yourself. I'm really lookin' forward to tonight, and I plan on havin' all sorts of fun!"

❧

It seemed as though all the Amish young people in the community were at the bonfire. They crowded into the Yutzys' barn for some game playing and singing. As usual, Rebekah sat off on the sidelines in her wheelchair, listening to the lively banter and watching the door for some sign of Daniel Beachy. She wondered if maybe he'd changed his mind about coming. Of course, something could've come up to detain him, she supposed.

She tried not to think any more about Daniel and forced her attention on the game of kickball several of the teenage boys were playing. Simon was among those involved, and he was laughing and running, trying to get control of that silly old ball. Several young girls sat on the sidelines, clapping and cheering the boys on. Rebekah supposed if she was much of a loyal sister, she'd be cheering Simon on, too. But somehow she couldn't seem to muster up the enthusiasm for it. If Daniel didn't show up a'tall, then she'd have made herself come for no purpose whatsoever, for he was the reason she'd agreed to come in the first place.

Rebekah slumped down in her wheelchair as her eyes drifted shut. She didn't have to try very hard in order to visualize Daniel's kind face. She could see those deep brown eyes gazing at her with such a look of love and devotion. It was a silly schoolgirl notion, but ever since her accident, dreaming the impossible had become a way of life for her. What harm was there in wishin' and dreamin' anyways? Why, if she thought hard enough, Rebekah could almost feel Daniel's warm breath on her upturned face.

"You aren't so bored that you've fallen asleep, I hope."

Rebekah's eyes snapped open, and she sat up with a start. Someone *had* been breathing on her!

Daniel stood directly in front of her, his head bent down so he was mere inches from her face.

Rebekah drew in a deep breath, trying to steady her unsettled nerves. "I was just restin' my eyes and doin' a little bit of daydreamin'," she murmured.

"Uh-huh. Well, since it's no longer daytime, I'd say you were doin' a little night-dreamin'. It's after eight o'clock, ya know," he said with a teasing grin.

She smiled up at him. "You've got me there, Daniel."

"I'm sorry I'm so late," he apologized. "I hope you didn't think I wasn't comin'."

She shrugged. "I wasn't too sure."

"I told ya I'd be here," he reminded.

"*Jah,* you did, but—"

"A promise is a promise, and I always try to keep my promises," he said with a nod. "Actually, I'm late because one of Pop's cows decided to give birth right before I left. She was havin' trouble, and my brothers had already gone, so that left only me to help out."

Rebekah smiled. She was sure his excuse was legitimate. She also knew he hadn't really promised he was gonna be here. He'd just said he planned to come. There was a big difference between promisin' and plannin'. Anyway, it didn't really matter now. He was here, and that's all she cared about.

"Have I missed much?" Daniel asked, squatting down on his haunches next to her chair.

She shook her head. "Not really. Just some games and a bit of singin'. We haven't had anything to eat yet, but some of the men started the bonfire, so we should be havin' the hot dog roast soon, I expect."

"Now that is good news," he said with a laugh. "Getting that calf born was a real job, and I'm a hungry man!"

Rebekah giggled. Daniel Beachy made her feel so lighthearted. In fact, she found a sense of peace and happiness just being here with him. *If only this feelin' could last,* she thought ruefully. *I need to prepare myself for the day when Daniel meets someone special, falls in love, and gets married. Then our friendship will be over for good.*

"Would ya like to go out by the fire?" Daniel asked, breaking into her thoughts. "Maybe if some of us wander out that way, the Yutzys will get the hint and set out the food."

Rebekah nodded. "You could be right. It's worth a try, anyway."

Daniel stood up. Lifting his elbows and flexing his broad shoulders, he stretched, then took hold of her wheelchair handles. He pushed her out the barn door and over to the bonfire.

The cool night air was chilly, and Rebekah suppressed a shiver.

"Are ya cold?" he asked with obvious concern. "We can move a bit closer to the fire, or I could get a quilt from my buggy."

She shook her head. "No, I'm fine. I think my shawl'll be enough." She pulled the heavy, woolen cloak a bit tighter around her shoulders.

"Have ya heard anything from the newlyweds?" he asked.

"Not firsthand, but I do know they'll be stayin' at my Aunt Crystal and Uncle Jonas's place tonight. I think they'll be at our home next Saturday," she replied.

"It was a *gut* weddin', wasn't it?" he remarked.

She nodded. *"Jah,* lots of food and plenty of merriment all day."

"Rebekah, there's somethin' I'd like to ask you," Daniel said in a serious tone.

She looked up at him expectantly. "Oh? What's that?"

"Well, I was wonderin'—"

Daniel's sentence was chopped right off when the group from the barn came laughing and hollering in their direction. Betty Yutzy, along with several other young women, was setting food on the nearby table, and someone yelled, "God is *gut,* and it's time to eat!"

Rebekah smiled at Daniel. "I guess this is what we've been waitin' for!"

"Jah, I guess," he responded with a look she thought might be one of disappointment. "Would ya like me to get you a hot dog and a stick for roastin'?"

"That'd be nice," she said gratefully. Her stomach was beginning to rumble, and she sure enough didn't want Daniel hearing it.

He disappeared into the crowd of clamoring young people but soon returned with two hot dogs and sticks for both of them. "Would ya like me to roast yours?" he asked Rebekah.

"Roasting a hot dog is one of the few things I can manage to do for myself." Rebekah's words sounded harsh, even to her own ears, and she felt awful about it. *"Es dutt mir leed*—I am sorry—Daniel. I didn't mean to sound ungrateful."

He smiled and handed her one stick and a hot dog. "It's all right; I understand."

Rebekah felt sure that he didn't understand. How could he? No one really understood what it felt like to be so helpless and dependent on others all the time. Whenever there was some simple task she could perform alone, Rebekah always felt so self-respecting.

Daniel moved the wheelchair a bit closer to the fire, so she could reach her stick into the sizzling coals. Besides the hot dogs and buns, there was also potato salad, coleslaw, potato chips, sweet pickles, baked beans, chocolate cake, and of course, plenty of marshmallows for roasting. They had a choice of either hot chocolate or apple cider to drink. Rebekah chose the hot chocolate and was thoroughly enjoying her meal when Simon sauntered up.

"Rebekah, I need to talk to you," he whispered.

"What? I can hardly hear you, Simon."

"I said, I need to talk to you," he hollered.

"*Wass wit du?*—what do you want?" she asked.

"I've asked Karen Sharp if I can give her a ride home in my buggy," he said, leaning closer to Rebekah's ear this time.

"That was nice of you," Rebekah replied with a nod. "I'm sure we can make room for her in the buggy."

Simon shook his head. "I don't think ya understand. I want to take her home—alone. I was wonderin' if you might be able to find another ride."

His words and the implication of their meaning finally registered in Rebekah's brain. "Well, I. . .that is. . . ," she stammered.

"I can give Rebekah a ride home," Daniel quickly put in.

"*Danki,* I'd sure appreciate that," Simon said with a grin. He walked away quickly, before Rebekah could say anything more.

Her heart sunk. Little brother was growing up—about to begin his own courtin' days. It wouldn't be fair to hold him back. It wasn't right to hold Daniel back, either. She studied him as he sat perched on a log, wondering how he must be feeling about now. "You're not obligated to see that I get home, Daniel. If you'd planned to ask someone else, then—"

Daniel held up one hand as he swiveled around to face her square on. "It wasn't just a favor to your brother, Rebekah. I was plannin' to ask if I could take you home tonight, anyways."

Rebekah blinked. "You were?"

"*Jah,* I was." He smiled so sweetly, she thought her heart might burst. "So how about it? Will you accept a ride home in my courtin' buggy tonight?"

Rebekah gulped. She probably should say no, but her heart was speaking now, not her head. Giving no more thought to the matter, she murmured, "*Jah,* Daniel, I would like a ride home in your buggy."

Chapter 15

D er Gaul is gross—your horse is big!" Rebekah exclaimed, once she and Daniel were settled inside his open buggy.

Daniel chuckled. "Jah, Toby's a good-sized one, all right. He handles well, though."

"Your buggy's right nice, too," Rebekah noted.

"I was pretty excited 'bout gettin' it when I turned sixteen," Daniel said enthusiastically. "I've had this buggy over four years now, and I think it still looks gut."

"I can see that you take great care with it," she said, letting her hand travel over the black leather seat.

Daniel answered with a smile and a nod, as he took up the reins and moved the horse forward.

They rode in silence awhile, with the only sounds being the steady clip-clop of the horse's hooves against the pavement and an occasional contented nicker from old Toby.

Rebekah felt such joy being in Daniel's courtin' buggy on such a beautiful, star-studded night. It's almost like a real date, she thought wistfully. But she reminded herself that it was merely one friend giving another friend a ride home from the singin'. There was no meaning attached, and she didn't even dare to hope that there was.

"Do you ever drive?"

Daniel's sudden question jerked her thoughts aside. "Papa taught me well, but he never allows me to take the horse and buggy out alone," she answered with a slight frown. "He says it would be takin' too much of a chance, 'cause something unexpected might occur."

Daniel nodded. "Jah, things have been known to happen, all right. Why, just the other day a buggy was run off the road by a bunch of rowdy teenagers, speedin' down Highway 6 in their fancy sports car." He shook his head slowly. "Some of them English boys don't seem to care 'bout our slow-movin' buggies a'tall."

"It does seem that way," Rebekah agreed.

"We need to be especially careful when we're out at night," he continued. "Even with our battery-operated lights and reflective tape, cars don't always see us so clearly."

"I remember once, my aunt Mim got caught in a storm. A car nearly hit her, and when she lost control of the buggy, it turned over on its side."

"I guess those two stories are reason enough for your papa not to let you drive alone," Daniel said with conviction. "None of us would want anything to happen to you, Rebekah."

Her heart did a flip-flop at Daniel's thoughtful words. Did "none of us" include him? Was he tryin' to tell her that he'd care if something bad happened to her? She shoved the thought aside, sternly reminding herself that Daniel was only a friend.

The ride to Rebekah's house was over much too soon. She was havin' such a *gut* time and wished it could just go on forever and ever.

When they pulled into the driveway, Daniel went around to get Rebekah's wheelchair from the back of the buggy. Then he lifted her down with ease and placed her in the chair as though she weighed no more than a child.

Her heart thumped like a rabbit's foot as his strong arms went around her waist and lowered her into the chair. She wondered if she could even find her voice in order to thank him properly. "I. . .I really appreciate the ride," she mumbled, refusing to look up at his face.

"It was my pleasure." Daniel offered her a warm smile before grabbing the handles and pushing the wheelchair up the path leading to her front porch. When they arrived at the wooden ramp, he moved to the front of her chair and bent over, so his face was mere inches from hers. The full moon sent a shaft of light shimmering down from the starry sky, and his deep mahogany eyes seemed to dance in the glow of it. "Rebekah, I was wonderin' if I might come a-callin' on you one night soon," he announced.

Daniel's words hammered in Rebekah's head, nearly giving her a headache. Was he askin' if he could court her? Oh, surely not. He must mean—

"Rebekah, did ya hear me?" Daniel asked, breaking into her thoughts.

Rebekah's chin quivered. "What are you sayin', Daniel?"

"We have so much in common, what with our love for flowers and all, and I want to court ya," he asserted.

The rhythm of Rebekah's heartbeat picked up again. She hadn't misunderstood after all. He really did want to court her. "Daniel, I'm honored that you'd ask me such a thing, but I—"

"You don't care for me?" he interrupted with a frown.

Rebekah shook her head, feeling the sting of hot tears at the backs of her eyes. "No, that isn't the problem. I. . .well, aren't you in love with Mary Ellen?" she blurted out without even thinking.

"Mary Ellen?" he sputtered. "Mary Ellen's a married woman, for goodness' sake!"

Rebekah gritted her teeth. What was wrong with Daniel anyways? Did he think she was a *Verhuddelt Meedel*—mixed-up girl? "I know my cousin's married," she fumed, "but before she and Johnny started courtin', it seemed as though you were quite smitten with her."

Daniel squatted down in front of Rebekah. "Now, why would ya go thinkin' somethin' like that? What have I ever done to make you believe such a thing?"

"Well, you were always hangin' around her, and—"

Daniel leaned his head back and laughed. "And you didn't know why?"

Rebekah sure didn't see what was so funny. She was feelin' *Verhuddelt* now. "I thought you, like so many other fellas, had your eye on my cute, outgoin' cousin."

"The only thing my eyes have ever wanted to look at is you, Rebekah Stoltzfus. I hung around Mary Ellen because you were usually with her. I wanted to be near you, but I never had the courage to say so before."

Rebekah swallowed against the unwanted lump in her throat. Tears began rolling down her cheeks. "Oh, Daniel, I'm so flattered by your words, but I can't agree to let you court me."

"Why not?" Daniel's poker face showed his obvious surprise by her response. "I think I've made it rather clear that I'm not in love with Mary Ellen, so there shouldn't be a thing wrong with us courtin'."

Rebekah's eyelids fluttered. "That isn't the problem, Daniel."

"What is the problem then?"

"Courtin' for us would be pointless," she stated flatly.

"Pointless?" he repeated. "What could be pointless 'bout two people who enjoy each other's company agreein' to court?"

Rebekah drew in a deep breath and reached up to wipe away another set of tears. "For most couples, courtin' often leads to a more permanent commitment."

"What's wrong with that? Love and marriage go well together, you know," he said with an impish smile.

Rebekah smiled, too, in spite of her tears. Daniel Beachy was everything a woman could want. He was all she wanted; that was for sure. Any normal girl would never have considered turning down his offer, either. However, that was the problem. Rebekah was not any normal girl. She was crippled and always would be. Her handicap didn't make her a good candidate as a wife. There were so many things she couldn't do. And children—she wanted *kinder* so badly. Daniel probably did, too. It was highly unlikely that she'd ever conceive. Even if by some miracle she could, how would a mother in a wheelchair, or walkin' stiff-legged with cumbersome crutches, ever care for a baby?

The very thing Rebekah wanted most—the love of a man—particularly this man, was being offered to her right now. As much as it hurt, she'd have to turn it down. She gazed into Daniel's beautiful brown eyes and blinked rapidly. "I'm a cripple, and I'll always be one. Our relationship could never go any further than just the fun of courtin'. As much as it pains me to say this, my answer has to be no. *Gut Nacht*, Daniel."

❧

It had been two weeks since Daniel asked to court Rebekah, but the pain she still felt made it seem like only yesterday. She dreaded facing him at preachin' today. There was no way she could get out of going, either, because it was to be held in their very own home.

"Oh, you're up," Mom said as Rebekah rolled into the kitchen. "We must hurry and get breakfast on if we're to be ready in time."

Rebekah glanced out the kitchen window. "It's startin' to snow. Maybe no one will come," she said hopefully.

Mom smiled. "It's not comin' down very hard. Besides, a little bit of snow won't keep any of our people from worshippin' God."

Rebekah sighed. "I suppose you're right." She wheeled away from the window. "What can I do to help?"

"You can set the table and cut the breakfast pie," Mom replied. "I'll have Nadine get out some cereal and milk when she comes in from collectin' eggs."

As if on cue, Nadine opened the back door and hustled into the kitchen. Her cheeks were pink from the cold, and she stamped snow off her feet. "Brr. . .it's mighty cold out there. I think winter's definitely on the way!"

Winter, Rebekah thought gloomily, *with its drab, gray days, and bitter chillin' winds. It always makes me feel sad. Oh, if only. . .*

"Rebekah, are you goin' to the singin' at the Rabers' tonight? Will your boyfriend be bringin' you home again?" Nadine asked, breaking into Rebekah's musings.

Rebekah nearly dropped the plate she was about to place on the table. "My what?"

"You heard me," Nadine said with a grin. "You might think it's a big secret, but we all know Daniel Beachy gave you a ride home in his courtin' buggy two Sundays ago. I think he's kinda sweet on you, Sister."

Rebekah's cheeks flamed. She hadn't said one single word to anyone in the family about Daniel bringing her home, much less mentioned his offer to court her. "You don't even know what you're talkin' about, Nadine!" she blustered. "Furthermore, you shouldn't go around spyin'!"

"I wasn't," Nadine retorted. "I just happened to be lookin' out my bedroom window when Daniel's buggy pulled into the yard. I saw him lift you down all cozylike." She giggled. "Why, I'll bet he even planted a big kiss right on your lips. Ain't it so, Sister?"

"He did no such thing!" Rebekah shouted. "How dare you even insinuate somethin' like that!"

"Girls, girls, this little discussion has gone on long enough," Mom admonished. "It's none of our business who brought Rebekah home from the singin'. When the time comes for her to make an announcement about any relationship she and Daniel might have, then she'll make it."

Rebekah's eyes filled with tears. "There'll never be a relationship between me and Daniel. Now, can we just get on with breakfast?"

Mom gave Rebekah a sympathetic look. *"Jah,* breakfast is on the way."

❧

At eight o'clock sharp the worship service began. Prior to the meeting, the large hinged doors that separated the living room from the rest of the house were flung open wide. The furniture was replaced with the traditional backless benches used in all Amish worship services.

The women and girls sat on one side, and the men and boys on the other. Out of the corner of her eye, Rebekah saw Daniel sitting on the end of a bench beside his brother, Abner. She looked away quickly when he turned and nodded in her direction. There was no point in giving him reason to believe she might have changed her mind.

The three-hour service seemed to take longer than usual, and Rebekah kept fidgeting in her wheelchair, wishing she could be anyplace else but here. In spite of the fact that the padded seat of her steel chair was a lot more comfortable than the hard, wooden benches, she was still getting mighty tired of sitting and thinking about Daniel Beachy. It was with great relief when she was finally able to wheel out of the room and into the kitchen to help with the noon meal.

Since it was too cold to eat outdoors, several tables were set up throughout the house. A tasty lunch of homemade brown bread, bologna, Swiss cheese, sour pickles, red beets, canned peaches, and deviled eggs was served to all the guests. For dessert, there was apple and shoofly pie, topped with plenty of fresh whipping cream. Lots of hot coffee and cold milk were set out in large pitchers, and everyone sat down to the tasty meal that had been furnished by Sarah Stoltzfus and her two daughters.

The men and boys were attended to first, and Rebekah made certain that the group she served were the ones farthest away from the table where Daniel, his father, and two brothers sat. Nadine had been assigned their table, and for that Rebekah was right grateful.

When the men were finished eating, they all went outside. Finally, the women and girls sat down to their meal. It was during lunch that Rebekah was able to visit with Mary Ellen for the first time since the wedding.

"How's it goin' with bein' a full-time wife and not teachin' school anymore?" she asked.

Mary Ellen shrugged. "I'm gettin' used to it now. Besides, Sarah Jane Beachy's doin' a fine job of fillin' my shoes, I hear tell."

"Marriage must agree with you," Rebekah whispered. "You look *wunderbaar gut.*"

"*Jah,* I never thought I could be so happy," Mary Ellen replied with a faint blush. "Being married to someone you love is *wunderbaar.*"

Rebekah didn't know quite how to respond. She wanted to express happiness for her friend. She would have liked to say that she, too, was in love and hoped to be married. However, she could say neither. She was jealous of Mary Ellen's happiness and knew she'd never marry or find the kind of pleasure Mary Ellen and Johnny obviously enjoyed.

"I hear you and Daniel Beachy have begun courtin,' " Mary Ellen said with a silly grin.

Rebekah's mouth fell open. "Where'd ya hear such a thing?"

Mary Ellen shrugged. "Someone who attended the last singin' said Daniel took you home." She poked Rebekah in the ribs and giggled. "I always did think he had an interest in you."

Rebekah frowned. "So he says."

"Then you've agreed to begin courtin'?"

"I told him no."

"You what?" Mary Ellen's wide-open eyes revealed her obvious surprise. "Oh, Rebekah, why? Don't you care for Daniel a'tall?"

Rebekah nodded. "I care very much for him."

"Then why won't you let him court you?"

"You, of all people, should know the answer to that, Mary Ellen. You've been my friend a long time, and I've shared so many things with you."

Mary Ellen patted Rebekah's hand. "It's about your handicap, right?"

Rebekah nodded, her eyes filling with familiar tears. "I care for Daniel, but if we start courtin', Daniel might want marriage—and later, children. I can't give him those things, and you know it."

"I know of no such thing, Rebekah, and neither do you." Mary Ellen shook her finger. "If you'll just trust God and give yourself half a chance—"

"A chance to do what?" Rebekah snapped. "I'm not a complete woman. I could never make Daniel happy."

"Don't say that," Mary Ellen admonished.

"Don't say what?" Nadine asked when she joined the young women at their end of the table.

Rebekah's head snapped up. "Nothin'. It was nothin' important a'tall."

"I think you two must have been talkin' about boys. Everyone always closes up like a star tulip whenever I come along. Mom especially does that. She thinks I'm way too young to be thinkin' about boys." She clucked her tongue. "It's just because I'm the *buppli* of the family, that's all!"

Rebekah shook her head, but Mary Ellen patted Nadine's arm. "Just hold on a bit longer, sweet girl. Your time's a-comin'. Soon you'll end up like me—an old married woman."

Nadine giggled and reached for a glass of milk. "You ain't old, Mary Ellen, but you're sure pretty. No wonder Johnny Yoder wanted to marry you." She glanced over at Rebekah. "My sister has a boyfriend, too, only she won't fess up to it."

Rebekah slammed her empty coffee cup down with such force that she thought it might be broken. When she realized it wasn't, she gave it a little shove, then pushed her wheelchair away from the table. "I'm goin' outside for some fresh air! I've had enough talk about boyfriends, love, and marriage!"

Chapter 16

Rebekah sat on the front porch, breathing in the crisp, cool, late afternoon air. The sun peeked out between fluffy white clouds, casting a golden tint on the gently rolling hills. There was a light dusting of powdery snow on the trees, but it had melted nearly everywhere else.

A group of boys played tug-of-war in the driveway, and a few men stood on the lawn visiting. *The rest of the* Mannsleit *must be out in the barn*, Rebekah decided. She was glad Daniel wasn't among those who were still outside, for sure as anything she didn't want to face him today.

She released the brake on her wheelchair and rolled slowly down the wooden ramp. Up the path leading to her greenhouse she went, so in need of solitude. A time to think and enjoy all the plants might help get her mind off love—and Daniel Beachy.

As soon as Rebekah entered the greenhouse, she lit a gas lantern for more light. It was cold as all outdoors, too, so she added a few logs to the burning embers inside the woodstove, thankful that Papa had placed them within easy reach.

Once the fire was going well, Rebekah moved into the glassed-in section of her greenhouse. Between the kerosene heater and the solar panels, this area was always plenty warm. She rolled her wheelchair up and down the aisles, drinking in the rich colors and fragrant smells coming from the variety of plants.

"If this is the only miracle You ever give me, then I'll learn to be content," Rebekah whispered in prayer. Even as she said the words, a feeling of emptiness settled over her soul. Was the greenhouse really enough? Could she learn to be content?

She reached for a lacy-edged, pink African violet and held the pot as though it were a baby. She thought about Aunt Grace, who'd be holdin' a real *buppli* in just a few months; and about Mary Ellen, recently married. Unlike her aunt or cousin, Rebekah's fingers might often caress a delicate plant but never a husband's bearded face. Like as not, her hands would change potting soil not dirty *Vindels*. As much as she enjoyed workin' with plants, they just weren't the same as a living, breathing human being, who could love in return.

Rebekah heard the front door of the greenhouse creak open, then snap shut. "Who's there?" she called out.

"It's me, Rebekah—Aunt Mim."

Rebekah expelled the breath she unknowingly had been holding. She was sure relieved it wasn't Daniel. She didn't think she could deal with facing him alone.

"I'm back here, Aunt Mim!" she hollered.

Mim poked her head through the doorway and smiled. "I haven't been in here since your opening day. I see you've made a few changes."

Rebekah nodded. *Jah,* I'm sellin' a few more items now, too. Daniel Beachy gave me plenty of *gut* ideas, and all the wooden items you see are his handmade creations."

"So, your business is doing well then?"

"Better than I ever expected." Rebekah placed the African violet back on the shelf. "Of course, winter's almost here, and I won't have nearly as many customers now."

"No, I suppose not," her aunt agreed. "But then, a young woman can certainly find other ways to fill the long winter hours."

Rebekah shrugged. "I s'pose I can always quilt or do some other type of handwork."

Aunt Mim gave her a wide smile and moved closer to the wheelchair. "It wasn't sewin' I had in mind, Rebekah."

"What did ya have in mind for someone like me?" Rebekah asked with a catch in her voice.

Mim pulled out a wooden stool and sat down beside her. "I was thinkin' more about courtin'. I hear tell you have a right fine suitor these days."

"Mary Ellen Hilty—I mean, Yoder!" Rebekah exploded. *"Du sin glene Bapel Meiler*—you are a blabbermouth!"

"Don't be so hard on Mary Ellen," Mim said softly. "She only cares about your happiness."

Jah, well, she can care without meddlin'. I suppose she saw me come here and asked you to talk with me."

Aunt Mim shook her head. "She shared her concerns, but it was my idea to speak with you." She placed a gentle hand on Rebekah's arm. "I believe I can help. I think you should hear my story."

"Your story?" Rebekah asked. "You used to read me stories when I was a *kinder.* Why do you think I need to hear one now?"

"Because, sweet niece, I think my story might teach you somethin' about love and faith."

Rebekah leaned her head against the back of her wheelchair and closed her eyes. "All right then, I'm ready to hear your story."

"Once there was a young woman named Miriam Stoltzfus. She fell in love with her childhood sweetheart, and he broke her heart when he moved away and married someone else. Miriam became bitter and angry. She didn't trust men a'tall and resolved never to marry. Miriam even blamed God for all her troubles. Her pupils at the one-room schoolhouse often talked behind her back, sayin' she had a heart of stone."

Rebekah nodded. She remembered hearing such talk.

"And so," Mim continued, "the bitter old-maid schoolteacher decided she could do everything in her own strength. She even forgot how to pray.

215

"One day there was a storm, and she dismissed the *kinder* to go home early. She told her six-year-old niece that she'd give her a ride home. A few minutes later, she heard a clap of thunder, then an awful, ear-piercin' sound, as the limb of a tree split right in two. Teacher Mim rushed outside, only to find her favorite niece lyin' on the ground."

Mim paused a moment, as though it pained her to relive the past. After inhaling a deep breath, she finally continued. "The doctor said Rebekah's spinal cord had been injured and that she'd probably never walk again. Miriam's heart was broken to bits, and she blamed herself somethin' awful for that tragic accident."

Rebekah's eyelids flew open. "You blamed yourself? I never knew that."

Mim nodded, her eyes filling with tears. "I'm the one who asked you to wait outside, and I felt responsible."

"I never faulted you for any of it, Aunt Mim," Rebekah said, her own eyes swimming with tears.

Aunt Mim leaned over and patted Rebekah's arm. "I know you didn't. You were always so happy and acceptin' of your limitations. However, as you grew, I saw a change come on. You began to withdraw and seemed kinda unsure of yourself. When you opened this new business, I thought things might be different. I was hopin' you'd see now that your handicap couldn't keep you from reaching your goals. I prayed God would send the right man into your life, too, so you'd find the kind of happiness you honestly deserve."

Rebekah shook her head slowly. "I couldn't put the burden of my handicap upon Daniel, Aunt Mim. It just wouldn't be fair."

Mim's forehead wrinkled. "I think we'd better get back to my story."

Rebekah shrugged, but this time she kept her eyes wide open. "All right then, I'm all ears."

"Well, Miriam Stoltzfus almost made a huge mistake. She met an English man, and he nearly talked her into leavin' the Amish faith."

Rebekah's mouth fell open. "An English man? You almost left the faith?"

Aunt Mim nodded. "Do you remember when a reporter came into your hospital room shortly after the accident?"

"The picture man?"

Jah, he took your picture and put it in the English newspaper."

Rebekah squinted her eyes. "What did you do?"

"I got plenty angry and told him off but good." Mim grimaced as she shook her head slowly. "I knew I could never give up the Amish religion, although I still wasn't right with God."

"So, what did you do then?" Rebekah prompted.

"I made the wisest decision of my life. I married Amos Hilty." Aunt Mim crinkled her nose a bit. "I turned him down at first, though."

"Why? Didn't you care for him?" Rebekah could hardly imagine such a thing. Aunt Mim and Uncle Amos seemed so *Asu Liebe*—with love.

Her aunt shrugged. "I didn't give myself a chance to find out whether I cared or not. I was so certain sure that Amos would let me down, too. I didn't think I could trust God to bring happiness into such an empty, bitter life as mine."

"But you did marry Uncle Amos, and you seem to be very happy," Rebekah reminded.

Aunt Mim's eyes filled with fresh tears, and she sniffed deeply. *Jah,* I'm happy. You see, one day God showed me somethin' mighty important."

"What was it, Aunt Mim?"

"He let me know that my bitterness and self-blamin' for so many things was of my own doing. He showed me that I could get rid of my doubts and hurts from the past. He can do that for you, too, Rebekah. God wants you to be happy, and if you'll only trust Him, He'll work a true miracle in your life."

A miracle. Wasn't that exactly what Rebekah had been looking for—an honest-to-goodness, true miracle from God? But could she take a leap of faith toward love and possibly marriage? She wanted to—more than anything—but she was so afraid of failing.

"Well, *Ich glauh Ich besser uff heere*—I think I'd better stop. Stories from my past are *gut,* but Rebekah, you'll never know what God can do until you give Him the chance. If Daniel loves you, then he'll be more than willin' to accept you—imperfections and all," Aunt Mim asserted.

Rebekah blinked back another set of tears. "I'll try to take the step of faith, Aunt Mim. Will you pray that I'll have the strength to do it?"

Mim nodded. "I'll be prayin', girl. *Da Herr sei mit du*—the Lord be with you."

Rebekah's wheelchair rattled down the path toward the barn. She could only hope Daniel and his family hadn't left for home yet. If she could just have the chance to speak with him alone for a few minutes, it might be that they could talk things out. If he hadn't changed his mind about them, maybe she'd allow him to come a-callin' after all.

When she reached the barn, Rebekah pushed open the side door and peered inside. There were several clusters of men and boys, talking and playing games. She didn't see any sign of Daniel or his family, though.

Papa spotted her and came over to the door. "What's up, Rebekah? Did ya need somethin'?"

She shook her head. "No, I was lookin' for Daniel Beachy, that's all."

"The Beachys left awhile ago," he said.

Rebekah frowned. "Well, do you know where Simon is, then?"

"I think he's outside. He and some other boys were gonna get a game of corner-ball goin'."

Rebekah wheeled back out into the chilly air. She knew what she had to do, but she'd better do it quicklike, before she lost her nerve.

Papa had been right. Simon was outside playing ball. Rebekah sat on the side-lines until Simon finally looked her way. She motioned for him to come on over.

He scowled at her but ambled over anyway. "What do ya want, and why are you sittin' out here in the cold? Don't ya know it might start snowin' again?" he snapped. "If you could run around like me and stay warm, that'd be one thing; but if you sit there in your wheelchair for very long, you'll likely catch your death of cold."

"I need your help," Rebekah said, ignoring his chastisement, and desperately clinging to Simon's arm.

He jerked it away impatiently. "What for?"

"Could you please hitch up our horse to the buggy and help me get inside?"

"Inside the buggy?" he asked with raised eyebrows.

Her head bobbed up and down. "Of course, inside the buggy. What else would I be talkin' about?"

"Where are you goin', and who's goin' with ya?" he asked suspiciously.

"It's none of your business," she replied evenly. "I just need to go, that's all."

Simon's jaw dropped. "I hope you're just jokin', Sister."

"No, I'm totally serious, Simon. I need to go someplace, and I know Papa won't allow me to head out alone, so I'm askin' for your help."

"You want me to go with ya?" Simon asked with a befuddled frown.

"No, I need to do this alone. I just want you to get the buggy ready and help me inside," she reaffirmed.

"Oh, sure, so I can be the one Papa punishes!" Simon exclaimed. "You know I'd be in awful big trouble if he finds out that I helped you do such a stupid thing."

"Then we'll have to be sure he don't find out," she said forcefully.

Simon shrugged and turned his palms up. "All right, then, but you'll owe me big for this one."

Chapter 17

Any other time, Rebekah might have been right nervous about driving the buggy all alone. But at this moment, she was plumb too excited about the prospect of seeing Daniel and telling him she'd changed her mind about them courtin'. Papa had taught her well about handling the horse, and just because she had no one with her didn't mean she should be afraid of a little old buggy ride.

The Beachy farm was about four miles away, and it wouldn't take too long to get there. However, one thing Rebekah hadn't counted on was bad weather. She'd only gone about a mile when it started to snow hard. The road was already turning slippery in spots, making it difficult to maintain control.

Rebekah gripped the reins tightly and talked soothingly to the horse. She had to remain calm and stay focused on the road ahead, or she could end up in mighty big trouble. She snapped on the switch for the battery-operated windshield wipers and did the same with the one for the lights. With icy snow pelting her windshield, she had to be sure she could see well enough, not to mention alerting any oncoming cars that her buggy was on the road.

Rebekah might not have been scared when she started this little trip, but she sure enough was feeling nervous now! What if she lost control, and her horse and buggy skidded off the road and into a ditch? The buggy could even overturn and end up on its side. *Who would help me then?*

Rebekah drew in a deep breath, hoping to steady her nerves; then she did what she should have done at the start of her ride. She prayed. Prayed for all she was worth. "Dear heavenly Father, I know I was wrong for takin' the horse and buggy out all alone. I probably don't even deserve Your help, but I'd sure be obliged if You'd get me to the Beachys' safely. When I get back home, I'll tell Mom and Papa what I've done and will accept responsibility for my reckless actions."

Rebekah was just about to the cross street leading to the road where the Beachy farm was located when she saw another Amish buggy. It was turned precariously on its side, just off the road a bit. The windows were all steamed up, and she couldn't see inside at all. Something deep inside her just didn't feel right about this whole thing. With her heart pounding and hands so sweaty she could hardly hold the reins, she pulled up next to the wreck. "Is anyone there? Are you hurt?" she shouted into the wind.

"We're okay, but the door's jammed," a man called out. When she realized it was the voice of Daniel Beachy, her heart slammed against her chest. Then it seemed as if it stopped beating altogether.

"Daniel, it's Rebekah. What happened here?" she screamed.

"We hit a patch of ice," he hollered. "Our horse broke free and bolted. My whole family's trapped inside this buggy!"

"*Ach,* my! What can I do to help?" She lifted a trembling hand to still her racing heart.

"Is Andrew with you?" It was Clarence Beachy speaking now, and he sounded almost as desperate as his son.

"No, I'm all alone," Rebekah replied in a shaky voice.

"Rebekah Stoltzfus, *was in der welt*—what in the world—are you doin' out by yourself in this horrible weather?" Daniel scolded.

"I was headin' for your place. I needed to speak with you, Daniel."

"Could ya possibly go for help?" This question came from Daniel's mother, Frieda, whose high-pitched voice gave clear indication as to her agitated state.

"*Jah,* I'll turn around and head back home right away," Rebekah answered.

"Be careful now, Rebekah!" Daniel called. "I'll be prayin' for ya."

"I'll be praying for you, too," Rebekah said, choking back a sob that seemed to be caught in her throat. Turning her buggy carefully around, she started back down the road. "Please, God," she prayed fervently, "I need You to guide me safely home. The Beachys are in real trouble, and I seem to be their only source of help right now."

The snow was falling harder now, a chilling wind was swirling in a frenzy, and the light of day was quickly fading. With great difficulty and a will of sheer determination, Rebekah managed to keep the horse and buggy on the road. "Steady, boy," she coaxed. "Together we can do this. We have the Lord on our side." A verse from the Book of Nahum popped into her mind. "The Lord is good, a strong hold in the day of trouble; and he knoweth them that trust in him."

A sense of peace settled over her, like a mantle of calm, and she knew instinctively that everything was going to be all right.

A short time later Rebekah pulled up in front of her own house. "Papa! Papa, come *schnell!*" she yelled into the night air.

Papa opened the front door and stepped onto the porch. Mom followed, along with several others who were still at the house. "Rebekah, what on earth are you doin' in that buggy?" Papa bellowed.

"I don't have time to explain things right now," she cried. "The Beachy buggy overturned not far from their house, and they're all trapped inside. Your help is needed right away!"

Papa wasted no time in grabbing his wool jacket. He called to Simon, "Get some rope from the barn!" Then he jumped into the buggy, pushing Rebekah into the passenger's seat. "You really should get into the house where it's warmer," he said with a stern look on his rugged face.

She shook her head determinedly. "No, Papa. I want to go along. I need to see with my own eyes that Daniel and his family are okay."

"All right then, but we'll be talkin' about this shenanigan of yours when we return home," he admonished with a deep frown.

Rebekah didn't argue. She knew Papa was right. It was a shenanigan she'd pulled, and they needed to talk, even if she was in for a strong tongue-lashing.

Simon came running out of the barn and jumped quickly into the backseat of the buggy. Uncle Amos and young Henry climbed into their buggy, too. "We'll go along to help," Uncle Amos called to Papa.

Papa nodded and moved the horse forward.

"Be careful now!" Mom called from the front porch. Aunt Mim was there, too, and when Rebekah looked back, she saw them both wave.

Rebekah's cheeks were flushed, and her hands were shaking so badly she had to stuff them into her apron pocket just to keep them still. "They're gonna be all right, aren't they, Papa?" she asked breathlessly.

With eyes straight ahead, Papa merely shrugged. "Did they say if any of 'em was hurt?"

"Daniel said they weren't," she responded. "But it's so cold, Papa, and what if a car comes along and doesn't see them there? They might be hit, and then—"

"Now don't you go borrowin' trouble, Daughter," Papa said calmly. "If ya want to make yourself useful, then you'd better start prayin'."

"I've been praying," Rebekah acknowledged. "I won't let up 'til everyone's safely out of that buggy neither."

They traveled in silence until they came upon the accident a short time later. "There it is! I see the buggy off to the left!" Simon shouted.

"I see it, too," Papa declared. He pulled his buggy as far off the road as possible, and Uncle Amos did the same. "Get out and set up some flares, Simon!" Papa called. "They're in my toolbox directly behind your seat."

Simon did as he was told, and Papa climbed down, reaching for the rope Simon had put into the buggy. He handed the reins over to Rebekah. "Hold that horse steady while I get the rope tied around the Beachy buggy."

Rebekah's hands were still trembling, and her heart pounded so hard she thought it might explode any minute. For some reason, she hadn't felt this nervous when she was driving the buggy alone. "Please let them be all right," she prayed softly.

Rebekah strained to see out the front window. Papa, Uncle Amos, and Henry were tying the rope to the back of the overturned buggy. When it was secured, Papa climbed back inside, while Simon joined the other men to help stand the Beachy carriage upright. Uncle Amos, Henry, and Simon put their full weight against the buggy as Papa backed up and pulled on the rope until it was taut. It took several tries, because the slippery road made things more difficult, but the buggy finally righted itself and was soon standing as it should be. The men quickly undid the rope, then tied it to the front of the other buggy.

Papa drove around until he was in front of the Beachy buggy; then the rope was tied to the back of the Stoltzfus buggy. In this manner, he towed Clarence and his family safely to their farm.

When they arrived, Papa halted the horse with a "Whoa now, boy!" Uncle Amos, who'd been following, also stopped. Everyone got out, except for Rebekah. She seemed to have been completely forgotten.

"Your door is stuck!" Papa called to the Beachys, when he pulled on it and nothing happened. "Are ya all okay?"

"We're fine," Clarence Beachy responded. "We'll push on this side of the door, and you can pull. If it still won't open, then you might want to look for a crowbar in my barn, so's you can pry it open."

Inside the buggy, Clarence and his three sons pushed, and outside, Papa, Uncle Amos, and their two boys pulled. It took two tries, but the door finally flew open, nearly spilling the Beachy men onto the snow-covered ground.

"We're free!" cried sixteen-year-old Harold Beachy as he clapped his hands.

"Danki!" Clarence said, pounding Papa on the back.

Papa nodded solemnly. "We're just glad everyone's all right." He glanced over at his own buggy then. "Actually, it's Rebekah who deserves the biggest thanks, for she's the one who found you and drove home to give us the news."

Everyone turned toward the Stoltzfus buggy. Rebekah was still sitting inside, listening, watching the scene unfold, and wishing like everything that someone would come help her down.

Chapter 18

Daniel raced around to Rebekah's side of the buggy and flung open the door. "Rebekah Stoltzfus, I should be furious with you for drivin' the buggy by yourself—and on a snowy day like this, no less," he barked. Lifting Rebekah into his arms, he held her close. "You're an angel of mercy, and even though you do deserve a good spanking, I sure have to thank ya for bein' so reckless."

Daniel gave her cheek a quick peck, and she let out a long sigh. "Oh, Daniel, I only did what I had to do."

"You might have saved our lives," he said in a voice raw with emotion. "Who knows what could have happened if some car had come along and hit us?"

Rebekah nodded soberly. "I was drivin' over to tell you that if you still want to court me, I'm willin'."

Daniel's face broke into a full-fledged smile. "Of course I still want to," he said with assurance. "I just can't believe you changed your mind. What happened?"

Rebekah was about to reply, but Daniel's mother, Frieda, stepped up beside them. "It's mighty cold out. Won't ya come inside, Rebekah? Maybe have a cup of hot chocolate or some coffee before you start for home? Your *daed* and the other menfolk have already gone to the house."

Rebekah was still being held securely by Daniel, and she couldn't help feeling rather flustered. What must Frieda Beachy think of her all cuddled up in her son's arms thataway? "I think I will join 'em," she said to Frieda. Looking up at Daniel, she added, "I'm probably gettin' kind of heavy anyways."

"To me, you're light as a feather," Daniel said with a grin. "However, I do wanna get you in out of this cold."

Rebekah let her head fall against Daniel's strong shoulder as she drank in the sweet nearness of him. He carried her across the yard as easily as one might transport a kitten. Up the steps he tromped, and into the house the two of them went.

Already gathered around the kitchen table were Daniel's father and his two brothers, along with Uncle Amos, Cousin Henry, Papa, and Simon. Frieda made hot water for coffee and cocoa, and Daniel's sister, Sarah Jane, got busy slicing huge pieces of spicy gingerbread for the hungry crew.

Daniel placed Rebekah in one of the empty chairs, then pulled the one next to it out for himself.

"Well, Rebekah Stoltzfus, you're the heroine of the day!" Clarence Beachy announced. "We're mighty thankful God sent you along to find our overturned buggy, that's for sure."

"My daughter took the horse and buggy out all alone—without my permission," Papa was quick to say. He gave Rebekah a frown and accentuated it with raised eyebrows. "Be that as it may," he continued, "I think she's learned somethin' kinda important today."

Rebekah averted her eyes from his gaze and studied the dark blue tablecloth instead. She was pretty sure one of Papa's stern lectures was forthcoming.

"Rebekah was able to do somethin' meaningful today, and it was all on her own, too, I might add," Papa said, puffing out his chest just a bit. "While it may have been rather foolish, it was also a brave thing to do. I don't have the foggiest notion why she took the buggy out, but I'm sure grateful that she was able to bring help to all of you."

"Jah, and we truly thank you, Rebekah," Frieda said as she handed her a cup of steaming hot chocolate.

Rebekah felt the heat of a blush coming on. She wasn't used to being the center of attention—at least not this way. The recognition she usually got was because she was an *eledich* cripple. It felt awful good to be praised for a capability and not her disability.

"I must say, I was gettin' pretty scared when the snow started comin' down hard, and then the road became all slicklike," Rebekah admitted. "I know I shouldn't have been drivin' the buggy all alone, but I thank God for watchin' over me so's I could get help."

"And I thank God that you changed your mind 'bout us," Daniel whispered in her ear. *"Wass Got tuht ist wohl getahn."*

❧

Winter had definitely come to Lancaster Valley. A thick blanket of pristine snow lay heavily on the ground, and all the trees were dressed in gleaming white gowns. Travel by horse and buggy became more and more difficult, and many Amish families exchanged their buggies for sleighs in order to accommodate the dangerously slick roads.

Rebekah loved riding in an open sleigh, especially when it was with Daniel Beachy. In spite of the bad weather, they'd managed to go to several more singings, and Daniel called on her as often as he could. They played board games, worked on puzzles, or just sat by the fire eating popcorn, drinking hot chocolate, and talking for hours on end. Sometimes, after school hours, he'd come to the greenhouse with his older sister, Sarah Jane, the new schoolteacher. They'd work on repotting plants, taking cuttings off larger ones, or starting flowers from seeds. The couple seemed to be drawing closer to each other, even with Sarah Jane acting as chaperone.

One evening in late February, Daniel stopped by her house. Everyone else in the family had already gone off to bed, but he and Rebekah sat in the kitchen, looking through a stack of nursery catalogs that had recently come in the mail.

Rebekah looked up from her studies and saw Daniel looking intently at her. *"Wass ist letz?"* she asked. "You look so thought-provoking."

"Nix ist letz—nothing is wrong. I was just thinkin' how lucky I am to have you as my girlfriend," he answered with a smile. "You're so sweet and kind, Rebekah."

"Me, sweet?" She quickly looked away. "I never thought anyone would think of me as sweet."

Daniel reached out and took her small hand. "Why not? You have a most generous spirit, and your eyes are always so sincere. I find everything about you to my liking," he said softly.

"Even my crippled legs?" She hated to spoil the moment by bringing up her disability, but she felt the question needed to be asked.

"Your legs only serve to remind me that you haven't allowed your disability to stop you from doin' *gut* things with your life." Daniel stroked the back of her hand lightly with his thumb. "I want to spend the rest of my days with you, Rebekah Stoltzfus. I want you to be my wife. Would ya be interested in marryin' me come fall?"

Rebekah felt like all the breath had been squeezed clean out of her. Just like when she was little and had taken a fall from the hayloft. She'd known she and Daniel were getting closer, but a proposal was the last thing she'd been expecting to hear.

"So, what's your answer?" Daniel prompted. "Will you agree to be my wife?"

Unwanted tears stung the corners of Rebekah's blue eyes. She'd never known such joy before Daniel came along. He made her feel whole and alive—so much so that she couldn't think clearly when he was around. Maybe this was the reason she didn't even hesitate to give her answer. *Jah*, Daniel Beachy, I'd be honored to be your wife."

Daniel leaned his face close to hers, until their lips nearly touched. Rebekah closed her eyes and waited expectantly. She'd never been kissed by a man before. Not in the real sense of the word, anyway. Hugs and quick pecks on the cheeks didn't count, and those had come from family and close friends.

Daniel's gentle kiss didn't last awfully long, but it took Rebekah's breath away, nonetheless. When he pulled back, Daniel was grinning from ear to ear. The look on his face reminded Rebekah of one of the barn cats after it had chased down a squirmy, little gray mouse. She suppressed a giggle as she again took up the seed catalog they'd been reading.

❧

Winter melted into spring, and spring blossomed into a promising summer. Everyone's life was busy as usual, and the new season was full of changes. Aunt Grace had given birth to a baby boy toward the end of March. About the same time, Mary Ellen announced that she, too, was expecting a baby, due the first part of November.

Holding her youngest cousin, baby Timothy, and hearing Mary Ellen's happy news caused Rebekah to have an ache in her heart for a child of her own. She was having second thoughts about whether marriage for her was really such a good idea after all.

What if she didn't make Daniel happy? What if she could never conceive? What if she got pregnant but couldn't take care of her baby? She kept these nagging doubts hidden from Daniel, as he seemed to be anxiously awaiting their wedding day, set to occur on the third Thursday of November.

It was already mid-August, which left only three short months 'til the wedding. If Rebekah didn't do something about her doubts and apprehension, she wondered if she could actually go through with this marriage. She still loved Daniel—probably more with each passing day. However, fear of the unknown was paralyzing her soul, and it was causing more discomfort than the partial paralysis of her lower body.

What's wrong with me? Rebekah silently moaned as she sat in her wheelchair, repotting a spider plant which had grown too large for its plastic container. *I thought I had all of this settled in my mind. I believed I could take the step of faith necessary for love and marriage. When I agreed to marry Daniel, I even thought it was God's will. I decided that He had brought the two of us together. Now, I'm not so sure.*

She patted some fresh potting soil around the roots of the plant, feeling downright jittery inside. "I need to stay busy, that's all. If I keep my mind occupied, I won't have time for second thoughts."

Rebekah's self-talk was cut short when a customer rang the bell and entered the greenhouse. She wheeled herself out to the front section of the building and was greeted by Johnny Yoder. As a married man, he was now growing a full beard and looked almost mature.

"*Gut Morgen,* Johnny. How are you today?" she asked, attempting to sound more cheerful than she felt.

Johnny took off his straw hat and wiped his forehead with the back of his hand. "*Ach,* my! It's hot out there. Only ten o'clock and already over eighty degrees!"

Rebekah nodded. "*Jah,* another hot and humid summer, that's for sure."

"I think the only critters who like this kind of weather are the lightnin' bugs," Johnny said with a laugh.

Rebekah smiled. "So, what brings you here today?"

"I thought I'd get a nice plant for Mary Ellen. It might make her feel a bit better."

"Oh? She's still not feelin' well?" Rebekah asked with concern.

"It's that awful mornin' sickness," Johnny answered. "Doc Manney says it should go away soon, but she's already in her sixth month, and still she fights it." He shook his head. "Her back hurts somethin' awful, too, and the poor thing can't stand or sit long neither."

Rebekah clicked her tongue. "That must be hard. I'll try to get over and see her real soon."

Johnny nodded. "*Jah,* that would be *gut.* You're her best friend, and I'm sure a visit would do her just fine."

"What kind of plant did ya have in mind?" Rebekah asked, changing the subject. "Somethin' for the flower garden or an indoor plant?"

Johnny scratched the back of his blond head. "I'm not too sure. Maybe somethin' for the garden. Mary Ellen spends a lot of time outdoors, since it's so hot inside durin' the days of summer. If I take her an outdoor plant to enjoy, she might sit out on the porch swing and relax more often."

Rebekah smiled. Johnny really did seem to care about Mary Ellen's needs. She was glad he made her friend so happy. "Let's go on back to where my plants are kept. I think I have a nice pot of mixed pansies she might like."

Johnny followed as she rolled into the other room, and a short time later he was at the cash register, paying for a large pot of yellow, white, and purple pansies.

As he opened the front door, Johnny nearly bumped straight into Daniel Beachy.

"That's a right beautiful bunch of pansies you've got there," Daniel said, stepping into the greenhouse, then hanging his hat on a wall peg.

Jah, and they're for a beautiful wife!" Johnny exclaimed. He waved and was gone before either Daniel or Rebekah could respond.

"Marriage sure seems to agree with him," Daniel said to Rebekah. "I think he's awful excited 'bout becomin' a father, too."

Rebekah nodded, and her lips turned into a frown.

Daniel knelt next to her wheelchair and reached out to take both of her hands. "Is somethin' wrong, Rebekah? You look so down in the mouth this mornin'."

Rebekah was about to reply when the doorbell rang again, and several English tourists entered her store. "I've gotta go wait on these people," she whispered to Daniel.

He nodded, and she wheeled away. "May I help you with somethin'?" Rebekah asked the two young couples.

"We were just wondering if you might sell anything cold to drink," one of the women asked. "It's so hot out today, and we're all quite thirsty."

Rebekah shook her head. "I don't sell any beverages, but I do have some cold water in the back room." She glanced at Daniel. "Would ya mind goin' and gettin' the pitcher, along with some glasses?"

"I can do that," he responded with a nod.

The group of "English" looked grateful, and offered their heartfelt thanks when Daniel reappeared a few minutes later with enough water for all.

"What do you sell here?" one of the young men asked Rebekah.

"It's a greenhouse. I sell plants, flowers, and all garden-related items," she explained. Some Englishers called the Amish "dumb Dutch," but Rebekah had to wonder just how smart these tourists were if they didn't even know what things were sold in a greenhouse, for goodness' sake.

"You could probably triple your profits if you sold some food and beverages, especially during the hot summer months," the young man asserted.

Jah, maybe so," Rebekah agreed.

The tourists finished their water, then turned to leave. They were about to exit the building when one of the women spotted a wooden whirligig shaped like a windmill. "Oh, look at this, Bill. Isn't it the cutest little thing? I'd sure like to have it for our backyard."

The man reached into his pants pocket and handed a wallet to his wife. "Here, help yourself," he said with a smile. He turned to Rebekah. "We're newlyweds, and I can't seem to say no."

Rebekah grinned, then moved to the cash register.

"This is so nice," the woman said. "You should sell more handmade Amish items here. Almost anything made by you Amish would probably retail quite well."

Rebekah smiled and merely muttered her thanks.

As soon as the customers left, Daniel moved over to her. "Those English tourists might have a good point 'bout you sellin' more things in here," he said.

Rebekah wrinkled her nose. "It wouldn't be much of a greenhouse if I began sellin' all sorts of trinkets and souvenirs just to please the tourists."

"It'd still be a greenhouse, Rebekah," Daniel argued. "It would just have a few added items for sale." His brown eyes fairly sparkled. "I sure can't wait 'til we're married. Then we'll finally be real business partners. Why, I have all sorts of new ideas I'd like to put into practice."

Rebekah felt like she'd just had a jolt of lightning shoot straight through her. She shivered, despite the warmth of the room. Was that all Daniel wanted—just a business partner? Had he proposed marriage just so he could become part owner of Grandma's Place?

Rebekah wrinkled her nose at him. "And what if there is no partnership, Daniel?"

He looked at her with questioning eyes. "No partnership? What do ya mean, Rebekah? Two heads are better'n one, ya know."

"That may be true, but what if I change my mind, and we don't get married after all?" The words seemed to jump right off her tongue, but there was no taking them back now.

"You're teasin' me, ain't it so, sweet Rebekah?" he said with a laugh.

She shrugged her shoulders and groaned softly. "I've been havin' some serious doubts 'bout marriage here of late, and what you just said only confirms my thinkin'."

"What? You can't mean that!" Daniel bent down and grabbed her by the shoulders. "Please say ya don't mean it."

She swallowed past the lump in her throat. "I do mean it. I'm thinkin' maybe you only want me for this business. Could be that the greenhouse is the only reason you ever showed any interest in me a'tall."

"Jumpin' frogs, Rebekah!" he cried. "I never thought anything of the kind! I care about you. Surely you can see that."

She bit her bottom lip so hard she could taste blood. "I'm not sure what I see anymore, Daniel. But I know one thing—I can't be a normal wife, and I'm pretty sure I can't have babies neither. I also know that—"

Daniel stopped her rush of words by placing one finger against her lips.

"Shh. . . Please don't say those things. We've talked about this stuff before—all except me wantin' to be your business partner more than your marriage partner, that is. I do want to be your business partner; I won't deny that, Rebekah. I've wanted it for a long time, but—"

Rebekah jerked her wheelchair to one side, and cutting him off in midsentence, she cried, "I've heard enough! Don't say anything more, Daniel. It's over between us, so just go on home and forget you ever knew me."

Daniel's face was red as a cherry. "Please, Rebekah, can't I have my say on this?"

She shook her head vigorously. "There's already been too much said. I should've never let things go on like this. My answer to your proposal should have been no from the beginnin'."

Daniel shuffled his feet a few times, jerked his straw hat off the wall peg, and marched out the door.

Chapter 19

Nadine and I have to go into town today. Would you like to go along?" Mom asked Rebekah the following morning as they were preparing breakfast. "We're gonna eat out again, and maybe it'll help lift your spirits some."

"I don't really need anything in town right now, but I would appreciate a ride to Mary Ellen's," Rebekah answered, making no reference to her "spirits." She'd already broken the news to her family about Daniel and her not getting married, and it was bad enough just doin' the tellin'. No use sulkin' about it or trying to make herself feel better with a lunch full of fattening food from the Better Is More Restaurant. No, the best thing for Rebekah would be to go callin' on her friend. *"Get your eyes off your own problem, and help someone else with theirs"*—that's what Grandma Stoltzfus always used to say.

"Taking you by Mary Ellen's won't be a problem a'tall, 'cause it's right on the way," Mom said, cutting into Rebekah's thoughts. "Are ya sure you wouldn't rather go to Lancaster, though? You can always visit your cousin some other time."

Rebekah shook her head. "Mary Ellen's not feeling well. I think a visit with her is more important than shoppin' or goin' out to lunch."

"What's wrong with Mary Ellen?" Nadine asked when she entered the kitchen.

"She's still havin' some mornin' sickness, and her back's hurtin', too," Rebekah answered.

Nadine wrinkled her nose and made a face that reminded Rebekah of a bull-dog. "I think bein' pregnant must be the worst thing any woman could ever go through. I'm sure not gonna have any children when I get married!"

Mom smiled and gave Rebekah a knowing look. "When you do get married, Nadine, children will come in God's time and not yours. It's God who'll give you the strength to get through it all, too."

"Jah, well, maybe I just won't get married, then!" Nadine folded her arms and plastered a determined look on her youthful face.

Rebekah laughed, even though her heart was aching like crazy. "You? My boy-crazy little sister, not ever get married? That's about as silly a notion as thinkin' robins won't come back to the valley every spring!"

"Don't make fun of me," Nadine pouted. "I don't like to be laughed at."

Rebekah sobered. "I'm sorry, Sister. No one likes to be laughed at. I should know that better'n anyone."

Nadine moved to the table where Rebekah was buttering a stack of toast. "I'd never laugh at you, Rebekah. I admire you too much."

Rebekah looked up at Nadine with tears in her eyes. "You do?"

"Of course," her sister replied. "You've done so much with your life. A business of your own is somethin' to feel real *gut* about."

"Nadine's right," Mom put in from her place at the stove. She was frying some fresh eggs in sweet, creamy butter, and had just flipped them over. "If anyone should laugh at you, then they truly don't know you a'tall."

Rebekah's mind pulled her back to that day at the market when the two English boys had teased and taunted her like crazy. They'd laughed right in her face and made all kinds of fun of her, not carin' in the least how she felt. Mom was right—they hadn't known her. She hadn't really known herself 'til she began to search the Scriptures for answers and until she'd taken a huge leap of faith by opening the greenhouse.

Rebekah said nothing to Mom or Nadine about that incident with the boys, nor did she mention anything about the awful pain she was feeling over breaking her engagement to Daniel. With God's help, she hoped to get through this horrible letdown and move on with her life—without Daniel Beachy! She added another piece of toast to the plate already stacked and stated, "We'd better get breakfast done and call Papa and Simon. I'm anxious to go see Mary Ellen."

❧

Mary Ellen and Johnny's home was set on the back side of Uncle Amos and Aunt Mim's property. It had been built by both fathers and was a two-story house with white siding and a long porch wrapped halfway around the building. Johnny had hung a two-seater porch swing under the overhang, and it was there that Rebekah saw Mary Ellen. She was holding a glass of iced tea in one hand, swinging to and fro, with her eyes closed and head leaning back against the wooden slats.

After helping Rebekah down from the buggy and making sure she was secure in her wheelchair, Mom climbed back into the driver's seat. "If you see Mim, tell her I'll be over for a visit one of these days," she called before pulling out of the driveway.

Rebekah waved and propelled herself up the wheelchair ramp.

Mary Ellen opened her eyes and smiled. "Oh, what a nice surprise. I'm so glad to see you today."

"Johnny was by the greenhouse yesterday and said you were still feelin' poorly," Rebekah explained. "I thought maybe a little visit might do us both *gut.*"

"Johnny and Pappy are out in the fields. Would you like me to call Mama Mim and see if she can help you into the swing?" Mary Ellen asked.

Rebekah shook her head. "No, that's not necessary." She eyed Mary Ellen's stomach. "You're gettin' pretty big round the middle these days. I think maybe you might need the swing all to yourself."

Mary Ellen grimaced. "Do I really look that big?"

"*Jah,* just like one of Papa's draft horses!" Rebekah giggled. "But you're still as beautiful as ever. I think bein' in a family way kinda becomes you. You look almost radiant, in fact."

"My radiance comes from bein' much too warm, I'm afraid," Mary Ellen said as she held the cool glass up to her flushed cheeks. "This late summer weather's sure gettin' to me, and my back—oh, it hurts somethin' awful!"

Rebekah winced. "Johnny said you're still fightin' the mornin' sickness, too."

Mary Ellen nodded. "It comes and goes, but when it comes, it can get pretty bad."

"Are ya drinking plenty of peppermint tea?" Rebekah questioned.

In response, Mary Ellen held up her glass. "Several glasses a day."

Rebekah shrugged. "Then all ya can do is pray that the sickness soon goes away."

Mary Ellen sighed deeply and gave Rebekah an anxious look. "I hope the baby comes in plenty of time before your weddin'. I sure wouldn't want to miss that big occasion."

Now it was Rebekah's turn to sigh. "I called the whole thing off."

"You what?"

"I told Daniel we weren't gettin' married," Rebekah declared. Her eyes were beginning to blur with unshed tears, and she looked away, hoping Mary Ellen wouldn't notice.

"You didn't say that for real, now did ya?" Mary Ellen's raised eyebrows clearly showed her disbelief.

Rebekah hung her head. "I was beginnin' to have doubts as to whether I could really be a *gut* wife to Daniel anyways."

"Because of your concerns about whether you can ever conceive?"

Rebekah only nodded.

"What does the doctor say?" Mary Ellen asked.

"He doesn't really know," Rebekah answered truthfully. "He said that in some cases of spinal cord injury, a woman can never conceive, but—well, some have actually been able to get pregnant and carry the baby to term."

"You might be one of those women," Mary Ellen contended. She tapped her fingers against the side of her glass. "That's sure no *gut* reason for you to go callin' off the weddin', for goodness' sake."

Rebekah's forehead knitted into a frown. "Oh, Mary Ellen, I do so want to be a wife and mother. God's already given me one miracle, so I don't know if I dare ask for yet another one."

"Of course you can ask," Mary Ellen asserted. "The Bible tells us in Luke, 'Ask, and it shall be given you; seek, and ye shall find; knock, and it shall be opened unto you.' Our heavenly Father wants to give us *gut* things."

Rebekah nodded. "*Jah,* I know. Sometimes I think I'm not deservin' of the *gut* things He gives to others, though."

"You are so," Mary Ellen said in earnest. "All God's children are deservin' of His love. He doesn't always give us everything we ask for, but He always gives us what He knows is best for us."

"My own capabilities aren't the only problem," Rebekah finally admitted.

Mary Ellen tilted her head, like she was pondering real hard. "What else is there?"

"It's Daniel," Rebekah said tersely.

"Daniel?" Mary Ellen repeated, wagging a finger. "How could Daniel be the problem? He's so much in love with you that it's downright sickenin'."

Rebekah laughed dryly. "I thought so, too—'til yesterday, that is."

"What happened yesterday?"

Rebekah quickly related the conversation she and Daniel had about him wanting to be her business partner, and the fact that she was certain this was the only reason he wanted to marry her.

"I hope he set you straight on that one," Mary Ellen scolded.

Rebekah started hem-hawing at first, then with a determined lift of her chin, she said pointedly, "He tried to deny it, but in the process, he admitted to wantin' the greenhouse real bad." She sniffed deeply. "That fact alone is mighty unsettlin' to me."

Mary Ellen shrugged. "Sometimes we draw the wrong conclusions because we want to."

"What are ya sayin'? Do you actually think I wanted to believe such things about Daniel?" Rebekah's voice had risen at least an octave, and her cheeks felt flushed.

Mary Ellen held up one hand. "Please, don't get defensive on me. I only meant that since you were already havin' some self-doubts about being a wife, maybe Daniel's comment was misunderstood. Might could be that you were just lookin' for a way out of what you felt wouldn't work a'tall."

"Now, listen here, Mary Ellen. Why, I'll have you know—"

"Hello there, Rebekah. How's my favorite niece today?" Aunt Mim asked as she stepped up to the porch.

"I. . .I'm, just fine, *danki,*" Rebekah stammered.

"Well, it didn't sound to me as if you were all that fine. You sounded pretty upset 'bout somethin' a moment ago."

"Rebekah thinks Daniel only wants to marry her so he can become her partner at the greenhouse," Mary Ellen was quick to say.

"It's true!" Rebekah shouted. "He sweet-talked me for months, just so's he could get his stocky hands on my business." Just thinking about it now got her to feeling all unsettled and *gridlich* again.

"Do you have time to hear another one of my little stories?" Aunt Mim asked, squeezing in beside Mary Ellen on the swing.

Rebekah shrugged. "I guess so. I'll be here 'til Mom picks me up this afternoon." She moved her shoulders up and down, trying to work out the kinks. "By the way, Mom says she'll be over to visit sometime soon."

Aunt Mim nodded, then began her story. "A long time ago, when Miriam Hilty was still Miriam Stoltzfus, she thought that a certain Amos Hilty wanted to marry her for reasons other than love."

"Really? I never knew that, Mama Mim," Mary Ellen said with wide eyes. "What other reasons might Pappy have had?"

Mim patted Mary Ellen's hand. "Well, I thought your *daed* only wanted a mother for his little girl." She shrugged. "I figured he probably wanted someone to do all his cookin' and cleanin', too. It wasn't 'til well after our marriage that I finally woke up and realized Amos cared deeply for me. What he really wanted all along was a companion and helpmate."

Mim pointed at Rebekah. "I've observed you and Daniel plenty of times, and I daresay that he loves you very much. While it might be true that young Mr. Beachy desires a partnership in your business, I'm convinced that he wants you as his wife even more."

Rebekah chewed thoughtfully on her bottom lip. "I do appreciate your sharin' another story with me, Aunt Mim. Only thing is, it doesn't change nothin' a'tall where me and Daniel are concerned."

Aunt Mim held her hands palms up. "Why not? It seems *en Sin une Schand*— a sin and a shame—for you to give up so early on love and marriage, dear girl."

"Daniel doesn't love me," Rebekah insisted. "He never even said he did, for pity's sake!"

"You're kidding, right?" asked Mary Ellen with a look of bewilderment.

Rebekah shook her head. "Nope, and he only wants my business. I know it, sure as day, and we're not gettin' married!"

Chapter 20

Rebekah moved restlessly about the kitchen on her crutches. She was feeling so fretful and fidgety this morning. She stopped pacing for a few moments and glanced out the window. A sparrow was eating from one of Daniel's handcrafted feeders. *Oh, Daniel, why'd ya hafta go and break my heart in two?* she silently wailed. *Didn't ya know how very much I loved ya?*

It had been two weeks since their breakup, and the pain was no less hurtful now than it had been on that terrible day when she discovered that her intended had only been usin' her to acquire a business sellin' flowers. Seeing Daniel at preachin' last week hadn't helped any neither.

Rebekah thought, maybe even hoped, that Daniel might try to win her back. She squinted her eyes so the tears wouldn't give way. *Not that I'd ever consider takin' him back.* No, she was through with men and all their sweet-talkin', connivin' ways. God had given her a business to run, and this summer it had done right well. If things kept on goin' as they were, why she'd be self-supportin' in no time a'tall. That was the miracle she'd been waiting for, wasn't it?

She trembled slightly as she thought about Daniel sittin' there at preachin', just across the room from her. He hadn't even so much as looked her way, let alone said anything. It just proved what she'd known as a fact—Daniel didn't love her now, and he never had.

Rebekah leaned her full weight against the windowsill. *"God takes care of the little bitty birds,"* she was reminded. *"So He'll most assuredly take care of you."* Grandma's words tumbled around in her mind like the clothes in Mom's old wringer washer on laundry day.

"I think what I need is a breath of fresh air," Rebekah said aloud, though no one was in the kitchen but her. Mom was outside hanging up clothes, Nadine was in the barn playing with a batch of new kittens, and the menfolk were out working in the fields.

Rebekah thought about casting off her leg braces and taking the wheelchair outside, but it was such a job to get them unhooked. Besides, as Mom always said, "The exercise will do your whole body some good."

With the crutches fastened securely to her arms by leather straps, Rebekah grabbed a light shawl from a wall peg and headed out the back door.

Mom was struggling with a sheet that the wind had caught in the clothesline, and she didn't seem to notice when Rebekah plodded down the path. Straight for the creek she headed, about one hundred yards from the house. A definite nip was in the air this morning, and Rebekah knew fall would be coming sooner or later. Autumn. The time for Amish weddings. Her own wedding was supposed to be in November. If only. . .

She shoved the familiar ache aside once again and attempted to pick up her speed just a bit. Walking so stiff-legged was such a chore, and she was beginning to wonder if she'd made a mistake by leaving the wheelchair parked in the kitchen. Already she was huffin' and puffin', and she was only halfway there. How was she ever gonna make it all the way at this rate?

" 'I can do all things through Christ which strengtheneth me,' " she quoted from the Scriptures. If she could just go another fifty yards or so, she'd be at the creek and could maybe find a log or something to sit on. Trips to the stream in the past had always been made in her wheelchair, which meant finding a place to sit and rest had never been a problem.

Methodically, Rebekah lifted first one foot, then the other, guiding herself along with the aid of her metal crutches. She could hear the running water gurgling over the rocky creek bottom. The melodic sound soothed her nerves and gave her the added incentive to keep on walking.

Soon, the rushing water came into view, meandering gracefully through a cluster of red maple and white birch trees. Rebekah scanned the banks, looking for something to use as a bench. Her back hurt like crazy, the muscles in her arms were all tight, and even her legs, which normally had little feeling, felt kind of tingly and pricklylike.

With great relief, she spotted a fallen tree, its branches stretched partway across the water and the trunk lying on dry land. A few more determined steps and she was there. Drawing in a deep breath for added strength, Rebekah lowered herself slowly to the stump. The bumpy surface offered little comfort for her backside, but at least she was sitting and could finally catch her breath. Even her hands were trembling, she noticed. The trek from the house had nearly been too much. Oh, how she wished she'd told someone where she was going. What if she couldn't make it back to the house on her own strength? The way she was feeling right now, she wasn't too sure she could even stand up again.

"What a dunce I was for thinkin' I could be so independent and go traipsin' on down here without my wheelchair," Rebekah chided herself. "It was just plain *kischblich*—silly—of me!"

She wrapped her shawl tighter around her shoulders and shivered. Not so much from the chilly morning, but rather from all her energy being used up. She didn't walk with her leg braces that much, and she knew now that she wasn't strong enough to take off on her own and go such a distance.

The rustling of fallen leaves caught Rebekah's attention. She glanced to the right and saw Brownie, their mixed-breed farm dog, running for all he was worth. Out in front of him was something fuzzy and small. A white ball of fur, that's what it surely looked like.

Rebekah squinted, trying to get a better look. What in the world? Brownie was chasin' one of those new baby kittens, for goodness' sake! Along the bank of the creek, the poor critter ran, with the old dog right on its tail.

"*Schpring*, kitty, *Schpring! Mach schnell*—run, kitty, run! Go quickly!" Rebekah cried. Of course the kitten couldn't understand what she was saying, so she turned her attention toward Brownie then. "Bad dog! You come here and leave that poor cat alone!"

Brownie cocked his head, as though he might actually plan to listen, but then he forged right ahead and kept on with the chase.

"Dumb dog!" Rebekah shouted. "You never did know when to hearken." She watched helplessly as the tired kitten began to lose ground. Brownie was just about ready to pounce when the unthinkable happened.

Plop! Right into that cold water poor kitty cat went sailing. Rebekah let out a gasp, and Brownie must have been a bit surprised, too, for the rebellious old mutt slammed on his brakes and nearly ran straight into a tree.

Rebekah stared in horror as the white ball of fur turned into a soggy little mass that resembled something akin to a roll of cotton when it's drenched in alcohol. Tiny paws began to flail helplessly about, making trivial headway through the swirling waters holding her in its grip.

"She's not strong enough to swim yet," Rebekah moaned. "The poor little critter will sure as anything drown." She couldn't just sit here and watch it happen. She had to do something to save that kitten's life!

Rebekah grasped the crutches tightly and with a grunt, she pulled herself up. "Hang on, little one. I'm a-comin'!"

Down the creek bank she went, inch by inch, step by step. At the water's edge, she bent over and let go of one crutch. It was strapped to her arm, and so it dangled precariously as she leaned across the swift current in an attempt to rescue the perishing cat.

Brownie was at her heels now, swishing his tail from side to side and barking to beat the band. It only seemed to frighten the pathetic little fur ball that much further. With eyes open wide and claws splashing against the water, it was swept further downstream. Rebekah saw it take in a mouthful of water; then down it went.

In a state of near panic, she took a few more steps, until she saw water rise over the top of her black high-top boots. No doubt it was stinging cold, but her unfeeling legs knew no pain. Further into the creek she trudged, lifting first one foot, then the other. The swift-moving current made it even more difficult to navigate, and soon she felt winded and emotionally spent.

"Help me, Lord," she prayed. "Allow me to reach the kitten in time." A few more steps, and she was almost there. A slight bend at the waist, a hand extended, and. . .

Splash! Facedown in the chilling water, Rebekah landed. She gurgled and gasped as her nose and mouth filled with unwanted fluid. She thrashed about with her arms and nearly smacked the side of her head with one of the crutches. All thoughts of the stranded kitten were gone from her mind now. All she wanted to do was save herself. The more she flailed against the stream's rapid flow, the deeper her body seemed to be sucked under.

Rebekah had never learned how to swim, and even if she had, her crippled legs would have been useless. If her arms had been stronger, maybe she could have paddled her way to the grassy banks. But no, she'd used all her strength just gettin' down to this silly creek. The panic she felt rising in her throat kept all clearheaded thinking away. She couldn't pray, she couldn't swim, and she couldn't consider any ways to get back on her feet.

"Rebekah! Grab my hand, *schnell!*"

Rebekah turned her head to the right, taking in another murky mouthful of water as she did so. She blinked rapidly. Was she dreamin'? Was there someone standing over her? No, it just couldn't possibly be.

She opened her mouth to cry out, but nothing more than a pitiful squeak came from her cold lips.

"Rebekah, listen to me now," the deep voice said sternly. "Quit your flounderin' and take hold of my hand." Daniel Beachy's concerned face was mere inches from hers, and she knew for certain that it wasn't an apparition a'tall.

She lifted one arm, the weight of the crutch working against her. A firm hand grasped hers, pulling with all the strength of an able-bodied man. Still, she couldn't seem to right herself, and instead of coming to her feet as she had hoped, Rebekah fell backward, dragging Daniel into the water as well.

He came up spitting and sputtering, with a look of sheer bewilderment spread all over his face.

"Well, Rebekah Stoltzfus," he mumbled, "you'd better have a mighty *gut* reason for all this!"

Chapter 21

Daniel swept Rebekah into his arms and carried her over his shoulder like she was a sack of grain. He plodded through the murky, swirling waters until he reached dry land. Then he placed her in a sitting position on the grassy bank and dropped down beside her. "Are ya okay, Rebekah? What were ya doin' in that creek? How come you're all alone and without the wheelchair?" The questions seemed to pour out of Daniel, until Rebekah finally interrupted him with a raised hand.

"Don'tcha think you should ask me only one question at a time?" she asked, coughing a few times and reaching up to pull her soggy head covering off. Her damp hair came loose from its usual bun, and long, thoroughly saturated hair came tumbling down her shoulders.

Daniel lifted his hand to her cheek and swiped at a splotch of mud. "You look like a drowned pup, ya know that?"

Rebekah sniffed deeply as she glared at him. "You don't look so *gut* yourself, Daniel Beachy!"

Daniel's lips twitched slightly, then turned up, as he burst into laughter. "No, I don't guess I do!" His face sobered after the laughter subsided. "So, are you gonna tell me why you're down here all alone, and how you ended up in that water or not?"

"I. . .I went for a walk," she replied with trembling lips. Her whole body was starting to shake a bit, too, and she wrapped her arms around her middle. "I was sittin' on a fallen tree when I noticed our dog chasin' one of Gretta's new kittens. The helpless little critter couldn't outrun the mutt, though, and the poor thing ended up fallin' into the creek."

Rebekah and Daniel both turned their heads toward the swiftly moving water again. "I. . .I can't believe it!" Rebekah exclaimed, pointing just across the creek bank. On the other side sat a waterlogged kitten, licking its tiny paws like it didn't have a care in the world. The yapping dog, who'd caused all the trouble, was nowhere to be found.

"Well, for goodness' sake!" Rebekah said with a groan. "I nearly drowned myself to save that silly creature, and here she is just fine and dandy!"

Unexpectedly, Daniel reached for her hand. "I'm so glad you didn't drown, Rebekah. I don't think I could stand it if somethin' bad happened to you."

Rebekah jerked her head back around to face him. His tender words were like healing balm to her soul. If only she could believe. . .

"What are you doin' here, anyways?" she asked in a none-too-friendly tone.

"I was out for a walk, when I heard a bunch of splashin' and carryin' on comin' from your creek." Daniel flashed her a warm smile. "In all honesty, I was headed to the greenhouse to see you."

Rebekah blinked several times. "You were?"

He nodded soberly. *Jah.* I thought it was time we got things aired out between us. I. . .well, I've been kind of like *Enwiedicher Hund*—a mad dog—for these last few weeks," he admitted with a frown. "I'm sorry to say that a bit of *Hochmut*—pride—got in my way, and I just couldn't face another tussle with ya."

Rebekah dropped her gaze to the ground, unable to look at the pain clearly written on Daniel's face. "You hurt me bad, Daniel Beachy. I thought you cared, but—"

He lifted her chin with a hand, so she was forced to look directly into his dark eyes. "I love you, Rebekah Stoltzfus. *Ich will Liebe du*—I will love you—forever, and *Ich Nix fer ungut*—I mean it well."

Rebekah felt the sting of tears flood her eyes. "Oh, Daniel, you've never said that to me before."

He hung his head sheepishly. "Guess I was a dumb *alte Kuh*—old cow—too scared to express my true feelin's."

"But, what about bein' partners and all?" she questioned. "You did say that you couldn't wait 'til you could help run the greenhouse, and—"

Daniel stopped her flow of words by planting a surprising warm kiss against her mouth. When he released her, Rebekah felt as though the breath had all been squeezed right out of her. Daniel had kissed her before, but never like that!

"If you'd have just listened to me that day at the greenhouse, instead of jumpin' to conclusions about my feelin's and all, I'd have told you that even though I wanted to run a greenhouse, that was never the reason for me wantin' to marry you, silly girl."

"It wasn't?" Rebekah squeaked. "But, I thought—"

"I know what ya thought," Daniel interrupted. "Ya thought I was just usin' ya, so's I could get my hands on that business of yours, right?"

She nodded. *Jah,* that's sure enough what I believed, all right."

"Well, it just ain't so, Rebekah," Daniel asserted. "I've been in love with ya ever so long. Way back when we first started goin' to singin's, and you'd sit there in your wheelchair, so sweet and sincere. Why, it was all I could do to keep from rushin' right up and declarin' my love for ya."

Rebekah stifled a giggle. She could hardly picture anything so silly as Daniel Beachy announcing his love thataway.

Daniel held her close, as though his very life depended on it. "Please say ya believe me, Rebekah. I want ya to be my wife, honest I do. It truly ain't for the business neither." He patted her back. "If it'll help anything, I'll even agree to let you run the greenhouse all by yourself. I won't be co-owner of Grandma's Place a'tall. I'll just keep on workin' with *Daed* and the dairy cows; that's what I'll do."

Rebekah choked on a sob. "Oh, sweet Daniel, I couldn't ask ya to do that.

I know how much you love flowers and all. Your love for cows in no way compares to that."

He leaned his head heavily on her shoulder. "That's right, but my love for flowers ain't nothin' compared to what I feel for you. So don't send me away again, for I just couldn't bear it. Will ya marry me, Rebekah, and love me forever?"

Daniel's eyes glistened with unshed tears, and it tore at Rebekah's tender heart. She reached out to stroke his clean-shaven face. "Oh, Daniel, I do love you so. I'm sorry for doubtin' your intentions and not givin' you the chance to explain."

"Does that mean you'll marry me, then?"

She nodded. *"Jah,* I'd be honored to be your wife."

❧

Rebekah was awakened by the irritating sound of someone knocking on her bedroom door. "Who is it?" she called groggily into her pillow.

Mom opened the door a crack and poked her head inside. "You're still in bed, Sleepyhead? I thought you'd be up with the chickens on your weddin' day."

Rebekah yawned and grabbed the sides of the bed, in order to pull herself into a sitting position. "I was havin' such a nice dream, I guess I must've hated to wake up."

"That's *gut,"* Mom said with a smile. "All brides should have pleasant dreams." She entered the room and poured fresh water into the basin on Rebekah's dresser. "It's time to rise and shine now, though. Breakfast is waitin', and it won't be long before the first of our guests begin to arrive."

Rebekah nodded. *Jah,* but Mary Ellen probably won't be one of them."

"Now, you don't know that a'tall," Mom said, handing Rebekah a damp washcloth. "Mary Ellen still hasn't gone into labor, so why wouldn't she be here for your special day?"

Rebekah shrugged. "She might not feel up to comin'. I can't speak firsthand, of course, but I hear that women are pretty miserable when they're this close to deliverin'."

Mom nodded. "That's true enough. At least it was for me. However, some women carry on as usual, right up to the beginnin' of their labor."

"Then I guess I can only hope Mary Ellen's one of 'em who can carry on as usual. I'll be mighty disappointed if she isn't here today."

❧

Rebekah sat straight and tall on a wooden bench, directly across from her groom. She'd chosen to wear her leg braces again today, so she could stand for her wedding vows, rather than sit in the confining wheelchair. She wore traditional Amish bridal clothes—a plain blue cotton dress, draped with a darker blue cape and matching apron, and a white prayer cap on her head. Daniel was dressed in a white shirt, black trousers, along with a black matching jacket and vest.

Rebekah glanced over her shoulder and smiled at Mary Ellen, who sat just two rows behind. She knew from the expression on her friend's face that she was probably not feelin' her best, but she cared enough to be here, and that meant a whole lot.

At nine o'clock sharp, the service began with singing from the *Ausbund*. A lengthy sermon from Bishop Benner followed, covering all aspects of the Christian marriage. Then he read several Scripture passages, including one from Colossians that said, " 'And whatsoever ye do in word or deed, do all in the name of the Lord Jesus, giving thanks to God and the Father by him.' "

In a booming voice, and with a most serious face, he quoted from yet another passage. " 'Wives, submit yourselves unto your own husbands, as it is fit in the Lord. Husbands, love your wives, and be not bitter against them.' "

Rebekah looked at Daniel and smiled shyly. He nodded slightly and graced her with a smile of his own. His serious brown eyes, so filled with adoration, told her all she needed to know. Daniel Beachy loved her; she knew that with all of her heart. As if to confirm that fact, he mouthed the words, *"Ich will Liebe."*

When the Bible reading was done, some of the church's deacons gave their testimonies. Rebekah fidgeted nervously, wondering if they'd ever finish. Finally, after nearly half an hour more, the bride and groom and their attendants were taken to another part of the house. Daniel and Rebekah were ushered into Grandma Stoltzfus's old room for counseling from the bishop. Rebekah's attendants, Sarah Jane Beachy, Nadine, and her cousin Peggy, stood outside in the hall, along with Daniel's two brothers, Harold and Abner, and Rebekah's brother, Simon.

The counseling consisted of several more scriptural references and a long dissertation from Bishop Benner on the importance of good communication, trust, and respect in all areas of marriage. He reminded the couple that divorce is not an option among those of their faith, and he emphasized the need to always work through their problems.

When they finally emerged from the bedroom, Rebekah let out an audible sigh. Even though she'd been allowed to sit during the counseling session, she felt all done in, and a bit shakylike.

Returning to the main room, Rebekah and Daniel sat down on their original benches, while the bishop gave a rather long prayer. At long last, he motioned them to step forward and stand directly in front of him.

Rebekah's heart pummeled, like one of Papa's hammers when he'd worked on the barn. It seemed as if this had been the moment she'd been waiting for her whole life. She was about to repeat her wedding vows before family and friends, and most importantly, before her heavenly Father. She could hardly believe it was actually happening to her, an *eledich* crippled woman, who spent most of her time confined to a wheelchair.

Daniel gave her another reassuring smile, and she steadied herself with the crutches strapped to her arms, waiting for the bishop to begin.

Following Bishop Benner's lead, Daniel repeated his vows. Then it was Rebekah's turn. Her quiet voice quivered as she said each word slowly, deliberately, taking the meaning fully to heart.

Out of the corner of her eye, she saw Mary Ellen leave the room, assisted by Aunt Mim and Aunt Crystal. *Maybe she's just tired from sittin' so long,* Rebekah reasoned. *Or could be it's too warm in here. There are nearly two hundred people crammed into our house today. Maybe this is a bad sign. Maybe. . .*

"Commit thy way unto the Lord; trust also in him; and he shall bring it to pass." The bishop pronounced a blessing over the bride and groom, jerking Rebekah's thoughts back to the ceremony at hand. She and Daniel returned to their respective benches as husband and wife.

As soon as the closing prayer was said, everyone who wasn't helping with the cooking or serving went outside to wait for the wedding meal. Tables were quickly set up in the living room and the adjoining room as well.

"We need to take our place at the *Eck,*" Daniel whispered to Rebekah.

She nodded. "I know, but I want to check on Mary Ellen first. She left the room durin' our vows, and I think somethin' might be amiss."

"Jah, all right then. While you're gone, I'll help set out more tables. We'll meet in ten minutes." Daniel gave Rebekah's arm a gentle squeeze, and she hobbled out to the kitchen. There she found Mom and several other women, scurrying about to get all the food dished up.

"Well, Frieda, *denks du die kinder Kenne hous Halde*—do you think these children can keep house?" Mom asked Rebekah's new mother-in-law.

"Well, *wann du die Rebekah so gut ufgezoge host es Ich der Daniel hab, glab Ich gehts*—well, if you raised Rebekah as well as I raised Daniel, I believe it will go," Frieda replied with a small laugh.

"Do ya know where Mary Ellen is?" Rebekah asked Mom as she stepped between the two women. "She left during the ceremony, and I'm a bit worried."

"Mary Ellen's water broke, that's all," Mom explained with a shrug. "I hear tell she's been in labor for several hours already. They've taken her upstairs, 'cause there's no time to get to the hospital now."

Rebekah's mouth dropped open. "Why'd she come here then, for goodness' sake? She should've had Johnny take her to the hospital right away, when her labor first started."

"Mim said Mary Ellen didn't wanna miss your weddin'. She thought, this bein' her first baby and all, that the labor would be a long one."

Rebekah trembled, and her hands felt sweaty. "Oh, Mom, if anything happens to Mary Ellen or the baby, I'll never forgive myself."

Mom draped an arm around Rebekah and led her to a chair at the kitchen table. "Don't go talkin' such foolishness, now. Ya can't take the blame for somethin' like this, Rebekah. Mary Ellen had a choice to make. You didn't force her to come to the weddin' today."

"I know, but she knew how much I wanted her here," Rebekah argued. "If only she would've had that baby on schedule. She's over two weeks late, and—"

"Hush, now," Mom said, interrupting Rebekah's rush of words by placing a finger against her lips. "Nothin' we say or do will change the fact that the baby was late or that Mary Ellen's here now. The best thing would be to carry on with the weddin' meal, so our guests don't go hungry. Women have been havin' babies for thousands of years, and we just need to pray that everything will be all right in the birthin' room upstairs." Mom rolled her shoulders. "I'm sure Mim and Crystal are quite capable of helpin' with the delivery, but Johnny's ridden into town to get Doc Manney, just in case any problems should occur."

Rebekah's hand trembled as she wiped a stray hair from her face. She bowed her head and silently petitioned the Lord for both Mary Ellen and the baby.

❧

The wedding meal consisted of fried chicken, roast beef slices, spareribs, bread filling, boiled red potatoes, sliced tomatoes, dilled green beans, red cabbage slaw, deviled eggs, gelatin salad, and several kinds of pies and cakes. There was also coffee, milk, and apple cider to drink.

Rebekah forced herself to sit at her and Daniel's corner table and visit with the many guests, who took turns sitting at the tables to be served. However, her mind was really upstairs, in that bedroom where a new life was about to be brought into the world.

This was Daniel's and her special day. She should be laughing and enjoying all the jokes and stories people were telling. She ought to be savoring the delicious foods and the love she could feel radiating from her new groom. Instead, she worried and prayed, 'til Mom finally came into the room and announced, "Mary Ellen Yoder's just given birth to a healthy baby girl! Doc Manney is with her right now, and the report is that both mother and daughter are doin' right well."

A cheer went up around the room, and Rebekah choked back a sob. With tears in her eyes, she turned to Daniel. "Would ya mind if I slipped out for a moment, so's I can see the new baby and her *mamm?*"

Daniel shook his head. "Of course not. Would ya like me to come along? Someone will have to carry ya up the stairs."

"Why don't you stay and enjoy our guests?" Rebekah replied, giving him a quick peck on the cheek. "I'll ask Papa to take me on up."

Daniel shrugged. "Okay then, do as ya like."

With the aid of her crutches, Rebekah made her way out of the crowded room. Soon Papa carried her upstairs, and she found Mary Ellen lying on the bed in Nadine's room. In her arms was cradled a small bundle of pure, sweet baby.

Mary Ellen's cheeks were flushed, and her voice filled with emotion as she whispered, "I'm sorry I missed the end of your weddin'."

Rebekah hobbled over to the bed, then leaned over to give her friend a kiss on the forehead. "You had a pretty good excuse, I'm a-thinkin'."

"Why don't you say hello to your second cousin, Martha Rose?" Mary Ellen murmured.

Rebekah's eyes clouded with tears, and she stroked the baby's downy head. "It's as soft as a kitten's nose," she noted. A small sigh escaped her lips as she blinked back tears. "Today's been such a perfect day. I'm married to a *wunderbaar* man, and now I'm lookin' down on a true miracle from God."

"*Jah*," Mary Ellen agreed. "God has surely blessed us with this *schnuck buppli* girl."

Rebekah nodded. "God is truly the God of miracles!"

Epilogue

Rebekah closed the drawer of the cash register as an English man and his two small children left the greenhouse carrying a large pot of petunias. It had been a *gut* year for their business, and for them as a married couple as well.

Their home, built by Rebekah's papa and Daniel's *daed*, was connected to her parents' house. It gave them a place of their own, yet they were near enough to family to have help available should it be needed.

Rebekah smiled to herself. She and Daniel had been married a little over a year now, and their love just seemed to keep on growing stronger with each passing day.

Daniel no longer helped his father in the dairy business. He was much too busy helping out at the greenhouse or building wooden gadgets to sell. He'd added weather vanes, wind chimes, and lawn furniture to the other items he sold in the store. Rebekah had also begun selling wicker baskets and plant stands for her flowers and plants.

In the summertime, they sold Papa's cold root beer and shoofly pies Mom had baked. In the wintertime, they offered coffee and hot chocolate, along with funny-cake pie and several kinds of cookies.

They were making enough money to live comfortably. Their meat and milk was supplied by Clarence Beachy, in exchange for fresh vegetables from the garden Daniel tended in the summer months. Mom saw that they had plenty of fresh eggs and chicken whenever they needed it, too. Setting her pride aside, Rebekah had learned to accept help from all available sources. She'd proven to herself that she could be financially self-sufficient, but it was no longer all that important. What truly mattered was the love of family and friends, and especially, God's love.

Rebekah was jolted by the shrill sound of a baby crying. She left the cash register and wheeled quickly into the back room. Next to her resting cot sat a wooden cradle, handmade with love by the little one's father.

Reaching into the cradle, Rebekah picked up her month-old baby daughter. "Little Anna, are ya hungry?" she crooned. The baby nestled against her mama's breast and began to nurse hungrily. "If your namesake, Grandma Anna Stoltzfus, could only have seen you," Rebekah whispered, "I'm sure she'd have loved you as much as we all do." She stroked the soft, downy hair on top of her baby's small head and closed her eyes.

"Mei, des is aver en sche buppli—my, isn't she a pretty baby? She's sure enough a miracle, sent straight from God, ain't it so?"

Rebekah's eyes flew open, and she gazed up at her tall, bearded husband. She blinked away the tears of joy that had crept into her eyes. *"Jah,* she certainly is. I never dreamed God would be so *gut* as to give us a child of our own. Someday I hope little Anna and her cousin, Martha Rose, will have a special friendship, like Mary Ellen and I've had for so many years."

Daniel bent down and touched his warm lips to Rebekah's mouth, causing little shivers to spiral up her arms. She never got tired of his kisses, nor that look of love that so often crossed his face.

"Your faith has become strong, and God has given our girl a blessed gift havin' you as a *Mudder*—mother." Daniel kissed her again. "Praise God for baby Anna. Praise God for our love, Rebekah, my *Frau*—wife."

Rebekah wiped more tears from her eyes and murmured, "And praise God for all of His miracles!"

Plain and Fancy

In loving memory of my good friend, Sharon Hanson, whose love for her "special" child was an inspiration to all.

Chapter 1

Laura Meade opened her laptop, entered the correct password to put her on-line, and began the E-mail she'd been meaning to write for the past week.

Dear Shannon,

I'm finally settled in at the Lancaster School of Design. I think I'm going to like it here. Not only is the college rated in the top ten, but the valley's beautiful, and the Amish in the area are unbelievable! The Plain women I've seen wear simple, dark-colored dresses, with little white hats on their heads. The men wear cotton shirts, dark pants with suspenders, and either a straw or black felt hat with a wide brim. They drive box-shaped, gray buggies pulled by a horse. They look like something out of the Dark Ages!

Tomorrow I'm going to the farmers' market. I hear it's a great place to get good buys on handmade Amish quilts. I may even be able to acquire some helpful decorating ideas.

Hope you're doing well. I'm looking forward to seeing you at Christmas.

Your friend,
Laura

Laura thought about sending an E-mail to her parents, but she'd talked to them on the phone an hour ago. Moving away from the desk, she picked up a brush from the dresser and began her nightly ritual of one hundred strokes through her long, thick tresses.

She glanced around. Even the smallest room at home was bigger than her dorm room, but she'd only be here two years. Then she could go home and redecorate the whole town of Minneapolis if she wanted to.

"It's stifling in here," Laura moaned. She dropped the hairbrush to the bed and opened a window. A slight breeze trickled through the screen, but it did nothing to cool the stuffy room. Here it was the first week of September, and the days were still hot and humid.

Fall had always been Laura's favorite time of the year. In fact, someday she hoped to decorate her own home with harvest colors. The kitchen windows would be outlined with sheer, yellow curtains. The living room, dining room, and bedroom floors would be covered with thick, bronze carpet. She wanted Early American furniture, and there would be plenty of paintings on the walls.

Mom and Dad had allowed her to travel halfway across the country to attend the Lancaster School of Design. There were several good schools closer to home, but when Laura heard about this one, so near to the heart of Amish land, she wanted to come. She was sure she could learn some unique decorating ideas from the interesting culture of the Plain People.

Laura glanced at the picture of Dean Carlson, sitting in a gold frame on top of her dresser. He was the newest partner at Meade Law Firm, and she and Dean had been dating off and on for the last six months. Dean hadn't been happy about her moving to Pennsylvania, even though it would only be for a few years.

A loud knock jolted Laura out of her musings. With a sigh, she crossed the room and opened the door.

A young woman with short, curly blond hair stood in the hallway. "Hi, I'm Darla Shelby, your next-door neighbor."

Laura shook her hand. "I'm Laura Meade."

"Since tomorrow's Saturday, I thought I'd hop in my sports car and drive to Philly for some serious shopping. Would you like to tag along?" Darla offered.

The mention of a car caused Laura to brood over her own expensive car, parked in the garage at home. She wished she would have driven it to Pennsylvania, but her parents had insisted on her flying.

"I realize we've only met," Darla continued, "but I figure what better way to get acquainted than in the middle of a Philadelphia shopping spree."

Laura leaned against the doorframe as she contemplated the tempting offer. "I appreciate the invitation, and I'd love to go some other time, but I've got my heart set on seeing the farmers' market at Bird-in-Hand tomorrow. I understand some of the Plain People go there."

Darla nodded. "Those Amish and Mennonites are quite the tourist attraction." She pointed at Laura. "I'll let you off the hook, but I hope you'll take a rain check."

"I promise, but tomorrow, why don't you go to the market with me?"

Darla wrinkled her nose. "No way! I'd rather be caught in the middle of rush-hour traffic on the turnpike than brush elbows with a bunch of farmers!"

Laura wiggled her eyebrows. "Those *farmers* do look pretty interesting."

"Maybe so, but they're not interesting enough for me to waste a whole day on." Darla turned toward her own room, calling over her shoulder, "Whatever you do, Laura Meade, don't let any of that Amish culture rub off on you!"

❧

A ray of sun filtered through the window, causing Laura to open her eyes. She peeked at the clock on the bedside table. It was nearly nine o'clock! She'd slept much later than she planned. Jerking the covers aside, she slipped out of bed and headed straight for the shower. Later, as she studied the contents of her closet, Laura had a hard time deciding what to wear. She finally opted for rust-colored slacks and a beige tank top. She accentuated the outfit with a gold necklace. Her long, auburn hair was pulled back on the sides and held in place with tan, pearl-studded combs.

"Nothing fancy, but presentable," she said to her reflection in the mirror. "Amish country, I hope you're ready, because here I come!"

When Laura stepped from the cab, she stood in awe of her surroundings. Part of the parking lot was full of Amish buggies. It looked odd to see them lined up, with modern-looking cars parked a few aisles away. She wished she'd remembered her camera, for this was a sight to behold!

Heat and humidity were already beginning to weigh the morning down, and she was relieved to step inside the farmers' market and find the building much cooler.

The first table Laura discovered was run by two young Amish women. They were selling an assortment of pies and cookies. Both wore their hair parted down the middle, then pulled back into a tight bun. Small, white caps were perched on top of their heads, and their dresses were long, blue cotton, with black aprons over the top. One of the women smiled and asked if she'd like to sample something.

Laura stared longingly at a piece of apple pie. "They look delicious, but I had breakfast not long ago." The truth was, she was always counting calories. One bite of those scrumptious pastries and she'd probably gain five pounds. She moved on quickly, before temptation got the better of her.

The next few tables were run by non-Amish farmers. Their things didn't interest Laura much, so she found another table, where an elderly Amish woman was selling handmade quilts.

"Those are gorgeous!" Laura exclaimed. "How much do they cost?"

The woman showed her each one, quoting the prices, which ranged from four to nine hundred dollars.

"I'm going to buy one," Laura said without batting an eyelash. "I don't want to carry it around while I shop, though. Can you hold this one for me?" She pointed to a simple pattern, using a combination of geometric shapes, done in a variety of rich autumn colors.

"What's this called?" she asked.

"That's known as 'Grandmother's Choice,' " the Amish woman replied, her hand traveling lightly over the material.

Laura nodded. "I like it—a lot. I'll be back for it before I leave, but I can pay now if you'd like."

The woman smiled. "Pay when ya come back." She placed the quilt inside a box, then slipped it under the table.

It was getting close to lunchtime, so Laura decided to look at one more table, then find something nonfattening to eat.

The next table was loaded with a variety of hand-carved items. Laura glanced around for the person in charge but didn't see anyone. She picked up one of the finely crafted birdhouses and studied the exquisite detailing. When a young Amish man popped up from behind the table, she jumped, nearly dropping the birdhouse. He was holding a box filled with more birdhouses and feeders. A lock of sandy brown hair fell across his forehead, and his deeply set, crystalline blue eyes met Laura's gaze with a look that took her breath away. Her cheeks grew hot, and she quickly placed the birdhouse back on the table. "I–I was just admiring your work."

A hint of a smile tweaked the man's lips, revealing a small dimple in the middle of his chin. "My name's Eli Yoder. I'm a wood-carver and carpenter, and I'm ever so thankful God gives me the ability to use my hands for somethin' worthwhile."

Though she had been to church a few times, Laura was not particularly religious. Nibbling on the inside of her cheek, she merely nodded in response.

"Are ya lookin' for anything special? I also have wooden flowerpots and ornamental things for the lawn." Eli lifted one up for her inspection.

Laura stared at his hand, clutching a windmill whirligig. Her gaze traveled up his muscular arm. Below his rolled-up shirtsleeve, his tanned arms were feathered with light brown hair. She licked her dry lips and forced her wayward thoughts to come to a halt. "I—uh—live in a dorm room at the Lancaster School of Design," she stammered. "So I really don't have a need for birdhouses or whirligigs."

"I don't think I've ever heard of that school."

"I'm learning to be an interior decorator," she explained, drawing her gaze to his appealing face, then back to the items on the table.

When he made no comment, she looked up again and saw that he was staring at her with a questioning look.

"My job will be to help people decorate their homes in attractive styles and colors."

"Ah, I see. Do ya live around here, then?"

She shook her head. "My name's Laura Meade, and I'm from Minneapolis, Minnesota. I've already studied some interior design at one of our local community colleges, and I'm here to complete my training."

There was an awkward silence as they stared at one another.

"Eli, there you are! I thought we were supposed to meet for lunch," a beseeching woman's voice called out. "I waited outside, but ya never showed. I figured I'd better come a-lookin'."

Eli turned to face a young, blond-haired Amish woman, dressed similar to the other Plain women Laura had seen earlier. "I'm sorry, Pauline," he said. "I got busy talkin' with this customer and forgot about the time." He considered Laura a moment. "Is there anything you're wantin' to buy?"

"I was just looking," she murmured.

"Well, *wass machts aus?*" Pauline said, frowning. "Eli, if you're finished here, can we go have lunch?" She took a few steps closer, brushing her hand lightly against Eli's arm.

Eli nodded. *"Jah,* Pauline." He glanced back at Laura. "It was nice chattin'. I wish ya the best with your studies." He turned away, and the Amish couple ambled off.

Laura tried to still her racing heart as she watched them disappear. *How did it get so warm in here? And how in the world could someone as plain as that Amish man be so adorable?*

❧

As Eli and Pauline exited the building, he glanced over his shoulder. The young English woman was still standing beside his table. *She's sure a fancy one. Fancy and very pretty. I wonder why someone like her would be so interested in birdhouses?*

"Eli, where do ya wanna eat lunch?"

Pauline's question and slight tug on his shirtsleeve brought Eli's thoughts to an abrupt halt.

"I thought you carried a picnic basket," he said peevishly.

"I did, but I wasn't sure where ya wanted to eat it."

He shrugged. "It makes no difference."

"Let's go to the park across the street. There's picnic tables and trees to shade us from the hot sun."

Eli gave no response, and she grabbed his sleeve again. "What's wrong? You're actin' kinda *naerfich.*"

"I'm not nervous," he assured her. "I've just got a lot on my mind."

Pauline slipped her hand through the crook of his arm. "After you've had a few bites of fried chicken, ya won't be thinkin' of nothin' but my good cookin'."

Eli feigned a smile. "Kissin' wears out, but cookin' don't." Truth be told, he really wasn't in the mood to eat just now, but he wouldn't let on to Pauline. He was sure she'd worked hard making the picnic lunch, and he'd promised to eat it with her. Besides, it was a silly matter that had turned his thoughts away from his date. A few drumsticks and a plate of potato salad would sure as anything get him thinking straight again!

❧

The expensive Amish quilt Laura purchased at the market was placed across the bottom of her bed, making it a definite focal point in the tiny dorm room. It reminded her of the young Amish man who'd been selling woodcrafted items. As she sat at her desk trying to study, Laura found herself wishing she'd bought one of his birdhouses.

Her fingers drummed restlessly across the desktop. As ridiculous as it might seem, Laura had been attracted to Eli Yoder. It was stupid, because she and the Amish man were worlds apart. Besides, the young woman he'd been with seemed awfully possessive. *She could even be his wife.*

Laura fought the urge to fantasize further and forced herself to concentrate on the monochromatic swatches of material lying before her. It wouldn't be good to get behind on her studies because of a passing fancy with someone she'd probably never see again.

❧

Laura was kept busy with classes and what seemed like never-ending homework. It had been several weeks since she'd ventured into Amish land, but today was Saturday, and she was determined to have some fun. She was fascinated by the

Plain People and decided to check out a few gift shops in a nearby Amish community. This time she made sure she had her camera.

Laura took a taxi to the village of Paradise. The first store she entered was a souvenir shop, filled with excited tourists. It had numerous shelves full of Pennsylvania Dutch trinkets, and a rack of postcards, with photos of Amish and Mennonite farms, Plain People, and horse-drawn buggies. Laura bought several, with the intent of sending them to family and friends back home.

Her next stop was the Country Store, which was set up something like a modern convenience store. It was stocked with gift items, groceries, and plenty of snack food.

Laura wandered toward the back of the store. To her amazement, the shelves were lined with oil lamps, bolts of plain cotton material, women's black bonnets, men's straw hats, boxes of plain handkerchiefs, and several pairs of work boots. One whole section was stocked with barrels full of whole grains, and along one wall were several straw brooms and a variety of gardening tools.

"The Amish must do their shopping here," Laura murmured, feeling suddenly self-conscious, like she didn't belong. She moved quickly toward the door.

Outside on the sidewalk, two Amish girls were playing jump rope. They took turns using the rope, sucking on lollipops while they awaited their turn.

They're so cute. I just have to get their picture. Laura pulled a camera from her purse, focused it on the children, and was about to snap the picture when someone grasped her shoulder.

"We don't approve of havin' our pictures taken."

Laura spun around. A pair of penetrating blue eyes bore down on her. Her heart skipped a beat. It was the same Amish man she'd met at the farmers' market a few weeks ago!

"I remember you," Eli stated. "You were at the market, lookin' at my birdhouses."

Laura offered Eli what she hoped was her best smile. "I'm sorry if I did wrong by trying to photograph those cute little girls."

"The Amish don't believe in havin' their pictures taken," he reaffirmed.

"What about all the pictures on postcards?" She withdrew one from her purse. "Isn't that an Amish man working in the fields?"

Without even glancing at the postcard, Eli shot back, "Photographers have many ways of gettin' the pictures they want. Sometimes they hire non-Amish to dress like us. Some use close-up lenses, so they can take pictures without us even knowin'. Others offer payment. This happens a lot with our *kinder.*"

"Your what?"

"The children."

Laura frowned. "I don't understand. If your religion doesn't approve, why would it be okay for kids to take money?"

"Not all Amish are as strict about the rules. A few believe it's all right for the *kinder* to have their pictures taken. Like many other religions, some of our people make certain worldly concessions." Eli shook his head. "Some even leave the faith in order to live like the English do."

Laura was tempted to ask if that would be such a bad thing, but she didn't want to say anything offensive to the Amish man.

Eli motioned toward a wooden bench near the building. "Would ya wanna sit awhile? I'll take my birdhouses inside; then we can have a glass of root beer. That is, if you'd like one."

Laura nodded enthusiastically. Of course she'd like a root beer! Especially when it would give her more time to question Eli. She dropped to the bench and leaned forward with her elbows resting on her jean-clad knees. She watched Eli head to the parking lot, where his horse and buggy stood waiting. He made two trips into the Country Store, shouldering large cardboard boxes filled with birdhouses and feeders. When he emerged for the last time, he was carrying huge mugs of foamy root beer. He handed one to Laura and sat down beside her.

"I noticed your buggy is open—sort of like a carriage," she remarked. "Most of the Amish buggies I've seen are closed and kind of box-shaped."

Eli grinned. "That's my courtin' buggy. Pop gave it to me on my sixteenth birthday."

"What's a courting buggy?"

"English boys get a driver's license, and maybe a car when they turn sixteen. We Amish get an open buggy, so's we can start courtin'. You English call it *datin',*" he explained.

"Have you been dating very long?"

"Are you wantin' to know my age?"

Laura felt the heat of embarrassment creep up her neck, but she nodded.

"It's okay. I don't mind ya askin' one bit. I'm twenty-three, and Pop says I oughta be married already." Eli chuckled and lifted the mug of root beer to his lips.

So, he's single, and just a year older than me. Laura wasn't sure why, but that bit of information gave her a great deal of pleasure. "How come you're not married?"

Eli shrugged. "Guess I haven't found anyone who can put up with me."

"I'm sure some young lady already has her eye on you." Laura was thinking of the Amish woman who'd been with Eli at the market. She'd seen the way that Plain gal looked at him.

Eli laughed. "I don't know 'bout that, but I do know I'm not ready to settle down to marriage yet." He smacked his lips and changed the subject. "Umm. . . this is sure *gut* root beer. Thomas Benner, the store owner, makes it himself."

Laura took a sip. "*Gut?* What does that mean?"

"It's the Pennsylvania Dutch word for *good,*" he explained.

She smiled. "It is *gut* root beer, and your buggy's sure nice-looking. How does it ride?"

Eli rewarded her with a warm smile. "Would ya like to find out?"

"I'd love that!" Laura jumped up, then whirled around to face him. "Would it be all right? It's not against your religion or anything?"

Eli's smile widened, causing the dimple in his chin to become more pronounced. "Many Mennonite and Amish Brethren take money from tourists in exchange for a buggy ride. So, I know of no rule sayin' ya can't take a ride in my buggy." He winked at her. "If someone should see us, they'll probably just think you hired me for a ride."

🙚

Eli helped Laura into the left side of the open buggy; then he climbed up on the right and gathered the reins. With a few clucks to the beautiful gray and black gelding, they were off.

A slight breeze caught the ends of Laura's golden bronze hair, whipping them gently around her face. Eli felt his chest constrict. *This English woman is sure appealin'. Why, it's almost sinful to be so beautiful. I'm wonderin' why she would even want to be seen with someone as plain as me.*

Eli felt a twinge of guilt for allowing himself the simple pleasure of admiring her beauty, but he couldn't quit thinking how it might be to know her better.

"This is awesome!" Laura exclaimed. "I never would have dreamed riding in a buggy could be so much fun!"

He glanced over at her and smiled. *"Jah,* I like it, too."

When they'd gone a short distance, Eli turned the buggy down a wide, dirt path, where there were no cars, just a carpet of flaxen corn on either side.

"Where are we going?"

"To Paradise Lake. It's wonderful *gut* this time of year." Eli flashed her another smile. "I think you're gonna love it!"

🙚

Laura leaned back in her seat, breathed deeply of the fresh air, and drank in the rich colors of the maple trees dotting the countryside. "I think the warm hues of autumn make it the loveliest time of the year," she murmured.

Eli raised his dark eyebrows. "Such fancy words you're usin'."

She laughed. "Should I have said, it's wonderful *gut?*"

"Jah, wonderful *gut!"* Eli pulled the horse to a stop in a grassy meadow near the small lake. "Here we are!"

"You were so right," she gasped. "It *is* beautiful here!"

Eli grinned like a child with a new toy. "In the summer it's a *gut* place for swimmin' and fishin'. We like to skate on the lake when it freezes over in wintertime, too."

Laura drew in another deep breath. "It looks like the perfect place for a picnic."

"My family and I have been here many times." Eli glanced over at Laura. "Would ya like to get out and walk around?"

"That sounds nice, but I rather like riding in your courting buggy," she said with a sigh of contentment. "Can't we just drive around the lake?"

"Sure, we can." Eli got the horse moving again.

As they traveled around the lake, Laura began to ply him with questions about the Amish. A gentle breeze rustled the trees, and she felt her heart stir with a kind of excitement she'd never known. She wasn't sure if it was the fall foliage, the exhilarating buggy ride, or the captivating company of one very cute Amish man that made her feel this way. One thing for sure, she felt a keen sense of disappointment when Eli turned the buggy back to the main road.

"Do you like wearin' men's trousers?" he asked suddenly.

She glanced down at her blue jeans and giggled. "These aren't men's trousers. They're made for a woman, and they're quite comfortable." When Eli made no comment, she decided it was her turn to ask a question. "What's your family like?"

He grinned. "I have a *gut* family. There's Pop and Mom, and I have an older sister, Martha Rose. She's married to Amon Zook, and they've got a three-year-old son. I also have two younger brothers who help Pop on the farm while I'm workin' at the Strausberg Furniture Shop in Lancaster."

"I'd like to see your farm sometime." The unexpected comment popped out of Laura's mouth before she had time to think about what she was saying.

When Eli's brows drew downward, and he made no response, she wondered if she'd overstepped her bounds. As much as she would like it, she'd probably never get to meet Eli's family or have another opportunity to ride in an Amish buggy.

It seemed like no time at all before they were pulling into the Country Store's parking lot. Eli jumped down and came around to help Laura out of the buggy. When his hands went around her waist, she felt an unexpected shiver tickle her spine. "Thanks for a wonderful *gut* ride. I'll never forget this day."

Laura started across the parking lot and was surprised to see Eli walking beside her. They both stopped when they reached the sidewalk. "I'd better find a telephone booth and call a taxi. I'm supposed to meet a friend for supper in about an hour," she said with a note of regret.

Eli clicked his tongue. "Your friend is some lucky fellow."

She gazed deeply into his eyes. "It's not a man I'm having supper with. It's a girl from school."

He smiled. "I was wonderin'—would ya be interested in goin' back to Paradise Lake next Saturday? We could take a picnic lunch."

Laura could hardly believe her ears. Had he really asked her on a date? Maybe not a date exactly, but at least another chance to see him.

"That would be nice," she said, forcing her voice to remain steady. "What should I bring?"

"Just a hearty appetite and a warm jacket. I'll ask Mom to fix the lunch, because she always makes plenty of food."

"It's a date." Laura felt the heat of a blush. "I mean—I'll look forward to next Saturday. Should we meet here in front of the Country Store, around one o'clock?"

"Jah, that'll be fine," he answered with a nod.

"Until next Saturday then." Just before Laura turned toward the phone booth, she looked back and saw him wave. She lifted one hand in response and whispered, "Eli Yoder, where have you been all my life?"

Chapter 2

Laura's eyelids drooped as she leaned against the headrest in the backseat of the taxi. A picture of Eli's clean-shaven face popped into her mind. His twinkling blue eyes, sandy brown hair, and that cute little chin dimple made him irresistible.

She opened her eyes with a start. What was she thinking? She couldn't allow herself to fantasize about Eli Yoder. He was off limits—forbidden fruit for a modern English woman. *Then why am I thinking about him? And why did I ever agree to go on a picnic with him next Saturday?*

As hard as she tried, Laura seemed unable to squelch the desire to see Eli one more time. She would learn a bit more about the Amish, they would enjoy a *gut* picnic lunch, soak up the beauty of Paradise Lake, and it would be over. They'd never see each other again. She would only have memories of the brief time she'd spent with an intriguing Amish man. It would be a wonderful story to tell her grandchildren someday. She smiled and tried to visualize herself as a grandmother, but the thought was too far removed. The only thing she could see was the face of Eli Yoder, calling her to learn more about him and his mysterious religion.

❧

The family style restaurant was crowded, and Laura was late. She stood in the clogged entryway, craning her neck to see around the people in front of her. Was Darla already in the dining room? Sure enough, she spotted her friend sitting at one of the tables.

When Laura arrived, Darla was tapping her fingers against her place mat. "Sorry to be late," Laura apologized. She pulled out a chair and sat down quickly.

"Were you caught in traffic?"

"Nope. I went for a ride in an Amish buggy this afternoon. I guess we lost track of time."

Darla's eyebrows furrowed. "We?"

"I was with Eli Yoder. He's the cute Amish guy I met at the market a few weeks ago. I'm sure I mentioned it."

Before Darla could comment, Laura rushed on. "We had a great time. The fall colors at the lake were gorgeous." She glanced down at her purse and frowned. "I had my camera with me the whole time, but I forgot to take even one picture."

Darla gazed at the ceiling a few seconds; then she looked back at Laura. "You're starstruck, but I hope you realize you're making a big mistake."

"What are you talking about?"

"I can see you're crazy about this Amish guy, and it can only lead to trouble."

"I'm not *crazy* about him!" When Laura noticed several people staring, her voice softened. "I did enjoy his company, and the buggy ride was exciting, but that's all there is to it. I hardly even know the man."

Darla studied her menu. "I hope you're not planning to see him again."

"We're going on a picnic next Saturday, but it's no big deal."

Darla leaned across the table. "Don't do it. Cancel that date."

Laura's mouth dropped open. "It's not a real date. It's just an innocent picnic. Besides, I can't cancel. I don't have his telephone number, so I have no way of getting in touch with him." She grabbed her menu, hoping this little discussion was finally over.

"Most Amish don't have telephones," Darla reminded. "Do you know they live like the pioneers used to? They don't use electricity, no phone, no cars—"

Laura held up her hand. "I get the picture. Can we change the subject now?"

Darla's voice dropped to a whisper. "I want to say one more thing."

Laura merely shrugged. Darla was obviously not going to let this drop until she'd had her say.

"I've lived in this area all my life, so I know a little something about the Amish."

"Such as?"

"They don't take kindly to outsiders involving themselves in their lives."

"Eli doesn't seem to mind."

Darla gritted her teeth. "His folks sure would mind if they knew he was seeing an English woman. I'll bet they don't, though, do they?"

Laura hated to be cross-examined. None of this was Darla's business. "I have no idea what Eli's told them."

"The Amish are private people. They live separate, extremely plain lives. They don't like worldly ways—or worldly women for their men." Darla shook her finger. "You'd be smart to nip this in the bud before it goes any further."

Laura remained silent. She didn't need Darla's unwanted advice, and she knew *exactly* what she was doing.

❧

Laura had been sitting on the wooden bench in front of the Country Store nearly an hour. *Where is he? Maybe he isn't coming. Maybe Darla's right and he's decided it's best not to have anything to do with a "worldly" woman. I'll give him another five minutes; then I'm leaving.*

She scanned the parking lot again. There were several Amish buggies parked there, but they were all the closed-in type. Eli's courting buggy was nowhere in sight. She watched as several Amish families went into the store. *How do those poor women stand wearing long, dark-colored dresses all the time? And their hair—parted straight down the middle, then pulled back into a tight bun. I wonder why they wear those little caps perched on top of their heads? I couldn't stand looking so plain!*

It was 1:50 when Eli's buggy finally pulled into the parking lot. Laura felt such relief, she was no longer angry. She waved and skittered across the parking lot.

Eli climbed down from the buggy. "Sorry to be so late. I had to help with chores at home, and it took longer than expected."

"It's okay. You're here now; that's all that matters."

Eli gave her a boost, then went around and took his seat. He glanced up. "There's not a cloud in the sky, so it should be a *gut* day for a picnic." He beamed at Laura, and her heart skipped a beat. "Did ya bring a jacket? The sun's out, but it's still pretty chilly."

Laura shook her head. "I'm wearing a sweater. I should be fine."

Eli picked up the reins and said something in Pennsylvania Dutch to the horse.

"What'd you say?"

His face turned crimson. "I told him I was takin' a beautiful young woman on a ride to the lake, so he'd better behave himself."

Laura's heart kept time to the *clip-clop* of the horse's hooves. "Thank you for such a nice compliment."

Eli only nodded in response.

They traveled in silence the rest of the way, but Laura found being in Eli's company made words seem almost unnecessary.

Paradise Lake soon came into view. If it were possible, the picturesque scene was even more beautiful than it had been the week before. Maple leaves were dispersed everywhere, like the colorful patchwork quilt lying on Laura's bed. The sun cast a golden tint against the surrounding hills, and a whippoorwill called from somewhere in the trees. Laura relished the sense of tranquility as it washed over her like gentle waves against the sand.

Eli helped her down, and she slid effortlessly into his arms. Raising her eyes to meet his, her breath caught in her throat at the intensity of his gaze. Her pulse quickened, and she grabbed her camera, hoping the action would get her thinking straight again. She photographed the scenery, being careful not to point the camera in Eli's direction. It was a sacrifice not to snap a few pictures of his handsome face. How fun it would be to send one to her friend, Shannon.

Eli pulled a heavy quilt and a huge picnic basket from under the buggy seat. He motioned Laura to sit on the ground, where he'd stretched the comforter. The contents of the basket revealed more food than two people could possibly eat, and Laura knew she'd be counting calories for the rest of the week. As Eli spread a green tablecloth over the quilt, she eyed the meal in anticipation. He set out containers of fried chicken, coleslaw, dill pickles, brown bread, Swiss cheese, baked beans, and chocolate cake. Then he handed Laura a glass of iced tea, some plastic silverware, and a paper plate.

Eli bowed his head in silent prayer, so she waited for him to finish before she spoke. "It was nice of your mother to prepare this. Especially since she doesn't even know me."

Eli reached for a drumstick. "I didn't tell Mom about you."

"Why not?"

He removed his straw hat and placed it on the quilt. "I don't think my folks would like me seein' someone outside the faith."

Laura couldn't hide her disappointment as she bit her bottom lip. "I guess I'll never get to meet them."

"I'd like you to see where I live and meet my family, but takin' you there might cause trouble."

She gave him a sidelong glance. "If you didn't tell your mother about me, then why'd she pack such a big lunch?"

"I told her I was goin' on a picnic, but I'm sure she was thinkin' it was with someone else." Eli reached for another piece of chicken. "Is there anything more you'd like to know about the Amish?"

Laura sighed deeply. Apparently, Eli Yoder wasn't that different from other men. If he didn't like the way the conversation was going, he simply changed the subject. "When did your religion first begin?" she inquired.

"Our church got its start in the late sixteen hundreds when a young Swiss Mennonite bishop, named Jacob Amman, felt his church was losin' some of its purity," Eli began. "He and several followers formed a new Christian fellowship, later known as 'Amish.' So, ya might say we're right-wing cousins of the Mennonites."

Laura nodded as Eli continued. "The Old Order Amish, which is what my family belongs to, believes in separation of church and state. We also expect Bible-centeredness to be an important part of our faith. A peaceful way of life and abidin' to all nonworldly ways are involved, too."

Laura frowned. "Like no telephones or electricity?"

Eli nodded. "We believe it's the way Christ meant for the church to be. A few Amish businessmen do have a phone," he amended. "They either keep it in the barn or in a small shed outside their home."

Laura ate in silence for a time, savoring the delicious assortment of food and trying to digest all that Eli had shared. She knew about some Protestant religions and had attended Sunday school a few times while growing up. However, the Amish religion was more complex than most. She found it rather fascinating, in a quaint sort of way.

The wind had picked up slightly, and Laura shivered, pulling her sweater tightly around her shoulders.

"You're cold," Eli noted. "Here, take my coat." He removed his jacket and draped it across her shoulders.

Laura fought the impulse to lean her head against his strong chest. The temptation didn't linger long, for the sound of horse's hooves drew her attention to an open buggy pulling into the grassy area near their picnic spot.

A young Amish woman, wearing a dark bonnet and an angry scowl, climbed down from the buggy. Laura thought she recognized the girl, and her fears were confirmed when Eli called, "Pauline, what're you doin' here?"

"I was lookin' for you, Eli Yoder! I stopped by your farm, but Lewis said you'd gone to Paradise Lake for a picnic. I couldn't think who ya might be with, but I see clearly who's taken my place." Pauline planted both hands on her hips and frowned. "I'm mighty disappointed, Eli. I thought this was *our* place. How could ya bring a foreigner here?"

Laura's mind whirled like a blender on full speed. She'd never thought of herself as a foreigner. After all, this was America, and she was an American through and through.

Eli jumped up and moved toward Pauline. He placed one hand on her shoulder, but she brushed it aside. "She's that Englisher you were showin' birdhouses to at the market, ain't it so?"

Eli glanced back at Laura. His face was bright red. "Pauline Hostetler, meet Laura Meade."

Pauline's lips were set in a thin line. She glared at Laura as though she were her worst enemy.

Laura didn't feel much like smiling, but she forced one anyway. "It's nice to meet you, Pauline."

"Ich will mit dir Hehm geh," Pauline said, looking back at Eli.

"I can't go home with you. I came with Laura, and I've gotta take her back to town after we finish our picnic," he explained.

Pauline turned away in a huff. "And to think, I borrowed my brother's buggy for this! I deserve much better." She scrambled into the buggy. "Enjoy your *wunderbaar schee* picnic!"

"Jah, des Kannich du!" Eli called.

Laura sat there, too stunned to speak and trying to analyze what had just happened. Pauline Hostetler was obviously Eli's girlfriend. Laura watched as she drove out of sight, leaving a cloud of dust in her wake.

As Eli dropped to the quilt, Laura offered him a tentative smile. "Guess I owe you an apology."

"For what? You did nothin' wrong."

"I caused a bit of a rift between you and your girlfriend."

Eli shifted on the blanket. "Pauline's not really my girlfriend, though I think she'd like it to be more. We've been friends since we were *kinder.*"

"But you saw how upset she got. She was clearly jealous."

Eli shrugged. "I'm sorry if she's jealous, but I've done nothin' wrong, and neither have you."

"Nothing but have a picnic with a *foreigner,*" Laura said sarcastically. "I couldn't understand the words you two were speaking. What were you saying?"

Eli toyed with the end of the tablecloth. "Let's see. . . She said, *'Ich will mit dir Hehm geh*—I want to go home with you.' Then she told us to enjoy our *'wunderbaar schee,'* or 'wonderful nice' picnic. To that, I said, *Jah, des Kannich du,'* which means, 'Yes, I will.' "

"She spoke some Pennsylvania Dutch to me at the market the other day, too."

"Do you remember the words?"

Laura squinted as she massaged the bridge of her nose. "I think it was something like, *'Wass machts us.'* She looked kind of irritated when she said it."

"Wass machts aus," Eli corrected. "It means, 'What does it matter?' "

"Pauline doesn't like me."

He frowned. "How can ya say that? She don't even know you."

Laura groaned. "She knows you, and she's obviously in love with you. I think she's afraid I might be interested, too."

Eli eyed her curiously. "Are ya?"

Laura scooted across the quilt until she was shoulder to shoulder with Eli. "Yes, I am interested. You're different from any man I've ever met." She slid in front of him, so she could gaze into his blue eyes. "I don't want to make trouble for you, so it might be better if we say good-bye and go our separate ways."

Eli reached for her hand. "You're the most beautiful, exciting woman I've ever met. I don't want ya to go walkin' out of my life." He rubbed his thumb slowly across her knuckles, causing little shivers to spiral up her arm.

"Me neither," she said softly.

"Even though it's not possible for us to start courtin', I don't see why we can't keep seein' each other as friends," Eli commented. "It wouldn't really be breakin' any rules."

Laura blinked. She hadn't expected him to offer that much. "How do you know your family won't disapprove? I mean, an Amish man making the acquaintance of a worldly English foreigner?"

Eli shrugged. "I don't know what they'd say for sure, but there's one way to find out."

Laura leaned closer, so her face was mere inches from Eli's. "What's that?"

"We can finish our picnic lunch, then drive over to my place. You can meet my family, before Pauline tells them her version of our picnic."

Laura's stomach clenched, and she willed herself to breathe normally. Was this what she really wanted? What if Eli's family didn't like her? If they made him stop seeing her, even as a casual friend, how would she ever convince him to leave the Amish faith?

Now where did that thought come from? I hardly even know Eli Yoder. Besides, he seems happy with his plain lifestyle. Why would he be willing to give it up for some fancy Englisher like me?

Laura made a conscious effort to concentrate on eating a bit more of the delicious assortment of picnic foods. She would worry about counting calories and changing Eli tomorrow. If she was going into the enemy camp today, it may as well be on a full stomach.

Chapter 3

The Yoders' farm was situated on sixty acres of dark, fertile land. The fields were planted in alfalfa, corn, and wheat, reminding Laura of a quilt—rich, lush, orderly, and serene. The expansive white house was surrounded by a variety of trees and shrubs, while an abundance of autumn blooms dotted the flower beds. A windmill not far from the home turned slowly in the breeze, casting its shadow over the tall white barn directly behind the house. There were no telephone or power lines on the property, but a waterwheel grated rhythmically in the creek nearby, offering a natural source of power. There was also a huge propane tank sitting beside the house. Laura assumed it was used for heat or to run some of the Amish family's appliances.

"This is it," Eli said with a sweeping gesture. "My home."

Laura's gaze traveled more thoroughly around the orderly looking farm. There were sheep and goats inside a fenced corral, and chickens ran about in a small enclosure. On the clothesline hung several pair of men's trousers, a few dark cotton dresses, and a row of towels, pinned in orderly fashion.

Eli put his hand against the small of Laura's back, leading her around the house and up the steps of a wide back porch. When they entered the kitchen, Laura's mouth fell open. She *had* stepped back in time—to the pioneer days.

The smell of sweet cinnamon and apples permeated the room, drawing Laura's attention to the black, wood-burning stove in one corner of the room. There were no curtains on the windows, only dark shades, pulled halfway down. Except for a small battery-operated clock and one simple calendar, the stark white walls were bare.

A huge table was in the middle of the kitchen. Long wooden benches were placed on either side, and two straight-backed chairs sat at each end. A kerosene lamp hung overhead, with a smaller one sitting in the center of the table. Against one wall was a tall wooden cabinet, with a sink and a hand pump sandwiched on the sideboard. Strategically placed near a massive stone fireplace were a rocking chair and a well-used couch.

Like a statue, Laura stood near the door. "Do all Amish live this way?"

Eli moved across the room. "What way?"

"So little furnishings. There aren't any pictures on the walls and no window curtains. Everything looks so bare."

"Our religion doesn't permit such things," Eli explained. "The Old Order Amish believe only what serves as necessary is needed in the home. The Bible forbids God's people from makin' graven images."

Laura didn't have a clue what Eli was talking about. All she knew was this home was like no other she'd ever seen. Here was a group of people, living in the modern world, yet having so little to do with it. It was unbelievable!

Eli grinned when a slightly plump Amish woman entered the room. Her brown hair, worn in the traditional bun and covered with a small white cap, was peppered with gray. Her hazel-colored eyes held a note of question when she spotted Laura.

"Mom, I'd like ya to meet Laura Meade," Eli said quickly. He motioned toward Laura, then back to his mother. "This is my *mamm*, Mary Ellen Yoder."

She hates me. The woman's just met me, and I can tell by her expression that she's decided I'm the enemy. Laura forced a smile. "It's nice to meet you, Mrs. Yoder."

Mary Ellen moved toward the stove and began to stir the big pot of simmering apples. "Do ya live around here?"

"No—"

"Has your car broken down, or are ya just another curious tourist who wants to check out the strange people livin' in the plain house?"

"I'm none of those things, Mrs. Yoder. I'm from Minneapolis, Minnesota, but I'm attending the Lancaster School of Design," Laura explained.

Mary Ellen whirled around, casting Eli a questioning look.

"We met at Farmers' Market a few weeks ago," he said. "Laura was interested in my birdhouses. I've been showin' her around."

Mary Ellen's gaze went to the wicker basket in Eli's hand. "You two have been on a picnic?"

Jah, we went to Paradise Lake," he answered.

"It's beautiful there," Laura put in. "The lunch you made was wonderful."

Before Eli's mother could respond, the kitchen door flew open, and two young men sauntered into the room. They were speaking in their native tongue but fell silent when they saw Laura standing beside Eli.

"These are my younger brothers, Lewis and Jonas," Eli said, motioning toward the rowdy pair. "Boys, this is Laura Meade. We met at Farmers' Market."

Lewis nudged Jonas and chuckled. *"Es gookt verderbt schee doh!"*

Jonas laughed and nodded. *"Jah*, it does look mighty nice here!"

Laura felt the heat of a blush stain her cheeks. "It's nice to meet you."

Turning to his mother, Jonas said, "Pop'll be right in. How 'bout some lemonade? We've worked up quite a thirst."

Mary Ellen nodded and moved across the room to the icebox.

Jonas, who had light brown hair and blue eyes like Eli's, pulled out one of the benches at the table. "Why don't ya set yourself down and talk awhile?"

Laura glanced at Eli to see if he approved, but he merely leaned against the cupboard and smiled at her. His mother was already pouring huge glasses of lemonade.

Laura had the distinct feeling Mrs. Yoder would be happy to see her leave, and she was about to decline the invitation when Eli spoke up. "We'd be glad to have a cold drink, and maybe some of those ginger cookies you made yesterday, Mom."

With a curt nod, Mary Ellen scooped several handfuls of cookies out of a ceramic jar. She piled them on a plate and brought them and the lemonade to the table.

Lewis and Jonas dropped to one bench, and Eli and Laura sat on the other one.

Eli made small talk with his brothers, and occasionally Laura interrupted with a question or two. She was getting an education in Amish culture that rivaled anything she'd ever read about or seen on any postcard.

The young people were nearly finished with their refreshments when the back door flew open. A tall, husky man with graying hair and a full beard lumbered into the room. He slung his straw hat over a wall peg, then went to wash up at the sink. All conversation at the table ceased, and Laura waited expectantly to see what would happen next.

The older man dried his hands on a towel, then took a seat in the chair at one end of the table. He glanced at Laura but said nothing.

Eli decided he needed to break the silence. "Laura, this is my *daed*, Johnny Yoder. Pop, I'd like ya to meet Laura Meade."

Laura nodded. "Mr. Yoder."

Pop turned to Mom, who was now chopping vegetables at the kitchen sideboard. "What's to eat?"

Mom's face was stoic as she replied in Pennsylvania Dutch, "The rest are havin' lemonade and cookies. Do you want some?"

Pop grunted, "All right, I am satisfied."

Mom brought another pitcher of lemonade to the table and placed it in front of her husband.

"Danki," Pop muttered.

Eli turned to his father again. "Laura's from Minneapolis, Minnesota. She's attendin' some fancy school in Lancaster."

"The wisdom of the world is foolishness," Pop grumbled in his native language.

Eli shot him an imploring look. "There's no need to be goin' rude on my guest."

"Ah, so the Englisher can't understand the Dutch. Is this the problem?" Pop asked with a flick of his wrist.

"What kind of fancy school is it?" Lewis questioned.

"I'm learning to be an interior decorator," Laura answered.

"It's so's she can help folks decorate their homes real fancylike," Eli interjected.

"It wonders me so that anyone could put such emphasis on worldly things," Mom commented while placing another plate of cookies on the table.

"Laura and I went to Paradise Lake for a picnic," Eli said, changing the subject to what he hoped was safer ground. "It sure is beautiful now. Some of the leaves are beginnin' to fall."

"I'll be glad when it's wintertime and the lake freezes over," Jonas added. "I love to go ice-skatin'."

Eli noticed that Laura's hands were trembling. He wasn't the least bit surprised when she hopped off the bench and announced, "Eli, I think I should be going."

He sprang to his feet as well. "I'm gonna drive Laura to the Country Store. I'll be back in plenty of time for chores and supper."

When no one responded, Eli jerked the back door open so he and Laura could make a hasty exit. "Well, that went well," he grumbled a few minutes later.

"I'm sorry for putting you through all that," she murmured as he helped her into the buggy. "Your family obviously doesn't approve of me."

"Don't worry about it. We're just friends."

"Your folks sure do talk funny," Laura commented.

"In the privacy of our homes, we often speak Pennsylvania Dutch," Eli explained.

Laura shook her head. "I wasn't talking about that."

"What then?" he asked, giving her a sidelong glance.

"Your mother said, 'It wonders me so,' and one of your brothers said, 'Set yourself down and talk awhile.' " Laura giggled. "That kind of talk sounds so uneducated."

Eli pulled sharply on the reins, guiding the horse to the side of the road. When the buggy came to a complete stop, he turned to face Laura. "Are you makin' fun of my family?"

"No, no, of course not," she stammered. "I just meant—"

Eli held up his hand. "You don't have to explain. I know how strange we Amish must seem to you English. We talk differently, dress differently, and *jah*, even think counter thoughts. It's who we are, and we don't care how the world chooses to view us."

Laura twisted the ends of her purse strap, biting down on her lower lip. "I–I'm sorry. I didn't mean to make light of the way you talk." She looked away. "Maybe it *would* be better if you never saw me again."

"No!" Eli was quick to say. He grabbed her hand. "I wanna be your friend. I'll be glad to show ya around more of our Amish villages whenever you like."

"Even if your parents disapprove?"

He nodded. "*Jah*, but I think I can make 'em see reason. Pop and Mom are really fun-lovin', easygoin' folks." He shrugged. "After all, we're not courtin' or anything. There's really nothin' for them to be concerned about."

Laura smiled sweetly. "How about next Saturday? Could you show me around then?"

He pursed his lips. "I think I could."

🙊

Eli returned home in time for supper. He'd no more than taken his seat when the lectures began. "You play with fire, and you're bound to get burned!" Pop shouted.

"There's always trouble somewhere, and that Englisher has trouble written all over her pretty little face."

Eli snorted and reached for a buttermilk biscuit. He ripped off a hunk and dipped it into his stew. "I've come of age. I should be allowed to make my own decisions. Don't you think it's time?"

Jonas grinned. "I'm thinkin' my big brother is *Asu Liebe.*"

"I am not in love!" Eli snapped. "Laura and I are just friends. I don't see how it could hurt for me to spend a little time showin' her around the countryside and sharin' a bit about our Amish ways."

"The Amish ways? Why would she be needin' to know our ways?" asked Mom. "The English who come nosin' around our community are usually nothin' but trouble. It has always been this way."

"Laura's not trouble, Mom," Eli defended. "She's just curious about our lifestyle, and I think—"

"You are mixed up!" Pop roared. "A few questions here, and a few trips around the country there, and soon that foreigner will be tryin' to talk you into leavin' the faith."

Eli felt his face flame. "No way, Pop!"

"Eli's secure in the faith," Lewis interjected. "He got baptized and joined the church much younger than either Jonas or I did. Ain't it so, Jonas?"

Before Jonas could open his mouth, Pop hollered, "You'd best be stayin' outta this, boy. If ya can't keep your opinions to yourself, then you'll be doin' double chorin' for the next two weeks!"

Lewis fell silent. Eli, however, couldn't keep quiet. He swallowed the last bit of food in his mouth. "Are ya forbiddin' me to see Laura again?"

Pop shook his head. "No, all Amish *younga* have the right to choose. However, you're already a church member. You must be careful not to let anything cloud your judgment. As long as ya don't get *Asu Liebe* for the Englisher or let her tear ya away from the faith, we won't interfere."

"We don't have to like it, though," Mom added.

Eli stood up. "I think I'll go out to my workshop and do some carvin'." He made a hasty exit out the back door, ignoring the concerned looks exchanged among those left at the table.

❧

Laura collapsed onto her bed. She felt as if she hadn't slept in days. Today had been exhausting. By the time Eli had dropped her off in front of the Country Store, all her energy was zapped. Until today, Laura had usually been able to charm anyone she'd met. Not only had she not charmed Eli's parents, but she was quite sure she'd actually alienated them.

Laura knew she would have to take things slow and easy. She didn't want to scare Eli off by making him think there was more to their relationship than mere friendship. After all, that's all there really was at this point, but she was hoping for more—so much more.

Chapter 4

Saturday dawned with an ugly, gray sky and depressing, drizzling rain. Laura groaned as she stared out the window of her dorm room. She figured Eli probably wouldn't show up for their rendezvous at all. If they went for another buggy ride, they'd be drenched in no time; and she seriously doubted that he'd want to pass the time sitting in some restaurant or wandering through a bunch of tourist-filled souvenir shops. They weren't supposed to meet until two o'clock, so with any luck, maybe the rain would be gone by then.

Laura turned from the window and ambled over to her desk, fully intending to get in a few hours of study time. Her mind seemed unwilling to cooperate, so she ended up pushing the books aside and painting her fingernails instead.

By noon, the drizzle had turned into a full-fledged downpour. Laura could only hope Eli Yoder would not stand her up.

❧

"From the way you're dressed, I'd say you're going out. What I want to know is where you're heading on an icky day like this."

Laura was watching out the downstairs window for her taxi, and she turned at the sound of Darla's voice. Laura offered a brief smile and held up her green umbrella. "I'm waiting for a cab to take me to the village of Paradise."

Darla's forehead wrinkled. "I thought you'd be up in your room studying. What do you want to do, drown in liquid sunshine?"

Laura laughed. "I can't concentrate on schoolwork today. Besides, I'm supposed to meet Eli at the Country Store."

Darla's frown deepened. "You may be gorgeous, but you sure don't have a lick of sense."

"What's that supposed to mean?" Laura moved away from the window and began to pace the length of the hallway.

"It means you're barking up the wrong tree, chasing after that Amish fellow."

"It's none of your business."

Darla started toward the visitors' lounge. "Do whatever you want, but don't come crying to me when you get your delicate little toes stepped on."

A honking horn turned Laura's attention back to the window. "My taxi's here. I've gotta go. See you later, Darla."

❧

Laura stepped from the cab just in time to witness a touching scene. Eli Yoder was standing in front of the Country Store, holding a black umbrella over his head. The minute he spotted Laura, he stepped forward and, like a true gentleman, positioned the umbrella over her.

She smiled up at him, her heart pounding with expectation. "I'm surprised to see you."

"We said we'd meet here," Eli said with a friendly grin.

She nodded. "Yes, but it's raining, so I know we can't go for a buggy ride."

"We Amish don't stay home just 'cause it rains." Eli steered her across the parking lot. "I brought one of our closed-in buggies today."

Laura's heart was beating a staccato rhythm as she felt the warmth of his hand on her elbow, and she realized it was something she could easily become accustomed to.

Eli helped her into the gray, box-shaped buggy, then went around to the driver's side.

"Where are we going?"

"Is there anything in particular you're wantin' to see?"

She shrugged and leaned her head against the padded leather seat. Her heart felt light, and she was content just being with Eli, so it didn't really matter where they went.

"The farmers' market is open today," Eli said, breaking into her thoughts. "Would ya like to go there?"

She smiled. "I'd love to go to the farmers' market. There are so many interesting things to see there."

"*Jah,*" he agreed, "and today they're havin' a craft show, so many Amish and English will be sellin' their wares."

"It sounds like fun." Laura stole a glance at Eli. "Are you selling any of your wooden creations?"

"*Himmel*—I mean, no, no. I just want to look around today. Maybe get a few ideas 'bout what I might carve."

"Good idea." Laura smiled. "Maybe I'll get some more decorating ideas, too."

❧

They entered the farmers' market and found a host of people roaming up and down the aisles. *The rain sure didn't keep anyone at home,* Laura noted. *Apparently, folks from Lancaster Valley appreciate a craft show as much as Eli and I do.*

"Let's start over here," Eli suggested, directing Laura's attention to a table on their left.

What a strange-looking couple we must make. Laura noticed several people staring at them. *Eli, dressed in his plain Amish clothes, and me, wearing designer blue jeans and a fancy monogrammed sweatshirt.* "Well, let them stare," she murmured.

"What was that?" Eli asked, moving close to the table of a Mennonite man who was selling small wooden windmills.

Laura shrugged. "Nothing. I was talking to myself."

Eli let out a low whistle as he picked up one of the windmills. "Finely crafted—very fine."

"It's nice," Laura agreed.

"Are ya hungry? Want somethin' to eat or drink?" he asked when they moved on.

"No, but if you're hungry, I'll drink a diet soda and watch you eat."

Eli pinched her arm lightly. "A diet soda for someone so skinny?"

"I am not skinny," she retorted. "I'm merely trying to keep my figure."

Eli's ears turned red as he looked her up and down. "Your figure looks right *gut* to me."

Laura giggled self-consciously. "Thanks for the nice compliment, but for your information, this shape doesn't come easy. I have to work at staying slender, and it means watching what I eat."

Eli raised his dark eyebrows as he continued to study her. "One so pretty shouldn't be concerned about gainin' a few pounds. Mom's pleasantly plump, and Pop says he likes her thataway."

Laura folded her arms across her chest. "You'll never catch me in any kind of plump state—pleasantly or otherwise."

Eli chuckled. "Someday you'll meet a great guy, get married, and have a whole house full of *kinder*. Then you won't even have a figure, much less have to worry 'bout keepin' it."

Laura flinched. "If I ever do get married, I have no intention of losing my shape!"

Eli steered her toward the snack bar at one end of the market. "I didn't mean to get your dander up. If ya ask me, you're way too touchy 'bout your weight."

"I don't recall asking you!" she snapped. "What would you know anyway? You're used to plain, fat women."

Eli jerked his head as though she'd slapped him across the face. "Maybe today wasn't such a *gut* idea after all. Maybe I should take you back to the Country Store."

Laura clutched at his shirtsleeve. "Please, Eli, can't we start over? I didn't mean to offend you."

They had reached the snack bar, and Eli turned to face her. "Our worlds are very different, Laura. I'm plain, and you're fancy. I see things differently than you do. I'm afraid it'll always be so."

Laura shook her head, her eyes filling with unwanted tears. "We're just getting to know each other. It's going to take a bit of time for us to understand one another's ways."

"Maybe we never will," he said with a frown. "I've been Amish all my life, and it's the only way I know."

She smiled up at him. "I can teach you modern things, and you can teach me Amish ways. I really want to learn, and I promise to be more tactful."

"I guess we can give it another try." Eli tapped Laura on the arm. "Can I interest ya in a glass of root beer and a giant, homemade pretzel?"

Afraid of hurting his feelings or getting into another discussion about her weight, Laura nodded. "Sure, why not." After all, she could count calories on her own time.

❧

Laura lay on the bed, her mind replaying the events of the day. As strange as it might seem, she was glad she and Eli had experienced their first disagreement. In spite of the dissension it had caused, it actually seemed to strengthen their relationship. For the remainder of the day, Eli had been compromising, and she'd done the same.

A soft knock on the door stirred Laura from her musings. "Who is it?"

"Darla."

Laura crawled off the bed. Jerking open the door, she wrinkled her nose at Darla. "If this little visit is going to be another lecture, you can save your breath."

Darla shook her head. "I wanted to apologize for this afternoon." She smiled brightly. "And see how your day went."

Laura motioned her inside. "Actually, it went well. Eli and I took in a craft show at Farmers' Market in Bird-in-Hand, and I got more decorating ideas."

Darla flopped onto the bed. "From what I've been told, the Amish don't believe in decorations or fancy adornments in their homes."

"True," Laura agreed, "but that's what makes it so unique."

"I don't follow."

Laura dropped down next to Darla. She ran her fingers across the quilt on her bed. "Take this, for example. It's plain, yet strikingly beautiful." She raised her eyebrows. "A quilt like this is in high demand, which is why it was so costly."

Darla shrugged. "To be perfectly honest, Amish decor doesn't do much for me. Neither do Amish men."

Laura clenched her jaw. This conversation was leading to another argument, and she was not in the mood. "It's been a long day, and I'm dog-tired. Do you mind if we continue this discussion some other time?"

Darla stood up and started for the door. "I almost forgot—you had a phone call while you were out exploring Amish land."

"Who was it?"

"Mrs. Evans took the call, and all she told me was that it was some guy, asking for you."

"Hmm. . .maybe it was Dad."

"I really couldn't say, but I think Mrs. Evans left a note in your mailbox."

"I'll go check, thanks," Laura said, following Darla out.

Darla waved and disappeared into her own room, and Laura ran down the steps. She found the note in her mailbox, just as Darla said. It read: *A man named Dean Carlson called around two o'clock. He wondered why he hadn't heard from you lately and wants you to give him a call as soon as possible.*

Laura sucked in her breath. So Dean was missing her. *Do I call him first thing in the morning, or should I make him wait a few days?*

Laura held the phone away from her ear and grimaced. She knew she'd made a mistake calling Dean so early in the morning. She should have remembered he was a bear before his third cup of coffee.

"What do you mean, you don't want me to come to Lancaster for a visit?" he barked.

"It's not that I don't want you to come," she said sweetly. "It's just that—I'll be coming home for Christmas, and—"

"Christmas? That's three months away!"

"I know, but—"

"I'm flying in next weekend, and that's all there is to it."

"No, no, it's not a good idea."

"Why not?"

Laura could almost see Dean's furrowed brows and the defiant lift of his chin. He was a handsome man, with jet-black hair that curled around his ears and eyes as blue as a summer sky.

Laura twisted the end of the phone cord around her finger as she struggled to find the right words. "It would be great to see you, Dean, but I always have lots of homework on the weekends, and—"

"Were you studying yesterday when I phoned?"

Laura sucked in her breath, knowing she couldn't possibly tell Dean about her Saturday date with Eli Yoder. "I—uh, went to the farmers' market."

"What's that got to do with homework?" he growled.

"I was researching the Amish culture."

"You're kidding, right?"

"No, I've been studying their quilts and getting some ideas for my next designing project." *I've been studying a fascinating Amish man, too.*

Dean cleared his throat. "How about next weekend? Can I come or not?"

Laura chewed on her lower lip. She liked Dean. . .or at least she had when they were seeing each other socially. Why was she giving him the runaround now? It only took a few seconds for her to realize the answer. She was infatuated with Eli Yoder and wanted to spend her weekends with him. Dean would only be a distraction, and if Eli found out about her English boyfriend, it might spoil her chances of getting him to leave the Amish faith.

"Laura, are you still there?"

Dean's deep voice drew Laura back to their conversation, and she sighed deeply. "Yes, I'm here."

"What's it gonna be?"

"I'd rather you didn't come."

"Is that your final word?"

"Yes. As I said before, I'll be home for Christmas."

Dean grunted, said good-bye, and hung up the phone. Laura breathed a sigh of relief. At least one problem was solved.

Chapter 5

Over the next several weeks, Eli and Laura saw each other whenever possible. In fact, Eli could hardly get Laura out of his thoughts. The vision of her beautiful face, smooth as peaches and cream, inched its way through his mind on more than one occasion. He had finally told his folks he was still seeing Laura, and the news hadn't gone over well, especially with Mom.

"She'll try to change you," she admonished one Saturday, as Eli was hitching the buggy for another trip to meet Laura. "Why, the first thing ya know, that English woman will be askin' you to leave the faith."

"*Ach*, Mom. No one could ever talk me into somethin' like that!"

Mom pursed her lips. "I wouldn't be so sure. Love does strange things to people."

Eli's eyebrows shot up. "Love? Who said anything about love, for goodness' sake?"

Mom gave him a knowing look. "I've seen the face of love before, Son. Every time ya come home after bein' with that fancy woman, I can see the look of love all over your precious face."

Eli felt himself blush. He would never admit it, especially not to Mom, but he was beginning to wonder if his fascination with Laura might be more than curiosity or friendship. What if he were actually falling in love with her? If she felt the same way about him, would she really expect him to leave the faith?

"Well, are ya headin' out or not?"

Mom's question drew Eli out of his musings. "*Jah*, I'm on my way."

As Eli stepped into the buggy, Mom waved. "Don't be too late, and remember what I said. We'd never live through a shunnin' in this family."

"There will be no shunnin'!" Eli called as he steered the horse down the driveway.

✲

Laura leaned her head out the buggy window and drew in a deep breath. "It smells like winter's coming!" she exclaimed.

Eli nodded. "I'm sorry it's so cold. Now we have to be content with one of Pop's closed-in buggies." He exhaled a groan. "I sure do miss my courtin' buggy."

"Don't you use it in the winter months at all?" she asked.

He shrugged. "Sometimes, on the milder days, but it's much warmer inside this buggy, don'tcha think?"

"*Jah*," she said with a giggle and a flip of her ponytail.

Eli grinned. "You look mighty *schnuck* today."

"*Schnuck?* What's that?"

"It means *cute*."

Laura's heart fluttered. "Thanks for the compliment."

Eli only nodded and made the horse go a bit faster.

"Where are you taking me today?" Laura asked.

"I thought ya might like to see one of our schoolhouses."

"Schoolhouses? You have school on Saturdays?"

He chuckled. "No, but Saturday's the best day for a tour of the schoolhouse. There won't be any *kinder* about, and no teacher wearin' a stern look or carryin' a hickory switch."

Laura shook her head. "Eli Yoder, you're such a big tease." She reached across the short span between them and touched his arm. "Maybe that's why I like you so well."

"Because I like to kid around?"

"Yes. I find your humor and wholesome view on life kind of refreshing. It's like a warm breeze on a sweltering summer day."

Eli scrunched up his nose. "I don't believe I've ever been compared to a warm breeze before."

She withdrew her hand and leaned back. "I've learned a lot from you."

"Is that *gut* or bad?"

"It's *gut*, of course." Her voice lowered to a whisper. "I could teach you a lot about English ways, if you'd let me. We could take in a movie sometime, or—"

Eli held up his hand. "No, thanks. I think I know more'n I need to know 'bout the fancy life."

"How can you say that? Have you ever given yourself a chance to find out what the modern world really has to offer?"

"I ain't blind, Laura," he muttered. "I see what's out there in the world, and I'm not the least bit interested in electrical gadgets, fancy clothes, or thinkin' I don't need God."

Laura's mouth dropped open. "Who ever said anything about not needing God?"

"I know some English folks do love God," Eli said, "but many are too self-centered to give Him anything more'n a few thoughts, and then it's only when they need somethin'."

"Where did you hear that?" she asked, her voice edged with irritation. Was this going to turn into a full-fledged disagreement? If so, she wasn't sure it was a good idea to give her opinion. After all, she was trying to appease, not aggravate, Eli.

Eli shrugged. "It don't matter where I got the notion. The important thing is, I'm content to be Amish, happy to be a child of God, and I don't need no worldly things to make me complete."

"My dad says religion is a crutch for weak men." The words were out before Laura even had time to think.

Eli pulled sharply on the reins and eased the horse and buggy to the side of the road. "Are you sayin' I'm a weak man?"

She turned to face him. "No, of course not. I just meant—"

"Maybe we've come too far," Eli said, his forehead wrinkling.

"Too far? You mean, we missed the schoolhouse?"

He shook his head. "Too far with this friendship we've been tryin' to build."

Laura's heart began to pound, and her throat felt like it was on fire. If Eli broke things off now, there would be no chance for them. She couldn't let that happen. She would not allow him to stay angry with her for something so ridiculous as a difference of opinion on religious matters.

She touched his arm again. "Eli, I respect your religious beliefs, but can't we just agree to disagree on some things?"

"It's kind of hard to have a friendship with someone when we keep arguin'."

She nodded. "I know, so let's not argue anymore. In fact, if it would make you feel better, I'll just sit here and listen to you narrate. How's that sound?"

He reached for the reins. "You're a hard one to say no to, Laura Meade."

She smiled. "I know."

❧

It was only the first week of December, but the valley had been hit with a heavy blanket of snow. Laura figured it would mean the end of her enjoyable rides with Eli. . .at least until spring. She'd be going home for Christmas soon, so that would put an end to their times anyway. Leaving Eli, even for a few weeks, wasn't going to be easy. However, she'd promised her parents and friends she would be coming for the holidays. Besides, even if she stayed in Pennsylvania, Eli would spend Christmas with his family, and she, the fancy English woman, would never be included in their plans.

Laura stared out her dorm room window. If only she had some way to get in touch with Eli. If they could just meet somewhere for lunch.

She finally curled up on her bed with a romance novel, surrendered to the fact that this Saturday would be spent indoors, without Eli Yoder.

Laura had only gotten to the second page when a loud knock drove her to her feet. "Who's there?"

"Darla. Are you busy?"

Laura opened the door. "What's up?"

Darla was wearing a pair of designer jeans and a pink angora sweater. A brown leather coat was slung over one arm, and a matching cap was perched on top of her short, blond curls. "I thought I'd drive into Philly today. I still have some Christmas shopping to do, and only the big stores have what I want."

"You're going shopping today?"

Darla nodded. "I was hoping you'd come along."

"In this weather?" Laura gestured toward the window. "In case you haven't noticed, there's a foot of snow on the ground!"

Darla shrugged. "I'm sure most of the main roads have been cleared." She nudged Laura's arm. "I'll treat you to lunch."

Laura released a sigh. "Oh, all right." It wasn't the way she really wanted to spend the day, but it was better than being cooped up in her room.

The ride to Philadelphia went well. They took the main highway, and just as Darla had predicted, it had been plowed and sanded. In spite of the weather, the stores were crowded with holiday shoppers.

Laura and Darla pushed their way through the crowds until they'd both purchased enough Christmas presents for everyone on their lists. Everyone except Eli. Laura wanted to get him something special, but since he lived such a plain life and was against worldly things, she couldn't find anything suitable.

They left the city around four o'clock, and by the time they reached the turnpike, it was snowing again.

"I know it's a little out of the way, but would you mind stopping at the Country Store on our way home?" Laura asked Darla.

"What for?"

"I want to get a Christmas present for Eli. I couldn't find anything appropriate in Philly, but I'm sure I can find something in Paradise."

Darla squinted her eyes. "I don't mind stopping, but I do mind what you're doing."

Laura looked away. "What are you talking about?"

"I can see no matter how much I've warned you, you've decided to jump into the deep end of the pool."

"Huh?"

"Don't be coy with me, Laura. I've warned you about the Amish, and you've forged ahead anyway. It doesn't take a genius to see you're head over heels in love with this Eli fellow."

"In love? Don't be ridiculous! Eli and I are just friends."

Darla gave the steering wheel a few taps with her gloved fingers. "Sure. . . whatever you say."

When they arrived in Paradise, the Country Store looked deserted. A sign in the window said they were open, so Darla parked her car, and Laura went in.

She soon realized that choosing a gift for an Amish man, even in a Plain store, wasn't going to be easy. There were shelves full of men's black felt hats, suspenders in all sizes, and a large assortment of white handkerchiefs. Laura wanted something more special than any of these things. It had to be something that would make Eli remember her.

She was about to give up when she spotted a beautiful set of carving tools. She paid for them and left the store feeling satisfied with her purchase. Now if she only had some way to get the gift to Eli.

When she returned to the car, Laura noticed the snow had turned to freezing rain.

"This isn't good," Darla complained as they pulled out of the parking lot. "I should have gone directly back to Lancaster and stayed on the main roads."

Laura groaned. "I'm sure we'll get back to the school in time for your favorite TV show."

"I wasn't thinking about TV," Darla snapped. "I'm concerned about staying on the road and keeping my car intact."

No sooner had she spoken the words than they hit a thick patch of ice. The car slid off the road, coming to a stop in the middle of a snowbank.

"Oh, great!" Darla moaned. She put the car in reverse and tried to back up. The wheels spun, but the car didn't budge. Darla tried several more times, but it was no use. They were stuck, and there was nothing they could do about it.

"Maybe we should get out and push," Laura suggested with a weak smile.

"And maybe I should call for help," Darla said, reaching into her purse for the cell phone. She started to dial but dropped it onto the seat with a moan.

"What's wrong?"

"It's dead." Darla opened the car door and got out. Laura did the same.

"Now we're really in a fix," Darla complained. "I should have checked my phone battery before we left Lancaster this morning."

"I guess it's my fault. If I hadn't asked you to go to Paradise—"

Laura stopped speaking when she heard the *clip-clop* of a horse's hooves approaching. "Do ya need some help?" a deep male voice called out.

She whirled around, and her heartbeat quickened. Eli Yoder was stepping down from an open sleigh. "Are we ever glad to see you!" she cried.

As soon as Eli joined them, Laura introduced Darla. Then, offering Eli a wide smile, Laura asked, "Would it be possible for you to give us a ride to Lancaster? We need to call a tow truck for Darla's car."

Eli surveyed the situation. "I can pull you outta that snowbank with my horse."

Darla shook her head. "You've got to be kidding!"

"My horse is strong as an ox," he asserted.

Darla shrugged. "Okay. Give it a try."

Laura and Darla stepped aside as Eli unhitched the horse and hooked a heavy rope from the animal's neck to the back bumper of Darla's car. He said a few words in Pennsylvania Dutch, and the gelding moved forward. The car lurched and was pulled free on the first try.

"Hooray!" Laura shouted with her hands raised.

Darla just stood there with her mouth hanging open.

"Why don't I follow you back to Lancaster?" Eli suggested. "That way I can be sure that you don't run into any more snowbanks."

"Thank you," Darla said.

"Would it be okay if I rode in your sleigh?" Laura asked Eli. "I've always wanted to go on a sleigh ride." She smiled at him. "Besides, I have something for you."

His brows arched upward. "You do?"

She nodded. "I'll get it from Darla's car and be right back." Laura raced off before Eli had a chance to reply. When she grabbed Eli's gift from the car, Darla, already in the driver's seat, gave her a disgruntled look but said nothing.

Laura made her way back to where Eli waited beside the sleigh. After he helped her up, she pulled the collar of her coat tightly around her neck. "Brr. . . It's sure nippy out."

Eli reached under the seat and retrieved a colorful quilt. He placed it across her lap, and she snuggled beneath its warmth, feeling like Cinderella on her way to the ball.

Eli followed Darla's car back to Lancaster. When they arrived in front of their dorm, Darla got out and came over to the sleigh. "Thanks again, Eli. You sure saved the day!"

"I'm glad I happened to be in the right place at the right time," he replied with a warm smile.

Darla looked up at Laura, still seated in the sleigh. "Are you getting out or what?"

She shook her head. "You go on. I need to speak with Eli."

Darla shrugged and walked away.

Laura turned to face Eli. "I'm glad you came along when you did. I'm leaving for Minneapolis in a few days, and I didn't think I'd get the chance to see you before I left."

"I went to the Country Store this mornin'," Eli said. "You weren't there, so I thought maybe you'd already gone home for the holidays."

Laura frowned. If she'd had any idea Eli was going to venture out in the snow just to see her, she'd have moved heaven and earth to get to Paradise this morning. "I really didn't think you'd be coming," she said softly. "I guess fate must have wanted us to meet today after all."

Eli raised one eyebrow. "Fate? You think fate brought us together?"

She nodded. "Don't you?"

He shook his head. "If anyone brought us together, it was God."

"I have something for you," Laura said, feeling a bit flustered. She handed him the paper bag, and her stomach lurched with nervous anticipation. "Merry Christmas, Eli."

Eli opened the sack and pulled out the carving set. He studied it a few seconds; then his forehead wrinkled. "It's a nice gift—much better than the carvin' set I use now." He fidgeted, and Laura was afraid he was going to hand it back to her.

"What's wrong? Don't you like it?"

"It's *wunderbaar*, but I'm not sure I should accept such a gift."

"Why not?" she asked, looking deeply into Eli's searching blue eyes.

"I have nothin' to give you in return."

Laura reached for his hand and gently closed her fingers around his. "Your friendship is the only Christmas present I need. Please say we can always be friends."

Eli swallowed hard, and she watched him struggle for composure. Several seconds went by; then he offered her a grin that calmed her fears and warmed her heart. "*Jah*, I'd like us to always be friends."

Chapter 6

Laura's first few days at home were spent thinking about Eli. When she closed her eyes, she could visualize his warm smile, little chin dimple, and those clear, blue eyes, calling her to reach out to him.

Ever since Laura had returned home, her mother had been trying to keep her occupied. "Why not join me for lunch at Ethel Scott's this afternoon?" she suggested one morning.

Laura was lying on the couch in the living room, trying to read a novel she'd started the day before. She set it aside and sat up. "I need to get my Christmas presents wrapped."

Mom took a seat next to Laura. Her green eyes, mirroring Laura's, showed obvious concern. "I'm worried about you, Dear. You haven't been yourself since you came home for the holidays." She touched Laura's forehead. "Are you feeling ill?"

Laura shook her head. "I'm fine. Just a little bit bored. I'm used to being in class every weekday."

"That's precisely why you need to get out of the house and do something fun." Mom tipped her head, causing her shoulder-length auburn hair to fall across her cheek. Even at forty-five, she was still lovely and youthful looking.

"Ethel's daughter Gail is home from college, and I'm sure she'd be thrilled to see you," Mom continued. "In fact, she'd probably get a kick out of hearing about that boring little town you're living in now."

Laura moaned. "Lancaster isn't little, and it sure isn't boring."

"The point is, you've been cooped up in this house for days. Won't you please join me today? It'll be much better than being home alone."

"I won't be alone," Laura argued. "Foosie is here, and she's all the company I need." She glanced at her fluffy, ivory-colored cat, sleeping contentedly in front of the fireplace. "After I'm done wrapping gifts, I thought I might give Shannon a call."

Mom stood up. "I would think it would be Dean Carlson you'd be calling." She shook her finger at Laura. "Dean's called at least four times in the past two days, and you always find some excuse not to speak with him."

Laura drew in her bottom lip. How could she explain her reluctance to talk to Dean? "I'll be seeing Dean on Christmas Day. That's soon enough."

Her mother shrugged and left the room.

Laura puckered her lips and made a kissing sound. "Here, Foosie, Foosie. Come, pretty lady."

The ball of fur uncurled, stretched lazily, then plodded across the room. Laura scooped Foosie into her lap and was rewarded with soft purring when the cat snuggled against her white angora sweater. "I've missed you. Too bad cats aren't allowed in the dorm rooms at school. If they were, I'd take you back with me."

The telephone rang and Laura frowned. "Just when we were getting all cozy." She placed the cat on the floor and headed for the phone that was sitting on a small table near the door. "Meade residence."

"Laura, is that you?" a familiar female voice asked.

"It's me, Shannon."

"When did you get home?"

"Last Saturday."

"And you haven't called? I'm crushed."

Laura chuckled. "Sorry, but I've been kind of busy." *Busy thinking about Eli Yoder.*

"Is it all right if I come over?"

"Sure, I'd like that."

After Laura hung up the phone, she headed for the kitchen. She had two cups of hot chocolate ready by the time her friend arrived.

"Have a seat, and let's get caught up," Laura said, handing Shannon a mug.

Shannon sniffed her drink appreciatively. "You got any marshmallows?"

Laura went to the cupboard to look, while Shannon placed her mug on the table, then took off her coat. "I think it's gonna be a white Christmas. I can smell snowflakes in the air."

Laura tossed a bag of marshmallows on the table and took the seat across from Shannon. "We've already had a good snowstorm in Lancaster."

"Really? Were you able to get around okay?"

"Oh, sure. In fact, I—"

"Say, you haven't said a word about my new hairstyle," Shannon cut in. She dragged her fingers through her bluntly cut, straight black hair. "Do you like it?"

Laura feigned a smile as she searched for the right words. "You—uh—look different with short hair."

Shannon blew on her hot chocolate, then reached inside the plastic bag and withdrew two marshmallows. She dropped them into the mug and grinned. "I kind of like my new look."

"I'm surprised you would cut your hair. I thought you'd always keep it long."

Shannon shrugged, then took a sip of her drink. "Long hair is too much work, and it takes forever to dry." She set the cup down and snapped her fingers. "I know! Why don't you make an appointment at Brenda's Beauty Boutique and get your hair cut and styled while you're home for Christmas?"

Laura trembled at the thought of losing her shining glory. "I don't think I could ever cut my hair. It took me too long to get it this way."

Shannon poked at the marshmallows with the tip of her finger as she studied Laura. "Have you met any cute guys out there in Lancaster County?"

Laura smiled. "Eli Yoder. I sent you an E-mail about him."

"You mean that Amish fellow?"

"He's the one."

"I thought that was just a passing fancy. Surely you're not really interested in this guy."

Laura felt the heat of a blush creep up the back of her neck and spread quickly to her face. "I've been fighting my attraction to Eli, but it's a losing battle." She drew in a deep breath and let it out in a rush. "To tell you the truth, I think I might be in love with him."

Shannon nearly choked on her hot chocolate. "You can't be serious!"

"I am."

Shannon leaned forward, as though she were sharing some dark secret. "Does he know how you feel?"

"I don't think so. We've only agreed to be friends, and I don't see how it could work for us to have a romantic relationship."

Shannon nodded. "Makes sense to me."

"Eli's really religious," Laura remarked. "We're worlds apart, with him being a plain kind of guy, and me being a fancy English woman." She laughed dryly. "At least that's how Eli sees me."

Shannon drummed her fingers along the edge of the table. "Hmm. . ."

"What?"

"Maybe he'll leave the Amish faith and become *fancy.*"

"I've thought about that—even hoped for it," Laura admitted. "Eli's religion and his plain lifestyle are very important to him. I doubt he'd be willing give to it up, though I am going to ask—when I get the nerve."

Shannon reached across the table and patted Laura's hand. "This is a fine fix you've got yourself into. Maybe you'll end up going over to the other side before it's all said and done."

Laura's eyebrows furrowed. "Other side? What are you talking about?"

"I was thinking you might join the Amish faith. People have done a lot stranger things in the name of love."

Laura's frown deepened. "I don't think I could do that, Shannon. It would be so hard to give up everything I have, and—"

The kitchen door flew open, chopping off Laura's sentence. Her father entered the room, carrying an overstuffed briefcase and frowning like there was no tomorrow. From the way his shoulders were sagging, and the grim look he was wearing, Laura figured he must either be exhausted or terribly agitated about something.

Dad was a small, thin man, with dark brown hair and a matching mustache. His mahogany eyes looked unusually doleful as he shuffled across the room and collapsed into a chair.

"Dad, is something wrong?" Laura asked with concern. "You look so tired."

"It's just this fast-paced world we're living in," he answered, lowering his briefcase to the table. "On days like today, I wish I could pull a magic handle and make everything slow down. Maybe the pioneer days weren't so bad. Life in the fast lane is pretty hectic, but I suppose I'll survive." He pursed his lips and looked right at Laura. "Whatever you do, young lady, never let 'all work and no play' become your motto."

Dad's words made Laura think of Eli and his Amish family. They worked hard, but they weren't living in the fast-paced world. They took time for fun and relaxation. She wondered if Dad were given the chance, whether he might trade in his briefcase for a hoe and the quiet life among the Plain People. She chuckled softly. *Naw, that could never happen.*

❧

Eli meandered toward his woodworking shop at one end of the barn. He didn't know why, but he wasn't in the mood to carve or build one single thing.

He looked down at the woodworking set Laura had given him and groaned. He wished she hadn't presented him with such a fine, expensive gift. In fact, he wished she hadn't bought him anything at all. He'd given her nothing in return, and accepting Laura's present only made it that much harder to distance himself from her.

Eli sank to the metal folding chair by his workbench and leaned forward, until his head was resting in the palm of his hands. "If only I hadn't told her we could always be friends. It just ain't right."

"What ain't right?"

Eli jerked upright at the sound of his younger brother's voice. "Jonas, what do ya think you're doin', sneakin' up on me thataway?"

Jonas chuckled and sauntered over to the workbench. "I thought you came out here to work on a Christmas present, not talk to yourself," he said, giving Eli's shoulder a good smack.

Eli frowned. "I was plannin' on finishin' up the planter box I'm makin' for Martha Rose, but I can't seem to get in the mood."

Jonas pulled a bale of straw over to the bench and plopped down on it. "Christmas is only a few days away. How do ya think our big sister will feel 'bout not gettin' a gift from you?"

Eli grabbed the planter in question, along with a strip of sandpaper, and began sanding it with a vengeance. "It'll be done on time."

Jonas touched Eli's arm. "Take it easy. You're gettin' all worked up."

"I ain't worked up," Eli snapped as he continued to run the coarse paper over the edges of the wooden box.

Jonas eyed Eli intently. "Is that so? Well, ya sure could've fooled me."

"Quit starin'!" Eli shouted.

"I was just checkin' to see if my big brother is *Asu Liebe.*"

Eli slapped the sandpaper down on the bench and stood up, nearly knocking over his chair. "I ain't in love! Now, if ya don't have nothin' sensible to say, why don'tcha get on outta here?"

"It's that fancy English woman, ain't it so?"

Eli's forehead was beaded with sweat, and he knew it wasn't from heat, for there was at least a foot of snow on the ground. If only he could get Laura out of his mind. . .

"You're not denyin' it, so it must be true," Jonas persisted. "She's gotten under your skin, huh?"

Eli whirled around to face his brother. "Laura and I are just friends." His eyelid began to twitch. "Even if I wanted it to be more, it could never happen."

"How come?"

"She's English."

"I know, but—"

"There's no buts," Eli said impatiently. "I'd never leave our faith, and I sure couldn't ask Laura to become one of us."

"Why not?"

Eli folded his arms across his chest and drew in a deep breath. He was getting mighty frustrated with his little brother and this ridiculous conversation they were having. "Let's put it this way—would ya throw a newborn baby kitten into the pigpen?"

Jonas looked at him as if he'd gone daffy. "Huh? What's a little bitty kitten got to do with Laura Meade?"

Eli shook his head. "Never mind. You're probably too *Verhuddelt* to understand."

"I'm not mixed up! Just say what ya mean, and mean what ya say!" Now Jonas's forehead was dripping with sweat.

"Calm down," Eli commanded. "This is a dumb discussion. I say we drop it."

Jonas elevated his chin defiantly. "Ya know what I think?"

Eli blew out his breath and lifted his gaze toward the rafters. "No, but I'm sure ya won't scram 'til you've told me."

"I think you're in love with Laura Meade, but ya know she's no good for you. I'm thinkin' the best thing for everyone is for you to hurry and get hitched up with Pauline Hostetler."

Eli clenched his fists. If Jonas didn't leave soon, he couldn't be sure what he might do. With a trembling finger he pointed to the door. "Just go—now!"

❧

Christmas Day turned out to be pretty much the way Laura had expected. Her father invited several people from his law firm to dinner, and most of them spent the whole time talking about trial dates, briefs, and who they thought might get out of going to jail.

Among the guests was Dean Carlson, seated right next to Laura. She studied him as he droned on and on about the new computer system they'd recently installed at the office. There was no denying it—Dean was handsome. The funny thing was, Laura used to enjoy Dean's company. Now he seemed superficial and self-absorbed. She kept comparing him to Eli, whose warm, sincere smile could melt her heart, and whose infectious laughter was genuine, not forced like Dean's. She didn't know why she'd never seen it before, but Dean's whole mannerism was brash, and he was certainly the most egotistical man she'd ever met. Eli, on the other hand, was gentle and genuinely humble.

"Laura, are you listening to me?" Dean asked, breaking into her thoughts.

She managed a weak smile. "I think Dad may have mentioned the new computer system."

"You *weren't* listening," he snapped. "The computer system was not the last thing I said."

She blinked. "It wasn't?"

"I was asking if you'd like to go to the New Year's Eve office party with me."

Laura stared at Dean. How could she even consider dating a man like him? Oh, sure, he had money, a good education, and a prestigious job, but he simply wasn't Eli Yoder.

"I want to take you to the party," Dean said again. "Will you go or not?"

Every fiber of her being shouted *"Not!"* She reached for her glass of water and took a few sips, hoping to buy some time.

When Dean began tapping the side of his glass with the tip of his spoon, she finally answered. "I appreciate the offer, but I hadn't planned on going to the party this year."

"Why not?"

Laura wasn't sure how to respond. She really had no legitimate reason for staying home. "I—uh—I'm leaving for Pennsylvania the day after New Year's, and I need to get packed."

Dean leaned his head back and roared. It was the first genuine laugh she'd heard out of him all day, but it didn't make her smile. "You have a whole week between now and the party. Surely that's time enough to pack a suitcase."

When Laura made no reply, he reached for her hand. "Come on, Honey, please say you'll go with me. After all, I do work for your dad, and I know he would approve."

Laura groaned inwardly. She knew she was losing this battle, and she didn't like it one bit. "Well, I—"

Dean leaned closer, and she could feel his warm breath against her ear. "If you don't have a wonderful time, I promise never to ask you out again."

Laura nodded in defeat. "Okay, I'll go."

❧

Mom had insisted Laura buy a new dress for the party. She couldn't understand what the fuss was about but decided she might as well enjoy the pampering. After all, she'd be leaving soon; then it would be back to the grindstone of school, homework, and. . .Eli. She hoped she could figure out a way to meet him again.

Standing before her full-length bedroom mirror, Laura smiled at the lovely young woman looking back at her. *If Eli could only see me now.*

Mom stood directly behind her, and she smiled into the mirror as well. "You look exquisite. I'm glad you decided to buy this beautiful silk gown. That shade of green brings out the color of your eyes so well."

Laura merely shrugged.

"I'm sure Dean will be impressed," her mother continued. "He's such a nice man."

"I suppose—just not my type."

"Not your type?" Mom's eyebrows furrowed. "How can you say that, Laura? Why, Dean is nice looking, has plenty of money, and—"

Laura turned away from the mirror. "Do you think my hair looks all right this way, or should I have worn it down?"

"Your hair looks lovely in a French roll," her mother responded. She gave Laura's arm a gentle squeeze. "I'm sure Dean will think so, too."

❧

The New Year's Eve party at the country club was already in full swing when Dean and Laura arrived. He'd been nearly an hour late picking her up, which had put her in a sour mood right from the beginning.

They'd no sooner checked their coats, when Dean pulled her into a possessive embrace. "You look stunning tonight, Laura. I'm so glad you decided to come."

Laura wished she could reciprocate with a similar remark, but the truth was, she wasn't glad to be here. In fact, she felt a headache coming on, and if it didn't let up soon, she knew she'd have a good excuse to leave the party.

"Would you like something to drink before we check out the buffet?" Dean asked.

She merely shrugged in response.

"What can I get you from the bar?"

"Nothing, unless they have diet cola."

"You're not driving," Dean reminded. "And if you're concerned about me drinking and driving, you shouldn't worry your pretty little head. I can handle a few drinks without any problem at all."

Laura gnawed on her bottom lip until it almost bled. If Dean was planning to have a few drinks, she could only imagine how the evening might end. She had to do something to get away from him now. "There's my friend, Shannon," she said. "I'm going over to say hi."

"Okay, I'll get our drinks; then I'll meet you at the buffet table in ten minutes." He sauntered off toward the bar.

Laura saw Shannon carrying her plate to one of the tables. "I'm glad to see you here," she said, taking a seat beside her friend.

"Why wouldn't I be?" Shannon asked. "My boyfriend, Clark, does work for your dad, you know." She glanced at the buffet table. "Clark's still loading up on food, but he'll be joining me soon."

Laura shrugged. If Shannon's comment was meant to chase her away, it wasn't going to work. "Listen, can you do me a big favor?" she asked.

"If it's within my power."

"I'm gonna call a cab and go home, so when Dean comes looking for me, would you tell him I had a splitting headache and left?"

"Tell him yourself. He's heading this way." Shannon pointed across the room, and Laura groaned.

"What's wrong? Did you two have a little disagreement?"

"Something like that." Laura decided it would be pointless to tell her friend the real reason she wanted to get away from Dean Carlson. The truth was, she wasn't just worried about his drinking. She didn't like that gleam in his eyes tonight. She was sure he wanted more than she was willing to give.

"Here's your diet cola," Dean said, handing Laura the cold drink. He nodded at Shannon. "How's it going?"

Shannon smiled. "Fine. How's everything with you?"

Laura set her glass on the table and tuned them both out as they engaged in small talk. Her thoughts turned naturally to Eli, and she couldn't help wondering how he was spending his New Year's Eve. She cringed when Dean pulled her thoughts away. "Tonight's going to be a great evening," he said, stroking the back of her neck.

She stood up quickly, knocking her soft drink over, and spilling some of it down the front of her new dress. "I–I'm not feeling well, Dean. I'm going to call a cab and go home."

Dean's eyebrows furrowed. "You can't be serious. We just got here, and I haven't had a chance to eat yet, much less show you off to my friends."

I don't want to be shown off. Laura thrust out her chin and looked at him defiantly. "I'm going home!"

"Okay, okay, don't get yourself in such a huff," Dean said. He set his drink on the table and steered her toward the coat closet. "I'll get my car."

"I'm calling a cab," she insisted. "There's no point in both of us missing the party. You stay and have a good time."

He smiled, and his eyes clouded over. "If you're dead set on going, then I may as well collect that stroke-of-midnight kiss." Before Laura could say anything, Dean bent his head and captured her lips in a kiss that would have left most women reeling with pleasure.

Laura drew back and slapped his face.

"What was that for?" he barked, reaching up to touch the red mark on his cheek. "I thought you wanted that kiss as much as I did."

Laura's face was so hot, she felt as though she were the one who'd been slapped. She wasn't in control of her emotions tonight, and that really bothered her.

"I'm sorry, Dean," she apologized. "Your kiss took me by surprise."

Dean's eyelids fluttered and he backed up a few steps. "I don't know what's come over you, Laura, but you haven't been the same since you left Minneapolis to attend that stupid school in Pennsylvania. If I were your father, I would never have allowed you to go there and would have insisted you finish your designing courses right here in town."

Laura's hands were trembling as she held them at her sides. If Dean kept goading her, she was liable to let him have it on the other cheek. "Good night, Dean," she said through clenched teeth. "Don't bother walking me out."

Chapter 7

The day after New Year's, Laura said good-bye to her parents at the airport. She was more than anxious to be on her way. It wasn't that she hadn't enjoyed being with them, but she wanted to get back to her studies. . .and Eli Yoder.

Laura hugged Mom and Dad, thanking them for the beautiful leather coat they'd given her for Christmas. Then, without so much as a backward glance, she boarded the plane, welcoming the butterflies doing a tap dance in her stomach.

Her time on the plane was spent sleeping and thinking about Eli. Laura couldn't decide if she should be straightforward and tell him that she'd come to realize how much she loved him, or if she should be coy, hoping to draw a declaration of love from him first.

By the time the plane landed in Philadelphia, she was a ball of nerves. The next flight to Lancaster wasn't for two hours, and she didn't relish the thought of sitting around the airport that long. If there hadn't been snow on the ground, she might have considered renting a car and driving to Lancaster.

She became absorbed in her newest romance novel but felt relief when the boarding call finally came. She still hadn't figured out how, but by this time tomorrow, she would have bared her soul to Eli.

❧

Laura awoke in her dorm room the following morning with a pounding headache. A warm shower and a cup of tea helped some, but when she knocked on Darla's door to ask for a ride to Eli's farm, Laura's headache worsened.

"I have other plans today," Darla informed her. "Besides, I wouldn't even consider being a party to you ruining your life."

"How can seeing Eli ruin my life?"

Darla opened the door wider and motioned Laura inside. "Have a seat, and I'll see if I can explain things to you."

Laura pulled out the desk chair, and Darla sat on the edge of her bed.

"I know you've got a thing for this guy, but the more you see him, the further your relationship will develop." Darla pursed her lips. "One of you is bound to get hurt, and it's my guess, you're gonna be the one."

"What makes you think I'll get hurt?"

"We've been through this before. You and Eli are from different worlds, and even if one of you were dumb enough to try the other's way of life, it wouldn't work."

"How do you know?"

"Trust me on this," Darla asserted. "You're living in a dream world if you think you can ever get Eli to leave his faith."

"Why is that so impossible?" Laura snapped. "People change religions all the time."

"If Eli turns his back on the Amish church, he'll be shunned. Do you understand what that means?"

Laura nodded and her throat tightened. "Eli has told me quite a bit about the Amish."

"Then you know how serious it is when someone leaves the faith and becomes part of the modern world."

"That will have to be Eli's decision." Laura stood up. "If you're not available to drive me to the Yoder farm, then I'll call a cab."

❧

Laura stepped out of the taxi and walked carefully up the slippery path leading to the Yoders' front porch. She was almost to the door when a sense of panic gripped her. What if Eli wasn't home? What if he was home but wasn't happy to see her?

It was too late to turn around, for the cab was already out of sight. Laura knocked on the door.

A few moments later, Mary Ellen Yoder answered. She was holding a rolling pin in one hand, and with the other hand she swiped at a wisp of hair that had fallen loose from her bun. Laura couldn't read the woman's stoic expression, but her silence was enough to remind her that she was on enemy territory.

"Is Eli at home?"

"He's out in the barn, workin' in his wood shop," Mary Ellen said in a cool tone.

Laura gritted her teeth and forced herself to smile. "Thanks; I'll go find him." She stepped quickly off the porch, before Eli's mother had a chance to say anything more. If the older woman's sour expression was meant to dissuade her, it hadn't worked. Laura was here now, and she was more determined than ever to speak with Eli.

❧

Eli was bent over his workbench, hammering a nail into the roof of a small birdhouse, when he heard the barn door open. He didn't think much of it, knowing his brothers were still busy with chores; but when a familiar female voice called out to him, he was so surprised, he smashed his thumb with the hammer.

"Laura? What are you doin' here? How'd ya get here?"

Slowly, she moved across the room, until she stood right in front of Eli. "I came in a cab. I had to see you."

"When did you get back from Minnesota?"

"Last night."

Eli wished she would quit staring at him. It was hard to think. Hard to breathe. He swallowed a couple of times. "How was your holiday?"

"It was okay. How was yours?"

"*Gut,*" he answered. *Though it would have been better if you'd been here.* Eli shook his head, trying to get himself thinking straight again.

"I've missed you," Laura said, leaning against him. "Did you miss me?"

A warning went off in Eli's head, but it was too late. Laura's hand was on his arm, and she was gazing into his eyes in a way that made his heart slam into his chest. How could he tell her it wasn't right for her to be here?

Eli couldn't voice any of his thoughts. In fact, he couldn't even think straight with her standing there so close and smelling so nice. "Paradise Lake is completely frozen now. Would ya like to go ice-skating?" he asked suddenly.

She tipped her head slightly. "Ice-skating? Eli, I have no skates."

He grinned. "I think my sister left her skates here in the barn when she married Amon Zook."

Laura smiled. "If your sister's skates fit, I'd be happy to go ice-skating."

Paradise Lake was covered with a thick layer of shimmering ice. Laura thought it was even more appealing than it had been in the fall. She drank in the beauty of the surrounding trees, dressed in frosty white gowns and shimmering in the morning sun like thousands of tiny diamonds.

Eli helped her into his sister's skates, which were only a tad too big. Hand in hand, they skated around the lake. Then Eli set off on his own, doing fancy spins and figure eights.

Laura shielded her eyes against the glare of the sun as she watched in rapt fascination, realizing with each passing moment how much she loved Eli Yoder. She tried skating by herself, but it was hard to concentrate on anything but the striking figure he made on the ice. He was wearing a pair of black pants, a light blue shirt, and a gray woolen jacket. He'd removed his black felt hat, and his sandy brown hair whipped against his face as he appeared to become one with the wind.

Laura's heart hammered in her chest when Eli waved and offered her a flirty wink. She tried to catch up to him, hoping they could take a break and sit awhile. They needed to talk. She needed to tell him what was in her heart.

Pushing off quickly, Laura lost her balance and landed hard on the ice. Eli was at her side immediately, his blue eyes looking ever so serious. "Are you okay? Ya didn't break anything, I hope."

"My knee hurts, but I don't think my leg's broken."

Laura winced as Eli pulled up her pant leg to examine the injury. "It looks like just a bad bruise," he remarked. "You probably should put some ice on it."

"I think I just did," she said with a giggle.

Eli helped Laura to her feet and over to the sleigh. "I'd better get you back to your school so you can rest that knee."

Laura gripped Eli's shoulders and, standing on tiptoes, she kissed him on the cheek.

He smiled at first, then jerked back like he'd been stung by a bee. "What was that for?"

"Just my way of saying thanks for being such a *gut* friend."

His blue eyes grew serious. "I–I think it'd be best if we didn't see each other anymore."

"Why?" Laura cried. "Haven't you enjoyed yourself today?"

He nodded soberly. *"Jah,* that's the problem."

Her chin quivered slightly. "I don't see how enjoying yourself can be a problem."

"I told you once we could always be friends, but now things have changed."

"How?"

"I can't be your friend, because I've fallen in love with you, Laura."

"Oh, Eli!" she exclaimed. "I love you, too!" She buried her face in his jacket, relishing the warmth and his masculine smell.

"What we feel for each other ain't right," Eli mumbled.

"It sure feels right to me."

"It won't work for us," he insisted. "We have to end this before we both get hurt."

"Nothing could hurt worse than never seeing you again," Laura said with a catch in her voice. "We can be together if we want it badly enough."

He eased her gently away. "I don't see how."

"You could leave the Amish faith. We'd be able to date then. When we both feel ready, we could get married, and—"

Eli's eyebrows arched. "Married? Are ya saying you'd marry me?"

Laura swallowed. Is that what she was saying? Did she really love Eli, or was he simply a prize she wanted and thought she couldn't have?

"In time we might be ready for marriage," she amended.

Eli shook his head. "I could never leave the Amish faith or move away from God. Please, don't ask me to do that."

She grasped his coat collar. "I'm not asking you to leave God. You can worship Him in any church. I'm only asking you to give up your plain lifestyle, with all its silly rules." She leaned close to him again. "I know you'd be happier if you could do a few worldly things. Won't you at least give it some thought?"

Eli stepped away from her, then motioned toward the sleigh. "It's time to go. This discussion is over."

Laura's eyes filled with tears as he helped her into the sleigh. When he picked up the reins and they began to move forward, she felt as though her whole world was falling apart. "Eli, you never said. Will you think about my proposal?"

He looked straight ahead.

"Please, don't shut me out. Won't you give our relationship a chance?" she pleaded.

Eli remained silent all the way back to Laura's school. When he stopped at the front gate, he came around to help her down. She clung to him, but he pushed her gently away. "Good-bye, Laura."

Tears of frustration trickled down her cheeks. Why wouldn't Eli listen to reason? What had gone wrong with her plan?

❧

January and February were cold. . .so cold and dreary Laura thought she would die. It wasn't just the weather making her feel that way. Her heart was broken because

Eli had rejected her. If he really cared, he should have agreed to leave his rigid faith and join the "real" world. Two months had passed since their final good-bye, but Laura still longed for something she couldn't have. Visions of the happy times they'd spent together danced through her mind. Losing Eli hurt so much, and she couldn't do anything to ease the pain. Shopping for clothes didn't help. Throwing herself into her studies made no difference. Even an occasional binge on hot-fudge sundaes and chocolate milkshakes did nothing to make her feel better. The barrage of E-mails and phone calls from Dean Carlson didn't soothe Laura's troubled spirit, either. She cared nothing for Dean, and she told him so.

As winter moved into spring, Laura moved on with her life. At least she thought she was moving on, until one of her teachers gave the class an assignment, asking each student to decorate a bedroom, using an Amish quilt as the focal point.

Laura had her own Amish quilt. . .the one she'd purchased at the farmers' market, the first day she'd meet Eli. When she and Eli broke off their relationship, she'd sent it home. She supposed she could call Mom and ask her to mail it back, but this assignment was due next week, and there would hardly be enough time for that. There was only one logical thing to do—go to the farmers' market and buy another quilt.

❧

Laura was glad Darla had agreed to join her this time. She didn't relish the idea of going to Farmers' Market alone. There were too many painful memories there. Too many reminders of Eli.

Darla parked her car, and they went inside the building. A normal Saturday would have been busy at the market, but there weren't many tourists in Lancaster Valley yet, so the majority of people were just local shoppers.

"I'm beginning to see why the country look fascinates you," Darla said as they browsed through a stack of colorful quilts. "The vibrant hues and various shapes in these comforters are actually quite pretty."

Laura nodded as she fingered a monochromatic blue quilt with a double-wedding-ring pattern. "I think I'll buy this one. I love the variance of colors and the interlocking rings."

"I think I'll keep looking awhile. No sense picking the first one I see," Darla said with a chuckle. When Laura didn't answer, she poked her in the ribs. "Did you hear what I said?"

Still no reply.

Laura stood frozen in her tracks. Her heart was pounding like a pack of stampeding horses, and her throat felt so dry she could barely swallow.

"Laura, what's wrong? You look like you've seen a ghost."

"It's Eli—and that woman," Laura said, her voice cracking. "I had no idea he would be here today. If I'd known, I sure wouldn't have come."

"Where is he, and what woman are you talking about?" Darla asked.

"She's Eli's girlfriend, and they're right over there." Laura pointed toward the root beer stand several feet away. "I shouldn't be surprised to see them together, but it still hurts."

Darla grabbed Laura's arm. "Come on. We've gotta get you out of here."

Laura jerked away. "I'm not going anywhere. This is a free country, and I have as much right to be here as they do."

"I'm sure, but you don't want Eli to know you're here. Do you?"

Laura hung her head. "Maybe."

"What? The guy threw you over for some Plain Jane, and you want to grovel in the dirt in front of him?"

"He didn't throw me over, and I wasn't planning to grovel. I was just thinking I should say hello."

"Now that's a brilliant idea." Darla turned back toward the stack of coverlets. "You do whatever you like, but I came here to look at Amish quilts. That *was* our assignment, you know."

Laura took a deep breath, glanced back at her friend, then marched straight up to Eli.

"Laura? What are you doing here?" he asked with a look of surprise.

"I'm looking at quilts," she answered, fixing her gaze somewhere near the center of his chest. "I have an assignment to do, and—"

"Come on, Eli, let's go," Pauline Hostetler interrupted. She gave his shirt-sleeve a good yank, then glanced over at Laura, bestowing her with an icy stare.

Laura's hands were shaking badly, and tension pulled the muscles in her neck. She had a deep sense she'd done the wrong thing asking Eli to leave his faith, and she couldn't ignore it a moment longer.

She took a guarded step forward. "Eli, could we talk? I need to tell you something." Her mouth went dry with trepidation. She stared into his deep blue eyes and recognized his hesitation.

He shrugged. "*Jah*, I guess it'd be all right." He glanced over at Pauline. "Could ya wait for me at your folks' table? I won't be long."

Pauline hesitated, then stalked off, muttering something under her breath.

"Should we go outside?" Eli suggested.

Laura followed as he led the way to the nearest exit. When they stepped out, he motioned toward a wooden bench near the building.

Once she was seated, Laura felt a bit more comfortable. At least now she could gulp in some fresh air, which she hoped might tame the brigade of bumblebees marching through her stomach.

"What did ya wanna talk about?" Eli asked.

"Us. I wanted to talk about us."

"There is no *us*, Laura," he said, shaking his head. "I thought you understood I can't leave my faith."

"I do understand, Eli," she said softly. "I'm sorry for asking you to give up your way of life."

Eli's lips curved into a smile. "Someday you'll meet the right man, and—"

Laura covered his mouth with her fingers. "I've already found the right man."

His eyebrows raised in obvious surprise. "You have? That's *gut*. I wish you all the best."

She compressed her lips in frustration. Was Eli deaf, dumb, and blind? Couldn't he see how much she wanted him? She grasped both of his hands and gave them a squeeze. "The man I've found is you, Eli. I want no other, and I never will."

"But, Laura—"

"I know, I know. You can't leave the Amish faith and become a fancy Englisher." She swallowed hard and took a deep breath. "That doesn't mean we can't be together, though."

He looked at her as if she'd lost her mind. "It don't?"

She shook her head. "I can come over to the other side."

"I'm afraid I don't get your meanin'," he said, a deep frown creasing his forehead.

"I'll join the Amish faith and become Plain."

"You don't know what you're sayin', Laura," he whispered. "A few folks have joined our faith, but not many. It ain't easy, ya know."

"I'm sure it's not," she agreed, "but I can do it, Eli. I can do anything for you."

❧

Eli couldn't believe Laura was offering to join his faith. During the time they'd been seeing each other, he'd often found himself wishing for such a miracle, but she'd asked him to join her in the fancy world. Now she wanted to become Plain? It made no sense at all. He studied her intently. She seemed sincere, but truth be told, Laura didn't have any idea what she was suggesting. "I do love you, and I probably always will," he acknowledged.

"I'm so glad to hear that," she said, leaning closer and placing her hand on his arm. "I was afraid you might turn me away."

Eli breathed in the strawberry scent of Laura's hair and reveled in the warmth of her touch. How could he make her understand, yet how could he say good-bye again?

"These last few months have been awful," Laura asserted. "I need to be with you."

Eli's voice shook with emotion. "You might not be happy bein' Amish. It would be a hard thing to change over and give up all the modern, worldly things you've become used to havin'. You'd have to learn our language and accept our religious views."

She nodded. "I know it won't be easy, but with your help, I can do it. You will help me, won't you, Eli?"

Filling his lungs with fresh air and struggling to make a decision, Eli lifted Laura's chin with his thumb and stared into her sea green eyes. They were meant for each other. He knew it in his heart. He pushed aside the niggling doubts. Nothing could go wrong. Laura would just need some time to adjust. *"Jah,* I'll help in every way I can," he murmured.

Chapter 8

Once Laura made her decision to become Amish, everything in her life changed as quickly as a leaf falls from a tree. The purchase of a second quilt had been forgotten when she decided to go back to the interior design school and withdraw. Next, she called her parents and told them what she had done. They were understandably shocked, and her mother threatened to fly right out to Pennsylvania to talk some sense into Laura. Her father seemed almost too understanding. Laura wondered if he wanted her to be happy, or if it was possible that Dad could actually identify with her desire to go Plain.

Laura would be living with Eli's sister, Martha Rose, so she gave her mother the address and asked her to send the quilt she'd originally purchased.

When they hung up the phone that afternoon, Laura's mother reminded her that she could always come home if things didn't work out. Laura figured her parents probably thought this was a lark—something she'd try on like a new pair of shoes, and when she decided they weren't to her liking, she would discard them. That was likely the reason they'd accepted her decision as well as they had.

"Be happy, Laura, and please keep in touch," were Dad's final words.

※

Eli was glad his sister had agreed to let Laura stay there, and even happier that Martha Rose was willing to mentor his fancy English woman who wanted to become Plain. Mom and Pop were another matter. They were no more thrilled about the idea of Laura joining the Amish faith than they had been about Eli seeing her when she was still English. It was hard to understand how Mom, who normally was so pleasant and easygoing, seemed almost rude to Laura when she'd visited their home. Even now, with her about to become Amish, there was a coolness in the way his mother spoke to Laura. He hoped things would change once Laura took her training and was baptized into the faith.

※

Martha Rose and Amon Zook lived in a typical Amish home. There were four bedrooms upstairs, and the one Laura was given was closest to the bathroom. For this, she was grateful, even though it didn't take long for her to realize there wouldn't be much time for primping or leisurely bubble baths. In fact, with only one bathroom in the house, she would have to hurry through her daily regime to allow others the use of the "necessary room."

When Eli's sister showed Laura her room, she was shocked. It was even smaller than her dorm room at the school had been. And plain. . .so very plain. There was a double bed, a chest of drawers with a washbowl and pitcher sitting on top, and a small cedar chest at the foot of the bed. Dark shades hung at the two windows, and, except for a small, braided throw rug, the hardwood floor was bare. Instead of a closet, her clothes would be hung on wooden pegs, connected to a narrow strip of wood along one wall.

"Here's a few dresses you can wear," Martha Rose said, handing Laura two long, cotton frocks. One was dark blue, the other a drab green. "You're a bit shorter than me, so they might be kinda long." She grinned. "Better too long than too short."

Laura stood there, too dumbfounded to speak. In her excitement to join the Amish faith and win Eli's heart, she'd forgotten that she would be expected to wear such colorless, outdated clothing. She glanced over at Martha Rose. She had a lovely face—creamy complexion, dark brown eyes—and it was framed by hair the color of chestnuts. She was tall and large-boned but certainly not fat. *She could be a beautiful woman if she didn't have to hide behind such plain clothes and that drab hairdo.*

"I have a white head coverin' and also a dark bonnet for you to wear," Martha Rose continued. "And you'll need a few aprons."

Laura nodded mutely as she was given the rest of her new wardrobe. *What have I gotten myself into?* She inhaled deeply and drew from her inner strength. She could do this. Her determination and love for Eli would see her through anything.

"We'll go to the Country Store tomorrow and buy you some black leather shoes for church and other special occasions," Martha Rose announced. "If you already own a pair of sneakers, you can wear them for everyday." She looked down at her own bare feet and smiled. "Of course, most of us just go barefoot around home, especially during the warmer weather. It saves our shoes, and it's much cooler."

Laura shifted uneasily. Barefoot? Sneakers and black leather shoes? Were those her only choices? In her new wardrobe, she would no doubt feel like a little girl playing dress-up. "Don't your feet get pretty dirty and sore, running around barefoot?" she questioned.

Martha Rose nodded. *"Jah,* but they toughen up, and we always wash our feet before goin' to bed."

Laura shrugged. What could she really say? She'd gotten herself into this predicament, and it was of her own choosing that she'd decided to go Plain. She would simply draw from her inner strength and do whatever was necessary in order to convince Eli and his family she was worthy of being part of their clan. After she and Eli were married, then she could ask again if he would consider leaving the Amish faith and join the "real world."

❧

The next few days were busy. . .busier than Laura ever imagined. She had so much to learn about cooking, sewing, baking, doing laundry and other household chores, not to mention the terrible outside jobs. Gathering eggs, slopping the hogs, and cultivating the garden were all things she'd never done before. It was dirty, backbreaking work, and she made so many foolish mistakes.

One morning, as Laura was getting dressed, she glanced at herself in the hand mirror she'd stuffed in the chest of drawers, along with her satchel of makeup. For some reason, she just couldn't part with these things, so she hadn't mailed them home with all her clothes.

Today was Saturday, and Laura knew Eli would be coming to take her for a buggy ride. They planned to go into Paradise and do some shopping, then stop for a picnic on the way home.

Laura stared longingly at the tube of lipstick she held in her hand. *What would it hurt to apply a little color to my pale lips? If I don't do something to keep myself attractive, Eli might lose interest in me and go back to Pauline.*

Laura blended the coral lipstick with the tips of her fingers, then reached inside the makeup case for some blush. A little dab blended on each cheek and she looked less pale. She added a coat of mascara to her eyelashes and filled in her brows with a soft cinnamon pencil.

"There now," she whispered to her reflection. "I almost look like my old self— not nearly so dowdy." She glanced down at her plain green dress and scowled. "What I wouldn't give to put on a pair of jeans and a T-shirt." She slipped her head covering on and sighed. "Guess I'd better get used to all this. . .at least until Eli and I are married. Then I'll have the freedom to do as I choose."

Downstairs in the kitchen, Laura found Martha Rose and Mary Ellen sitting at the table drinking a cup of tea and eating shoofly pie. Just the smell of the molasses-filled pastry made Laura's stomach churn. No matter how long she was forced to stay Amish, she didn't think she would ever acquire a taste for this particular dessert.

"*Gut Morgen,*" Martha Rose said cheerfully when Laura joined them.

"*Gut Morgen* to you, too," she responded with a slight nod. Learning Pennsylvania Dutch was another challenge for Laura, along with studying the Bible and learning the church rules, which the Amish called the *Ordnung*.

Mary Ellen studied Laura intently. "What's that you've got on your face?"

Laura shrugged and reached for an apple from the ceramic bowl in the center of the table. "Just a little color to make me look alive," she mumbled as she bit into the succulent fruit.

"Makeup's not allowed," Eli's mother persisted. "Surely you know that."

Laura looked pointedly at Mary Ellen, challenging her with her eyes. "I think it's a silly rule. What harm is there in trying to make yourself a bit more attractive?"

" 'Favour is deceitful, and beauty is vain: but a woman that feareth the Lord, she shall be praised,' " Mary Ellen quoted.

Laura squinted her eyes. "Where'd you hear that?"

"It's in the book of Proverbs," Martha Rose answered, before her mother had a chance to respond.

"Jah, that's true," Mary Ellen agreed. She looked right at Laura. "Face powder may catch some men, but it takes bakin' powder to hold him."

Martha Rose giggled, and her mother chuckled behind her hand, but Laura sat there stony-faced. She didn't see what was so funny. Besides, she had the distinct impression these two Plain women were laughing at *her*.

Laura pushed her chair away and stood up. She realized that among the Amish, women all looked pretty much the same. "I'll go wash the makeup off." *But I don't have to like it,* she added silently.

Eli whistled as he hitched his horse to the open buggy. He was looking forward to his date with Laura, but he still couldn't believe she'd actually agreed to become Plain. She was beautiful, talented, and smart. He was sure she could have any man she wanted, yet it was him she'd chosen. Him and his Amish way of life.

"I'll make her happy," he mumbled. The horse whinnied and nuzzled the back of Eli's arm.

"At least *you* ain't givin' me a hard time," Eli remarked. "If Mom and Pop had their way, I'd be courtin' Pauline."

Eli knew his parents had his best interests at heart, but they didn't understand how much he loved Laura.

"It just ain't right, her bein' so fancy and all," Mom had said the day he'd given them the surprising news.

"Jah," Pop had agreed. "It's not gonna be easy for her to give up all the modern things she's been used to and start livin' as we do."

"Laura wants this," Eli had insisted. "She knows what she's givin' up, and it's her decision to do so. Won'tcha please give her a chance?"

His folks had agreed, but he was sure it was only to please him. Deep in his heart, Eli felt they were just waiting to say, "I told you so."

Eli climbed into the driver's seat and gathered up the reins. He knew Mom had gone over to Martha Rose's this morning, so she'd be seeing Laura even before he did.

He clucked to the horse and it moved forward. "Let's just hope things went well between Laura and Mom," he muttered. "If they didn't, I'm likely to have a cross woman on my hands the rest of the day."

When Laura greeted Eli at the back door, he thought she looked like she'd lost her best friend. "What's wrong? Aren't ya happy to see me this mornin'? Do you still wanna go to Paradise, then on a picnic?"

"I do want to go, Eli, but—well, I'll tell you about it on the ride to town," she whispered.

Eli glanced at his mother and sister, sitting at the kitchen table. Mom merely shrugged, and Martha Rose offered him a weak smile.

"Would ya like to come in and have a piece of shoofly pie?" Mom asked.

Eli licked his lips and started across the room.

"I think we should be on our way," Laura said, stepping between Eli and the table.

He frowned. "What's your hurry?"

"I've got quite a bit of shopping to do, and we don't want to get to the lake too late." She rushed past him, pulled a dark blue sweater from the wall peg by the back door, and grabbed the wicker picnic basket sitting on the cupboard.

Eli looked at Laura, standing by the door, tapping her foot. He glanced back at the table, and his mouth watered just thinking about how good a hunk of that pie would taste.

As though sensing his dilemma, Martha Rose said, "Why don'tcha take a few pieces along? You and Laura can have it with the picnic lunch she made."

Eli shrugged. *Jah,* okay. I guess I can wait that long to sample some of your *gut* cookin', Sister."

He reached for the pie, but Martha Rose was too quick for him. She'd already begun slicing it by the time he got to the table. "If you really wanna help, get some waxed paper from the pantry," she instructed.

He did as he was told, not caring in the least that his big sister was bossing him around. He'd grown used to it over the years. Besides, she really didn't mean to sound so pushy. Martha Rose was and always had been a take-charge kind of person. She was pleasant and kind, so he could tolerate a little ordering about now and then.

"You two have a *gut* day," Martha Rose said as Eli and Laura started out the back door.

"Jah, and be sure to be home in time for chorin' and supper," Mom called.

"I will," Eli said, closing the door behind them.

Laura stopped at the bottom of the stairs, and Eli nearly ran straight into her. "What'd ya stop for? I could have knocked ya to the ground."

She scowled at him. "You're henpecked. Do you know that?"

His eyebrows furrowed. "You don't know what you're sayin', Laura."

Her nose twitched and she blinked her eyes. "Those two women have you eating out of the palms of their hands."

Eli started walking toward his open buggy. "They do not. I just happen to like pleasin' them, that's all. I love Mom and Martha Rose, and they're both mighty good to me."

"Well, they're not so good to me!"

Eli whirled around to face Laura. She looked madder than one of Pop's mules when a big old horsefly took a bite out of its ear. "How can ya say they're not good to you? Martha Rose took ya in, didn't she?"

Laura opened her mouth, but before she could respond, Eli rushed on. "She gave ya some of her dresses to wear, took ya shoppin' for shoes and the like, and both she and Mom have taken time out of their busy days to teach ya about housekeepin', cookin', Bible readin', and so many other things you'll be needin' to know before ya can be baptized."

Laura's lip protruded as she handed Eli the picnic basket. "I should've known you wouldn't understand. You're one of *them.*"

"What's that supposed to mean?" Eli asked as he climbed into the buggy and took up the reins.

Laura was still standing on the other side of the buggy with her arms folded.

"It means, you're Amish, and I'm not. I'm still considered an outsider, and I don't think any of your family will ever accept me as anything else."

"Of course they will." He glanced at her out of the corner of his eye. "Are ya gettin' in or not?"

"Aren't you going to help me up?"

He groaned. "I might have, if ya hadn't been naggin' at me. Besides, if you're gonna be Amish, then you'll need to be learnin' how to get in and out of our buggies without any help."

❧

Laura was so angry she was visibly shaking. In fact, if she hadn't been sure she'd be forced to work all day, she would have turned around and marched right back to the house. It would serve Eli Yoder right if she broke this date!

"Time's a-wastin'," Eli announced.

She sighed deeply, lifted her skirt, and practically fell into the buggy.

Eli chuckled, then snapped the reins. The horse jerked forward, and Laura was thrown against her seat. "Be careful!" she cried. "Are you trying to throw my back out?"

Eli's only response was another deep guffaw, which only angered her further.

Laura smoothed her skirt, reached up to be sure her head covering was still in place, then folded her arms across her chest. "I'm glad you think everything's so funny! You can't imagine what I've been through these past few weeks."

"Has somethin' bad happened?" Eli's voice was laced with obvious concern, and he reached over to gently touch Laura's arm.

She moaned. "I'll say."

"What was it? Did ya get hurt? How come I didn't hear about it?"

She shook her head. "No, no, I wasn't hurt. At least not in the physical sense."

"What then?"

"I've nearly been worked to death every day since I moved from the Lancaster School of Design to your sister's house. It seems as though I just get to sleep and it's time to get up again." She frowned. "And that stupid rooster crowing at the top of his lungs every morning sure doesn't help things, either."

"Pop says the rooster is nature's alarm clock," Eli said with a grin.

How can he sit there looking so smug? Laura fumed. *Doesn't he care how hard I work? Doesn't he realize I'm doing all this for him?*

"In time, you'll get used to the long days," Eli maintained. "Someday you'll come to find pleasure in that old rooster's crow."

"Humph! I doubt that!" She held up her hands. "Do you realize that every single one of my nails is broken? Not to mention embedded with dirt I'll probably never be able to scrub clean? Why, the other morning, Martha Rose had me out in the garden, pulling weeds and spading with a rusty old hoe. I thought my back was going to break in two."

"You *will* get used to it."

She scrunched up her nose. "If I live to tell about it."

Chapter 9

Laura's days at the Zook farm flew by. As spring quickly turned into summer, each day became longer, hotter, and filled with more work. Instead of "becoming used to it," she found herself disliking each new day. How did these people exist without air-conditioning, ceiling fans, and swimming pools? How did the women stand wearing long dresses all summer, when they would have been so much cooler in a pair of shorts?

Laura had seen Amon and little Ben play in the creek near their home, and she longed to join them. Anything to get cooled off and have some real fun. Eli's mother's idea of fun was going to a quilting party or making shoofly pies.

To make matters worse, Laura had to attend church every other Sunday and sit with the women on unyielding, wooden, backless benches. She couldn't visit with Eli until the three-hour service was over, lunch had been served, and everything was cleaned up. The women waited on the men, of course, and they did all the cleaning, too. If Laura ever thought life as an Amish woman was going to be easy, she'd been sorely mistaken. On days like today, she wondered if she'd made the biggest mistake of her life by asking to join the Amish church.

"It's not too late to back out," she muttered as she set a basket of freshly washed laundry on the grass underneath the clothesline. "I can go back to the school in Lancaster. Better yet, I can go home to Mom and Dad in Minneapolis. At least they don't expect me to work from sunup to sunset every day but Sunday."

Laura heard a pathetic *mooo*, and she looked up to see several black-and-white cows lining the fence, a few feet from where she stood. They were swishing their tails. . .and looking right at her.

"Just what I need—a cheering section. Go away, cows! Get back to the field, grab a hunk of grass, start chewing your cuds, then go take a nice, long nap." She bent down, grabbed one of Amon's shirts, gave it a good shake, then clipped it to the clothesline. "At least you bovine critters are allowed the privilege of a nap now and then. That's more than I can say for any of the humans who live on this farm!"

"Maih gayn fa di kee?" a small voice asked.

Laura looked down. There stood little Ben, gazing up at her with all the seriousness of a three year old. He'd said something in Pennsylvania Dutch, but she had no idea what he was talking about. She'd been studying the Amish dialect for a few months, but there were still many unfamiliar words.

"Maih gayn fa di kee," the child repeated. This time he pointed toward the cows, still gawking at Laura like she was free entertainment.

"Ah, the cows. You're talking about the cows, aren't you?" she said, dropping to her knees beside the little boy. *"Maih gayn fa di kee."* Laura smiled. "We go for the cows!"

Ben looked up at her and grinned. *"Jah."* He really was a cute little thing, with his blond, Dutch-bobbed hair, big blue eyes, and two deep dimples framing his smile.

"The clothes are washed," Laura said in Pennsylvania Dutch. She pointed to the heap of laundry in the basket, hoping the change of subject would take the boy's mind off cows that couldn't be let out of the corral, no matter how much he may have wanted it.

Ben studied the basket a few seconds; then he frowned.

"Wass ist letz—what is wrong?" she asked.

"Es hemm mitt en loch," he said, grabbing one of his daddy's shirts.

Laura smiled when she realized that the child was telling her about his father's shirt with a hole. She patted the top of Ben's head. "No doubt that shirt will end up in *my* pile of mending."

Ben made no comment, but then, she knew he couldn't understand. He would be taught English when he started school. With an impish grin, the boy climbed into the basket of wet clothes.

Laura was about to scold him, but Ben picked up one of his mother's dark bonnets and plunked it on top of his head. She sank to her knees and laughed so hard she had tears running down her face. The cows on the other side of the fence mooed, and the little boy giggled.

Maybe life on this humble, Amish farm wasn't all bad.

❧

Laura sat at the kitchen table, reading the Bible Martha Rose had given her. Why did it seem so confusing? She'd been to Sunday school and Bible school a few times when she was growing up. She'd even managed to memorize some Bible passages in order to win a prize. Why couldn't she stay focused now?

"You've been at it quite awhile. Would ya like to take a break and have a glass of iced tea with me?" Martha Rose asked, pulling out a chair and sitting beside Laura.

Laura looked up and smiled. She really did need a break. "Thanks, I'd like that."

Martha Rose poured two glasses of iced tea and piled a plate high with peanut butter cookies.

"Are you trying to fatten me up?" Laura asked when the goodies were set on the table.

Martha Rose chuckled. "As a matter of fact, you are pretty thin. I figured a few months livin' with me, and you'd have gained at least ten pounds."

Laura shrugged. "Your cooking is wonderful, but I'm trying to watch my weight."

"You need to eat hearty in order to keep up your strength," Martha Rose chided. She pushed the cookie plate in front of Laura. "Please, have a few."

Laura shrugged. "I guess two cookies wouldn't hurt."

"How are your studies comin' along?" Martha Rose asked. "Has little Ben been stayin' outta your way?"

"He's never been a problem," Laura answered honestly. "In fact, your little boy is a real sweetheart."

"*Jah*, well, he can also be a pill." Martha Rose shook her head. "Only this mornin' I found him playin' in the toilet, of all things. Said he was goin' fishin', like he and his pa did last week."

Laura laughed and shook her head. "Where is the little tyke now?"

"Down for a nap. I'm hopin' he stays asleep awhile, 'cause I've got a bunch of ripe tomatoes waitin' to be picked. Not to mention fixin' supper and gettin' a bit more cleanin' done. Church will be here this Sunday, ya know."

"I'd almost forgotten. Guess that means we'll have to do more cooking than normal," Laura said, already feeling the ache in her back from standing long hours at the stove.

Martha Rose shook her head. "Not really. Most of the women bring something to share, so I'll mostly be responsible for beverages and a big pot of bean soup."

"Isn't it kind of hot for soup?"

"We enjoy soup most any time of the year, and my *daed* always says, 'a little somethin' hot on the inside makes the outside heat seem much less.'"

Laura's brows knitted together. The Plain folk sure did have a funny way of looking at things. She wondered if she would ever truly feel a part of them.

Maybe I won't have to, she mused. *After Eli and I are married, I might be able to convince him to leave the Amish faith. Once I'm his wife, he'll have to listen to me. After all, I just read in the Bible this morning that husbands are supposed to love and nurture their wives. If Eli truly loves me, then he should be willing to do anything to make me happy.*

"How's the Pennsylvania Dutch comin'?" Martha Rose asked, breaking into Laura's thoughts.

"Not so good. I can understand more now, but I'm still having trouble speaking the words right."

"Practice makes perfect," Martha Rose said. "I think it might help if we spoke less English to you."

Laura nearly choked on the piece of cookie she'd just put in her mouth. "You're kidding."

"I think you need to hear more Dutch and less English. It'll force ya to study harder and try sayin' more words yourself."

Laura groaned. Wasn't it enough that she was being made to wear plain, drab clothes, labor all day on jobs she hated, conform to all kinds of rules she didn't understand, and get along without modern conveniences? Must she now be forced to speak and hear a foreign language most of the time?

As if she could read her thoughts, Martha Rose reached over and patted Laura's hand. "You do wanna become Amish, don'tcha?"

Tears welled up in Laura's eyes. "I love Eli, and I'd do anything for him, but

I never dreamed it would be so hard."

"You say ya love my brother, but what about your love for God? It's Him you should be tryin' most to please, not Eli."

Laura swallowed hard. How could she tell Martha Rose that, while she did believe in God, she'd never really had a personal relationship with Him? She wasn't even sure she wanted one. After all, what had God ever done for her? If He were on her side, then wouldn't Eli have been willing to leave his religion and become English? They could have worshipped God in any church.

"Laura?" Martha Rose prompted.

She nodded. "I do want to please God. I just hope He knows how hard I'm trying and rewards me for all my efforts."

Martha Rose frowned. "We should never have to be rewarded for our good deeds or service to God. We're taught to be humble servants, never prideful, never wantin' more. There's joy in lovin' and servin' the Lord, as well as serving others."

Laura thought on that a few seconds. The Amish people she was living among did seem to emanate a certain kind of peaceful, joyful spirit. She couldn't figure out why, since they did without so many things.

Martha Rose pushed away from the table. "I think we should end this discussion and get busy pickin', don't you?"

Laura eased out of her chair. While she had no desire to spend the next few hours out in the hot sun bent over a bunch of itchy tomato plants, at least she wouldn't be forced to hear any more of Martha Rose's lectures. Unless, of course, the woman decided to carry the conversation with them into the garden.

Laura wasn't looking forward to another long, boring church service, but the promise of a "singing" that night gave her some measure of joy. It would be held in the Beachys' barn, and Eli had promised to take her. Since he'd be coming to Amon and Martha Rose's for preaching, he would probably stick around all day, then later escort Laura in his courting buggy to the singing.

As much as Laura hated all the chores she was expected to do, and didn't care for the way she was forced to dress, she never got tired of spending time with Eli. In fact, the more they were together, the more she was convinced she'd done the right thing by asking to become Amish. Even though Eli could get under her skin at times, he made her feel loved, nurtured, and happy. He treated her with respect—nothing like Dean Carlson had when they were dating.

Laura rarely thought about Dean anymore, and when she did, it was only to compare him to Eli. She did think about her parents, though. She wrote letters whenever she found time, but she wished she had her computer so she could type a quick E-mail instead of writing everything in longhand. She'd even managed to call them a few times, when she went to town and could use a pay phone.

Mom and Dad were doing fine, but she knew they missed her. She was also aware that neither of them understood her decision to become Amish. Dad was the most indulgent, since he admittedly wished for a simpler life. Mom, on the other hand, thought the whole idea of living like the pioneers was utterly foolish. Whenever they talked, she always reminded Laura that she could come home.

"I'm not going home until Eli is ready to come with me," Laura muttered as she dressed for church that morning. "If things go as planned, I should be baptized into the Amish church sometime next month; then Eli and I will get married in November." She slipped into her dark blue dress. "If I have my way, we'll be living in Minneapolis by Christmas."

🌿

Eli felt a mounting sense of excitement over his date with Laura tonight. They'd been on plenty of other dates, but tonight he planned to kiss her.

Guess I really shouldn't be plannin' such a thing, he thought as he helped Laura into the buggy. Even though he'd told her awhile back that she should learn to get in by herself, he had decided to act gentlemanly tonight. He didn't want their date to end up in an argument, like it had a few other times this summer. Truth be told, he was a bit worried that Laura might not take to the Amish way of life, and if she were displeased with him, it could be that she'd leave—head straight back to that fancy school in Lancaster, or worse yet, go home to Minnesota.

"I've been looking forward to tonight," Laura murmured as she settled against the buggy seat.

"*Jah,* me too," Eli agreed. He glanced over at her and smiled. "You're sure pretty, ya know that?"

Laura lifted her hand to touch her head covering. "You really think so?"

He nodded. "I do."

"But my hair's not long and beautiful anymore," she argued.

Eli frowned. "Your hair's still long. You're just wearin' it up in the back now."

"I know, but it looks so plain this way."

He reached over to gently touch her arm. "You may become one of us Plain folk, but you'll never *be* plain, Laura."

She shrugged her shoulders. "I'll always feel plain wearing long dresses that don't even fit me right. And I miss not wearing makeup. I look so pale without lipstick, blush, and eye shadow."

Eli clicked his tongue. "You're a very *Shee Meedel,* with or without makeup."

Laura gave him a satisfied smile. "Thanks. I'm glad you think I'm a pretty girl."

🌿

When they arrived at the Beachy farm, the barn was already filled with young people. The huge doors were swung open wide, allowing the evening breeze to circulate and help cool the barn.

Soon the singing began, and the song leader led the group in several slow hymns, followed by a few faster tunes. There were no musical instruments, but the singsong chant of voices permeated the air with a pleasant symphony of its own kind. Even Laura got caught up in the happy mood, and she was pleasantly surprised to realize she could actually follow along without too much difficulty.

When the singing was done, the young people paired off, and the games began. Laura was breathless by the time she and Eli finished playing several rounds of Six-Handed Reel, which to her way of thinking was similar to square dancing.

"Would ya like a glass of lemonade and some cookies?" Eli asked as he led Laura over to one of the wooden benches along the wall.

She nodded. "That sounds wonderful. I mean, *wunderbaar.*"

Eli disappeared into the crowd around the refreshment table, and Laura leaned her head against the wooden plank behind her. She caught a glimpse of Pauline Hostetler, who appeared to be watching her.

It wasn't hard to see that Pauline was not fond of Laura. In the months since she'd been part of the Amish community, Pauline hadn't spoken one word to her. *She's jealous because Eli loves me and not her.* Laura knew it probably wasn't right, but she felt a sense of pleasure knowing she'd won Eli's heart. Someday he would be all hers.

"Here ya go," Eli said, handing Laura a tall glass of cold lemonade. "I was gonna get us some cookies, but the plate was empty. I didn't wanna wait around 'til one of the Beachy girls went to get more."

"That's okay," Laura said, flashing him a smile. "I ate a few too many of your sister's peanut butter cookies earlier this week, and I don't want to gain any weight."

Eli frowned. "You could use a few extra pounds."

Why? So I can end up looking like your slightly plump mother? Laura didn't vocalize her thoughts. Instead, she quietly sipped her lemonade. They'd be going home soon, and she didn't want to say anything to irritate Eli, for tonight was the night she planned to give him a *real* kiss.

Chapter 10

I f you're ready to go home now, I'll get the horse and buggy," Eli told Laura after they'd finished their refreshments.

She smiled. "I'm more than ready."

Eli offered her a quick wink. "I won't be long. Come outside when you see my horse pull up in front of the barn." He chuckled. "No point in us both gettin' bit up by all the swarmin' insects out tonight." He strolled out the door, leaving Laura standing by the refreshment table alone. She caught sight of Pauline, who exited the barn only moments after Eli had.

"She'd better not be looking for my man," Laura muttered under her breath.

"Were you speakin' to me?" a pleasant female voice asked.

Laura whirled around and was greeted with a friendly smile from a young woman about her age, whom she'd seen before but never personally met.

"I was talking to myself," Laura admitted, feeling the heat of a blush creep up her neck.

The other woman nodded. "I do that sometimes." She extended her hand. "My name's Anna Beachy, and you're Laura, right?"

"Yes, I live with Martha Rose Zook and her family."

"I know. Martha Rose and I are *gut* friends. Have been since we were *kinder*." Anna's green eyes gleamed in the light of the kerosene lanterns hung from the barn rafters. "Our moms were friends when they were growin' up, too."

Laura nodded mechanically. While this was interesting trivia, she was most anxious to get outside and see if Eli had the buggy ready. What was taking him so long, anyway?

"Yep, our families have been linked together for quite a spell," Anna continued. "Martha Rose's *mamm*, Mary Ellen, is the stepdaughter of Miriam Hilty. The dear woman's gone on to heaven now, but Miriam, who everyone called 'Mim,' was a real *gut* friend of Sarah Stoltzfus, Rebekah Beachy's mother. Rebekah is my *mamm*, and she's partially paralyzed. She either uses a wheelchair or metal leg braces in order to get around. Has since she was a young girl, I'm told." Anna drew in a deep breath and rushed on. "Now, Grandma Sarah is livin' with my aunt Nadine, and—"

Anna's voice droned on and on, and Laura tapped her foot impatiently, wondering how she could politely excuse herself. "I see," she said in the brief seconds Anna came up for air. "It does sounds like you have a close-knit family." She cleared her throat a few times. "It's been nice chatting with you, Anna, but Eli's outside getting his horse and buggy ready to take me home. I'd better not keep him waiting."

Jah, okay. You go ahead," Anna said cheerfully. "Tell Eli I said hello, and let him know he should inform his big sister she owes me a visit real soon."

"I'll be sure he gets the message." Laura hurried away before Anna could say anything more.

Once outside, she headed straight for the long line of buggies parked alongside the Beachys' barn. She stopped short when she saw Eli. He was talking to Pauline Hostetler!

Eli backed against the buggy when Pauline reached up and stroked the side of his face. What was going on here? This didn't set well with him at all. Didn't Pauline know he was courting Laura Meade?

"That English woman will never make you happy, Eli," Pauline murmured. "Take *me* home tonight, and let *her* find another way."

Eli brushed Pauline's hand aside. "I can't do that. I brought Laura to the singin', and I'll see that she gets home." He sniffed. "Besides, I love her, and just as soon as she joins the church, I'm gonna ask her to be my wife."

Pauline's face was pinched like a dried-up prune. "You're not thinkin' straight, Eli. You haven't been right in the head since that fancy woman came sashayin' into your life."

He was about to respond, but his words were cut off when Pauline kissed him full on the mouth. It took him completely by surprise, and he wasn't sure what to do. He didn't have to think long, because Laura came sauntering up, and he could tell right away she was hopping mad.

"What's going on here?"

Pauline pivoted toward Laura. "What's it look like? Eli was kissin' me."

Eli felt his face flame. "Pauline, that just ain't so."

"I was remindin' Eli how good we are together, and he just up and kissed me," Pauline declared.

Eli could see Laura's face in the moonlight, and it was about as red as his felt. How was he ever going to make her understand the way things really happened? He knew she was a bit insecure in their relationship, and this escapade of Pauline's sure wouldn't help any.

"I should have known you were up to no good when I saw you leave the barn," Laura shouted in Pauline's face.

"Me?" Pauline countered. "All I did was talk to Eli, and he—"

Eli touched Pauline's arm, and she whirled back around to face him. "I know you're not happy 'bout me and Laura, but lyin' ain't gonna help ya none," he stated.

Pauline shrugged his hand away and stalked off. "You'll be sorry you chose her and not me. Just wait and see if you're not," she hollered over her shoulder.

Laura was fit to be tied. Did Eli really make the first move, or had Pauline deliberately kissed him just to stir up trouble? Even if it broke her heart, she had to know what transpired.

"Are ya ready to go home?" Eli asked, giving her a sheepish look.

"I was ready half an hour ago," she snapped. "And don't go thinking you can soft-soap me with that cute, little-boy look of yours, either."

"You remind me of *Enwiedicher Hund*," Eli said with a deep chuckle. "You've got quite a temper, but seein' how you acted when ya saw me and Pauline together lets me know how much ya love me."

Laura folded her arms and scowled at him. "I'm beginning to know more of your language, and I'll have you know, Eli Yoder, I do not look like a mad dog."

He tickled her under the chin. "You do love me, right?"

She groaned softly. "You know I do. That's why it always makes me angry whenever I see that woman with you." She leaned a bit closer to him. "Tell me the truth, Eli. Did she kiss you, or was it the other way around?"

Eli pursed his lips. "She kissed me. Honest."

"But why? Did you encourage her in any way?"

He shook his head. "She knows I love you, Laura. She's just jealous and wants to make ya think there's somethin' goin' on with us." He helped her into the buggy. "Think about it. Who's the woman I've been courtin' all summer?"

"As far as I know, only me," she replied coolly.

Eli went around and took his own seat, then picked up the reins and got the horse moving. "Let's stop by Paradise Lake on the way home. It's a *wunderbaar* night, and—"

"I don't think so, Eli," she said, flipping the ties of her head covering to the back of her neck. "I'm sure a trip to the lake would be real romantic, but to be perfectly honest, I was kind of hoping it would be me you'd be kissing tonight, not Pauline."

Eli reached over and took her hand. "*Jah,* I was wantin' that, too."

Laura sighed deeply and gazed up at the night sky. It was a beautiful evening, and the horizon was lit by hundreds of twinkling fireflies. The buggy ride should have been magical for both of them. Instead, Pauline had thrown a damper on things.

"I'm not much in the mood for love or romance now, so I think it would be good if we head straight to your sister's house," Laura said regrettably.

Eli moaned. "I'm not the least bit happy 'bout it, but, *jah,* okay. Maybe our next date'll go better."

❧

With the exception of Eli, Laura felt closer to her future sister-in-law than she did the rest of his family. Martha Rose had patiently taught her to use the old treadle sewing machine, showed her how to bake those dreadful shoofly pies, and had given her lessons in milking, gathering eggs, and slopping the pigs. It was none of those things that made Martha Rose seem special, though. It was her friendly attitude and the way she'd accepted a complete stranger into her home. Laura wasn't sure if it was Martha Rose's hospitable nature, or if she was only doing it to please her brother. Either way, living with this young woman for the past few months had helped Laura understand the true meaning of friendship.

Having been raised as an only child, in a home where she lacked nothing, Laura knew she was spoiled. The Amish lived such a simple life, and yet they seemed happy and content with their lot. It was a mystery she couldn't explain. Even more surprising was the fact that on days like today, she almost felt one with the Plain People. Their slow-paced, quiet lifestyle held a certain measure of appeal. Although Laura still missed modern conveniences and the freedom to dress as she pleased, she also enjoyed some things about being Amish.

Little Ben Zook was one of the things she enjoyed most. He often followed her around, asking questions and pointing out things she'd never noticed before. He was doing it now, out in his mother's herb garden.

"*Es gookt verderbt schee doh,*" the child said, pointing to a clump of mint.

Laura nodded. "*Jah,* it looks mighty nice here." She plucked off a leaf and rubbed it between her fingers, the way she'd seen Martha Rose do on several occasions. "*Appeditlich*—delicious," she said with a chuckle.

Ben sniffed deeply and smiled. "*Appeditlich!*"

Laura was amazed at his appreciation for herbs, flowers, and all the simple things found on the farm. Most of the English children she knew needed TV, video games, and hordes of mechanical toys to keep them entertained. Was this really a better way of life? Would it be a mistake to ask Eli to become fancy?

She shook her head, as though trying to knock some sense into it. Of course she would ask him to leave someday. After all, it was ridiculous to think she could completely adjust to the Amish way of life. It would strip away her identity. If she remained Plain, she would miss out on all the good things the world had to offer. After all, she had needs, desires, and goals. Those didn't include a life of hard work or a house full of *kinder*. The truth was, in spite of Laura's fascination with little Ben, she had no desire to have children of her own. If she ever were to get pregnant, she would be fat and even dowdier than she was now. No, she could never let that happen.

❧

The baptismal ceremony and introduction of new members was scheduled for early October. Laura kept reminding herself that she needed to be ready by then, since Amish weddings were usually held in late November, after the harvest was done. If she wasn't able to join the church before then, it would be another whole year before she and Eli could be married. Of course, he hadn't actually proposed yet, but she was hopeful it would be soon.

For that matter, Eli still hadn't kissed her. She worried he might have lost interest in her. Maybe he was in love with Pauline and just wouldn't admit it. If only she could be sure. She'd given up a lot to be with him, so why didn't he show some appreciation?

Laura saw more of Eli's sister than she did him these days. His job in town at the furniture store kept him busy enough, but now he was also helping his father and brothers with the harvest. Over the last month she'd only seen him twice, and that was on biweekly church days.

"So much for courting," Laura complained as she trudged wearily toward the chicken coop. "If I weren't so afraid of losing Eli to Pauline, I'd put my foot down and give him an ultimatum. I'd tell him either he'd better come see me at least once a week, or I'm going home to Minnesota."

There was just one problem. Laura didn't want to go home—at least not without Eli. She would endure a bit longer, but if things didn't change by the time she was baptized, she planned to have a long talk with Eli Yoder and set him straight on a few things!

❧

The big day finally arrived. This was the Sunday for baptism and church membership.

Laura was nervous as a cat about to have kittens, as she paced back and forth across the kitchen floor, waiting for Amon to pull the buggy out front.

Little Ben jerked on his mother's apron while she stood at the cupboard, packing jars of pickled beets into a cardboard box. "These will go *gut* with our Sunday lunch," she told Laura.

"Ich will mit dir," Ben whined.

"I know you wanna go," Martha Rose said. "As soon as Papa gets the buggy ready."

Ben smiled; then he reached up and touched his mother's stomach. *"Buppli."*

Laura stopped pacing and whirled around to face Martha Rose. *"Buppli?* Are you pregnant, Martha Rose?"

Martha Rose nodded. *"Jah.* I found out for sure a few days ago."

"How is it that Ben knew and I didn't?"

"He was there when I told Amon. I planned to tell you soon."

"Oh," was all Laura could manage. Maybe she wasn't as much a part of this family as she'd believed.

Amon stuck his head through the open doorway and grinned at them. A short thatch of blond hair hung across his forehead, and his brown eyes seemed so sincere. "All set?"

Martha Rose nodded. "I've got my lunch contribution packed." She smiled at Laura. "Let's be off then, for we sure wouldn't wanna be late for Laura's baptism."

❧

Eli paced nervously across the front porch of their farmhouse. Today's preaching service would be held here, and he could hardly wait. This was the day Laura would become one of them. This was the day he. . .

The sight of Amon Zook's buggy pulling into the yard halted Eli's thoughts. He skirted around a wooden bench and leaped off the porch, skipping over all four steps.

Laura offered him a tentative smile as she stepped down from the buggy. He took her hand and gave it a squeeze. "This is the day we've both been waitin' for, Laura."

She nodded, and he noticed there were tears in her eyes.

"What's wrong? You ain't havin' second thoughts, I hope."

"No, I'm just a bit nervous. What if I don't say or do the right things? What if—"

He hushed her words by placing two fingers against her lips. "You went through the six weeks of religious trainin' just fine. Today's only a formality. Say and do whatever the bishop asks. Everything will be okay; you'll see."

"I hope so," she whispered.

The service started a few minutes after Eli and Laura entered the house. He took his seat on the men's side, and she sat with the women.

The song leader led the congregation in several hymns, all sung in the usual singsong fashion; then everyone stood for Scripture reading. Next, Bishop Weaver gave the main message. When he finished, he cleared his throat a few times and said in a clear, booming voice, "Today, twenty young people have expressed their faith in Christ by requestin' baptism and membership into this church."

He motioned to the applicants, who all stood and filed to the front of the room.

Laura's legs were shaking as she knelt before the bishop. He poured a small amount of water from a ceramic pitcher and let it drip onto her head. "Do you believe Jesus is the Son of God, and that He died for you?"

"I do," she replied. *"Do you really?"* a little voice niggled at the back of her mind. *"Do you truly know Me as your Lord and Savior?"*

Laura chose to ignore the silent reproof. She would have plenty of time to think about her relationship to God. Right now, all she wanted was to be with Eli. Her love for him was all that mattered.

Chapter 11

The service was finally over, and Laura felt such relief as she stepped outside into the crisp fall air. It was official. She was no longer a fancy English woman. For as long as she and Eli chose to remain Amish, she would be Plain.

Most of the women were busy getting the lunch meal set out, but Laura didn't care about helping. All she wanted to do was find Eli. It didn't take her long to spot him, talking with the bishop over near the barn.

Are they talking about me? Is Eli asking Bishop Weaver if he thinks I'm sincere? Laura grabbed the porch railing and gripped it as if her very life depended on it. *What if the bishop knows I'm not a true believer? What if he's counseling Eli to break up with me?*

"We could use another pair of hands in the kitchen," Martha Rose said as she stepped up behind Laura. "The *Mannsleit* are waitin' to eat."

Laura spun around to face her. "Why don't the *menfolk* fix the meal and wait on us women once in awhile?"

Martha Rose poked Laura's arm. "You're such a kidder. Everyone knows it's a woman's duty to serve the men."

Laura opened her mouth, fully intending to argue the subject, but something stopped her. She had just joined the Amish church. It wouldn't be good to say or do anything that might get her in trouble. Especially not with Eli out there talking to Bishop Weaver. She might be reprimanded or even shunned if she messed up now.

"What do you need help with?" Laura asked.

"Why don'tcha pour coffee for the men and milk for the boys?" Martha Rose suggested. "The pitchers are over there, on the long wooden plank we're usin' as a servin' table."

Laura shrugged and started down the porch steps. *"Jah,* okay. Whatever you say," she muttered under her breath.

❧

Lunch was over, and everyone had eaten until they were full. Laura was just finishing with the cleanup when she caught sight of Eli heading her way.

"Come with me for a walk," he whispered, taking Laura's hand and leading her away from the house.

"Where are we going?" she asked breathlessly.

"You'll see."

A few minutes later, they were standing under a huge weeping willow tree, on one side of the house, away from curious stares. Eli's fingers touched Laura's chin, tipping her head back until they were staring into each other's eyes. "You're truly one of us now," he murmured.

She nodded, feeling as though her head might explode from the anticipation of what she felt certain was coming.

Eli bent his head, and his lips touched hers in a light, feathery kiss. She moaned softly as the kiss deepened.

When Eli pulled away, she leaned against him for support, feeling as if her breath had been snatched away. It seemed as though she'd waited all her life to be kissed like that. Not a kiss of passion, the way Dean Carlson had done, but a kiss with deep emotion. Eli Yoder loved her with all his heart. She was sure of it now.

"I can finally speak the words that have been in my heart all these months," Eli said, gazing deeply into her eyes. "I love you, Laura, and I want ya to be my wife."

Tears welled up in her eyes and spilled over onto her cheeks. "Oh, Eli, I love you, too." She hugged him tightly. "Yes. . .I will marry you!"

"I just spoke with Bishop Weaver," Eli said. "At the next preachin', he's gonna tell the congregation we're officially published. We're to be married on the third Thursday in November."

Laura blinked away another set of tears. "I'm so happy I could dance."

His eyebrows furrowed. "The Amish don't dance, Laura."

She slapped him playfully on the arm. "I know that, Silly. It was just an expression."

Eli's frown remained firmly in place. "If you're gonna be one of us, you'll need to get rid of your English expressions and learn to speak, think, and act as we do."

Laura swallowed hard. She knew his request was legitimate, but it wasn't going to be easy. It wasn't in her nature to be submissive or look plain. While she might have agreed to become Amish for a time, her ultimate goal was to marry Eli and convince him to become part of her world. She would bide her time, obey all the rules, and even try to speak and act like an Amish person. Deep inside, she would always be fancy, though, and she hoped someday Eli would be as well.

❧

Eli thought his heart would burst from the sheer joy of knowing Laura would soon be Mrs. Eli Yoder. She loved him; he was sure of it. Why else would she have thrown her old life aside and agreed to become Plain? He would never have admitted it, but *his* feet felt like dancing today. He wanted to shout to the world that he was the luckiest man alive and had found a most special woman.

While he wasn't able to shout it to the world, Eli knew he could share his news with the family. Grabbing Laura by the hand, he started to run.

"Where are we going?"

"To tell my folks our *gut* news."

Laura skidded to a halt. "Do you think that's such a good idea? I mean, can't you wait and tell them later. . .after you go home?"

Eli grimaced. "Now why would I wanna wait that long? The family deserves to hear our news now, when we're together."

"They may not want you marrying a foreigner," Laura argued. "Your mother doesn't like me, and—"

Eli stopped her words with another kiss. When he stepped back, he said softly, "You're not a foreigner anymore, Laura, and I'm sure Mom likes ya just fine."

Laura drew in a deep breath, releasing it with a moan. "Okay. Let's get this over with so we can spend some quality time together."

They found Eli's parents sitting on the porch, visiting with Martha Rose and Amon. Little Ben was playing at their feet, dragging a piece of yarn in front of the yellow barn cat's nose.

Eli led Laura up the steps and motioned her to take a seat in one of the empty chairs. He pulled out another one and sat down beside her.

"Today's baptism was *gut*," Mom said, looking over at Laura. "We welcome you into our church."

Jah, you're one of us now," Pop agreed.

"Thank you, Mr. and Mrs. Yoder," Laura said, offering them a smile that seemed almost forced.

In an attempt to reassure her, Eli took her hand. "Laura has agreed to become my wife," he said, looking first at his parents, then his sister and brother-in-law. "We plan to be married in November."

Mom and Pop exchanged glances, and Eli was afraid they might say something negative about his plans. Much to his relief, Mom smiled and nodded. "We hope you'll be happy bein' Amish, Laura, and we hope you will make our son happy as well."

Pop nodded. *Jah*, for Eli's a fine man, with much love to give. He'll make a *gut* husband and father; just you wait and see."

Martha Rose got up from her seat and bent down to give Laura a hug. "Congratulations. Soon we'll be like sisters."

Amon extended his hand to Eli and added his well-wishes.

Eli grinned. "Laura was a bit nervous 'bout tellin' ya the news, but I knew you'd all share in our joy."

Laura shot him a look that could only be defined as exasperated. Maybe he'd said too much. It could be that he shouldn't have said anything about the way she was feeling.

He was trying to think up something to make her feel better, when Pop commented, "Say, Eli, if you're gonna marry this little gal, then don'tcha think you should try to fatten her up some?"

Eli looked at Laura, then back at his father. "Why would I do that, Pop?"

"Yes, why would he?" Laura echoed.

"I've seen her at mealtime, and she don't hardly eat anything," Pop contended. "Why, she'll waste away to nothin' if she don't start eatin' more."

Laura stood up quickly, nearly knocking over her chair. "I have no intention of becoming fat, Mr. Yoder!"

Pop tipped his head back and howled. "She's a feisty one, now ain't she, Son?" When he finally quit laughing, he looked at Laura and said, "If we're gonna be kinfolk, then I think you should start callin' me Johnny. Mr. Yoder makes me feel like an old man." He glanced over at Mom and gave her knee a few pats. "I'm not old yet, am I, Mary Ellen?"

Mary Ellen clicked her tongue as she pushed his hand aside. "Go on with ya, now, Johnny Yoder. You've always been a silly boy, and I guess you always will be."

Mom and Pop started howling to beat the band. Soon Martha Rose and Amon were chuckling pretty good, too.

Laura was standing there, tapping her toe against the wooden porch, and Eli figured it was time to end it all before she said or did something that would probably embarrass them both.

He stood up and grabbed her hand. "I think Laura and I should take a walk down to the creek. She needs to get cooled off, and I need to figure out how I ended up with such a laughable family."

❧

Two weeks later, Laura and Eli were to be officially published at the close of the preaching service. Church was held in the Zook home, so it made things easy for Laura, who, according to Amish custom, had to wait upstairs in her room until the conclusion of the service. Any other time, this arrangement would have suited her just fine, but today she was a ball of nerves and wanted to know what was going on.

She paced back and forth in front of the window. Every once in awhile she would go to the door and listen. She could hear the steady hum of Bishop Weaver's deep voice, but she couldn't quite make out his words.

Finally, after what seemed like an eternity, she heard the congregation sing their closing hymn. It was over. She could finally go downstairs and help with the meal.

In the kitchen, she found Martha Rose, Mary Ellen, Anna and Rachel Beachy, as well as their mother, Rebekah. Everyone had a job to do, even crippled Rebekah, who sat at the table in her wheelchair, buttering huge stacks of bread.

Laura offered Martha Rose a cheery smile. "Is it official? Did the bishop announce the date for our wedding?"

Martha Rose nodded and handed Laura a jar of pickled beets. "It'll be the third Thursday of November, and here's somethin' for you to do."

Laura glanced at the other four women, but they all seemed focused on their job of making ham-and-cheese sandwiches. She shrugged and took the jar over to the cupboard, wondering why no one seemed to care much about her upcoming marriage.

As Laura forked out beet slices and placed them on a platter, her nose wrinkled. She hated the smell of pickled beets. If she lived to be a hundred, she'd never figure out what anyone saw in those disgusting, pungent things! She had just finished putting the last one on the plate when Pauline Hostetler entered the kitchen.

"The tables are set up, and all the other women are busy settin' out things," she said, looking at Martha Rose. "Do ya have anything ready for me to carry out?"

"You can take this plate of sandwiches." Mary Ellen held up a tray, and Pauline took it from her.

She was just about to the door when Martha Rose spoke. "Laura, why don'tcha go with Pauline? You can take the beets, then stay to help pour beverages."

Laura drew in a deep breath and let it out in a rush. The last thing she needed was another close encounter with her rival. She didn't wish to make a scene, however, so she followed Pauline out the back door.

They had no more than stepped onto the porch when Pauline whirled around and faced Laura. "You think you've won Eli's heart," she hissed, "but you're not married yet, so there's still some hope. You may have fooled Eli, but I can see right through ya."

Laura took a few steps back, wanting to get away from Pauline, and wondering if the young woman really did know she wasn't being completely honest with Eli. Sure, she loved him and wanted to get married. She had become Amish, too, but deep down inside, she was still Laura Meade, a fancy English woman who wanted modern things and didn't think she needed God. After all, she'd managed to get Eli, hadn't she? She'd done that all by herself. God had nothing to do with it.

"I'm sure Eli will come to his senses soon," Pauline continued. "He's blinded by romantic notions right now, but one of these days he'll realize you're not really one of us." She gazed into Laura's eyes, making her feel like a young child who'd been caught stealing pennies from a piggy bank. "I don't trust you, Laura Meade. When Eli sees the real you and casts ya aside, I'll be there, ready and willin' to become his wife."

Laura's mind whirled as she tried to think of an appropriate comeback. All she could think to do was run—far away from Pauline's piercing gaze. She practically flew down the stairs, dropped the platter of beets on the table, and sprinted off toward the creek.

🌺

Eli was just rounding the corner of the house when he caught sight of Laura running off. He was about to call out to her, but Pauline stopped him. "Let her go," she insisted. "Come sample the chocolate chip cookies I made."

Eli's forehead wrinkled. "What's goin' on, Pauline? Did you and Laura have words?"

Pauline placed the plate of sandwiches on the table and motioned him to follow her around the side of the house. When they were out of earshot and scrutinizing eyes, she stopped and placed both hands on Eli's shoulders.

He shrugged them away. "What's this all about?"

"That English woman will never make you happy. She's an outsider and she always will be. She doesn't belong here, so you'd better think twice 'bout marryin' her."

Eli felt his face flood with color. How dare Pauline speak to him that way! Who did she think she was, trying to turn him against Laura?

"I love Laura," he said through clenched teeth, "and she's not an outsider. Do I need to remind you that she joined the church and has agreed to abide by our

Ordnung?"

Pauline shook her finger in his face. "You're the most pigheaded man I've ever met, Eli Yoder! You're blinded by her beautiful face and smooth-talkin' words, but I know what's in her heart."

"Is that so?" he shouted. "What gives ya the right to try and read someone else's mind?"

"I didn't say 'mind,' Eli. I said, 'heart.' I have a sixth sense about things, and my senses are tellin' me—"

"I don't care what your senses are sayin'," Eli interrupted. He drew in a deep breath to steady his nerves and tried to offer her a smile. "Look, Pauline, I'm sorry things didn't work out between us, but if you'll search your own heart, instead of tryin' to see what's in others', I'm sure you'll realize we could never be anything more than friends."

Pauline planted her hands on her hips, and her blue eyes flashed angrily. "We could've been more than friends if she hadn't come along and filled your head with all sorts of fancy English ideas."

Eli was trying so hard to be civil, but he'd had just about enough of Pauline's meddling. He had to get away from her. He needed to be with Laura.

"I never meant to hurt ya," he said sincerely, "but I love Laura with all my heart, and she loves me. She gave up bein' English so's we could be together, and nothin' you say is gonna change my mind. Is that clear enough?"

Pauline's eyes filled with tears, making Eli feel like a big heel. He really was sorry for hurting her, but it didn't change anything. He didn't love her now and never had. Even when they'd been courting, he'd only seen her as a friend.

Eli gently touched her arm. "I pray you'll find someone else to love." He walked away quickly, hoping she wouldn't follow. His life was with Laura, and she needed him now.

❧

Laura leaned heavily against the trunk of a tree as she gazed at the bubbling creek. *Maybe I made a mistake thinking I could become part of a world so plain and simple. Maybe Pauline is right and Eli does belong with her.*

She sucked in her bottom lip, and a fresh set of tears coursed down her cheeks. Could Pauline really see through her? Did the accusing young woman know Laura was only pretending to have changed?

How could she? Laura reasoned. *No one knows what's in my heart or mind. I've taken my biblical training classes, studied the Amish language, and learned how to cook, sew, and keep house. I wear plain clothes and no makeup, and I'm living without electricity or any other modern conveniences. What more is there? Why would Pauline think I'm not to be trusted?*

"Because you're not," a little voice reminded. *"You're lying to Eli, and you're lying to yourself."*

Laura dropped to the ground and sobbed. She *was* lying to Eli, but to herself? She knew exactly what she wanted out of life. A big, beautiful home, lots of money, and Eli Yoder. She wanted him more than anything. If she had to lie a little in order to make him think she really had become Amish, what harm had been done? It would only be until after the wedding. Then she could tell him how unhappy the Plain life made her and beg him to become English.

Laura jerked her head when someone touched her shoulder. She looked up and saw the face of the man she loved staring down at her.

"What's wrong? Why are ya cryin'?" he asked, helping Laura to her feet.

"I–I had a little encounter with your ex-girlfriend," she said, sniffing and reaching up to wipe the tears from her face. "Pauline hates me, and she's gonna try to come between us."

"No, she's not," he said firmly. "I just spoke with Pauline, and I put her in her place, but good."

"You did?"

He pulled her into his arms. "I told Pauline it's you I love, and nothin' she says will ever change my mind."

"You mean it?"

Jah, I do. Pauline and I have never been anything more'n friends, and she knows it. I don't know why she's bent on makin' trouble, but don't you worry, 'cause I'll never stop lovin' ya, Laura." Eli bent to kiss her, and Laura felt like she was drowning in his love. Everything would be all right. Things were working according to plan, and soon she'd have all she'd ever wanted.

Chapter 12

Laura was excited about the wedding and had been given permission for her parents to attend. The bishop made it clear he wanted no other English invited to the solemn occasion, so this meant neither Shannon nor Darla could come.

Leaving Darla out didn't really bother Laura, since her school chum probably would not find much enjoyment being around "farmers." Besides, the last letter she'd gotten from Darla said she'd finished school and was working in Philadelphia, doing window designing for one of the big department stores. Darla would no doubt be working on the day of Laura's wedding.

Laura did feel bad about not inviting Shannon, though. They'd been best friends since they were kids, and each had promised the other they'd someday be in one another's weddings.

Laura decided to ask Eli's sister to be her main attendant, and her other two attendants were going to be Martha Rose's friends, Anna Beachy and Nancy Frey, the schoolteacher. The ceremony would be held at Amon and Martha Rose's house, since Laura was still living with them.

With only a few weeks until the wedding, there was much to be done. Martha Rose helped Laura sew a simple wedding dress, and they spent many hours baking and cleaning house. Several ladies in the community offered their help, and a few men volunteered to set up tables, benches, and move furniture out of the way.

"When are your parents arrivin'?" Martha Rose asked Laura as the two of them scrubbed the kitchen floor.

"Day before the wedding," Laura answered, swiping the back of her hand across her damp forehead.

"They're more than welcome to stay here. We have plenty of room," Martha Rose said.

Laura nodded. "I know you do, and it's a very kind offer, but Mom and Dad are hotel kind of people. I don't think they'd last five minutes without TV or a microwave."

Martha Rose pursed her lips. "You're managin'."

That's because I have a purpose. I won't always be stuck looking like a frump or wearing my nails down to a nubbin. Laura feigned a smile. "I'm learning."

❧

Laura and Martha Rose were seated at the kitchen table, with little Ben playing on the floor nearby. Martha Rose was mending a pair of Amon's trousers, and

Laura was hemming her wedding dress. "My folks should be here soon," she remarked.

"You said they were flyin' in and would be rentin' a car to drive out?" Martha Rose asked.

Laura nodded. "I wanted them to meet all of you before the wedding, so tomorrow won't be too much of a shock."

Martha Rose frowned. "Why would they be shocked?"

"The Amish lifestyle is a bit different from what they're used to." Laura sighed deeply. "I just hope they don't try to talk me out of marrying Eli."

"Why would they do that? I'm sure you've told 'em how much you love my brother."

"Oh, yes, and Dad said if I was happy, then he was, too." Laura grinned. "I think it gives him pleasure to see me get what I want."

"Havin' one's way is not always of the Lord, Laura," Martha Rose admonished. "We're taught to be selfless, not self-centered. Surely you learned that from your religious trainin' prior to baptism."

"Yes, yes, of course," Laura stammered. "I just meant, when I was younger and didn't know much about religious things, I was rather spoiled." She chuckled. "Dad still thinks of me as his little girl, but I know he and Mom want my happiness."

"So, you're happy bein' Amish?"

"Of course. Why wouldn't I be?"

Their conversation was interrupted when a car came up the graveled driveway, causing the two farm dogs to carry on.

Laura jumped up and darted to the back door. "It's them! My folks are here!" She jerked the door open and ran down the steps.

Her father was the first to step from the car, and the bundle of fur in his hands brought a squeal of delight from Laura's lips. "Foosie!" Her arms went around Dad's waist, and she gave him a big hug.

"Your mother and I thought you might like your cat, now that you're about to be married and will soon have your own home."

Mom stepped out of the car and embraced Laura. "It's so good to see you." She frowned and took a few steps back. "Oh, dear, you've changed! What happened to our beautiful, vibrant daughter? What have these Plain People done to you?"

Laura had expected some reservation on her parents' part, but her mother's rude comment took her by surprise. If she wasn't beautiful anymore, did that mean she was ugly?

"Laura is still beautiful. . .in a plain sort of way," Dad said, handing the cat to Laura.

Laura rubbed her nose against Foosie's soft fur and sniffed deeply. At least someone still loved her. She could feel tears stinging the back of her eyes. "I–I don't think I can keep Foosie."

"Why not?" Mom asked.

"Eli and I will be living with his parents until their addition is complete,"

Laura explained. "They might not appreciate having an inside cat underfoot."

"That's nonsense!" Dad exclaimed. "I thought the Amish liked animals." He gazed around the farmyard, until he spotted the cows in the field. "See, there's a bunch of animals."

"And don't forget those dreadful dogs that barked at us when we pulled in," Mom added.

"Those are farm animals," Laura reminded. "They're not pampered pets."

"Be that as it may, I would think your husband would want you to be happy," Mom said.

Before Laura could respond, Martha Rose was at her side. "I'm Martha Rose Zook." She extended her hand toward Laura's mother.

Mom smiled and shook the offered hand, and Dad stepped forward to greet Martha Rose. "I'm Wesley Meade, and this is my wife, Irene."

"I'm glad to meet ya."

"Nice place you've got here. I always did have a hankering for the country life," Dad said, sounding a bit wistful.

"Won'tcha please come inside? It's kinda nippy out, and I've got plenty of hot coffee and some freshly baked brownies waitin'," Martha Rose offered.

"Sounds good to me," Dad replied enthusiastically.

Everyone followed Martha Rose to the house. When they stepped onto the back porch, Laura stopped. "Uh, what would you like me to do with my cat?"

Martha Rose blinked. "*Ach*, my! I didn't realize you were holdin' a cat. Where'd it come from?"

"We brought it from Minnesota," Dad answered. "Foosie is Laura's house pet."

Laura rocked back and forth on her heels. What if Martha Rose made her throw Foosie out in the barn? She knew the cat would never get along with farm cats. Besides, she might get fleas!

"Bring the cat inside," Martha Rose said, opening the door. "I'm sure Ben would love to play with her awhile."

Once her folks were seated at the kitchen table, Laura placed Foosie on the floor beside Ben. He squealed with delight and hugged the cat around the neck.

"Now don't *knutsche* too hard," Martha Rose admonished her son. She quickly poured mugs of steaming coffee, and Laura passed around a plate of brownies.

"What's a *knutsche*?" Mom asked.

"It means 'cuddle,'" Laura explained.

"*Schnuck! Schnuck!*" Ben hollered as Foosie licked the end of his nose.

"Ben thinks Foosie is cute," Laura said, before either of her parents could raise the question.

"Laura says you plan on stayin' at a hotel in Lancaster while you're here," Martha Rose said as she handed Dad a mug.

He nodded. "That's right. We made our reservations as soon as Laura phoned and told us about the wedding."

"You're welcome to stay here."

Mom smiled sweetly. "That's kind of you, Martha Rose, but I think it would be less hectic if we stay at the hotel."

Martha Rose shrugged. "Whatever ya think best."

"I made my own wedding dress," Laura said, holding up the pale blue dress she'd been hemming earlier.

Mom frowned. "Oh, my! It doesn't look anything like a traditional wedding gown."

"It's a traditional Amish dress," Martha Rose stated.

Mom shrugged. "I see."

Laura could see by the look on her mother's face that she was anything but happy about this plain wedding. For that matter, she was probably upset about Laura marrying an Amish man. Mom most likely thought her only daughter had completely lost her mind. However, she had no idea Laura was planning to marry Eli, gain his trust, then ask him to leave the Amish faith and move back to Minnesota. If Mom had known, she might not look quite so grief-stricken.

I don't want Mom and Dad to let my secret out. So I'll tell them my plans when the time is right. Until then, they'll just have to accept what is going on. Laura turned to look at her dad. He was grinning like a Cheshire cat, and obviously enjoying the homemade brownies, for he'd already eaten three.

"Eli and his parents are coming over for supper," Laura said, changing the subject again. "I'm so anxious for you to meet him."

"*Jah,*" Martha Rose agreed. "Eli's right excited 'bout meetin' your folks, too."

The back door opened, and Eli, his brothers, and their folks entered the house. Laura rushed to his side. "My parents are here, and I'm so glad you came!"

Introductions were soon made, and everyone took seats at the table. Laura and Martha Rose served a scrumptious supper of ham, bread stuffing, mashed potatoes, green beans, chowchow, and homemade bread.

All heads bowed in silent prayer, and Laura was relieved when her parents followed suit. Even though they only went to church at Christmas and Easter, they did know social graces.

"Laura tells me you work in a law office," Eli said as he passed Laura's dad the platter of ham.

"Sure do. In fact, I have several other lawyers working for me." Dad grinned and forked two huge pieces of meat onto his plate. "Umm. . .this sure looks tasty."

"Pop raises hogs," Lewis spoke up. "He's always got plenty of meat to share with Martha Rose and Amon."

Johnny Yoder nodded and spooned himself a sizable helping of bread stuffing. "Yep, I'm not braggin' now, but I think I've got some of the finest hogs around."

Mary Ellen patted her husband's portly stomach. "*Jah,* and some pretty *gut* milkin' cows, too."

Laura moved the fork slowly around her plate, wishing this conversation would take a turn. Just talking about food made her feel fat.

As if he knew what she was thinking, Eli's father glanced over at her dad and frowned. "Wesley, how much influence do ya have on that daughter of yours?"

Dad gulped down some milk before he answered. "I'm not altogether sure. Why do you ask?"

Johnny pointed a finger at Laura. "She eats like a bird. Just look at her plate. Hardly a thing on it!"

Laura knew everyone was looking at her, and her face flooded with the heat of embarrassment. "I eat enough to sustain myself. I just don't think one needs to become chubby in order to prove one's worth."

The room became deathly quiet, and she knew she'd said too much. By Amish standards, elders were not to be argued with. . .especially not the parents of your betrothed.

"I—um—meant to say, I prefer to watch my weight," she quickly amended. "If others choose to overeat, that's their right." *Not much better,* she realized a little too late.

"Laura, what are ya sayin'?" Eli whispered. "Are ya tryin' to make some kinda trouble tonight?"

She shook her head. "I'm sorry. I don't know what came over me."

Tonight was supposed to be a happy occasion. . .a time for Laura's folks to get to know Eli and his family. Things had been going so well, but now there was tension, and she was the cause. Would she ever learn to keep her big mouth shut?

"I think our daughter might be a bit nervous," Laura's mother said, offering one of her most pleasant smiles. "It isn't every day she introduces her father and I to her future husband and in-laws, you know."

Martha Rose nodded. "I think you could be right, Irene. Laura's been jittery as a dragonfly all day. Haven't ya, Laura?"

Laura shrugged. "I suppose."

"In fact, Laura did most of the work today, just to keep her hands busy," Martha Rose added.

"I did work pretty hard, but that's because I wanted Martha Rose to rest." Laura glanced at her mother. "Martha Rose is in a family way."

Mom's eyebrows furrowed. "Family way?"

"She's pregnant, Hon," Dad said with a chuckle. "I haven't heard that expression since I was a boy growing up on the farm, but I sure can remember what 'being in a family way' means."

"Your folks were farmers?" The question came from Johnny, who leaned his elbows on the table as he scrutinized Laura's dad.

"My parents farmed a huge spread out in Montana," her father answered. "Dad sold the farm several years ago, since none of us boys wanted to follow in his footsteps." His forehead wrinkled. "Sometimes I wonder if I made the wrong choice, becoming a fancy city lawyer instead of an old cowhand."

Little Ben, who up until this moment had been busy playing with the bread stuffing on his plate, spoke up for the first time. *"Meislin!"* he shouted, pointing to the floor and disrupting the conversation.

"*Meislin?* Where?" Martha Rose screeched. She was immediately on her feet.

"*Schpring, bussli!*" Ben hollered as he bounced up and down in his chair.

"What on earth is going on?" Laura's mother asked with a note of concern.

"Aw, it's just a few little mice, and Ben's tellin' the kitty to run," Jonas said with a deep chuckle. "That fluffy white cat will take 'em in a hurry, too, I'll bet."

"Fluffy white cat?" Mary Ellen's eyes were wide. "When did ya get an indoor cat, Martha Rose?"

Martha Rose had a broom in her hand and was running around the kitchen, swinging it this way and that. If Laura hadn't been so concerned about Foosie, she might have thought the whole scene was rather funny.

Foosie was busy dodging the broom and leaping into the air as two tiny, gray field mice scooted across the floor at lightning speed. Everyone at the table was either laughing or shouting orders at Martha Rose.

"Open the door!" Amon hollered. "Maybe they'll run outside."

"No, don't touch that door!" Laura shrieked. "Foosie might get out, and I'd never be able to catch her once the dogs discovered she was on the loose."

Foosie was almost on top of one mouse, but just as her paw came down, the critter darted for a hole under the cupboard. The other mouse followed, leaving a very confused cat sitting in front of the hole, meowing for all she was worth.

Laura's dad was laughing so hard, he had tears rolling down his cheeks. "Well, if that doesn't beat all. In all the years we've had that cat, I don't believe I've ever seen her move so fast." He wiped his eyes with a napkin and started howling again.

Laura stood up. "I don't see what's so funny, Dad. Poor Foosie has never seen a mouse before. She could have had a heart attack, tearing around the room like that."

Another round of laughter filled the room. Even Martha Rose, who only moments ago had been chasing the mice with her broom, was back in her seat, holding her sides and chuckling as hard as everyone else.

Laura just shook her head. Was all this silliness a good sign, or did it merely mean Eli's family and her parents had taken leave of their senses?

Eli reached for Laura's hand. "I think you were nervous for nothin'," he whispered in her ear. "The cat and mice game sure enough got everyone in a happy kinda mood. *Wass Got tuht ist wohl getahn*—what God doeth is well done."

❧

"Today's the big day," Martha Rose said when Laura entered the kitchen bright and early the next morning. "Did ya sleep well?"

Laura yawned and reached for a mug to pour herself some coffee. "Actually, I hardly slept a wink. I was too nervous about today."

Martha Rose pulled out a chair and motioned for Laura to take a seat. "I understand how ya feel. I was a ball of nerves on my weddin' day."

"Really? You mean, it's not just me?"

Martha Rose got another chair and seated herself beside Laura. She touched her outstretched arm. "I think all brides feel the same. Even though we love our grooms like everything, we're still kinda jittery 'bout tyin' the knot."

Laura took a long, slow drink from her cup. "I hope I can make Eli happy."

"You will. Ya love him, don'tcha?"

"Of course, but—"

"Just do your best to please him. Always trust God to help ya, and your marriage will go fine."

Laura nodded, but she wasn't sure it would be as easy as Martha Rose made it seem. Especially since she didn't have any idea how she was going to put her trust in God.

❧

The wedding began at nine o'clock sharp. Laura and her three attendants sat on one bench, directly in front of Bishop Weaver. On the bench across from them sat Eli and his two brothers, along with a friend, Dan, his other attendant. Laura's mother and Eli's mom sat behind Laura, and behind Eli sat his dad, Laura's father, and Amon, holding little Ben on his lap. All the other wedding guests filled the rest of the benches, making a total of a hundred and fifty in attendance.

Laura, wearing her light blue, full-skirted dress, covered with a white organdy apron, sat rigid on her backless bench. *Am I really doing the right thing? Will I ever be able to convince Eli to leave the Amish faith? And if he refuses, can I possibly spend the rest of my life as a Plain woman?*

Laura knew divorce was not an option among the Amish, so no matter what Eli decided about going English, she would have to accept it and be willing to live with his decision. She glanced over at her groom, sitting straight and tall, and looking so happy. He was awfully handsome, dressed in a pair of black trousers, a matching vest, and a collarless, dark jacket. Accentuating his white cotton shirt was a black bow tie, making Eli look every bit as distinguished as any of the lawyers who worked for her father's law firm.

Bishop Weaver's booming voice drew Laura out of her musings. He was asking the wedding party to follow him and two church deacons to another part of the house. They were led upstairs and down the long hall. When they came to Laura's bedroom, the bishop opened the door. Signaling the bride's and groom's attendants to wait outside, he ushered Laura and Eli inside.

As they sat in two straight-backed chairs, the bride and groom were given instructions on the responsibilities and obligations related to marriage. Each of the deacons said a few words, quoting Scripture and admonishing the young couple to remain faithful to one another.

Half an hour later, they returned to the living room, where the congregation was singing a traditional Amish hymn. When the singing ended, one of the deacons delivered a lengthy sermon, alluding to more Bible verses related to marriage.

Laura was beginning to feel a headache coming on. She was getting mighty tired of hearing how a wife should behave. . .be faithful, loving, obedient, always looking to her husband's needs. What about her needs? Didn't they matter at all?

When the sermon was over, Bishop Weaver stepped forward and motioned

Eli and Laura to join him at the front of the room. Laura felt the touch of Eli's hand, and she squeezed his fingers in response. This was it. This was the moment they'd been waiting for.

There was no exchange of rings, like in most English weddings, but there were vows. "Vows not to be taken lightly," the bishop said. "Vows to be kept, for better or worse, for rich or poor, in sickness and health, 'til death do you part."

Feeling much like a toy robot, Laura repeated her vows and listened as Eli did the same. His eyes were brimming with tears, and he wore a smile that stretched from ear to ear. Eli Yoder really did love her. Now all he had to do was prove it.

Chapter 13

Eli and Laura moved outside to the front lawn. Even though there was a chill in the air, the sun was shining and the sky was clear blue. It was a perfect day for a wedding, and Eli was content in the knowledge that Laura Meade was now Mrs. Eli Yoder.

A reception line was formed, with those in attendance coming by to offer Eli and Laura their congratulations. When Wesley and Irene Meade hugged their daughter, they both had tears in their eyes. For one brief moment, Eli felt a pang of guilt. He knew he was the cause of Laura leaving her fancy life and becoming one of the Plain People. Because of her love for him, she wouldn't see much of her family, and she'd given up all the modern things her rich father could offer.

Eli shook hands with Laura's parents and said, "I'll take *gut* care of your daughter. I hope ya know that."

Wesley nodded. "I believe you're an honest man, Eli, and I can tell by the look on your face how much you love Laura."

"Please, let her keep Foosie," Irene put in. "She needs a touch from home."

Eli grinned. *"Jah,* I'll speak to Mom and Pop 'bout the cat. I'm sure they won't mind havin' a pet inside, just as long as it's housebroke."

"Oh, she is," Laura asserted. "Foosie's never made a mess in the house. Not even when she was a kitten."

Mom and Martha Rose came through the line next. They hugged Eli and Laura, then excused themselves to go help in the kitchen. Pop, Amon, and little Ben followed, with both men shaking Eli's hand and welcoming Laura into the family with a hug and a kiss on the cheek. Not to be outdone, Ben insisted on kissing the bride, too. In fact, it was all Amon could do to tear his son out of Laura's arms and send him off to play. It was obvious the child was enamored with Laura, and she seemed to like him equally well.

She'll make a gut *mother,* Eli mused. *Lord willin', maybe we'll have a whole house full of* kinder.

❧

The wedding meal was a veritable feast. Long tables had been set up in the living room, dining room, parlor, and for hardier individuals, some were placed outside on the lawn. Several Amish women served up platters of fried chicken, baked ham, bread filling, mashed potatoes, a variety of cooked vegetables, plenty of chowchow, and a fine array of cookies, pies, and cakes. There was also coffee, milk, and homemade root beer.

Laura and Eli sat at their corner table, along with their attendants. There was plenty of joke telling and friendly banter going on, and Laura was thoroughly enjoying herself.

"Eat hearty, *Frau*," Eli said, needling Laura in the ribs with his elbow. "Today's our weddin' day, and this is no time to diet."

She leaned closer to him and smiled. "I might splurge and try a little bit of everything, but tomorrow's another day. I'll probably have five pounds to shed after this feast!"

Laura glanced across the room and saw her parents sitting at a table with Eli's folks. They seemed to be having a good time, despite the fact they hardly knew anyone.

Pauline Hostetler was among the women acting as servers. Laura hadn't expected to see her at all today, much less helping out. For one brief moment, she felt pity for Pauline. She'd lost Eli to a fancy English woman, and now her heart was obviously broken.

"Wanna sneak away with me?" Eli's tender words, and the wiggling of his eyebrows, drew Laura out of her contemplations.

"Sneak away? As in leave this place?" she asked, offering him a smile.

Eli reached for her hand. "I think it's time for my bride and me to get some fresh air," he announced to those at their table. "I hope you'll excuse us."

"I'll race you to the creek," Laura said as soon as they were outside.

"You're on!" Eli shouted, then took off at a run.

Laura was breathless by the time she reached the water, and she didn't get there much behind Eli. They collapsed on the grass, ignoring the chill and laughing and tickling each other until Laura finally called a truce.

"So, it's peace you're wantin', huh?" Eli teased. "All right, but you'll have to pay a small price for it."

Laura squirmed beneath his big hands. "Oh, yeah? What kind of payment must I offer the likes of you, Eli Yoder?"

"This," he murmured against her ear. "And this." He nuzzled her neck with his cold nose. "Also this." His lips trailed a brigade of soft kisses along her chin, up her cheek, and finally they came to rest on her lips. As the kiss deepened, Laura moaned softly and snuggled closer to Eli.

When they finally pulled away, she gazed deeply into his dazzling blue eyes. "I love you, Husband, and I always will."

"And I love you, my *seelich*—blessed gift."

❧

Laura and Eli spent their first night as husband and wife at Martha Rose and Amon's house. Tomorrow they would be moving to Eli's parents' and sharing their home until the addition was built. This smaller home, added onto the main house, was where Johnny, Mary Ellen, and their two younger sons would live. Laura and Eli would remain in the larger home, since they were a new family. The building wouldn't begin until spring, and this caused Laura some concern. What would it be like living under the same roof with her in-laws? Would Mary Ellen scrutinize her every move? Would she be expected to do even more work than she had while living at the Zooks'?

Forcing her anxiety aside, Laura stepped into the kitchen. Eli had already gone to work at his job in town, and she knew her folks would be here soon to say good-bye.

Martha Rose was busy baking bread, but she looked up and smiled when Laura entered the room. "How's the *Hochzeit?* Did ya sleep well?"

Laura shuffled across the kitchen, still feeling the effects of sleep. She nodded and yawned. "The newlyweds are fine, and I'm sorry I overslept. Eli left for work without waking me."

"Guess he thought ya needed to rest. Yesterday was a pretty big day," Martha Rose reminded.

Laura reached for the pot of coffee on the back of the wood-burning stove.

"There's still some scrambled eggs left in the warmin' oven," Martha Rose said, gesturing with her head. "Help yourself."

Laura moaned. "After all I ate yesterday, I don't think I need any breakfast."

"Oh, but breakfast is the most important meal of the day," Martha Rose argued. "And now that you're a married woman, you'll be needin' to keep up your strength."

Laura dropped into a chair at the table. "What's that supposed to mean?"

"Just that you'll soon be busy settin' up your own house."

"Not really. Eli and I will be living with your folks, remember?"

Martha Rose nodded. *Jah,* but not for long. If I know my brother, he'll be workin' long hours on that addition." She winked at Laura. "He's a man in love, and I think he'd kinda like to have ya all to himself."

Laura felt the heat of a blush stain her face. "I–I'd like that, too," she admitted.

"So, dish up some eggs, and while you're at it, why not have some of that left-over apple pie from the weddin'?"

Laura opened her mouth to offer a rebuttal, but the sound of a car pulling into the yard drew her to the window instead. "It's my parents. They've come to say good-bye." She jerked open the door and ran down the stairs. If she was going to get all teary-eyed, she'd rather not do it in front of Eli's sister.

As soon as Mom and Dad stepped from the car, the three of them shared a group hug.

"I'll miss you," Laura said tearfully.

"Be happy," her mother whimpered.

"If you ever need anything. . .anything at all, please don't hesitate to call," Dad said. He grinned at her. "I know you Amish don't have phones in your houses, but I hear tell it's acceptable for you to use a pay phone."

Laura nodded. "That's true, but some Amish have phones outside. Mostly those who have a home business."

"We should really go inside and say good-bye to your new sister-in-law," Mom said as she started for the house.

Laura reached out to stop her. "Martha Rose is kind of busy this morning. She said to tell you good-bye." *Why did I lie about that? Why don't I want Mom and Dad to come inside?*

Dad broke into her thoughts before she could come up with any kind of reasonable answer. "Where's Eli? We do get to tell our son-in-law good-bye, I hope."

"Eli works at a furniture store in Lancaster," Laura explained. "He left early this morning."

Mom's mouth dropped open. "The day after your wedding? Why, I've never heard of such a thing! The two of you should be on a honeymoon at some resort, not him working, and you stuck on this dreary old farm."

Laura hung her head. How could she argue with that? Especially when she'd been thinking the same thing.

Dad slipped his arm around her waist. "The Amish have some pretty strange ways, but this man you've married is a rare one. He's a hard worker, and I'm convinced he loves you."

A few tears slipped under Laura's lashes and dribbled down her cheeks. She sniffed deeply. "I love him, too, Dad, but someday I'm hoping—"

Laura's words were halted by a piercing scream. At least she thought it was a scream. She turned toward the sound coming from the front porch. Foosie was clinging to one of the support beams, and Amon's dogs were below, yapping and jumping up and down. Poor Foosie was hissing and screeching for all she was worth.

"Oh, no," Laura moaned. "Foosie must have slipped out the door behind me." She turned back to face her parents. "I'd better go rescue her, and you two had better get to the airport. You don't want to be late for your flight."

Mom gave Laura a quick peck on the cheek, then climbed into the rental car. Dad embraced Laura one final time, and just before he took his seat on the driver's side, he said, "Don't forget. . .call if you need us."

Laura nodded and blinked back tears. She offered one final wave, then raced toward the house. Even if she couldn't fix her own problems today, she could at least save her cat!

❧

Laura had visited Eli's parents' home several times, but she'd never had occasion to use the rest room. It wasn't until she and Eli moved her things to his house and were settled into their own room that Laura was hit with a sickening reality. Johnny Yoder had never installed indoor plumbing! Most of the Amish farms in the valley had indoor bathrooms, but the Yoders still used an outhouse.

When Laura expressed her dislike of the smelly facilities, Eli promised as soon as the addition was done, he would see about turning one of the upstairs closets into a bathroom.

"How am I supposed to bathe?" Laura wailed as she paced back and forth in front of their bedroom window.

"We have a galvanized tub for that," Eli answered from his seat on the bed.

"You'll heat water on the stove, and—"

"And nothing!" Laura shouted. "Eli Yoder, I can hardly believe you would expect me to live under such barbaric conditions!"

Eli looked at her like she'd taken leave of her senses. "Calm down. You'll wake up the whole house, shoutin' thataway." He joined her at the window. "You've gotten used to livin' without other modern things, so I'd think you could manage this little inconvenience. After all, it's really not such a *greislich.*"

She squinted her eyes at him. "It's a terrible thing to me, Eli. And this is not a 'little' inconvenience. It's a major catastrophe!"

He clicked his tongue. "Such big words you're usin', and such resentment I see on your face." He brushed her cheek lightly with his thumb. "You've done so well adjustin' to bein' Amish, and I'm right proud of you."

How could she stay mad with him looking at her that way? His enchanting eyes were shining like the moonlight, and his chin dimple was pronounced by his charming smile.

She leaned against his chest and sighed deeply. "Promise me you'll build us a decent bathroom as soon as you can?"

"*Jah*, I promise."

❧

The next few weeks flew by as Laura settled into her in-laws' home during weekdays, and she and Eli honeymooned at various relatives' and friends' homes every weekend. There wasn't much privacy for the newlyweds, and Laura always felt obligated to help out wherever they stayed. At least they were sent home with a gift from their hosts every Sunday evening. They'd already received some bedding, several jars of home-canned fruit, and a huge sack of root vegetables. Laura's favorite gift was an oval braided rug in rich autumn hues. This she placed on the bare, wooden floor in their bedroom. The room they shared had been Eli's, and as she spread it near her side of the bed, he informed her that he'd never seen the need for a rug before.

"Look how well it goes with the quilt I purchased at the farmers' market last fall," she said, motioning toward the lovely covering at the foot of their bed. "It can be the focal point of our room."

Eli raised his eyebrows. "Don't know nothin' about *focal* points in the room, but it does looks right *gut.*" He pulled Laura to his chest and rubbed his face against her cheek. "Almost as *gut* as my beautiful wife."

"Eli, you're hurting me," she complained. "Your face is so scratchy!"

He stepped back, holding her at arm's length. "It'll be better once my beard grows fully."

She thrust out her chin. "I don't see why you can't shave anymore. I think it's a silly rule that married Amish men have to wear a beard."

Eli scowled at her. "You knew it was a rule before you agreed to marry me. I don't see why you're makin' such a fuss over it now."

Laura shrugged and turned away. "Forget it. There's nothing I can do about it anyway." *At least, not now.*

❧

"I hear your sister's in a family way," Maude Hostetler said to Eli as he and Laura sat at the Hostetlers' kitchen table during one of their "visiting" weekends.

Eli grinned. "That's right, she is."

Maude glanced at Laura, sitting beside Eli. "How many *kinder* are you hopin' to have?"

Laura's face grew warm, and she looked over at Eli. "As many as the good Lord allows," he replied.

Laura's feelings turned from embarrassment to shock. Her mouth opened, but the only word that came out was, "Huh?"

Eli squeezed her hand under the table. "I like *kinder*. . .you like *kinder*. . .we'll have a whole house full!"

Pauline, who had been silent until now, spoke up. "I think Laura will be a great *mamm*. Can't ya just see her chubby little body runnin' around chasin' *kinder* all day?"

Everyone at the table stared at Pauline. She didn't seem to care, for she laughed and went right on with her tirade. "Before long, Laura will look like an *alte Kuh*—old cow, instead of all prim and proper, tryin' to keep her fancy ways without no one noticin'."

Matt Hostetler's fist came down hard against the table, and everyone jumped. "That'll be enough, Daughter! What's gotten into you?"

Pauline wrinkled her nose and leveled her gaze at Laura. "Why don'tcha ask *her*?"

Laura scooted her chair back and stood up. "I think we should go, Eli. It's obvious we're not wanted here."

"That just ain't so," Maude insisted. "It's only our daughter who's bein' rude, and if she was a few years younger, she'd be taken out back to the woodshed and given a sound *bletching*. I think her bein' the baby of the family and the last one to leave the nest might've made her a bit spoiled."

Ignoring her mother's comment, Pauline pointed at Laura. "You stay and finish your supper. I'll leave!" With that, she jumped up and marched out of the room.

Eli grasped Laura's hand and pulled her gently back to her seat. "We won't be spendin' the night, but I think we should finish eatin' before we head for home."

Maude nodded. "And don't forget your weddin' gift. Matt made you a straw broom, and I have several jars of home-canned pickled beets."

Eli felt a sense of relief when Laura picked up her fork and began to eat the potpie on her plate. He knew it had been a mistake coming here, but what else was he to do? After all, the Hostetlers *had* extended an invitation.

On the buggy ride home, Eli kept glancing at Laura, slouched in her seat with her eyes closed. Truth be told, he was worried sick about his new bride. She

335

hadn't been acting right ever since they moved in with Mom and Pop. Was it the folks she was having trouble with, or did Laura resent *him?* He had to know what was wrong, and he had to know soon.

🌹

Laura kept her eyes shut, hoping Eli would think she was asleep and wouldn't try to make conversation. The last thing she wanted was another argument, and she was pretty sure they would quarrel if she told him all the things on her mind.

As they pulled into the Yoders' driveway, Laura opened her eyes. She sat up with a start when Eli pulled the buggy over, just as he'd done many times before when he thought they needed to work things out.

"What are you doing?"

"I'm stoppin' here so we can talk."

"There's nothing to talk about."

"I think there is," he replied stiffly.

She drew in a deep breath and released it with a shudder. "What do you think we need to talk about?"

"This business between you and Pauline, for one thing," he said. "How come there's so much hostility still goin' on?"

Laura groaned. "Eli, Eli, are you really so blind? Pauline's still in love with you, and she's angry with me for taking you away from her."

Eli scrunched up his nose. "If I've told ya once, I've told ya a hundred times. . . Pauline and I were never more than friends."

"She wanted it to be more," Laura argued. She balled her hands into fists. "I think your mother did, too."

"Mom?"

Laura shook her head. "Oh, Eli, don't look so wide-eyed and innocent. We've been living with your folks several weeks now. Surely you can feel the tension between me and your mother."

He merely shrugged in response.

"She's mentioned Pauline a few times, too. I think she believes Pauline would have made you a better wife."

Even in the darkened buggy, Laura could see a vein on the side of Eli's neck begin to bulge. It often did that whenever he was upset.

"Your mom is always criticizing me," Laura continued. "I can never do anything right where she's concerned."

Eli pursed his lips. "I don't believe that."

"Are you calling me a liar?"

"No, but I think I know Mom pretty well."

"You don't know her as well as you think!" Laura shouted. "She scrutinizes my work, and she—"

Eli shook his finger in front of her face. "Enough! I don't want to hear another word against my mom!"

Chapter 14

Christmas was fast approaching, and Laura looked on it with dread. Nothing seemed to be going right these days. She and Eli argued all the time, Foosie was an irritant to Eli's mother, Laura detested the extra chores she was expected to do, and worst of all, she hated that smelly outhouse! She was on her way there now and none too happy about it.

On previous trips to the privy, she'd encountered icky spiders, a yellow jackets' nest, and a couple of field mice. She was a city girl and hated bugs. She shouldn't have to be subjected to this kind of torture.

Laura opened the wooden door and held it with one hand as she lifted her kerosene lantern and peered cautiously inside. Nothing lurking on the floor. She held the lamp higher and was just about to step inside when the shaft of light fell on something. It was dark and furry—and it was sitting over the hole!

Laura let out a piercing scream and slammed the door. She sprinted toward the house and ran straight into Eli, coming from the barn.

"Laura, what's wrong? I heard ya hollerin' and thought one of Pop's pigs had gotten loose again."

Laura clung to Eli's jacket. "It's the outhouse. . .there's some kind of monstrous animal in there!"

Eli grinned at her. *"Kumme*—come now, it was probably just a little old mouse."

"It wasn't," she sobbed. "It was dark and furry. . .and huge!"

Eli slipped his hand in the crook of her arm. "Let's go have a look-see."

"I'm not going in there."

He chuckled. "You don't have to. I'll do the checkin'."

Laura held her breath as Eli entered the outhouse. "Be careful."

She heard a thud, followed by a loud whoop. Suddenly, the door flew open and Eli bolted out of the privy, chased by the hairy creature Laura had seen a few moments ago. It was a comical sight, but she was too frightened to see the full humor in it.

"What was that?" she asked Eli as the two of them stood watching the critter dash into the field.

"I think it was a hedgehog," Eli said breathlessly. "The crazy thing tried to attack me, but I kicked him with the toe of my boot. . .right before I walked out of the outhouse."

Laura giggled. "Don't you mean, 'ran out of the outhouse'?"

Eli's face turned pink and he chuckled. *"Jah,* I guess I was movin' pretty fast."

The two of them stood there a few seconds, gazing into each other's eyes.

Then they both started giggling. They laughed so hard, they had tears streaming down their faces, and Laura had to set the lantern on the ground for fear it would fall out of her hand. It felt good to laugh. It was something neither of them did much anymore.

When they finally got control of their emotions, Eli reached for her hand. "I'll see about indoor plumbing as soon as spring comes. I promise."

❧

Christmas morning dawned with a blanket of pristine snow covering the ground and every tree in the Yoders' yard. It looked like a picture postcard, and despite the fact that Laura missed her parents, she felt happier today than she had in weeks.

She let the dark shade fall away from the living room window and took a seat in the wooden rocker by the fireplace. Even though there was no Christmas tree or twinkle lights on the house, there were a few candles spaced around the room, along with several Christmas cards from family and friends. *Guess I did end up with an Early American look. It's just a little plainer than I had wanted.*

Laura spotted the Christmas card they'd received from her parents, along with a substantial check. She closed her eyes and sighed deeply. *I thought I'd be back home by Christmas. Oh, well. . .maybe next year.*

❧

Eli had been looking forward to Christmas for weeks. He'd made Laura a special gift, and this afternoon his sister and her family would be joining them for Mom's traditional holiday feast.

"Life couldn't be any better," he said to the horse he was grooming. "Maybe later we'll hitch you up to the sleigh and I'll take my beautiful wife for a ride to Paradise Lake."

The horse whinnied as if in response, and Eli chuckled. "You kinda like that idea, don'tcha, old boy?"

When Eli entered the house a short time later, he was holding Laura's gift under his jacket. "Where's my *Frau?*" he asked Mom, who was scurrying around the kitchen.

She nodded toward the living room. "In there. I guess she thinks I don't need any help gettin' dinner on."

Eli merely shrugged and left the kitchen. No point getting Mom more riled than she already was. He found Laura sitting in the rocking chair, gazing at the fireplace. *"En freh-licher Grischtdaag!"*

"A Merry Christmas to you, too," she replied.

Eli bent down and kissed the top of her head. "I have somethin' for ya."

Laura jumped up. "You do? What is it?"

Eli held his jacket shut. "Guess."

She wrinkled her nose. "I have no idea. Tell me. . .please."

Eli chuckled and withdrew an ornate birdhouse, painted blue with white trim.

"Oh, Eli, it's just like the one you showed me at Farmers' Market the day we first met."

He smiled. "And now you do have a place for it."

She accepted the gift, and tears welled up in her eyes. "Thank you so much. It's beautiful."

"Does my pretty *Frau* have anything for her hardworkin' husband?" Eli asked in a teasing tone.

Laura hung her head. "I do, but I'm afraid it's not finished."

"You made me somethin'?"

She nodded. "I've been sewing you a new shirt, but your mom's kept me so busy, I haven't had time to get it hemmed and wrapped."

Eli took the birdhouse from Laura and placed it on the small table by her chair. He pulled her toward him in a tender embrace. "It's okay, my love. You'll get the shirt finished soon, and I'll appreciate it then every bit as much as I would if you'd given it to me now."

Laura rested her head against his shoulder. "I love you, Eli. Thanks for being so understanding."

Silent prayer had been said, and everyone sat around the table with expectant, hungry looks on their faces. Mary Ellen had outdone herself. Huge platters were laden with succulent roast beef and mouthwatering ham. There were bowls filled with buttery mashed potatoes, candied yams, canned green beans, and coleslaw. Sweet cucumber pickles, black olives, dilled green beans, and red beet eggs were also included in the feast, as well as buttermilk biscuits and cornmeal muffins.

Everyone ate heartily. Everyone except for little Ben and Laura. Their plates were still half full when Mary Ellen brought out three pies—two pumpkin and one mincemeat—along with a tray of chocolate donuts.

Ben squealed with delight. *"Fettkuche!"*

"No donuts until you eat everything on your plate," Martha Rose scolded.

Ben's lower lip began to quiver, and his eyes filled with tears.

"Bein' a crybaby won't help you get your way," Amon admonished.

"He's only a child," Laura put in. She pulled one of the pumpkin pies close to her and helped herself to a piece. "Surely he can have one little donut."

All eyes seemed to be focused on Laura; and Ben, who'd moments ago been fighting tears, let loose with a howl that sent Laura's cat flying into the air.

"Now look what you've gone and done," Amon said, shaking his finger in Ben's face. "You've scared that poor cat half to death."

Foosie was running around the table, meowing and swishing her tail. Laura bent down and scooped her up, but the look on Mary Ellen's face was enough to let her know that in this house, cats didn't belong at the table. She mumbled an apology and deposited Foosie back on the floor.

"You're not settin' a very good example for the boy, Laura." This reprimand came from Eli's father, who was scowling at her. "If you're not gonna eat all your food, then I don't think ya should be takin' any pie." Johnny looked pointedly at Eli then. "What do you think, Son? Should your wife be allowed to pick like a bird, then eat pie in front of Ben, who's just been told he can't have any *Fettkuche* 'til he cleans his plate?"

Laura squirmed uneasily as she waited to see how Eli would respond. She felt his hand under the table, and her fingers squeezed his in response.

"Don'tcha think maybe you should eat everything else first, then have some pie?" Eli's voice was tight, and the muscle in his jaw quivered.

"I don't see why," she shot back. "I'm watching my weight, and the only way I can keep within my calorie count is to leave some food on my plate."

"You could pass up the pie," Mary Ellen suggested.

And I could leave this place and never come back, Laura fumed. Why was everything she did always under scrutiny? Why did she have to make excuses for her behavior all the time? She consoled herself with the thought that soon this would be *her* home, and Eli's parents would only be guests. Things would go the way *she* wanted when that time came.

Laura pushed away from the table. "I'm not really hungry enough for pie, anyway. I think I'll go outside for a walk." She threw Eli what she hoped was a scathing look and stomped out of the room. What in the world had she done by marrying a foreigner?

❧

Spring came to the valley early, and with it, the reality that Eli had no plans to leave the Amish faith. Although Laura hadn't come right out and asked, she knew from some of his comments that he was content to remain Plain. Laura would either have to accept her plight in life or leave. Every time she thought about going home to Minnesota without Eli, she felt sick. She would stick it out a bit longer, in the hopes she could eventually get through to him.

The building of the addition began as soon as the snow melted. It couldn't be finished soon enough, as far as Laura was concerned. Mary Ellen Yoder was a pain! In fact, since today was Saturday, and the men were all working on the addition, Eli's mom had suggested she and Laura do some baking.

Martha Rose had taught Laura the basics of baking breads, pies, and cakes, but Mary Ellen seemed to think there was more she should learn. "Today I thought we'd make a brown sugar sponge roll," she said, giving Laura a little nudge toward the cupboard where all the baking supplies were kept.

Laura groaned. "Do we have to? I'm really tired this morning, and I thought it would be nice to sit out on the front porch and watch the men work."

Mary Ellen's forehead wrinkled. "Are ya feelin' poorly?"

Before Laura could respond, her mother-in-law rushed on. "If ya aren't quite up to snuff, then maybe a good spring tonic is what you're needin'." She opened the cupboard near Laura and plucked out a box of cream of tartar, some sulfur, and a container of Epsom salts. "All we've gotta do is mix some of these in a jar of water. You'll take two or three swallows each mornin' and be feelin' like your old self in no time a'tall."

Laura nearly gagged. She couldn't imagine anything tasting worse than the mixture Mary Ellen had just suggested. "I'm fine, really. Just didn't sleep well last night. A few cups of coffee, and I'll be good to go."

Mary Ellen shrugged and stepped aside. "Suit yourself, but remember the spring tonic, just in case you're still not up to par come mornin'."

Laura nodded and feigned a smile. "Thanks, I'll remember."

Preaching was to be held at the Hostetlers' the following day. Laura wasn't looking forward to going, but she saw no way to get out of it. She was tempted to say she was sick, but the thought of Mary Ellen's spring tonic was enough to keep her quiet.

I'll just have to avoid Pauline, Laura told herself as she dressed for church. *Besides, what can that woman say or do to hurt me?*

Several hours later, Laura had her answer. After the service, she and Pauline somehow ended up alone in the kitchen.

"Married life must be agreein' with you," Pauline said in a sarcastic tone.

Laura grabbed a stack of paper plates and headed for the dining room.

"You've put on a few pounds, I see," Pauline called after her.

Laura skidded to a stop and whirled around to face her enemy. "I haven't gained any weight." She raised her chin, so she was looking Pauline right in the eye. "Even if I have, it's none of your concern."

"Eli might not want a plump wife."

Laura held her ground. "I am not plump!"

Pauline shrugged. "Why don't ya quit while you're ahead?"

"What's that supposed to mean?"

"Give Eli his freedom. You'll never make him happy."

Laura was so angry she was visibly shaking, but she couldn't back down now. Pauline Hostetler needed to be put in her place. "I'll have you know, Eli and I are very happy. He tells me how much he loves me every day."

"He probably doesn't want to hurt your fancy feelin's."

Silently, Laura began counting to ten. She couldn't let her temper get the better of her. If someone got wind of it, Eli would be told; then they'd be arguing again. The last thing she needed was for Pauline to hear them quarreling.

"I'm sure you're aware that the Amish don't believe in divorce," Pauline went on. "You're probably countin' on Eli stickin' with you no matter what."

Laura shook her head slowly. "I feel sorry for you, Pauline."

"Well, ya needn't waste your time feelin' sorry for me. You're the one who's headed for trouble." Pauline shook her finger. "When Eli gets fed up and realizes you're not truly one of us, he'll probably ask Bishop Weaver for an annulment. After all, it's not like you're *really* Amish."

Laura set the plates on the table and planted both hands on her hips. "You're wrong about that. Eli will never ask for an annulment, because he loves me. Not you, Pauline. . .me!" Laura stalked out of the room, banging the door as she went.

Laura managed to avoid Pauline the rest of the day, but that was probably because Pauline gave her a wide berth. She served one group of tables, and Laura served another. When it was time for visiting, Pauline excused herself to go to her room, saying she had a headache.

Laura smiled to herself. *Perfect. It couldn't have worked out better if I'd planned it myself.*

❧

As they rode home from church that day, Eli worried. Laura seemed so pensive. Had someone said or done something to upset her? He offered her a smile. "Sure was a *gut* day, wasn't it? So nice we could eat outside again. The only trouble with winter is havin' to cram all our tables into the house or barn where we have worship."

"Uh-huh," Laura mumbled.

"*Wass ist letz?* Is there somethin' troublin' ya?" Eli asked with concern. "You seem kinda down in the dumps."

She shrugged. "Nothing's wrong. Everything's fine. I'm just getting tired of going to other people's houses and seeing they have indoor plumbing, while our bathroom is yet to be started."

"I said I'd build one just as soon as the addition is done."

"I know, but that might be awhile. Besides, I hate that stupid outhouse!"

Eli squinted his eyes. "Why must ya always find somethin' to complain about? Can't ya just learn to be patient? The Bible says, 'the trying of your faith worketh patience.' It's in the book of James."

"Look," Laura shouted, "I'm a slave to piles of laundry, dirty dishes, and holey socks. My faith in things getting better has definitely been tried, and so has my patience!"

Eli blinked. Was there no pleasing this woman? He'd said he would install indoor plumbing as soon as the addition was finished. That ought to be good enough.

❧

Laura sat on the edge of her seat, pouting. Should she tell Eli about her encounter with Pauline? Sure, she wanted the bathroom done, and she was fed up with working all the time, but that wasn't the real reason she was acting so cross.

Choosing her words carefully, Laura said, "Eli, could I ask you a question?"

He blew out his breath. "Not if it's about indoor plumbin'."

"It's not."

He shrugged. "Okay, ask the question."

She reached across the seat and touched his arm. "Do you think Pauline Hostetler would have made you a better wife?"

Eli lifted one eyebrow and glanced over at Laura. "Pauline? What's she got to do with anything?"

"I just want to know if you think—"

"I can't believe you'd ask me that, Laura. You should know I love ya."

Her eyes filled with unexpected tears. "I thought I did. . .until today."

"What happened?"

342

"Pauline and I had a little discussion." Laura wiped the tears from her face. "Actually, it was more like an argument."

A look of bewilderment spread across Eli's face. "What were you arguin' about?"

"You."

"Me? Why would you be discussin' me with Pauline?"

"She's the one who brought the subject up," Laura was quick to say. "She thinks I'm no good for you."

"That's ridiculous!"

Laura swallowed hard. "We do argue quite a bit, Eli."

He nodded soberly. *"Jah,* it's true, but Pauline don't know that."

"She's still in love with you."

He groaned. "I've never said or done anything to make Pauline believe I loved her. Not even when she and I were courtin'."

"Well, be that as it may, she's definitely in love with you." Laura sniffed deeply. "She thinks you should see the bishop about an annulment."

Eli pulled sharply on the reins and steered the buggy to the side of the road. "This is more serious than I realized."

Laura's eyes filled with fresh tears. "You—you want to end our marriage?"

He grabbed her around the waist and pulled her close. "Of course not! While we might not see eye-to-eye on everything, you're my wife, and I love you. I plan on us on stayin' married 'til death parts us."

"You don't know how happy I am to hear you say that," Laura said, snuggling against his jacket. "That doesn't take care of things with Pauline, though."

Eli touched her chin lightly with his thumb. "Leave that up to me."

Chapter 15

I'm not feeling well. I think I'll stay home from church today," Laura mumbled when Eli tried to coax her out of bed.

"You were feelin' all right last night."

"That was then. This is now."

"If you're worried about Pauline, I've spoken with her *daed*, and he's had a talk with her."

Laura shook her head. "It's not that. Pauline hasn't said a word to me since our last confrontation."

"That's *gut*," Eli murmured against her ear. "Now get up and go help Mom with breakfast."

"I don't feel like helping today," she said with a deep moan.

Eli touched her forehead. "You ain't runnin' a fever."

"I'm not sick. . .just tired."

"Laura, get up!" Eli said sternly. "You're actin' like a lazy *alte Kuh*."

Laura bolted upright. "I am not a lazy old cow! I work plenty hard around here. Harder than anyone should be expected to work."

Eli pulled back the covers, hopped out of bed, and stepped into his trousers. He walked across the room to where the water pitcher and bowl sat on top of the dresser. After splashing a handful of water on his face and drying it with a towel, he grabbed his shirt off the wall peg and started for the door. "See ya downstairs in five minutes."

"How dare you order me around!" Laura shouted at the door as it clicked shut. "Maybe I should go home to my parents for awhile. I wonder how you'd like that, Eli Yoder!"

❧

Laura was quiet on the buggy ride to preaching, and during the service, she didn't even sing.

Bishop Weaver gave the last of the three sermons, using Mark 11:25 as his text. "Jesus' own words said, 'And when ye stand praying, forgive, if ye have ought against any: that your Father also which is in heaven may forgive you your trespasses.'"

How can I forgive Eli when he didn't even say he was sorry? Laura fumed. *That verse doesn't make sense to me.*

Laura was still pouting on the trip home. Eli kept looking at her, and finally he broke the eerie silence between them. "I thought Bishop Weaver's sermon was *gut*, didn't you?"

Laura merely shrugged in response.

"If we don't forgive others, we can't expect God to forgive us."

Laura held her breath, hoping this conversation was leading to an apology. Eli certainly owed her one after this morning.

"I'm not angry anymore, Laura. I forgive ya for bein' so cross this mornin', too."

"Me? It was you shouting orders and not understanding how tired I was," she reminded.

Eli nodded slowly. *"Jah,* I was unkind, and for that I'm sorry. Will ya forgive me?"

A sob caught in her throat, and she slid closer to Eli. "I forgive you," she whispered.

Holding the reins with one hand, Eli took Laura's hand with the other. "Is that all you've got to say?"

She sat there several seconds; then a light dawned. "Oh, yeah. I'm sorry, too."

He grinned and gave her hand a gentle squeeze. "You're forgiven."

Laura leaned her head on his shoulder and sighed. Everything would be all right now.

❧

Johnny and Mary Ellen's new home was finally ready. Since Lewis and Jonas would probably be out of the nest in a few years, it wasn't necessary for the addition to be nearly as large as the main house, so it only had three small bedrooms, a compact bath, roomy kitchen, and an adequate-sized living room. Laura envied Mary Ellen for her indoor plumbing, but it never occurred to her that Eli's mother had waited a long time for such a luxury.

Mary Ellen had been kind enough to leave Eli and Laura some furniture, and Laura was glad to finally have the house all to herself. It would be a welcome relief not to have Eli's mom analyzing everything she said and did. As far as Laura was concerned, the completion of the addition was the best thing to happen since she moved onto the Yoders' farm.

On her first morning as the new mistress of the house, Laura got up late. When she entered the kitchen, she realized Eli was already outside doing his chores. She hurried to start breakfast and was just setting the table when he came inside.

"Your cereal is almost ready," she said with a smile.

He nodded. "Is my lunch packed? I have to leave for work in five minutes."

"Oh, I forgot. I'm running late this morning. Usually your mom gets breakfast while I make your lunch."

"It's okay. I'll just take a few pieces of fruit and some cookies." Eli opened his metal lunch pail and placed two apples, an orange, a handful of peanut butter cookies, and a thermos of milk inside. He took a seat at the table, bowed his head for silent prayer, and dug into the hot oatmeal Laura handed him.

"Can you stop by the store and pick up a loaf of bread on your way home tonight?" Laura asked, taking the seat beside him.

Eli gave her a questioning look.

"I won't have time to do any baking today," she explained. "I have clothes to wash, and I want to spend most of the day organizing the house and setting out some of our wedding gifts."

Eli gulped down the last of his milk and stood up. "Guess this one time we can eat store-bought bread. I know it's important for you to set things up." He leaned over and kissed her cheek.

"Ouch! You're prickly!"

"Sorry." Eli grabbed his lunch pail and headed for the door. "See ya later."

Laura waved at his retreating form. When he shut the door, she sighed deeply and surveyed her kitchen. "This house is so big. Where should I begin? I wouldn't want Mary Ellen back again, but a maid sure would be nice."

🌺

Laura fretted as she stood at the kitchen sink doing the breakfast dishes. Eli had changed since their marriage. He not only looked different, what with his scratchy beard and all, but he was often snippy and demanding. He still hadn't started the indoor bathroom yet, either, and that exasperated her to no end.

"Work, work, work, that's all I ever do," she muttered. "If Eli tended me the way he does his garden, I'd be in full bloom by now! Whatever happened to romance and long buggy rides to the lake?"

A single tear rolled down her cheek, and she wiped it away with a soapy hand. "Life is so unfair. I gave up a lot to become Eli's wife, and now he won't even listen to me."

The only reminder of Laura's past was her cat, Foosie, who lay curled at her feet. She glanced down at the pampered pet and mumbled, "Too bad Mom and Dad can't come for a visit." She sniffed deeply. "No. . .they're too busy. Dad has his law practice, and Mom runs around like a chicken hunting bugs, trying to meet all her social obligations."

The cat purred contentedly, seemingly unaware of her frustrations.

"You've got life made, you know that?" she scolded.

A knock at the back door drew Laura's attention away from Foosie. *Oh, no. I hope that's not Mary Ellen.*

She dried her hands on her apron and dabbed the corners of her eyes with a handkerchief, then went to answer the door.

To her surprise, Martha Rose and little Ben stood on the porch, each holding a basket. Martha Rose's held freshly baked apple muffins, and Ben's basket was full of ginger cookies.

Laura smiled. She was always glad to see her sister-in-law and that adorable little boy. "Come in. Would you like a cup of tea?"

Martha Rose, her stomach now bulging, lowered herself into a chair. "That sounds mighty *gut*. We can have some of the muffins I brought, too."

Ben spotted Foosie, and he darted over to play with her.

"What brings you by so early?" Laura asked, as she pulled out a chair for herself.

"We're on our way to the Country Store, but we wanted to stop and see you first," Martha Rose answered. "We have an invitation for you and Eli."

Laura's interest was piqued. "What kind of invitation?"

"Since tomorrow's Saturday, and the weather's so nice, Amon and I have decided to take Ben to Paradise Lake for a picnic. We were wonderin' if you and Eli would like to come along."

Laura dropped several tea bags into the pot she'd taken from the stove before she sat down. "Would we ever! At least, I would. If Eli can tear himself away from work long enough, I'm sure he'd have a good time, too."

Martha Rose nodded. "We'll meet ya there around one o'clock. That'll give everyone time enough to do all their chores." She waved her hand. "Speaking of chores—you look awfully tired. Are ya workin' too hard?"

Laura pushed a stray hair back under her head covering and sighed. "I have been feeling a little drained lately. I'll be fine once I get this house organized."

Martha Rose opened her mouth to say something, but Laura cut her off. "What should I bring to the picnic?"

"I thought I'd fix fried chicken, two different salads, and maybe some pickled beet eggs. Why don't ya bring dessert and some kind of beverage?"

"That sounds fine," Laura answered, feeling suddenly lighthearted. They were going on a picnic, and she could hardly wait!

The lake was beautiful, and Laura drank in the peacefulness until she felt her heart would burst.

Martha Rose was busy setting out her picnic foods, and the men were playing ball with little Ben. Laura brought out the brownies and iced mint tea she'd made, and soon the plywood table they brought from home was brimming with delectable food.

Everyone gathered for silent prayer; then the men began to heap their plates full. Laura was the last to dish up, but she only took small helpings of everything. When she came to the tray of pickled beet eggs, a surge of nausea rolled through her stomach like angry ocean waves. Pickled eggs were sickening—little purple land mines, waiting to destroy her insides.

Laura dropped her plate of food and dashed for the woods. Eli ran after her, but he waited until she'd emptied her stomach before saying anything.

"You okay?" he asked with obvious concern.

Laura stood up on wobbly legs. "I'm fine. It was the sight of those pickled eggs. They're disgusting! How can anyone eat those awful things?"

Eli slipped his arm around her waist. "Maybe you've got the flu."

She shook her head. "It was just the eggs. Let's go back to the picnic. I'm fine now, honest."

The rest of the day went well enough, and Laura felt a bit better after drinking some tea. She even joined a friendly game of tag, but she did notice the looks of concern Eli and his sister exchanged. Nobody said anything about

347

her getting sick, and she was glad. ❧

A few days later, Laura was outside gathering eggs from the henhouse when she had another attack of nausea. She hadn't eaten any breakfast, so she figured that was the reason. Besides, the acrid odor of chicken manure was enough to make anyone sick!

Mary Ellen was outside, hanging laundry. She waved to Laura when she started toward the house with her basket of eggs. Laura waved back and hurried on. She was in no mood for a confrontation with her mother-in-law this morning, and she certainly didn't want to get sick in front of her.

"I'm almost finished here," Mary Ellen called. "Come have a cup of coffee."

Laura's stomach lurched at the mere mention of coffee, and she wondered how she could graciously get out of the invitation.

Mary Ellen called to her again. "I know you're busy, but surely you can take a few minutes for a little chat."

"I'll set these eggs inside, then be right over," Laura agreed in defeat. *May as well give in, or Mary Ellen will report to Eli that his wife is unsociable.*

Laura entered the house and deposited the brown eggs in the icebox. Then she went to the sink and pumped enough water for a cool drink. She drank the water slowly and took several deep breaths, which seemed to help some.

"Here goes nothing," she said, opening the back door.

She found Mary Ellen seated at her kitchen table. There were two cups sitting there, and the strong aroma of coffee permeated the air.

Laura's stomach did a little flip-flop as she took a seat. "Uh, would you mind if I had mint tea instead of coffee?"

Mary Ellen stood up. "If that's what you prefer." She went to the cupboard and retrieved a box of tea bags, then poured boiling water from the teapot on the stove into a clean mug.

"You're lookin' kinda peaked this mornin'," Mary Ellen said as she handed Laura the tea.

"I think I might have a touch of the flu."

"You could be in a family way. Have ya thought about that?"

Laura shook her head. "It's the flu. Nothing to worry about."

Mary Ellen eyed her suspiciously. "Would ya like some shoofly pie or a buttermilk biscuit?"

"I might try a biscuit."

Mary Ellen handed her a basket of warm biscuits. "So, tell me. . .how long's this flu thing been goin' on?"

"Just a few days."

"If it continues, you'd better see Doc Wilson."

Laura grimaced. *There she goes again. . .telling me what to do.* She plucked a biscuit from the basket and spread it lightly with butter. "*Jah,* I'll see the doctor if I don't feel better soon."

❧

Laura's nausea and fatigue continued all that week, but she did her best to hide it from Eli. She didn't want him pressuring her to see the doctor, or worse yet, asking a bunch of questions, the way his mother had.

One morning, Laura decided to go into town for some supplies. She asked Eli to hitch the horse to the buggy before he left for work. As soon as her morning chores were done, she donned her dark bonnet and climbed into the waiting buggy.

When Laura arrived in town, her first stop was the pharmacy. She scanned the shelves until she found exactly what she was looking for. She brought the item to the checkout counter and waited for the clerk to ring it up. He gave her a strange look as he placed the small box inside a paper sack. Laura wondered if she was the first Amish woman who'd ever purchased a home pregnancy kit.

The test couldn't be taken until early the next morning, so when she got home later in the day, Laura found a safe place to hide the kit. The last thing she needed was for Eli to discover it and jump to the wrong conclusions. He would surely think she was pregnant, and she was equally sure she wasn't. She couldn't be. She'd been so careful. Of course, her monthly time was late, but that wasn't too uncommon for her.

Laura waited until Eli left for work the following morning before going to her sewing basket and retrieving the test kit. She slipped it into her apron pocket and rushed to the outhouse.

Moments later, Laura's hands trembled as she held the strip up for examination. It was bright pink. The blood drained from her face, and she steadied herself against the unyielding wall. "Oh, no!" she cried. "It can't be!"

She studied it longer, just to be sure she hadn't read it wrong. It was still pink. "I can't be pregnant. I *won't* be pregnant!"

When she hurried back to the house, Laura's eyes were sore and swollen from crying. She went straight to the kitchen sink and splashed cold water on her face.

I need time to think. No one must know about this—especially not Eli. It will have to remain my secret.

"How long can I keep a secret like this?" she moaned. After some quick calculations, she figured she must be about eight weeks along. In another four to six weeks, she might be starting to show. Besides, if she kept getting sick every day, Eli would either suspect she was pregnant, or decide she was definitely sick and send her to the doctor.

"Oh, Foosie, what am I going to do?" she wailed, looking down at the cat, asleep at her feet. "If I only knew Darla's new phone number, I'd drive back to town and call her."

Laura snapped her fingers. "I do have her address, so I can write a letter."

She moved over to the desk and took out a piece of paper and a pen. She could keep the secret a little longer. Just until Darla responded to her letter.

❧

A whole week went by before Laura heard anything from Darla. Her reply was sympathetic, and she'd devised a plan. Darla would take next Friday off, and Laura was to meet her in Lancaster, in front of a restaurant they both knew well. She would leave the buggy parked there, and Darla would drive her to Philadelphia. She'd already scheduled an appointment for Laura at one of the abortion clinics there.

The following week, Laura pulled her horse and buggy into the restaurant parking lot. Darla was waiting in her sports car. "You've sure gotten yourself into a fine fix," she scolded as Laura climbed into the passenger's seat. "I knew marrying that Amish guy would bring you nothing but trouble."

"I don't need any lectures," Laura snapped.

Darla reached for a paper sack, lying on the floor by Laura's feet. "Here, you'd better put these on, and let your hair down."

Laura peeked into the bag and frowned. Inside were a navy blue blazer, a few pieces of jewelry, an indigo-colored belt, and a pair of navy pumps. "What are these for?"

"Don't you think it might look a little odd for an Amish woman to go to an abortion clinic? You could even become tomorrow's newspaper headlines," Darla said, shaking her head.

"I hadn't thought about that." Laura untied the strings from her head covering, then pulled the pins out of her bun. Her long hair fell loosely past her shoulders, and she ran her fingers through the ends. Next, she removed the black apron and shoes. She slipped the jacket over her blue, cotton dress, secured the belt around her waist, and stepped into the pumps. The finishing touch was a string of pearls and a matching bracelet.

How ironic. I've longed for these fancy things, yet right now, I feel strangely guilty about wearing them.

As though she could read her thoughts, Darla touched Laura's hand. "You're doing the right thing."

Laura nodded soberly. "I suppose."

"That didn't sound too convincing," Darla chided. "Your letter said you didn't want this baby."

"I don't. It's just that—"

"You'll feel better once this is all behind you."

Laura shrugged. "I don't see how I could feel much worse."

Chapter 16

Laura lifted the teakettle from the back of the stove and poured herself a cup of raspberry tea. This morning she felt better than she had in days. Maybe it was because of the decision she'd made the week before.

She took a seat at the table and let her mind drift back to the drive she and Darla had made to Philadelphia. . . .

Darla had been parking the car at the abortion clinic when a young man carrying a small child walked past. He looked so happy, and the toddler was smiling, too. It caused Laura to think about Eli, and how much he wanted children. He would be a good father, and maybe even a better husband if she gave him what he wanted.

She thought about little Ben—always playful and curious, so full of love, all cute and cuddly. Laura had never cared much for children until she met Ben. She loved that little boy and was sure he loved her in return.

If she were to abort this baby and Eli ever found out, it would be the end of their marriage. Pauline would get her wish, because Eli would probably have their marriage annulled. She'd be banned from the Amish church.

Laura could still see the look on her friend's face when she'd told her she wasn't going to have an abortion. Darla had argued, of course. She'd even tried to make Laura feel guilty for wasting her time. Laura had held firm, realizing that she would do anything to keep Eli—even give birth to his child.

The screen door creaked open, pulling Laura out of her musings. Eli hung his straw hat on a wall peg and went to wash up at the sink. "I hope breakfast's about ready, 'cause I'm hungry as a mule!"

"Pancakes are warming in the oven," Laura said, offering him a smile. "I was wondering if we could talk before we eat, though."

He shrugged. "Sure, what's up?"

She motioned him to sit down, then poured him a cup of tea. "How do you really feel about children, Eli?" she asked, keeping her eyes focused on the cup.

"I've told ya before, someday I hope to fill our house with *kinder.*"

She looked up at him. "Would November be soon enough to start?"

His forehead wrinkled.

"I'm pregnant, Eli. You're gonna be a father in about seven months."

Eli stared at her, disbelief etched on his face. "A *buppli?*"

She nodded.

He jumped up, circled the table, pulled Laura to her feet, and kissed her soundly. "The Lord has answered my prayers!" He pulled away and started for the back door.

"Where are you going?" she called after him.

"Next door. I've gotta share this *gut* news with Mom and Pop!"

❧

Laura hung the last bath towel on the line and wiped her damp forehead with her apron. It was a hot, humid June morning, and she was four months pregnant. She placed one hand on her slightly swollen belly and smiled. A tiny flutter caused her to tremble. "There really is a *buppli* in there," she murmured. So much for calorie counting and weight watching.

She bent down to pick up her empty basket, but an approaching buggy caught her attention. It was coming up the driveway at an unusually fast speed. When it stopped in front of the house, Amon jumped out, his face all red, and his eyes huge as saucers. "Where's Mary Ellen?" he asked Laura.

She pointed toward the addition. "Is something wrong?"

"It's Martha Rose. Her labor's begun, and she refuses to go to the hospital. She wants her *mamm* to deliver this baby, just like she did Ben."

Laura followed as Amon ran toward the addition. They found Mary Ellen in the kitchen, kneading bread dough. She looked up and smiled. "Ah, so the smell of bread in the makin' drew the two of you inside."

Amon shook his head. "Martha Rose's time has come, and she sent me to get you."

Mary Ellen calmly set the dough aside and wiped her hands on a towel. "Laura, would ya please finish this bread?"

"I thought I'd go along. Martha Rose is my friend, and—"

"There's no point wastin' good bread dough," Mary Ellen said, as though the matter was settled.

Amon was standing by the back door, shifting his weight from one foot to the other. Laura could see he was anxious to get home. "Oh, all right," she finally agreed. "I'll do the bread, but I'm comin' over as soon as it's out of the oven."

It was several hours later when Laura arrived at the Zook farm. She found Amon pacing back and forth in the kitchen. Ben was at the table, coloring a picture. *"Buppli,"* he said, grinning up at her.

Laura nodded. *"Jah,* soon it will come." She glanced over at Amon. "It's not born yet, is it?"

He shook his head. "Don't know what's takin' so long. She was real fast with Ben."

"How come you're not up there with her?" Laura asked.

Amon shrugged. "Mary Ellen said it would be best if I waited down here with the boy."

"Want me to go check?"

"I'd be obliged."

Laura hurried up the stairs. The door to Martha Rose and Amon's room was open a crack, so she walked right in.

Mary Ellen looked up from her position at the foot of the bed. "It's gettin' close. I can see the head now. Push, Martha Rose. . .push!"

Laura's heart began to pound, and her legs felt like two sticks of rubber. She leaned against the dresser to steady herself.

A few minutes later, the lusty cry of a newborn babe filled the room. Laura felt tears stinging her eyes. This was the miracle of birth. She never imagined it could be so beautiful.

"Daughter, you've got yourself a mighty fine girl," Mary Ellen remarked. "Let me clean her up a bit; then I'll hand her right over."

Martha Rose was crying, but Laura knew they were tears of joy. She slipped quietly from the room, leaving mother, daughter, and grandmother alone to share the moment of pleasure.

❧

Laura had seen Doc Wilson several times, and other than a bit of anemia, she was pronounced to be in good condition. The doctor prescribed iron tablets to take with her prenatal vitamins, but she still tired easily.

"I'm gonna ask Mom to come over and help out today," Eli said as he prepared to leave for work one morning.

Laura shuffled across the kitchen floor toward him. "Please don't. Your mom's got her hands full helping Martha Rose with the new baby. She doesn't need one more thing to worry about."

Eli shrugged. "Suit yourself, but if you need anything, don't think twice 'bout callin' on her, ya hear?"

She nodded and lifted her face for his good-bye kiss. "Have a *gut* day."

Eli left the house and headed straight for his folks' addition. Laura might think she didn't need Mom's help, but he could see how tired she was. Dark circles under her eyes and swollen feet at the end of the day were telltale signs she needed more rest.

He found Mom in the kitchen, doing the breakfast dishes. "Shouldn't you be headin' for work?" she asked.

He nodded. "*Jah*, but I wanted to talk with you first."

"Anything wrong?" she asked with a look of concern.

He shrugged and ran his fingers through the back of his hair. "Laura's been workin' too hard, and I think she could use some help."

"Want me to see to it, or are ya thinkin' of hirin' a *maut*?"

"I'd rather it be you, instead of a maid, if ya can find time."

She smiled. "I think I can manage."

"Thanks." Eli grasped the doorknob, but he pivoted back around. "Do ya think Laura's happy, Mom?"

She lifted an eyebrow in question. "Why wouldn't she be? She's married to you, ain't it so?"

He chuckled. "*Jah*, but I ain't no prize." His tone became serious then. "Do ya think she's really content bein' Amish?"

Mom dried her hands on a towel and moved toward him. "Laura chose to become Amish. You didn't force her, neither."

"I know, but sometimes she looks so sad."

"Ah, it's just bein' in a family way. All women get kind of melancholy durin' that time." She patted his arm. "She'll be fine once the *buppli* comes."

Eli gave her a hug. "You're probably right. I'm most likely worryin' over nothin'."

❧

Laura wasn't due until the end of the November, but five days before her and Eli's first anniversary, she went into labor. When Eli arrived home from work that afternoon, he found her lying on the couch, holding her stomach and writhing in pain.

"What is it, Laura?" he asked, rushing to her side.

"I think the baby's coming."

"When did the pains start?"

"Around noon."

Eli grasped her hand. "What does Mom have to say?"

Laura squeezed his fingers. "She doesn't know."

"What?" Eli could hardly believe Laura hadn't called on Mom. She'd delivered many babies, so she was bound to know if it was time.

"I wasn't sure if it even was labor at first," Laura explained. "But then my water broke, and—"

Eli jumped up and dashed across the room.

"Where are you going?" she called.

"To get Mom!"

❧

Laura leaned her head against the sofa pillow and stiffened when another contraction came. "Oh, God, please help me!" It was the first real prayer Laura had ever uttered, and now she wasn't sure God was even listening. Why would He care about her when she'd never really cared about Him? She'd only been pretending to be a Christian. Was this her punishment for lying to Eli and his family?

Moments later, Eli came bounding into the room, followed by his mother.

"How far apart are the pains?" Mary Ellen asked as she approached the couch.

"I—I don't know for sure. About two or three minutes, I think," Laura answered tearfully. "Oh, it hurts so much! I think Eli should take me to the hospital."

Mary Ellen did a quick examination, and when she was done, she announced, "You waited too long. The *buppli* is comin' now."

Eli started for the kitchen. "I'll get some towels and warm water."

"Don't leave me, Eli!"

"Calm down," Mary Ellen chided. "He'll be right back. In the meantime, I want you to do exactly as I say."

Laura's first reaction was to fight the pain, but Mary Ellen was a good coach, and soon Laura began to cooperate. Eli stood nearby, holding her hand and offering soothing words.

"One final push and the *buppli* should be here," Mary Ellen said.

Laura did as she was instructed, and moments later the babe's first cry filled the room.

"It's a boy! You have a son, Eli," Mary Ellen announced.

Laura lifted her head from the pillow. "Let me see him. I want to make sure he has ten fingers and ten toes."

"In a minute. Let Eli clean him a bit," Mary Ellen instructed. "I need to finish up with you."

"Mom, could ya come over here?" Eli called from across the room. His voice sounded strained, and Laura felt a wave of fear wash over her.

"What is it? Is something wrong with our son?"

"Just a minute, Laura. I want Mom to take a look at him first."

Laura rolled onto her side, trying to see what was happening. Eli and Mary Ellen were bent over the small bundle wrapped in a towel, lying on top of an end table. She heard whispering but couldn't make out their words.

"What's going on?" she called. "Tell me now, or I'm going to come see for myself."

Eli rushed to her side. "Stay put. You might start bleedin' real heavy if ya get up too soon."

Laura drew in a deep breath and grabbed hold of Eli's shirtsleeve. "What's wrong?"

"The child's breathin' seems a bit irregular," Mary Ellen said. "I think we should take him to the hospital."

"*Jah,*" Eli agreed. "It might not be a bad idea for Laura to be seen, too."

❧

Laura had only gotten a glimpse of her son before they rushed him into the hospital nursery, but what she did see concerned her greatly. The baby *wasn't* breathing right. He looked kind of funny, too. He had a good crop of auburn hair, just like Laura's, but there was something else. . .something she couldn't put her finger on.

"Relax and try to rest," Eli said as he took a seat in the chair next to Laura's hospital bed. "The doctor's lookin' at little David right now, and—"

"David?" Laura repeated. "You named our son without asking me?"

Eli's face flamed. "I—uh—thought we'd talked about namin' the baby David, if it was a boy."

She nodded slowly. "I guess we did. I just thought—"

Laura's sentence was interrupted when Dr. Wilson and another man entered the room. The second man's expression told her all she needed to know. There *was* something wrong with the baby.

"This is Dr. Hayes," Dr. Wilson said. "He's a pediatrician and has just finished examining your son."

"Tell us. . .is there somethin' wrong with David?" Eli asked, jumping to his feet.

Dr. Hayes put a hand on Eli's shoulder. "Sit down, Son."

Eli complied, but Laura could see the strain on his face. She felt equally uncomfortable.

"We still need to run a few more tests," the doctor said, "but we're fairly sure your boy has Down's syndrome."

"Are ya sayin' he's retarded?" Eli asked.

"Quite possibly, only we prefer to call it 'handicapped' or 'disabled.' The baby has an accumulation of fluid on his lungs. It's fairly common with Down's. We can clear it out, but he will no doubt be prone to bronchial infections—especially while he's young."

Laura was too stunned to say anything at first. This had to be a dream—a terrible nightmare. This couldn't be happening to her.

"Once we get the lungs clear, you should be able to take the baby home," Dr. Hayes continued.

"Take him home?" Laura pulled herself to a sitting position. "Did you say, 'take him home'?"

The doctor nodded, and Eli reached for her hand. "Laura, we can get through this. We—"

Laura jerked her hand away. "Are you kidding? We've just been told our son has Down's syndrome, and you're saying 'we can get through this'?" She shook her head slowly. "The baby isn't normal, Eli. He doesn't belong with us."

Eli studied Laura a few seconds. "Who does he belong with?"

"If he's handicapped, he belongs in a home."

Chapter 17

The baby was brought to Laura the following day, and she could barely look at him. The nurse held David up and showed her he had ten fingers and ten toes.

Fingers that are short and stubby, Laura thought bitterly. She noticed the child's forehead. It sloped slightly, and his skull looked broad and short. The distinguishing marks of Down's syndrome were definitely there. The doctor had explained that David might also be likely to have heart problems, hearing loss, or poor vision. He said Down's syndrome was a genetic disorder, resulting from extra chromosomes.

How could this have happened? Laura screamed inwardly. She looked away and told the nurse to take the baby back to the nursery. Swiping at her tears, she reached for the telephone next to her bed. It was time to call Mom and Dad. They needed to know the baby had been born.

"How am I going to tell them their first grandchild is handicapped?" she moaned.

Mom answered the phone, and she was understandably shocked when Laura gave her the news. Laura had hoped she might offer to come to Pennsylvania, but after Mom said how sorry she was, she made some excuse about her hectic schedule, said the baby should be put in a home for special children, and hung up the phone. Dad hadn't been at home, so she had no idea how he would have reacted.

Laura was crying when Eli entered the room carrying a potted plant. "I got ya an African violet from the Beachys' greenhouse, and—" He dropped it to the nightstand and moved quickly to the bed. *"Wass ist letz?* Is it something about David?"

She hiccupped loudly and pulled herself to a sitting position. When she felt she could speak without crying, Laura plunged ahead. "I just got off the phone with my mother."

"What did she say?"

"She said she was sorry to hear our sad news and that David should be put in a home."

Eli sank to the edge of her bed and reached for her hand.

"She's right, Eli. A disabled child takes a lot of work."

Eli frowned deeply. "David has just as much right to live a normal life as any other child."

"But he's not normal," Laura argued.

"Mom will be there to help whenever you need her."

The full meaning of Eli's words slammed into her chest. Laura shook her head, and another set of tears streamed down her cheeks. "I can't do this, Eli. Please don't ask it of me."

Eli rubbed his thumb gently back and forth across her knuckles. "God gave us David. He must have a reason for choosin' us as his parents, so we'll love him. . . cherish him. . .protect him."

Laura's eyes widened. "God was cruel to allow such a thing!"

"God knows what's best for each of us. The book of Romans tells us that all things work together for good to them that love God," Eli said softly. He pointed to the African violet. "Just like this plant needs to be nourished, so does our son. God will give us the strength and love we need to raise him."

She looked away. It was obvious Eli planned to have the last word. Apparently, her thoughts and feelings didn't matter one bit. For the first time since she'd laid eyes on Eli Yoder, Laura wished they had never met.

❧

Laura went home from the hospital the following morning, but the baby would have to stay a few more days. The doctors thought he might be ready to take home next week, so this gave Laura a short reprieve. She needed some time to decide what to do about the problem.

Eli had taken a few hours off work in order to pick her up at the hospital, but he'd already gone back to his job in Lancaster. Laura was alone and hoped to find some answers before he returned home.

She poured herself a cup of chamomile tea and curled up on the living room couch. Reliving her dialog with Eli at the hospital, Laura's heart sank to the pit of her stomach. Eli thought they should keep David.

She closed her eyes and tried to shut out the voice in her head. *God is punishing me for pretending to be religious. I tricked Eli into marrying me by making him think I'd accepted his beliefs.*

Laura's eyes snapped open when she heard a distant clap of thunder. She stared out the window. Dark clouds hung in the sky, like a shroud encircling the entire house.

"The sky looks like I feel," she moaned. "My life is such a mess. I should have listened to Darla and gone into that abortion clinic."

The realization of what she'd said hit Laura with such intensity, she thought she'd been struck with a lightning bolt. "Oh, no! Dear, Lord, no!" she sobbed. "You're punishing me for wanting an abortion, not just for lying to Eli about my religious convictions." She clenched her fists into tight little balls. "That's why David was born with Down's syndrome!"

Laura fell back on the sofa pillows and cried until there were no more tears. Nearly an hour later, she sat up again, dried her eyes, and stood up. She knew what she had to do. She scrawled a quick note to Eli, placed it on the kitchen table, and went upstairs.

❧

"Laura, I'm home!" Eli set his lunch pail on the cupboard. No sign of Laura in the kitchen. He moved through the rest of the downstairs, calling her name. She wasn't in any of the rooms.

She must be upstairs restin'. She's been through a lot this week. I'd better let her sleep awhile.

Eli went back to the kitchen. He'd fix himself a little snack, then go outside and get started on the evening chores.

There was an apple-crumb pie in the refrigerator, which Mom had brought over last night. He grabbed a piece, along with a jug of milk, and placed them on the table. Not until he took a seat did Eli see the note lying on the table. He picked it up and read it.

> Dear Eli,
>
> It pains me to write this letter, even more than the physical pain I endured in childbirth. I know you don't understand, but I can't take care of David, so I'm going home to my parents.
>
> I have a confession to make. I'm not who you think I am—I'm not really a believer. I only pretended to be one so you would marry me. The truth is, I had hoped that once we were married you might decide to leave the Amish faith and become part of my world. I tried to be a good wife, but I could never measure up.
>
> Pauline was right when she said she would be better for you. It would have saved us all a lot of heartache if you'd married her instead of me.
>
> Do what you need to about ending our marriage. I know divorce is not acceptable, but maybe once you've explained things to Bishop Weaver, he will agree to an annulment. Our marriage was based on lies from the very beginning, so it was never a true marriage at all.
>
> I'm not deserving of your forgiveness, but please know, I do love you.
>
> Always,
> Laura

The words on the paper blurred. Eli couldn't react. Couldn't think. He let the note slip from his fingers, and a deep sense of loss gnawed at his insides. *Laura wouldn't pack up and leave without speaking with me first. . .without trying to work things out.*

He propped his elbows on the table and cradled his head in his hands as a well of emotion rose in his chest. "Oh, Laura. . .I didn't know."

During her first few days at home, Laura slept late, picked at her food, and tried to get used to all the modern conveniences she'd previously taken for granted. Nothing seemed to satisfy her. She was exhausted, crabby, and more depressed than she'd ever been in her life. Things had changed at home. Maybe it was she who'd changed, for she now felt like a misfit.

Today was her and Eli's first anniversary, and she was miserable. As she sat at the kitchen table toying with the scrambled eggs on her plate, Laura thought about their wedding day. She could still hear Bishop Weaver quoting Scriptures about marriage. She could almost feel the warmth of Eli's hand as they repeated their vows. She'd promised to love, honor, and obey her husband. A painful lump lodged in her throat as she realized that she'd done none of those things. She deserved whatever punishment God handed down.

Mom came into the kitchen, interrupting Laura's thoughts. "This came in the mail," she said, handing Laura a letter. It was postmarked Lancaster, Pennsylvania.

Laura's fingers shook as she tore open the envelope, then began to read.

Dear Laura,

I knew you were upset about the baby, and I'm trying to understand. What I don't get is how you could just up and leave, without even tryin' to talk to me first. Don't ya realize how much David and I need you? Don't ya know how much I love you?

David's breathin' better now, and the doctors let him come home. Mom watches him when I'm at work, but it's you he's needin'. Won't ya please come home?

Love,
Eli

Tears welled up in Laura's eyes and spilled over onto the front of her blouse. Eli didn't seem angry. In fact, he wanted her to come home. He hadn't even mentioned her lies. Had he forgiven her? Did Eli really love her, in spite of all she'd done?

Maybe he doesn't believe me. He might think I made everything up, because I couldn't deal with our baby being born handicapped. He might want me back just so I can care for his child.

Laura swallowed hard. No matter how much she loved Eli and wanted to be with him, she knew she couldn't go back. She was a disgrace to the Amish religion, and she had ruined Eli's life.

❧

The days dragged by, and Laura thought she would die of boredom. The weather was dreary and cold, and even though Mom tried to encourage her to get out and socialize, Laura stayed to herself most of the time. She thought modern conveniences would bring happiness, but they hadn't. Instead of watching TV or playing computer games, she preferred to sit in front of the fire and knit or read a book.

It was strange, but Laura missed the familiar farm smells—fresh-mown hay stacked neatly in the barn, the horses' warm breath on a cold winter day, and even the wiggly, grunting piglets, always squealing for more food. Laura was reminded of something Eli had once said, for much to her surprise, she even missed the predictable wake-up call of the rooster each morning.

By the middle of December, Laura felt stronger physically, but emotionally she was still a mess. Would she ever be able to pick up the pieces of her life and go on without Eli? Could she forgive herself for bringing such misery into their lives?

If God was punishing her, why did Eli have to suffer as well? He was a kind, Christian man who deserved a normal, healthy baby. He'd done nothing to warrant this kind of pain. How could the Amish refer to God as "a God of love and life"?

Laura sat on the living room couch, staring at the Christmas tree, yet not really seeing it. *What's Eli doing right now? No doubt he and the baby will be spending the holiday with his parents.*

She glanced at her parents. They were sitting in their respective recliners, Dad reading the newspaper and Mom working on Christmas cards. They didn't seem to have a care in the world. Didn't they know how much she was hurting? Did they think this was just another typical Christmas?

A sudden knock at the front door drew Laura out of her musings. She looked over at the mantel clock. Who would be coming by at nine o'clock at night, and who would knock rather than use the doorbell?

Dad stood up. "I'll get it."

Laura strained to hear the voices coming from the hall. She couldn't be sure who Dad was talking to, but it sounded like a woman. *Probably one of Mom's lady friends, or someone from Dad's office.* She leaned against the sofa pillows and tried not to eavesdrop.

"Laura, someone is here to see you," Dad said as he entered the living room with a woman.

Laura's mouth dropped open and she leaped from the couch. "Martha Rose! What are you doing here? Is Eli with you?" She stared at the doorway, half expecting, half hoping Eli might step into the room.

Martha Rose shook her head. "I've come alone. Only Amon knows I'm here. I left him plenty of my milk, and he agreed to care for baby Amanda and little Ben so I could make the trip to see you." She smiled. "The bus ride only took a little over twenty-seven hours, and Amon knows I won't be gone long. Besides, if he runs into any kind of problem with the *kinder,* he can always call on Mom."

Laura's heart began to pound as she tried to digest all that Martha Rose had said. "What's wrong? Has someone been hurt? Is it Eli?"

Martha Rose held up her hand. "Eli's fine. . .at least physically." She glanced at Laura's folks, then back at Laura. "Could we talk in private?"

Laura looked at Mom and Dad. They both shrugged and turned to go. "We'll be upstairs if you need us," Mom said.

"Thanks," Laura mumbled. Her brain felt like it was in a fog. Why had Martha Rose traveled all the way from Pennsylvania to Minnesota if there was nothing wrong at home? Home—was that how she thought of the farmhouse she and Eli had shared for the past year? Wasn't this her home—here with Mom and Dad? She studied her surroundings. Everything looked the same, yet it felt so different. It was like trying to fit into a pair of shoes that were too small.

"Laura, are you okay?" Martha Rose asked, placing a hand on Laura's trembling shoulder.

"I—uh—didn't expect to see you tonight." Laura motioned toward the couch. "Please, have a seat. Let me take your shawl. Would you like some tea or hot chocolate?" She was rambling but couldn't seem to help herself.

Martha Rose took off her shawl and draped it over the back of the couch, then she sat down. "Maybe somethin' to drink but after we talk."

Laura sat beside her. "What's so important that you would come all this way by bus?"

"My brother has been so upset since you left. He told me he wrote a letter, askin' you to come home."

"Did he also tell you I've been lying to him all these months?"

"About bein' a believer?"

Laura nodded.

"*Jah*, he mentioned that, too."

"Then you understand why I can't go back." Laura swallowed hard. "I asked Eli to see the bishop about an annulment, but I've heard nothing from him on the subject."

Martha Rose reached inside her apron pocket and pulled out a small Bible. She opened it and began reading. " 'If any brother hath a wife that believeth not, and she be pleased to dwell with him, let him not put her away.' " She smiled. "That's found in the book of First Corinthians."

Laura's eyes widened. "Are you saying Eli could choose to stay with me, even though I'm not a believer?"

Martha Rose nodded. "It doesn't have to be that way, though."

"What do you mean?"

"You could give your heart to Jesus right now. He wants you to accept His death as forgiveness for your sins. First John 3:23 says, 'And this is his commandment, that we should believe on the name of his Son Jesus Christ, and love one another, as he gave us commandment.' "

As Martha Rose continued to read from the Bible, Laura fell under deep conviction—she was finally convinced of the truth in God's Word—and soon tears began streaming down her face. "Oh, Martha Rose, you have no idea how much I've sinned. I did a terrible thing, and now God is punishing me. How can I ever believe He would forgive me?"

"Romans 3:23 says, 'For all have sinned, and come short of the glory of God.' If we ask, God will forgive any sin." Martha Rose clasped Laura's hand.

"I—I—didn't even want our baby. When I first found out I was pregnant, I had an English friend drive me to Philadelphia—to an abortion clinic."

The shocked look on her sister-in-law's face told Laura all she needed to know. Eli and his family thought this was a terrible sin, and so must God.

"Why, Laura? Why would ya do such a thing?"

"I was afraid of having a child. I know it's a vain thing to say, but I wanted to keep my trim figure." She gulped. "Even more than that, I wanted Eli all to myself. I couldn't go through with it, though. I loved Eli too much, and I wanted to give him a child." Laura closed her eyes and drew in a shuddering breath. "God's punishment was David. He gave us a disabled child."

"God don't work thataway," Martha Rose insisted. "He loves you, just as He loves the special child He gave you and Eli. God wants you to ask His forgiveness and surrender your life to Him."

"I want to be forgiven," Laura admitted. "I want to change, but I don't know if I have enough faith to believe."

Martha Rose took hold of Laura's hand. "All ya need to do is take that first little step by acceptin' Jesus as your Savior. Then, through studyin' His Word and prayin', your faith will be strengthened. Would ya like to pray right now and ask Jesus into your heart?"

Laura didn't even hesitate. "Would you help me? I don't really know how to pray."

As Martha Rose and Laura prayed, Laura found the forgiveness she so desperately needed. When she went to bed that night, a strange warmth crept through her body. She felt God's presence for the very first time and knew without reservation that she was a new person, because of His Son, Jesus. Martha Rose was sleeping across the hall in the guest room, and Laura thanked God she had come.

Laura clung tightly to Martha Rose's hand as they stepped down from the bus. She was almost home, and even though she still had some doubts about her ability to care for a handicapped child, it was comforting to know she would have God to help her. She scanned the faces of those waiting to pick up passengers. There was no sign of Eli or Amon.

"Are you sure they knew we were coming?" Laura asked Martha Rose, feeling a sense of panic rise in her throat.

"I sent the telegram, so I'm certain they'll be here," Martha Rose said, leading Laura toward the bus station. "Let's get outta the cold and wait for 'em inside."

The women had no more than taken seats when Amon walked up. He was alone.

Laura felt like someone had punched her in the stomach. "Where's Eli? Didn't he come with you?" *Maybe he's changed his mind about wanting you back. Could be that he's already gotten the marriage annulled,* a troubling voice taunted.

"Eli's at the hospital," Amon said, placing a hand on Laura's shoulder.

Her stomach churned like whipping cream about to become butter. "The hospital? Is it the baby? Is David worse?"

Amon shook his head. "There was an accident today."

"An accident? What happened?" Martha Rose asked, her face registering the concern Laura felt.

"Eli cut his hand at work, on one of them fancy electric saws."

Laura covered her mouth with her hand. "How bad?"

"He lost part of one finger, but the doc said he should still be able to use the hand once everything heals."

"Oh, my dear, sweet, Eli!" Laura cried. "Haven't you already been through enough? If only I hadn't run away. If only—"

Martha Rose held up her hand. "No, Laura. You can't go blamin' yourself. Just as David's birth defect is no one's fault, this was an accident, plain and simple. In time, Eli will heal and be back at work."

Laura looked down at her clasped hands, feeling like a small child learning to walk. "Guess my faith is still pretty weak. I'd better pray about it, huh?"

Martha Rose nodded. "*Jah,* prayer is always the best way."

Eli was lying in his hospital bed, fighting the weight of heavy eyelids. Against his wishes the nurse had given him a shot for pain, and now he was feeling so sleepy he could hardly stay awake. Amon had left for the bus station over an hour ago. What was taking so long? Maybe Laura had changed her mind and stayed in Minneapolis. Maybe. . .

"Eli? Eli?" A gentle voice filled his senses. Was he dreaming or was it just wishful thinking?

He felt the touch of a soft hand against his uninjured hand, and his eyes snapped open. "Laura?"

She nodded, her eyes filled with tears. "Oh, Eli, I'm so sorry!" She rested her head on his chest and sobbed. "Can you ever forgive me for running away. . . for lying about my relationship to God. . .for wanting you to change when it was really me who needed changing?"

Eli stroked the top of her head, noting with joy that she was wearing her covering. "I've already forgiven you, my love, but I must ask your forgiveness, too."

She raised her head and stared into his eyes. "For what? You've done nothing."

He swallowed against the lump in his throat. "For not bein' understanding enough." He touched her chin with his good hand. "I think I expected too much, and sometimes I spoke harshly, instead of tryin' to see things from your point of view. If I'd been a better husband, maybe you would've found Christ's love sooner."

Laura shook her head. "It wasn't your fault. I was stubborn and selfish. That's what kept me from turning to God. I believed I could do everything in my own strength. I thought I could have whatever I wanted, and it didn't matter who I hurt in the process." She sniffed deeply. "When I finally turned away from sin and found forgiveness through Christ, I became a new creature." She leaned closer, so their lips were almost touching. "I love you, Eli Yoder."

He smiled. "And I love you, Laura Yoder. Christmas is only a few days away, and I'm convinced it's gonna be our best Christmas ever." He sealed his promise with a tender kiss.

"Ich wehl dich," Laura whispered.

"I choose you, too," he murmured, then drifted off to sleep.

Epilogue

Laura stood at the sink, peeling potatoes for the stew they would have for supper. She gazed out the window at Eli and their two-year-old son as they romped in the snow. David was doing so well, and she praised and thanked God for him every day. He was such an agreeable, loving child. How could she have ever not wanted him? Eli had been right all along. David was special—a wonderful gift from God.

A soft "meow" drew Laura's attention from the window. She turned toward the sound, and her lips formed a smile. Foosie was running across the kitchen floor, and their nine-month-old daughter, Barbara, was in fast pursuit.

Laura chuckled at the sight of her perfect little girl, up on her knees, chasing that poor cat and pulling on its tail. No wonder Foosie preferred to be outdoors these days.

"Life couldn't be any better," Laura whispered. "I've made peace with Pauline Hostetler. My parents live on a small farm nearby. I've learned that Eli's folks really do care about me. I have two *wunderbaar* children and a *gut* husband who loves us all more'n anything, and—" She looked up. "And I have You, Lord. Thank You for takin' a fancy, spoiled English woman and turnin' her into a plain Amish wife, who loves You so much. God, You've truly blessed me!"

The Hope Chest

To my mother, Thelma Cumby.
Thanks for giving me your special hope chest,
so I could pass it down to my daughter, Lorine,
who will someday give it to one of her girls.

Chapter 1

Rat-a-tat-tat! Rat-a-tat-tat! Rachel Beachy would have recognized that distinctive sound anywhere. She tipped her head back, shielded her eyes from the glare of the late afternoon sun, and gazed up at the giant birch tree. Sure enough, there it was—a downy woodpecker. Its tiny claws were anchored to the trunk of the tree, its petite head bobbing rhythmically in and out.

Hoping for a better look, Rachel decided to climb the tree. As she threw her leg over the first branch, she was glad she was alone and no one could see how ridiculous she looked. She'd never really minded wearing long dresses. After all, that was what Amish girls and women were expected to wear. However, there were times, such as now, when Rachel wished she could wear a pair of men's trousers. It certainly would make climbing trees a mite easier.

Rachel winced as a piece of bark scratched her knee, leaving a stain of blood that quickly seeped through her dress. To Rachel, it was worth the pain if it would allow her to get a better look at that cute little wood-tapper.

Pik-pik-pik! The woodpecker's unusual call resonated against the trunk. *Rat-a-tat-tat!*

"Such a busy little bird," Rachel said softly as it came into view, just two branches above where she sat straddling the good-sized limb. *Sure do wish I had my notebook along so's I could write down a few things about this beautiful creature the Lord made. God knows every bird in the mountains and the creatures of the field. It says so in Psalm 50.*

Rachel was about to move up one more limb, but a deep male voice drew her attention to the ground. "Hey, Anna, slow down once, would ya?"

Rachel dropped so her stomach was flat against the branch. She lifted her head slightly and peeked through the leaves. Her older sister sprinted across the open field, and Silas Swartley was a few feet behind. He ran like a jackrabbit, with his hands cupped around his mouth, yelling to beat the band. "Anna! Wait up!"

Rachel knew she'd be in big trouble if Anna caught her spying, so she held real still and prayed the couple would soon move on.

Anna stopped near the foot of the tree and Silas quickly joined her. "I wanna talk to ya, Anna," he panted.

Rachel's heart slammed into her chest. *Why couldn't it be me Silas wants to talk to? If only he could see that I'd be much better for him. If he knew how much I cared, would it make a difference?* Rachel knew Silas only had eyes for Anna. He'd been in love with her since they were *kinder*, and Rachel had loved Silas nearly that long as well. He was all the things she wanted in a man—good-looking, kindhearted, interested in birds, and he enjoyed fishing. . . .

She was sure he had many other attributes that made him so appealing, but with Silas standing right below her tree, she could barely breathe, much less think of all the reasons she loved him so much.

Rachel looked down at her sister, arms folded across her chest, standing there like a wooden statue. It was almost as if she couldn't be bothered with talking to Silas. It made no sense, for Anna and Silas had been friends a long time, and Silas had been coming over to their place to visit ever since Rachel could remember.

Silas reached for Anna's hand, but she jerked it away. "Just who do ya think you are, Silas Swartley?"

"I'm your boyfriend, that's who. Have been since we were *kinder*, and you know it."

"I don't know any such thing, so don't go tryin' to put words in my mouth."

Rachel stifled a giggle. *That sister of mine. . .she's sure got herself a temper.*

Silas tipped his head to one side. "I don't get it. One minute you're sweet as cherry pie and the next minute ya act as if ya don't care for me a'tall."

Rachel knew Silas was speaking the truth. She'd seen with her own eyes the way Anna led that poor fellow on. Why, just last week she'd let him bring her home from a singing. There had to be some kind of interest on her part if she was willing to accept a ride in his courting buggy.

Rachel held her breath as Silas reached out to touch the ties on Anna's *Kapp*. Anna jerked her head real quick, causing one of the ribbons to tear loose. "Now look what you've done!" Anna jerked the covering off her head and stuffed it inside the pocket of her black apron.

Silas removed his broad-brimmed straw hat, revealing a crop of dark, Dutch-bobbed hair. He planted the hat on top of Anna's head. "Here, you can wear my hat now."

Anna yanked it right off, but in so doing, the pins holding her hair in a bun must have been knocked loose, for a cascade of soft, tawny brown fell loosely down her back.

Rachel wished she could see the look on Silas's face. She could only imagine what he must be thinking as he reached up to scratch the back of his head. "I know Amish women aren't supposed to wear their hair down in public, but I sure wish you could, Anna." He groaned softly. "Why, you're prettier than a field full of fireflies at sunset!"

Rachel nearly gagged. It was sickening the way Silas got so sappy over Anna. Especially when she didn't seem to appreciate all his attentions.

Anna rocked from side to side, kind of nervouslike. "Sometimes I wish I could cut my hair short, the way many English women do. Long hair can be such a bother, and anyways, it serves no real purpose."

"It does when ya wear it like that," Silas murmured.

Rachel gulped. *What I wouldn't give to hear Silas talk to me thataway. Maybe if I keep on hopin'. Maybe if. . .*

Rachel's thoughts took her to the verse she'd read in the book of Psalms that morning. *"But I will hope continually, and will yet praise thee more and more."*

Rachel would gladly offer praises to God if she could only win Silas's heart. Truth be told, the verse she should call her own might best be found in the book of Job. *"My days are swifter than a weaver's shuttle, and are spent without hope."* She'd most likely end up an old maid, while Anna would have a *wunderbaar* husband and a whole house full of *kinder*.

"It don't make much sense to have long hair when you have to wear it pinned up all the time," Anna said, handing the straw hat back to Silas and pulling Rachel out of her musings.

"Are you questionin' the Amish ways, young lady?" Silas scolded playfully. "Now, what would your *mamm* and *daed* have to say about that?" Before Anna could answer, he added, "You've always been a bit of a rebel, haven't ya, now?"

Anna leaned against the tree, and Rachel dug her fingernails into the bark of the branch she was lying on. *What will my sister say to that comment?*

"I know there's some things about the Amish ways that are *gut*, but I feel so restricted," Anna said with a deep sigh.

Silas knelt on the grass beneath Anna's feet. "Can ya give me an example of what you're talkin' about?"

Rat-a-tat-tat! Rat-a-tat-tat! Pik! Pik!

"Say, that sounds like a woodpecker to me," Silas said, leaning his head back and looking up into the birch tree where Rachel was hiding.

She froze in place. If Silas should spot her instead of the bird, she'd be caught like a piggy trying to get into Mom's flower garden. Anna would sure as anything think she'd climbed the tree just to spy on her and Silas.

"Forget about the dumb old woodpecker," Anna said impatiently. "I'm trying to tell you why I don't like bein' Amish no more."

Silas stood up and peered into the branches. "Hmm. . .I know I heard him, but I sure don't see that old rascal anywhere."

"You and your dopey bird-watchin'! One would think you've never seen a woodpecker before." Anna moaned. "Rachel's fascinated with birds, too. Why, I believe she'd rather be watchin' them eat from one of our feeders than eatin' a meal herself."

Silas looked away from the tree and turned to face Anna. "Birds are interestin' little creatures, but you're right. . .I can do my bird-watchin' some other time." He touched her shoulder. "Now what were ya gonna say about bein' Amish?"

"Take these clothes, for example," Anna announced. "Women shouldn't have to wear long dresses all the time. They only get in the way."

Rachel sucked in her breath. Where was this conversation headed? If Anna wasn't careful, she'd be saying something plumb stupid and maybe even getting into all kinds of trouble for shooting off her big mouth. Especially if the bishop got wind of it. Anna had been acting a bit strange here of late—disappearing for hours at a time and saying some mighty peculiar things. Her conversation with

Silas was only confirming what Rachel already suspected. Anna was dissatisfied with the Amish way of life. It wasn't like Anna climbed trees and saw her dress as a hazard. No, Rachel's prim and proper sister wouldn't be caught dead up in a tree. Rachel knew there was a lot more that bothered Anna about being Amish than wearing long dresses. She'd heard her complain about other things as well.

"What would you suggest women wear—trousers?" Silas asked, jerking Rachel's attention back to the conversation below.

"I think it's only fair that women and girls should have the freedom of wearin' long pants if they want to," Anna replied stiffly.

"Are ya sayin' you'd wear men's trousers if ya could?"

"Maybe I would, and maybe I wouldn't. I sure could do my chores much easier if I didn't have a long skirt gettin' in the way all the time." Anna paused, and Rachel shifted her legs, trying to get a bit more comfortable. "Maybe I'd be a whole lot happier if I'd been born English."

Oh, great! Now you've gone and done it, Rachel fumed. *Why can't ya just be nice to Silas instead of tryin' to goad him into an argument? Can't ya see how much the fellow cares for you? If anyone should be wantin' to wear men's trousers, it's me—Rachel, the tomboy. At least I've got the sense not to announce such a thing. And sayin' you should have been born English is just plain stupid.*

"I, for one, am mighty glad you're not English!" Silas said, his voice rising an octave.

"Humph! If I weren't Amish, I could wear whatever I please whenever I wished to do so."

"Listen here, Anna," he argued, "you shouldn't even be thinkin' such thoughts, much less speaking 'em. Why, if your *daed* ever heard ya say anything like that, you'd be in big trouble, and that's for certain sure!"

Anna moved away from the tree. "Let's not talk about this anymore. I need to be gettin' home. Rachel was way ahead of me when we left the river, so she's probably already there and has done half my chores by now. Mom let me have the afternoon off from workin' in the greenhouse, so I don't want her gettin' after me for shirking my household duties."

Rachel watched as Silas plopped the straw hat back on his head. "Yeah, well, I guess I need to be headin' for home, too." He made no move to leave and she had to wonder what was up.

Anna rolled and pinned her hair into place. Then she reached inside her pocket and retrieved the head covering, securing it back in place. She started walking away, but Silas stepped right up beside her. "I still haven't said what I wanted to say."

"What'd ya wanna say?"

Silas shuffled his feet a few times, gave his suspenders a good yank, then cleared his throat real loud. "I. . .uh. . .was wonderin' if I might come a-callin' one evenin' next week."

Rachel's heart skipped a beat, and she focused real hard on getting it to work right again. Silas had been sweet on Anna a good many years, so she should have known the day would come when he'd ask to start courting her. Only trouble was, if Anna started courting Silas, Rachel's chances would be nil. Oh, she just couldn't bear to think about it!

"Callin'? You mean, call on *me?*" Anna asked in obvious disbelief.

"Of course, Silly. Who'd ya think I meant—your little sister, Rachel?"

That's what I wish you meant. Rachel's pulse quickened at the thought of her being Silas's girlfriend. She drew in a deep breath and pressed against the tree limb as though she were hugging it. No sense hoping and dreaming the impossible. She knew Silas didn't care about her in the least. Not in the way he did Anna, that's for sure. To him, Rachel was just a girl, five years younger than he at that.

"We've known each other for many years, and ya did take a ride in my courtin' buggy," Silas continued. "Now I think it's high time—"

"Hold on to your horses," Anna cut in. "You're a nice man, Silas Swartley, and a *gut* friend, but I can't start courtin' you."

Rachel could only imagine how Silas was feeling about now. Her tender heart went out to him. She wondered how her sister could be so blind. Couldn't Anna see how *wunderbaar* Silas was? Didn't she realize what a *gut* husband he would make? *At least for me,* Rachel lamented.

"I'm sorry if I've hurt your feelin's." Anna spoke so softly that Rachel had to strain to hear the words. "It's just that I have lots of dreams, and—"

"There's no need to explain," Silas said, cutting her off in midsentence. "You may think I'm just a big dumb Amish boy, but I'm not as stupid as I might look, Anna Beachy."

"I never meant to say you were stupid. I just want ya to understand that it won't work for the two of us." There was a long pause. "Maybe my little sister *would* be better for you."

Yes, yes, I would! Rachel's heart pounded with sudden hope. She held her breath, waiting to hear what Silas would say next, but disappointment flooded her soul when he turned on his heels and started walking away.

"I'll leave ya alone for now, but when you're ready, I'll be waitin'," he called over his shoulder. *"Wann du mich mohl brauchst, dan komm Ich*—when you need me, I will come." He broke into a run and was soon out of sight.

Rachel released her breath and flexed her body against the unyielding limb. Hot tears pushed against her eyelids, and she blinked several times to force them back. At least Silas and Anna hadn't known she was here, eavesdropping on their private conversation. That would have ruined any chance she might ever have of catching Silas's attention. Not that she had any, really. Besides their age difference, Rachel was sure she wasn't pretty enough for Silas. She had pale blue eyes and straw-colored hair. Nothing beautiful about her. Anna, on the other hand, had been blessed with sparkling green eyes and hair the color of ripe peaches. Rachel was certain Anna would always be Silas's first choice, because she was *schnuck. Too bad I'm not cute. I wish I hadn't been born so plain.*

❧

When Rachel arrived home several minutes behind her sister, she found her brother Joseph working on an old plow out in the yard. A lock of sandy brown hair lay across his sweaty forehead, and his straw hat was lying on a nearby stump.

He looked up and frowned. "You're late! Anna's already inside, no doubt helpin' Mom with supper. You'd better get in there quicklike, or they'll both be pretty miffed."

"I'm goin'," Rachel said with a shrug. "And don't you be thinkin' you can boss me around." She scrunched up her nose. "You may be twenty-one and three years older than me, but you're not my keeper, Joseph Beachy."

"Don't go gettin' your feathers ruffled. You're crankier than the old red rooster when his hens are fightin' for the best pieces of corn." Joseph's forehead wrinkled as he squinted his blue eyes. "Say, isn't that blood I see on your dress? What happened? Did ya fall in the river and skin your knee on a rock?"

Rachel shook her head. "I skinned my knee, but it wasn't on a rock."

Joseph gave her a knowing look. "Don't tell me it was another one of your tree-climbin' escapades."

She waved a hand and started for the house. "Okay, I won't tell ya that."

"Let Mom know I'll be in for supper as soon as I finish with the plow," he called after her.

As Rachel stepped onto the back porch, she thought about all the chores she had to do. It was probably a good thing. At least when her hands were kept busy, it didn't give her nearly so much time to think about things—especially Silas Swartley.

❧

Silas kicked a clump of grass with the toe of his boot. What had come over Anna Beachy all of a sudden? How come she was friendly one minute and downright rude the next? Worse than that, when had she developed such a dissatisfaction with being Amish? Had it been there all along, and he'd been too blind to notice? Was Anna just going through some kind of a phase, like many *younga* did when they sowed their wild oats?

Silas clenched his fists and kept trudging toward home. *Lord, I love Anna, but is she really the woman for me? I could never hold to foolish notions 'bout women wearin' men's pants or cuttin' their hair off, and she knows it. I care for Anna, but she's sure mixed up in her thinkin'. Why, she even suggested I start courtin' her little sister.* He shook his head and muttered, "Is that woman simpleminded? Rachel's just a *kinder,* for goodness' sake. Guess I'd best be prayin' about all this, for Anna surely does need some help."

As Silas rounded the bend, his farm came into view. A closed-in buggy sat out front in the driveway, and he recognized the horse. It belonged to Bishop Weaver.

"Hmm. . .wonder what's up?" He shrugged. "Maybe Mom invited the bishop and his family for supper tonight."

Silas entered the kitchen a few minutes later and found his folks and Bishop Weaver sitting at the kitchen table, drinking tall glasses of lemonade.

"How's things?" Silas asked. "Is supper ready? I'm starved!"

Mom gave him a stern look over the top of her metal-framed reading glasses, which were perched on the middle of her nose. "Where's your manners, Son? Can't you say hello to our guest before ya start frettin' over food?"

Silas was none too happy about his mother embarrassing him that way, but he knew better than to sass her back. Mom might be only half his size, but she could still pack a good wallop to any of her boys' backsides, and she didn't care how old they were!

"Sorry," Silas apologized as he smiled and nodded at the bishop. "When I saw your buggy, I thought maybe you had the whole family along."

Bishop Weaver shook his head. "Nope. Just me."

"The bishop came by to have a little talk with you," Pap said, running a hand through his slightly graying hair, then motioning Silas to take a seat.

"Me? What about?"

"Your friend, Reuben Yutzy," Bishop Weaver answered with a curt nod.

Silas took off his straw hat and hung it on a wall peg near the back door, then took a seat at the table. "What about Reuben?"

Bishop Weaver leaned forward and leveled Silas with a piercing gaze. "As you already know, Reuben works for a fancy English paint contractor in Lancaster."

Silas merely nodded in response.

"I hear tell Reuben's been seen with some worldly folks."

"As you just said, he works for the English."

"I'm talkin' about Reuben's off hours," the bishop said, giving his long, gray beard a few good yanks. "Word has it that he's been goin' to some picture shows and hangin' around with a group of English *younga* who like to party and get all liquored up."

Silas frowned deeply. "I see."

"You know anything 'bout this, Son?" Pap spoke up.

"No, why would I?"

"Reuben and you have been *gut* friends since you was *kinder*," Mom reminded.

Silas shrugged. "That's true, but he don't tell me everything he does."

"So, you're sayin' you don't know nothin' about Reuben bein' involved in the things of the world?" Bishop Weaver questioned.

"Not a thing." Silas scooted his chair back and stood up. "Now, if you'll excuse me, I'd best see to my chores before supper."

Outside, on the back porch, Silas drew in a deep, cleansing breath. What in the world was going on here? First Anna acting *Ab im Kopp*—off in the head—and now all these questions about Reuben? It was enough to make him downright nervous!

Chapter 2

Mom was sitting in her wheelchair at the table, tearing lettuce into a bowl. "You're late, Rachel." She wiped her hands on a paper towel and reached for a tomato. "Anna said you left the river way before she did. What kept ya, Daughter?"

"I'm really sorry," Rachel said sincerely. "I did a little bird-watchin' on the way home, and Anna must have missed me somehow." *Of course she missed you. You were up in a tree,* a little voice reminded. Pushing the thought aside, Rachel went to the kitchen sink and pumped enough water to fill the pitcher she'd just plucked off the counter.

"It seems you and Anna have both been livin' in a dream world lately. Is this what summer does to my girls?"

"I can't help it if I enjoy studyin' God's feathered creatures," Rachel replied.

Anna turned from her job at the stove. "Sure is funny I never saw you on the way home. If you were lookin' at birds, then where exactly were you—up in a tree?"

Rachel felt her face flame. Up in a tree was exactly where she'd been, but she sure didn't want Anna to know that. She glanced down at the bloodstain on her dress, hoping it would go unnoticed. "It don't matter where I was," she said defensively. "The point is—"

"I know, I know. . .you were lookin' at some stupid bird." Anna snickered. "Silas is such a *kischblich* man. He likes watchin' birds, too, but I think it's a big waste of time."

Rachel bristled at her sister's insensitivity. Who did she think she was, calling Silas a silly man? Just because Anna didn't appreciate birds didn't mean Rachel or Silas shouldn't. Truth of the matter, Anna didn't appreciate anything about Silas. In fact, she deserved to be reminded of how *wunderbaar* he was.

"Have ya heard anything from Silas Swartley lately?" Rachel asked. *See how Anna likes that topic of conversation.* "I happen to know he brought you home from a singin' awhile back. Seems to me he might wanna start courtin' pretty soon."

Mom's pale eyebrows lifted in obvious surprise. "Is that so, Anna? Might could be that you'll soon be makin' a weddin' quilt for your hope chest." She smiled sweetly. "Or would ya prefer I make one?"

Anna started stirring the pot of savory stew like there was no tomorrow. "It was just one ride in his buggy. Nothin' to get all excited about, so there's no need for either one of us to begin a weddin' quilt."

"Why not be excited?" Mom asked. "Silas has been hangin' around our place for years now, and your *daed* and I both think he's a right nice fellow. Besides, you're twenty-three years old already. Don'tcha think it's time ya begin thinkin' about marriage?"

Anna moved away from the stove and opened the refrigerator door. She withdrew a bunch of celery and took it over to the sink. "I'm thinkin' the stew needs a bit more of this," she said, conveniently changing the subject.

Rachel had begun setting the table, but she couldn't let the matter drop. "Silas is really sweet on Anna," she commented, giving her older sister a sidelong glance.

"Is that so?" Mom said, shifting her wheelchair to one side, making it easier for Rachel to reach around her. "A lovely quilt would sure as anything make a fine addition to someone's hope chest." She stared off into space, like she might be thinking about her own hope chest and the days when she'd been preparing for marriage.

"I'm really sorry if Silas thinks he's sweet on me," Anna said with a frown. "I just can't commit to someone I'm not in love with."

Mom clicked her tongue. *"Ach,* I didn't mean to interfere. Guess I jumped to the wrong conclusion, but seein' as how you and Silas have been friends for so long, and since ya let him bring ya home from a singin', I thought things were gettin' kinda serious."

"Anna has other things she wants to do with her life. I heard her say so," Rachel blurted out. The sudden realization of what she'd just said hit her full in the face, and her hand went straight to her mouth.

"When did ya hear me say such things?" Anna asked, turning to face Rachel and leveling her with a look of concern.

Rachel shrugged and kept placing the silverware on the table. "I'm sure you said it sometime."

"What other things are ya wantin' to do with your life?" Mom asked, pushing the salad bowl to the center of the table.

Anna merely shrugged in response.

"If I had someone as *wunderbaar* as Silas Swartley after me, I'd sure marry him in an instant," Rachel asserted. Her face felt suddenly warm, and she scurried across the room, hoping nobody had noticed the blush that was surely staining her cheeks.

"My, my," Anna said with a small laugh. "If I didn't know better, I'd be thinkin' my little sister was in love with Silas."

"Rachel's only eighteen—too young for such thoughts!" Mom declared.

"How old were you when you fell in love with Dad?" asked Anna.

"Guess I wasn't much more'n nineteen," Mom admitted. "Still—"

The back door flew open, interrupting Mom's sentence. Twelve-year-old Elizabeth burst into the kitchen. Her long brown braids, which were supposed to be pinned at the back of her head, were hanging down her back and had come partially unbraided. "Perry won't let me have a turn on the swing. He's been mean to me all day!"

Mom shook her head. "You know your twin brother likes to tease. *Der gleh Deihenge*—the little scoundrel. I wish you would try to ignore it."

"But, Mom, Perry—"

Mom held up one hand to silence Elizabeth. "Run outside and call Dad and your brothers in for supper."

A short time later, the family was gathered around the huge wooden table. Dad sat at the head, with Joseph beside him, and Perry in the next seat. Mom was at the other end of the table, and Rachel, Anna, and Elizabeth sat directly across from the boys.

"Did ya get that old plow fixed today, Joseph?" Dad asked as he filled his plate with a generous helping of stew.

Joseph shrugged. "I can't be sure 'til I try it out in the fields, but I think it's probably workable again."

Dad pulled thoughtfully on his long brown beard, lightly peppered with gray. "No matter what those English neighbors of mine may think, I say ya just can't replace a reliable horse and plow!"

"Horses can be unreliable, too," Anna put in. "In fact, I've known 'em to be downright stubborn at times."

Dad gave her a curious look, but he made no comment.

"I've been wonderin'. . .don'tcha think we need to modernize a bit?" Anna asked. "I mean, workin' the greenhouse would go much better if we had electricity and a telephone. . .even one outdoors on a pole."

"We're Old Order Amish, Anna. Don't ever forget that," Dad reminded. "God's Word commands us to be separate. Although some in our community make a few concessions, I don't choose to live as the English do, and I never shall!"

Everyone was silent, but Rachel knew her sister well. She could sense the frustration Anna was feeling and wondered if she should say something on her behalf—before Anna spoke again and got herself into trouble. Rachel drew in a deep breath. What could she really say, though? She sure didn't agree with Anna's worldly thinking. In fact, Rachel loved everything about being Amish—especially one Amish man in particular.

Anna folded her arms across her chest in a stubborn, unyielding pose, and a contrite look crossed her face. "I'd like to be excused."

Dad nodded, but Mom protested. "You've hardly eaten a thing."

"I'm not hungry." She lowered her head, causing her long lashes to form crescents against her pale cheeks.

Rachel looked down at her own plate. How could anyone not be hungry with a helping of Mom's delicious savory stew sitting before them?

"Let her go," Dad said. "Just might could be that goin' without supper is what she needs to help clear her head for better thinkin'."

Anna jumped up, nearly knocking over her glass of lemonade, and stormed out of the room.

Rachel moved back against her chair, her shoulder blades making contact with the hard wood. *Such a silly one, my sister is. She just don't know how good she's got it, and that's for certain sure.*

After supper, Rachel helped her mother and Elizabeth wash and dry the dishes, then clean up the kitchen. "Many hands make light work," Mom always said. Too bad Anna was upstairs sulking in her room. If she'd been helping, they probably could have been done already.

When the last dish was finally put away, Rachel turned to her mother. "I think I'll go up and see how Anna's doin'. Unless you've got somethin' more for me here."

Mom shook her head. "Nothin' right now. In fact, I was just thinkin' about goin' outside to check on my garden." She glanced up at Elizabeth, who was drying her hands on a terry cloth towel. "How'd ya like to join your old *mamm* outside?"

Elizabeth wrinkled her freckled nose. "You ain't old."

Rachel glanced over at her mother. She was smiling from ear to ear—that sweet smile that made her so special. Even with her disability, Mom never complained. From all Rachel had been told, their mother had been confined to a wheelchair most of her life. The story was that when Mom was a *kinder*, a tree branch fell during a bad storm. It hit her across the back and neck, and part of her spinal cord had been damaged. Ever since then, Mom had either been in a wheelchair or strapped to a pair of crutches that made her walk all stiff-legged, like a wooden doll. However, she didn't let her disability hold her back much. In fact, Mom had been right independent when she was a *younga* and had first opened the greenhouse she'd named Grandma's Place.

Rachel smiled to herself as she thought of the stories Dad and Mom often told about their courting days and how they almost didn't marry. Mom had been convinced Dad only wanted her because he loved flowers so much and hoped to get his hands on her business. It took some doing, but Dad finally made her believe it was her he loved most. They got married, ran the greenhouse together, and a year later, little Anna was born. Mom thought it was a true miracle, the way God had allowed her to give birth. Rachel could only imagine how her mother must have felt when she kept having one miracle after another. First Anna, then two years later Joseph was born. Another three years went by, and Rachel came onto the scene. Mom must have thought she was done having *kinder*, because it was another six years before the twins made their surprise appearance.

Wow! Five miracles in all, Rachel mused. *I'll surely feel blessed if God ever gives me five children.* She drew in a deep breath and released it with such force that Mom gave her a strange look.

"You okay, Rachel? Ya looked kinda like you were daydreamin' again."

Daydreaming was nothing new for Rachel. As far back as she could remember, she'd enjoyed fantasizing about things.

"I'm fine, Mom," she said with a nod. "Guess I *was* doin' a bit of dreamin', all right."

"Say, how'd ya get that blood on your dress?" Mom asked suddenly.

"Oh, just scraped my knee," Rachel replied with a shrug.

"Want me to take a look-see?"

"No, it's nothin'." Rachel smiled. "I'm ready to go up and see Anna now."

"*Jah*, you go ahead," Mom said. "Maybe you can talk some sense into her about courtin' Silas."

Upstairs, Rachel found Anna lying on her bed, staring at the plaster ceiling. "Mind if I join ya?"

"Why's Dad so stubborn?" Anna asked, not even bothering to answer Rachel's question. "Can't he see there's a place for some modern things? He's the reason I get so upset, ya know." A stream of tears ran down her cheeks, and she swiped at them with the back of her hand.

Rachel took a seat near the foot of Anna's bed. "People often blame things on the previous generation 'cause there's only one other choice."

Anna sat up, swinging her legs over the side of the bed. "What's that supposed to mean?"

"The other choice would be to put the blame on yourself."

Anna sucked in her protruding lip and blinked several times. "How dare you speak to me thataway! I can do whatever I like, and Dad can't make me do otherwise!" With one quick motion, she jerked off her head covering, and her golden brown locks came tumbling down the back of her dark green dress.

Rachel couldn't help but think of the things Silas had said when Anna's hair had been down earlier that day. It made her feel almost ill to realize Silas was in love with such a spiteful, rebellious woman.

Anna paced the room with quick, nervous steps. Suddenly she pointed to a pair of scissors, lying next to the sewing basket on her dresser. "Maybe I should cut my hair short." She leaned over, and her fingers were just inches from the scissors when Rachel's gasp stopped her.

"What do ya think you're doin'?" Rachel shouted. "Amish women don't have short hair and you know it!"

Anna pulled her hand slowly away. "If I weren't Amish, then I could do whatever I wanted with my hair, and my clothes, and—"

"But you are Amish, and you should be happy bein' such."

"Why? Why must I be happy bein' Amish?" Anna squinted her green eyes at Rachel. "Didn't God give each of us a mind of our own? Shouldn't I have the right to choose how I wanna live?"

Rachel nodded. "Of course you should, but you're already baptized into the church, and if you were to go against the *Ordnung* now, you'd be shunned, and that's a fact!"

Anna sniffed. "Don'tcha think I know that, Rachel? I feel like an impostor sometimes. I've thought long and hard on all of this, too."

"Then I hope you've come to the right conclusion. You've gotta learn to be happy with the Amish faith."

❧

Silas shielded his eyes from the glare of the morning sun as he strolled through the small town of Paradise. He'd come in early today with the intent of speaking to his friend, Reuben, who was painting on a new grocery store in town.

He found Reuben around the back of Larsen's Supermarket, holding a paintbrush in one hand and a giant oatmeal cookie in the other.

"I see you're hard at work," Silas said with a grin.

Reuben chuckled. "I do need to keep up my strength."

"*Jah*, I'm sure."

"What brings you to town so early?" Reuben asked as he applied a glob of paint to the side of the wooden building.

"I came to see you."

"So, now ya see me. What do ya think?"

Silas shook his head. "You're such a strange one. Always kiddin' around."

Reuben's blue eyes fairly sparkled, and he ran a hand through his blond hair, which was growing much too long for any self-respecting Amish man. Silas had to wonder how come his friend wasn't wearing his straw hat, either, especially on a day when the sun was already hot as fire. He was about to voice that question when Reuben asked a question of his own.

"You heard any good jokes lately?"

Silas shook his head. "Nope. You?"

Reuben nodded but kept right on painting. "My boss, Ed, told me a real funny one the other day, but I don't think you'd like it much."

"How come?"

"It was kinda off-color."

Silas chewed on his lower lip. He wondered what Reuben's folks would have to say about that.

"How come ya don't give up this paintin' job and go back to helpin' your *daed* on the farm? I'm sure he could use the extra pair of hands, and—"

"I don't like farmin'," Reuben asserted. "In fact, there ain't much about the Amish ways I do like anymore."

Silas rocked back and forth on his heels, trying to think of the right thing to say. He'd been helping his pap work the land ever since he finished his eighth-grade education. That was seven years ago, and he was still happy staying at home. It didn't make sense to him that an Amish man, born and raised on a farm, preferred to be painting houses, stores, and the like.

"I'm sorry you feel thataway," Silas said. "Sure hope you're keepin' your opinions to yourself."

Reuben stopped painting and turned to face Silas. "What's that supposed to mean?"

Silas shrugged. "Bishop Weaver was at our place yesterday. He's heard some things, and he's gettin' mighty concerned."

"Things about me?"

Silas nodded. "Is it true?"

"Is what true?"

"That you have been runnin' around with some English fellows?"

Reuben's brows furrowed. "You plannin' on tellin' the bishop whatever I say to you now?"

"*Himmel*—no, no," Silas was quick to say. "I just thought I'd ask, that's all."

Reuben snorted. "All right then. . . *Jah*, I've done a few worldly things with some of the fellas I work with."

"Like what?"

Reuben shrugged. "Let's see now. . . We've gone to a couple of R-rated movies, had a few beers with our boss after work, and—"

Silas held up his hand. "Don'tcha know better than that? In Proverbs 23:20 it says, 'Be not among winebibbers.' And chapter six, verse fourteen of 2 Corinthians reminds us about not bein' unequally yoked with unbelievers."

"Yeah, I know all that, but I ain't no dummy. I've been readin' some books about other beliefs, and I'm not so sure I swallow all that Bible teachin' anymore."

"My pap told me once, 'Never mistake knowledge for wisdom. One might help you make a livin', but the other helps you make a life.' "

Reuben flicked a fly off his paintbrush and frowned. "Let's just say I've learned there's more to this world than sittin' in church for hours on end and followin' a bunch of silly rules. We only live once, and regardless of what your pap says, I aim to have me some fun!"

Hearing the way his friend was talking gave Silas a deep ache in his heart, just the way it had when he'd spoken with Anna yesterday. He didn't understand why so many of the *younga* were getting dissatisfied with the old ways. He closed his eyes and drew in a deep breath. He might not be able to do much about Reuben, but Anna was another matter. She needed him to intervene on her behalf, and if there was any way he could get her thinking straight again, he was determined to do it.

Chapter 3

The following morning, Rachel awoke to the soothing sound of roosters crowing in the barnyard. She loved that noise—loved everything about their farm, in fact. She yawned, stretched, and squinted at the ray of sun peeking through a hole in her window shade. Today the family was planning to go to Farmers' Market, where they would sell some of their garden produce, as well as plants and flowers from Mom and Dad's greenhouse.

Dad, Joseph, and Perry were outside getting the larger market buggy ready when Rachel came downstairs to help with breakfast. The sweet smell of maple syrup greeted her as she entered the kitchen. Mom was mixing pancake batter, Anna was frying sausage and eggs, and Elizabeth was setting the table, which included a huge pitcher of fresh syrup.

"*Gut Morgen,*" Rachel said cheerfully. "What can I do to help?"

Mom glanced up at Rachel, then back to the batter. "You can go outside and tell the *Mannsleit* we'll be ready with breakfast in ten minutes."

Rachel nodded, then made a hasty exit out the kitchen door. Dad and Perry were loading the back of their larger, four-sided market buggy, and Joseph was hitching the brawny horse that would pull it.

"Mom says breakfast in ten minutes," Rachel announced.

"You can go get washed up," Dad told Perry.

The young, freckle-faced boy pointed to the boxes of green beans sitting on the grass. "What about those?"

"You stay, and you go," Dad said, indicating his wish to speak to Rachel alone. "I'll see to the boxes."

Perry straightened his twisted suspenders and took off on a run. From behind, his long legs made him appear much older than a boy of twelve. From the front, his impish grin and sparkling blue eyes made him look like a child, full of life and laughter, mischief and fun.

Rachel stood quietly beside her father, waiting for him to speak. His shirt-sleeves were rolled up to the elbows, and she marveled at how quickly his strong arms loaded the remaining boxes of beans. When the last box was put in place, Dad straightened and faced Rachel. "Do ya think you could do me a favor?"

Rachel twisted one corner of her apron and stared down at the ground. Dad's favors usually meant some kind of hard work. "I suppose so. What did ya have in mind?"

Dad bent down so he was eye level with Rachel. "Well, now. . .I know how close you and Anna have always been. I was hopin' ya might let your *mamm* and me know what's goin' on with her these days."

Rachel opened her mouth to respond, but Dad cut her right off. "Fact of the matter is, Anna's been actin' mighty strange here of late, and we can't be sure we can trust her. We need your help findin' out what's up."

Rachel wrinkled her nose. Was Dad saying what she thought he was saying? Did he actually want her to spy on her sister? If Dad thought she and Anna were close, he was surely mistaken. Here of late, Rachel and Anna didn't see eye-to-eye on much of anything. Rachel knew if Anna's talk about learning more of the English ways ever reached Mom's or Dad's ears, they'd be plenty miffed. That was obvious by the way Dad had reacted last night when Anna mentioned they should modernize some. Rachel sure didn't want to be the one to tell them what was going on inside Anna's stubborn head.

"So, what do ya say?" Dad asked, pulling Rachel out of her troubling thoughts.

Rachel flicked her tongue across her dry lips. "What exactly am I expected to do?"

"To begin with, your *mamm's* been tellin' me that Anna has a suitor, yet she's not the least bit interested in courtin' the poor fellow."

"You must mean Silas Swartley," Rachel said with a frown. "He's sweet as molasses on Anna, but she won't give him the time of day." She shook her head. "Such a shame it is, too. Poor Silas is tryin' ever so hard to win her over."

Dad glanced toward the front of the market buggy, where Joseph was still hitching the horse. "Kinda reminds me of your *mamm* when I was tryin' to show her I cared."

Rachel listened politely as her father continued. "Sometimes a man shows his feelin's in a strange sort of way." Dad nodded toward Joseph and chuckled softly. "Now take that big brother of yours—we all know he's sweet on Pauline Hostetler, but do you think he'll do a thing about it? *Himmel.* . .Joseph's gonna fool around, and soon some other fellow's bound to come along and win her heart. Then it'll be too late for my boy."

Rachel knew all about Joseph's crush on Pauline. He'd been carrying a torch for Pauline ever since Eli Yoder dropped her to marry Laura, the fancy, English woman from Minnesota. The fact that Pauline was three years older than Joseph didn't help things, either. Rachel had to wonder if the age difference bothered Pauline the way it did her brother. It seemed rather strange that the twenty-four-year-old woman still wasn't married. Either she'd never gotten over Eli, or Pauline just wasn't interested in Joseph. He sure wasn't going to take the initiative; Rachel was pretty sure of that.

"Well, I'm thinkin' that if anyone can talk to Anna about givin' Silas a chance, it would be you," Dad said, cutting into Rachel's contemplations one more time.

Rachel swallowed hard. *If Dad only knew what he was askin'. It's hard enough to see Silas hangin' around Anna all the time. How in the world can I be expected to talk Anna into somethin' she really don't wanna do?* Truth be told, Rachel would just as soon slop the hogs every day as to tell Anna how stupid she was for snubbing Silas.

She let her gaze travel over their orderly farmyard, then back to her father. *"Jah,* okay. I'll have a little talk with Anna 'bout Silas."

"And you'll tell us if anything strange is goin' on with your sister?"

Rachel nodded, feeling worse than pond scum in late August. "I'll tell."

❧

Farmers' Market was on the outskirts of Bird-in-Hand. It was only a twenty-minute ride from the Beachy farm, but today the trip seemed especially long. The cramped quarters in the buggy and the hot, sticky weather didn't help much, so Rachel was feeling kind of cross.

Dad and Mom rode in the front of the buggy, with Elizabeth sitting between them. There were two benches in back where Rachel, Anna, Joseph, and Perry sat. Behind them were the boxes filled with produce, plants, and fresh-cut flowers. Mom's wheelchair was scrunched in as well.

The temperature was in the nineties, with humidity so high Rachel could feel her damp dress and underclothes sticking to her body like flypaper. When they finally pulled into the graveled parking lot, she was the first to jump down from the buggy.

Perry tended to the horse, while Joseph and Dad unloaded the boxes and carried them inside the market building. Elizabeth and Rachel followed, with Anna a few feet behind, pushing Mom's wheelchair.

Everyone helped set up their table, and soon the Beachys were open for business. Whenever they were between customers, the children were allowed to take turns wandering around the market.

Rachel took a break around noontime and went to a stand where they were selling homemade ginger ale. A tall, gangly Amish fellow waited on her. He had freckles covering his nose and looked to be about nineteen or twenty. Rachel didn't recognize him and figured he must be from another district.

"It's a mighty hot day, ain't it so?" he asked, giving her a wide grin that revealed a mouthful of stained teeth.

Rachel had to wonder if the young man was among the Amish teenagers who liked to sow his wild oats. Could be that this fellow was hooked on cigarettes, which would explain the ugly yellow teeth. She thought it such a pity that so many of the *younga* became dissatisfied with their religion and wanted to see how the English lived. Her mind went immediately to her older sister. How she hoped Anna would never stoop so low as to start drinking and smoking, the way some in their district did. It would be a sin and a shame to waste her life that way.

Rachel smiled cordially at the man selling ginger ale. Even if he was sowing his oats, he still deserved to be treated with kindness. *"Jah,* it surely is warm," she said, handing him a fifty-cent piece. In return, he gave her a paper cup full of mouthwatering soda pop.

Rachel moved on to another table, where Nancy Frey, the schoolteacher who taught at the local Amish one-room schoolhouse, was selling a variety of pies.

Nancy smiled at Rachel. "Are ya here with your family?"

"*Jah.* We're sellin' produce and lots of flowers and plants from my folks' greenhouse," Rachel replied. "Our stand's at the other end of the building."

"I sure hope business is better for you than it has been here. Pies aren't doin' so well today."

"That's too bad." Rachel licked her lips. "Yum! Apple-crumb, shoofly, and funny-cake are all my favorite pies."

Nancy laughed. "Would ya like to try a slice? I already have an apple-crumb cut."

"It's right temptin', but I'd better not spoil my appetite, or I won't be able to eat any of the lunch I brought along." She held up her cup of ginger ale. "Besides, I've got this to finish yet."

"How is your dear *mamm* these days?" Nancy asked. "Does she still get around on those crutches of hers?"

Rachel nodded. "She does some, though I think it's kinda hard for her to walk like a stiff-legged doll. She uses her wheelchair more often than the braces—probably because it's a mite easier."

"*Jah,* I can imagine."

"Well," Rachel said with a shrug, "guess I'll be movin' on. It's awful stuffy in here, so I think I'll step outside for a breath of what I hope will be fresh air."

Nancy nodded. "I know what ya mean. If I weren't here alone, I'd be goin' outside, too."

"I'd be more'n happy to watch your table," Rachel offered.

"*Danki,* but my sister Emma will probably be along soon. I'm sure she'll be willin' to let me take a little break."

"All right then." Rachel waved and moved away from Nancy's table, heading in the direction of the nearest exit.

Soon Rachel found the solace she was looking for under an enormous maple tree growing in the park right next to the market. She was about to take a seat at one of the picnic tables when she caught sight of Silas Swartley. Her heart slammed into her chest as she realized he was heading her way.

❧

Silas gritted his teeth. He'd just come from the Yutzys' table, and talking to Reuben's folks had made him feel downright sick. They knew what their son was up to. . .or at least some of it. Silas was pretty sure Reuben hadn't told them everything he was doing. But then, he hadn't really told Silas all that much.

Silas figured he should be minding his own business, but he couldn't stand by and watch two of his best friends get in trouble with the elders of the church for disobedience to the *Ordnung.* He knew Reuben was already doing some worldly things, but Anna was another matter. He was pretty sure she was only *thinking* on the idea. She was obviously discontent with her life, but he was hoping to change all that. If Anna would agree to court him, then maybe he could persuade her to give up all her silly notions about wanting to taste what the world had to offer.

Silas had come outside for a breath of fresh air and was headed over to the park when he noticed Anna's little sister Rachel. "Hmm. . .she might be just the one I need to talk to."

✌

Silas plunked down beside Rachel, without even bothering to ask if she minded or not. Of course, truth be told, it tickled her pink that he'd even want to be seen with her, much less sit right on the same bench.

"Whatcha doin' out here by yourself?" Silas asked as he took off his straw hat and began fanning his face with the brim.

"Tryin' to get cooled off," Rachel said, kind of breathlesslike. For one moment, she had an impulse to lean her head on Silas's shoulder and confess her undying love for him. She didn't, of course, for she knew he would either become angry or laugh and call her a *kinder* who was much too young for someone as mature as him.

"I know what ya mean," Silas responded to her comment about the weather. "Whew! I thought it was hot inside, but I don't think it's a whole lot better out here."

So Silas had come from inside the market. *Funny thing*, Rachel mused as her lips turned slightly upward. *I never saw him once all mornin'.* It was a surprise to her that Silas wasn't hanging around their table making googly eyes at Anna, the way he usually did.

"Rachel, I was wonderin' if we could talk," Silas said, breaking into her private thoughts.

"I thought we were talkin'."

He chuckled and dropped his hat to his knees. *"Jah,* I guess we were at that. What I really meant to say was, can we talk about your sister?"

Rachel's smile turned upside down. She might have known Silas hadn't planned to talk about her. She shrugged, trying not to let her disappointment show. "What about Anna? It was *that* sister you were referrin' to, right?"

Silas shifted his gaze toward the sky. "Of course I meant Anna. It sure enough couldn't be Elizabeth. I ain't no cradle robber, ya know."

Rachel felt as though Silas had slapped her right across the face. Even though he was speaking about her twelve-year-old sister, she still got his meaning. She knew Silas wouldn't dream of looking at her, since she was five years younger than he was and all. Besides, what chance did she have against the beauty of her older sister? She stared off into space, hoping he wouldn't notice the tears that had gathered in her eyes.

In a surprise gesture, Silas touched Rachel's chin and turned her head so she was looking directly at him. Her chest fluttered with the sensation of his touch, and it was all she could do to keep from falling right off the bench. "So, what is it ya wanted to say 'bout Anna?" she asked with a catch in her voice.

"You and your sister are pretty close, ain't it so?"

She gulped and tried to regain her composure. "I used to think so."

"Anna probably talks more to you than anyone else, right?"

Rachel shook her head. "I think she tells her friend Martha Rose a whole lot more'n she tells me."

387

Silas lifted one eyebrow in question. "Martha Rose?"

Rachel nodded. "Yep. They have been *gut* friends for a long time."

Several seconds went by before Silas spoke again. "Hmm. . .I suppose I could talk to Martha Rose, but I don't know her all that well. I'd feel a mite more comfortable talkin' to you 'bout Anna than I would to her best friend."

Rachel supposed she should have been flattered that Silas would want to avail her as a confidant, yet the thought of him only using her to learn more about Anna irked her to no end.

"Okay," she finally conceded, "what do you wanna know 'bout my sister?"

"Can you tell me how to make her pay me some mind?" Silas asked, looking ever so serious. "I've tried everything but stand on my head and wiggle my ears, yet still, she treats me like yesterday's dirty laundry. I tell you, Rachel, it's got me plumb worn out tryin' to get sweet Anna to court me."

Sweet Anna? Rachel thought ruefully. *Silas, you might not think my sister's so sweet if you knew all the things she's been sayin'. . .about you and the Amish way of life.*

Rachel felt sorry for poor Silas, sitting here all woebegone, pining for her sister's attention. If she wasn't so crazy about the fellow herself, she might pitch in and try to set things right between him and Anna. With a slight shrug, she responded to Silas's question. "I think only God can get my sister thinkin' straight again." She looked away, studying a row of trees on the other side of the park.

"You're kinda pensive today," Silas noted. "Is it this oppressive heat, or are ya just not wantin' to help me with Anna?"

Rachel tipped her head forward, the whole while praying for something to say that wouldn't be a lie and wouldn't hurt Silas's feelings. Finally, she lifted her chin and faced him again. "I think a man who claims to care for a woman should speak on his own behalf. Even though Anna and I don't talk much anymore, I still know her fairly well, and I don't think Anna would like it if she knew you were plottin' like this."

Silas twisted his hands together. "I ain't plottin', Rachel. I'm just tryin' to figure out some way to make Anna commit to courtin' me, that's all. I thought maybe you could help out, but if you're gonna get all peevish on me, then just forget I even brought up the subject."

Now I've gone and done it. Silas will never come to care for me if I keep on makin' him mad. Rachel placed her trembling hand on Silas's bare arm, and the sudden contact with his skin caused her hand to feel like it was on fire. "Maybe it wouldn't hurt if I had a little talk with Anna."

A huge grin spread across Silas's handsome face. "You mean it, Rachel? You'd really go to bat for me?"

She nodded slowly, feeling like she was one of her father's old sows being led away to slaughter. First she'd promised Dad to help Anna and Silas get together, and now she was promising Silas to speak to Anna on his behalf. It made no sense, since she didn't really want them to be together. But a promise was a promise, so she smiled and said, *"Jah,* I'll do my best."

Chapter 4

It was Sunday morning, and church was to be held at eight-thirty in the home of Eli and Laura Yoder. They only lived a few farms away from the Beachys, so the horse and buggy ride didn't take long at all.

Many buggies were parked near the side of the Yoders' house, but Dad managed to find an empty spot on the side where Eli's folks' addition had been built. Joseph helped Mom into her wheelchair; then everyone else climbed out and scattered, hoping to find friends and relatives to visit with during their free time before church started.

Rachel noticed Silas Swartley standing on one end of the front porch, and she silently berated herself for loving him. She was almost certain he would never love her in return. She wasn't sure he even liked her. *I either need to put him out of my mind or figure out some way to make him take notice of me.*

Silas seemed to be focused on Anna, who was talking with her friends Martha Rose Zook and Laura Yoder at the other end of the porch. *Guess I'd better speak to Anna soon, before Silas comes askin' if I did.* Rachel joined her sister and the other two women but made sure she was standing close enough to Anna so she could whisper into her ear. "Look," she said softly, "there's Silas Swartley. He seems to be watchin' you."

Anna shrugged. "So?"

"Don'tcha think he's good-lookin'?"

Anna nudged Rachel in the ribs. "Since you seem so interested, why not go over and talk to him?"

Rachel gasped. "I could never do that!"

"Why not?"

"It's you he's interested in, not me."

"I think we'd better hurry and get inside. Preachin's about to begin," Anna said, conveniently changing the subject.

Rachel followed her sister into the Yoders' living room, where several rows of backless, wooden benches were set up. She'd have to try speaking to Anna about Silas later on.

The men and boys took their seats on one side of the room and the women and girls on the other. Rachel sat between her two sisters, with Mom sitting in her wheelchair at the end of their bench, closest to Elizabeth.

All whispering ceased as the hymnals were passed out by one of the deacons. In singsong, almost chantlike voices, the congregation recited several traditional Dutch hymns. Next, one of the ministers delivered a short message, followed by a longer sermon by Bishop Weaver.

Rachel noticed that Elizabeth was fidgeting, obviously growing restless. Mom reached over and placed a firm hand on the child's knee. "Sit still," she whispered. "Even the little ones like David Yoder and his baby sister aren't fussin', so you shouldn't be neither."

"I'm hungry," Elizabeth whined. "When's church gonna be over?"

Mom gave her a cross look. "You're not too old for a visit to the woodshed, ya know."

Elizabeth sat up straight and never gave another word of complaint.

The next hour was spent in silent prayer and Bible reading. Rachel glanced over at Anna. She was twiddling her thumbs and staring out the window.

What's that willful sister of mine thinkin' about? Rachel had a terrible feeling that Anna's curiosity over worldly things and her dissatisfaction with their Old Order ways would only lead to trouble. What if Anna were to up and leave the faith?

Rachel clenched her teeth. *No, that can't happen. It would break Mom's and Dad's hearts, not to mention upsettin' the whole family. Why, we'd have to shun our own flesh and blood!* Rachel shuddered just thinking about it. Right then, she vowed to pray more, asking the Lord to change her sister's mind about things. She would even make herself be happy about Anna and Silas courting if it meant Anna would alter her attitude and be happy being Amish.

Rachel felt a sense of relief when the preaching service was finally over. It wasn't that she didn't enjoy church, but all those troubling thoughts rolling around in her head were enough to make her feel downright miserable.

Outside in the front yard, several large tables were set up, and soon each of them was laden with an abundance of tasty food. There were large platters of roast beef, bowls of mashed potatoes, bread stuffing, pickled red beets, hot cabbage slaw, fresh cucumbers, steamed brown bread, butter, apple jelly, pitchers of cool milk, and for dessert, tart cherry pie topped with homemade vanilla ice cream.

Rachel and Anna joined several other young women as they began to serve the menfolk. After that, the women and children took their places at separate tables.

When the meal was over and everything had been cleared away, men and women of all ages gathered in small groups to visit. The younger children were put down to nap, while the older ones started playing games of hide-and-seek, tag, and corner-ball. The young adults also gathered. Some joined the games, while others were content to just sit and talk.

Rachel didn't feel much like playing games or engaging in idle chitchat, so she decided to take a walk. Walking always seemed to help her relax and think more clearly. She left Anna talking with a group of women and headed off in the direction of the small pond near the end of the Yoders' alfalfa field.

The pool of clear water was surrounded by low-hanging willow trees, offering shade and solitude on another hot, sticky day in July. Feeling the heat bear down on her, Rachel slipped off her shoes and socks, then waded along the water's edge, relishing the way the cool water tickled her toes. When she felt somewhat cooler, she plunked down on the grass. Closing her eyes, Rachel found herself thinking about the meeting she'd had with Silas the day before. She'd only made one feeble attempt to talk to Anna about him and knew she really should try again. It was the least she could do, since she had made a promise.

A snapping twig caused Rachel to jump. She jerked her head in the direction of the sound and was surprised to see Silas standing under one of the willow trees. He smiled and winked at her. It made her heart beat faster and was just enough to rekindle her hope that he might actually forget about Anna and come to love her instead.

"I didn't know anyone else was here," Rachel murmured as Silas moved over to where she was sitting.

"I didn't know anyone was here, either." Silas removed his straw hat and plopped down on the grass beside her. They relaxed in silence for a time, listening to the rhythmic birdsong filtering through the trees and an occasional *ribbet* from a noisy bullfrog.

Rachel thought about all the times Silas had visited their farm. She remembered one day in particular when a baby robin had fallen from its nest in the giant maple. Silas had climbed that old tree like it was nothing, then put the tiny creature back in its home. That was the day Rachel gave her heart to Silas Swartley. Too bad he didn't know it.

"I just talked to Reuben Yutzy," Silas said, breaking into Rachel's thoughts. "He's been workin' for a paint contractor in Lancaster for some time now."

She nodded but made no comment.

"Reuben informed me that he's leavin' the Amish faith." Silas slowly shook his head. "Can you believe it, Rachel? Reuben's been my friend since we were *kinder,* and now our friendship is gonna be over."

Rachel's mouth dropped open. "I'd never have guessed Reuben would leave. I always thought he was settled into our ways. As I recall, he never even joined his brothers when they decided to sow their wild oats."

The lines in Silas's forehead deepened. "Well, he's sowin' them now. Since he started workin' for that English man, Reuben's been hangin' around the wrong crowd and doin' all sorts of worldly things. I tried talkin' to him the other day, but I guess nothin' I said got through his thick skull. Reuben's made up his mind about leavin', and he seems bent on followin' that path."

"Many of our men work in town for paint contractors, carpenters, and other tradesmen," Rachel reminded. "Most of them remain in the faith in spite of their jobs."

"I know, but like I said, Reuben got mixed up with the wrong sort of English folks." Silas gave his earlobe a few tugs. "Reuben told me that he bought a fancy truck awhile back, but he's been keepin' it parked outside his boss's place of business so none of his family would know."

Rachel fidgeted with her hands. She wanted so badly to reach out and touch Silas's disheartened face. It would feel so right to smooth the wrinkles out of his forehead. She released a deep sigh instead. "Things are sure gettin' *Verhuddelt* here of late."

Silas nodded. "You're right about things bein' mixed up. I think there's somethin' else goin' on with Reuben, too."

"Like what?"

"I'm not sure. He dropped a few hints, but when I pressed him about it, he closed up like a snail crawlin' into its shell. Said he didn't want to talk about it." Silas grimaced. "I'm thinkin' maybe there's a woman involved."

"An Englisher?"

"Might could be. It wouldn't be the first time an Amish man fell for an English gal." Silas shrugged. "That's what happened to Eli Yoder a few years back, ya know."

Rachel nodded. *"Jah,* but Laura joined the Amish faith, so Eli never was shunned." She pulled a hanky from her apron pocket, dried her bare feet on it, then slipped her socks and shoes back on before she stood up. "I should be gettin' back to the house. My folks are likely to miss me, and they'll probably send Joseph out lookin'." She shook her head. "I'm not in any mood to deal with my cranky brother today."

"Joseph's not happy?"

"Nope. He's got a big crush on Pau—" Rachel's hand flew to her mouth when she realized she'd almost let something slip. "Like as I was sayin'," she mumbled, "I need to head back."

"Wait!" Silas jumped to his feet. "I was wonderin' if you've had a chance to speak with Anna yet."

Rachel felt her cheeks flame as she turned to face him. She worried that he might be able to see right through her. Could Silas possibly be reading her mind? She hoped not, because she really didn't want him to know what she was thinking right now.

"Silas, I still believe it would be best if you spoke with her yourself." Rachel touched his arm lightly. "And my advice is, you'd better do it soon, before it's too late."

❧

Rachel and her family were packing up to leave the Yoders' place when she noticed Silas had Anna cornered next to his courting buggy. Her sister didn't look any too happy about it, and Rachel could only wonder why. She inched a bit closer, hoping to catch a word or two. Eavesdropping was becoming a habit, it seemed, but she couldn't seem to help herself. Besides, it wasn't like she was doing it on purpose. People just seemed to be in the wrong place at the wrong time.

"I think it would be best if you'd forget about me," she heard Anna say. "Ya really should find someone more suited to you."

Silas shuffled his feet a few times, turning his hat over and over in his hands. "Don't rightly think there's anyone more suited to me, Anna."

Anna shrugged. "If ya think about it, you'll realize that we don't have much in common. Never have, really. On the other hand, I know who would be just right for you."

Me. . .me. . . Rachel squeezed her eyes shut, waiting to hear Silas's next words.

"Who might that be?" he asked.

"Rachel."

"Don't start with that again, Anna."

Rachel's eyes snapped open. She had to give up this silly game of bouncing back and forth from hope to despair. It only proved her immaturity, which was exactly why Silas saw her as a mere child.

"She likes a lot of the same things you like, Silas," her sister asserted. "Besides, I think she's crazy about you." Anna nodded toward her family's buggy, where Rachel stood, dumbfounded and unable to move. She'd probably never be able to look Silas in the face again.

Silas didn't seem to even notice Rachel, for he was looking straight at Anna. "As I've said before, Rachel's not much more'n a *kinder*. I need someone who's mature enough for marriage and ready to settle down."

"Rachel is *eighteen*, soon to be *nineteen*," Anna said, emphasizing the words. "Give her a few more months, and she'll be about the right age for marryin'."

"But it's you I love, Anna." Silas's tone was pleading, and if Rachel hadn't been so angry at her sister for embarrassing her, she might have felt pity for the man she loved.

"Rachel, are ya gettin' in or not?" Dad's booming voice jerked Rachel around to face him.

"What about Anna? She's still talkin' to Silas over by his buggy." Rachel pointed in that direction, but Dad merely grabbed up the reins.

"I'm sure Silas will see that Anna gets home," Mom put in. "After all, you did mention that he's sweet on her."

Rachel's throat ached from holding back tears, and she reached up to massage her throbbing temples. Silas thought she was just a *kinder*, and he was in love with Anna. At the rate things were going, she might never get to use her hope chest. She glanced Silas's way one last time, then hopped into the buggy and took her seat at the rear.

"Why are you lookin' so down in the mouth?" Joseph asked.

She folded her arms and scowled. "It is none of your business."

"I'll bet she'll tell me," Elizabeth piped up. "I'm a girl, and girls only share their deepest secrets with another girl. Ain't that right, Sister?"

Before Rachel could answer, Perry put in his two cents worth. "Aw, Rachel's probably got a bee in her *Kapp* 'cause she don't have a steady boyfriend yet. She's most likely jealous of Anna gettin' to ride home with Silas Swartley." He gave Rachel an impish smile. "That's it, ain't it? You're green with envy, huh?"

"Leave Rachel alone," Mom hollered back. "If she wants to talk about whatever's botherin' her, she will. Now, let's see how quiet we can make the rest of this ride home."

Chapter 5

The following day, Rachel felt more fretful than ever. She'd hardly said more than two words to anyone all morning and was sorely tempted to tell Anna she'd overheard most of her conversation with Silas yesterday. In fact, she was working up her courage and praying for just the right words as she hung a batch of laundry on the line.

Anna came out of the greenhouse and headed in Rachel's direction. *Guess this is as good a time as any,* Rachel decided. She waved and called her sister to come over. Anna merely waved back and kept right on walking toward the barn. A short time later, she emerged with one of the driving horses, then began to hitch the mare to the buggy.

"Where are ya goin'?" Rachel asked, dropping one of Perry's shirts into the wicker basket and moving toward Anna.

"Gotta run some errands in town; then I may stop by and see Martha Rose for a bit."

"You be careful now," Mom called. She was sitting on the front porch in her wheelchair, shelling peas into an bowl.

"I will," Anna hollered as she stepped into the buggy.

"And don't be out too late, neither," Mom added. "There was a bad accident last week along the main highway. It was gettin' dark, and the car driver didn't see the horse and buggy in time."

"I'll be careful." Anna flicked the reins, and the horse and buggy were soon out of sight.

Rachel bent down and snatched a pair of Dad's trousers from the wicker basket. "Guess I'll have to catch Anna later," she grumbled.

"Rachel!" Mom called.

"Jah?"

"When you're done with the laundry, I'd like ya to go over to the greenhouse and help your *daed.* I've got several things here at the house needin' to be done, so I won't be able to work out there today."

"What about Anna? She's the one who likes workin' with flowers."

"She's runnin' errands in Paradise."

Rachel already knew that. What she didn't know was why. Couldn't *she* have gone to town so Anna could have kept working in the greenhouse? Life wasn't always fair, but she knew there was no point in arguing. Rachel cupped her hands around her mouth. *"Jah,* okay, Mom! I'll go over to the greenhouse as soon as I'm done here."

Silas's morning chores were done, but he had a few errands to run for Pap. He decided this would be a good time to stop by the Beachys' greenhouse and have a little talk with Anna. Maybe he'd even buy Mom a new indoor plant or something she could put out in her garden. That would give him a good excuse for stopping at Grandma's Place, and it might keep Anna from suspecting the real reason for his visit.

Half an hour later, Silas stepped inside the greenhouse and was surprised to see Rachel sitting behind the counter, writing something on a tablet. *"Gut Morgen,"* he said, offering her a smile. "Is Anna about?"

She shook her head. "Nope. Just me and my *daed* are here today." She motioned toward the back room. "He's repottin' several African violets that have outgrown their containers."

Silas's smile turned upside down. "I thought Anna usually worked in the greenhouse. She ain't sick, I hope."

Rachel tapped her pencil along the edge of the counter. "She went to Paradise. Had some errands to run."

Silas scratched the back of his head. "Hmm. . .guess maybe I can try to catch up with her there. I have some errands to run today, too." He turned toward the door, all thoughts of buying a plant forgotten. If he hurried, he might make it to Paradise in time to find Anna there. The town wasn't very big, so if she was still running errands, he was bound to spot her. "Have a nice day. See ya later, Rachel," Silas called over his shoulder.

Anna. . .Anna. . .Anna, Rachel fumed. *Is that all Silas ever thinks about? He didn't bother to ask how I was doing or even make small talk about the weather.*

"I heard the bell ring above the door," Dad said as he entered the room. "Did we have a customer, or were ya just checking to see how things look outside?"

Rachel was about to answer when she felt a sneeze coming on. She grabbed a hanky out of her apron pocket, leaned her head back, and let out a big *ker-choo!*

"Bless you, Child."

"Danki."

"You're not comin' down with a summer cold, I hope," Dad said, giving her a look of concern.

She shook her head. "I think I'm allergic to all these flowers. I do okay with the ones growing outside, but bein' cooped up with 'em is a whole different matter."

"Guess workin' in the greenhouse isn't your idea of fun, huh?"

She turned her head away and mumbled, "Truth is, I would rather be outside."

Making no mention of her preference, Dad asked, "How come the doorbell jingled and we have no customers?"

"It was Silas Swartley," Rachel replied. "He was lookin' for Anna, and when I told him she was runnin' errands in Paradise, he hightailed it outta here, lickety-split."

Dad chuckled. "Ah, love is in the air; there's no doubt about it."

Rachel nibbled on the end of her pencil, remembering the way Silas looked whenever he spoke of Anna. It made her sick to her stomach, knowing Anna didn't love Silas in return.

Dad grinned like an old hound dog. "Someday your time will come, Rachel. Just be patient and have hope that God will send the right man your way."

❊

It was after nine o'clock, and still Anna hadn't returned home. Dad and Mom were sitting on the front porch, talking about their workday and doing a bit of worrying over their eldest daughter, while Rachel kept Elizabeth entertained with a game of checkers on the little table at one end of the porch. Joseph and Perry were out in the barn, grooming the horses and cleaning Joseph's courting buggy.

Rachel had just kinged her last red checker and was about to ask her little sister if she wanted to give up the game and have another piece of funny-cake pie when a horse and buggy came up the graveled drive. It was Anna, and before she even got the horse reined in, Dad was on his feet.

"Why are you so late, Daughter?" he called as he ran toward the buggy. "You sure couldn't have been runnin' errands all this time."

The porch was bathed in light from several kerosene lanterns, but the night sky was almost dark. Rachel knew Anna wasn't supposed to be out after the sun went down because there was too much risk of an accident, even with the battery-operated lights on the buggy.

Rachel peered across the yard and strained to hear what Anna and their father were saying. *Sure hope that sister of mine hasn't done anything foolish today.* An unsettled feeling slid through Rachel as she watched Anna step from the buggy.

"Your *mamm* and me were gettin' worried," Dad's deep voice announced.

Mom coasted down the wheelchair ramp. "Oh, thank the Lord! I'm so glad to see you're safe!"

"Sorry. I didn't realize that it was gettin' so late," Anna apologized.

"Well, you're home now, and that's what counts," Dad said. "We can talk about where you've been so long after I get the horse and buggy put away." He quickly unhitched the mare and led her off toward the barn.

"Anna, where's your apron and *Kapp?*" Mom asked as Anna stepped in front of the wheelchair.

Rachel studied her sister closely. Sure enough, Anna wasn't wearing anything over her dark blue cotton dress. No cape. No apron. No head covering! What in the world was that girl thinking?

Anna glanced down at her dress. "I—uh—guess I must have left it somewhere."

"Genesis 3:7!" Elizabeth hollered. " 'And they sewed fig leaves together, and made themselves aprons.' Ain't that what the Bible says? Ain't that why Amish women wear *Kapps* and aprons?"

Anna shot Elizabeth a look that could have stopped the old key-wound clock in the parlor, but she pushed past her little sister and started to open the front screen door without any comeback.

"Wait a minute, Anna." Mom propelled herself back up the ramp. "We need to talk about this, don'tcha think?"

Anna shrugged. "Can't it wait 'til tomorrow? I'm kinda tired."

Rachel gulped. If Anna were a few years younger, she'd have had a switch taken to her backside for talking to their mother that way. What in the world had come over her?

"It may be gettin' late, and you might be tired, but this is a serious matter and it won't wait 'til tomorrow," Mom asserted.

Anna pointed at Rachel, then Elizabeth. "Can't we talk someplace else? No use bringin' the whole family into this."

Mom folded her arms and set her lips in a straight line, indicating her intent to hold firm. "Maybe your sisters can learn somethin' from this discussion. I think it would be a *gut* idea if they stay—at least 'til your *daed* returns. Then we'll let him decide."

Rachel sucked in a deep breath and held it while she waited to see what Anna's next words would be.

"Guess I don't have much say in this," Anna said, dropping to the porch swing with a groan.

"Are ya gonna make your next move?" Elizabeth asked Rachel. "I just took one of your kings while you were starin' off into space."

Rachel jerked her thoughts back to the checkerboard. "I don't see how you managed that. . .unless you were cheatin'. I *was* winnin' this game, ya know."

Elizabeth thrust out her chin. "I wasn't cheatin'!"

Rachel was planning to argue the point further, but the sound of her father's heavy boots on the steps drew her attention away from the game again.

"Joseph's tendin' the horse," Dad said, looking down at Anna, who was pumping the swing back and forth like there was no tomorrow. "Now, are ya ready to tell us where you've been all day?" A muscle in Dad's cheek began to twitch, and Rachel knew it wasn't a good sign.

"Why aren't ya wearin' your apron and *Kapp*, Anna?" he shouted.

Rachel flinched, right along with her older sister. Their father didn't often get angry, but when he was mad enough to holler like that, everyone knew they'd better listen.

"I—uh. . ." Anna hung her head. "Can't we talk about this later?"

Dad slapped his hands together, and everyone, including Mom, jumped like a bullfrog. "We'll talk about it now!"

Anna's chin began to quiver. "Dad, couldn't I speak to you and Mom in private?"

He glanced down at Mom, who had wheeled her chair right next to the swing. "What do you think, Rebekah?"

She shrugged. "I guess it might be best." She turned her chair around so she was facing Rachel and Elizabeth. "You two had better clear away the game. It's about time to get washed up and ready for bed anyway."

"But, Mama," Elizabeth argued. "I'm almost ready to skunk Rachel and—"

Rachel shook her head. "Do as Mom says. You can skunk me some other time." She grabbed up the checkerboard, let the pieces fall into her apron, folded it up, then turned toward the front door. As curious as she was about where Anna had been and why she was dressed in such a manner, Rachel knew it was best to obey her parents. She'd have a heart-to-heart talk with her rebellious sister tomorrow morning. Until then, she'd be doing a whole lot of praying!

❧

Mom and Anna were preparing breakfast when Rachel came downstairs the following morning. "You're late," Anna complained. She was stirring the oatmeal so hard, Rachel feared it would come flying right out of the pot.

"How do you think you're gonna run a house of your own if ya can't be more reliable?" Anna continued to fume.

"Anna Beachy, just because you got up on the wrong side of the bed, it don't give ya just call to be *gridlich* with your sister this mornin'," Mom scolded. She was sitting at the kitchen table, buttering a huge stack of toast, and the look on her face told Rachel that her mother would not tolerate anyone being cranky this morning.

Rachel hurried to set the table, knowing it would be best to keep quiet.

Anna brought the kettle of oatmeal to the table and plopped it on a pot holder, nearly spilling the contents. "Like as not, you'll be gettin' married someday, Rachel, and I was wonderin' if you'd care to have my hope chest."

Rachel glanced at her mother, but Mom merely shrugged and continued buttering the toast. Anna was sure acting funny. Of course, she'd been acting pretty strange for several weeks now. Rachel could hardly wait until breakfast was over and she had a chance to corner Anna for a good talk. She was dying to know where her sister had been last night and what had happened during her little discussion with their folks.

"I've already got a start on my own hope chest, but thanks anyways," Rachel said, giving Anna the briefest of smiles.

"I'd sure like to go to Emma Troyer's today," Mom said, changing the subject. "She's feelin' kind of poorly and could probably use some help with laundry and whatnot." She sighed deeply. "Trouble is, I've got too much of my own things needin' to be done here and out at the greenhouse."

"I'll go," Anna said as she went to the refrigerator and took out a pitcher of milk.

Mom nodded. "If ya don't dally and come straight home, then I suppose it'd be all right. You'll hafta wait 'til this afternoon, though. I need help bakin' pies this mornin'."

Rachel could hardly believe her ears. Wasn't Anna in any kind of trouble for coming home late last night and not wearing her *Kapp* and apron? What sort of story had she fed the folks so that Mom would allow her to take the buggy out again today? Worse yet, if Anna went gallivanting off, it would probably mean Rachel would be asked to help in the greenhouse for the second day in a row. She had planned to do some bird-watching this afternoon, and maybe, if there was enough time, she would go fishing at the river. From the way things looked, she'd most likely be working all day.

"Did I hear someone mention pies?" Elizabeth asked excitedly. Rachel hadn't even noticed her younger sister enter the room. She'd been too upset over Anna's request to leave the farm again.

"I sure hope you're plannin' to make a raspberry cream pie, 'cause you know it's my favorite!" Elizabeth went on.

Mom gave the child a little pat on the backside when she sidled up to the table. "If you're willin' to help Perry pick raspberries, it might could be that we'll do up a few of your favorite pies." Her forehead wrinkled slightly. "Our raspberry bushes are loaded this summer, and if they're not picked soon, the berries are liable to fall clean off. Now that would surely be a waste, don'tcha think?"

Elizabeth's lower lip came jutting out. "I don't like to pick with Perry. He always throws the green berries at me."

"I'll have a little talk with your twin brother 'bout that," Mom stated. "Now, run outside and call the *Mannsleit* in for breakfast."

Rachel was glad when the morning meal was over. Anna had gone out to feed the hogs, and Rachel was on her way to gather eggs in the henhouse. Maybe they could finally find time for that little chat she'd been waiting to have.

With basket in hand, Rachel started across the yard, wishing she could go for a long walk. The scent of green grass kissed by early morning dew and the soft call of a dove caused a stirring in her heart. There was no time for a walk or even lingering in the yard. Rachel had chores to do, and she'd best get to them.

A short time later, Rachel reached under a fat hen and retrieved a plump, brown egg. A few more like that and she'd soon have the whole basket filled. When she finished, there were ten chunky eggs in the basket, and several cranky hens pecking and fussing at Rachel for disturbing their nests.

"You critters hush now," she scolded. "We need these eggs a heap more'n you, so shoo!" Rachel waved her hands, and the hens all scattered.

When an orange-and-white barn cat brushed against Rachel's leg and began to purr, she placed the basket on a bale of straw and plopped down next to it. Rachel enjoyed all the barnyard critters. They seemed so content with their lot in life. Not like one *person* she knew.

"What am I gonna do, Whiskers?" Rachel whispered. "I'm in love with someone, and he don't even know I'm alive. All he thinks about is my older sister." Her eyes drifted shut as an image of Silas Swartley flooded her mind. She could see him standing in the meadow, holding his straw hat in one hand and running the other hand through his dark chestnut hair. She imagined herself in the scene, walking slowly toward Silas with her arms outstretched.

"Sleepin' on the job, are ya?"

Rachel's eyes popped open, and she snapped her head in the direction of the deep male voice that had pulled her out of her reverie. "Joseph, you 'bout scared me to death, sneakin' up thataway."

He chuckled. "I wasn't really sneakin', but I sure thought you'd gone off to sleep there in your chair of straw." He sat down beside her. "What were you thinkin' about, anyways?"

Rachel gave Joseph's hat a little yank so it drooped down over his eyes. "I'll never tell."

Joseph righted his hat and jabbed her in the ribs with his elbow. "Like as not, it's probably some fellow you've got on your mind. My guess is maybe you and Anna have been bit by the summer love bug."

Rachel frowned deeply. "What do you know 'bout Anna? Has she told ya she's in love with someone?"

Joseph leaned over to stroke the cat's head, for Whiskers was now rubbing against *his* leg. "She hasn't said nothin' to me personally, but she's been actin' mighty strange here lately. I hear tell she got in pretty late last night, and there's been other times when Anna's whereabouts haven't been accounted for. What other reason could she have for actin' so secretive, unless some man's involved?"

Rachel remembered Silas saying he was going to Paradise yesterday and hoped to find Anna. Could she possibly have spent the day with him? She grabbed the basket of eggs and jumped up. "I've gotta get these back to the house. See ya later, Joseph!"

Rachel tore out of the barn and dashed toward the hog pen, where she hoped to find Anna still feeding the sow and her new brood of piglets. In her hurry, she tripped over a rock and nearly fell flat on her face. "*Ach,* my!" she complained. "The last thing I need this mornin' is to break all the eggs I've gathered."

She walked a little slower, but disappointment flooded her soul when she saw that Anna wasn't at the pigpen. Rachel had to wonder if she'd already left for Emma Troyer's.

Back at the house, Rachel was relieved to see Mom, Anna, and Elizabeth rolling out pie dough at the kitchen table. Each held a wooden rolling pin, and Rachel noticed that Elizabeth had more flour on her clothes than she did on the heavy piece of muslin cloth used as a rolling mat.

"You're just in time," Mom said with a nod of her head. "Why don't ya add some sugar to the bowl of raspberries on the cupboard over there?"

Rachel put the eggs in the refrigerator, then went to the sink to wash her hands. "Elizabeth, it sure didn't take you and Perry long to pick those berries. How'd ya get done so fast?"

"Mama helped," Elizabeth replied. "Her wheelchair fits fine between the rows, and she can pick faster'n anybody I know!"

Mom chuckled. "When you've had as many years' practice as me, you'll be plenty fast, too."

Rachel glanced at Anna. She was rolling her piecrust real hard—like she was taking her frustrations out on that clump of sticky dough. Rachel figured this probably wasn't a good time to be asking her sister any questions. Besides the fact that Anna seemed a might testy, Mom and Elizabeth were there. It didn't take a genius to know Anna wouldn't be about to bare her soul in front of them.

Rachel reached for a bag of sugar on the top shelf of the cupboard. She'd have to wait awhile yet. . .until she had Anna all to herself.

The pie baking was finished a little before noon, and Anna, who seemed right anxious to be on her way, asked if she could forgo lunch and head over to Emma's.

"*Jah,* I suppose that'd be okay," Mom said. "I could fix ya a sandwich to eat on the way."

Anna waved her hand. "Don't trouble yourself. I'm sure Emma will have somethin' for me to eat."

Mom nodded but sent Anna off with a basket of fresh fruit and a jug of freshly made iced tea. "For Emma," she stated.

Rachel finished wiping down the table, then excused herself to go outside, hoping her sister hadn't left yet. She saw Anna hitching the horse to the buggy, but just when she was about to call out to her, Dad came running across the yard. "Not so late tonight, Anna!"

Anna climbed into the buggy. "I'll do my best to be back before dark."

Dad stepped aside, and the horse moved forward.

Rachel's heart sank. *Not again! Am I ever gonna get the chance to speak with that sister of mine?* With a sigh of resignation, she turned and headed back to the house. Today was not going one bit as she'd planned!

Chapter 6

Rachel gripped the front porch railing, watching as Anna climbed out of the buggy and began to unhitch the horse. It was almost dark. She could hardly believe Anna would be so brazen as to disobey their parents two nights in a row. *What kind of shenanigan is Anna pullin' now?*

Before Rachel had a chance to say anything to her sister, Dad was at Anna's side, taking the reins from her. "Late again," he grumbled. "You know right well we don't like ya out after dark." He shook his finger in her face. "You'd better have a good excuse for this, Daughter. Somethin' better'n what ya told us last night."

Rachel wanted to holler out, "What did ya tell them last night?" Instead, she just stood there like a statue, waiting to hear Anna's reply.

Anna hung her head. "I—uh—need to have a little heart-to-heart talk with you and Mom."

"Fine. I'll do up the horse, then meet ya inside." Dad walked away, and Anna stepped onto the porch. She drew Rachel into her arms.

"What was that for?" Rachel asked. A feeling of bewilderment, mixed with mounting fear, crept into her soul.

Anna's eyes glistened with tears. "No matter what happens, always remember that I love you."

Rachel's forehead wrinkled. "What's goin' on, Anna? Are you in some kinda trouble?"

Anna's only response was a deep sigh.

"I've been wantin' to talk to you all day—to see why you have been actin' so strange—and to find out how come you were late last night."

Anna drew in a shuddering breath. "Guess you'll learn it soon enough, 'cause I'm about to tell Dad and Mom the truth about where I was then and tonight."

"Weren't ya runnin' errands in Paradise yesterday?"

Anna shook her head.

"And today—did ya spend the day at Emma Troyer's?"

"I went to Lancaster—both times," Anna admitted as she sank into a rocking chair on the front porch. "I know you probably won't understand this, but I'm gonna have to leave the faith."

Rachel's mouth dropped open. "Oh, no. . .that just can't be! How could ya even think of doin' such a thing?"

A pathetic groan escaped Anna's lips and she began to cry.

Rachel knelt in front of the rocker and grasped her sister's trembling hand. "I'm guessin' the folks don't know," she said, hoping this was some kind of a crazy mistake and that as soon as Anna was thinking straight again, she'd make it all right.

"I made up some story about why I was late last night. I said I was with Silas all day, and the reason I wasn't wearin' my apron was because I spilled ice cream down the front of it."

"And the *Kapp?*" Rachel questioned. "How come ya weren't wearin' that last night?"

Anna winced, as though she'd been slapped. "I lied about that, too. Said Silas wanted to see me with my hair down, so I took it off and forgot to put it back on before I headed home."

Rachel's mind was whirling like Mom's gas-powered washing machine running at full speed. First Anna had said she wasn't interested in Silas; then she'd lied and said she was. It made no sense at all. The words she wanted to speak stuck in her throat like a wad of chewing gum.

"You—you—really lied to the folks about all that?" she squeaked.

Anna nodded.

"And they believed you? I mean, you said the other day that you had no interest in Silas."

"I know, but I wanted to throw them off track." Anna swallowed hard. "I've gotta tell them the truth now; there's no other way."

Rachel rubbed her fingers in little circles across the bridge of her nose. This wasn't good. Not good at all. Anna was lying to Mom and Dad and saying *Verhuddelt* things about leaving the Amish faith. How could she be so mixed up? What in the world was happening to their family?

Rachel had every intention of questioning her sister further, but Dad stepped onto the porch. "Let's go into the kitchen, Anna." He pointed at Rachel. "You'd better go on up to bed."

Obediently, Rachel stood up, offering Anna a feeble smile. At this rate, she'd never find out the whole story.

When Rachel entered the kitchen, she discovered her mother working on a quilt. A variety of lush greens lay beside vivid red patches spread out on the table like a jigsaw puzzle.

"Ain't it nice?" Mom asked as she glanced up at Rachel. "This is gonna be for Anna's hope chest, seein' as to how she's got herself an interested suitor and all. Why, did you know that she sneaked off yesterday just to be with Silas Swartley? The little scamp told us she wasn't interested in him, but it seems she's changed her mind."

Before Rachel could comment, Dad and Anna entered the room. "*Gut Nacht,* Rachel," Dad said, nodding toward the hallway door.

"*Gut Nacht,*" Rachel mumbled as she exited the room, only closing the door partway. She stopped on the stairwell, out of sight from those in the kitchen. She knew it was wrong to eavesdrop, but she simply couldn't go to bed until she found out what was going on.

"Anna, you said ya had somethin' to say," Dad's voice boomed from the kitchen. "Seems as though ya oughta start by explainin' why you're so late."

"She was probably with Silas again," Mom interjected. "Anna, we don't have a problem with him courtin' you, but we just can't have ya out after dark. It's much too dangerous."

Rachel knew Anna was taking the time to think before she spoke because there was a long pause. Suddenly, her sister blurted, "I lied about me and Silas. He's not courtin' me, and I'm leavin' the faith!"

Rachel peered through the crack in the doorway and saw Mom's face blanch.

"You're what?" Dad hollered.

"I—I got married today," Anna stammered.

"You were supposed to be at Emma's," Mom said as though the word *married* had never been mentioned.

"What are you talkin' about, Girl?" Dad sputtered.

"Me and Reuben Yutzy got married today by a justice of the peace in Lancaster," Anna announced, her voice sounding stronger by the minute. "We've been seein' each other secretly for some time now, and yesterday we went to get our marriage license."

Rachel's hand flew to her mouth as she stifled a gasp.

"What would cause you to do such a thing?" Dad bellowed. His back was to Rachel, and she could only imagine how red his face must be.

"If it's Reuben ya love and wanted to marry, why'd ya hide it?" Mom questioned. "Why didn't ya speak with the bishop and have him announce in church that ya wanted to be published? We could have had the weddin' this fall, and—"

"Reuben and I are leavin' the Amish faith," Anna interrupted.

"You can't be serious about this!" Dad hollered.

"Daniel, you'll wake the whole house," Mom said, sounding close to tears. "Can't we discuss this in a quiet manner?"

Dad cleared his throat and shuffled his feet a few times, the way he always did when he was trying to get himself calmed down. A chair scraped across the kitchen floor. "Sit down, Daughter, and explain this rebellious act of yours."

Rachel stood there, twisting the corners of her apron, too afraid to even breathe. Nothing like this had ever happened in the Beachy home, and she couldn't imagine how it would all turn out.

"Reuben and I have been in love for some time, but we both feel as though the Amish rules ain't right for us no more. We didn't want anyone to know our plans, so I pretended I was seein' Silas yesterday."

Rachel leaned against the wall, feeling as if her whole world was caving in. How could she have been so blind? Anna had been telling her that she didn't love Silas, yet she'd been leading the poor fellow on. She'd been acting secretive and kind of pensive lately, too.

"As you probably know, Reuben's got himself a job workin' for a paint contractor in Lancaster," Anna continued. "That's where we plan to live. I just came home tonight to explain things and gather up my belongings. Reuben's comin' to get me tomorrow mornin'."

"I won't hear this kind of talk in my house!" There was a thud, and Rachel was pretty sure her father's hand had connected with the kitchen table.

"Oh, Daniel, now look what you've gone and done," Mom said tearfully. "All my squares are *Verhuddelt.*"

"Our daughter's just announced that she's gotten married today and plans to leave the faith, and all you can think about is your mixed-up quiltin' squares? What's wrong with you, *Frau?*"

"But. . .but. . .Anna was raised in the Amish faith," Mom blubbered. "She knows we don't hold to bein' one with the world."

Rachel chanced another peek, just to see how things were looking. Dad was pacing back and forth across the faded linoleum. Mom was gathering up her quilting pieces. Anna was just sitting there with her arms folded across her chest.

"I know ya don't understand, but I've not been happy with our way of life for some time now," Anna asserted.

Dad slapped his hands together, and Rachel jumped back behind the door. "I'll not have ya talkin' thataway! You're our firstborn child, Anna, and it's gonna break your *mamm's* heart if ya run off and leave your faith behind."

"It's not *my* faith I'd be leavin'," Anna said, sounding even more sure of herself. "I'd be turning from my Amish upbringing because it's not somethin' I believe in anymore."

"You were baptized into the church," Mom said softly.

"I know," Anna replied, "but I've come to think the reason I've been feelin' so discontent is because I'm not meant to be one of you. Reuben feels the self-same way."

"Maybe I should have a little talk with Reuben Yutzy," Dad threatened. "Might could be that he'll come to his senses once I set him straight on a few things."

"You'd have to give up your way of dress if ya left," Mom put in. "You'd be expected to become part of the world. Surely ya must realize the seriousness of all this."

Dad's fist pounded the table again. "You can't do this, Anna. I forbid it!"

Rachel shuddered. Whenever their father forbade anyone in the family to do anything, that was the end of it, plain and simple. No arguments. No discussion. Nothing. The Beachy children had been taught to believe in the Scripture, "Children, obey your parents." Rachel knew that to do anything less meant a sound *bletching* when they were *kinder* and a harsh tongue-lashing, confinement to one's room, or a double dose of chores when they were older. Surely Anna would come to her senses and do what was right.

A muffled sob, followed by, "I'm sorry, Dad, but my mind's made up," told Rachel all she needed to know. Her oldest sister was about to be shunned!

❧

Morning came much too quickly as far as Rachel was concerned. She awoke feeling like she hadn't slept at all. Part of her heart went out to her sister, for she seemed so sincere in her proclamation about loving Reuben and wanting to leave the Amish faith. Another part of Rachel felt sorry for poor, lovesick Silas. What was he going to say when he got wind of this terrible news? He'd been friends with Anna a long time and had brought her home from a singing not long ago. He must believe he had a chance with her.

And what about the greenhouse? Who would help Mom and Dad with that? Anna had been working there for several years, and the folks sure weren't getting any younger. Eventually they'd need someone to take it over completely.

Rachel slipped out of her nightgown and into a dress, feeling like the weight of the world was resting on her shoulders. She'd be the one asked to fill in for Anna at the greenhouse; she was sure of it. Joseph liked flowers well enough, but he was busy working the fields, and Dad often helped out in the fields—especially during harvest season. If Rachel were forced into the confines of the stuffy, humid greenhouse, she'd hardly have any time for watching birds, hiking, or fishing. She knew it was selfish, but she was more than a little miffed at Anna for sticking her with this added responsibility.

A sudden ray of hope ignited in Rachel's heart. *With Anna leavin', Silas might begin to take notice that I'm alive.* She poured water from the pitcher on her dresser into the washing bowl and smiled. *Guess I could even tolerate workin' with flowers all day if I had a chance at love with Silas.*

Rachel splashed some water on her face, hoping the stinging cold might get her thinking straight. As the cool liquid made contact, she allowed her anxiety to fully surface. Silas wasn't going to turn to her just because Anna was no longer available. Besides, even if by some miracle he did, Rachel would be his second choice. She'd be like yesterday's warmed-over stew.

Her shoulders drooped with anguish and a feeling of hopelessness. She wasn't sure she wanted Silas's love if it had to be that way. But then, she *was* a beggar, and beggars couldn't be choosy.

Rachel hung her nightgown on a wall peg and put her head covering in place. She looked ready enough to face the day, but in her heart she sure wasn't. She hated the thought of going downstairs. After Dad had yelled some more last night, then sent Anna to her room to think things over and pray on it, Rachel had a pretty good notion what things would be like with the start of this new day.

A sudden knock pulled Rachel out of her troubling thoughts. "Rachel, are ya up?" Anna called through the closed door.

"Jah. Just gettin' dressed. Tell Mom I'll be right down to help with breakfast."

"Could I come in? I need to talk."

"Sure, you're more'n welcome."

When Anna opened the door, Rachel could see that she'd been crying. Probably most of the night, truth be told. She also noticed that her sister's hope chest was at her feet.

Anna bent down and pushed the cumbersome trunk into Rachel's room. "I can't stay long," she said in a quavery voice. "I'll be leavin' soon, but I wanted you to have this."

Rachel's heart slammed into her chest. She'd really hoped that after a good night's sleep her stubborn sister might have changed her mind about leaving home. Of course, as far as Anna knew, Rachel hadn't heard what she'd told the folks last night.

"You're leavin'? Where are ya goin'?" Rachel asked, making no mention of the hope chest Anna had slid to the end of her bed.

"Last night after ya went upstairs, I told Mom and Dad that I've been secretly seein' Reuben Yutzy." Anna took a seat on the edge of Rachel's bed. "We got married yesterday," she murmured. "Reuben went home to tell his folks, and I came here to tell ours. Last night was the final time for me to sleep in my old room because this mornin' Reuben's comin' for me, and we're leavin' the faith."

Rachel sucked in her breath and flopped down beside her sister. "Leavin' the faith? But where will you go?"

"We'll be livin' in an apartment in Lancaster."

"What'd the folks say about all this, Anna?"

"They're upset, of course. Last night Dad even forbade me to go. Said I had to go up to my room to think and pray on the matter." Anna sniffed. "Guess maybe he hoped I'd see things in a different light come mornin'."

"And do ya?"

Anna shook her head and reached over to pat Rachel's arm. "No, Silly. I love Reuben, and my place is with him."

"What about your hope chest?" Rachel's voice dropped to a near whisper. "Won'tcha be needin' all your things now that you're married and about to set up housekeepin'?"

Anna shook her head. "The apartment Reuben rented is fully furnished. Besides, the things in that chest would only be painful reminders of my past." She nodded at Rachel. "Better that you have 'em."

Rachel was sorely tempted to tell her sister there wasn't much point in her having one hope chest, much less two, since she would probably never marry. She thought better of it, though, because she could see from the look on Anna's face that saying good-bye was hurting her real bad.

"If you renounce your faith, you and Reuben will be shunned. . .probably excommunicated. You've both been baptized into membership, Anna. Have ya forgotten that?"

Anna blew out her breath. "Of course I haven't forgotten. Leavin' home and family is the sacrifice we're gonna have to make. There ain't no other way."

Rachel jumped up. "Yes, there is! You can forget all this nonsense 'bout becomin' an Englisher. You can stay right here and marry Reuben again, in the Amish church." Strangely enough, Rachel found herself wishing Anna had accepted Silas's offer to court her. With him, at least, she knew Anna would be staying in the faith.

What am I thinkin'? Rachel fretted. *Here I am, so in love with Silas that my heart could burst, and I'm wishin' my sister could be makin' plans to marry him. Maybe I am silly, after all.*

Rachel looked at Anna, and her eyes filled with tears. "What about Silas? You rode home with him in his courtin' buggy from a singin' not long ago. Didn't that mean anything a'tall?"

"I didn't mean to lead Silas on," Anna said sincerely. "I love Reuben, and that's all that matters."

Rachel clenched her fists. It wasn't all that mattered! What about Silas's feelings, and what about their family? Didn't Anna care that her leaving would tear the family apart? How could she be so unfeeling?

"Even if I weren't plannin' to leave, I wouldn't have married Silas," Anna continued. "I don't love him. I never have."

Rachel planted her hands on her hips and looked into Anna's darkened eyes. What had happened to her pleasant childhood playmate? "Silas is a wonderful man, and he loves you. Don't that count for anything?" she shouted.

Anna frowned. "I'm sorry for Silas, but I've gotta go with my heart." She closed her eyes and drew in a deep breath. "What do *you* want out of life, Rachel?"

Rachel swallowed hard. "That's easy. I want love. . .marriage. . .and lots of *kinder.*"

"Since you're so worried over Silas, why don'tcha try to make him happy? I know ya care for him, so go after Silas. Might could be that the two of you will marry, and he'll give you a whole houseful of *kinder.*"

Rachel hung her head. "I can't make Silas happy. He don't love me."

Chapter 7

Not one word was said during breakfast about Anna's plans to leave. It was almost as if nothing had even gone on last night. Rachel figured her folks were hoping Anna's thinking would have righted itself during the night, and this morning life would be just as it always had been in the Beachys' home.

When breakfast was over, Dad went outside. Rachel was at the sink doing dishes, and when she glanced out the window, she saw him hitch up the buggy and head down the road. She thought it was odd that he hadn't even said where he was going.

A short time later, Dad returned with Bishop Weaver. Rachel and Elizabeth were out in the garden when she saw the two men climb out of their buggies.

Rachel straightened and pressed a hand against her lower back to ease some of the kinks. The bishop nodded at her. "Where's your sister Anna? I hear tell she's given this family some rather distressin' news."

Before Rachel could reply, Anna came out of the house lugging an old suitcase down the steps.

Bishop Weaver marched over to her and shook his finger right in her face. "I understand you're thinkin' of leavin' the Amish faith."

Rachel dropped the beet she'd just dug up and held her breath. She feared the worst was coming, and there was nothing she could do about it.

"I'm afraid you're a bit confused, Anna," Bishop Weaver said. "Your folks have raised you well—of that much I'm sure."

"Mom and Dad had nothin' to do with my decision to marry Reuben and leave home," Anna said quickly. "It was my own choice to do so."

The bishop's face flamed, and Rachel felt a sudden need to stand up for her sister. She took a deep breath and walked right over to where they were standing. "I'm sure Anna must have a powerful *gut* reason for wantin' to become English," she boldly proclaimed.

Dad, who'd been standing quietly next to the bishop, finally spoke up. "Rachel Beachy, you had your chance to talk Anna into courtin' Silas, and ya didn't succeed. So, this matter is none of your business!"

Rachel blinked. She guessed it had been a mistake to say anything on Anna's behalf.

"I don't like disappointin' my family," Anna put in, "but I'm a married woman now, and I've gotta be with my husband."

The bishop crossed his arms. "And you're both plannin' to leave the faith?"

Anna nodded.

"Is that your final answer?"

"It has to be."

Bishop Weaver turned toward Dad. "I'm sorry, Daniel. Guess there's nothin' more to be said, unless Anna and Reuben change their minds." With that, he marched back to his buggy.

Anna looked up at her father with tears in her eyes. "Sorry, but I won't be changin' my mind, and I don't think Reuben will neither."

Dad said nothing in return. He stared at Anna a few seconds, like he was looking right through her; then he stalked off.

Rachel didn't know what she could say, either. She felt sick at heart over the way things were going. If Anna left the faith, nothing would ever be the same at home.

A few minutes later, Reuben pulled up in a fancy, red truck. Anna climbed into the passenger's seat, and without even a wave, they were gone.

Rachel felt like breaking down and sobbing, but she didn't. Instead, she got busy and finished up in the garden, then spent the rest of the day helping Mom and Elizabeth can several jars of pickled beets. It kept her hands busy enough, but her mind kept going over the sorrowful events of the last twenty-four hours. Rachel couldn't believe her big sister had actually moved out of the house.

⚜

Rachel tossed and turned in her bed that night. Knowing Anna wasn't in her room across the hall left a huge empty spot in Rachel's heart. Even though she was five years younger than her older sister, Rachel and Anna had always been close. They had played together when they were small and worked side by side as they grew up. Until recently, they'd shared secrets and similar hopes for their future. Rachel had known Anna was becoming dissatisfied with the Amish way of life, but she hadn't realized how far things had gone. It amazed her that Anna had been able to keep such a secret and not have any of the family suspect anything.

Rachel closed her eyes and tried to picture Anna married to Reuben Yutzy, making their home in Lancaster, wearing English clothes, and living the fancy, modern life. It was all too much to comprehend.

"Does Silas know?" Rachel whispered into the night. *Surely his heart will be broken over this. He's not only lost Anna to the modern world, but to his best friend.* Thinking about Silas helped Rachel feel a little less sorry for herself. She would have to remember to pray for him often.

Ping! Ping! Rachel rolled over in bed. What was that strange noise? *Ping! Ping!* There it was again. She sat up and swung her legs over the side of the bed. It sounded like something was being thrown against her bedroom window.

She hurried across the room and lifted the window's dark shade. In the glow of the moonlight she could see someone standing on the ground below. It was a man, and he was tossing pebbles at her window!

"Who'd be wantin' to get my attention at this time of night?" Rachel muttered as she grabbed her robe off the end of the bed.

Quietly, so she wouldn't wake any of the family, Rachel tiptoed barefoot down the stairs. When she reached the back door, she opened it cautiously and peered out. She could see Silas Swartley, bathed in the moonlight, standing on the grass.

Rachel slipped out the door and ran across the lawn. "Silas, what are ya doin' out here in the dark, throwin' pebbles at my window?"

Silas whirled around to face her. "Rachel?"

She nodded. *Jah*, it's me. What's up, anyhow?"

Silas shifted his long legs. "I—uh—thought it was Anna's window I was throwin' stones at. I've been wantin' to speak with her but never seem to get the chance."

Rachel's heartbeat quickened. So Silas didn't know. He couldn't have heard the news yet, or else he would have realized Anna wasn't here. She took a few steps closer and impulsively reached out to touch his arm. "Anna's not in her room, Silas."

"She's not? Where is she then?"

Rachel knew her lower lip quivered, but she seemed powerless to stop it. She pressed her lips tightly together, trying to compose herself. This was going to be a lot harder than she'd thought. "I hate to be the one tellin' ya this," she began slowly, "but Anna ran off and got married last night. She left home this mornin'."

Silas's mouth dropped open like a window with a broken hinge. "Married? Left home?" He stared off into space as though he were in a daze, and Rachel's heart went out to him. She had to tell Silas the rest. He had the right to know. Besides, if he didn't hear it from her, he was bound to find out sooner or later. News like this traveled fast, especially when an Amish church member left the faith to become English.

"Anna married Reuben Yutzy. They're leavin' the church, and—"

"Reuben? My *gut* friend?"

Rachel nodded. The motion was all she could manage, given the circumstances. Even in the darkness she could see the pained expression on Silas's face.

"This can't be. It just can't be," he muttered.

Rachel swallowed against the lump in her throat. If only she could take away his pain. If she could just think of a way to make her sister come home. *But what good would that do? Anna's already married to Reuben and nothin' is gonna change that fact.*

Silas began to pace. "I knew Reuben was dissatisfied with our way of life. I also knew he was hangin' around some English fellows who were leadin' him astray." He stopped, turned, and slowly shook his head. "I just had no idea Anna was in on it."

Rachel felt herself tremble. She didn't know if her shivering was from the cool grass tickling her bare feet or if it stemmed from the anger she felt rising in her soul. There was only one thing she was certain of—Silas was trying to lay part of the blame on her sister's shoulders.

"Listen here," she said with a tremor in her voice, "Anna wasn't *in* on this. She became *part* of it because she loves Reuben and wanted to be with him."

"Did she tell you that?"

"Not in so many words, but she did say she and Reuben have been secretly seein' each other and that they're in love."

Silas snorted. "She probably influenced him to make the break. Anna always has been a bit of a rebel."

Rachel's heart was thumping so hard she feared it might burst. How dare Silas speak of her sister that way! She gasped for breath, grateful for the cool night air to help clear her head. "Anna might have a mind of her own," she snapped, "but she's not the kind of person who would try to sway someone else to leave the church. I have a pretty good notion Reuben wanted to go English as much as Anna did. Maybe even more."

❧

Silas drew in a deep breath, trying to get control of his emotions. It seemed like his whole world was falling apart, but he knew he had no right to blame Anna for everything. He'd just talked to Reuben a few days ago, and his friend had made it clear that he wanted many of the things the world had to offer. He was working for an English man, was running around with the English doing all sorts of worldly things, and Reuben had even told Silas he wasn't happy being Amish anymore. Truth be told, Silas had been expecting Reuben to leave the faith. What he hadn't expected was that Anna Beachy would be leaving, too—especially not as Reuben Yutzy's wife!

"If I could make things different, I would," Rachel said, breaking into Silas's troubling thoughts. He looked down at her and noticed that her chin was quivering. For one brief moment, Silas was tempted to take Rachel into his arms and offer comforting words. Trouble was, he had no words of comfort. . .for Rachel or himself. All he was feeling was anger and betrayal. His best friend had taken his girl, and Anna had led him on all these years. How could he ever come to grips with that knowledge?

Silas dipped his head in apology. "Sorry for snappin' at ya, Rachel. I know none of this is your fault. It's just such a shock to find out you've lost not one, but two special friends in the same day." He sniffed. "This had to be goin' on between Reuben and Anna for some time, and I was too blind to see it. What a dunce I've been, thinkin' Anna and I had a future together. Why, I chased after her like a horse runnin' toward a bucket of fresh oats, even though she kept pushin' me away. She must have thought I was *Ab im Kopp.*"

Rachel grabbed his arm and gave it a good shake. "Stop talkin' thataway! You're not off in the head for lovin' someone. Reuben had you fooled, and Anna had our whole family fooled." She shook her head. "No one's to blame but Anna and Reuben. They should've been honest with everyone involved. They shouldn't have waited so long to tell us their plans."

Silas nodded. "You're right, Rachel. They deserve to be shunned."

Rachel grimaced. "That's the part I dislike the most. It's hard enough to have Anna leave home, knowin' she'll be livin' as one with the world. To realize we have to shun our own kin is the worst part of all."

Silas blew out his breath. "*Jah*, but we have no other choice. It's the old way of doin' things, and it will most likely always be so." He took a few steps backward. "Guess I should be gettin' on home. My mission here is over. As much as it pains me to say it, Anna's outta my life for good."

Rachel rubbed her hands briskly over her arms, like she might be getting cold, and for the second time tonight, Silas was tempted to embrace her. He caught himself in time, remembering Anna's words the other day when she'd said she thought Rachel might be interested in him. If he hugged her, even in condolence, she might get the wrong idea. No, it would be better if he didn't say or do anything to lead young Rachel on. Things were messed up enough. No sense making one more mistake.

"See ya at the next preachin'," Silas said before he turned and sprinted up the driveway, where his horse and buggy stood waiting. Rachel Beachy would have to find comfort from her family, and he would find solace through his work on the farm.

Chapter 8

It was the first day of August, and an unreal stillness hung in the hot, sticky air. It was like an oven inside the house, so Rachel wandered outside after lunch, hoping to find a cool breeze. She found, instead, her younger brother and sister, engaged in an all-out water skirmish.

Squeals of laughter permeated the air as the twins ran back and forth to the water trough, filling their buckets and flinging water on one another until they were both drenched from head to toe.

Rachel chuckled at their antics and stepped off the porch, thinking she might join them. The flash of a colorful wing caught her attention instead. Her gaze followed the flitting bird to a nearby willow tree. Like a magnet, she followed the goldfinch as it sailed from tree to tree, finally stopping at one of the feeders in the flower garden. When it had eaten its fill, it flew over to the birdbath. Dipping its tiny black head up and down, the finch drank of the fresh water Rachel had put there early that morning.

Rachel loved watching the birds that came into their yard. Loved hearing their melodic songs. Loved everything about nature.

Per-chick-o-ree, the finch called.

"Per-chick-o-ree," Rachel echoed.

She watched until the bird flew out of sight; then she moved across the yard toward the clothesline. In this heat, she knew the clothes she'd washed and hung this morning would definitely be dry.

Rachel heard a small voice, and she looked down. Apparently Elizabeth had given up her water battle with Perry, for she was crouched next to the basket of clothes. Her usually pinned-up braids hung down the back of her sopping wet dress like two limp rags. "Dad says Anna will come to her senses and return home again. What do you think, Rachel?" the child asked.

Rachel knelt next to her sister and wrapped her arms around the little girl's small shoulders. "We're all hopin' Anna will return to us, but it might never happen."

"How come?"

"Anna has it in her mind that she wants to live as the English do. I hear tell she's workin' as a waitress at a restaurant in Lancaster. She and Reuben are married now, and they've settled into an apartment there."

"Why can't they live here with us?" Elizabeth asked, her blue eyes looking ever so serious.

Rachel drew in a deep breath. How was she going to explain something to her little sister that she didn't understand herself? "Well," she began, "Reuben and

Anna don't think our ways are so good anymore."

"Why not?"

"It's like this—"

"Rachel Beachy, what do ya think you're doin', fillin' Elizabeth's head with such talk?" Dad's deep voice cut through the air like a knife, cutting Rachel off in midsentence. He grabbed Elizabeth's arm and pulled her to her feet. "Get on up to the house and change outta those wet clothes. Your *mamm's* been lookin' for ya, and I'm sure she's got somethin' useful you can be doin'."

As soon as Elizabeth was gone, Dad turned to face Rachel. "You oughta be ashamed, talkin' to Elizabeth like that. She's young and don't understand things of the world just yet. She might think what Anna's done is perfectly okay."

"Elizabeth meant no harm in askin', and I didn't think it would hurt to try to explain things a bit." Rachel's eyes filled with unwanted tears, and she bit her lip, hoping to keep them at bay. Things were bad enough around here; she sure didn't want any hard feelings between her and Dad.

"*Jah,* well, be careful what you say from now on," Dad said, his voice softening some. "We've lost one daughter to the world, and I sure don't want any of my other *kinder* gettin' such crazy thoughts." He turned toward the greenhouse, calling over his shoulder, "When you're done with the laundry, I could use your help. We're likely to have lots more customers today!"

Rachel grabbed another towel from the wicker basket and gave it a good snap. "*Immer Druwel ergitz*—always trouble somewhere," she mumbled.

It was another warm day, and Rachel, accompanied by Elizabeth, had gone into town to buy some things their mother was needing. Since Dad paid Rachel a little something for working in the greenhouse, she bought a few new things for her hope chest—just in case.

"How 'bout some lunch?" Rachel asked her sister when they finished shopping. "Are ya hungry?"

Elizabeth giggled and scrambled quickly into the buggy. "You know me, Rachel. . .I'm always hungry."

"Where would ya like to go?" Rachel asked, tucking her packages behind the seat, then taking up the reins.

"I don't care. Why don't you choose?"

Rachel nodded and steered the horse in the direction of the Good 'n Plenty, a family style restaurant located on the other side of town.

The restaurant was crowded with summer tourists, and the girls had to wait to be seated. Elizabeth needed to use the rest room, so Rachel waited for her in the hallway outside the door. A man walked by wearing a baseball cap with an inscription on the front that read "Born to Fish. Forced to Work!"

Yep, that's me, Rachel thought ruefully. *I'd love to go fishin' every day and never have to work in the greenhouse again.*

As the fisherman disappeared, Rachel caught a glimpse of an Amish man coming from the kitchen, but she thought nothing of it until she got a good look at him. It was Silas Swartley, and he was heading her way.

"It's good to see you, Rachel. How are things?"

Rachel swiped her tongue across her parched lips. Except for biweekly preaching services, she hadn't seen much of Silas since that night he'd come to the house looking for Anna. The fact that she'd been the one to give him the shocking news about her sister running off with his best friend still stuck in Rachel's craw. It should have been Reuben or Anna doing the telling. But no, they left without thinking of anyone but themselves. Seeing Silas standing here now, looking so handsome, yet unapproachable, gave Rachel a funny feeling way down deep inside.

Silas was holding a wooden crate in his hands. "Well, has the cat got your tongue, or are ya gonna answer my question?" he teased.

"W—what question was that?"

"I asked how things are."

"About the same as usual, I guess," she replied with a slight nod. "How's it at your place?"

"Everything's about the same with us, too," he said with a silly grin. "I brought in a crate of fresh potatoes from our farm. This restaurant buys a lot of produce from us." Silas tipped his head toward Rachel. "How come you're here?"

"Elizabeth and I came to town for a few things. We're here for lunch." She suppressed a giggle. "Why else would we be at the Good 'n Plenty?"

Silas's tanned face turned red like a cherry tomato, and he stared down at his black work boots. "I don't suppose you've heard anything from Anna."

Rachel swallowed against the nodule that had lodged in her throat. Of course Silas would ask about Anna. He was still in love with her. Truth be told, Silas was probably hoping Anna would give up her silly notion about being English and come back to the valley again. But then, even if she did, what good would that do him? Anna was a married woman now—out-of-bounds for Silas Swartley.

"Anna's made no direct contact with us," Rachel said flatly. "She did send Martha Rose a letter, though."

Silas looked a bit hopeful. "What'd it say?"

"Just that she and Reuben are settled now. She got herself a job as a waitress, and Reuben's still paintin' houses and all." Rachel's nose twitched. "Guess they've gotta have lots of money, since they're livin' in the modern world and will probably be buyin' all sorts of fancy gadgets."

Silas's dark eyebrows furrowed. "*Jah*, I reckon so. Sure wish Anna would've waited awhile to marry Reuben and not run off like that. Maybe if she'd given it more thought and given me more time, I coulda won her heart."

Rachel shrugged. "She's gone now, and I'm pretty sure she's never comin' back."

Silas squinted his dark eyes. "How do ya know that?"

"I just do, that's all. My sister's walkin' a different path now, and she made it real clear that it was her choice."

Silas shook his head. "I've known Anna since we were *kinder*, and I always thought we were *gut* friends. It's awful hard to accept the idea that there's no future for me and her."

Rachel's heart ached for Silas, but more than that, it ached for herself. She was sure he would always love Anna, even if they couldn't be together. So much for hoping he might ever be interested in plain little Rachel. Hopeless, useless daydreams would get her nowhere, yet no matter how hard she tried to push it aside, the dream remained. "The future rests in God's hands," she mumbled, turning away.

Silas left the Good 'n Plenty feeling like someone had punched him in the stomach. Anna wasn't coming home. Rachel had confirmed his worst fears. Old memories tugged at his heart. He'd trusted Anna, and she had betrayed that trust. Could he ever trust another woman? *Even if she does change her mind and come back, she'll never be mine. She's a married woman now. . .married to my best friend!*

Deep in his heart, Silas knew he had to accept things as they were and get on with life, but no matter how hard he tried, he just couldn't imagine any kind of life without Anna Beachy.

Poor Rachel—she looked so sad. Anna's leavin' must have hurt her nearly as much as it did me. He would have to remember to pray for her and all the Beachys. No Amish family ever really got over one of their own running off to become English, and from the look on Rachel's face, he figured she had a long ways to go in overcoming her grief.

"Was that Silas Swartley you were talkin' to?" Elizabeth asked when she stepped out of the ladies' room.

Rachel nodded. "It was him."

Elizabeth looked up at her expectantly, like she thought Rachel should say something more.

Rachel merely shrugged. "He was askin' about Anna."

"He was real sweet on her, ain't it so?"

"Jah, he was. I'm afraid he is very much broken up over her leavin'."

Elizabeth grabbed Rachel's hand and gave it a squeeze. "Anna's never comin' back, is she?"

"Probably not, unless it's just for a visit."

"Could we go to Lancaster sometime? I'd surely like to see my big sister again."

"That wouldn't be a *gut* idea," Rachel said, pulling her sister along as they made their way down the hall.

"Why not?" the child persisted. "I miss Anna a lot."

Rachel felt sick at heart because she missed her older sister, too. How could she explain it to Elizabeth when she couldn't make sense of it herself? If they went to Lancaster to see Anna, Dad would be furious. Not only that, but Elizabeth might like the modern way Anna was living and decide to seek after worldly things herself. No, it would be better for all if they never paid a visit to Anna.

"Your table is ready now," a young Mennonite waitress said as they approached the dining room.

Rachel smiled, glad for the diversion. Maybe after they were seated, Elizabeth's mind would be on her empty stomach and not on Anna. Might could be that the discussion would be dropped altogether and they could eat a quiet, peaceful lunch.

Much to Rachel's chagrin, no sooner had they placed their orders, when the questions began again.

"Are Mom and Dad mad at Anna?" Elizabeth blinked several times. "They never talk about her anymore."

Rachel drew in a deep breath and offered up a silent prayer. She needed God's wisdom just now, for sure as anything she didn't want to make things worse by telling her sensitive, young sister something that might upset her even more. "It's like this," she began, carefully choosing her words, "Mom and Dad love Anna very much, but they also love bein' Amish. They believe in the *Ordnung* and want to abide by the rules of our church."

Elizabeth nodded soberly. "I've tried talkin' about Anna several times, but Dad always says it would be best if I'd just forget I ever had an older sister. How can I do that, Rachel? Anna's still my big sister, ain't it so?"

Rachel reached across the table and gently touched Elizabeth's small hand. "Of course she's your sister. Nothin' will ever change that." She sighed deeply. "The thing is, Anna's moved away now, and she's wantin' to live like the English."

Elizabeth's lower lip trembled. "She really don't wanna be Amish no more?"

"I'm afraid not. But we can surely pray that someday she and Reuben will change their minds and be willin' to reconcile with the church through repenting and confession before the bishop and the congregation." Rachel was grateful that their district's rules for shunning weren't as strict as some, where absolutely all contact with banned church members was forbidden. Bishop Weaver had made it clear that, as outcasts, Reuben and Anna should be avoided, although limited contact with them would be allowed. But he was firm in stating that church members were not to do any business with them or eat at the same table with them unless they repented and returned to the faith.

Rachel felt hot tears stinging the backs of her eyes. Today had started off well enough, but after seeing Silas and talking about Anna with him and now trying to make Elizabeth understand, she felt all done in. She had no answers. Not for Silas, not for Elizabeth, and not for herself. As far as Rachel was concerned, life would never be the same. She lifted her water glass and took a sip. If only there was some way she could get Silas to notice her now that Anna was out of his life. If only God would make Silas love her and not Anna.

As she set the glass back down, a little voice in Rachel's head reminded her that God never forced a person to love anyone—not even Him. If Silas was ever going to get over losing Anna, it would have to be because *he* chose to do so.

I can still hope, Rachel mused. *The Bible says in Psalm 71:14, "But I will hope continually, and will yet praise thee more and more."*

Chapter 9

The Beachys were all sitting on the front porch because it was still too hot inside to go to bed. Mom was in her wheelchair, mending one of Joseph's shirts. Dad sat beside her in the rocker, reading the Amish newspaper called the *Budget*. Joseph and Perry were sitting on the steps, playing a game, and Rachel shared the porch swing with Elizabeth. It was a quiet, peaceful night, in spite of the sweltering August heat.

Rachel mechanically pumped her legs as she gazed out at the fireflies rising from the grass. An owl hooted from a nearby tree, and the sun dipped slowly below the horizon, transforming the sky into a hazy pink. If not for the fact that she still missed Anna so much and had been forced to take her place in the greenhouse several hours a day, Rachel would have felt a sense of contentment as she soaked up the aura of beauty God's hand had provided.

Of course, I've lost Silas, too. Ever since Anna and Reuben had left, Rachel sensed that Silas was mourning his loss. She'd seen him at preaching services several times, and no matter how hard she tried to be friendly, he remained aloof. *Maybe I should give up the hope of him ever seein' me as a woman he could love.* "It's all just a silly dream," she murmured.

"What'd ya say?" Elizabeth asked, nudging Rachel with her elbow.

Rachel felt her face flush. "Nothin'. I was just thinkin' out loud."

"Daydreamin' is probably more like it," Joseph said with a chuckle. "I've never known anyone who could stare off into space the way you do and see nothin' a'tall. A daydreamin' little tomboy, that's our Rachel."

Rachel grimaced. Was Joseph looking for an argument tonight? Maybe he'd had a rough day out in the fields. Could be that Perry had been goofing around and didn't help much. Or the hot weather might be making her big brother a bit cross.

"If ya ever plan on any man marryin' you, then you'd better turn in your fishin' pole for a broom," Joseph continued. "A grown woman ain't supposed to climb trees, wade in the river, and stand around for hours gawkin' at dumb birds."

Rachel folded her arms across her chest and squinted at Joseph. "I refuse to let you ruffle my feathers."

He snickered. "Aw, I wasn't tryin' to upset ya. I was just funnin', that's all."

Rachel shrugged. "I thought maybe you were *gridlich* 'cause ya had a rough day."

"I think we're all a bit cranky," Dad spoke up. "A few more swelterin' days like this, and everything in the garden will dry up, like as not."

Mom nodded. *"Jah,* I've had to water things in the greenhouse a lot more'n usual, too."

"Everyone has their share of troubles," Perry added. "Did ya hear 'bout Katie Swartley breakin' her arm?"

Rachel's ears perked right up. "Silas's *mamm?*"

Perry nodded. "Yep, I heard it from her son Sam this mornin' when we went fishin' in the pond near Swartleys' place."

"When did this happen?" Mom questioned. "And how?"

"Sometime yesterday," Perry answered. "Sam said she fell down the stairs."

Mom clicked her tongue. *"Ach,* poor Katie. How's she gonna manage with only one good arm?"

"Guess her boys will have to chip in and help out more," Dad commented. "It's a downright shame she don't have no girls."

"I could give her a hand," Rachel volunteered, trying to keep her excitement out of her voice. She did feel bad about Katie's arm, but if she could go over there every day, it would give her a chance to see Silas.

"That's a nice thought, Rachel," Dad said, "but you're needed here, especially in the greenhouse. August is a busy time, what with so many tourists comin' by and all. I'm helpin' Joseph and Perry in the fields part of each day, and we sure can't expect your *mamm* to handle things in the greenhouse all by herself."

"How 'bout me?" Elizabeth chimed in. "I like flowers. Can't I help in the greenhouse?"

Mom looked over at Elizabeth and smiled. "I appreciate the offer, but I need someone at the house to get the noon meal fixed."

Joseph turned to face his mother. "Say, I've got an idea."

"And what might that be?" she asked.

"Why don't ya ask Pauline Hostetler to help out with the greenhouse? I know for a fact that she loves flowers."

"And how would ya be knowin' that?" Dad asked, giving Joseph a quick wink.

His face turned beet red and he started squirming a bit.

"Joseph's sweet on Pauline," Perry interjected. "I seen him talkin' to her at the last preachin' service."

Rachel couldn't believe her bashful brother had finally taken the initiative with Pauline. She thought this bit of news might be beneficial to her as well. She jumped off the swing and raced over to her mother's wheelchair. "I really would like to help out at the Swartleys'," she said sincerely. "If Pauline agrees to work at the greenhouse, I'd even be willin' to pay her with some of the money I've already made this summer."

Mom's brows drew together. "Now why would ya do somethin' like that? It's your *daed* and I who should be payin' any hired help, not you, for goodness' sake."

Rachel giggled nervously. If she weren't careful, she'd be giving away her plans to win Silas. "I—I just thought, since you'd have to pay someone to take my place, I'd be obliged to help with their wages."

Mom smiled. "That's very generous of you, Daughter, but it surely won't be necessary."

"I can help Katie Swartley?"

"If it's okay with your *daed*, then it's fine by me," Mom said with a nod.

"Won't bother me none, as long as Pauline agrees to the terms," Dad stated. He looked over at Joseph, who seemed to be studying the checkerboard real hard. "Son, since this was your idea, how 'bout you drivin' over to the Hostetlers' place tomorrow mornin' and askin' Pauline if she'd like to work in the greenhouse for a few weeks?"

Joseph smiled from ear to ear. "Sure, I can do that."

Rachel smiled, too. If things went well, by tomorrow afternoon she might be on her way to winning Silas Swartley's heart.

Silas and his younger brothers, Jake, age seventeen, and Sam, who was twelve, had just returned from the fields. Silas spotted a horse and buggy parked in the driveway, but before he could say anything, Jake hollered, "Looks like we've got company!"

"Probably one of Mom's friends come to see if she needs any help," Silas replied with a shrug.

"I hope they brought somethin' good to eat," Sam put in. "Now that Mom's arm is busted, she sure won't be doin' much bakin'."

Silas flicked his little brother's straw hat off his head. "It's the same old story with you, Boy. Always hungry, ain't ya?"

Sam flashed him a freckle-faced grin and bounded up the porch steps. "Last one to the table is a fat cow!"

Silas and his brothers raced into the kitchen, laughing and grabbing at each other's shirts, hoping to be the first ones washed up and seated on their bench at the table.

Jake and Sam were already at the sink, pumping water and lathering up their hands, but Silas stopped short just inside the door. His gaze was fixed on Rachel Beachy, who was busy setting the table. She glanced over at him and smiled, and his heart seemed to stop beating for a few seconds. He'd never noticed it, but Rachel had two little dimples—one in each cheek. Had she never smiled at him before, or had he just been too busy to notice? Today she almost looked like a mature woman. Could she have changed that much since he'd last seen her?

"Guess that's your buggy outside," Silas said, feeling kind of nervous all of a sudden.

"*Jah*, it's mine, all right," she answered. "I'm here to help your *mamm* 'til her arm gets better."

Silas's mouth dropped open. "You're gonna stay with us?"

"No, Silly. Rachel will be comin' over every mornin' and stayin' until after supper," Mom said.

Silas really felt stupid. Here his mother was standing at the stove, stirring a pot of soup with her one good arm, and he hadn't even noticed her until she spoke up.

He swallowed hard, removed his hat, and hung it on a wall peg. "That's right nice of you, Rachel. Nice of your folks to let you come, too."

Rachel placed a loaf of bread on the table. "If Pauline Hostetler hadn't been willin' to take my place at the greenhouse, I probably couldn't have come."

"Did ya bring anything *gut* to eat?" This question came from young Sam, who had already taken his place at the table.

"Samuel, where are your manners? Sometimes I don't know what gets into my boys," Mom scolded. "Rachel came to help, not furnish the likes of you with all kinds of fattenin' goodies."

Rachel smiled at Sam. "Actually, I did bring some chocolate chip cookies." She motioned toward a basket on the cupboard.

Sam started to get up, but Silas placed a restraining hand on his shoulder. "You'd better eat lunch first, don'tcha think?"

"What is for lunch, and where's Pap?" Jake asked as he joined his brothers at the table.

"Vegetable soup and ham sandwiches, and he's not back from town yet," Mom answered.

Silas and his brothers waited until Rachel and Mom took their seats, then all heads bowed in silent prayer. A short time later everyone had eaten their fill, and Rachel offered the cookies as dessert.

Silas smacked his lips after the first bite. "Umm. . .these are right tasty. You didn't bake 'em yourself, did ya, Rachel?" He laughed, but she didn't.

"Of course," Rachel replied a bit stiffly. "I may be just a little tomboy in some folks' eyes, but I can cook, bake, sew, clean, and do most everything else around the house."

Silas didn't have a clue what he'd said to make Rachel go all peevish on him, but for some reason, she seemed kind of miffed. He shrugged and reached for another cookie. *She sure don't look like no* Hausfrau *to me.*

❧

As Rachel cleared away the dishes, her mind was on Silas, who'd gone back out to the fields with his brothers. She sure wished she could figure him out. One minute he was smiling and saying how nice it was for her to help out, and the next minute he was making fun of her.

Was Silas really making fun of you? a little voice niggled at the back of her mind. *He did say your cookies were good, and he only asked if you'd baked them.* Maybe she was overly sensitive where Silas was concerned. Might could be that she had tried too hard to make him take notice of her by smiling real sweet and bringing those cookies. Maybe she should play hard to get, like some of the other young Amish women often did when they were trying to get a man's attention.

"No, that wouldn't be right," Rachel mumbled as she placed the dirty dishes in the sink. Besides, she was not Anna, so if Silas was going to take notice, then it wouldn't be because she was playing hard to get.

"Did you say somethin'?" Katie asked, drawing Rachel out of her musings.

"I was talkin' to myself," Rachel admitted. She grinned at Katie, whose plump face always seemed to be wearing a smile.

"If you ever need someone to talk to, I've got *gut* ears for listenin'," the older woman said as she wiped down the tablecloth.

Rachel smiled. "I'll remember that." She moved over to the stove to retrieve the pot of water she'd heated to wash the dishes. "I can finish up in here. I'm sure you've gotta be tired by now. Why don'tcha go rest awhile?"

Katie handed Rachel the dishrag. "I think I'll take ya up on that offer. My arm's kinda hurtin', so some aspirin and a good nap might do me some good."

"What else are ya needin' done today?" Rachel asked.

"Let's see now. . .it's too hot to do any bakin', but if you're feelin' like it, maybe you could mix up a ribbon salad." Katie waved her good hand toward the pantry. "I think there's a few packages of gelatin, some walnuts, a can of crushed pineapple, and a bag of marshmallows in there. Last time I checked the refrigerator, we had plenty of whipping cream, milk, and cream cheese, so you should be able to put it together in time for supper."

A short time later, Rachel had prepared the ribbon salad and was just placing it inside the refrigerator when the back door swung open. Thinking it was probably Herman Swartley returning from town, Rachel turned toward the door and smiled. Her smile was quickly replaced with a frown when she saw Silas standing there, holding his hand and grimacing in obvious pain.

She hurried to his side, feeling as if her breath had been snatched away. "What is it? Are ya hurt?" Her frown faded to surprise when she heard Silas's answer.

"I got a big old splinter in my thumb, and it's all your fault."

Rachel's hands went straight to her hips. "My fault? How can gettin' a splinter be my fault?"

Silas hung his head, kind of sheepishlike. "I took a handful of your cookies out to the fields, and after I ate a few, I forgot to put my gloves back on. Next thing I knew, I was grabbin' hold of the wagon, and here's what I've got to show for it!" He held up his thumb for her inspection.

Rachel bit back a smile, even though her stomach did a little flip-flop just thinking about how much the sliver must hurt. "So, it's my fault ya weren't wearin' your gloves, huh?"

He nodded and looked her right in the eye, which made her stomach take another nosedive. "If you weren't so *gut* at makin' cookies, I wouldn't have grabbed a handful. And if I'd had my gloves on, I sure wouldn't have all this pain."

Silas's voice had a soft quality about it, yet he spoke with assurance. Rachel thought she could sit and listen to him talk for hours on end. "Take a seat at the table and I'll have a look-see," she instructed, pulling her wayward thoughts back to the need at hand. "Do you know where your *mamm* keeps her needles and such?"

Silas's eyes were wide, and his mouth hung open just a bit. "You're not plannin' to go pokin' around on my thumb, are ya?"

She tipped her head to one side. "Now, how else did ya expect me to remove that old splinter?"

Silas swallowed hard. "Guess you've got a point." He nodded toward the old treadle sewing machine positioned along the wall nearest the stone fireplace. "I think you'll find all your doctorin' tools over there."

Rachel went immediately to the sewing machine and opened the top drawer of the wooden cabinet. Sure enough, there were plenty of needles, a pair of tweezers, and even a magnifying glass. Katie Swartley must have had some experience taking out slivers, her having three boys and a husband.

"It might be best if you close your eyes," Rachel said as she leaned close to Silas and took his big hand in hers. This was the closest she'd ever been to him, and it took all her willpower and concentration to focus on that nasty sliver and not his masculine scent or the feel of his warm breath blowing softly against her face.

"I ain't no *buppli*," Silas said between clenched teeth. "So, I'll keep my eyes open; thank you very much."

"As you like," Rachel replied. She jabbed the needle underneath the sliver and pushed upward.

"Yow! That hurts like crazy!" Silas's face was white as a sheet, and Rachel feared he might be about to pass out.

Rachel clenched her teeth to keep from laughing out loud. So Silas didn't think he was a baby, huh? "Hang your head between your knees and take some deep breaths," she ordered.

As soon as Silas had his head down, Rachel grabbed his hand again and set to work. It was hard to ignore his groans and yowls, but in short order she had the splinter out. "Let me pour some peroxide over it and give you a bandage," she said. "Do you know where those are kept?"

Silas sat up and took several deep breaths before he answered. "In the cupboard, just above the sink."

Soon the wound was cleansed and a bandage was securely in place. Silas smiled at Rachel, and she thought her heart had stopped beating. *How could Anna have turned Silas away in exchange for the likes of Reuben Yutzy, who is doin' all that worldly stuff?*

"*Danki*, Rachel," Silas said, offering her a crooked grin. "That splinter was a nasty one, and I don't rightly think I coulda taken it out myself."

She licked her lips and smiled back at him. "You're welcome."

Silas stood up and started for the door, but suddenly he pivoted back around. "Say, I was wonderin'. . .that is. . ."

"What were you wonderin'?"

He shook his head and turned toward the door. "Never mind. It weren't nothin' important."

The door clicked behind him and Rachel sank into a chair. Was there any hope for her and Silas, or had she just imagined that he'd looked at her with interest?

Chapter 10

Over the next few weeks, Rachel helped Katie nearly every day but Sunday. She would get up an hour early in order to get her own chores done at home; then right after breakfast she'd head over to the Swartleys'. Katie's arm was hurting less, but she would have to wear the cast for another three weeks, which meant she still had the use of only one arm.

Things weren't going as well with Silas as Rachel had hoped. Ever since the day she'd removed his splinter, Silas had seemed kind of distant. She had to wonder if he was trying to avoid her, although she couldn't think why, since she'd made every effort to be pleasant. It might be that Silas's aloofness was just because he was so busy in the fields. On most days, she only saw him during lunch and supper, and even then he appeared tired and withdrawn.

Today was Saturday, and Katie Swartley had enlisted the help of some neighboring Amish women so Rachel could work in the greenhouse with Pauline. Dad had taken Mom, Elizabeth, and Perry to Bird-in-Hand, where they would be selling some of their plants and fresh-cut flowers at the farmers' market. Since Saturday was always a big day at the greenhouse, they didn't want to leave Pauline alone to deal with the tourists, who would no doubt be stopping by. Joseph was also left behind to finish up some chores in the barn.

As Rachel began watering plants, the musty scent of wet soil assaulted her senses, causing her to sneeze and making her wish she could be outside instead of cooped up inside a much-too-warm greenhouse. She glanced over at Pauline, who was waiting on some English customers. The tall, blond-haired woman certainly had changed of late. Instead of being distant and sometimes cross, Pauline had become outgoing and cheerful. Rachel could remember a few years ago, back when Pauline had been jilted by Eli Yoder, she hadn't even tried to hide her bitter feelings. Every chance Pauline got, she told tales about the woman who had stolen Eli's heart. Rachel had often been tempted to tell Pauline that she'd better keep her own garden free of weeds instead of worrying over someone else's, but she never said anything. Pauline was six years older than her and probably wouldn't have listened to any advice from a *kinder*.

Rachel couldn't be sure what had brought about such a dramatic change in Pauline, but she suspected it had something to do with working in the greenhouse. *Of course, my brother Joseph might have had a little influence on her attitude.* Joseph seemed to have set his reservations aside about his and Pauline's age difference. Rachel noticed the way he hung around Pauline every chance he got. Pauline would have to be blind and just plain dumb not to be flattered by all his attention.

When the customers exited the greenhouse, Rachel moved over to the counter. "You can take your lunch break now if ya want. I'll wait on anyone who might come by during the next hour."

Pauline nodded and grabbed her lunch basket from underneath the counter. "Think I'll eat outside. Might as well enjoy the *gut* weather while it lasts. Fall's almost upon us; can ya tell?"

"Jah. Mornin' and evenin' seem much cooler now. Won't be no time a'tall 'til the leaves start to change," Rachel remarked.

Pauline was just about to open the door when Rachel called out, "I think Joseph's still in the barn. Would ya mind goin' there and lettin' him know I made a sandwich for him and it's in the refrigerator?"

Pauline smiled. "I think I can do better than that. I'll go on up to the house, fetch the sandwich and somethin' cold to drink, then take it out to Joe myself."

Ah, so it's "Joe," now, is it? Rachel hid her smile behind the writing tablet she'd just picked up. "See you later, Pauline. Tell *Joe* I said hello, and I hope he enjoys his lunch."

The door clicked shut and Rachel moved over to the window and watched Pauline walk down the path toward their house. "I wonder if I should give Anna's old hope chest to her." She shrugged. "Guess maybe I should hang on to it. . .just in case Anna changes her mind and returns home for some of her things."

❧

Silas wasn't sure it was such a good idea to be going to the greenhouse Rachel's mother had named Grandma's Place, but his buggy was already pulling into the graveled parking lot, so he figured he may as well carry out his plans.

When he entered the greenhouse, Rachel greeted Silas from behind the front counter, where she sat reading a book.

"I thought you'd be swamped with customers," he said, removing his straw hat and offering her a smile.

Rachel jumped off her stool and moved swiftly to the other side of the counter. "We were busy earlier, but I think everyone must be eatin' their lunch about now." She took a few steps toward Silas. "I'm surprised to see ya here today."

He shuffled his feet a few times and glanced around the room. "Uh, where's Pauline? I thought she was workin' here now."

Rachel nodded curtly, and her eyebrows drew together.

Have I said somethin' wrong? Silas wondered.

"Pauline does work here, but she's on her lunch break right now. Want me to see if I can find her?" Rachel asked, moving toward the door.

Silas stopped her by placing his hand on her arm. *"Himmel*—no, no. I didn't come by to see Pauline."

"You didn't?"

He shook his head.

"What did ya come for?"

He rocked back and forth on his heels, with one hand balled into a fist and the other one hanging on to his hat real tight. "I—um—was wonderin'. . . That is—"

"Are ya needin' a plant or some cut flowers?" Rachel interrupted. "Mom and Dad took quite a few to the market this mornin', but I think there's still a good supply in the back room."

Silas cleared his throat a few times, trying to decide the best way to broach the subject that had brought him here in the first place. *It sure is gettin' mighty warm.* He fanned his face with his hat, hoping the action might give him something to do with his hands, as well as get him cooled down some.

"You okay, Silas?" Rachel asked with a note of concern. "You're lookin' kinda poorly. Wanna sit down awhile?"

"*Jah*, maybe that would be a *gut* idea," he said, pulling up an empty crate and plunking down with a groan. "Whew! Don't know what came over me, but I was feelin' a little woozy for a minute."

"Maybe you're comin' down with the flu or somethin'," Rachel said, placing her hand against his forehead. Her fingers felt cool and soft, making it even harder for Silas to think straight.

"I'm not sick," he asserted. "It's just warm in here, that's all."

Rachel nodded and took a few steps back. "It always is a bit stuffy in the greenhouse, which is one of the reasons I don't like workin' here."

"What would you rather be doin'?"

"Fishin'. . .bird-watchin'. . .almost anything outdoors," she answered, giving him another one of her dimpled smiles.

Silas swallowed hard. If he was ever going to ask her, he'd better do it quick, because right now he felt like racing for the door and heading straight home.

"The reason I stopped by was to see if ya might wanna go to Paradise Lake with me tomorrow. Your brother Joseph and me were talkin' the other day, and he mentioned that ya like to fish. So, I thought maybe we could do a bit of fishin', and if we're lucky, get in some bird-watchin', too." There, it was out. Now all he had to do was wait for her answer.

Rachel stood there, staring at him like she was in some kind of a daze. For a minute he wondered if he would need to repeat himself.

"Since tomorrow is an off Sunday and there won't be no preachin' service, I guess it'd be as good a time as any for some outdoor fun," she said in a quavery voice.

He jumped up. "You mean you'll go?"

She nodded. "I'd be happy to. How 'bout I fix us a picnic lunch to take along? Fishin' always makes me real hungry, and later tonight I was plannin' to bake some more of those chocolate chip cookies you like so well."

Silas licked his lips in anticipation of what was to come. He was mighty glad he'd finally gotten up the nerve to ask Rachel to go fishing. "Let's meet at the lake around nine o'clock. How's that sound?"

"Sounds *gut* to me," she said, walking him to the door.

❧

Rachel stood at the window, watching Silas's buggy disappear down the lane. When it was well out of sight, she hugged herself real tight and started whirling around the room. "I can't believe it! Silas Swartley and I are goin' fishin'!"

She couldn't help but wonder, and yes, even hope that this sudden invitation was a sign that Silas was beginning to care for her. *Guess maybe he's not interested in Pauline after all.* She laughed out loud. "Maybe I'd better start fillin' my hope chest with a few more things. If Silas enjoys my company tomorrow, he might even offer to take me home from the next singin'. Now that would mean we were courtin'!" She would have to remember to thank Joseph for letting Silas know how much she liked to fish.

❧

As soon as Silas returned home, he went straight to the barn to get out his fishing gear. Tomorrow he would be meeting Rachel at Paradise Lake. Besides the fishing pole, several fat worms, extra tackle, and line, he'd decided to take along his binoculars and the new book he'd recently bought on bird-watching.

He grinned as he grabbed his pole off the wall. It amazed him that any woman would actually like to fish and study birds, but he was glad he and Rachel had that in common. None of his brothers showed the least bit of interest in either birds or fishing with him, and now that Reuben was gone, he had been forced to fish alone.

Silas frowned deeply. He hadn't thought about Reuben for several weeks, and he wished he wasn't thinking of him right now. Reminders of Reuben always made him think about Anna, and he wasn't sure he was completely over her yet. He had loved her a lot, and she'd hurt him real bad, running off with his best friend and all. A fellow didn't get over being kicked in the gut like that overnight. Matters of the heart took time to heal, and until a moment ago, he thought his heart was on the way to mending.

"I'll feel better once I'm seated on the dock at Paradise Lake with my fishin' pole in the water and the warm sun against my back," he muttered.

"Who ya talkin' to, Silas?"

Silas whirled around. There stood his youngest brother, Sam, looking up at him like he was a fly on the wall. "I ain't talkin' to no one but myself, and you shouldn't go around sneakin' up on others," he scolded.

Sam scrunched up his freckled nose. "I weren't sneakin'. Just came out to the barn to feed the cats, and I heard you talkin' about goin' fishin'."

Silas nodded. "That's right. I'll be headed to Paradise Lake in the morning."

"Can I go along?" Sam asked eagerly.

Silas gave his brother a little pat on the arm. "Naw, I'd rather go alone. Besides, you don't even like to fish."

"I know, but it might be better than hangin' around here all day. Ever since Mom got that cast on her arm, she's been askin' me to do more chores."

"Ball wollt's besser geh—soon it will go better," Silas said with a grin. "Mom

won't always be wearin' her arm in a sling."

Sam shrugged. "I guess you're right." He turned to go, calling over his shoulder, "If it's a girl you're meetin' tomorrow, could ya save me a piece of cake from the picnic?"

Silas ran his fingers through the back of his hair. That little brother of his was sure no dumb bunny. Only thing was, it wouldn't be cake he'd be bringing home tomorrow, because Rachel had said she was going to bake his favorite kind of cookie.

Chapter 11

Rachel had a hard time getting away Sunday morning without telling her family she was meeting Silas at the lake. She tried to be discreet when she packed the picnic lunch, hoping no one would notice how much she had stashed inside the wicker basket. Both Elizabeth and Perry asked if they could go along, and she almost felt guilty telling them no. If she and Silas were going to get better acquainted, the last thing she needed was her rowdy brother and nosy sister tagging along.

The morning sun slid from behind a cloud as Rachel hitched the horse to the buggy. It was a bit chilly out, but the day held a promise of sunshine. She was about to climb into the driver's seat when Dad called out to her. "I'm not so sure I like the idea of you goin' to the lake by yourself."

"I've been fishin' there since I was a *kinder,* and I've never had a problem," she replied. "Besides, there's usually plenty of people around, so I probably won't be alone."

Dad shook his head. "That may be, but it ain't *gut* for a young woman to be runnin' around by herself. I really think you should take your sister or one of your brothers along."

Rachel placed the picnic basket under the front seat and turned to face her father. "I'm meetin' someone."

He gave his beard a few good yanks. "Ah, so my daughter has a beau now, does she?"

Rachel felt the heat of a blush stain her cheeks. "He's not a beau, just a friend."

Dad chuckled. "So it is a fellow you're meetin', then?"

She nodded. *"Jah."*

"Mind if I ask who?"

"It's Silas Swartley."

Dad's smile widened. "A fine young man, Silas is." He winked at Rachel. "Should I be askin' your *mamm* to start makin' a weddin' quilt?"

"Himmel!" Rachel exclaimed. "I knew I shouldn't have said anything. Like I stated before, Silas and I are just friends."

"Then why the big secret 'bout meetin' him?"

Rachel hung her head. "I—I—just didn't want anyone jumpin' to conclusions."

Dad gave her arm a gentle pat. "Your secret's safe with me, Daughter. Now run along and catch plenty of fish, will ya? Some nice, tasty trout would look mighty *gut* on the supper table!"

Rachel smiled and climbed into the buggy. She was ever so glad her *daed* was such a thoughtful man.

❧

Silas was sitting on the dock with his fishing line dangling in the water. There were several small boats on the lake, but no one else was on the dock or shoreline. Maybe he and Rachel would be alone all day. Did he really want to be alone with her? He'd thought he did yesterday when he asked her to meet him here. Now that he'd had ample time to think about it, he worried that he might have been a bit hasty making the invitation. What if Rachel thought he was interested in her as more than a friend? What if she thought this was a real date?

Silas stared out across the lake, his gaze settling on a crop of trees where several crows sat, making their distinctive call of *caw, caw, caw!* Truth be told, he really did enjoy Rachel's company. The fact that she liked birds and fishing was a benefit, but it was her sweet spirit and appreciation for the simple things in life that really captured his attention.

"She ain't too bad-lookin', either," Silas said aloud. He closed his eyes, and Rachel's pleasant face flashed into his mind. Her pale blue eyes and soft, straw-colored hair made her appear almost angelic. And whenever she smiled, those cute little dimples made him want to reach right out and touch her cheeks.

Silas shook his head. *What am I thinkin'? Rachel is Anna's little sister. She's five years younger than me and ain't much more'n a* kinder. *Of course, I do know of some married couples where one is older than the other.* He sighed deeply. *Guess five years ain't really all that much.*

Silas was driven from his inner conflict when he heard a horse and buggy come plodding up the road. He turned and waved as Rachel's buggy pulled into the grassy spot near the dock.

❧

Rachel smiled and waved at Silas, who was sitting on the edge of the dock holding a fishing pole. He looked so eager. Was it possible that he was as happy to see her as she was to see him? She prayed it was so.

"Catch anything yet?" she asked as she stepped down from the buggy.

Silas shook his head. "Not yet, but then I haven't been here very long."

Rachel grabbed her fishing pole from the back of the buggy, along with the can of night crawlers she'd caught last night. When she walked onto the dock, Silas slid over, making room for her to sit beside him. "Sure is a nice day," he remarked. "Should have our share of trout in no time." He winked at Rachel and her heart skipped a beat.

Does he have some feelings for me? she asked herself. It was a glimmer of hope she would cling to.

The sun was shining brightly, the sky was a clear aquamarine, and the lake was smooth as glass. Rachel felt a sense of peace settle over her as she cast out her line. It felt so right being here with Silas. *If only. . . No, I mustn't allow myself to start daydreamin'. Today, I'm just gonna relax and enjoy the company of the man I could surely spend the rest of my life with.*

By noon, Silas had caught six trout and four bass, and Rachel had five of each. They both cleaned their own catch, then put the fish inside the small coolers they'd brought along.

"I don't know about you, but I'm starvin'," Silas said, eyeing the picnic basket Rachel had taken from the buggy and placed upon the quilt she'd spread on the ground.

"I made plenty, so I'm glad you're hungry," she said with a smile.

Silas dropped to the quilt. "What'd ya bring?"

Rachel knelt next to the picnic basket and opened the lid. "Let's see now. . . ham-and-cheese sandwiches, dill pickle slices, macaroni salad, cheese curds, pickled beet eggs, iced tea to drink, and for dessert. . .chocolate chip cookies."

Silas licked his lips. "Yum. Let's pray; then we'll eat ourselves full!"

Rachel and Silas shared stories, told jokes, and got to know each other better. By the time they finished eating the last of the cookies, Rachel felt as though she'd known Silas all her life. Actually, she had, but not on such a personal level. Silas, being five years her senior, had always hung around her older sister, so she'd never had the chance to learn what many of his likes and dislikes were. Today he'd shared his aversion to liver and onions, a dish his *mamm* seemed intent on fixing at least once a month. He also revealed his objection to so many Amish parents who chose to look the other way when their rebellious teenagers sowed their wild oats. Silas talked about his relationship to God and how he'd been praying for the Lord to have His will in his life.

"Yep, I believe strongly in prayer," Silas said with obvious conviction. "It's the key to each new day and the lock for every night."

Rachel smiled. "You're right about that." Even as she said the words, Rachel wondered if she was being sincere. Oh, she believed in prayer, all right. The problem was, she didn't pray as often as she should anymore. Since she'd been busy helping Silas's mother, Rachel had let her personal devotions and prayer time slip. It was something she needed to work on, and right then she promised herself and God that she would.

Silas chewed on a blade of grass as he began telling Rachel what he thought about so many *younga* who, because they were allowed to taste some worldly things, had gone English.

"I think it's a sin and a shame," he said with feeling. "If I ever have any *kinder*, I'm gonna hold a tight rein on 'em so's they don't ever leave the faith."

Rachel leaned back on her elbows and let his words digest fully before she answered. "You might be right, but then again, holdin' a tight rein could turn someone's head in the opposite direction." She sat up and pivoted to face him. "Take a baby robin, for example. If its *mamm* never taught it to fly and always kept it protected inside the nest, do you think that *buppli* would ever learn to soar in the air?"

Silas scratched the back of his head and squinted his dark eyes. "I guess you've got a point. You're pretty bright for someone so young."

Rachel felt as though Silas had slapped her on the face with a wet rag. *Why'd he have to go and bring up my age? And just when we were beginnin' to have such a good time.* "I'll have you know, Silas Swartley," she asserted, "I'll be nineteen next Saturday. My *mamm* was married by the time she was my age, and—"

Silas held up one hand. "Whoa, now! Don't get your feathers all ruffled. I sure didn't mean to offend ya."

Rachel grabbed their empty paper plates and the plastic containers the food had been in and began slinging them into the picnic basket. Her face felt hot, her hands were shaking, and tears were stinging the backs of her eyes. She had so wanted this day to be perfect. Maybe she was too sensitive. Might could be that Silas hadn't meant to upset her at all. She stood and proceeded to move toward her buggy. "Guess I should be gettin' back home."

Silas jumped up and ran after her. "You can't go now, Rachel. We haven't spent any time lookin' at birds."

She shrugged. "Maybe some other time. I'm not much in the mood anymore."

Silas placed a restraining hand on Rachel's arm. "Please, don't go. I'm awful sorry for makin' ya mad."

She swallowed hard, struggling to keep her tears at bay. Silas was looking at her with those big brown eyes, and he really did look sorry. "I'm not exactly mad," she admitted. "I just get tired of everyone thinkin' I'm still a *kinder*." Her arms made a wide arc as she motioned toward the lake. "Could a child catch as many fish as I did today?" Before Silas had a chance to answer, she rushed on. "Could a little girl have fixed such a tasty picnic lunch or baked a batch of cookies you couldn't eat enough of?"

Silas studied her a few seconds, then in an unexpected gesture, he pulled her to his chest. "No, Rachel, only a feisty young woman coulda done all those things."

Rachel held her breath as he moved his fingers in gentle, soothing circles across her back. Was Silas about to kiss her? She wrapped her arms around his neck and nestled her head against his shoulder.

Then, as quickly as he'd embraced her, Silas pulled away. "Now that we've got that cleared up, how's about I get my binoculars and bird identification book, and the two of us can spend the next hour or so lookin' for some unusual feathered creatures?"

Rachel nodded as a sense of embarrassment rattled through her. Silas's sudden shift in mood hit her like a blow to the stomach, and she cringed, wondering what he must have thought about her brazen actions. Even though it was Silas who initiated the hug, she had taken it one step further. Truth be told, Silas had never led her to believe he had any romantic feelings for her. The embrace was probably just a friendly, brotherly gesture.

"You get your gear, and I'll put away the picnic stuff," she said, scooting away quickly, before he could see how red her face must be.

A short time later, Silas and Rachel were seated on the grass, taking turns looking through his binoculars, as though their physical encounter had never even taken place. In no time at all they'd spotted several gray catbirds, a brown thrasher, a few mourning doves, and several species of ducks on the lake. Silas looked each one up in his bird identification book, and they discussed the various traits and habitats of those they'd seen.

"Do you have a bird book or binoculars of your own?" Silas asked.

Rachel shook her head. "Whenever I save up enough money, some other need always seems to come along, so I just jot notes on a paper about all the interestin' birds I see." She was tempted to tell him that here lately, she'd spent most of her money buying more things for her hope chest, but she thought better of bringing that subject up. Silas might think she was hinting at marriage, and she wasn't about to say or do anything that would spoil the rest of the day. Except for that one misunderstanding, their time together had been almost perfect. Even if she never got to be alone with Silas again, she would always cherish the memory of this day.

Closing her eyes, Rachel uttered a brief, silent prayer. *It's been a* wunderbaar *day, Lord.* Danki.

Chapter 12

After their enjoyable day at the lake, Rachel expected Silas to be friendlier the following week. He wasn't. In fact, she saw very little of him, and when he did come to the house for meals, he seemed aloof and kind of cranky whenever someone spoke to him. Something wasn't right. She felt it in every fiber of her being. She wanted to ask him what was wrong, but there never seemed to be a good time, what with his family always around.

By Saturday, Rachel was fit to be tied. She'd been forced to stay home from the Swartleys' again because Mom and Dad went to town for more supplies. That meant she was needed at the greenhouse, and even worse, it appeared as though her family had forgotten all about her birthday. Not one person said "Happy birthday" during breakfast, and there was no sign of any gifts, either. It was such a disappointment not to be remembered on her special day.

Elizabeth and Perry had been left home this time, and they were still up at the house when Rachel walked out to the greenhouse. She put the Open sign in the window, lit all the kerosene lanterns, and made a small fire in the wood-burning stove to take the autumn chill out of the room.

Rachel studied her surroundings, letting her gaze travel from the plants hanging by the rafters on long chains to the small wooden pots and lawn figurines sitting on shelves. Dad had made most of those things, and his expertise with wood was quite evident. Rachel knew her folks loved this greenhouse, and she was also aware that it had been one of the things that brought them together. Even so, she had no desire to spend so much time helping out here. Today, of all days, she would much rather be outside.

"It's my birthday," she fumed. "I should at least be allowed the pleasure of a walk to the river." She plunked down on the stool behind the counter, placed her elbows on the hard wood, and rested her chin in the palms of her hands.

Pauline showed up a few minutes later, and Joseph was with her.

"I thought you were out in the barn," Rachel said, giving her brother a knowing look.

He shrugged, and his face turned kind of pink. "I was 'til I saw Pauline's buggy come down the lane."

"Are ya plannin' to help out here today?" Rachel asked hopefully. "If so, maybe I won't be needed."

"I wish I could, but it's not possible today." Joseph cast a quick glance in Pauline's direction, then looked back at Rachel with a silly grin on his face.

"What are ya doin' here, if it's not to work?" Rachel asked impatiently.

435

"I came to see Pauline. That is, if you have no objections."

Pauline chuckled and elbowed Joseph in the ribs. He laughed and jabbed her right back.

At least somebody's happy today, Rachel thought ruefully. "I think I'll go in the back room and see if any of the plants need waterin'," she announced.

"Okay, sure," Joseph said, never taking his eyes off Pauline.

"Sickenin'. Downright sickenin'," Rachel muttered under her breath as she headed for the middle section of the greenhouse. *This day can't be over soon enough to suit me!*

❧

Silas paced back and forth in front of his open courting buggy. Should he or shouldn't he make this trip? Would his intentions be misrepresented? What exactly were his intentions, anyway? He'd spent the last week trying to sort out his feelings, and yet he felt more confused now than ever.

Pushing his troubled thoughts aside, he tried to pray. God seemed so far away today, but he knew it was his own fault. He'd been negligent in reading the Bible this morning, and his only prayer had been the silent one before breakfast.

I won't allow myself to move away from You, Lord, Silas prayed. *I'd never want to end up like Reuben and Anna, who obviously fell away.* Silas was reminded that up until six months ago, he and Reuben had been close. It was as much a surprise to Silas as it had been to Reuben's folks when they discovered Reuben had gone "fancy."

Then there was Anna. Beautiful, spirited, stubborn Anna. Silas had been in love with her since the first grade, when they'd started attending school in the Amish one-room schoolhouse. In his mind's eye, he could still see the back of her cute little head. He'd sat in the desk behind her for all of the eight years they'd gone to school. Anna, with her dazzling green eyes and hair the color of ripe peaches. She'd stolen his heart when he was six years old, and she'd broken it in two when he was twenty-three. Would he ever be free of the pain? Would the image of her lovely face be forever etched in his mind? Could he learn to trust another woman?

"It does no good to pine for what you can't have," a little voice reminded. *"Get on with your life and follow Me."*

Silas moved to the front of the buggy, where his faithful horse waited patiently. He leaned against the gelding's side and stroked his silky ears. "What do ya say, old boy? Do we take a little ride, or do we stay home?"

The horse whinnied as if in response, and Silas smiled. "All right then, let's be on our way."

❧

Rachel had just put the Closed sign in the window and was about to turn down the lights when she heard a horse and buggy pull up in front of the greenhouse. Pauline had gone home fifteen minutes ago, and Rachel was anxious to head home herself. She sighed deeply. "Guess I can handle one more customer."

Rachel opened the front door, and her mouth dropped open when she saw

Silas standing there holding a paper bag in one hand and a bouquet of orange and yellow chrysanthemums in the other.

"Well, well," she said with a giggle, "it isn't every day someone shows up at the greenhouse carryin' a bunch of flowers."

Silas chuckled. "Guess that's true enough. Most folks leave here with flowers, but it ain't likely they'd be bringing 'em in."

Rachel stepped aside to allow Silas entrance. "So what brings you here at closin' time, Silas Swartley?"

He cleared his throat real loud, then handed her the flowers and paper sack. "Just wanted to give you these. Happy birthday, Rachel."

Rachel felt as though all the breath had been squeezed clean out of her lungs. This was such a surprise. Never in a million years had she expected a gift from Silas, especially since he'd been so distant all week. "*Danki,*" she murmured. "How'd ya know today was my birthday?"

"You said somethin' about it when we went fishin' last Sunday," he replied.

Rachel placed the flowers on the counter and opened the paper sack. She let out a little squeal when she looked inside. "Binoculars and a bird-watchin' book? Oh, Silas, this is my best present!" The truth was, it was her only birthday present, but she wasn't about to tell him that. It was bad enough her whole family had forgotten her special day; she sure didn't want to talk about it.

"I was hopin' ya might like it," Silas said, taking a few steps closer to Rachel. "Now, whenever you see some unusual bird, you can look it up in the book and find out all about its habits and whatnot."

Rachel withdrew the binoculars. "These will sure come in handy, too."

Silas nodded. "*Jah,* I often put my own binoculars to *gut* use."

Rachel swallowed hard. Why was Silas looking at her so funny? Did that gentle expression in his dark eyes and the agreeable smile on his clean-shaven face mean anything more than just friendship? She sure couldn't come right out and ask, but she needed to know if she dared to hope.

As if he sensed her dilemma, Silas reached out and took Rachel's hand. "I really enjoyed our time of fishin' and lookin' at birds the other day. If the weather holds out, maybe we can find time to do it again."

Rachel flicked her tongue back and forth across her lower lip. The sensation of Silas's touch did funny things to her insides. "I'd surely like that," she murmured. "I had a *gut* time last week, too."

Silas let go of her hand, then turned and moved slowly toward the door. "Well, guess I should be gettin' on home. Mom's probably got supper ready."

Rachel nodded. "I need to go up to the house and see about fixin' our supper as well. My folks went to town this mornin', and they still aren't back yet, so I'd better be sure there's somethin' ready to eat when they do get home."

When Silas got to the door, he turned and said, "I hear tell there's gonna be a singin' over at Abner Lapp's place two weeks from tomorrow. Do ya think ya might go?"

"Maybe." Rachel shrugged. "If I can get Joseph to take me."

Silas grinned. "From what I hear, your brother's got a pretty *gut* reason to bring his courtin' buggy to a singin'. My guess is, he'll be there."

Rachel nodded. "You're probably right."

Silas opened the door. "Well, see ya at preachin' tomorrow, Rachel." He bounded off the porch and climbed into his buggy before Rachel could say anything more.

She smiled to herself. "Guess this wasn't such a bad birthday after all."

❧

Holding her bouquet of flowers and the paper sack Silas had given her, Rachel stepped into the darkened kitchen. She had barely closed the door when a kerosene light flickered on and a chorus of voices yelled, "Happy birthday!"

"What in the world?" Rachel's mouth fell open as she studied her surroundings. Mom, Dad, Joseph, Perry, and Elizabeth all sat at the table, which was fully set for supper. On one end of the cupboard was a chocolate cake, and beside it were several gifts wrapped in plain brown paper.

"Elizabeth, did you do all this?" Rachel asked her sister.

Elizabeth smiled. "I helped, but Mama did most of it."

Rachel's eyebrows drew together. "How could that be? Mom and Dad have been gone all day."

Mom grinned like a cat that had just chased down a fat little mouse. "Came back early. Just so we could surprise ya."

"But I never heard your buggy come down the lane," Rachel argued. "I don't see how—"

Dad chuckled. "We used the old road comin' into the back of our property."

Tears stung the back of Rachel's eyes, and she blinked to keep them from spilling over. Her folks really did care. They hadn't forgotten it was her birthday after all.

"What's that you've got in your hands?" The question came from Perry, and Rachel felt her face heat with embarrassment.

"It's—uh—a birthday present."

"From who?" Joseph asked, giving her a discerning look.

"Silas Swartley," she said, trying to keep her voice from quivering.

"Rachel's got a boyfriend! Rachel's got a boyfriend!" Elizabeth taunted.

"I do not!"

"Do so!"

"Silas is just a *gut* friend," Rachel argued. "That oughta be clear as anythin'."

Joseph raised his eyebrows. "Oh, sure—about as clear as mud. He's a *gut* friend, all right. One who gives you a birthday present and takes you fishin'."

Rachel turned to face her father, and her forehead wrinkled in accusation. He shook his head. "He didn't hear it from me."

Mom shook her finger at Dad. "You knew our daughter had gone fishin' with Silas Swartley and you never said a word?"

"Rachel asked me not to say anything."

"If Dad didn't mention it, then how'd you know?" Rachel asked, looking back at Joseph.

He shrugged. "There were some other folks out at Paradise Lake, ya know."

"We never talked to anyone else," Rachel said quickly. "In fact, we were the only ones on the dock."

"That may be true, but there were some boats out on the water," Joseph reminded.

"Spies, don'tcha mean?" Rachel declared. "Humph! Some folks need to keep their big mouths shut where others are concerned."

"Now, don't go gettin' yourself into a snit," Mom said soothingly. "There was no harm done, so come sit yourself down and eat your favorite supper."

Rachel had to admit, the fried chicken and mashed potatoes did look mighty good. She was real hungry, too. She may as well eat this special supper Mom and Elizabeth had worked so hard to prepare. She would have a serious talk with Joseph later on. Then she'd find out who the informer had been.

Chapter 13

Rachel sat on the edge of her bed, looking over the presents she'd received earlier that day. It had been a *gut* birthday, even if Joseph had let the cat out of the bag about her and Silas going fishing together. Joseph told her later that it was Amon Zook who'd spilled the beans. He'd been fishing on the lake with his son, Ben.

She chuckled softly. "Guess ya can't keep anything secret these days."

Focusing on her gifts again, Rachel studied the set of handmade pillowcases Mom had given her and insisted must go straight into Rachel's hope chest. Dad's gift was a new oil lamp—also a hope chest item, since she already had two perfectly good lamps in her bedroom. Joseph and Perry had gone together on a box of cream-filled chocolates, which Rachel had generously shared with the family. Elizabeth had made several handkerchiefs. Then there was her favorite gift of all—the binoculars and bird identification book Silas had given her. The candy was almost gone. The handkerchiefs would be useful in the days to come. The oil lamp and pillowcases might never be used if Rachel didn't get married. Silas's gift, on the other hand, was something she would use whenever she studied birds in their yard and the surrounding area.

Rachel scooted off the bed and stepped around the cedar chest at the end of her bed, opened the lid, and slipped the pillowcases and lamp inside. She hadn't given her hope chest much thought until recently. Now that Silas was being so friendly, there might be a ray of hope for her future. " 'But I will hope continually, and will yet praise thee more and more,' " she murmured. "Thank You, Lord, for such a *gut* day."

As Rachel closed the lid of the chest, she caught sight of Anna's hope chest in the corner of her room. She was tempted to open it and look through its contents, but she thought better of it. It belonged to her sister, and she still didn't feel right about snooping through Anna's personal things.

She did give the hope chest to you, her inner voice reminded. Rachel was about to go over and open it up, but she changed her mind. What if Anna should ever return to the Amish faith? Wouldn't she want her hope chest back?

Someday, if Rachel should ever become published, then there would be a use for the things in both hers and Anna's hope chests. She would wait awhile to see what was inside. In the meantime, she planned to start adding even more things to her own hope chest.

❦

Silas felt a sense of excitement as he prepared to go to the singing that was to be held in Abner Lapp's barn. There would be a big bonfire and enough eats to fill even the hungriest man's stomach. Neither the singing, bonfire, nor even all the food was the reason he was looking forward to going. Simply put, Silas wanted to see Rachel again.

Silas climbed into his freshly cleaned courting buggy. His heartbeat quickened as he picked up the reins. The more time he spent with Rachel, the more he was drawn to her. Was it merely because they had so much in common, or was there something more going on? Could he possibly be falling for little Rachel Beachy, in spite of their age difference or the fact that she was the sister of his first love?

He shook his head and moved the horse forward. "I'd better take my time with Rachel, hadn't I, old boy? Elsewise, there might be *Kein Ausgang*—no exit for either one of us."

❧

Fifty young people milled about the Lapps' barn, eating, playing games, and visiting. The singing had already taken place, so the rest of the evening would be spent in pleasant camaraderie.

Rachel and Joseph had gone their separate ways as soon as they arrived, she with some other woman her age, and Joseph with Pauline Hostetler. That really wasn't such a big surprise, since he'd been hanging around her so much lately.

Rachel had just finished eating a sandwich and had taken a seat on a bale of straw, planning to relax and watch the couples around her. She was pretty sure her brother would be asking to take Pauline home tonight, and it had her kind of worried. What if he wanted to be alone with his date? What if he expected Rachel to find another way home? It would be rather embarrassing if she had to go begging for a ride.

She scanned the many faces inside the barn, trying to decide who might be the best choice to ask, should it become necessary. Her gaze fell on Silas Swartley, talking with a group of young men near the food table. It would be bold to ask him for a ride, even if they had become friends over the past few months. It was a fellow's place to invite a girl to ride in his courting buggy, not the other way around. Besides, she hadn't seen much of Silas lately. Every day last week, when she'd been at his place helping out, Silas had been busy with the fall harvest. They hadn't had a real conversation since a week ago Saturday, when Silas dropped by the greenhouse to give her a birthday present.

Rachel noticed Abe Lapp sitting by himself, eating a huge piece of chocolate cake. Abe was the same age as Rachel, and they'd known each other a long time. She could ask him for a lift home, but there was just one problem. . .Abe lived right here. He wouldn't be driving his horse and buggy anywhere tonight.

"Seen any interestin' birds lately?"

The question took Rachel by surprise. She'd been in such a dilemma over who to ask for a ride, she hadn't even noticed that Silas Swartley was standing right beside her. She glanced up and smiled. *"Jah."*

Silas pulled up another bale of straw and sat down. "You like my birthday present?"

She nodded. "A whole lot."

"Mom's gettin' her cast off soon. Guess ya won't be comin' around so much anymore," he said, looking down at his hands, clasped together in his lap.

Rachel studied him a moment before she answered. Did she detect a note of sadness in his voice when he mentioned her not coming over anymore, or was it just wishful thinking? If Silas knew how much she loved him yet didn't have feelings for her, the humiliation would be too great to bear. "I–I'm glad I could help out, but things will soon be back to normal at your house, so—"

"Rachel, would ya like some hot chocolate and then go sit with me out by the bonfire?" Abe Lapp interrupted as he plunked down on the same bale of straw Rachel was sitting on.

Silas's jaw clenched, and he shot Abe a look that could only be interpreted as one of irritation. "Rachel and I were havin' a little talk, Abe. If she wants anything, I'll be happy to fetch it for her."

Rachel stirred uneasily. What was going on here? If she hadn't known better, she'd have believed Silas was jealous of Abe Lapp. But that was ridiculous. Abe and Rachel were just friends, the same as she and Silas. Abe was only being nice by asking if she wanted some hot chocolate. Surely he wasn't interested in her in a romantic kind of way.

Abe poked Rachel on the shoulder. "What do you say? Would ya like me to get ya somethin' to drink?"

Silas jumped up quickly, nearly tripping over his bale of straw. "Didn't ya hear what I said? If Rachel wants anything, I'll get it for her!"

Rachel's heart was thumping so hard she feared it might burst wide open. Why was Silas acting so upset? It made no sense at all.

Abe stood up, too. "Don'tcha think that's Rachel's decision?"

Silas pivoted toward Rachel. "Well? Who's gonna get the hot chocolate?"

Rachel gulped. Were they really going to force her to choose? She cleared her throat, then offered them both a brief smile. "Me. I'll get my own drink; thank you very much." With that said, she hopped up and sprinted off toward the refreshment table.

❧

Silas looked at Abe and chuckled. "Guess we've been outsmarted."

Abe shrugged and reached up to rub the back of his neck. "I think so." He started to move away but stopped after he'd taken a few steps. "Look, Silas, if Rachel and you are courtin', I'll back off. If not, then she's fair game, and I plan on makin' my move."

Silas's eyes widened. "Your move?" Heat boiled up his spine as jealousy seared through him like hot coals on the fire.

Abe nodded. "I thought I might ask her to go fishin' with me sometime."

"Fishin'?"

"Yeah. I hear tell Rachel likes to fish."

"Where'd ya hear that?"

"Someone saw her at Paradise Lake a few weeks ago. She was sittin' on the dock with her fishin' pole."

Silas leveled Abe with a look he hoped would end this conversation. "That was me she was fishin' with."

"So, you two *are* courtin'."

Silas clenched his fists. It wasn't in his nature to want to hit someone, and everything about fighting went against the Amish way, but right now he was struggling with the impulse to punch Abe Lapp right in the nose. What was the fellow trying to do—goad him into an argument or a fistfight? He'd always considered Abe to be nice enough, but up until a few moments ago he hadn't realized Abe was interested in Rachel.

Silas was still trying to decide how to deal with Abe Lapp when Rachel returned, carrying a mug of steaming hot chocolate and a piece of shoofly pie. She smiled sweetly at both of them, then seated herself on the bale of straw.

Silas leaned over so his face was mere inches from Rachel's. Her pale blue eyes seemed to probe his innermost being, and Silas felt his heart begin to hammer. With no further thought, he blurted out, "I'd like to take ya home in my courtin' buggy tonight, Rachel. Would ya be willin' to go?"

She took a little sip of her drink, glanced up at Abe, then back over at Silas and replied, *"Jah,* I will."

Now that Rachel had accepted his invitation, Silas wasn't sure how he felt. Had he asked merely to get under Abe's skin? He looked down at Rachel, sitting there so sweet and innocent, and he knew the answer to his troubling question. He really did want to take her home. He enjoyed her company, maybe a bit more than he cared to admit. The truth was, Anna had hurt him real bad, and there was still a part of him that was afraid Rachel might do the same thing.

Silas's disconcerting thoughts were jolted away when Abe slapped him on the back. *Jah,* well, *Ich bins zufreide*—all right, I am satisfied." With that, Abe walked away, leaving Silas and Rachel alone.

"What time were you plannin' to head for home?" Rachel asked as Silas took a seat on the other bale of straw.

He shrugged. "Whenever you're done eatin' your pie and hot chocolate, I suppose."

"Aren't ya gonna have some?"

He chuckled. "I already had enough food for three fellows my size."

Rachel finished the rest of her dessert and stood up. "Guess I'd better find Joseph and tell him I won't be riding home in his buggy tonight."

Silas reached for her empty plate and mug. "I'll put this away for you while you go lookin' for him."

"Danki," she said, offering him a heart-melting smile. He sure hoped he hadn't made a big mistake asking to take her home. What if she jumped to the

wrong conclusions? What if she thought that one buggy ride meant they were officially courting?

You didn't have to ask her, a voice in him reminded. *You could have conceded to Abe Lapp.* Silas gritted his teeth. *Never!*

Rachel found her brother outside by the bonfire, talking with Pauline Hostetler. She quickly explained that she'd be riding home with Silas, and Joseph seemed almost relieved.

"No problem. No problem a'tall," he said, looking down at his boots.

Rachel bit back a smile. She knew it would probably rile Joseph if she questioned him about whether he planned to escort anyone home, but she had to ask.

"You takin' anyone special home tonight?" she whispered in his ear.

In the light of the fire, she saw his face flame as he nodded. *"Jah,* Pauline."

"That's *gut.* I'm glad to hear it." She turned and waved. "See you at home."

Joseph waved back. "Yeah, later."

Rachel practically skipped back to the barn. Joseph had a girlfriend, and she was going home in Silas's courting buggy. Life was *wunderbaar,* and she felt deliriously happy!

Chapter 14

A sense of exhilaration shot through Rachel as she sat in Silas's open buggy with the crisp wind whipping against her face. She chanced a peek at her escort, hoping he, too, was enjoying the ride.

Silas grinned back at her. "I think I smell winter in the air. Won't be too awfully long and we can take out the sleigh."

We? Does he mean me and him goin' for a sleigh ride? Rachel closed her eyes and tried to picture herself snuggled beneath a warm quilt, snow falling in huge, white flakes, and the sound of sleigh bells jingling in the chilly air.

"What are you thinkin' about?" Silas asked, breaking into her musings.

Rachel's eyes snapped open. "Oh, winter. . .sleigh bells. . .snow."

Silas chuckled. "Don't forget hot apple cider and pumpkin bread. Nothin' tastes better after a sleigh ride than a big mug of cider and several thick hunks of Mom's spicy pumpkin bread."

"My favorite winter snack is popcorn, apple slices, and hot chocolate with plenty of marshmallows," Rachel interjected.

"I like those things, too." Silas snickered. "Guess there ain't much in the way of food I don't like." Reaching into his jacket pocket, he withdrew a chunk of black licorice. "Want some?"

Rachel shook her head. "No thanks." She studied him as he began chewing the candy. In spite of his hearty appetite, there wasn't an ounce of fat on Silas. He was all muscle—no doubt from doing so many farm chores. *I'd love him no matter how he looked.* It wasn't hard to picture herself and Silas sitting on the front porch of their own home, looking through binoculars and talking about all the birds nesting in their backyard.

She shook her head, as though to bring some sense of reason into her thinking. Silas was a friend, and he'd offered her a ride home from the singing. That sure didn't mean he had thoughts of romance or marriage on his mind. She couldn't allow herself to fantasize about it, even if she did want more than friendship. She loved Silas so much, and each moment they spent together only made her more sure of it. She didn't want to feel this way; it wasn't safe for her heart. But no matter how hard she tried, Rachel couldn't seem to keep from hoping that Silas would someday declare his love for her.

As they pulled into Rachel's farmyard, she released a deep sigh, wishing the ride didn't have to end so soon. If only they could keep on going. If only. . .

Silas halted the horse near the barn and turned in his seat to face Rachel. "Thanks for lettin' me bring ya home tonight. I enjoyed the ride a whole lot more than if I'd been alone."

"Me, too," she freely admitted.

"You're a special girl, Rachel. I can see why Abe Lapp would be interested in you."

Rachel's breath caught in her throat, and her cheeks burned with embarrassment. The admiration in Silas's voice sounded so genuine. His gaze dropped to her lips. For one heart-stopping moment, Rachel had the crazy idea of throwing herself into his arms and begging him to love her. She knew better than to let her emotions run wild. She had too much pride to throw herself at him.

"Sure you don't want some licorice?" Silas asked, giving her a crooked grin.

All she could do was shake her head, her thoughts so lost in the darkness of his ebony eyes, where the moonlight reflected like a pool of clear water.

Rachel's heart pulsated as Silas slipped his arms around her waist and pulled her closer. She tipped her head back and savored the sweet smell of licorice as his lips met hers in a kiss so pleasing it almost lifted her right off the buggy seat. This was her first real kiss, and she could only hope her inexperience wasn't evident as she kissed him back with all the emotion welling up within her soul.

Silas pulled away suddenly, looking shaken and confused. "Rachel, I'm so sorry, I—"

Rachel held up her hand, feeling as though a glass of cold water had been dashed in her face. "Please, don't say anything more." She hopped down from the buggy and sprinted toward the house, as the ache of humiliation bore down on her like a heavy blanket of snow. She wasn't sure why Silas had kissed her, but one thing was certain—he was sorry he had.

🌺

All the way home Silas kept berating himself. *Why did I kiss Rachel like that? She must think I'm off in the head to be doin' something so brazen on our first buggy ride.*

As Silas thought more on it, he realized as much as he'd enjoyed the kiss, it hadn't been fair to lead Rachel on. She might think because he took her home, then went so far as to kiss her, it meant they were a couple and would be courting from now on.

"Is that what it means?" he said aloud. Did he want to court Rachel Beachy? Was he feeling more than friendship for her, or did he only want to be with her because she reminded him of Anna?

Silas slapped the side of his head. "What am I sayin'? Rachel's nothin' like her older sister. Nothin' a'tall. Guess I'd better commit the whole thing to prayer. I sure enough wasn't expecting this to happen tonight, and I definitely don't have any answers."

🌺

For the next two weeks, Rachel helped out at the Swartleys', and for the next two weeks, she did everything she could to avoid Silas. It made her sick to her stomach to think that he'd actually kissed her and felt sorry about it. She really must be a little *kinder* if she thought she had any chance of winning his heart. After that night, she was sure he would never ask her to go fishing again, and he certainly wouldn't be inviting her to take another ride in his courting buggy.

Silas had tried talking with Rachel on several occasions, but she kept putting him off, saying she was too busy helping his mother. Rachel knew her time of avoidance was almost over, for today's preaching service was being held at the Beachys' home, and Silas and his family had already arrived.

Rachel was amazed at how quickly the three-hour service went by. Usually it seemed to take forever, but today was different. Maybe it was because Silas was sitting across the aisle and kept sending glances her way. Beyond the flicker of a smile, she had no idea what he was thinking. Was it the kiss they'd shared two weeks ago? Was he waiting for church to be over so he could corner Rachel and tell her he didn't want to see her anymore? If she kept busy in the kitchen, maybe she could avoid him again today. That's just what she planned to do. . .stay busy and out of sight.

Things went well for awhile, but tables had been set up out in the barn for eating, and shortly after the noon meal was served, Rachel went back to the house. She planned to get another pot of coffee for the menfolk and carry out one of the pies she and Mom had baked the day before.

Much to Rachel's surprise, she discovered Silas leaning against the cupboard, arms folded across his chest, a silly grin plastered on his face. "I was hopin' you'd come to the kitchen," he said, taking a few steps in her direction.

She made no reply but moved quickly toward the stove and grabbed the pot of coffee.

"How's about goin' for a walk with me, so we can talk?" he asked, following her across the room.

Rachel averted her gaze and headed for the door, forgetting about the apple pie she was planning to take back to the barn. "As you can probably see, I'm kinda busy right now," she mumbled.

"You won't be helpin' serve all day," he reminded. "How about after you're done?"

"I really don't think we have anything to talk about."

Silas stepped in front of her, blocking the door. "Please, Rachel. . .just for a few minutes? I've wanted to talk to you for the last two weeks, but there never seemed to be a good time." He smiled. "Besides, I had some stuff to pray about."

Rachel nodded slowly. *"Jah,* me, too."

"So, can we meet out by the willow tree, say, in one hour?"

She shrugged. "Okay."

❧

At the appointed time, Rachel donned a heavy sweater and stepped onto the front porch. The afternoon air had cooled considerably, and a chill shivered through her. She caught sight of Silas out in the yard, talking to one of his cousins. She started across the lawn but stopped just before she reached the weeping willow tree. Silas was saying something to Rudy, and her ears perked up. She was sure he had mentioned her sister's name. *Why would Silas be talking to his cousin about Anna?*

A group of *kinder* ran past, laughing and hollering so loud she couldn't make out what either Silas or Rudy were saying anymore.

David Yoder, a child with Down's syndrome, waved to Rachel, and she waved back, hoping he wouldn't call out her name. The last thing she needed was for Silas to catch her listening in on his conversation.

The children finally wandered off, and Rachel breathed a sigh of relief. She leaned heavily against the trunk of the tree and turned her attention back to Silas and his cousin.

"So you're in love with her?" she heard Rudy ask.

"Afraid so," Silas answered. "Don't rightly think I'll ever find anyone else I could love as much."

Rachel's heart slammed into her chest. Even after all these months, Silas still wasn't over Anna. *That's probably why he said he was sorry for kissin' me,* she fumed. *Most likely, he was wishin' it had been Anna and not me in his courtin' buggy.*

Tears burned the back of Rachel's eyes. She should have known better than to allow her emotions to get carried away. Silas cared nothing about her, and he never had. He still loved Anna and probably always would, even though she was married and had left the Amish faith. She knew many people carried a torch for lost loves, and because of their pain, they never found love again. Mom had told her once that it almost happened to her great-aunt Mim. She was jilted by her first love, and for many years she carried a torch for him. Finally, she set her feelings aside and learned to love again. But that was only because she'd allowed the Lord to work on her bitter spirit. Rachel wasn't so sure Silas wanted to find love again—especially with a *kinder* like her.

Tired of trying to analyze things, Rachel spun around. She was about to head back to the house when she felt someone's hand touch her shoulder. "Where ya headin'? I thought we were goin' for a walk."

Rachel shrugged Silas's hand away. "I heard ya talkin' to Rudy. If you're still pinin' for Anna, then why bother takin' a walk with a little *kinder* like me?"

Rudy raised his eyebrows and moved away, but Silas kept walking beside her. When she didn't slow down, he grabbed her around the waist and pulled her to his side. "We need to talk."

Like a tightly coiled spring, Rachel released her fury on him. "Let go of me!" Her eyes were burning like fire, and she almost choked on the knot lodged in her throat.

"*Wass ist letz?*"

"Nothin's wrong!" she shouted.

Silas opened his mouth as if to say something more, but she cut him off. "Save it! I've heard all I need to know." She darted away without even a backward glance. She'd been a fool to think she could ever make Silas forget about Anna and fall in love with her. She'd been stupid to get caught up in a dumb thing like this. . .letting herself hope for the impossible. The one thing she'd enjoyed most about her friendship with Silas was how comfortable they seemed with each other.

Not anymore, though. That all ended when she'd heard him tell Rudy that he was still in love with Anna. If Silas wanted to pine his life away for a love he'd never have, then that was *his* problem. Rachel planned to get on with her life!

❧

Silas groaned as he watched Rachel race up the steps and disappear into her house. One of the Beachys' dogs howled, and the mournful sound echoed in his soul. Rachel had heard something he'd told Rudy, but she refused to let Silas explain. Now everything was ruined between them, and it was a bitter pill to swallow. There was no chance of a relationship with Rachel Beachy because she didn't trust him. Maybe with good reason. He hadn't been so good at trusting lately, either. He'd said he never wanted to move away from God, but he felt himself slipping into despair.

He turned toward his horse and buggy. There was no point in hanging around here. Maybe he should accept things as they were and get on with his life.

Chapter 15

Rachel felt such relief when Katie Swartley's cast finally came off, and she was able to stay home, even if it did mean spending more time helping Pauline in the greenhouse. Anything would be better than facing Silas every day. Knowing he was still in love with Anna and unable to quit loving him herself, Rachel felt a sense of hopelessness. Everything looked different now—the trees weren't as green, the birdsong wasn't as bright. She had nothing to praise God for anymore, and her times of prayer and Bible study became less and less.

The next singing was planned for the second Sunday in November and was to be held at the Hostetlers' place. Joseph had already made it clear that he would be going, and it was obvious that he and Pauline were officially courting. Even though Rachel was happy for them, she couldn't help but feel sorry for herself.

"Are you goin' to the singin' tonight?" her brother asked as they met in the barn that morning before church.

She shook her head. "I don't think so."

"Why not? It could be the last one for awhile, now that the weather's turnin' colder."

She shrugged. "I plan to work on my hope chest tonight."

Joseph grabbed her arm as she started to walk away. "It's Silas Swartley, ain't it? You haven't been actin' right for the last few weeks, and I have a hunch it's got somethin' to do with your feelin's for him."

Rachel felt a familiar burning at the back of her eyes, and she blinked rapidly, hoping to keep the tears from falling. "I'd rather not talk about Silas, if ya don't mind." She shrugged his hand away. "I need to feed the kittens, and if I'm not mistaken, you've got a few chores to do as well."

Joseph moved into the horse's stall without another word, and Rachel let out a sigh of relief. She and Joseph might not always see eye-to-eye, but at least he cared enough about her feelings to drop the subject of Silas Swartley.

As Rachel rounded the corner of the barn, she noticed Dad, down on his knees beside the woodpile. His face was screwed up in obvious pain, and his deep moan confirmed that fact. Rachel rushed to his side and squatted beside him. "*Wass ist letz?* You look like you're hurtin' real bad."

"I strained my back tryin' to lift a big hunk of wood. Must've bent over wrong." Dad groaned. "Don't think I can get up on my own, Rachel. Can ya go get Joseph?"

Rachel gently patted her father's shoulder. "*Jah,* sure. Just hang on a few more minutes and try to relax." She jumped up and bolted for the barn.

Joseph was still feeding the horses, and she hurried into the stall where he was forking hay. "*Mach schnell*—go quickly! Dad needs your help."

Joseph lifted his brows in question. "I'm busy, Rachel. Can't he get Perry to do whatever needs doin'?"

Rachel clutched his arm as he was about to jab the pitchfork into another bale of hay. "Dad's hurt his back and can't even stand up. Perry ain't strong enough to get him on his feet, much less help him into the house."

Joseph's blue eyes widened, and he dropped the pitchfork immediately. "Where is he?"

"Out by the woodpile."

Joseph raced from the barn, and Rachel was right behind him. They found their father in the same position as he'd been in when Rachel left him, only now, little beads of sweat covered his forehead. Rachel knew he must be hurting something awful, and she felt deep compassion for him.

Joseph grabbed Dad under one arm, and Rachel took hold of the other one. "On the count of three," Joseph instructed. "One. . .two. . .three!"

Dad moaned as they pulled him to his feet. Walking slightly bent over, he allowed Joseph and Rachel to support most of his weight as they slowly made their way to the house.

They found Mom in the kitchen, sitting in her wheelchair at the table, drinking a cup of tea. Elizabeth and Perry sat across from her, finishing up their bowls of oatmeal.

"*Ach*, my!" Mom cried. "What's wrong, Daniel? It appears you can barely walk."

Dad grunted and placed his hands on the edge of the cupboard for support. "Fool back went out on me, Rebekah. Happened when I was gettin' more wood." He swallowed real hard, like he was having a hard time talking. "Guess I'll have to make a trip to town tomorrow and see Doc Landers for some poppin' and crackin'. He'll have me back on my feet in no time a'tall."

Rachel glanced over at Joseph, and he gave her a knowing look. The last time Dad's back went out, it took more than a few days' rest or a couple of treatments with the chiropractor to get him back on his feet. There was no doubt about it; Dad wouldn't be going to church this morning, and more than likely he'd be flat on his back in bed for the next several weeks.

❧

Silas had just arrived at the singing, and he was hoping to find Rachel there as well. She'd seemed so distant lately—nothing like the fun-loving Rachel he'd gone fishing with a few weeks ago. Maybe he'd have a chance to clear things up with her. Even if there was no possibility for a future with Rachel, they had a lot in common, and he would still like to be her friend. He remembered how much fun they'd had fishing and studying birds, and his heart skipped a beat at the thought of their first kiss.

Silas caught sight of Joseph sitting on one side of the Hostetlers' barn. He was sharing a bale of straw with Pauline, which was no surprise to Silas. He hurried over and squatted down beside them. "Did Rachel come with you tonight? I haven't seen any sign of her."

Joseph shook his head. "She stayed home. Said somethin' about workin' on her hope chest."

"Hmm. . ." was all Silas could manage.

"Besides, our *daed* hurt his back this mornin', and Rachel probably figured Mom would be needin' her."

Silas wrinkled his forehead. "Sorry to hear that. Will he be able to help you finish the harvest?"

"I doubt it. He's in a lot of pain—could barely make it up the stairs and into bed," Joseph answered. "Guess that means Perry will have to stay home from school and help out. I sure can't put the hay up by myself."

Silas shook his head. "No, I guess not." He thought he should say more, but Joseph had turned his attentions to Pauline, so Silas let his thoughts shift back to Rachel.

Wonder why she would be workin' on her hope chest? After the way she acted the other night, it was fairly obvious she was done with me. Sure as anythin', Rachel isn't stocking her hope chest with the idea of marryin' me.

Suddenly, a light seemed to dawn. *Unless she and Abe Lapp are more serious about each other than I realized.* He groaned softly and stood up. Maybe it was for the best. Rachel would probably be better off with Abe anyway. They were closer in age, and Abe hadn't said or done anything to make Rachel mistrust him.

Silas looked down at Joseph and Pauline. "Well, guess I'll head over to the refreshment table and see what's good to eat."

"Jah, okay," Joseph muttered, although Silas was pretty sure Rachel's brother hadn't heard a word he'd said. He was too busy flirting with his date.

❧

When Rachel finished helping Mom and Elizabeth clear things away and wash the supper dishes, she excused herself to go to her room.

"You're not sleepy already, are ya?" Mom asked, rolling her wheelchair across the kitchen to where Rachel stood by the hallway door. "Since your *daed's* in bed and Perry's upstairs readin' to him, I thought maybe we three women could work on a puzzle or play a game."

Elizabeth jumped up and down. "Yes! Yes! And let's make a big batch of popcorn!"

Rachel felt terrible about throwing cold water on their plans, but she had work to do upstairs. Besides, she wasn't fit company for anyone tonight. "Maybe some other time," she said apologetically. "I had planned to work on my hope chest tonight."

Mom's eyes brightened. "I'm right glad to hear that, Rachel. I was beginnin' to wonder if you were ever gonna take an interest in marriage or that hope chest your *daed* made for your sixteenth birthday."

I've got an interest, all right. Trouble is, the man I want is in love with my married

452

sister. Rachel sure couldn't tell Mom what she was thinking. She knew that even though her mother rarely spoke of Anna anymore, she still missed her firstborn and was terribly hurt by her decision to go "fancy." There was no point in bringing up a sore subject, so Rachel smiled and said, "See you two in the mornin'."

When Rachel got to her room, she quickly knelt on the floor in front of her hope chest. The last time she'd opened it, she had been filled with such high hopes. Back then she and Silas seemed to be getting closer, and she'd even allowed herself to believe he might actually be falling in love with her. For a brief time she'd been praising God like crazy. Her hopeful dream had been dented when Silas said he was sorry for kissing her, and it had been smashed to smithereens when she'd overheard him telling his cousin Rudy that he still loved Anna. "What's the use in havin' a hope chest if you aren't plannin' to get married?" she murmured. "I could never marry anyone but Silas, because he's the only man I'll ever love."

Rachel lifted the lid and studied the contents of her cedar chest. There was the lamp Dad had given her, along with the pillowcases Mom had made. She'd purchased a few new items as well—a set of dishes, some towels, and a tablecloth. She'd also made a braided throw rug, some pot holders, and had even been thinking about starting a quilt with the double-ring pattern. There was no point in making one now. In fact, the best thing to do was either sell off or give away most of the things in her hope chest. She pulled out the set of pillowcases and the braided throw rug, knowing she could use them in her room. The other things she put in a cardboard box, planning to take them to the greenhouse the following day.

Since Christmas wasn't far off, she was fairly certain she could sell some things to their customers. Anything that didn't sell, she would take to Thomas Benner, the owner of the Country Store in Paradise, and see if he might put them out on consignment. Maybe she would use the money she made to buy a concrete birdbath for Mom's flower garden. If she got enough from the sales, she might also buy several bird feeders from Eli Yoder, which would bring even more birds into their yard. At least she could still take some pleasure in bird-watching—even though it would have to be without Silas Swartley. As long as she was able to get away by herself to enjoy the great outdoors, Rachel could endure anything—even losing Silas to the memory of her sister.

Rachel's only concern was what her mother would think when she saw her things for sale in the greenhouse. Mom had seemed so hopeful about Rachel adding items to her hope chest. If she knew what was really going on, she'd probably get all nervous, thinking she'd have to wait until Elizabeth grew up before she could plan a wedding. Of course, if things kept on the way they were with Joseph and Pauline, Mom could be in on their wedding plans.

Rachel closed the empty chest, and in doing so, she spotted Anna's hope chest. All these months it had been in the corner of her room, and never once had she opened it. It was all she had left of her sister. If she opened it now, memories of Anna and reminders of how much she missed her would probably make her cry. She already felt enough pain and didn't think she could bear any more right now.

Rachel ran her fingers along the top of Anna's cedar chest as tears slipped from her eyes and rolled down her cheeks. "Oh, Anna, wasn't it bad enough that you broke Silas's heart by marryin' his best friend? Did ya really have to move away and go English on us?" Rachel choked on a sob as she turned away from Anna's hope chest. *Will I ever see Anna again? Will I ever marry and become a mama?*

Chapter 16

Silas tossed and turned most of the night. He had to see Rachel again and try to explain things. Even if she never wanted to court him, he needed to clear the air and make her understand the way he was feeling. If only they could spend more time together. As he drifted off to sleep, visions of Rachel's sweet face and two little dimples filled up his senses. If only. . .

When Silas awoke the next morning, he had a plan. Rachel had been kind enough to help out at their place when Mom broke her arm, so now he could return the favor. If he helped Joseph get in the hay, he'd be busy out in the fields most of the day, but mealtimes would be spent in the Beachys' kitchen. It would be a good chance to see Rachel and maybe get in a word or two with her. It was worth a try. Besides, Daniel Beachy was laid up right now. He was sure the man would welcome his help.

Rachel had just finished washing and drying the breakfast dishes when she heard a horse and buggy pull into the yard. She peeked out the kitchen window and gulped when she saw who it was. Silas Swartley had climbed out of his buggy and was heading toward the house.

Joseph and Perry were in the fields. Elizabeth was at school. Dad and Mom had gone into town to see Doc Landers. That left Rachel all alone at the house. Silas had seen her through the window and waved. She had no other choice but to open the door.

"*Gut Morgen,*" Silas said when Rachel answered his knock. "I missed you at the singin' last night."

"I had other things to do," she replied stiffly.

"So I heard." Silas's forehead wrinkled. "I also heard your *daed* hurt his back."

Rachel nodded. "It goes out on him now and then. He's at the chiropractor's right now." She still hadn't invited Silas inside, and since she didn't plan to, Rachel stepped out onto the porch, hoping he would take the hint and be on his way.

"I came to help with the harvest," Silas surprised her by saying. "Joseph said your *daed* won't be up to it now, and since we're all done harvestin' over at our place, I figured I'd offer my services here."

Rachel flicked an imaginary piece of lint off the sleeve of her dress and tried to avoid his steady gaze. "That's right nice of you," she murmured. "Perry stayed home from school to help Joseph today. But it won't be good if he misses too many days."

"That's what I thought." Silas shifted from one foot to the other. "I—uh—was kinda hopin' you and I could have a little talk before I head on out to the fields."

Rachel blinked. "There ain't nothin' to talk about. Besides, I've gotta get to the greenhouse and open up."

"I thought Pauline worked in the greenhouse."

"She does, but she's got chores at her house to do every mornin', so she usually doesn't get here 'til ten or after."

Silas cleared his throat. "Okay, I'll let ya get to it then." He pivoted and started down the steps, but when he got to the bottom, he halted and turned back around. "Maybe later we can talk?"

She raised her gaze to his and nodded slowly. *"Jah,* maybe."

Silas saw tears clinging like dewdrops to Rachel's long, pale lashes. It was all he could do to keep from pulling her into his arms. Before their misunderstanding, he'd been drawing closer to Rachel, and some of his old fears had been sliding into a locked trunk of unwanted memories. Now he wondered why they had drifted apart. Maybe the real issue was trust. Did she trust him? Did he trust her?

A deep sense of longing inched its way through Silas's body. He'd missed seeing Rachel every day, and if the look on her sweet face was any indication of the way she felt, then he was fairly certain she'd been missing him, too.

"See you later, Rachel." Silas offered her his best smile, lifted a hand to wave, then headed for the fields.

"Later," she mumbled.

Rachel entered the greenhouse, carrying her box of hope chest items in her arms and a lot of confusion in her brain. It was kind of Silas to offer his help with the hay harvest, but how would she handle him coming over every day? She'd tried so hard to get him out of her mind, and now him wanting to talk had her real concerned. Was he planning to tell her again how sorry he was for that unexpected kiss of a few weeks ago? Did he want to explain why he still loved Anna, even though they could never be together? Well, Rachel already knew that much, and she sure as anything didn't need to hear it again. She'd made up her mind—she was not going to say anything more to Silas than a polite word or two—no matter how many days he came to help out. Somehow she must keep her feelings under control.

Rachel shivered as goose bumps erupted on her arms, and she knew it wasn't from the chill in the greenhouse. "Get busy," she scolded herself. "It's the only thing that will keep you sane."

Rachel quickly set to work pricing her hope chest items; then she placed them on an empty shelf near the front door. She had no more than put the Open sign in the window when the first customer of the day showed up. It was Laura Yoder, and Rachel breathed a sigh of relief when she saw that the pretty redhead was alone. The last time Laura came to the greenhouse, she'd brought both of her children along. Barbara, who was two and a half, had pulled one of Mom's prized African violets off the shelf, and the little girl had quite a time playing in all that rich, black dirt. Laura's four-year-old son, David, had been so full of questions. The child's handicap didn't slow him down much, and, like most children his age,

David was curious about everything.

As much as Rachel loved *kinder,* it sorely tried her patience when they came in with their folks and ran about the greenhouse like it was a play yard. If it was disturbing to her, she could only imagine how her other customers might feel. Most Amish parents were quite strict and didn't let their children get away with much, but Laura seemed to be more tolerant of her children's antics. However, Rachel was pretty sure she would step in and discipline should it become absolutely necessary.

"I see you're all alone today," Rachel said as her customer began to look around the store.

Laura nodded. "I left the little ones with Eli's *mamm.* I've got several errands to run, and I figured I could get them done much quicker if I was by myself." She chuckled. "Besides, Mary Ellen seems to like her role as Grandma."

Rachel smiled. "I guess she would. Let's see. . .how many grandchildren does she have now?"

"Five in all. Martha Rose has three, as I'm sure you know. And of course, there's my two busy little ones. Mary Ellen's son, Lewis, and his wife are expectin' most any day, so soon there'll be six." Laura moved over by the shelf where Rachel had displayed her hope chest items. "There's some right nice things here. If I didn't already have a sturdy set of dishes, I'd be tempted to buy these," she said, fingering the edge of a white stoneware cup.

"Guess the right buyer will come along sooner or later," Rachel remarked, making no reference to the fact that they were her hope chest dishes. Mom hadn't been very happy when she learned that Rachel was bringing them here, but Rachel was relieved when she chose not to make an issue of it. Truth be told, her mother was probably praying that Rachel's things wouldn't sell and some nice fellow would come along and propose marriage real soon.

"How's the flower business?" Laura asked, pulling Rachel out of her reflections.

"Oh, fair to middlin'," she replied with a nod. Rachel didn't feel the inclination to tell Laura that except for the need to help out, she really didn't care much about the flower business. Laura Yoder seemed like such a prim and proper sort of lady. She probably wouldn't understand Rachel's desire to be outdoors, enjoying all the wildlife God had created.

Sometimes Rachel wished she'd been born a boy, just so she could spend more time outside. Even baling or bucking hay would be preferable to being cooped up inside a stuffy old greenhouse all day.

"Have you got any yellow mums?" Laura asked, once more breaking into Rachel's thoughts.

"Mums? Oh, sure, I think we've got several colors," Rachel answered with a nod. "Come with me to the other room and we'll see what's available."

Rachel studied Laura as she checked over the chrysanthemums. Even though her hair was red and her face was pretty, she looked plain, just like all other Amish women. It was hard to imagine that she was ever part of the fancy, English world. Rachel had been a girl when Eli Yoder married Laura, and she'd only met her after

Laura had chosen to become Amish. She had no idea how Laura used to look dressed in modern clothes or even how the woman felt about her past life. *Maybe I should ask her a few questions about bein' English. It might help me better understand why Anna left home.*

Taking a deep breath for courage, Rachel plunged ahead. "Say, Laura, I was wonderin' about somethin'."

Laura picked up a yellow mum plant and pivoted to face Rachel. "What is it?"

"I know you used to be English."

Laura nodded.

"You've probably heard that my sister Anna married Reuben Yutzy awhile back, and the two of them left the faith and moved to Lancaster."

Laura's expression turned solemn. *"Jah,* I know about that."

"Except for one letter Anna sent to your sister-in-law, Martha Rose, we haven't heard a word from her," Rachel said with a catch in her voice. "It sure hurts knowin' she's no longer part of our family."

Laura gently touched Rachel's shoulder. "I'm sure it's not easy for any of you. . .not even Anna."

Rachel's eyes filled with unexpected tears, and she sniffed. "Ya really think it pains her, too?"

"I'm almost certain of it." Laura drew in a deep breath and let it out with a soft moan. "It hurt my folks when I left the English world to become Amish. They never quit lovin' me or offerin' their support, though. We stayed in touch, and pretty soon my *daed* surprised me real good by sellin' his law practice and movin' out to a small farm nearby." She smiled. "My folks are still English, of course, but they're livin' a much simpler life now, and me and the *kinder* get to see lots more of them."

"Do you think there's a chance that Anna and my folks will ever mend their fences—even if Anna and Reuben never reconcile with the church? Maybe even come to the point where they can start visitin' each other from time to time?"

Laura clasped Rachel's hand. "I'll surely pray for that, as I'm sure you're already doin'."

"Jah, that and a whole lot of other things."

Laura followed Rachel back to the front of the greenhouse, where Rachel wrapped a strip of brown paper around the plant and wrote up a bill. Laura paid her, picked up the mum, and was just about to open the front door when Pauline came rushing in. Her cheeks were pink, and a few strands of tawny yellow hair peeked out from under her *Kapp.* "Whew! It's gettin' a bit windy out there!" she exclaimed.

Laura laughed. "I can tell. You look like you've been standin' underneath a windmill, for goodness' sake."

Pauline giggled and reached up to readjust her covering, which was slightly askew. "Sure is a *gut* day to be indoors. I'm mighty glad I have this job workin' at Grandma's Place."

Wish I could say the same, Rachel thought ruefully. *"For I have learned, in whatsoever state I am, therewith to be content."* The verse from Philippians that Mom often liked to quote came popping into Rachel's mind. *Okay, Lord, I'll try harder.*

Pauline asked about Laura's *kinder,* and Laura spent the next few minutes telling her how much they were growing. She even told how her cat, Foosie, had paired up with one of the barn cats. Now the children had a bunch of fluffy brown-and-white kittens to occupy their busy little hands.

It amazed Rachel the way the two women visited, as though they'd always been friends. She knew from the talk she'd heard that it wasn't so. Truth be told, Pauline used to dislike Laura because she had stolen Eli Yoder's heart and he'd married her and not Pauline.

Rachel could relate well to the pain of knowing the man you loved was carrying a torch for someone else and didn't see you as anything more than a friend. She couldn't imagine how Pauline had gotten through those difficult years after Eli had jilted her and married an English woman. It amazed her to see that there was no animosity between the two women now.

Laura finally headed out, and Pauline got right to work watering plants and repotting some that had outgrown their containers. She was so happy doing her work that she was actually humming.

"I was wonderin' if you'd mind me askin' a personal question," Rachel asked when Pauline took a break and sat down on the stool behind the cash register.

"Sure, what is it?"

Rachel leaned on the other side of the counter and offered Pauline a brief smile. She hoped her question wasn't out of line and wouldn't be taken the wrong way. "I know you and Laura were at odds for awhile, and I was wonderin' what happened to make you so friendly with one another."

Pauline smiled. "I used to be jealous of Laura because I felt she stole Eli away from me. After she had David and went home to her folks, I was even hopin' Eli and I might still have a chance. But then she came back to Lancaster Valley, and when she did, she was like a changed person. She'd found Jesus, and one day she came callin' on me. Said we needed to have a little talk."

Rachel's interest was definitely piqued. "Really? Mind if I ask what was said?"

Pauline shrugged. "Nothin' much except Laura apologized for making me so miserable, and I told her I was sorry, too." She frowned deeply. "The thing was, I knew in my heart that Eli had never been in love with me. He and I were only *gut* friends. From the very beginning, I should have been Christian enough to turn loose of him and let him find the kind of happiness with Laura that he deserved. Truth be told, Eli probably did me a favor by marryin' Laura."

Rachel's eyebrows shot up. "Really? How's that?"

Pauline smiled. "If he'd married me, I never would have gotten to know Joe so well, and we. . ." Her words trailed off, and she blushed a deep crimson. "Guess you've probably figured out that I'm in love with your big brother."

Rachel grinned back at Pauline. "*Jah,* and I'm positive he feels the selfsame way about you." She turned and glanced across the room at her hope chest items. "Say, ya think ya might be interested in some things for your hope chest?"

Chapter 17

Daniel Beachy's back took nearly two weeks to heal, and Silas came over every day but Sunday to help with chores and the last of the harvesting. In all that time, he never had his heart-to-heart talk with Rachel. It wasn't because he hadn't tried. He'd made every effort to get her alone, but she always made up some excuse about being too busy. Silas was getting discouraged and had about decided to give up when he devised a plan. Yesterday had been his last day helping out. Daniel had assured him that he was feeling well enough to start doing some light chores, and the hay had been baled and put away in the barn. Silas wouldn't be going back to the Beachy farm—at least not to help out. However, that didn't mean he couldn't pay a little visit to the greenhouse.

❧

Since none of Rachel's hope chest items had sold yet, she decided it might be time to take them into town and see if Thomas Benner would sell them in his store. There had been storm clouds brewing that morning, and Dad wouldn't let Rachel take the horse and buggy to town because he was worried she might get caught in a snowstorm. She'd really been hoping to get her things into the Country Store in time for the busy Christmas shopping season. Now she'd have to wait until the weather improved. Besides, Mom had come down with a cold, and it wouldn't be fair to expect her to work with Pauline in the greenhouse while Rachel went to town.

Rachel donned her woolen cape and headed for the greenhouse. She'd talked her mother into going back to bed and had left a warm pot of fenugreek tea by her bedside. Mom would be resting, and Rachel would be all by herself until Pauline showed up. If the weather got real bad, Pauline might not come today. For that matter, they might not even have any customers. Who in their right mind would want to visit a greenhouse when the weather was cold and threatening to snow?

Shortly after she opened the greenhouse and stoked up the wood-burning stove, Rachel heard a horse and buggy pull up. Figuring it was probably Pauline, she flung open the door. To her astonishment, Abe Lapp stepped down from his closed-in buggy. She hadn't seen Abe since the last preaching service, and then she'd only spoken a few words to him when she was serving the menfolk.

"Looks like it could storm," Abe said when he entered the greenhouse. He was wearing a dark wool jacket, and his black felt hat was pulled down over his ears.

Ears that are a mite too big, Rachel noticed. An image of Silas sifted through her mind. *Abe's not nearly as good-looking as Silas, but then—as Dad often says—looks ain't everythin'.*

"What can I help you with, Abe?" Rachel asked as she slipped behind the counter and took a seat on her stool.

Abe took off his hat, and it was all Rachel could do to keep from laughing out loud. A bunch of his hair stood straight up. It looked as though he hadn't bothered to comb it that morning.

"I really didn't come here to buy anything," Abe said, looking kind of embarrassed. He jammed his free hand inside his coat pocket and offered her a crooked grin.

"What did ya come for?"

"I—uh—was wonderin' if you'd like to go to the next singin' with me."

Rachel frowned. "There's gonna be another one? I thought with the weather turnin' bad and all, there would be no more singin's 'til spring."

Abe shrugged. "There's supposed to be one this Sunday night, out at Herman Weaver's place. Guess if the weather gets real nasty, they'll have to cancel it."

Rachel wasn't sure what to say next. She didn't want to go to any singing—with or without Abe Lapp. She'd known Abe and his family a good many years and knew Abe was a nice enough fellow. He just wasn't Silas Swartley, and if she couldn't be courted by the man she loved, she didn't want to be courted at all. *Of course, you could just go as friends,* a little voice reminded. Still, that might lead Abe on, and she didn't want him to start thinking there was any chance for the two of them as a couple.

"So, what's your answer?" Abe asked, breaking into Rachel's disconcerting thoughts. "Can I come by your place Sunday night and give you a lift to the Weavers'?"

Rachel chewed on her lower lip as she searched for the right words. She didn't want to hurt Abe's feelings, but her answer had to be no. "I'm flattered that you'd want to escort me to the singin', but I'm afraid I can't go."

Abe's dark eyebrows drew downward. "Can't or won't?"

She swallowed hard. "My *mamm* has a bad cold, and Dad just got on his feet after a bout with his back. I think it's best for me to stick close to home."

Abe nodded and slapped his hat back on his head. "Good enough. I'll see you around then." With that, he marched out the door.

Rachel followed, hoping to call out a friendly good-bye, but Abe was already in his buggy and had taken up the reins. *Maybe I made a mistake,* she lamented. *Maybe I should have agreed to go with him. Wouldn't Abe be better than no one?*

She bowed her head and prayed, "Lord, if I'm not supposed to love Silas, please give me the grace to accept it."

As if on cue, she noticed there was another buggy parked in the driveway, and she recognized the driver. Rachel's heart started hammering real hard, and her hands felt like a couple of slippery trout as she watched Silas Swartley step down from his buggy and start walking toward the greenhouse. She couldn't imagine why he would be here. The harvest was done, and Dad's back was much better.

Silas rubbed his hands briskly together as he entered the greenhouse. His nose was red from the cold, and his black felt hat was covered with tiny snow-flakes. Dad had been right. . .the snow was here.

Rachel moved over to the counter, her heart riding on the waves of expectation. Silas followed. "It's mighty cold out. Guess winter's decided to come a bit early." He nodded toward the door. "Say, wasn't that Abe Lapp I saw gettin' into his buggy?"

"*Jah*, it was Abe."

"Did he buy out the store?"

She shook her head. "Nope, didn't buy a thing."

Silas raised his eyebrows. "How come?"

"Abe stopped by to ask me to the singin' this Sunday night," Rachel said with a shrug. "Can I help ya with somethin', Silas?"

He squinted his dark eyes, and Rachel wondered why he made no comment about Abe's invitation.

"I came by to see if you have any poinsettias. Mom's sister lives in Ohio, and she's comin' to visit soon. Mom thought since her birthday's soon, she'd give her a plant," Silas mumbled.

Rachel stepped out from behind the counter. "I believe we still have one or two poinsettias in the other room. Shall we go take a look-see?"

Silas followed silently as they went to the room where a variety of plants were on display. Rachel showed him several poinsettias, and he selected the largest one.

Back at the manually operated cash register, Rachel noticed her hands were trembling as she counted out Silas's change. Just the nearness of him took her breath away, and it irked her to think he had the power to make her feel so weak in the knees.

"Seen any interestin' birds lately?" Silas asked when she handed him the plant.

Glad for the diversion, she smiled. "I saw a great horned owl the other night when I was lookin' up in the tree with my binoculars. The critter was sure hootin' like crazy."

Silas chuckled; then he started for the door. Just as he got to the shelf where Rachel's hope chest items were placed, he stopped and bent down to examine them. "These look like some mighty fine dishes. Mind if I ask how much they cost?"

"The price sticker is on the bottom of the top plate," she answered.

Silas picked it up and whistled. "Kind of high, don'tcha think?" His face turned redder than the plant he was holding. "Sorry. Guess it's not my place to decide how much your folks should be sellin' things for."

Rachel thought about telling him that it wasn't Mom or Dad who'd priced the dishes, but she didn't want Silas to know she was selling off her hope chest items. She forced a smile and said, "I hope your aunt enjoys the poinsettia."

Silas nodded and opened the front door. "I hope Abe Lapp knows how lucky he is," he called over his shoulder.

Rachel slowly shook her head. "Now what in the world did he mean by that? Surely Silas doesn't think me and Abe are courtin'." Of course, she hadn't bothered to tell him that she'd turned down Abe's offer to escort her to the singing. But then, he hadn't asked, either.

Rachel moved over to the window and watched with a heavy heart as Silas drove out of sight. She glanced over at the dishes he'd said were too high-priced and wondered if he had considered buying them, maybe as a gift for his mother or aunt.

"Guess I should lower the price some." Rachel felt moisture on her cheeks. She'd been trying so hard to be hopeful and keep praising God, but after seeing Silas again, she realized her hopes had been for nothing. He obviously had no interest in her. Rachel wondered if God even cared about her. Hadn't He been listening to her prayers and praises all these months? Didn't He realize how much her heart ached for Silas Swartley?

Chapter 18

I t snowed hard for the next few days, but on Saturday the weather improved some, so Rachel convinced Joseph to hitch up the sleigh and drive her to the Country Store. It was only the second week of December, but there was still a chance people would be looking for things to give as Christmas presents. She had finally sold some towels and a few pot holders to customers at the greenhouse, but she still needed to get rid of the dishes, the kerosene lamp, and a tablecloth.

Thomas Benner was more than happy to take Rachel's things on consignment, although he did mention that they would have had a better chance of selling if she'd brought them in a few weeks earlier.

By the time Rachel left the store and found Joseph, who'd gone looking for something to give Pauline for Christmas, it was beginning to snow again.

"We'd best be gettin' on home," Joseph said, looking up at the sky. "If this keeps on, the roads could get mighty slippery. I wouldn't want some car to go slidin' into our sleigh."

"You're right; we should leave now," Rachel said as she climbed into the sleigh. She reached under the seat and withdrew an old quilt, wrapping it snugly around the lower half of her body. "Brr. . .it's gettin' downright cold!"

Joseph picked up the reins and got the horse moving. "Yep, sure is."

Rachel glanced over at her brother. He seemed to be off in some other world. "So, what'd you get for Pauline?"

He smiled. "I bought her a pair of gardening gloves and a book about flowers."

"She should like that, since she enjoys working in the greenhouse so much."

Joseph nodded. "She's sure changed, don'tcha think?"

Rachel bit back the laughter bubbling in her throat. "I think you've been *gut* for her."

His dark eyebrows lifted. "You really think so?"

"I do."

"Well, she's been *gut* for me, too."

"She's not worried about your age difference anymore?"

He shook his head. "Nope, doesn't seem to be."

"And you're okay with it?"

"Yep."

"I'm glad."

"Come spring, I'm thinkin' about askin' her to marry me." Joseph glanced over at Rachel. "Don't you goin' sayin' anything now, ya hear?"

"Oh, I won't," she assured him. "It's not my place to tell."

"I'm sorry things didn't work out for you and Silas," Joseph said sincerely.

Rachel grimaced. "It wasn't meant to be, that's all. I just have to learn to be content with my life as it is. There's no point in hopin' for the impossible. Job in the Bible did, and look where it got him."

"Think about it, Rachel. Even through all his trials, Job never lost hope," Joseph reminded. "And in the end, God blessed Job with even more than he'd lost."

Rachel drew in a deep breath. "I guess you're right, but it's not always easy to have hope. Especially when things don't go as we've planned."

"Life is full of twists and turns," Joseph remarked. "It's how we choose to deal with things that makes the difference in our attitudes. Our hope should be in Jesus, not man, and not on our circumstances."

Rachel stared straight ahead. She didn't want to talk about Job, hope, or even God right now. She was too worried about the weather. The snow was coming down harder, and the road was completely covered. She watched the passing scenery, noting that the yard of the one-room schoolhouse was empty. No bicycles. No scooters. No sign of any children. "School must have been dismissed early today. Nancy Frey probably thought it would be best to let the *kinder* go before the weather got any worse," she commented.

They rode along in silence awhile, until a rescue vehicle came sailing past, its red lights blinking off and on and the siren blaring to beat the band.

"Must be an accident up ahead," Joseph said, pulling back on the reins to slow the horse down.

Rachel felt her body tense. She hated the thought of seeing an accident, and she prayed one of their Amish buggies wasn't involved. So often horse-drawn buggies had been damaged by cars that either didn't see them or had been traveling too fast. Lots of Amish folks had been injured from collisions with those fast-moving automobiles.

Their sleigh had just rounded the next bend when they saw the rescue vehicle in the middle of the road. There were flares along the highway, a car pulled off on the shoulder, and rescue workers bent over a small figure. Several Amish children were clustered around, and a policeman was directing traffic.

"We'd better stop," Joseph said. "It could be someone we know." He pulled the buggy off the road; then he and Rachel jumped out.

They had only taken a few steps when a familiar voice called out, "Joseph! Rachel! Over here!"

Rachel glanced to her right. Elizabeth was running across the slippery snow, and she nearly knocked Rachel off her feet when she grabbed her around the middle. "It's Perry! He was hit by that car!"

The next several hours were like a terrible nightmare for the Beachy family. Perry had been killed instantly when the car hit a patch of ice and swerved off the road. All the other Amish children who'd been walking home from school had witnessed the accident, and most of them were in shock.

Rachel went through the motions of getting supper on, as Mom and Dad took care of the funeral arrangements and answered all sorts of questions for the authorities. No one could believe that young, impetuous Perry, who'd been making jokes at breakfast that same morning, was dead. He was up in heaven now, with relatives and friends who'd gone on before him. Rachel found some comfort in knowing he was with Jesus, but oh, how she would miss his smiling, often mischievous face. She knew the rest of the family felt the same way—especially Mom, who had lost her youngest child.

Rachel stirred the pot of lentil soup she was making for supper, and her thoughts went instinctively to Anna, whose favorite soup was lentil. *Anna needs to be told about Perry. She's still part of this family, even if she has moved away. She will probably want to come home for the funeral.*

Several women had come to the house with food and offers of help, and one of them was Martha Rose Zook. She'd received a few letters from Anna, so she would be the logical one to ask about getting word to her.

Rachel hurried to the living room just as Martha Rose and Laura Yoder were about to head out. "Wait, Martha Rose!" she called. "I need to speak with you."

Martha Rose moved away from the door, and Rachel motioned her into the kitchen. She didn't want anyone to overhear their conversation, especially not Mom or Dad.

"What is it, Rachel?" Martha Rose asked, offering her a sympathetic look. "Is there somethin' more I can do?"

Rachel nodded, as stinging tears clung to her lashes. "Could ya let Anna know what's happened today? She'll no doubt wanna be here for the funeral. It wouldn't be goin' against the ban to—"

Martha Rose hugged Rachel, interrupting her plea. "Of course I'll let her know. I have her address and phone number, so I'll just go to the nearest pay phone and give her a call."

Rachel smiled through her tears. *"Danki,* I'd sure appreciate that." She glanced toward the door leading to the living room. "Just the same, it might be best if ya didn't say anything to anyone about this."

Martha Rose held up her hand. "I won't say a word."

The funeral for Perry was two days later, and friends, relatives, and neighbors quickly filled up the Beachy house for the service. A plain pine coffin sat in one corner of the room, displaying young Perry's body, all dressed in white.

It sent shivers up Rachel's back to see her little brother lying there so still and pale. In this life, she would never again have the pleasure of seeing him run and play. Never again hear his contagious laugh or squeals of delight when a calf or kitten was born. It wasn't fair! She wondered why God allowed so much hurt to come into the world and had to keep reminding herself that even though Perry's days on earth were done, he did have a new life in heaven.

Rachel glanced around the room, noting that Silas and his family were in attendance. Silas caught her looking his way and offered a sympathetic smile. She only nodded in response and gulped back the sob rising in her throat.

Rachel was miserable without Silas as a friend, and now they'd lost another family member. *Anna may as well be dead,* she silently moaned. *She's not one of us anymore, and even though Martha Rose called her on the phone and told her about the funeral, she chose not to come.* Unbidden tears slipped out of Rachel's eyes and rolled down her cheeks in rivulets that stung like fire. *If only things could be different. If only. . .*

Rachel barely heard the words Bishop Weaver spoke. Her thoughts lingered on her selfish sister and how much she'd hurt the family by going English. She'd hurt Silas, too, and because of it, he'd spurned Rachel's love.

The service was nearly over, and the congregation had just begun the closing hymn when Rachel caught a glimpse of her sister coming in the back door. She had to look twice to be sure it really was Anna. Her modern sister was dressed in English clothes—a pair of black trousers and a royal blue slipover sweater. The biggest surprise was Anna's hair. She'd cut it real short, just like she'd threatened to do before she left home.

Anna slipped quietly onto one of the benches near the back of the room, and Rachel noticed that she was all alone. Apparently Reuben hadn't come. He might have had to work today, or maybe he was afraid to face everyone after all he'd done. Worse yet, maybe he and Anna had split up. What would happen if Anna left Reuben and returned to the Amish faith? Would their marriage be annulled by the bishop? Would Silas. . . ?

Rachel jerked her wayward thoughts aside. No point in borrowing trouble. . . at least not until she knew the facts.

When the benediction was pronounced, Rachel stood up. She knew the funeral procession to the cemetery would begin soon, and she wanted a chance to speak with her sister, just in case she didn't plan on staying.

She'd only taken a few steps when she was stopped by Silas. "I'm real sorry about Perry." He paused, his gaze going to the ceiling, then back again. "It just don't seem right, him bein' so young and all."

Rachel numbly stared at him. When Silas said nothing more, she started to move away. To her surprise, Silas grabbed her around the waist and gave her a hug. She held her arms stiffly at her side and waited until he pulled back. She was sure his display of affection was nothing more than a brotherly hug. Besides, it was too little too late as far as she was concerned. Rachel knew she needed to weed out the yearning she felt for Silas. It would only cause her further pain to keep pining away and hoping for something that never could be.

She bit her bottom lip in order to keep from bursting into tears, then turned away quickly.

Chapter 19

Rachel caught up with Anna as she was about to leave the house. "Anna, hold up a minute. I wanna talk to ya."

Anna turned to face Rachel, her green eyes filled with tears. "I probably shouldn't have come, but Perry was my baby brother, and I just couldn't stay away. Thanks for askin' Martha Rose to get word to me."

"It's only right that you should be here." Rachel nodded toward the door. "Let's go outside so's we can talk."

Once they were on the porch, Rachel led Anna over to the swing and they both sat down.

"Do you think this is a good idea?" Anna asked. "I'm still under the ban. You might be in trouble for talkin' to me."

Rachel shrugged. "Accordin' to Bishop Weaver, there's really no rule sayin' we can't talk to you a'tall. We're just not supposed to eat at the same table or do any kind of business with ya."

"Guess that's true enough." Anna swallowed hard. "Martha Rose said Perry was hit by a car, but she didn't know any of the details. Can ya tell me how this horrible thing happened?"

Rachel drew in a shuddering breath. "Joseph and me were headin' home from town in the sleigh. As we came around the bend near our driveway, we saw the accident. There was a rescue vehicle, a police car, and—" She choked on her next words. "Perry was lyin' in the road, and we were told that he probably died upon impact."

Anna reached for her hand. "The roads were icy, huh?"

Rachel nodded. "I'm sure the driver of the car didn't mean to run off the road and hit Perry. It was just an accident, but still—" She sniffed deeply. "Perry was so young. It don't seem right when a child is killed."

"I know," Anna agreed. "Sometimes it's hard to figure out why God allows bad things to happen to innocent people."

Rachel let go of Anna's hand and reached up to wipe her eyes. "Mom would remind us that the Bible says God is no respecter of persons, and that rain falls on the just, same as it does the unjust."

"How are Mom and Dad?" Anna asked, taking their conversation in another direction. "I only saw them from a distance, and I didn't think it would be wise to try to talk to them right now." She glanced away. "I'm sure they must hate me for leavin' the faith and all."

Rachel shook her head. *"Himmel!* They don't hate ya, Anna. They're disappointed, of course, but you're still their flesh and blood, and if you were to come back, they'd welcome ya with open arms."

Anna flexed her fingers, then formed them into tight balls in her lap. "I won't be comin' back, Rachel. Reuben and me are happy livin' the modern life. He likes his paintin' job, and I'm content to work as a waitress."

So they're not separated. Guess that's somethin' to be grateful for. "You could have done those things and still remained Amish," Rachel reminded.

"I know, but Reuben really needed a truck to get him back and forth to work, not to mention travelin' from job to job." Anna sighed deeply. "Besides, we both felt the *Ordnung* was too restrictive. We enjoy doin' some worldly things, and—"

"Anna, I hope you're not caught up with drinkin' or drugs!"

Anna shook her head. "No, I—"

"Silas told me Reuben had been runnin' with a wild bunch of English fellows before he married you, and Reuben even admitted to gettin' drunk a few times."

"Jah, he does like a few beers now and then. But he don't get drunk anymore," Anna added quickly.

Rachel wasn't sure what else to say. She knew what Bishop Weaver's concerns about drinking would be. *One drink can lead to another, and pretty soon you can't quit.* That's what he'd have to say.

"How's Silas Swartley these days?" Anna asked, breaking into Rachel's thoughts. "If he told you about Reuben, then I guess the two of you must be gettin' pretty close."

Rachel shifted uneasily. How much should she tell Anna about her relationship with Silas? Would it be best to say nothing, or did Anna have the right to know that Silas was still in love with her?

"Are ya gonna tell me or not?" Anna pried. "I can see by the look on your face that you're in love with him."

Yeah, and he still loves you. Rachel bit back the words and answered, "Silas and I are friends, nothin' more."

"Has he asked you out?"

"We've done a few things together, but there wasn't anythin' to it."

Anna shrugged. "I was kinda hopin' that after I left home, Silas's eyes would be opened and he'd see how good you'd be for him."

Well, he hasn't! Just thinking about Silas's rejection made Rachel feel cranky. Surely he had to know he wasn't going to get Anna back. Why couldn't he be happy with Rachel? *Guess I've reminded myself before that I wouldn't want his love secondhand.*

"You never really said—how's the rest of the family takin' Perry's death?" Anna asked, imposing on Rachel's thoughts one more time.

Rachel felt a fresh set of tears pool in her eyes. "It's been mighty hard—especially for Mom and Elizabeth. Perry was still Mom's little boy, and even though Elizabeth and her twin fought like cats and dogs, I know she still loved him."

Before Anna could reply, Joseph poked his head through the doorway. He shot Anna a look of irritation. "Kinda late, aren't ya?"

"I caught the bus partway here, then walked the rest of the way," Anna explained. "I came in during the closing hymn."

Joseph shrugged his broad shoulders. "Rachel, I came to tell ya that everyone went out the back door and they're climbin' into their buggies. We'll be headin' for the cemetery now."

Rachel stood up, but when Anna didn't join her, she turned back toward the swing. "Aren't ya comin'? You can ride with me and Joseph."

Anna stared down at her clasped hands. "I'm not sure I should. Some folks might see it as an intrusion."

"How could they?" Rachel questioned. "You're part of our family. You have every right to be at Perry's burial."

Anna looked up at Joseph, and Rachel could see that he was mulling things over. He finally nodded. "You're welcome to ride in the buggy with me and Rachel."

Anna stood up, and Rachel reached for her hand. They stepped off the front porch together and followed Joseph around the back of the house.

❧

A horse-drawn hearse led the procession down the narrow country road, with the two Beachy buggies following. Behind them was a long line of Amish carriages, and Silas Swartley's was the last. He felt sick to the pit of his stomach thinking how it would feel to lose one of his younger brothers. Even if they didn't always see eye-to-eye, they were kin, and blood was thicker than water.

At the cemetery everyone climbed out of their buggies and gathered around the hand-dug grave, then Bishop Weaver said a few words.

Silas stood near his own family, directly across from the Beachys. He was surprised to see Anna standing between Rachel and Joseph. On one hand, it made sense that she would be here, since she was part of their family. On the other hand, she'd gone English and had been shunned by her Amish friends and family, so he thought maybe she'd stay away.

It made his heart stir with strange feelings when he saw her wearing modern clothes. Her hair was cut short, and she was even wearing makeup. Such a contrast from the Anna Beachy he'd grown up and fallen in love with.

Silas glanced over at Rachel. Her shoulders drooped and tears rimmed her eyes; she looked exhausted. His heart twisted with the pain he saw on her face. If only she hadn't shut him out, he might be of some comfort to her now.

He shook his head slowly. Maybe it was best this way. She didn't trust him anymore, and he wasn't sure she should. After all, what had he ever done to make her believe he cared for her and not her sister? The truth was, until this very moment, he'd never seen Anna for what she really was—a modern woman who seemed much more comfortable in men's pants than she did in a long dress. She, who wanted his best friend—a drinking, loose-talking man, seeking out the fancy life and not caring who he hurt in the process.

Silas forced his attention to Bishop Weaver's words. "For as much as it has pleased the Almighty God to take unto Himself the soul of young Perry Beachy, we offer the body to this place prepared for it, that ashes may return to ashes. . . dust to dust. . .and the imperishable spirit may forever be with the Lord. Amen."

Rebekah Beachy sat slumped over in her wheelchair, audibly weeping. She clutched her husband's hand on one side, and her youngest daughter stood on her other side next to Joseph. The child was sobbing hysterically, and when her twin brother's coffin was lowered into the ground, Joseph lifted Elizabeth into his arms and carried her back to the buggy.

Silas felt strongly that he should speak to Rachel and Anna, too, for that matter. Now didn't seem the right time, though. There were too many others crowded around the grieving family, and he wanted the chance to speak with them in private.

I'll wait 'til later, he decided. *Maybe right after the funeral dinner.*

Chapter 20

Since it was bitterly cold and there was snow on the ground, dinner had to be served inside the house. This meant everyone would be fed in shifts—the men first, then the women and children.

Rachel knew Anna would not be welcome to eat at any of the tables with her Amish friends and relatives, so she set a place for her in the kitchen at a small table near the fireplace. At first Anna argued, saying she wasn't hungry, but Rachel won out and Anna finally agreed to eat a little something.

When the meal was over, Rachel returned to the kitchen, hoping to speak to her sister before she returned home. When she saw Anna and their mother talking, she came to a halt just inside the kitchen door. Mom had tears in her eyes, and she was pleading with Anna to return home and reconcile herself with the church.

Anna shook her head and muttered, "I can't. My place is with Reuben now."

Rachel slipped quietly away, knowing Anna and Mom needed this time alone. She scurried up the steps and went straight to her room, realizing that she, too, needed a few minutes by herself. She'd been so busy helping with the funeral dinner and trying to put on a brave front in order to help others in the family who were grieving that she hadn't really taken the time to properly mourn.

Rachel stood in front of the window, staring out at the spiraling snowflakes. Her thoughts kept time with the snow—swirling, whirling, falling all around, then melting before she had the chance to sort things out.

"Why'd You have to take my little brother, God?" she murmured. "Why did Anna have to hurt our family by leavin' the faith?" She trembled involuntarily. "How come Silas has to pine away for Anna and can't see me as someone he could love?"

Deep in her heart Rachel knew none of these things were God's fault. He'd allowed them all right, but certainly He hadn't caused the bad things to happen. God loved Perry and had taken him home to heaven. Anna hadn't left home to be mean, either. She was obviously confused about her faith in God and was blinded by her love for Reuben. Love did strange things to people. Rachel knew that better than anyone. *Look how I wasted so many months hoping Silas would fall in love with me. It's not his fault he can't seem to get over his feelings for Anna. She hurt him real bad, and he might always hunger for his lost love.*

Rachel knew she would have to get on with her life. Maybe God wanted her to remain single. Might could be that her job was to run the greenhouse and take care of Mom and Dad. It was a bitter pill to swallow, but if it was God's will, she knew she must.

Rachel walked to the corner of her room. Maybe there was something in

Anna's hope chest that she would like to have. Surely there were a few things she could put to good use in her new English home.

Rachel opened the lid and slowly began to remove each item. There were several hand towels, some quilted pot holders, and a few tablecloths—all things she was sure Anna could use. Next, she lifted out the beginning of a double-ring wedding quilt. Its colors of depth and warmth, in shades of blue and dark purple, seemed to frolic side by side.

Rachel's eyes filled with tears as she thought about her own hope chest, now empty and useless. She'd never even started a wedding quilt, and the few items she'd stored in the chest had either been sold or were on display at Thomas Benner's store. Rachel had no reason to own a hope chest anymore, for she would probably never set up housekeeping with a husband and have *kinder*. Maybe God never planned for her to become a wife and mother.

Shoving her pain aside and reaching farther into the chest, Rachel discovered an old Bible and an embroidered sampler. Attached to the sampler was a note:

> *This was made by Miriam Stoltzfus Hilty. Given to my* mamm,
> *Anna Stoltzfus, to let her know that God has changed my heart.*

Rachel knew that Miriam Stoltzfus was Great-Aunt Mim and that Anna Stoltzfus was her great-grandma. She noticed there was also a verse embroidered on the sampler: *"A merry heart doeth good like a medicine,"* Proverbs 17:22.

A sob caught in Rachel's throat as she read the words out loud. She clung to the sampler like it was some sort of lifeline. The yellowing piece of cloth gave her a strange, yet comforting, connection to the past.

Rachel's gaze came to rest on the old Bible. She laid the sampler aside and picked the Bible up, pulling open the inside cover. In small, perfectly penned letters were the following words: *"This* Biwel *belonged to Anna Stoltzfus. May all who read it find as much comfort, hope, and healing as I have found."*

Rachel noticed several crocheted bookmarks placed in various sections of the Bible. She turned the pages to some of the marked spots and read the underlined verses. One in particular seemed to jump right out at her. Psalm 71:14: "But I will hope continually, and will yet praise thee more and more." This was the very same verse Rachel had been reciting for the last several months. Was God trying to tell her something?

Rachel was about to turn the page when another underlined verse from Psalm 71 caught her attention. Verse 5 read: "For thou art my hope, O Lord God: thou art my trust from my youth."

Hot tears rolled down Rachel's cheeks as the words on the page burned into her mind. All this time Rachel had been hoping to win Silas's heart. She'd been praising God for something she hoped He would do. Never once had it occurred to her that the heavenly Father wanted her to put all her hopes in *Him*. She was to trust Him and only Him, and she should have been doing it since her youth.

She'd been trying to do everything in her own strength because it was what *she* wanted. When Silas didn't respond as she'd hoped, Rachel's faith had been dashed away like sunshine on a rainy day.

Rachel broke down, burying her face in her hands. "Dear Lord, please forgive me. Help me learn to trust You more. Let my hope always be in You. May Your will be done in my life. Show me how best to serve You. Amen."

Rachel picked up the precious items she'd found in Anna's hope chest, slipped them into her apron pocket, and headed downstairs. The *Biwel* belonged to Anna's namesake, and she should have it. The sampler belonged to Great-Grandma Anna's daughter, Miriam, and Anna should have that as well.

Anna wasn't in the kitchen when Rachel returned. Mom was sitting at the table with her head bowed. Not wishing to disturb her mother's prayer, Rachel slipped quietly out the back door. She found Joseph and Pauline on the porch, sitting side by side on the top step. *They look so gut together. I'm happy Joseph has found someone to love.*

Joseph turned around when Rachel closed the screen door. "Oh, it's you, little sister. Nearly everyone's gone home, and we didn't know where you were. Anna was lookin' for ya."

Rachel felt panic surge through her. "Did Anna leave?"

Joseph shook his head. "Naw, she said she wouldn't go without talkin' to you first."

"I think she took a walk down by the river," Pauline interjected. She removed her shawl and handed it to Rachel. "If you're goin' after her, you'd better put this on. It's mighty cold out today."

Gratefully, Rachel took the offered shawl. *"Danki.* I think I will mosey on down to the water and see if Anna's still there. I've got somethin' I wanna give her."

Rachel started out walking but soon broke into a run. The wind stung her face, but she didn't mind. Her only thought was on finding Anna.

The rest of Silas's family had already gone home, but he wasn't ready to leave just yet. He wanted to hang around and see if he could offer comfort to Rachel. She hadn't looked right when he'd seen her earlier, and after lunch he'd gone looking for her, but she seemed to have disappeared. He figured she must be taking Perry's death pretty hard, and it pained him when she hadn't even responded to his hug. She felt small and fragile in his arms—like a broken toy he was unable to fix. It was as if Rachel was off in another world—in a daze or some kind of a dream world.

He remembered hearing his mom talk about her oldest sister and how she'd gone crazy when her little girl drowned in Paradise Lake. He didn't think Rachel would actually go batty, but she was acting mighty strange, and he couldn't go home until he knew she was going to be okay.

Silas decided to walk down to the river, knowing Rachel often went there to fish or look for birds. Just as he reached the edge of the cornfield, he spotted someone standing along the edge of the creek. His heart gave a lurch when he saw the figure leaning over the water. Surely, she wasn't thinking of—

Silas took off on a run. When he neared the clearing, he skidded to a halt. The figure he'd seen was a woman, but it wasn't Rachel Beachy. It was her sister. He approached Anna slowly, not wanting to spook her.

She turned to face him just as he stepped to the water's edge. "Silas, you scared me. I thought I was all alone."

"Sorry. I sure didn't mean to frighten ya. I was lookin for—"

"I used to love comin' down here," she interrupted. "It was a good place to think. . .and to pray." Anna hung her head. "Sorry to say, I haven't done much prayin' since I left home. Guess maybe I should get back to it."

"Prayin' is *gut*," Silas agreed. "I think it goes hand in hand with thinkin'."

Anna smiled and pointed to the water. "Look, there's a big old catfish."

"Rachel likes to fish," Silas muttered.

Anna grinned. "I think you and my sister have a lot in common. She likes to spend hours feedin' and watchin' the birds that come into our yard, too."

Silas nodded. "I bought her a bird book and a pair of binoculars for her birthday."

"I'm sure she liked that."

"I thought so at the time, but now I'm not sure."

Anna touched the sleeve of Silas's jacket. "How come?"

He stared out across the water. "She thinks I don't like her. She thinks I'm still in love with you."

❧

Rachel stood behind the trunk of a white birch tree, holding her breath and listening to the conversation going on just a few feet away. She'd almost shown herself, but then she heard her own name mentioned, and she was afraid of what Anna and Silas were saying. Was Silas declaring his love for her sister? Was he begging her to leave Reuben and return to the Amish faith? Surely Silas must know the stand their church took against divorce.

"Who are you in love with, Silas?" she heard Anna ask.

Rachel pressed against the tree and waited breathlessly for his response. She was doing it again—eavesdropping. It wasn't right, but she could hardly show herself now, with Silas about to declare his love for Anna and all. Her thoughts went back to that day, many months ago, when Silas had said to Anna, "When you're ready, I'll be waitin'." Was he still waiting for her? Did he really think they had a chance to be together?

"I used to love you, Anna," she heard Silas say. "At least I thought I did." There was a long pause. "Guess maybe we'd been friends so long I never thought I'd fall in love with anyone but you."

"Have you, Silas?" Anna asked.

Rachel chanced a peek around the tree. Silas was standing so close to Anna he could have leaned down and kissed her. He didn't, though. Instead, he stood tall, shoulders back, and head erect. "You were right when you told me once that Rachel would be *gut* for me. I love her more'n anything, but I don't know what I can do to prove that love."

Feeling as if her heart could burst wide open, Rachel jumped out from behind the tree and leaped into Silas's arms, knocking them both over and just missing the water. "You don't have to do anything to prove your love!" she shouted. "What you said to Anna is proof enough for me!"

Silas looked kind of embarrassed as they scrambled to their feet, but Rachel didn't care. She turned to Anna with a wide smile. "I've got somethin' for ya."

"What is it?"

Rachel reached inside her apron pocket and withdrew the sampler and their great-grandma's Bible. "I found these at the bottom of your hope chest, and I think ya should have 'em."

Anna's eyes flooded with tears. "Great-Aunt Mim's Merry Heart sampler and Great-Grandma's *Biwel*. Mom gave them to me for my hope chest several years ago. I'd forgotten all about them."

Rachel handed the items over to her sister. "I read some passages in Great-Grandma Stoltzfus's *Biwel*. I found real hope in your hope chest, as I was reminded to put my hope in the Lord and keep trusting Him." She turned back to face Silas. "I thought I'd have to learn to live without your love, but now—"

Silas hushed her by placing two fingers against her lips. "Now you'll just have to learn to live as my wife." He leaned down to kiss her, and Rachel felt as if she were a bird—floating, soaring high above the clouds—reveling in God's glory and hoping in Him.

Epilogue

Rachel stood on the lawn, her groom on one side, her brother Joseph and new sister-in-law Pauline on the other. It had been a *gut* wedding. Two double-ring wedding quilts were presented to the brides by their mothers, along with a double portion of happiness for both sets of newlyweds.

The only thing that could have made my day more complete would have been to share it with my older sister. On an impulse, Rachel glanced across the yard. To her amazement, Anna was walking toward her, holding a brown paper bag.

"Excuse me a minute," Rachel whispered to Silas. "There's someone I need to see."

Silas squeezed her hand. "Hurry back, *Frau.*"

Rachel smiled and slipped quietly away. She drew Anna off to one side, and they exchanged a hug. "It's so *gut* to see you. I was hopin' you'd receive my note about the weddin'."

"I didn't think I should come inside for the ceremony, under the circumstances and all. I did want to wish you well and give ya this." Anna handed the sack to Rachel.

"What is it?"

"Look inside."

Rachel opened the bag and reached in. Surprise flooded her soul as she withdrew a sampler. At first she thought it was the same one she'd given Anna last year, but when she read the embroidered words, she knew it wasn't. " 'For thou art my hope, O Lord God: thou art my trust from my youth,' Psalm 71:5."

"I thought it would be somethin' you could hand down to your children and grandchildren," Anna explained. She placed her hand against her stomach. "That's what I plan to do with the Merry Heart sampler Great-Aunt Mim made."

Rachel's eyes widened. "You're in a family way?"

Anna nodded and smiled. "The baby will come in the spring."

"Do Mom and Dad know they're gonna be grandparents?"

"I told them a few minutes before you came outside." Anna's eyes filled with tears. "They said they still love me, Rachel. They want me and Reuben to come visit after the baby is born." She glanced around the yard as though someone might be watching. "It's not really goin' against Bishop Weaver's ban for me to visit here or talk with my family now and then. Besides, Reuben and I had a long talk awhile back. We both want to stay English, but we've found a good church. We're readin' our Bibles again and prayin' together."

Rachel embraced her sister one more time. "I'm so happy to hear that, Anna, and I thank you for coming today." She held the sampler close to her heart. "I'll always cherish this, and every time I look at it, I'll not only be reminded to put my hope in Jesus, but I'll think of my English sister, who is also trustin' in God."

Anna smiled and ran her fingers through her short hair. "That's so true."

"Well, I'd best be gettin' back to my groom, or he'll likely come a-lookin' for me," Rachel said with a giggle.

Anna nodded. "Tell him I said to be happy and that he'd better treat my little sister right, or I'll come a-lookin' for *him.*"

Rachel squeezed Anna's hand, then hurried toward Silas. She was so glad she'd opened her sister's hope chest last December, for if she hadn't, she might never have found the special sampler and the *Biwel* with God's Word, so full of hope.

When Rachel reached her groom, he pulled her to his side and whispered in her ear, *"Ich Leibe du*—I love you, and with you as my wife, I'll always be happy."

Rachel drew in a deep breath and leaned her head against his shoulder. "And I'll always love you."

A Letter to Our Readers

Dear Readers:

In order that we might better contribute to your reading enjoyment, we would appreciate you taking a few minutes to respond to the following questions. When completed, please return to the following: Fiction Editor, Barbour Publishing, Inc., P.O. Box 719, Uhrichsville, OH 44683.

1. Did you enjoy reading *Lancaster Brides?*
   ❏ Very much—I would like to see more books like this.
   ❏ Moderately—I would have enjoyed it more if _____
   _____
   _____

2. What influenced your decision to purchase this book?
   (Check those that apply.)
   ❏ Cover   ❏ Back cover copy   ❏ Title   ❏ Price
   ❏ Friends   ❏ Publicity   ❏ Other

3. Which story was your favorite?
   ❏ *A Merry Heart*   ❏ *Plain and Fancy*
   ❏ *Looking for a Miracle*   ❏ *The Hope Chest*

4. Please check your age range:
   ❏ Under 18   ❏ 18–24   ❏ 25–34
   ❏ 35–45   ❏ 46–55   ❏ Over 55

5. How many hours per week do you read? _____

Name _____

Occupation _____

Address _____

City _____ State _____ Zip _____